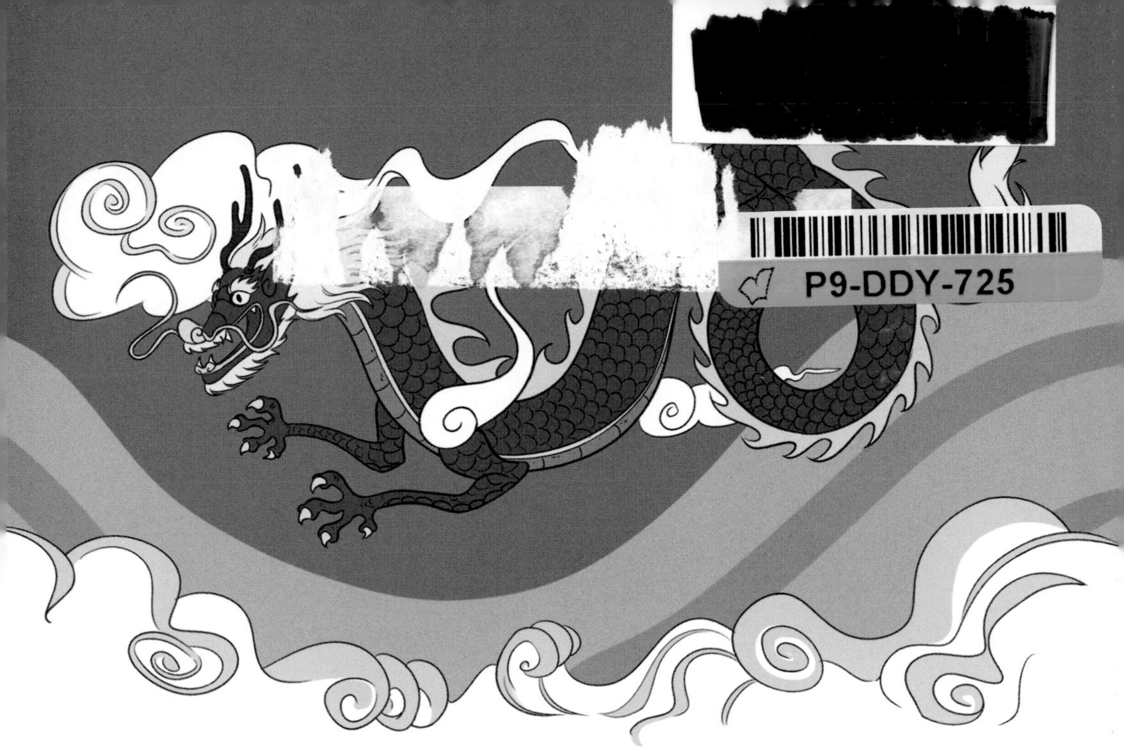

CITY OF DRAGONS

THE AWAKENING STORM

JAIMAL YOGIS & VIVIAN TRUONG

graphix
AN IMPRINT OF
SCHOLASTIC

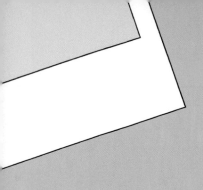

FOR FIN, EBEN, AND KAIFAS —J. Y.

TO MY PARENTS, FAMILY, AND FRIENDS — THIS BOOK WOULDN'T HAVE BEEN
COMPLETED WITHOUT THEIR ETERNAL LOVE AND SUPPORT. THANK YOU FOR
ALWAYS MAKING SURE I TOOK CARE OF MYSELF.

AND TO MY LATE UNCLE, WHO SPARKED THIS JOURNEY BY DRAWING STICK
FIGURES IMITATING MY SIBLINGS AT THE BACK OF A RESTAURANT TO CHEER
UP THE WHINY, THREE-YEAR-OLD ME. —V. T.

Library of Congress Control Number: 2020943284

ISBN 978-1-338-66043-2 (hardcover)
ISBN 978-1-338-66042-5 (paperback)

10 9 8 7 6   23 24 25

Printed in the U.S.A.   40
First edition, September 2021

Book design by Steve Ponzo
Creative Director: Phil Falco
Publisher: David Saylor

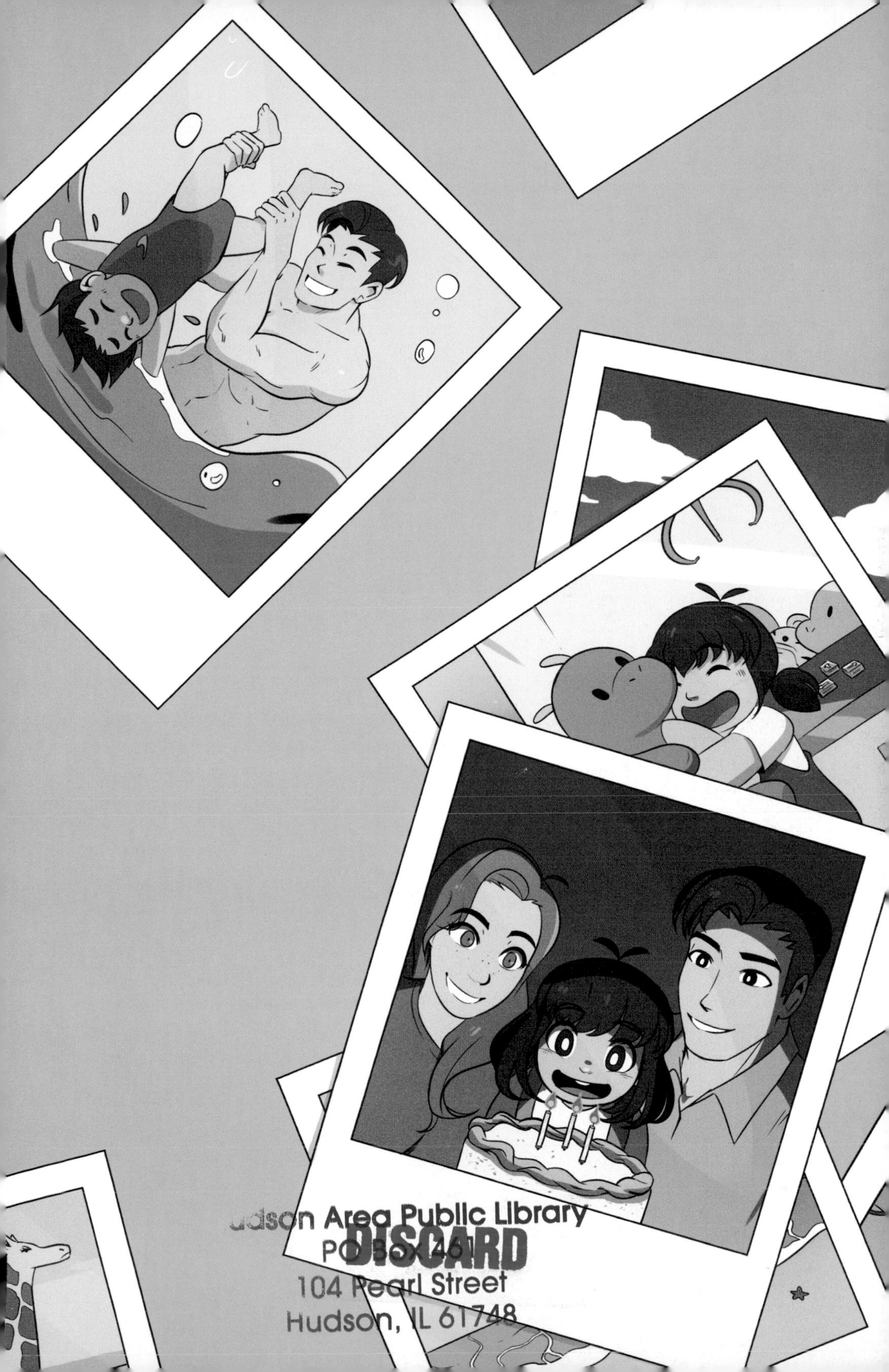

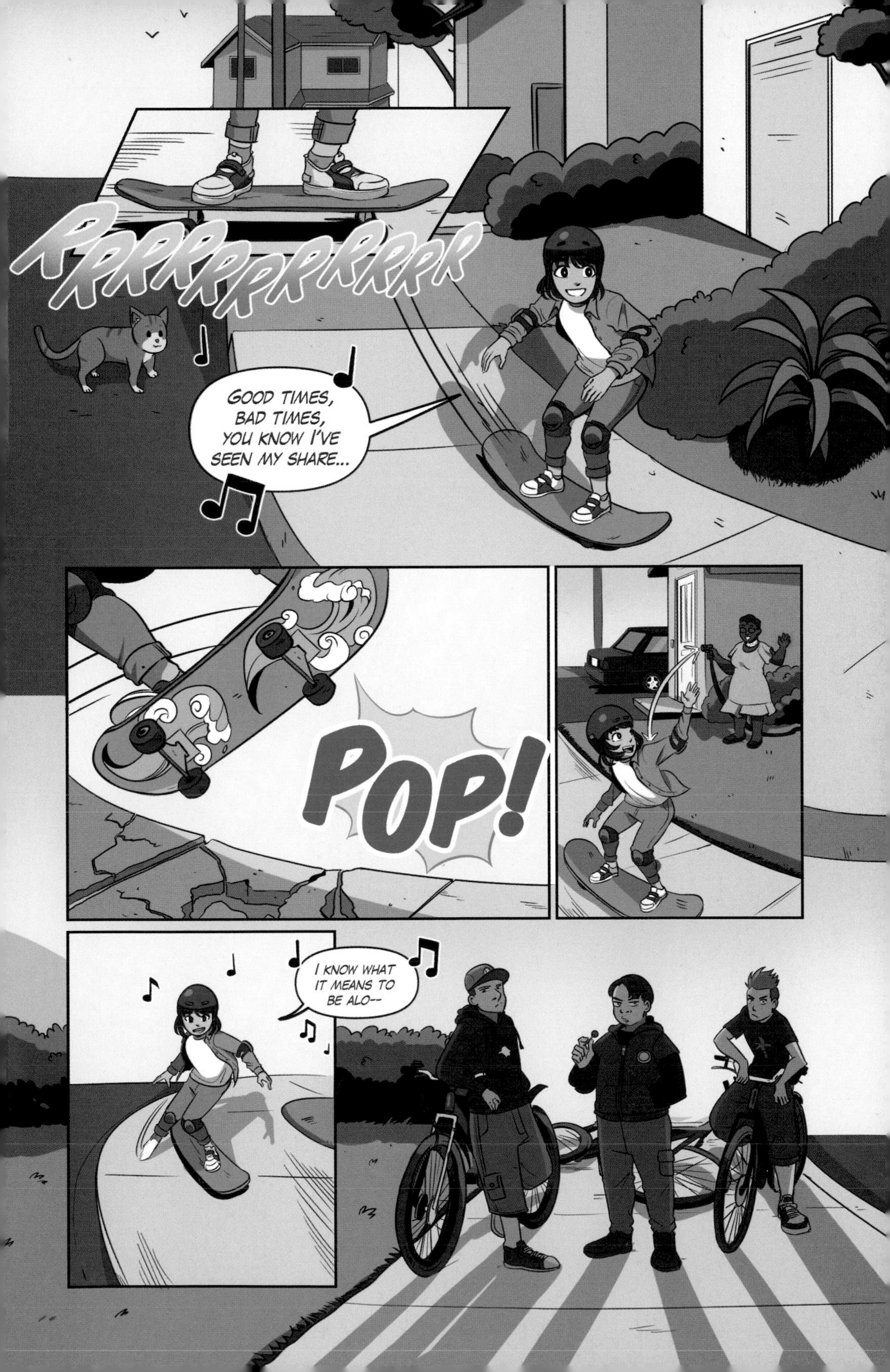
RRRRRRRRRRRRR
GOOD TIMES, BAD TIMES, YOU KNOW I'VE SEEN MY SHARE...
POP!
I KNOW WHAT IT MEANS TO BE ALO--

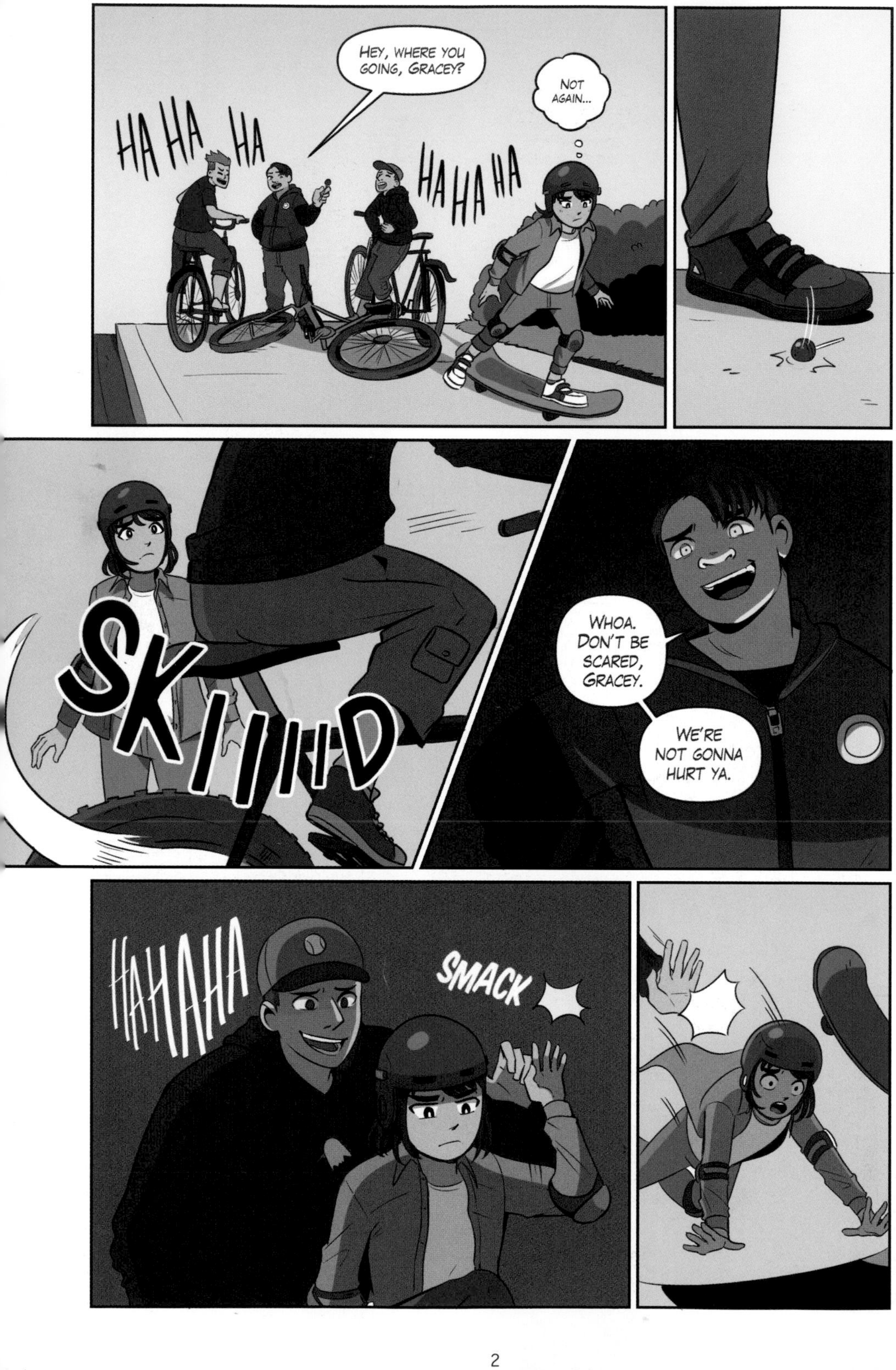
HA HA HA
HEY, WHERE YOU GOING, GRACEY?
HA HA HA HA
NOT AGAIN...
SKIIIID
WHOA. DON'T BE SCARED, GRACEY.
WE'RE NOT GONNA HURT YA.
HAHAHA
SMACK

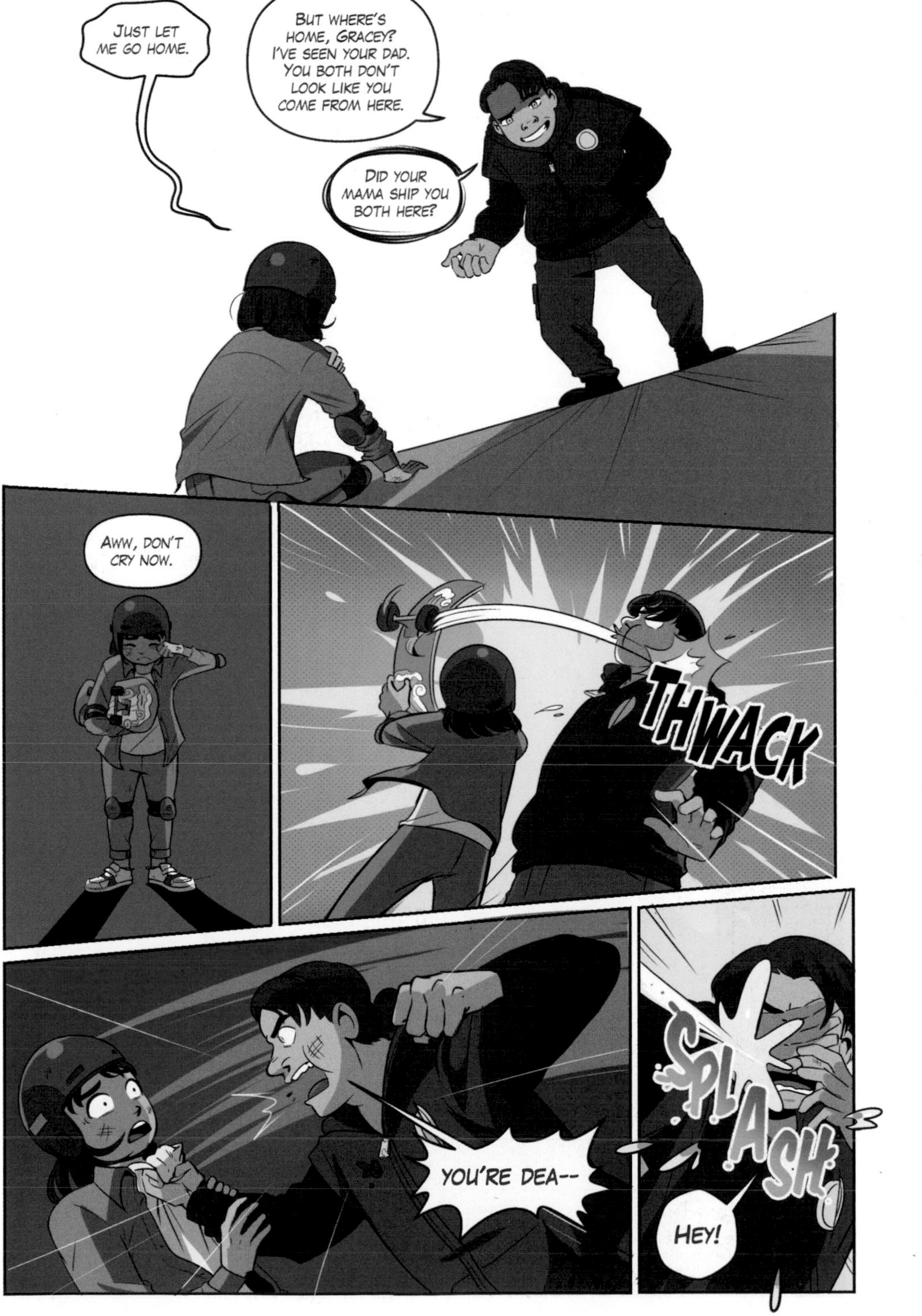
JUST LET ME GO HOME.
BUT WHERE'S HOME, GRACEY? I'VE SEEN YOUR DAD. YOU BOTH DON'T LOOK LIKE YOU COME FROM HERE.
DID YOUR MAMA SHIP YOU BOTH HERE?
AWW, DON'T CRY NOW.
THWACK
YOU'RE DEA--
SPLASH
HEY!

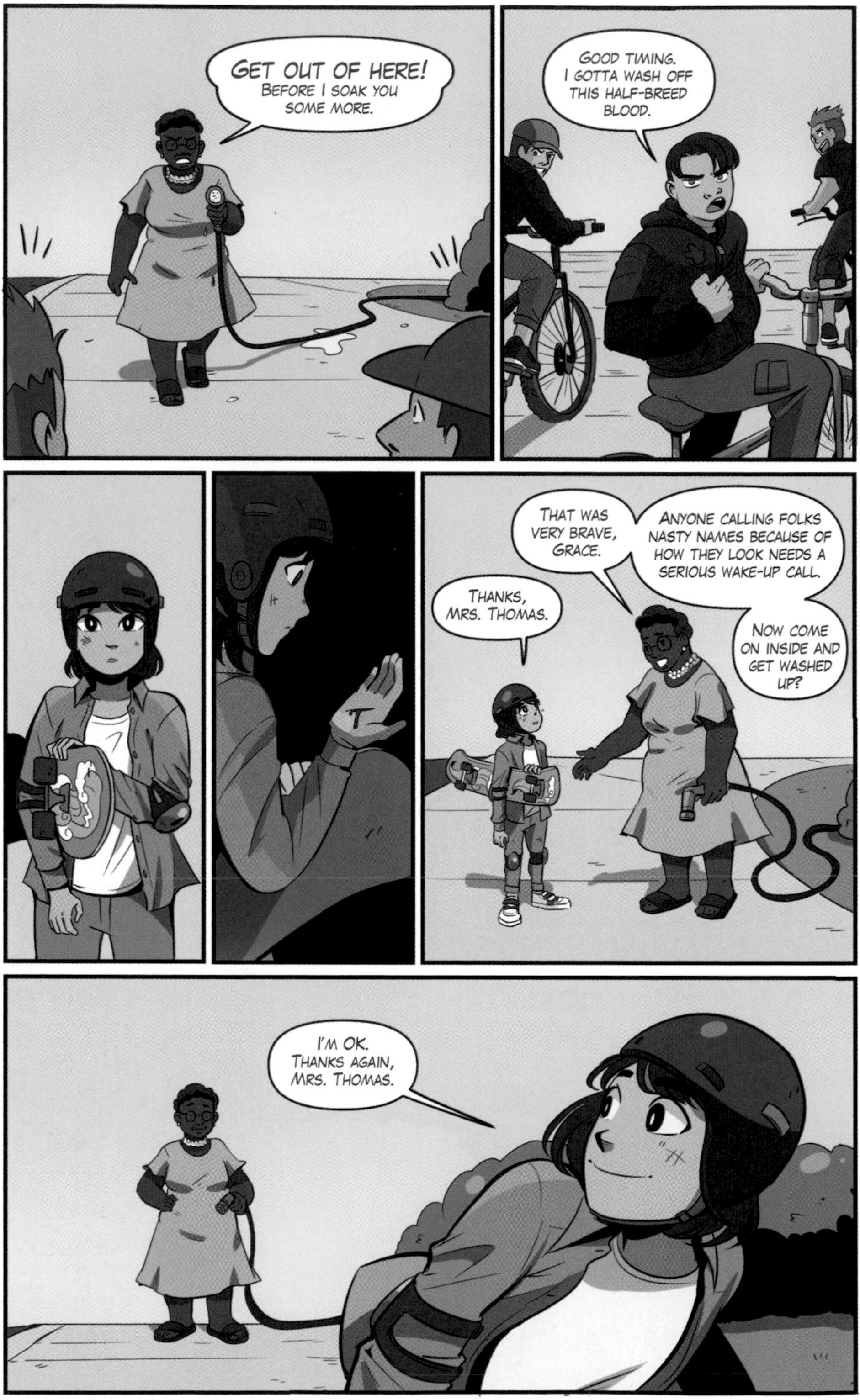
GET OUT OF HERE! BEFORE I SOAK YOU SOME MORE.
GOOD TIMING. I GOTTA WASH OFF THIS HALF-BREED BLOOD.
THAT WAS VERY BRAVE, GRACE.
ANYONE CALLING FOLKS NASTY NAMES BECAUSE OF HOW THEY LOOK NEEDS A SERIOUS WAKE-UP CALL.
THANKS, MRS. THOMAS.
NOW COME ON INSIDE AND GET WASHED UP?
I'M OK. THANKS AGAIN, MRS. THOMAS.

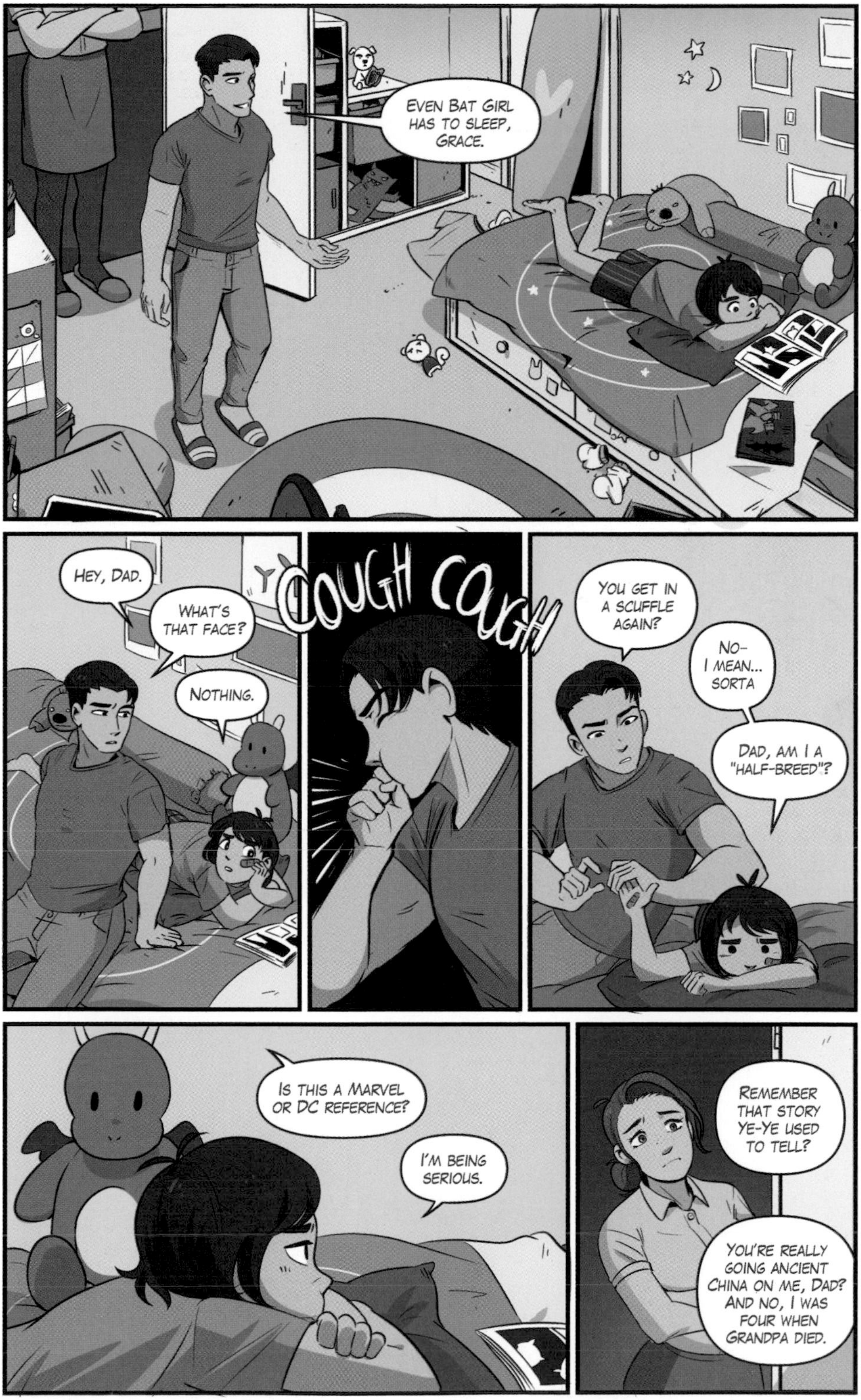

EVEN BAT GIRL HAS TO SLEEP, GRACE.
HEY, DAD.
WHAT'S THAT FACE?
NOTHING.
COUGH COUGH
YOU GET IN A SCUFFLE AGAIN?
NO– I MEAN... SORTA
DAD, AM I A "HALF-BREED"?
IS THIS A MARVEL OR DC REFERENCE?
I'M BEING SERIOUS.
REMEMBER THAT STORY YE-YE USED TO TELL?
YOU'RE REALLY GOING ANCIENT CHINA ON ME, DAD? AND NO, I WAS FOUR WHEN GRANDPA DIED.

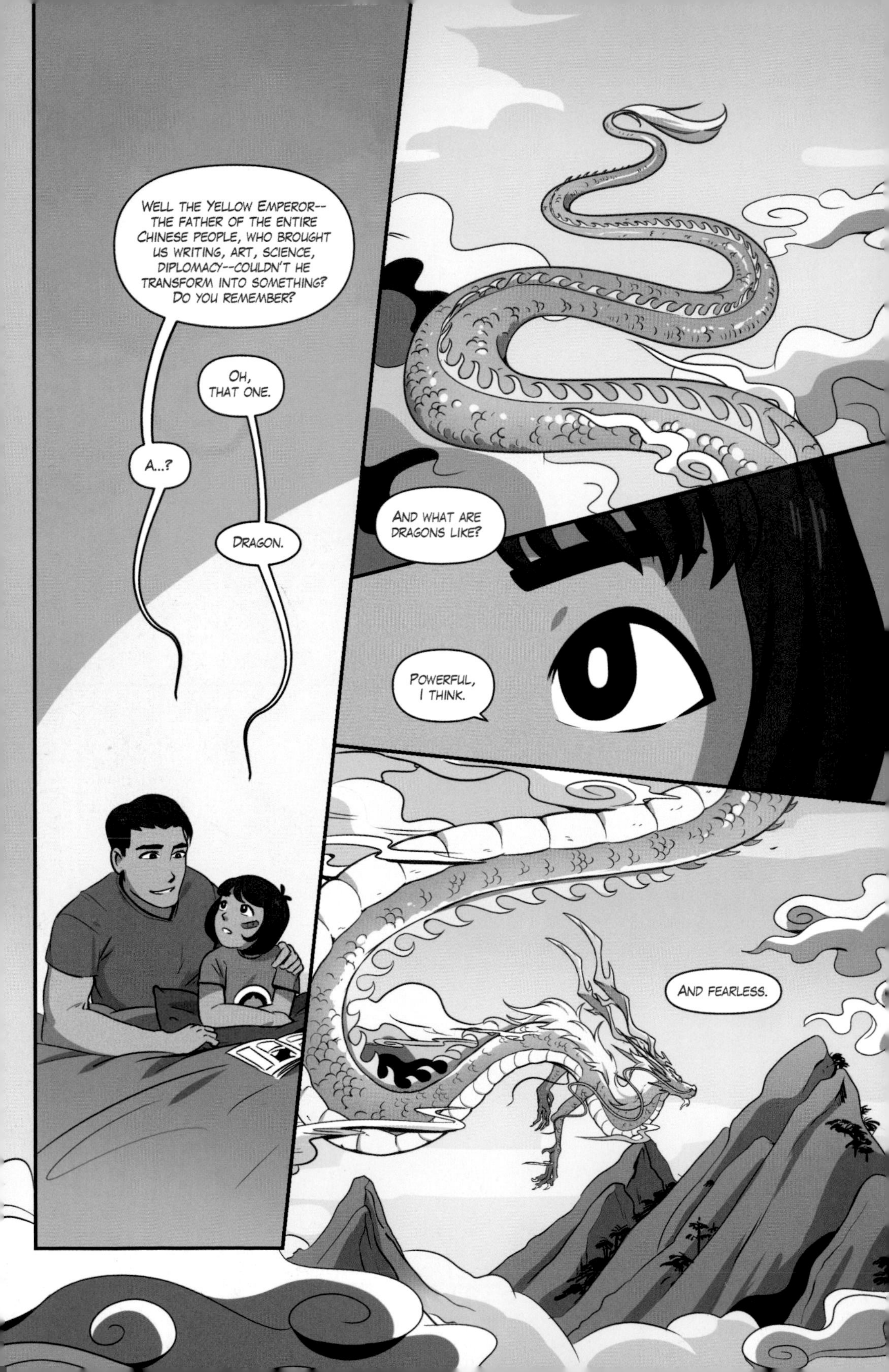
WELL THE YELLOW EMPEROR-- THE FATHER OF THE ENTIRE CHINESE PEOPLE, WHO BROUGHT US WRITING, ART, SCIENCE, DIPLOMACY--COULDN'T HE TRANSFORM INTO SOMETHING? DO YOU REMEMBER?
OH, THAT ONE.
A...?
DRAGON.
AND WHAT ARE DRAGONS LIKE?
POWERFUL, I THINK.
AND FEARLESS.

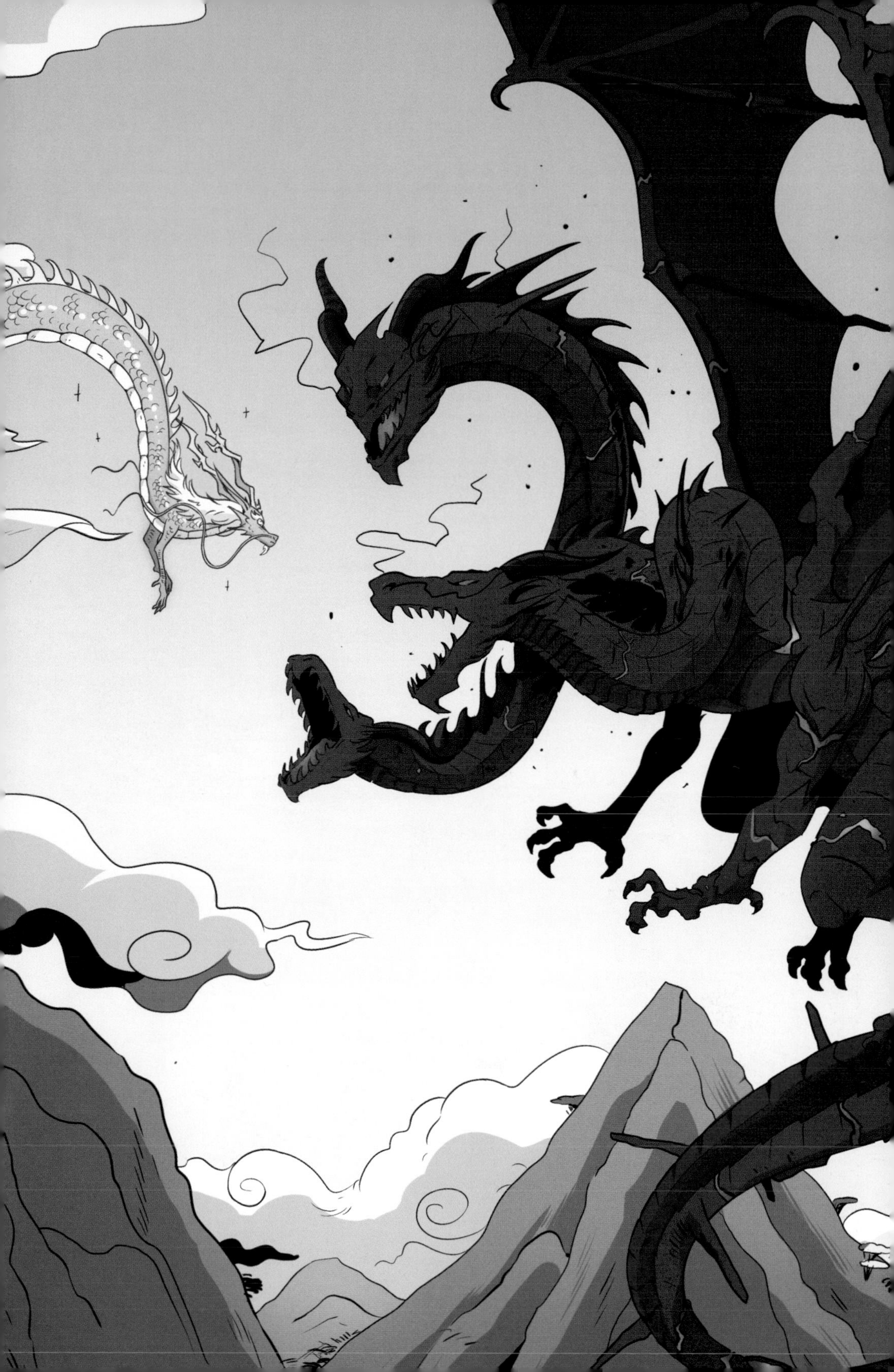

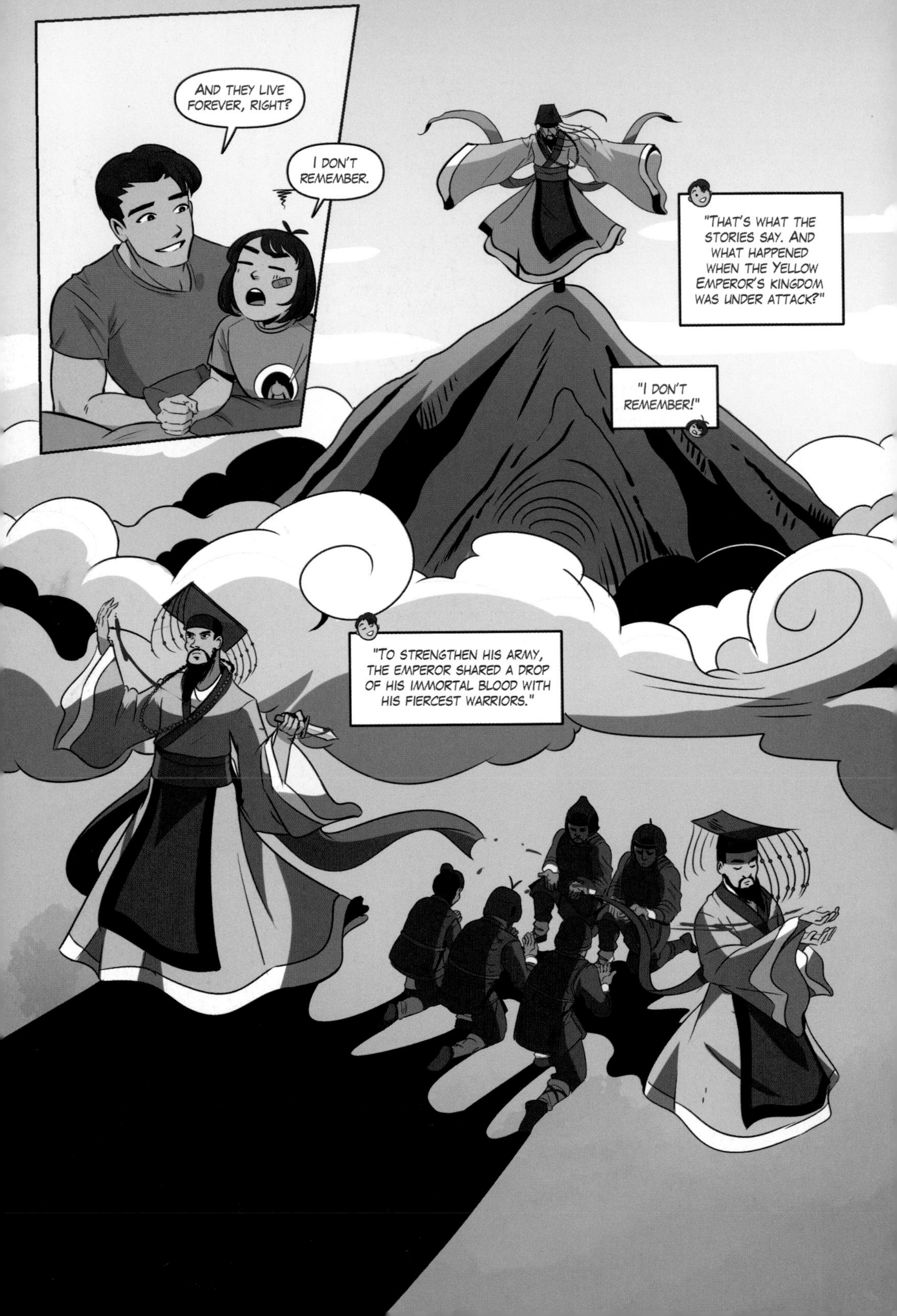
AND THEY LIVE FOREVER, RIGHT?
I DON'T REMEMBER.
"THAT'S WHAT THE STORIES SAY. AND WHAT HAPPENED WHEN THE YELLOW EMPEROR'S KINGDOM WAS UNDER ATTACK?"
"I DON'T REMEMBER!"
"TO STRENGTHEN HIS ARMY, THE EMPEROR SHARED A DROP OF HIS IMMORTAL BLOOD WITH HIS FIERCEST WARRIORS."

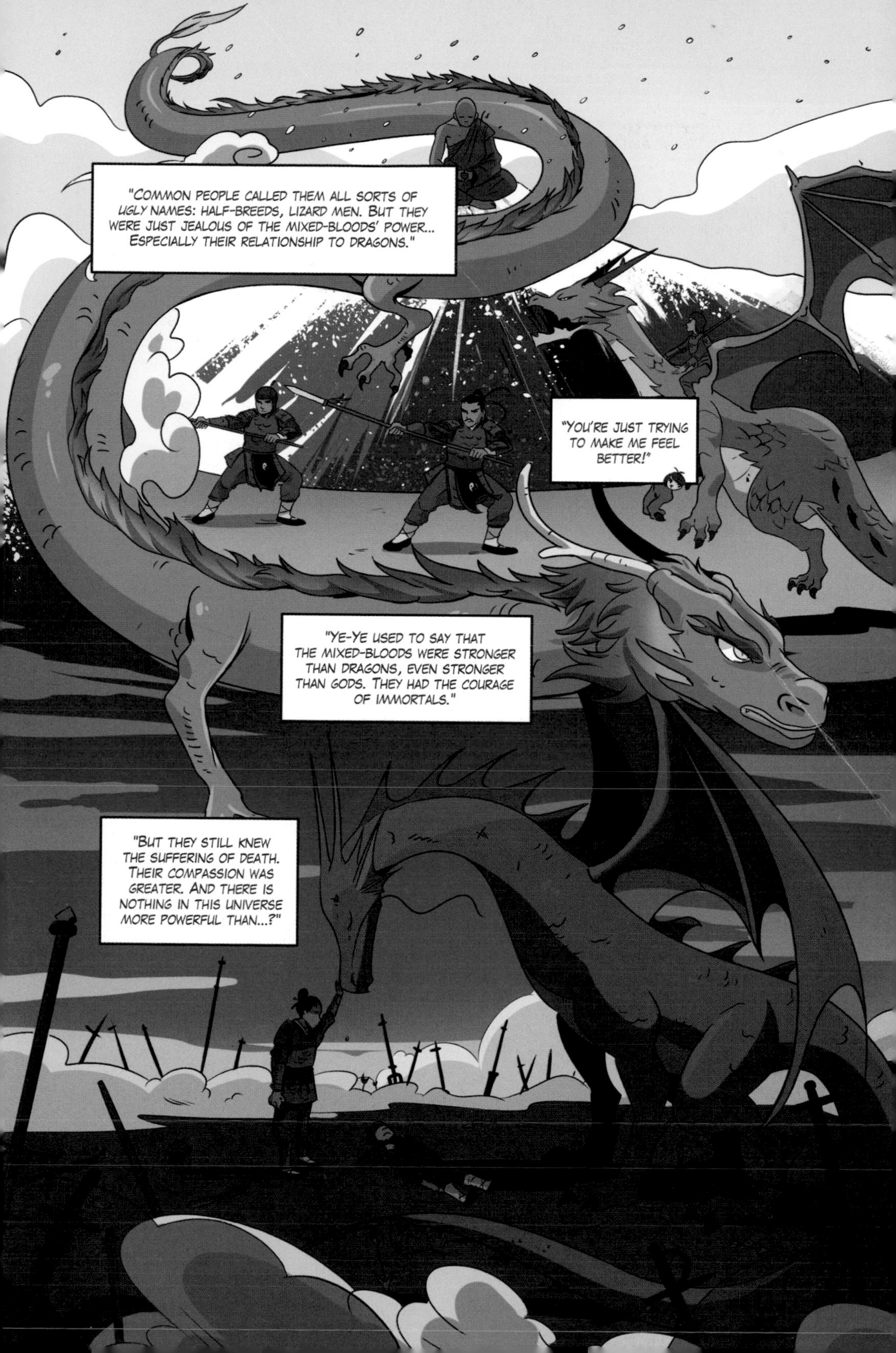
"COMMON PEOPLE CALLED THEM ALL SORTS OF UGLY NAMES: HALF-BREEDS, LIZARD MEN. BUT THEY WERE JUST JEALOUS OF THE MIXED-BLOODS' POWER... ESPECIALLY THEIR RELATIONSHIP TO DRAGONS."
"YOU'RE JUST TRYING TO MAKE ME FEEL BETTER!"
"YE-YE USED TO SAY THAT THE MIXED-BLOODS WERE STRONGER THAN DRAGONS, EVEN STRONGER THAN GODS. THEY HAD THE COURAGE OF IMMORTALS."
"BUT THEY STILL KNEW THE SUFFERING OF DEATH. THEIR COMPASSION WAS GREATER. AND THERE IS NOTHING IN THIS UNIVERSE MORE POWERFUL THAN...?"

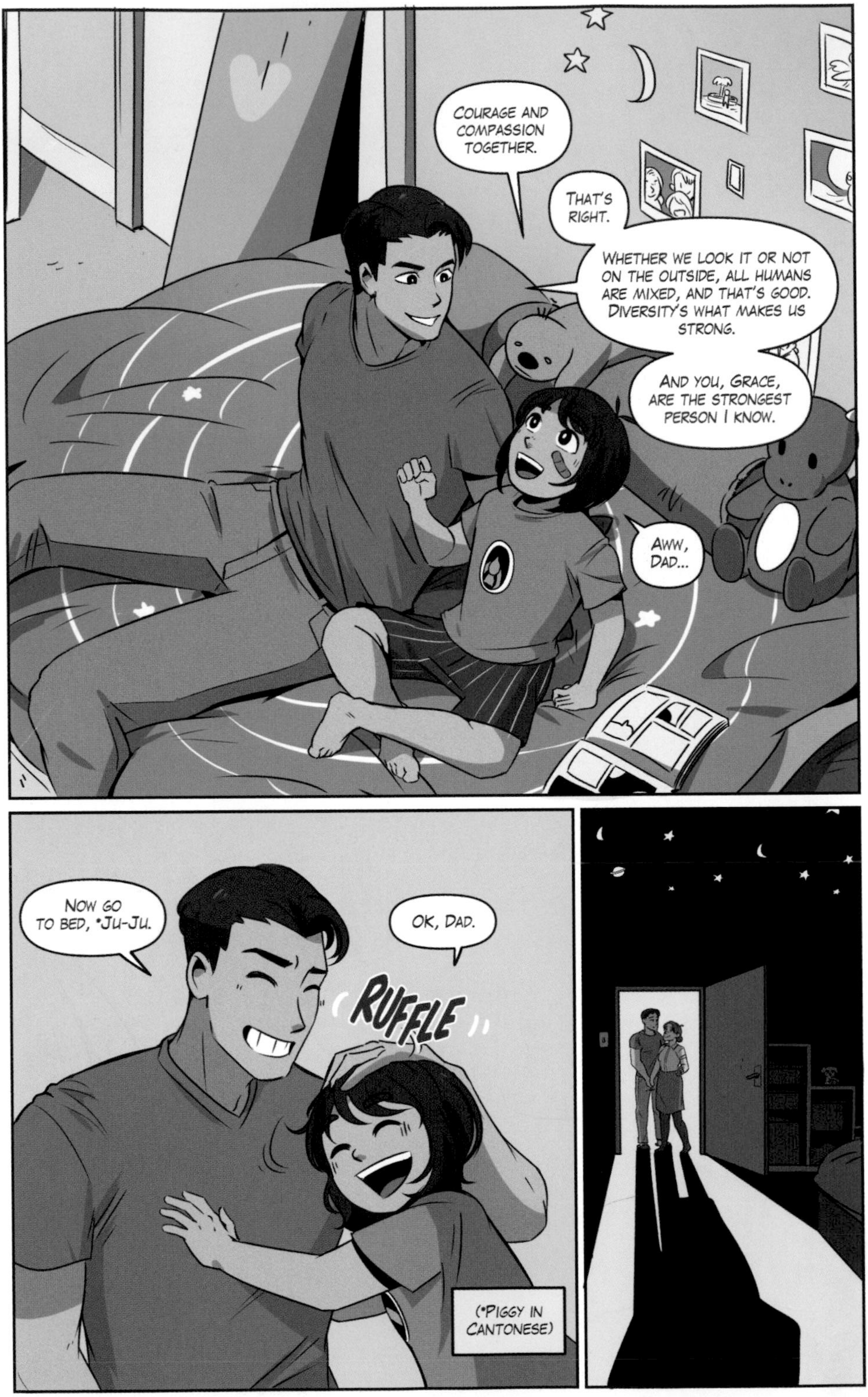
COURAGE AND COMPASSION TOGETHER.
THAT'S RIGHT.
WHETHER WE LOOK IT OR NOT ON THE OUTSIDE, ALL HUMANS ARE MIXED, AND THAT'S GOOD. DIVERSITY'S WHAT MAKES US STRONG.
AND YOU, GRACE, ARE THE STRONGEST PERSON I KNOW.
AWW, DAD...
NOW GO TO BED, *JU-JU.
OK, DAD.
RUFFLE
(*PIGGY IN CANTONESE)

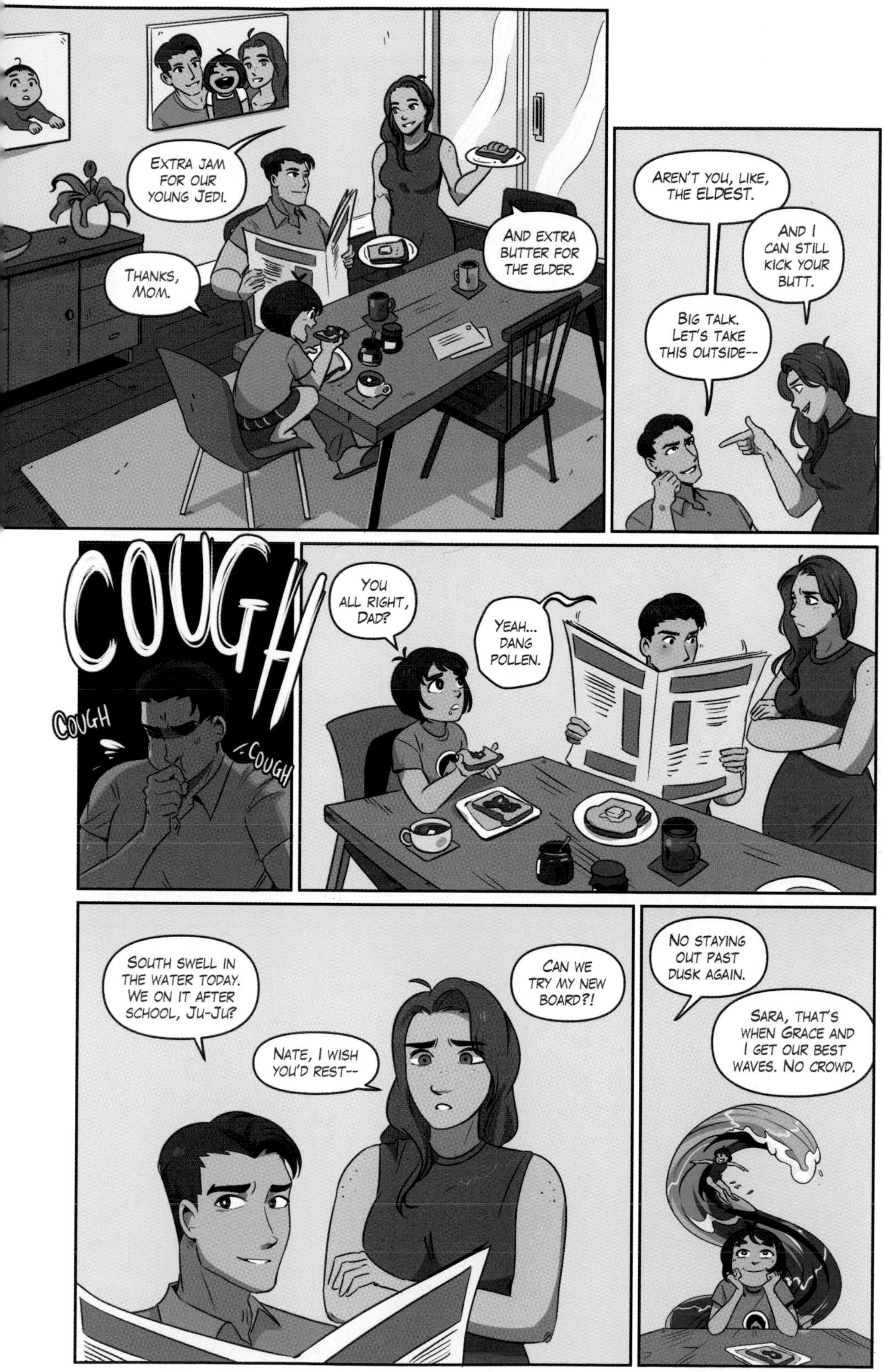
EXTRA JAM FOR OUR YOUNG JEDI.
AND EXTRA BUTTER FOR THE ELDER.
THANKS, MOM.
AREN'T YOU, LIKE, THE ELDEST.
AND I CAN STILL KICK YOUR BUTT.
BIG TALK. LET'S TAKE THIS OUTSIDE--
COUGH
COUGH
COUGH
YOU ALL RIGHT, DAD?
YEAH... DANG POLLEN.
SOUTH SWELL IN THE WATER TODAY. WE ON IT AFTER SCHOOL, JU-JU?
CAN WE TRY MY NEW BOARD?!
NATE, I WISH YOU'D REST--
NO STAYING OUT PAST DUSK AGAIN.
SARA, THAT'S WHEN GRACE AND I GET OUR BEST WAVES. NO CROWD.

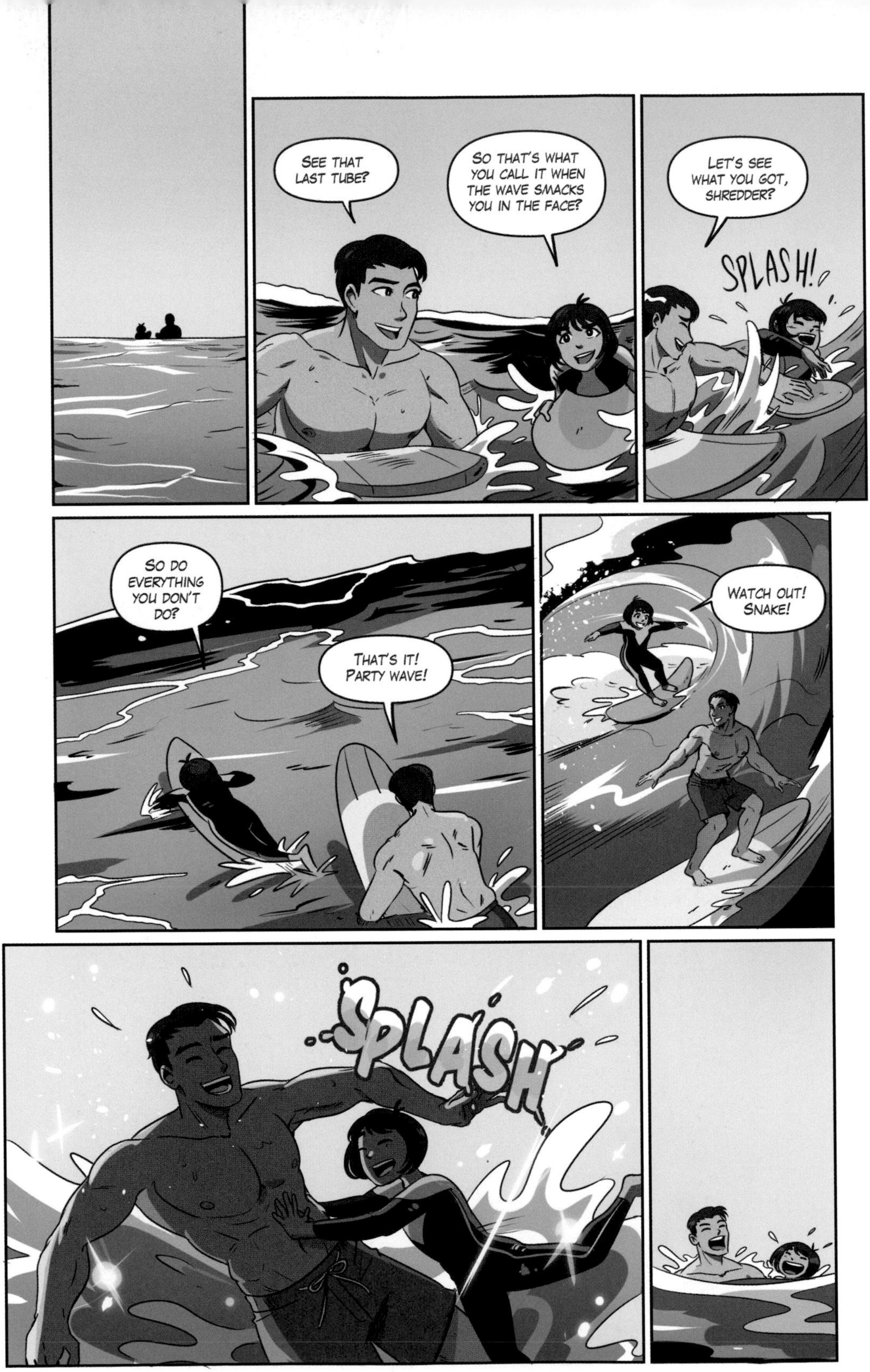
SEE THAT LAST TUBE?
SO THAT'S WHAT YOU CALL IT WHEN THE WAVE SMACKS YOU IN THE FACE?
LET'S SEE WHAT YOU GOT, SHREDDER?
SPLASH!
SO DO EVERYTHING YOU DON'T DO?
THAT'S IT! PARTY WAVE!
WATCH OUT! SNAKE!
SPLASH

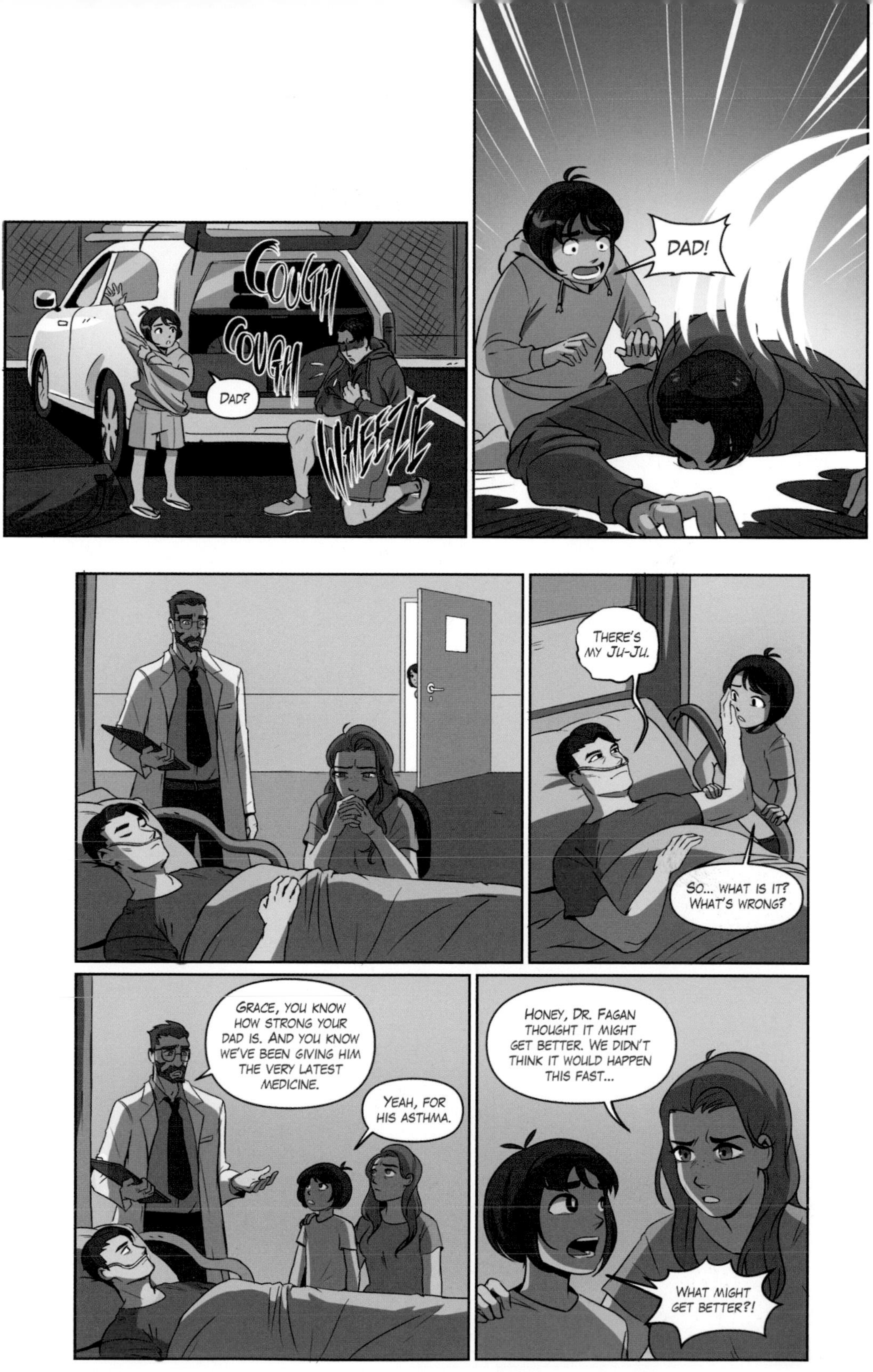
COUGH
COUGH
DAD?
WHEEZE
DAD!
THERE'S MY JU-JU.
SO... WHAT IS IT? WHAT'S WRONG?
GRACE, YOU KNOW HOW STRONG YOUR DAD IS. AND YOU KNOW WE'VE BEEN GIVING HIM THE VERY LATEST MEDICINE.
YEAH, FOR HIS ASTHMA.
HONEY, DR. FAGAN THOUGHT IT MIGHT GET BETTER. WE DIDN'T THINK IT WOULD HAPPEN THIS FAST...
WHAT MIGHT GET BETTER?!

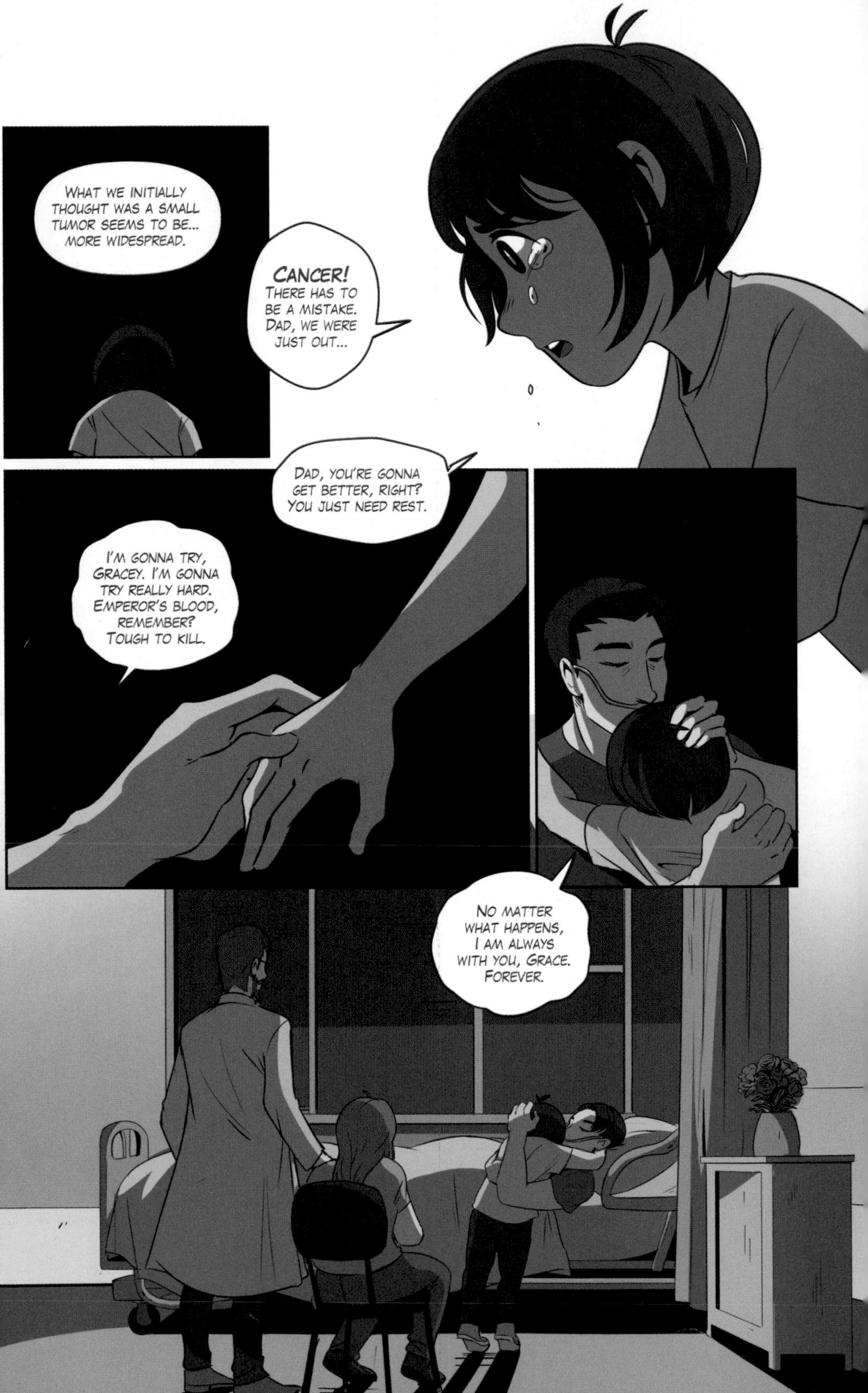
WHAT WE INITIALLY THOUGHT WAS A SMALL TUMOR SEEMS TO BE... MORE WIDESPREAD.
CANCER! THERE HAS TO BE A MISTAKE. DAD, WE WERE JUST OUT...
DAD, YOU'RE GONNA GET BETTER, RIGHT? YOU JUST NEED REST.
I'M GONNA TRY, GRACEY. I'M GONNA TRY REALLY HARD. EMPEROR'S BLOOD, REMEMBER? TOUGH TO KILL.
NO MATTER WHAT HAPPENS, I AM ALWAYS WITH YOU, GRACE. FOREVER.

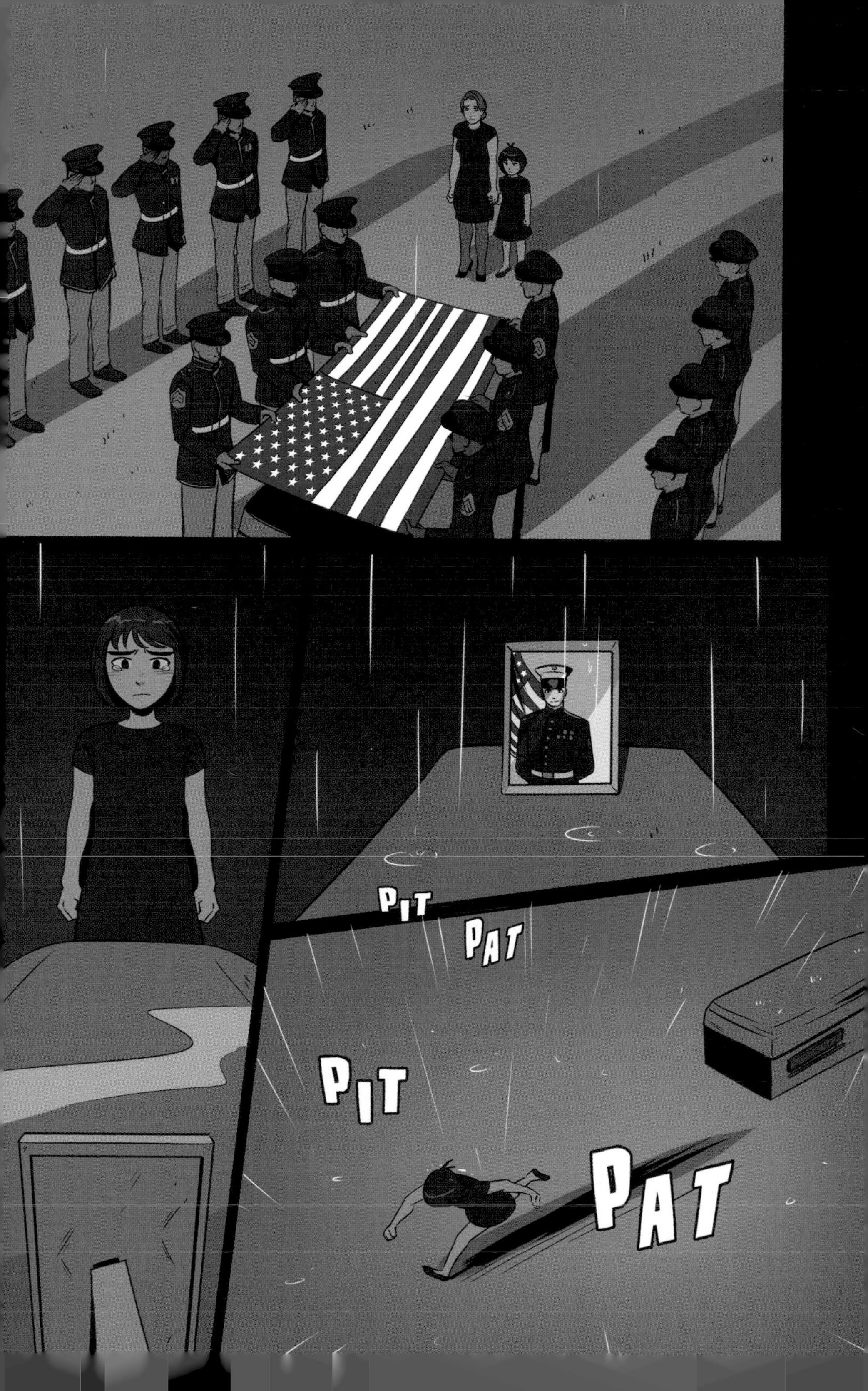
PIT
PAT
PIT
PAT

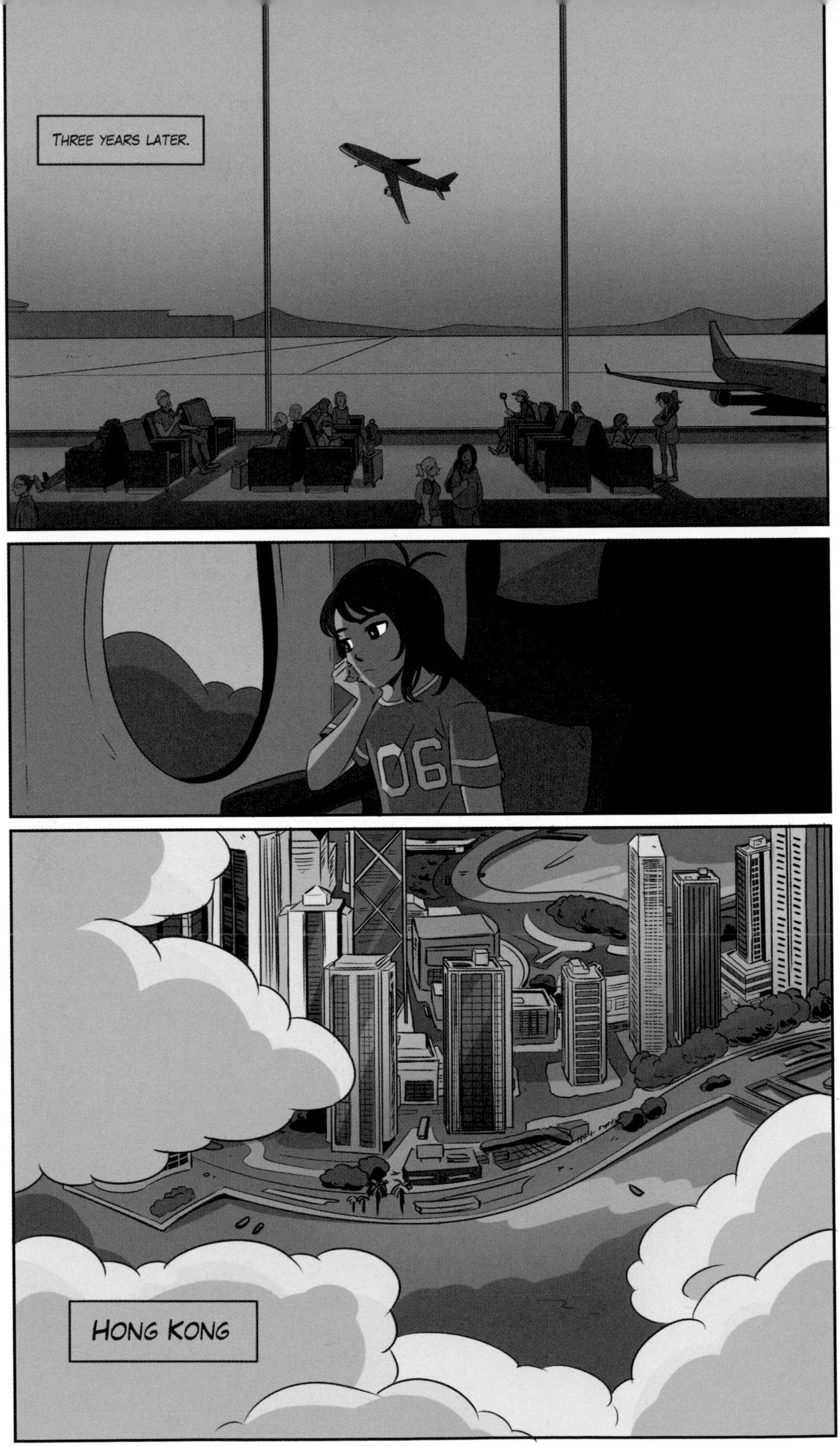
THREE YEARS LATER.
06
HONG KONG

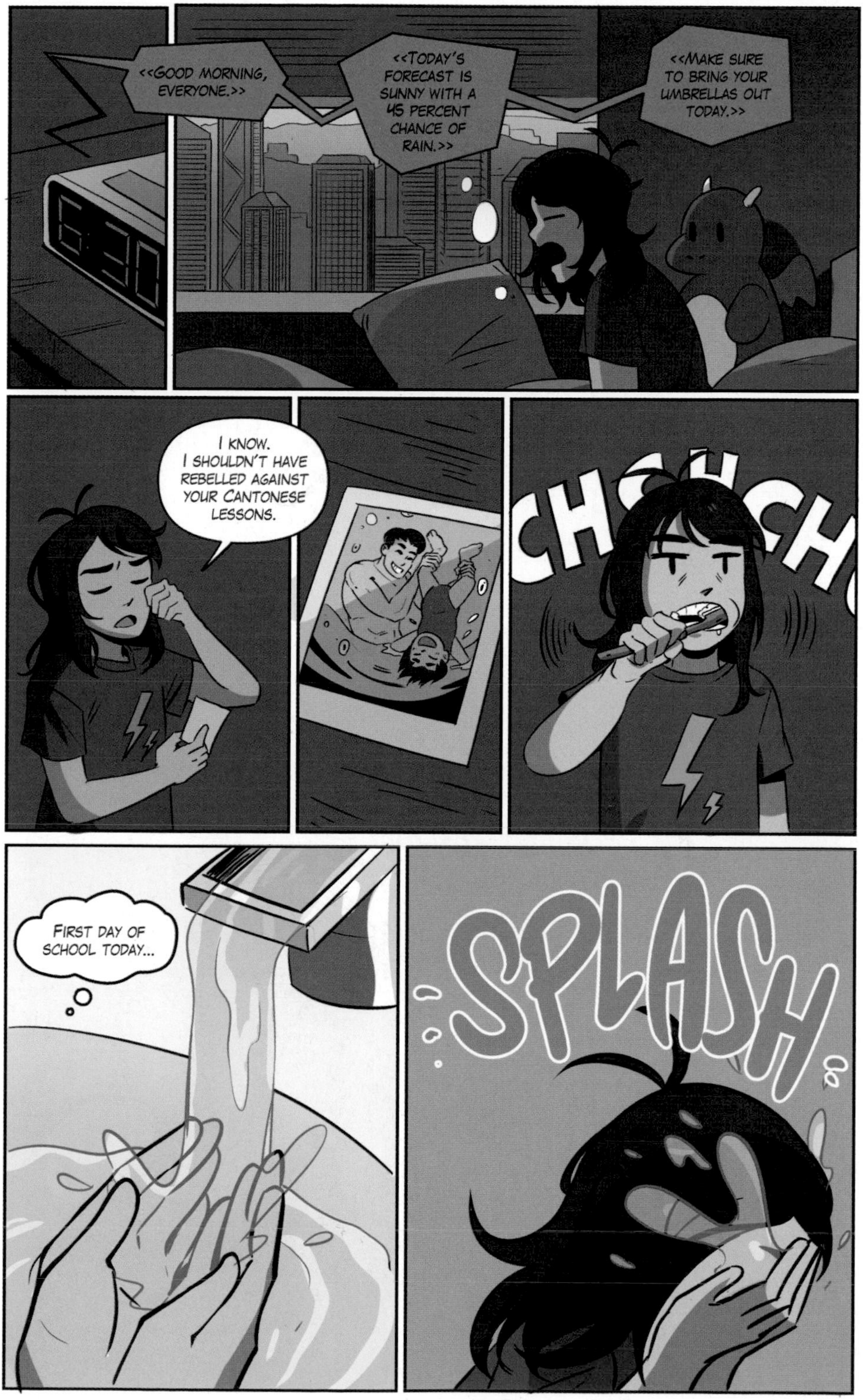
<<GOOD MORNING, EVERYONE.>>
<<TODAY'S FORECAST IS SUNNY WITH A 45 PERCENT CHANCE OF RAIN.>>
<<MAKE SURE TO BRING YOUR UMBRELLAS OUT TODAY.>>
I KNOW. I SHOULDN'T HAVE REBELLED AGAINST YOUR CANTONESE LESSONS.
CHCHCH
FIRST DAY OF SCHOOL TODAY...
SPLASH

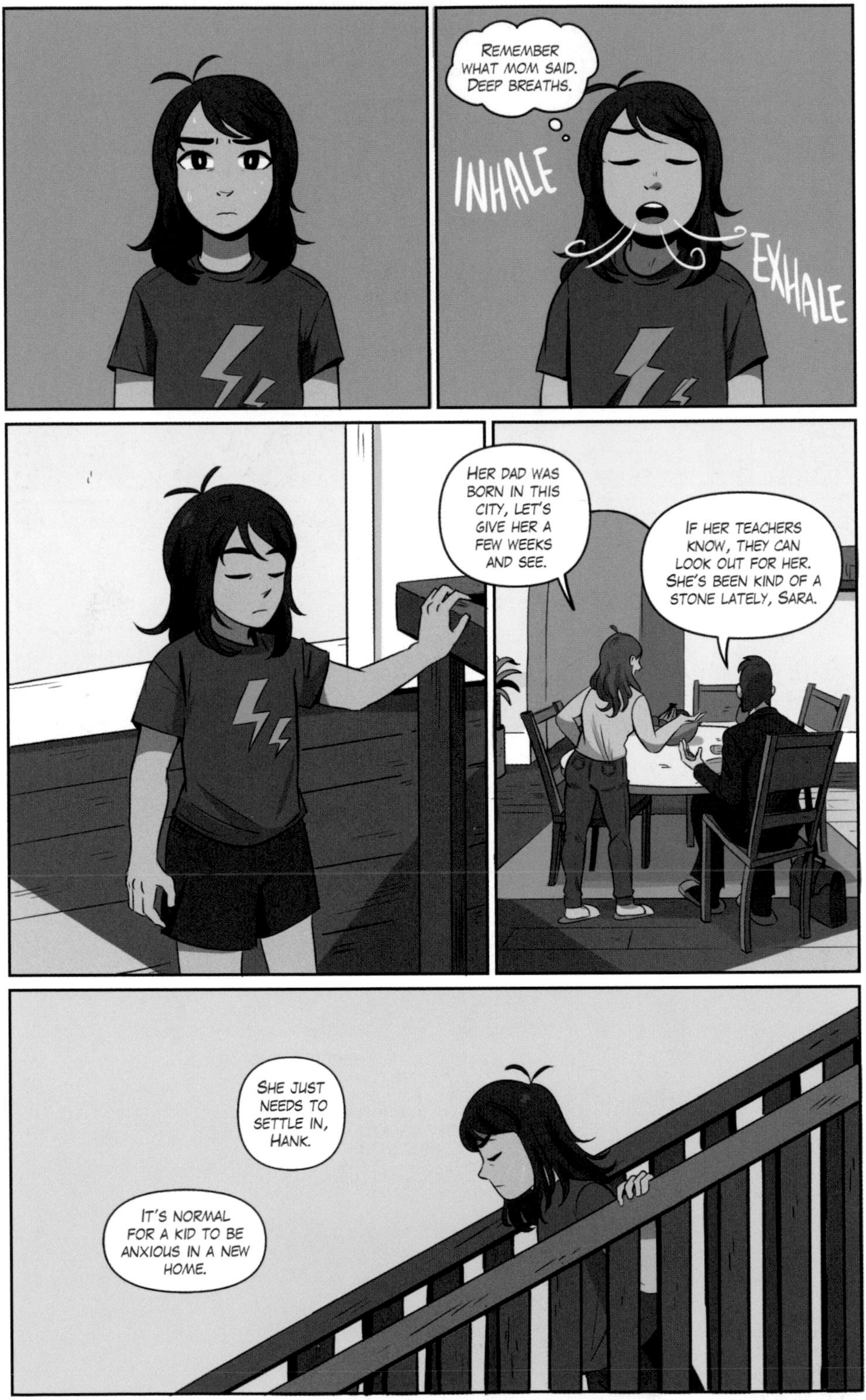
REMEMBER WHAT MOM SAID. DEEP BREATHS.
INHALE
EXHALE
HER DAD WAS BORN IN THIS CITY, LET'S GIVE HER A FEW WEEKS AND SEE.
IF HER TEACHERS KNOW, THEY CAN LOOK OUT FOR HER. SHE'S BEEN KIND OF A STONE LATELY, SARA.
SHE JUST NEEDS TO SETTLE IN, HANK.
IT'S NORMAL FOR A KID TO BE ANXIOUS IN A NEW HOME.

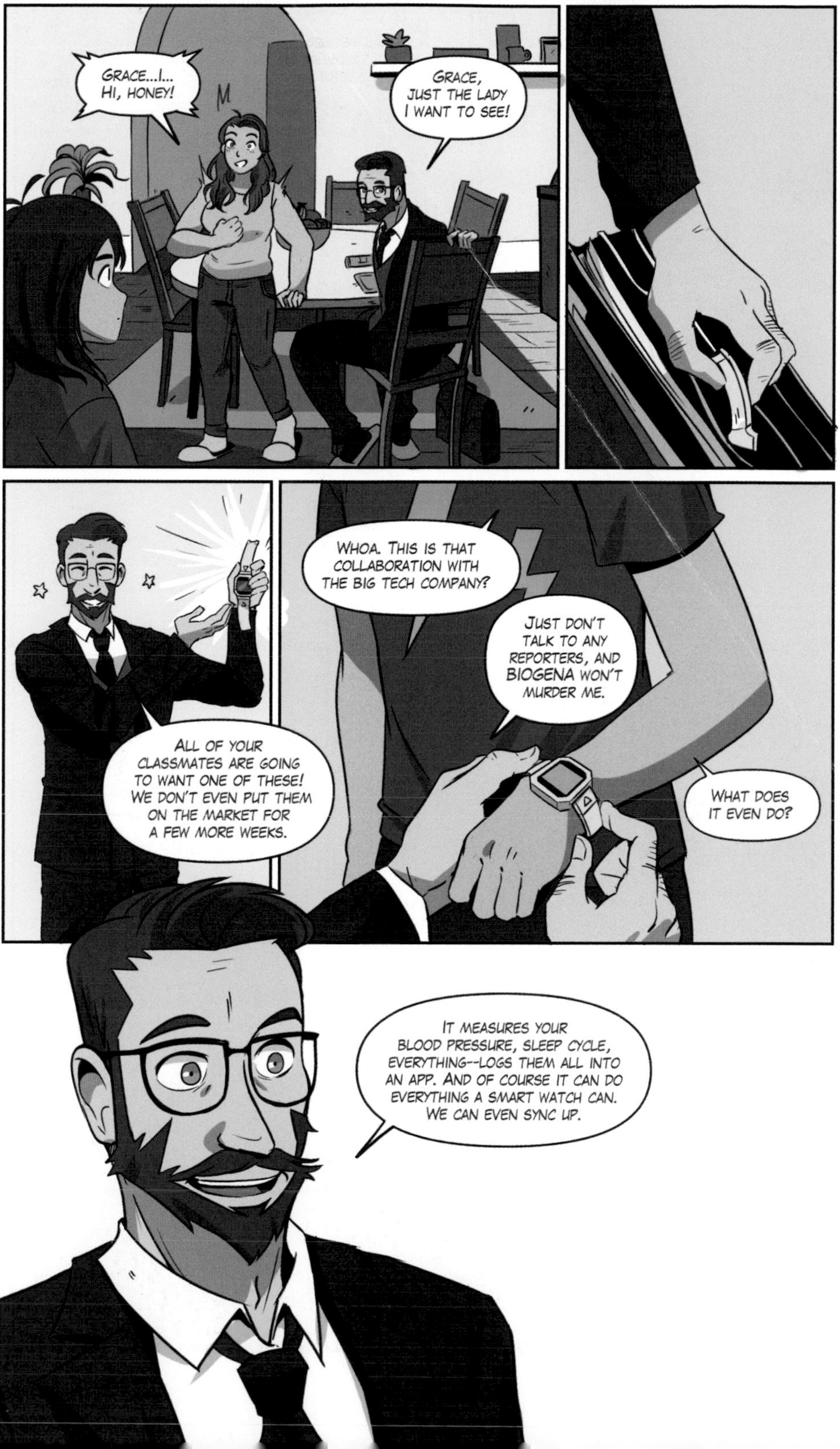
GRACE...I... HI, HONEY!
GRACE, JUST THE LADY I WANT TO SEE!
WHOA. THIS IS THAT COLLABORATION WITH THE BIG TECH COMPANY?
JUST DON'T TALK TO ANY REPORTERS, AND BIOGENA WON'T MURDER ME.
ALL OF YOUR CLASSMATES ARE GOING TO WANT ONE OF THESE! WE DON'T EVEN PUT THEM ON THE MARKET FOR A FEW MORE WEEKS.
WHAT DOES IT EVEN DO?
IT MEASURES YOUR BLOOD PRESSURE, SLEEP CYCLE, EVERYTHING--LOGS THEM ALL INTO AN APP. AND OF COURSE IT CAN DO EVERYTHING A SMART WATCH CAN. WE CAN EVEN SYNC UP.

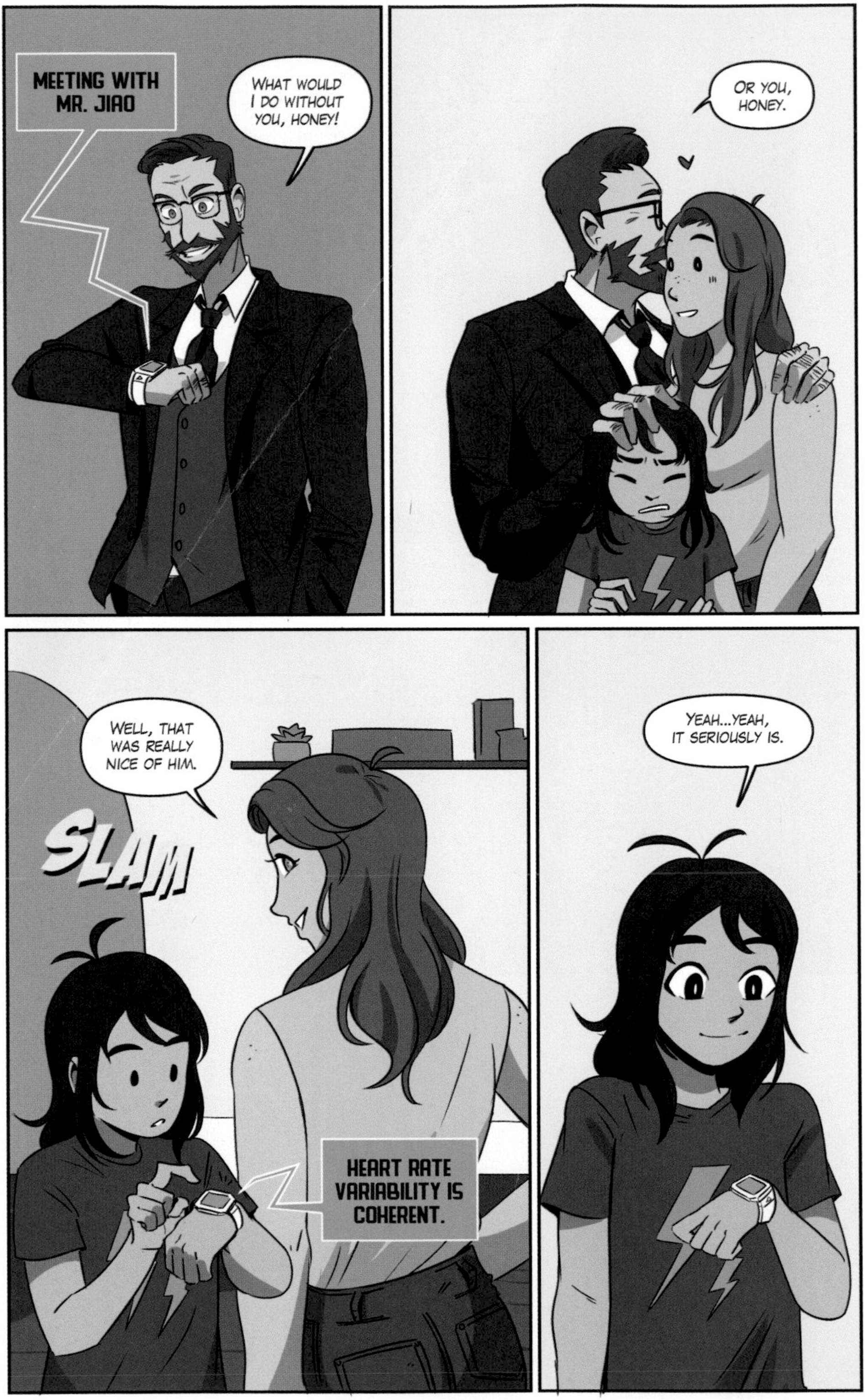
MEETING WITH MR. JIAO
WHAT WOULD I DO WITHOUT YOU, HONEY!
OR YOU, HONEY.
WELL, THAT WAS REALLY NICE OF HIM.
SLAM
HEART RATE VARIABILITY IS COHERENT.
YEAH...YEAH, IT SERIOUSLY IS.

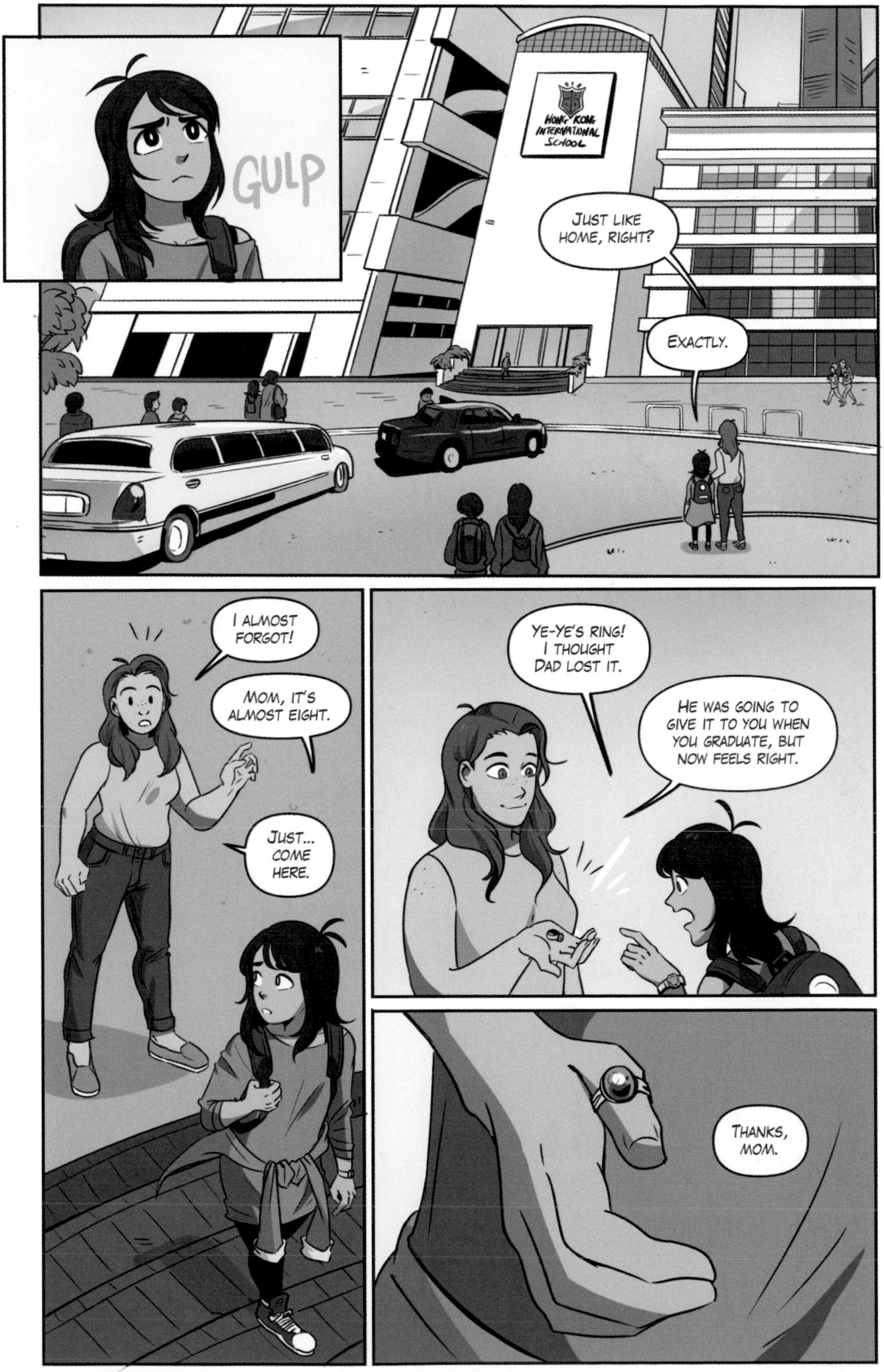
GULP
HONG KONG INTERNATIONAL SCHOOL
JUST LIKE HOME, RIGHT?
EXACTLY.
I ALMOST FORGOT!
MOM, IT'S ALMOST EIGHT.
JUST... COME HERE.
YE-YE'S RING! I THOUGHT DAD LOST IT.
HE WAS GOING TO GIVE IT TO YOU WHEN YOU GRADUATE, BUT NOW FEELS RIGHT.
THANKS, MOM.

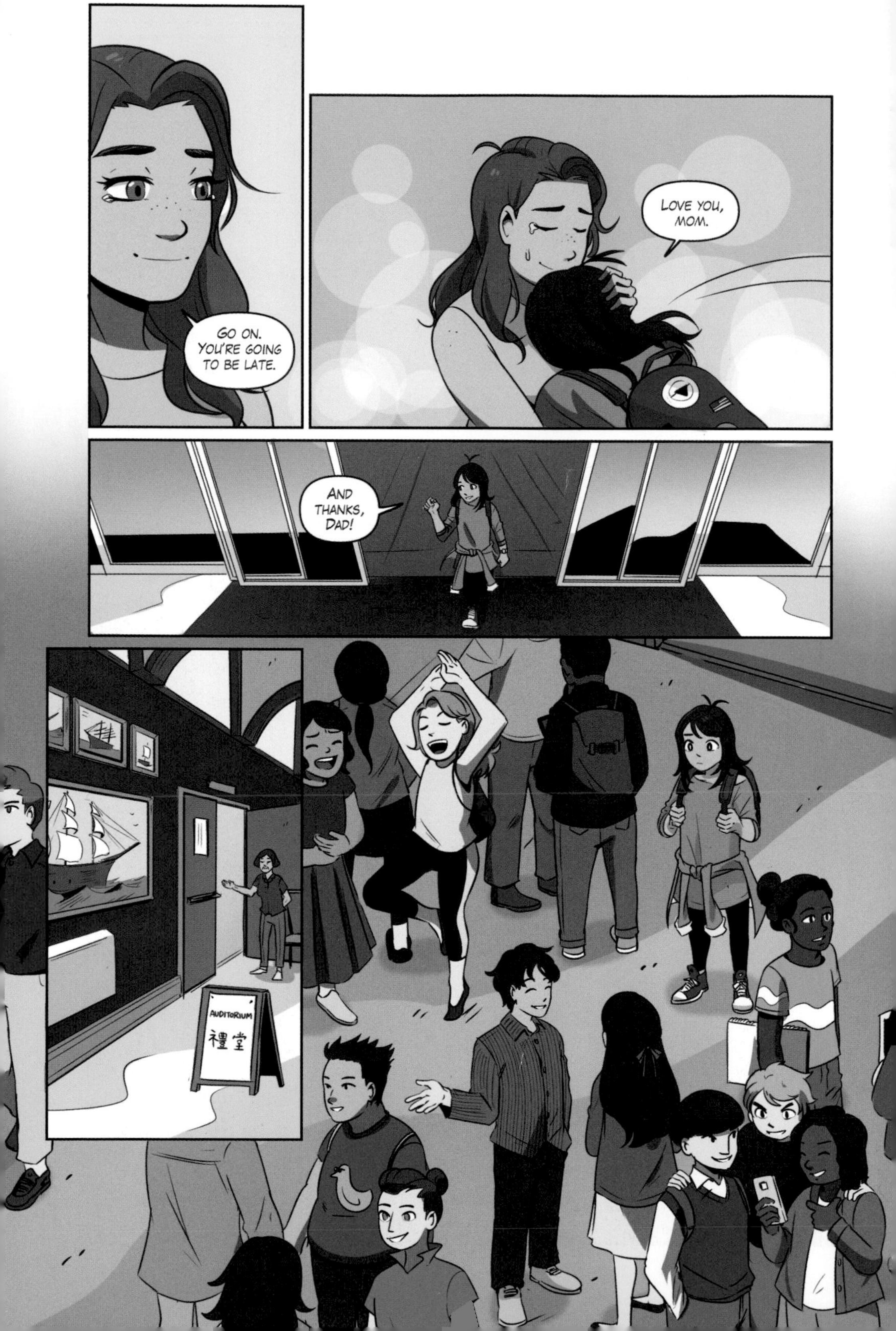
GO ON. YOU'RE GOING TO BE LATE.
LOVE YOU, MOM.
AND THANKS, DAD!
AUDITORIUM
禮堂

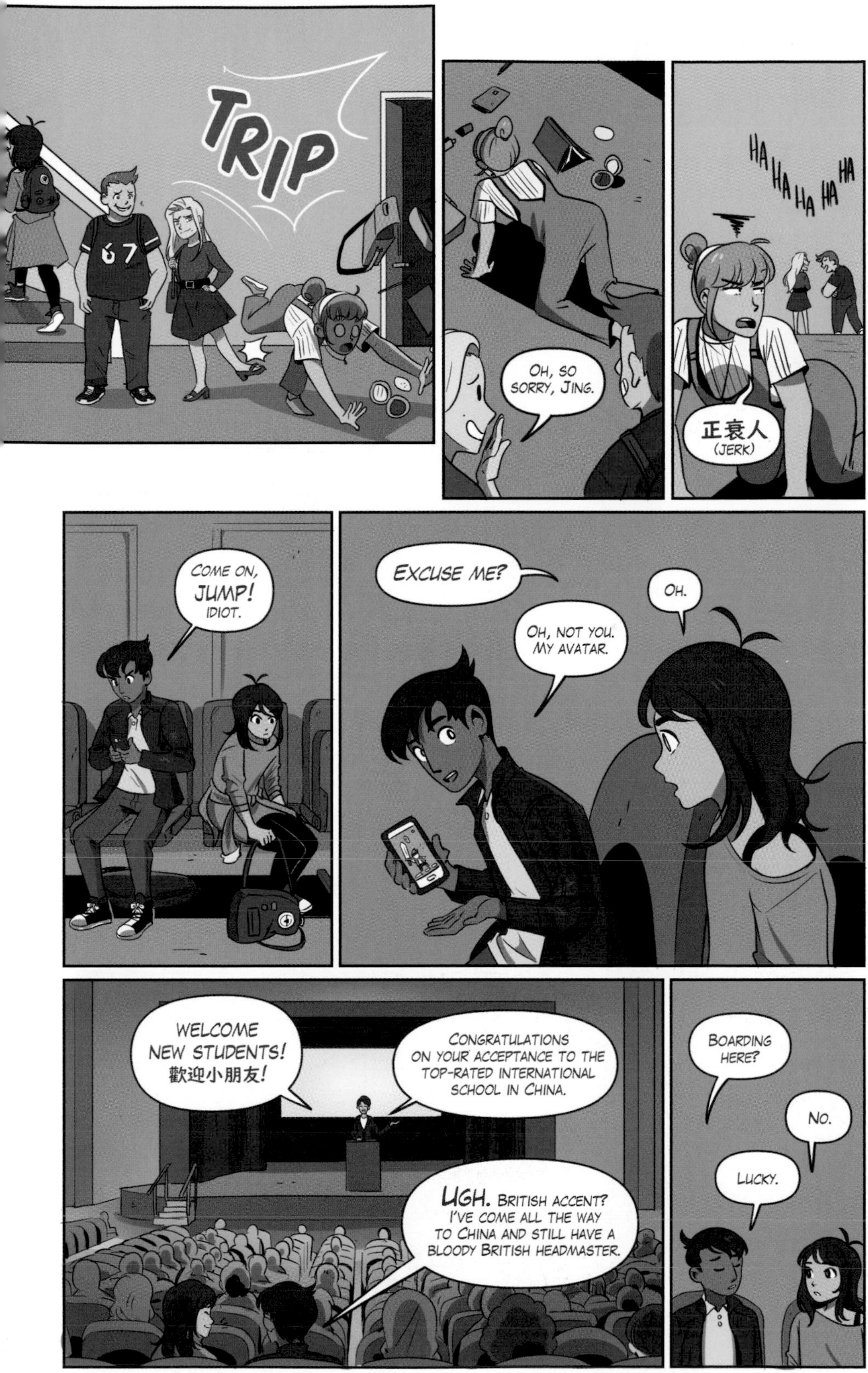
TRIP
OH, SO SORRY, JING.
HA HA HA HA HA
正衰人 (JERK)
COME ON, JUMP! IDIOT.
EXCUSE ME?
OH, NOT YOU. MY AVATAR.
OH.
WELCOME NEW STUDENTS! 歡迎小朋友!
CONGRATULATIONS ON YOUR ACCEPTANCE TO THE TOP-RATED INTERNATIONAL SCHOOL IN CHINA.
UGH. BRITISH ACCENT? I'VE COME ALL THE WAY TO CHINA AND STILL HAVE A BLOODY BRITISH HEADMASTER.
BOARDING HERE?
NO.
LUCKY.

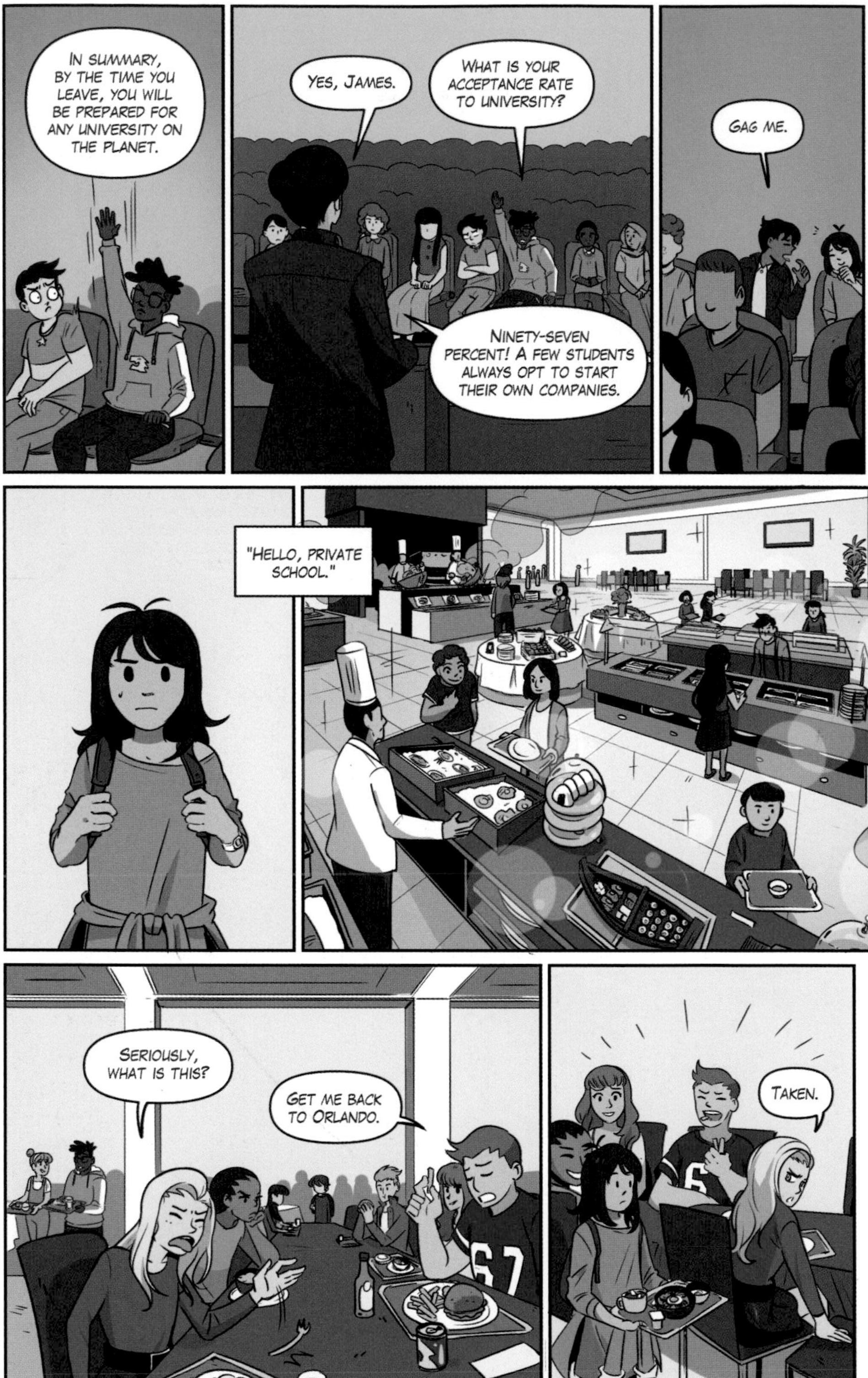
In summary, by the time you leave, you will be prepared for any university on the planet.
Yes, James.
What is your acceptance rate to university?
Ninety-seven percent! A few students always opt to start their own companies.
Gag me.
"Hello, private school."
Seriously, what is this?
Get me back to Orlando.
Taken.

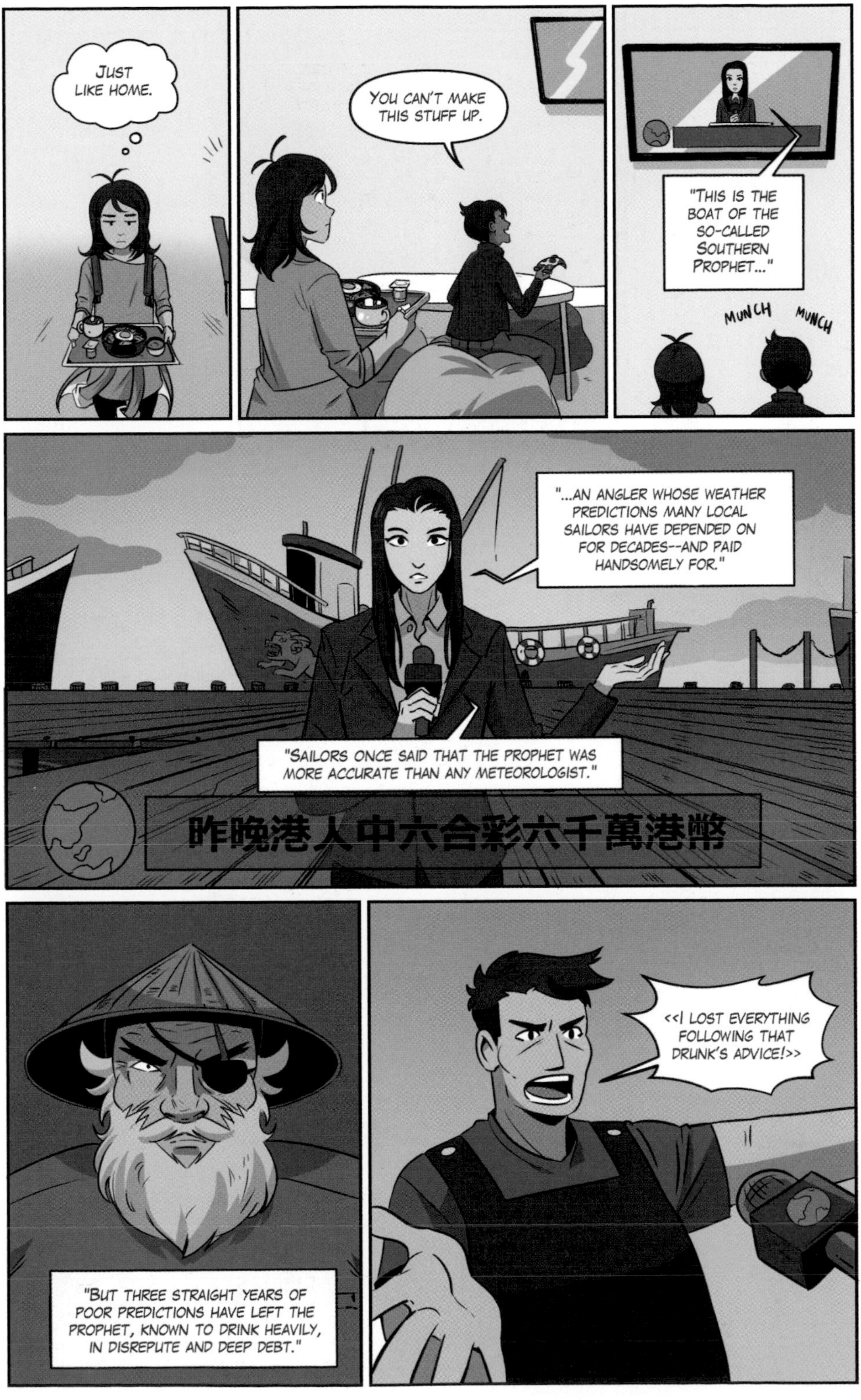

JUST LIKE HOME.
YOU CAN'T MAKE THIS STUFF UP.
"THIS IS THE BOAT OF THE SO-CALLED SOUTHERN PROPHET..."
MUNCH
MUNCH
"...AN ANGLER WHOSE WEATHER PREDICTIONS MANY LOCAL SAILORS HAVE DEPENDED ON FOR DECADES--AND PAID HANDSOMELY FOR."
"SAILORS ONCE SAID THAT THE PROPHET WAS MORE ACCURATE THAN ANY METEOROLOGIST."
昨晚港人中六合彩六千萬港幣
"BUT THREE STRAIGHT YEARS OF POOR PREDICTIONS HAVE LEFT THE PROPHET, KNOWN TO DRINK HEAVILY, IN DISREPUTE AND DEEP DEBT."
<<I LOST EVERYTHING FOLLOWING THAT DRUNK'S ADVICE!>>

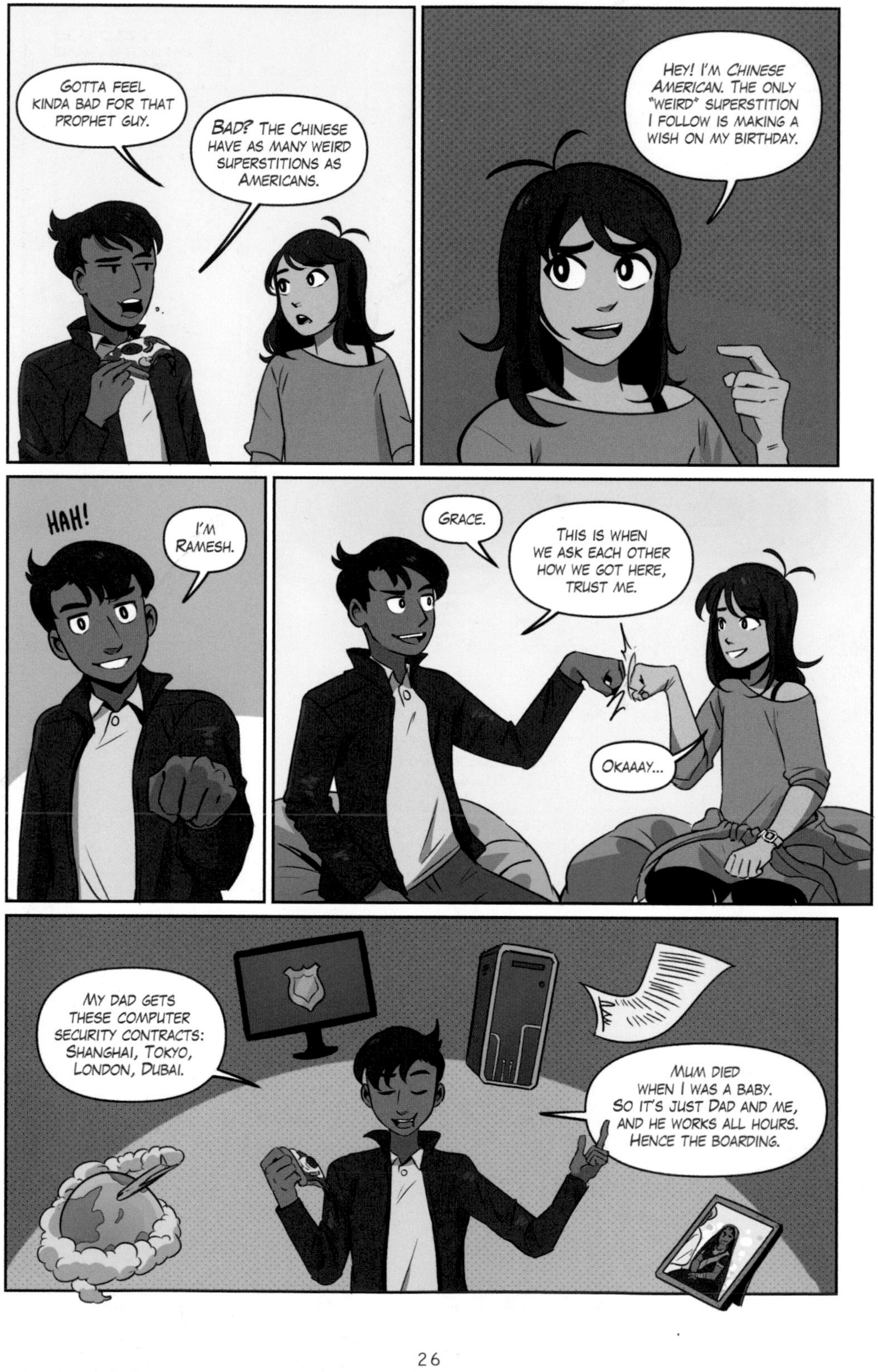
GOTTA FEEL KINDA BAD FOR THAT PROPHET GUY.
BAD? THE CHINESE HAVE AS MANY WEIRD SUPERSTITIONS AS AMERICANS.
HEY! I'M CHINESE AMERICAN. THE ONLY "WEIRD" SUPERSTITION I FOLLOW IS MAKING A WISH ON MY BIRTHDAY.
HAH!
I'M RAMESH.
GRACE.
THIS IS WHEN WE ASK EACH OTHER HOW WE GOT HERE, TRUST ME.
OKAAAY...
MY DAD GETS THESE COMPUTER SECURITY CONTRACTS: SHANGHAI, TOKYO, LONDON, DUBAI.
MUM DIED WHEN I WAS A BABY. SO IT'S JUST DAD AND ME, AND HE WORKS ALL HOURS. HENCE THE BOARDING.

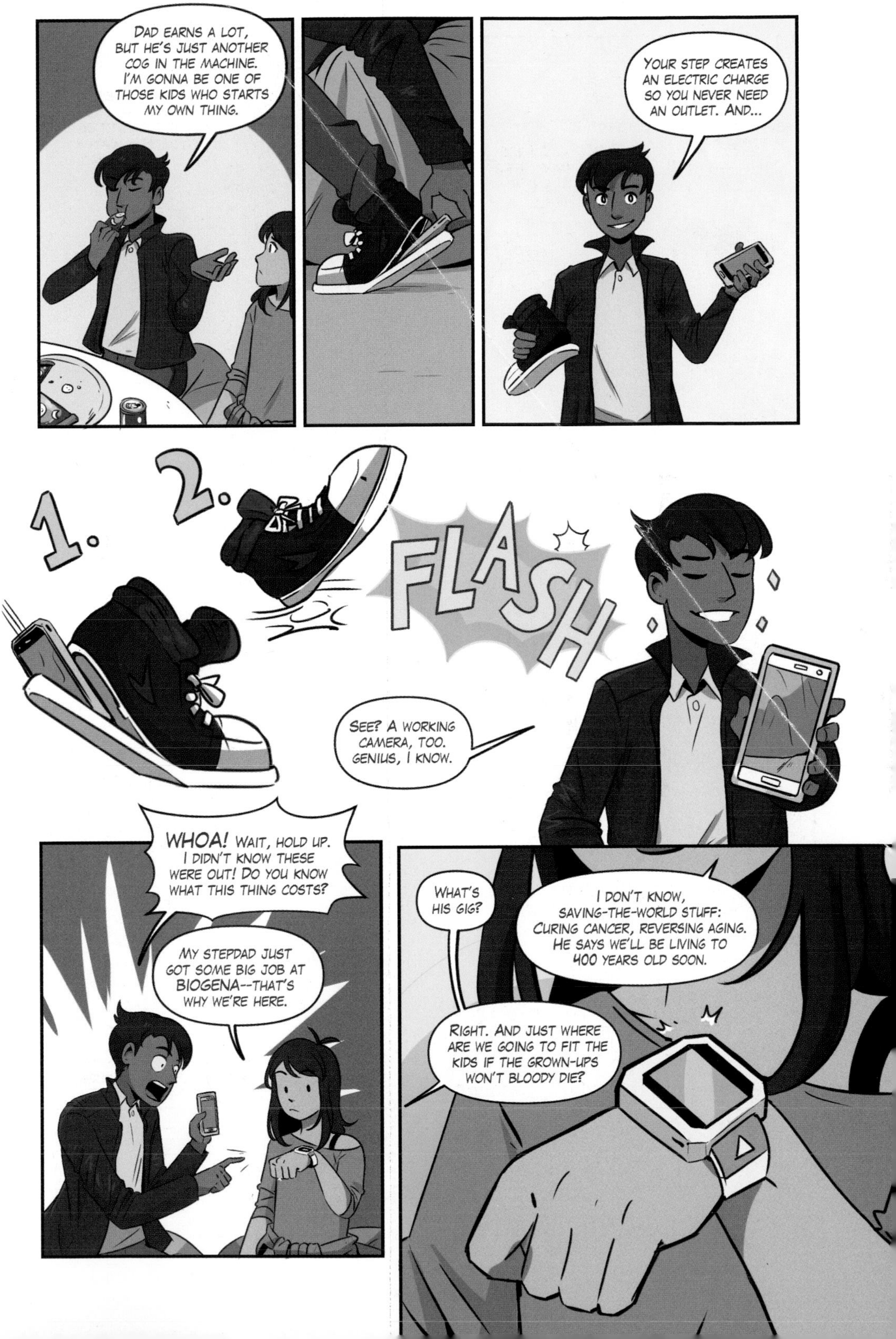
DAD EARNS A LOT, BUT HE'S JUST ANOTHER COG IN THE MACHINE. I'M GONNA BE ONE OF THOSE KIDS WHO STARTS MY OWN THING.
YOUR STEP CREATES AN ELECTRIC CHARGE SO YOU NEVER NEED AN OUTLET. AND...
1.
2.
FLASH
SEE? A WORKING CAMERA, TOO. GENIUS, I KNOW.
WHOA! WAIT, HOLD UP. I DIDN'T KNOW THESE WERE OUT! DO YOU KNOW WHAT THIS THING COSTS?
MY STEPDAD JUST GOT SOME BIG JOB AT BIOGENA--THAT'S WHY WE'RE HERE.
WHAT'S HIS GIG?
I DON'T KNOW, SAVING-THE-WORLD STUFF: CURING CANCER, REVERSING AGING. HE SAYS WE'LL BE LIVING TO 400 YEARS OLD SOON.
RIGHT. AND JUST WHERE ARE WE GOING TO FIT THE KIDS IF THE GROWN-UPS WON'T BLOODY DIE?

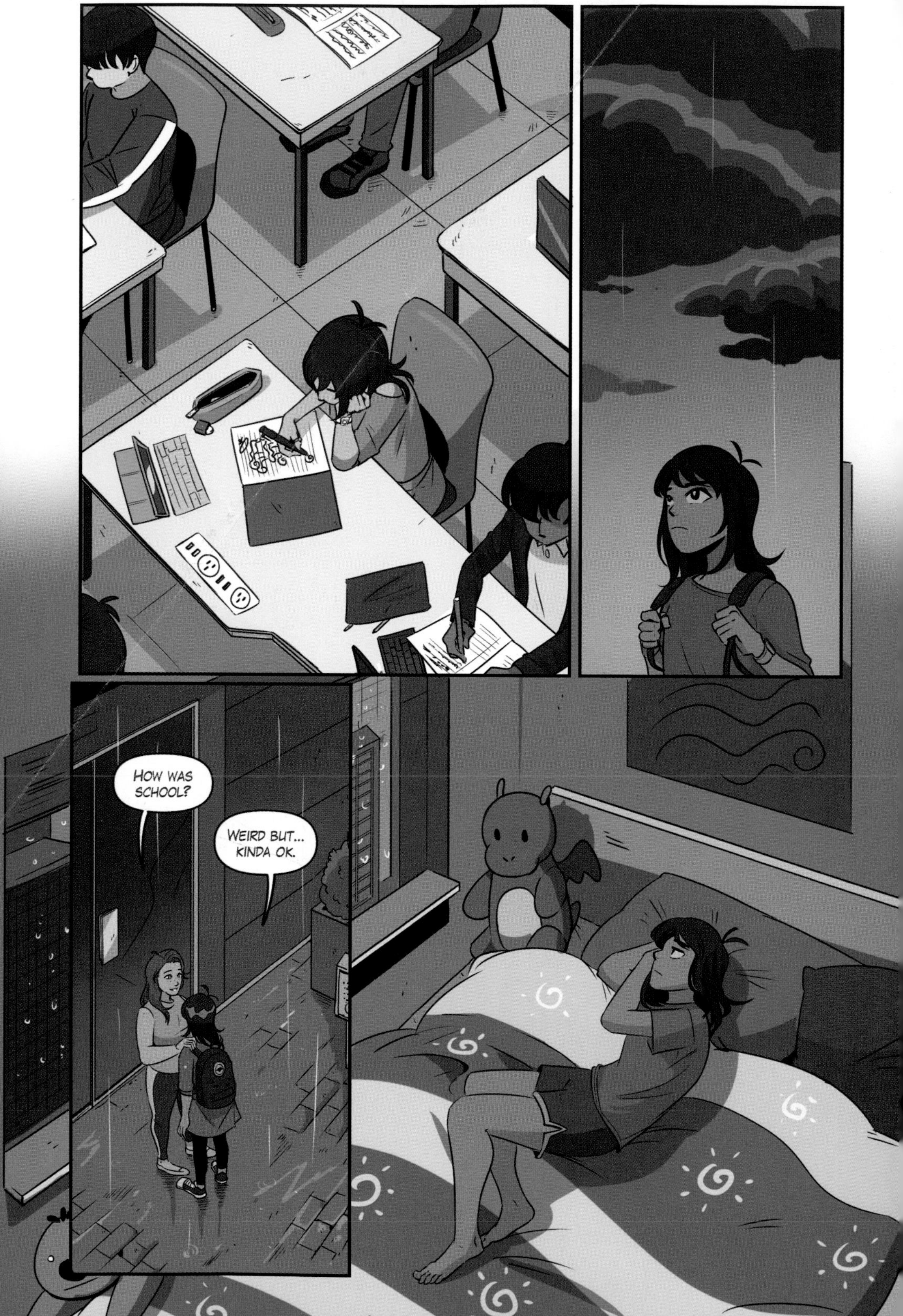
HOW WAS SCHOOL?
WEIRD BUT... KINDA OK.

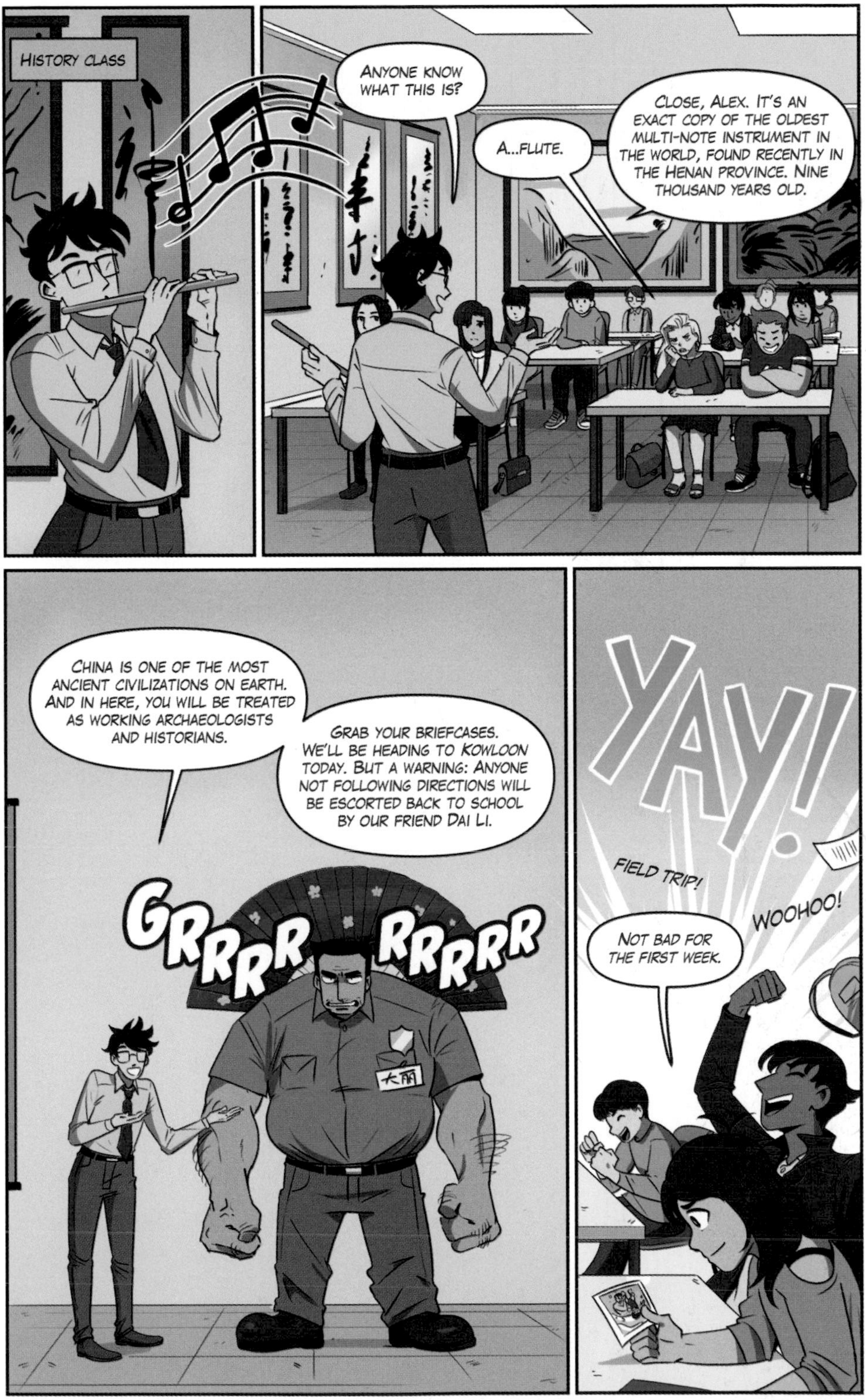
HISTORY CLASS
ANYONE KNOW WHAT THIS IS?
A...FLUTE.
CLOSE, ALEX. IT'S AN EXACT COPY OF THE OLDEST MULTI-NOTE INSTRUMENT IN THE WORLD, FOUND RECENTLY IN THE HENAN PROVINCE. NINE THOUSAND YEARS OLD.
CHINA IS ONE OF THE MOST ANCIENT CIVILIZATIONS ON EARTH. AND IN HERE, YOU WILL BE TREATED AS WORKING ARCHAEOLOGISTS AND HISTORIANS.
GRAB YOUR BRIEFCASES. WE'LL BE HEADING TO KOWLOON TODAY. BUT A WARNING: ANYONE NOT FOLLOWING DIRECTIONS WILL BE ESCORTED BACK TO SCHOOL BY OUR FRIEND DAI LI.
GRRRR RRRRR
大丽
YAY!
FIELD TRIP!
WOOHOO!
NOT BAD FOR THE FIRST WEEK.

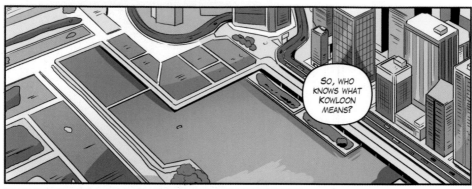

SO, WHO KNOWS WHAT KOWLOON MEANS?

HOW MANY MOUNTAINS DO YOU SEE?

EIGHT!

QUICK COUNTING, JAMES! A FACT THE EMPEROR PING NOTICED EIGHT CENTURIES AGO.

HOWEVER, KOWLOON MEANS "NINE DRAGONS." ANYONE?

HE WANTED TO NAME THE AREA EIGHT DRAGONS, BASED ON THE BELIEF THAT DRAGONS INHABITED MOUNTAINS, CAUSING VOLCANOES AND EARTHQUAKES.

THERE ARE ACTUALLY NINE MOUNTAINS?

BACK THEN, EVERY EMPEROR WAS SAID TO BE A DRAGON, TOO. SO WHEN PING COUNTED EIGHT, HIS COURTIER POINTED OUT THAT PING WAS THE NINTH.

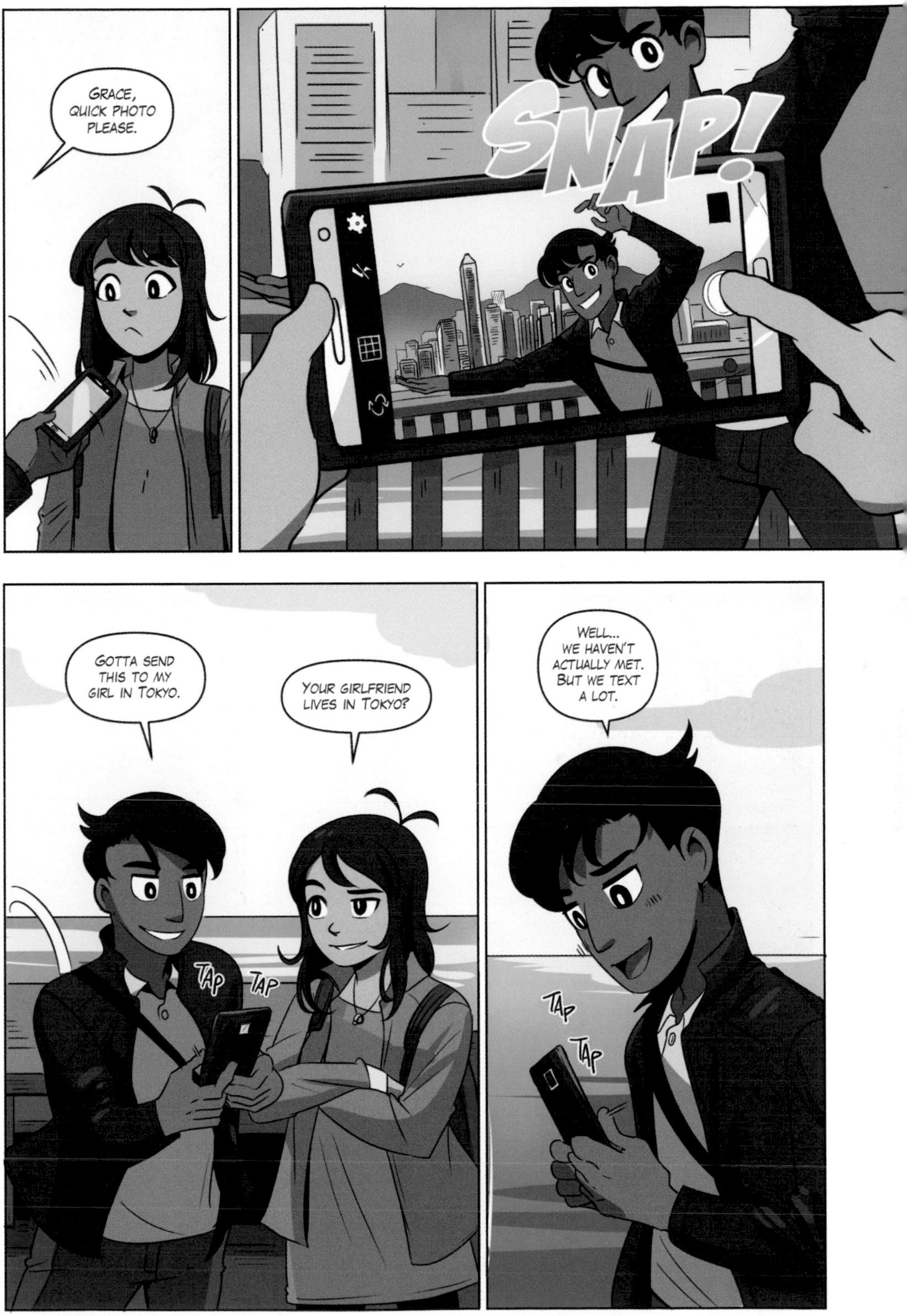
GRACE, QUICK PHOTO PLEASE.
SNAP!
GOTTA SEND THIS TO MY GIRL IN TOKYO.
YOUR GIRLFRIEND LIVES IN TOKYO?
TAP TAP
WELL... WE HAVEN'T ACTUALLY MET. BUT WE TEXT A LOT.
TAP TAP

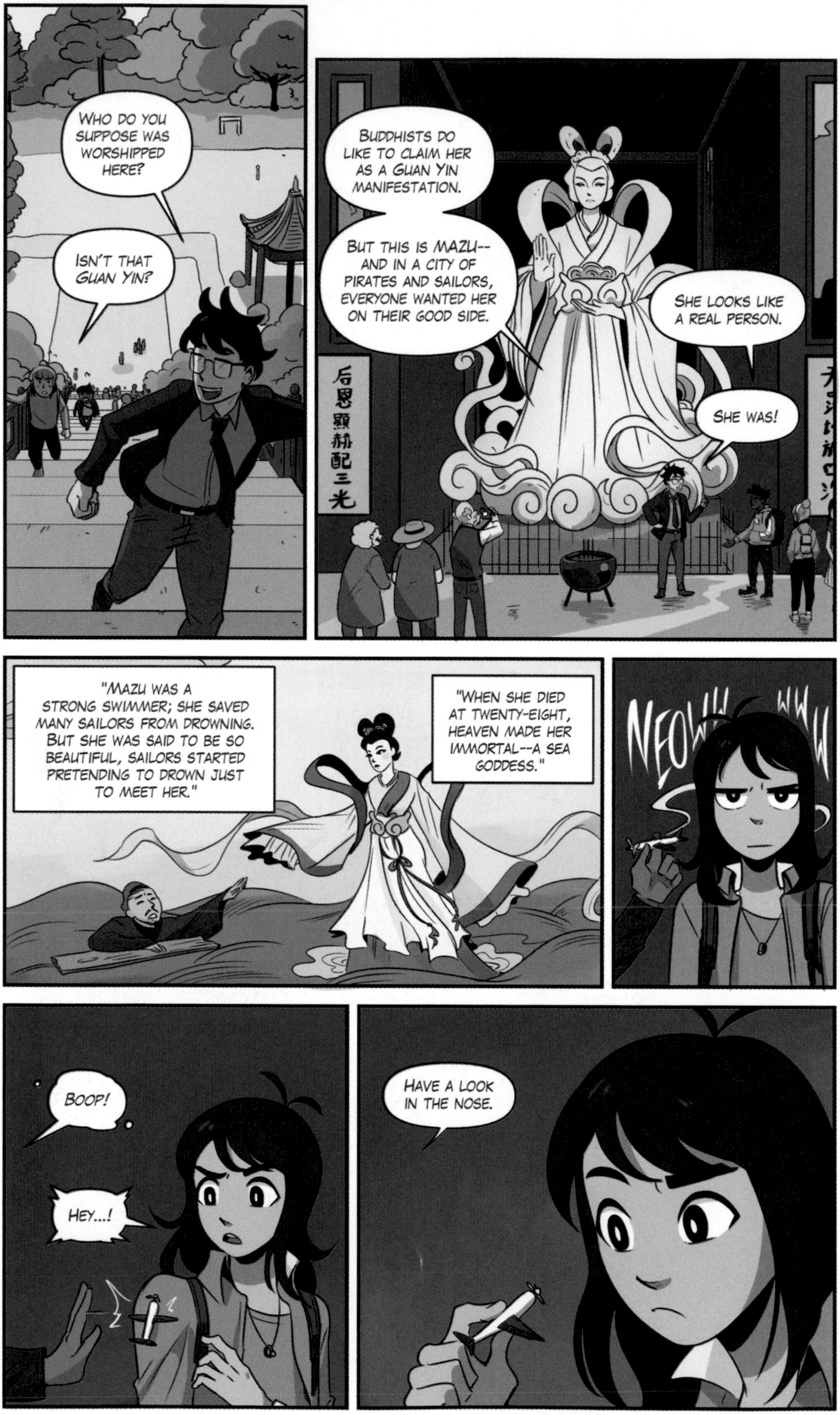
WHO DO YOU SUPPOSE WAS WORSHIPPED HERE?
ISN'T THAT GUAN YIN?
BUDDHISTS DO LIKE TO CLAIM HER AS A GUAN YIN MANIFESTATION.
BUT THIS IS MAZU-- AND IN A CITY OF PIRATES AND SAILORS, EVERYONE WANTED HER ON THEIR GOOD SIDE.
后恩顯赫配三光
SHE LOOKS LIKE A REAL PERSON.
SHE WAS!
"MAZU WAS A STRONG SWIMMER; SHE SAVED MANY SAILORS FROM DROWNING. BUT SHE WAS SAID TO BE SO BEAUTIFUL, SAILORS STARTED PRETENDING TO DROWN JUST TO MEET HER."
"WHEN SHE DIED AT TWENTY-EIGHT, HEAVEN MADE HER IMMORTAL--A SEA GODDESS."
BOOP!
HEY...!
HAVE A LOOK IN THE NOSE.

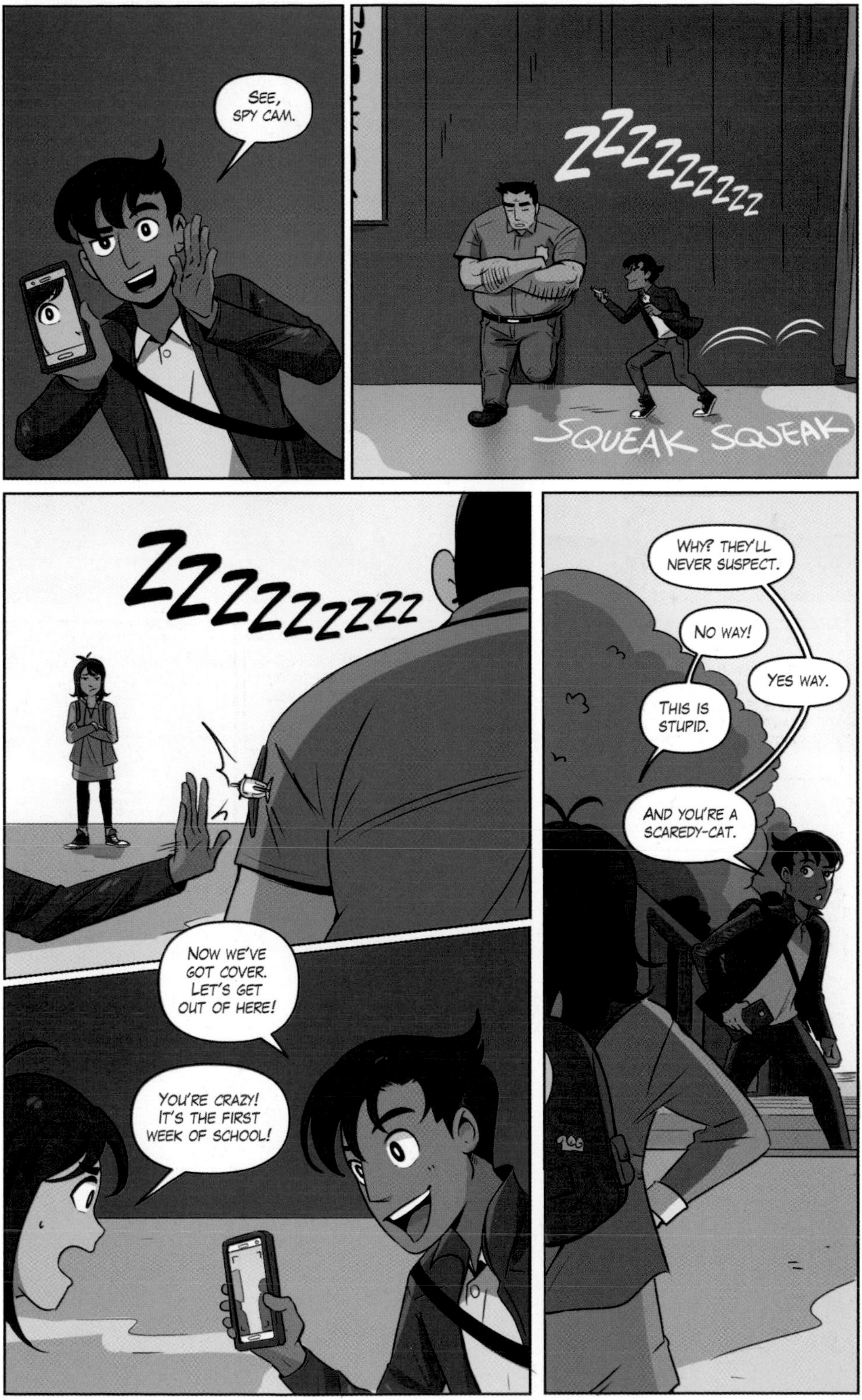
SEE, SPY CAM.
ZZZZZZZZZZ
SQUEAK SQUEAK
ZZZZZZZZZZ
NOW WE'VE GOT COVER. LET'S GET OUT OF HERE!
YOU'RE CRAZY! IT'S THE FIRST WEEK OF SCHOOL!
WHY? THEY'LL NEVER SUSPECT.
NO WAY!
YES WAY.
THIS IS STUPID.
AND YOU'RE A SCAREDY-CAT.

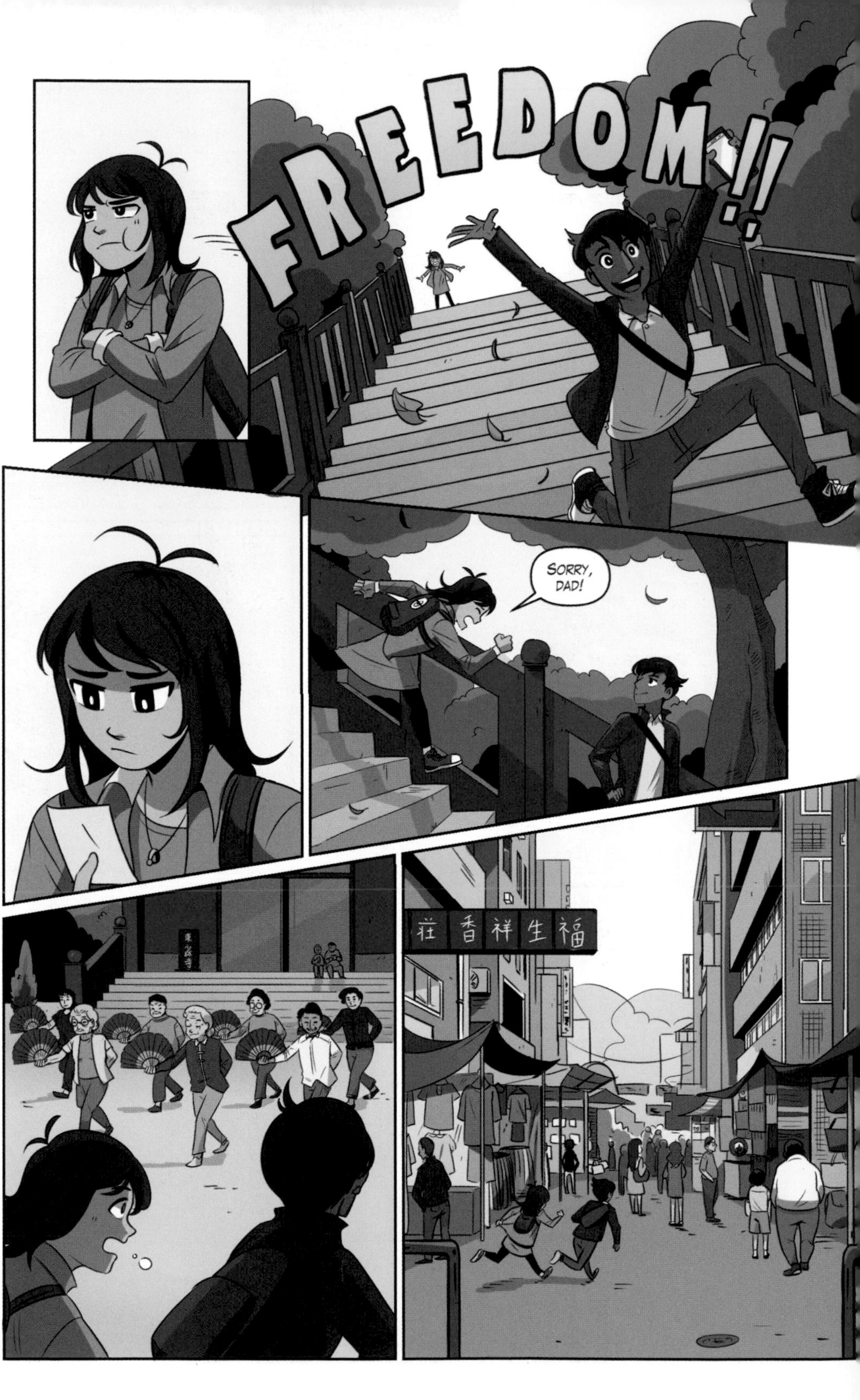
FREEDOM!!
SORRY, DAD!
莊香祥生福

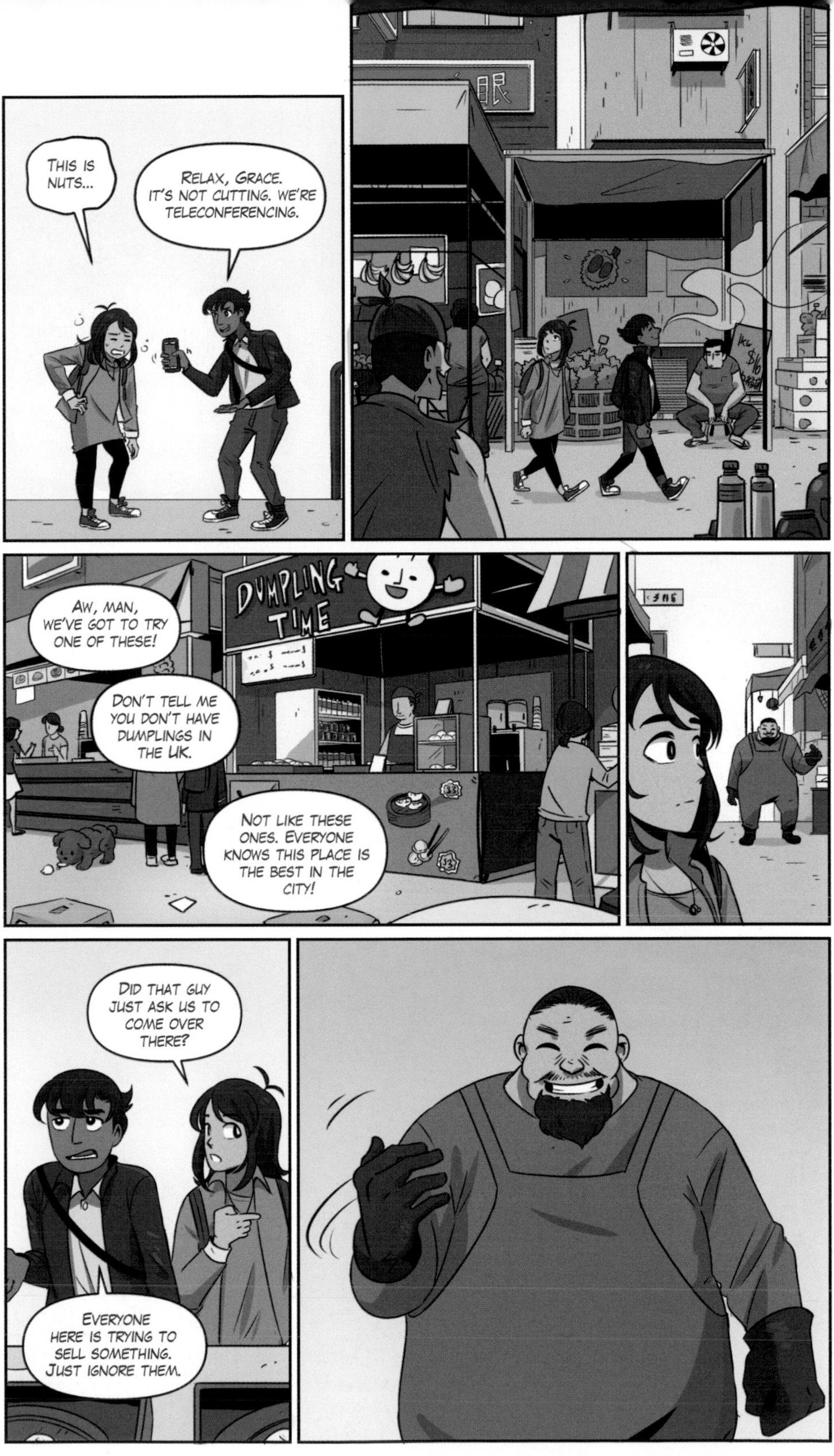

THIS IS NUTS...
RELAX, GRACE. IT'S NOT CUTTING. WE'RE TELECONFERENCING.
DUMPLING TIME
AW, MAN, WE'VE GOT TO TRY ONE OF THESE!
DON'T TELL ME YOU DON'T HAVE DUMPLINGS IN THE UK.
NOT LIKE THESE ONES. EVERYONE KNOWS THIS PLACE IS THE BEST IN THE CITY!
DID THAT GUY JUST ASK US TO COME OVER THERE?
EVERYONE HERE IS TRYING TO SELL SOMETHING. JUST IGNORE THEM.

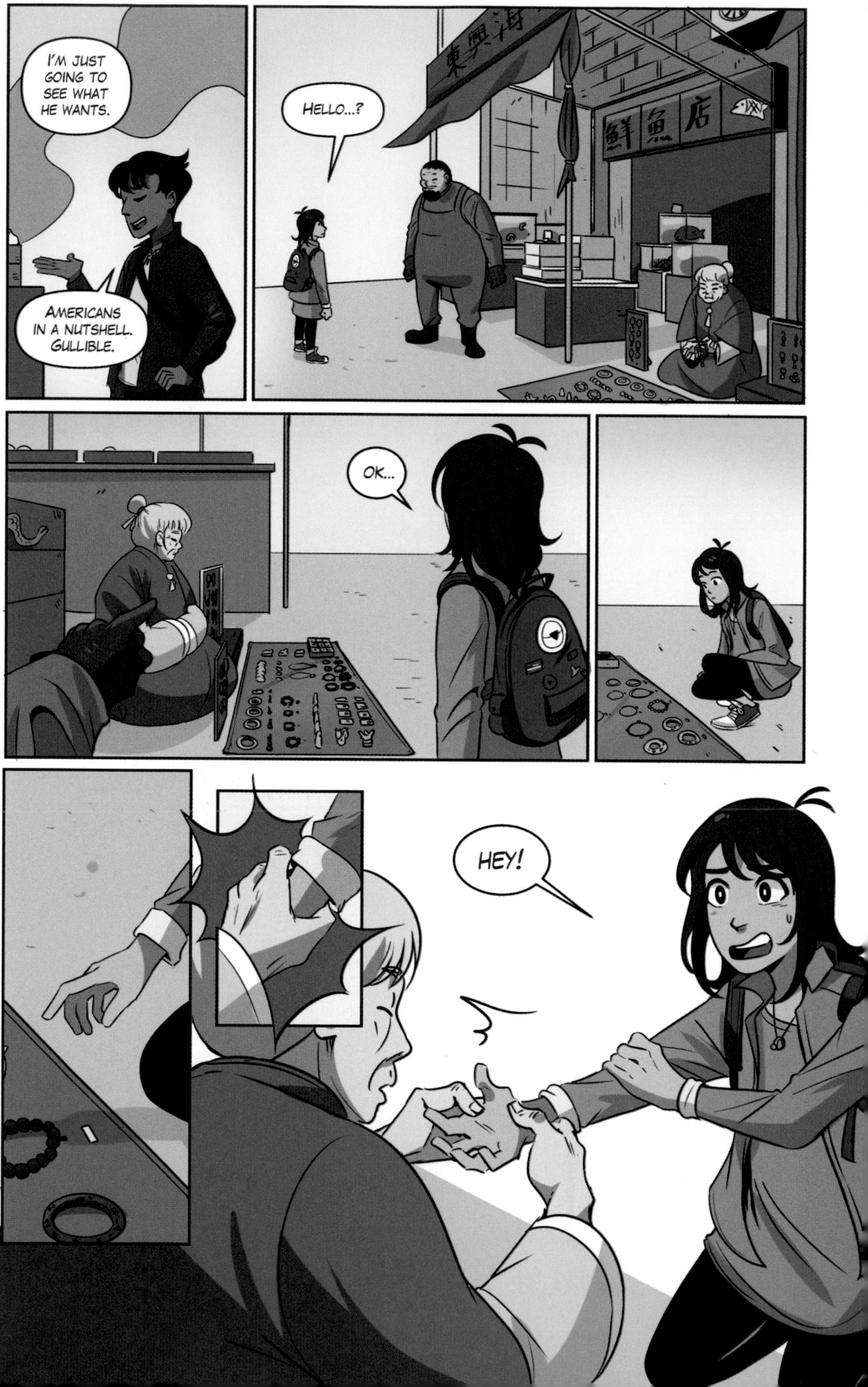
I'M JUST GOING TO SEE WHAT HE WANTS.
AMERICANS IN A NUTSHELL. GULLIBLE.
HELLO...?
鮮魚店
OK...
HEY!

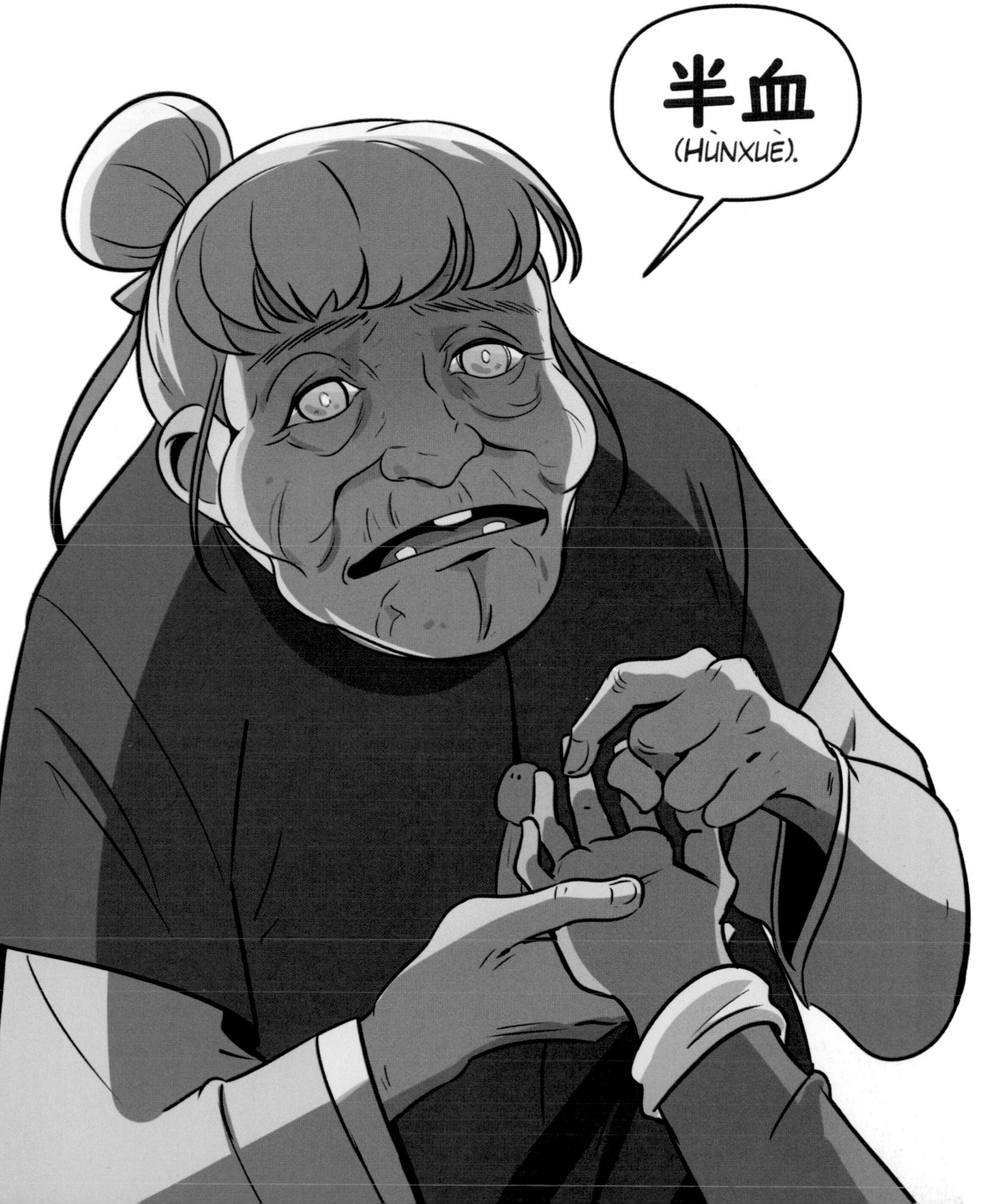
半血
(HÙNXUÈ).

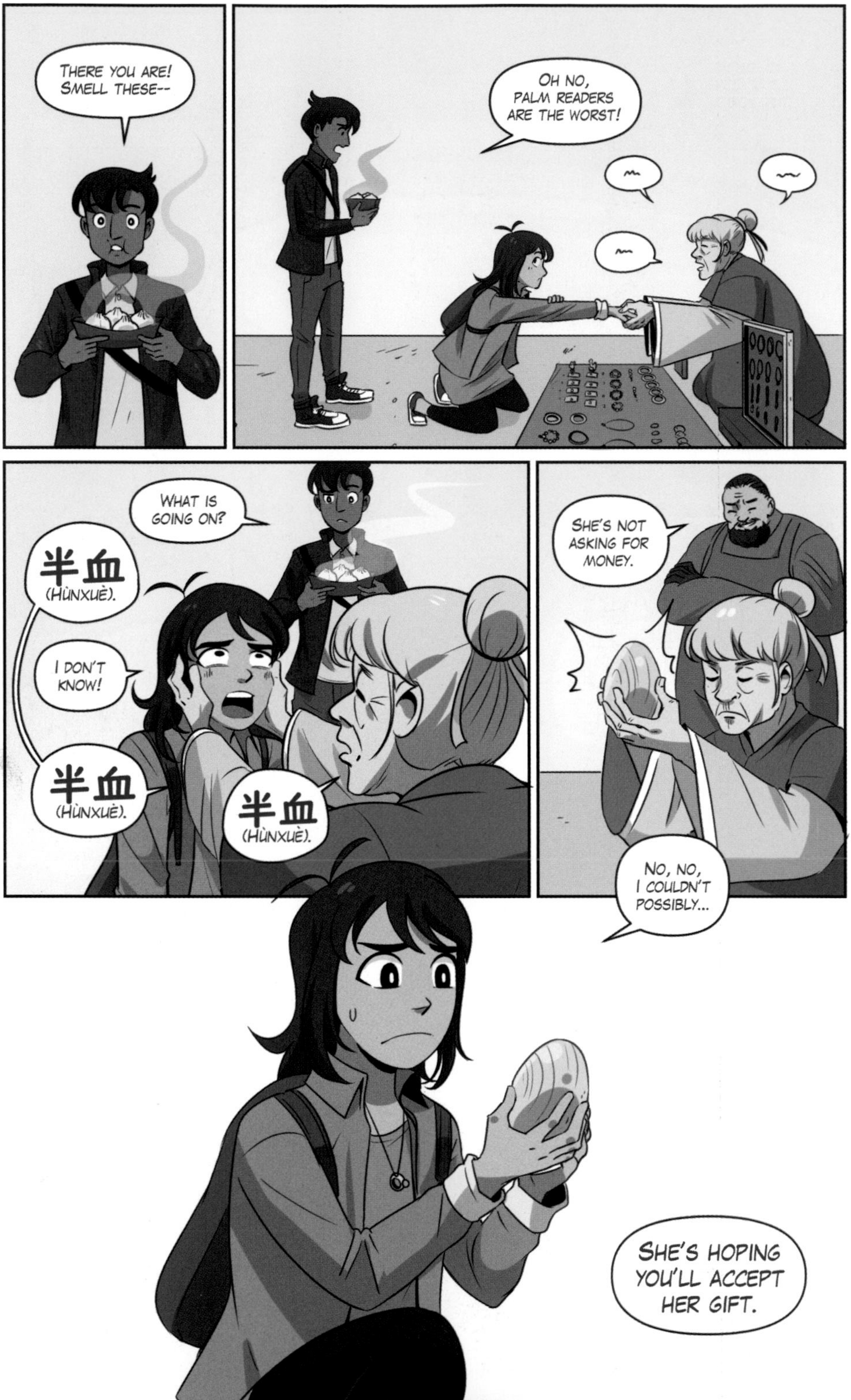
THERE YOU ARE! SMELL THESE--
OH NO, PALM READERS ARE THE WORST!
WHAT IS GOING ON?
半血 (HÙNXUÈ).
I DON'T KNOW!
半血 (HÙNXUÈ).
半血 (HÙNXUÈ).
SHE'S NOT ASKING FOR MONEY.
NO, NO, I COULDN'T POSSIBLY...
SHE'S HOPING YOU'LL ACCEPT HER GIFT.

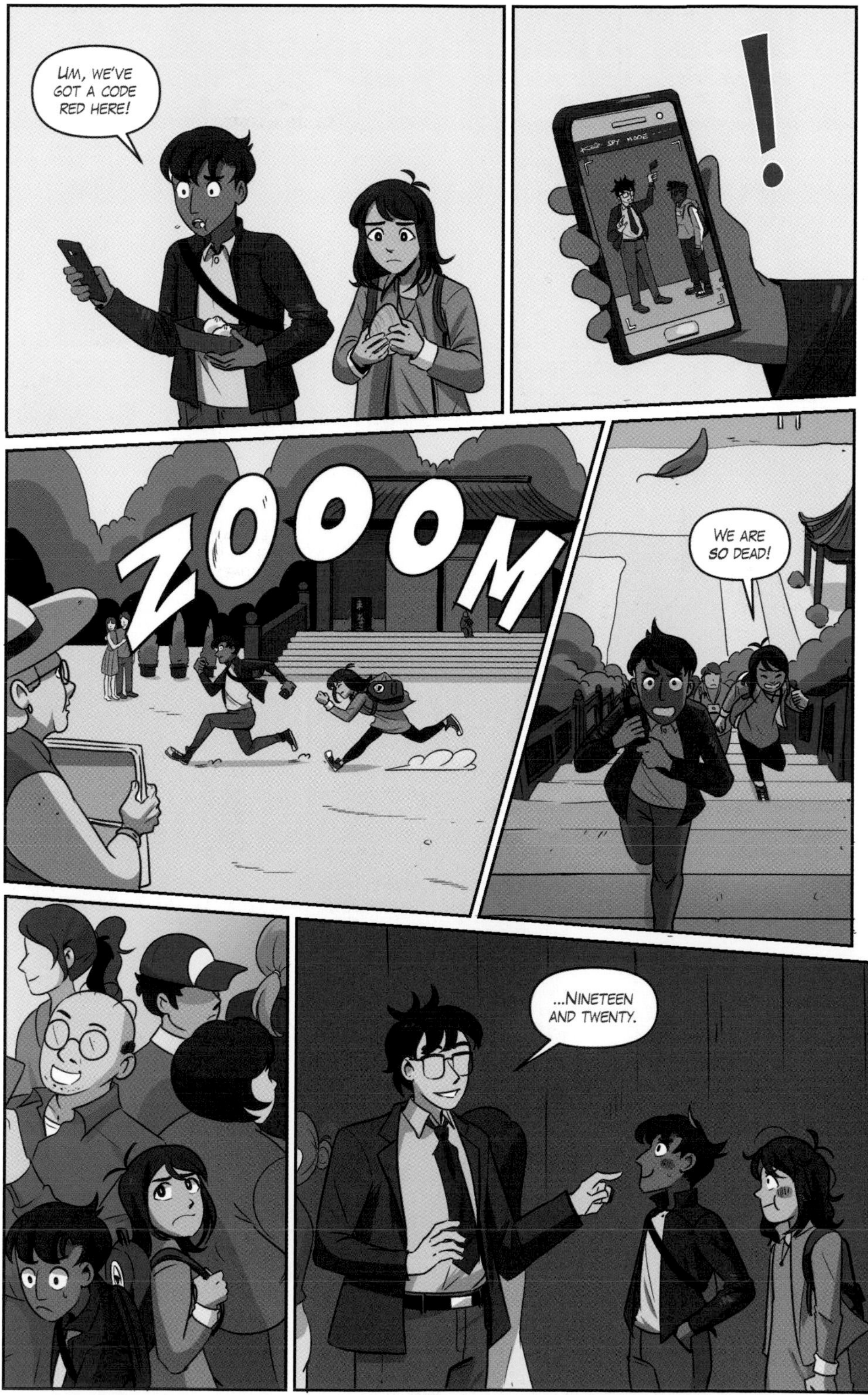
UM, WE'VE GOT A CODE RED HERE!
!
ZOOOM
WE ARE SO DEAD!
...NINETEEN AND TWENTY.

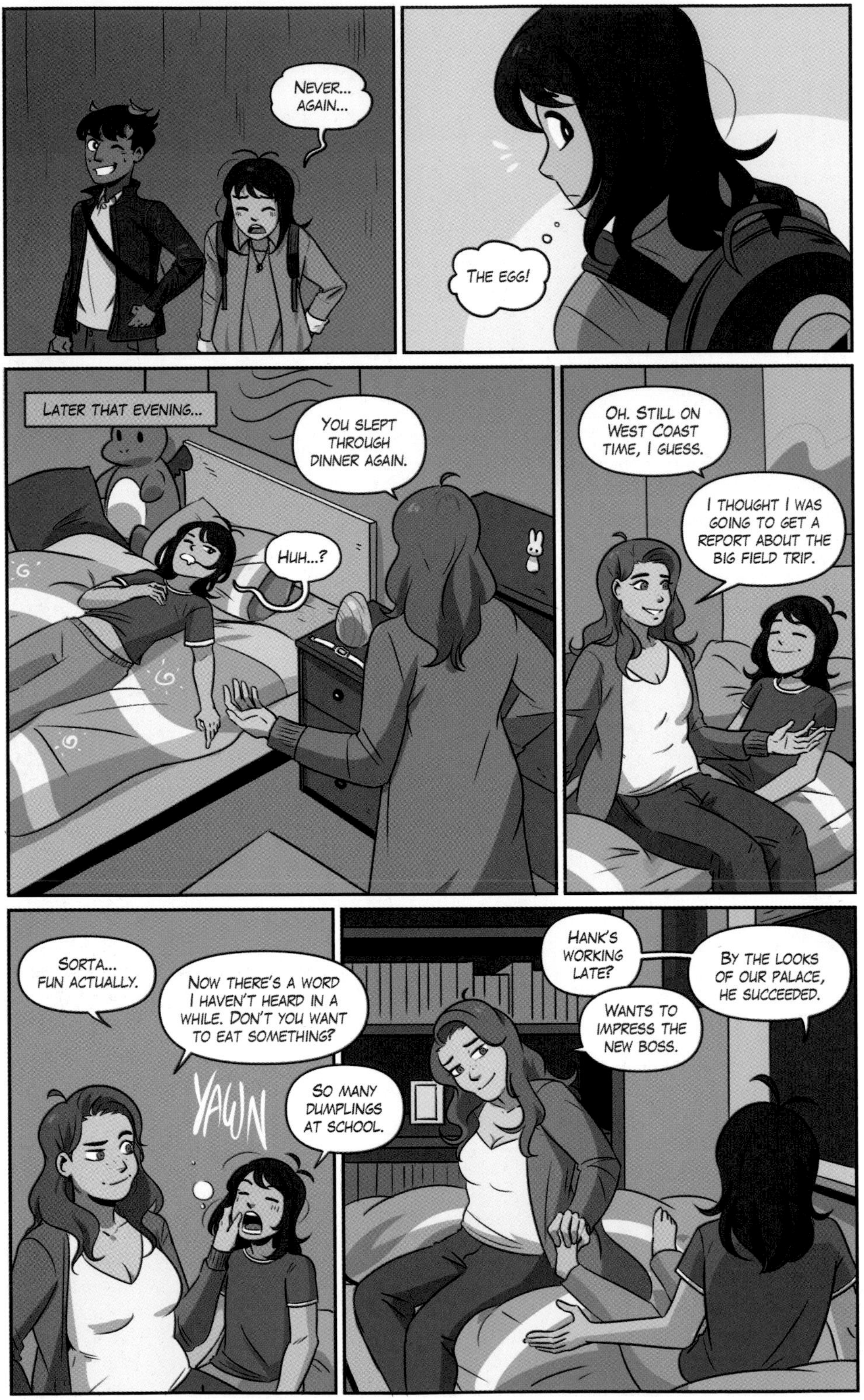
NEVER... AGAIN...
THE EGG!
LATER THAT EVENING...
YOU SLEPT THROUGH DINNER AGAIN.
HUH...?
OH. STILL ON WEST COAST TIME, I GUESS.
I THOUGHT I WAS GOING TO GET A REPORT ABOUT THE BIG FIELD TRIP.
SORTA... FUN ACTUALLY.
NOW THERE'S A WORD I HAVEN'T HEARD IN A WHILE. DON'T YOU WANT TO EAT SOMETHING?
YAWN
SO MANY DUMPLINGS AT SCHOOL.
HANK'S WORKING LATE?
WANTS TO IMPRESS THE NEW BOSS.
BY THE LOOKS OF OUR PALACE, HE SUCCEEDED.

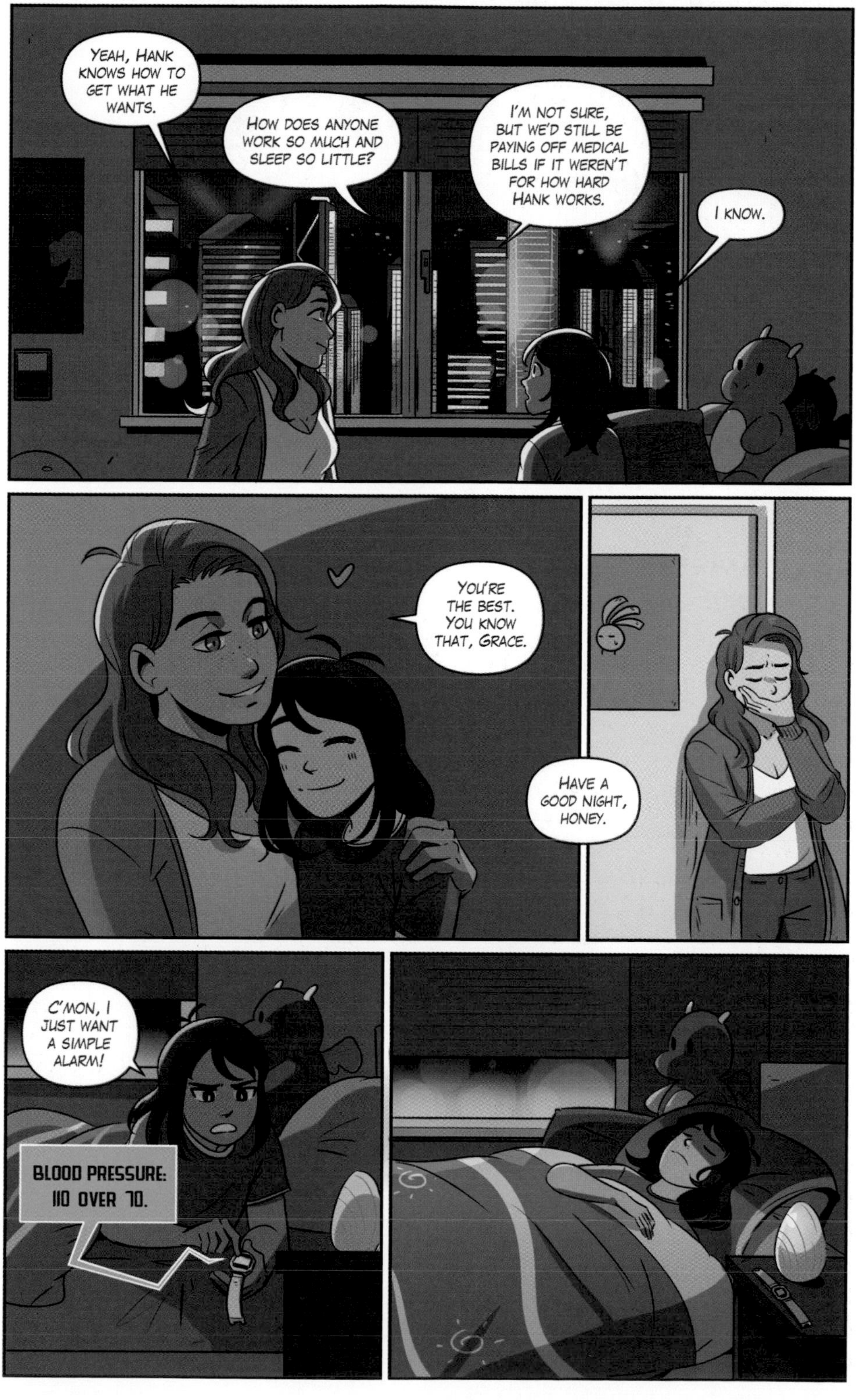
YEAH, HANK KNOWS HOW TO GET WHAT HE WANTS.
HOW DOES ANYONE WORK SO MUCH AND SLEEP SO LITTLE?
I'M NOT SURE, BUT WE'D STILL BE PAYING OFF MEDICAL BILLS IF IT WEREN'T FOR HOW HARD HANK WORKS.
I KNOW.
YOU'RE THE BEST. YOU KNOW THAT, GRACE.
HAVE A GOOD NIGHT, HONEY.
C'MON, I JUST WANT A SIMPLE ALARM!
BLOOD PRESSURE: 110 OVER 70.

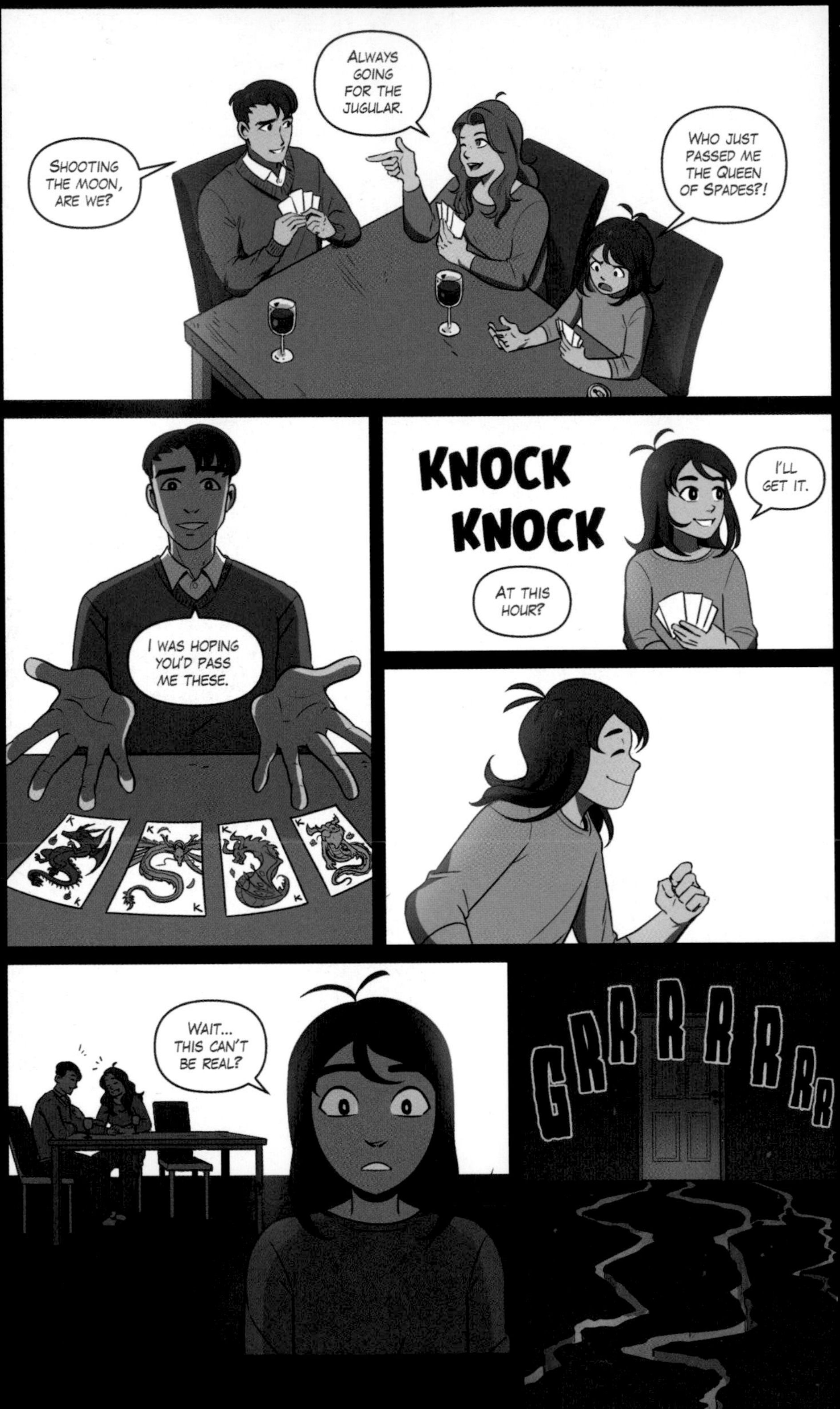
SHOOTING THE MOON, ARE WE?
ALWAYS GOING FOR THE JUGULAR.
WHO JUST PASSED ME THE QUEEN OF SPADES?!
I WAS HOPING YOU'D PASS ME THESE.
KNOCK KNOCK
I'LL GET IT.
AT THIS HOUR?
WAIT... THIS CAN'T BE REAL?
GRRRRRRR

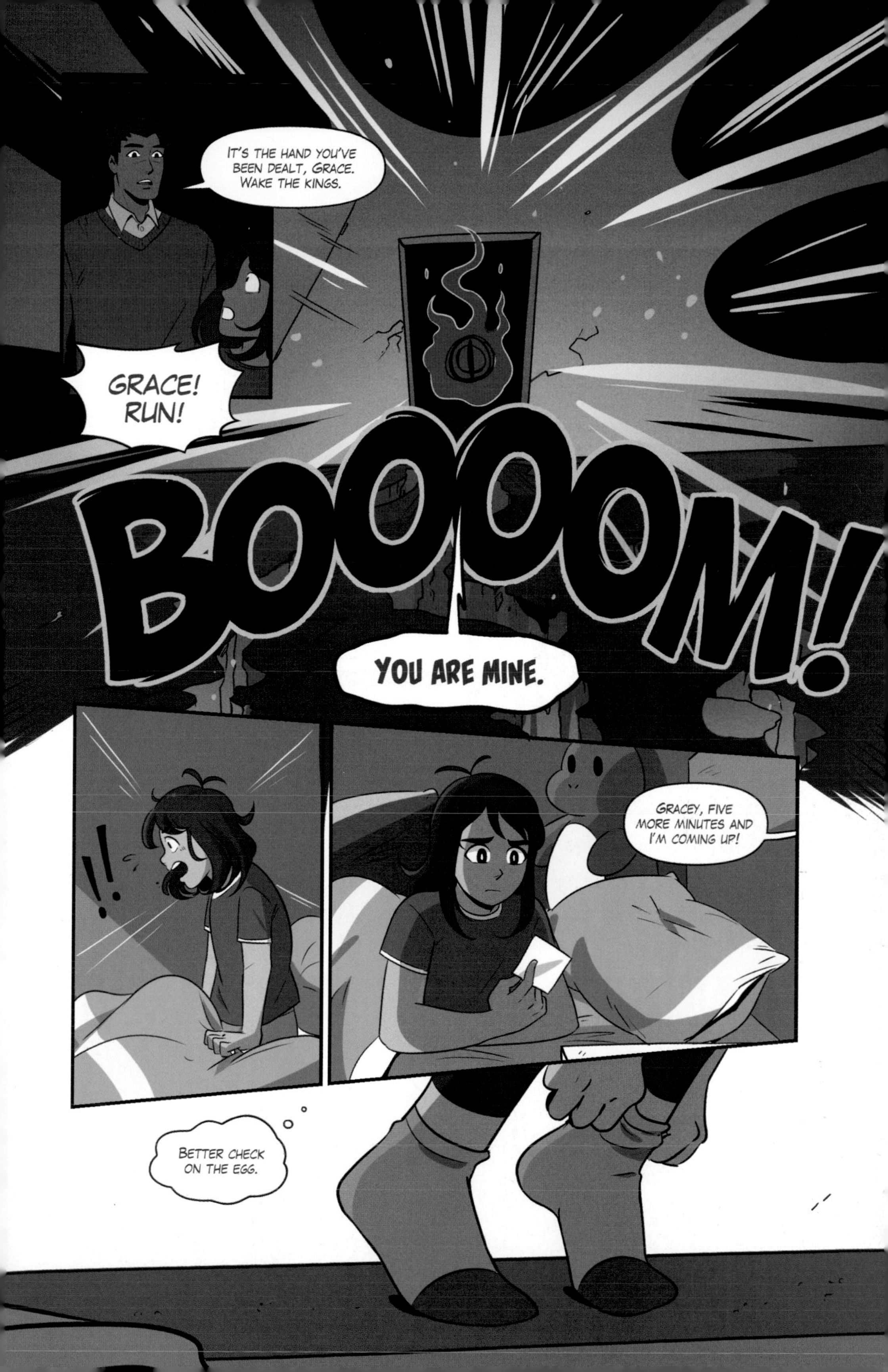
IT'S THE HAND YOU'VE BEEN DEALT, GRACE. WAKE THE KINGS.
GRACE! RUN!
BOOOOM!
YOU ARE MINE.
GRACEY, FIVE MORE MINUTES AND I'M COMING UP!
BETTER CHECK ON THE EGG.

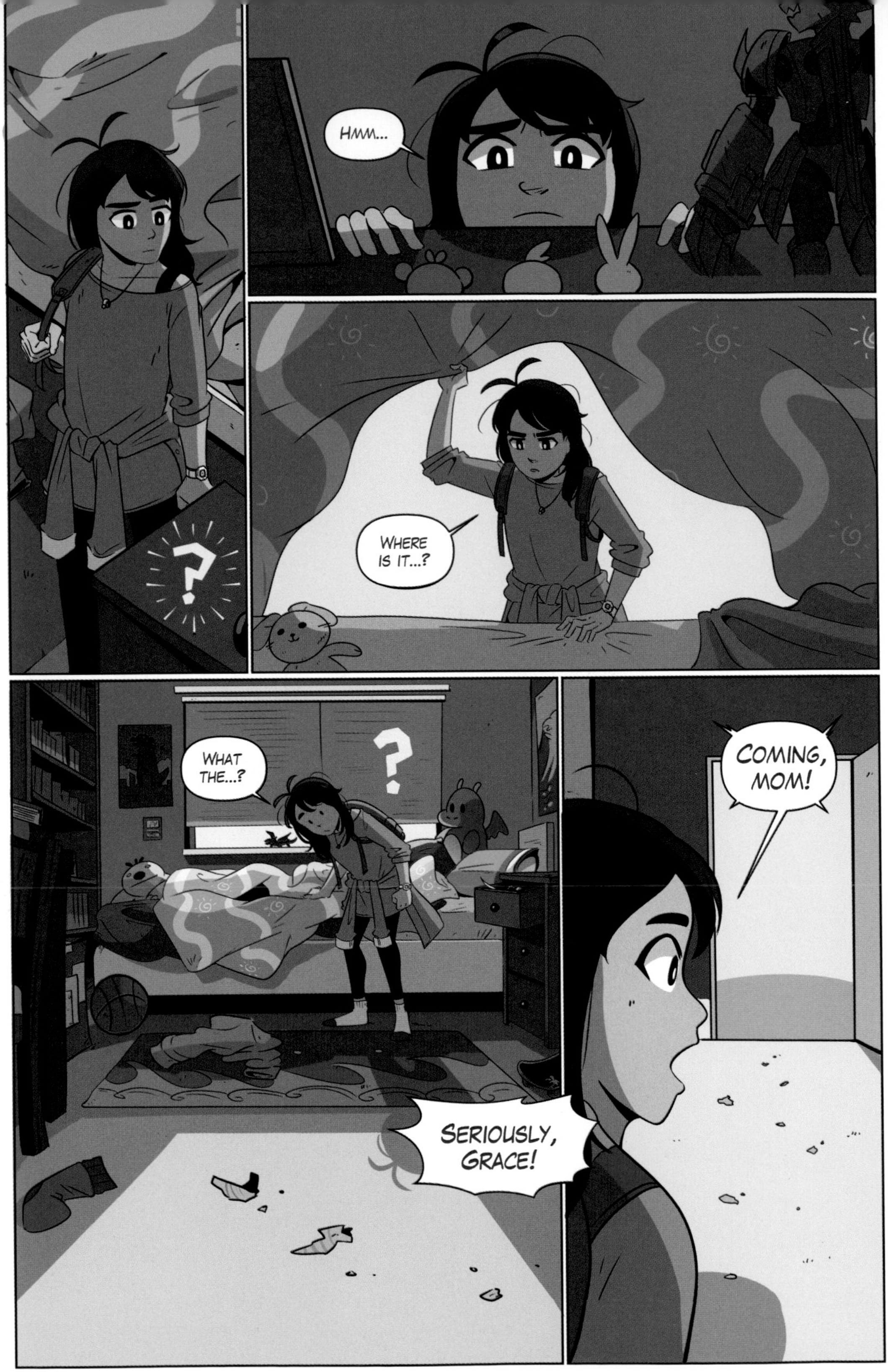
?
HMM...
WHERE IS IT...?
WHAT THE...?
?
SERIOUSLY, GRACE!
COMING, MOM!

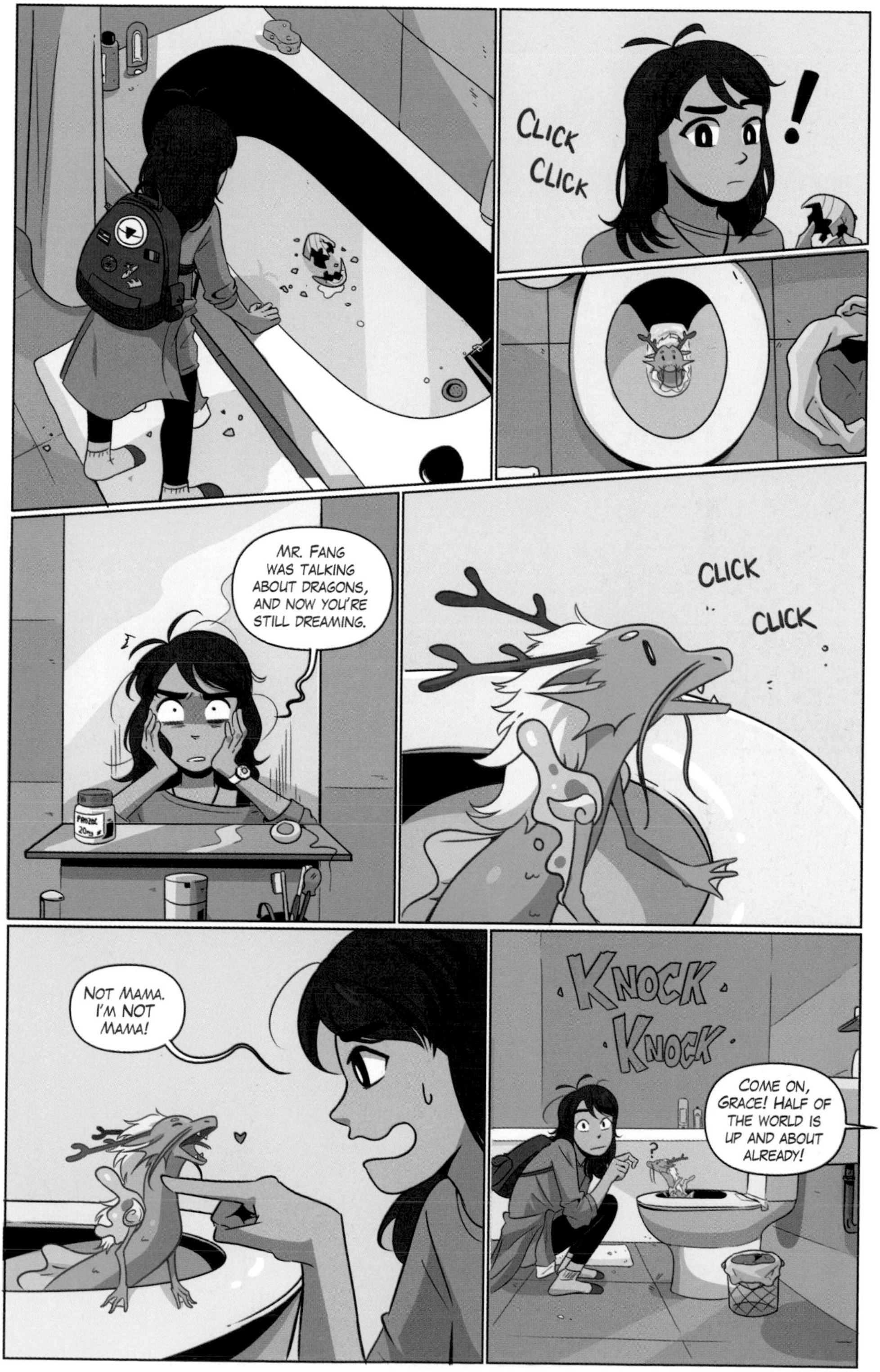

CLICK CLICK
!
MR. FANG WAS TALKING ABOUT DRAGONS, AND NOW YOU'RE STILL DREAMING.
CLICK
CLICK
NOT MAMA. I'M NOT MAMA!
KNOCK KNOCK
COME ON, GRACE! HALF OF THE WORLD IS UP AND ABOUT ALREADY!

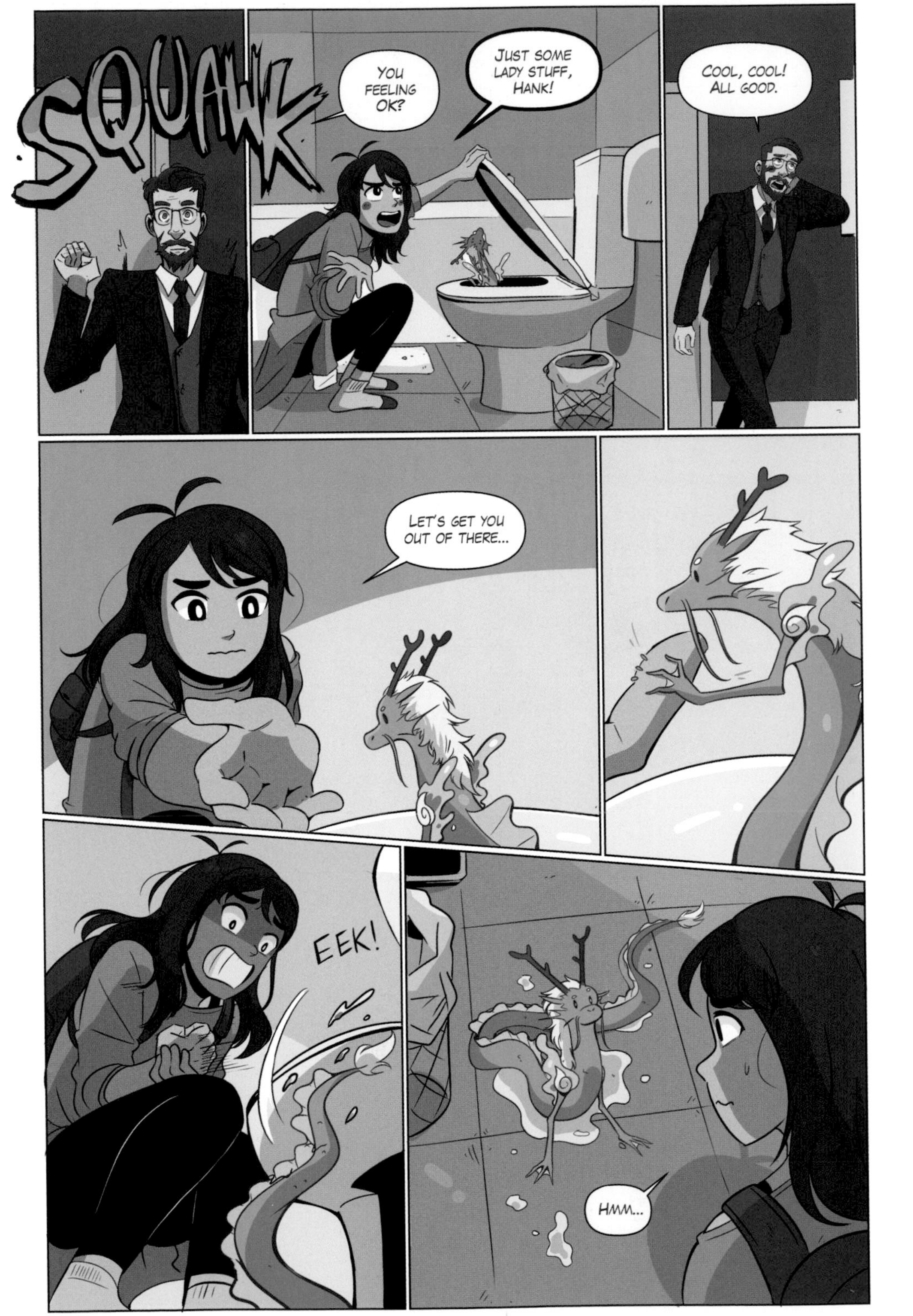
SQUAWK
YOU FEELING OK?
JUST SOME LADY STUFF, HANK!
COOL, COOL! ALL GOOD.
LET'S GET YOU OUT OF THERE...
EEK!
HMM...

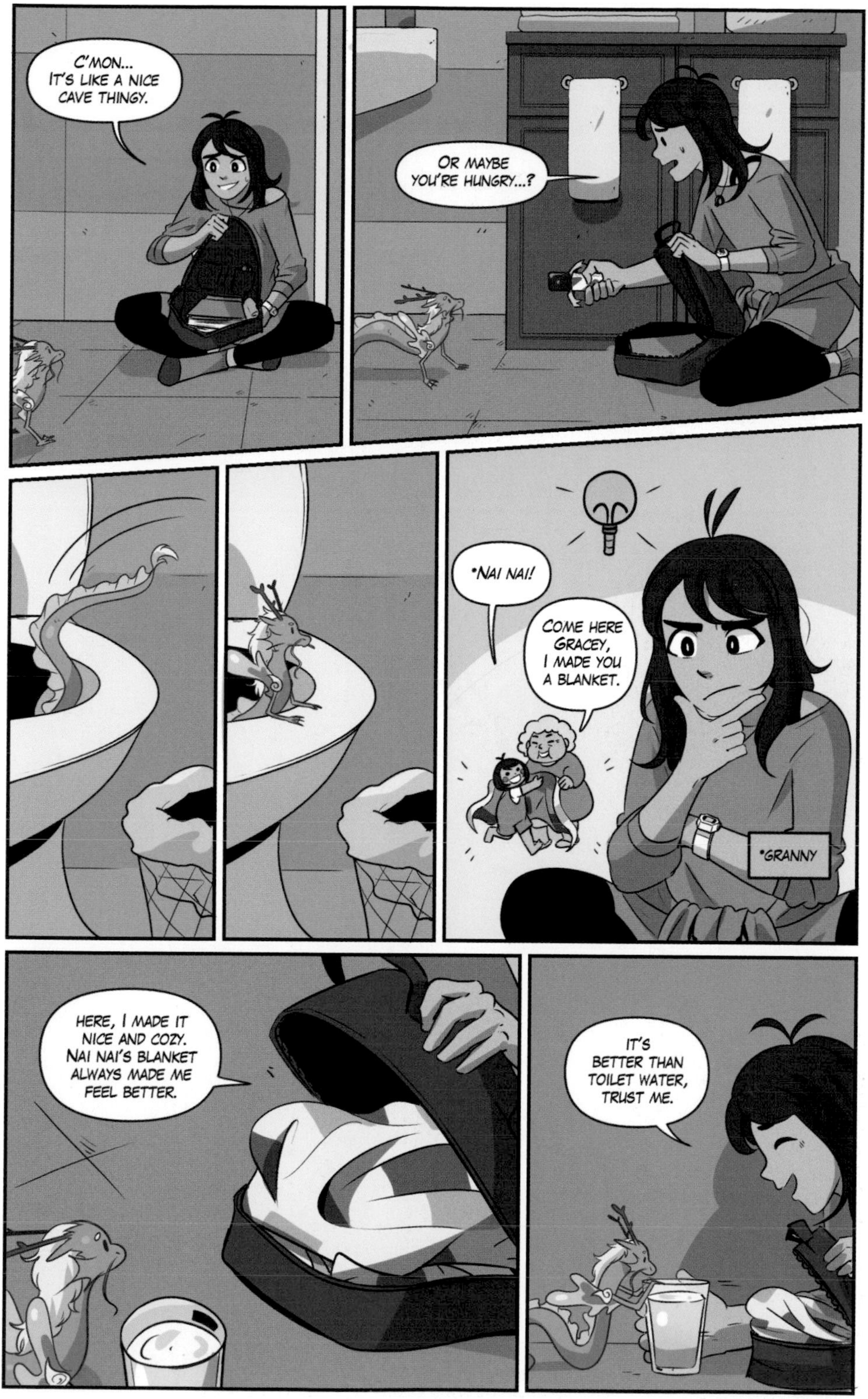
C'MON... IT'S LIKE A NICE CAVE THINGY.
OR MAYBE YOU'RE HUNGRY...?
*NAI NAI!
COME HERE GRACEY, I MADE YOU A BLANKET.
*GRANNY
HERE, I MADE IT NICE AND COZY. NAI NAI'S BLANKET ALWAYS MADE ME FEEL BETTER.
IT'S BETTER THAN TOILET WATER, TRUST ME.

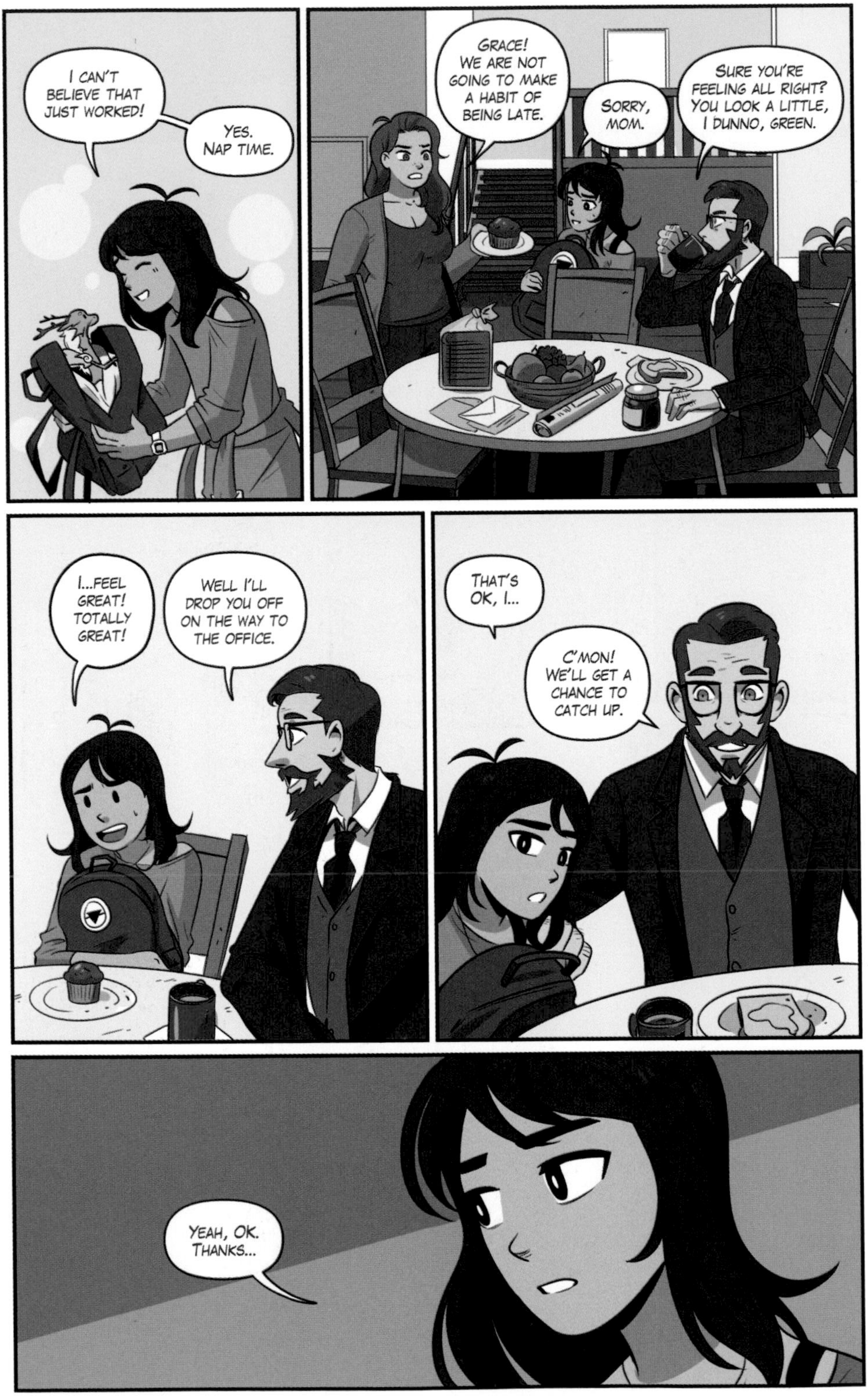
I CAN'T BELIEVE THAT JUST WORKED!
YES. NAP TIME.
GRACE! WE ARE NOT GOING TO MAKE A HABIT OF BEING LATE.
SORRY, MOM.
SURE YOU'RE FEELING ALL RIGHT? YOU LOOK A LITTLE, I DUNNO, GREEN.
I...FEEL GREAT! TOTALLY GREAT!
WELL I'LL DROP YOU OFF ON THE WAY TO THE OFFICE.
THAT'S OK, I...
C'MON! WE'LL GET A CHANCE TO CATCH UP.
YEAH, OK. THANKS...

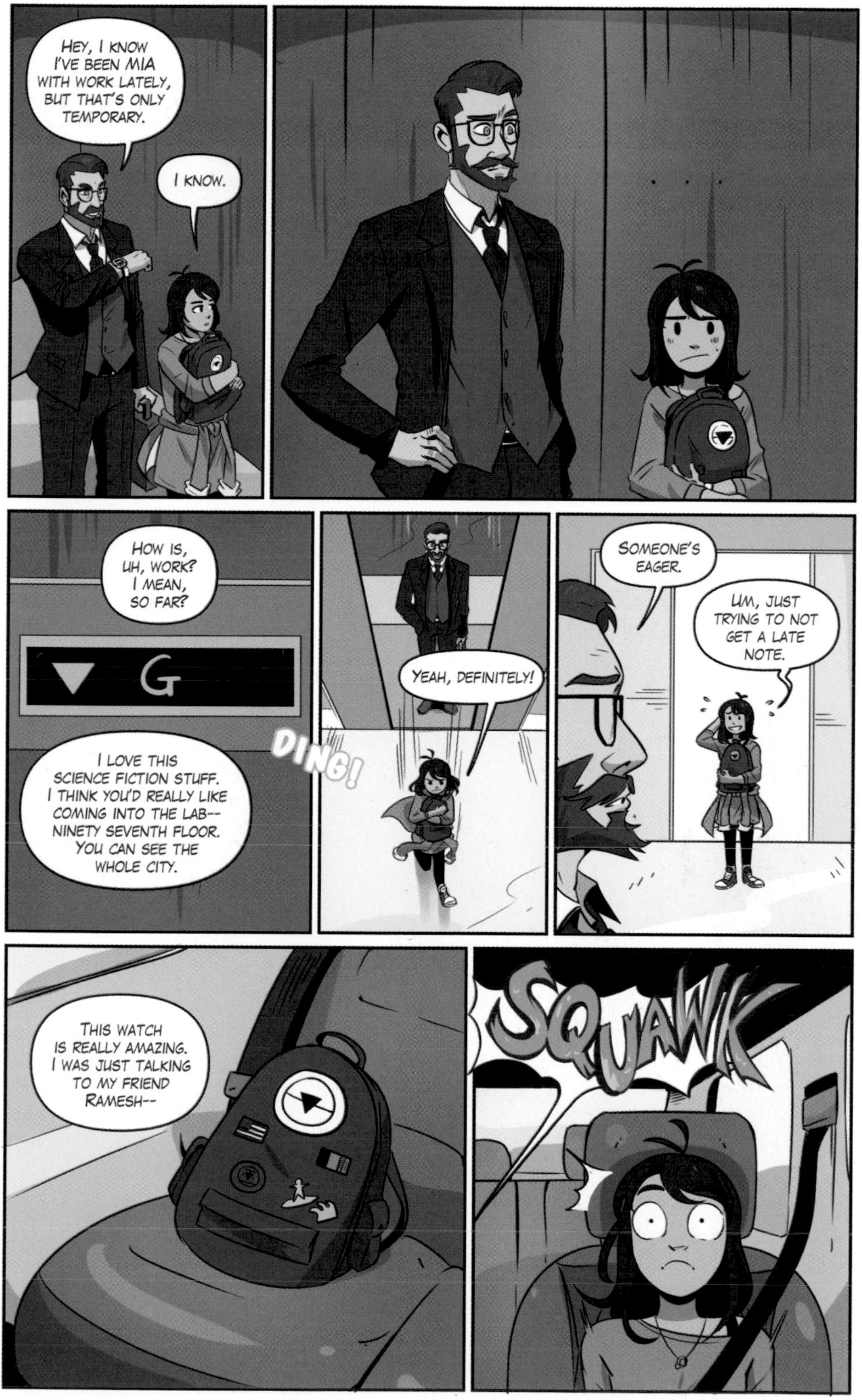
HEY, I KNOW I'VE BEEN MIA WITH WORK LATELY, BUT THAT'S ONLY TEMPORARY.
I KNOW.
. . .
HOW IS, UH, WORK? I MEAN, SO FAR?
G
I LOVE THIS SCIENCE FICTION STUFF. I THINK YOU'D REALLY LIKE COMING INTO THE LAB-- NINETY SEVENTH FLOOR. YOU CAN SEE THE WHOLE CITY.
DING!
YEAH, DEFINITELY!
SOMEONE'S EAGER.
UM, JUST TRYING TO NOT GET A LATE NOTE.
THIS WATCH IS REALLY AMAZING. I WAS JUST TALKING TO MY FRIEND RAMESH--
SQUAWK

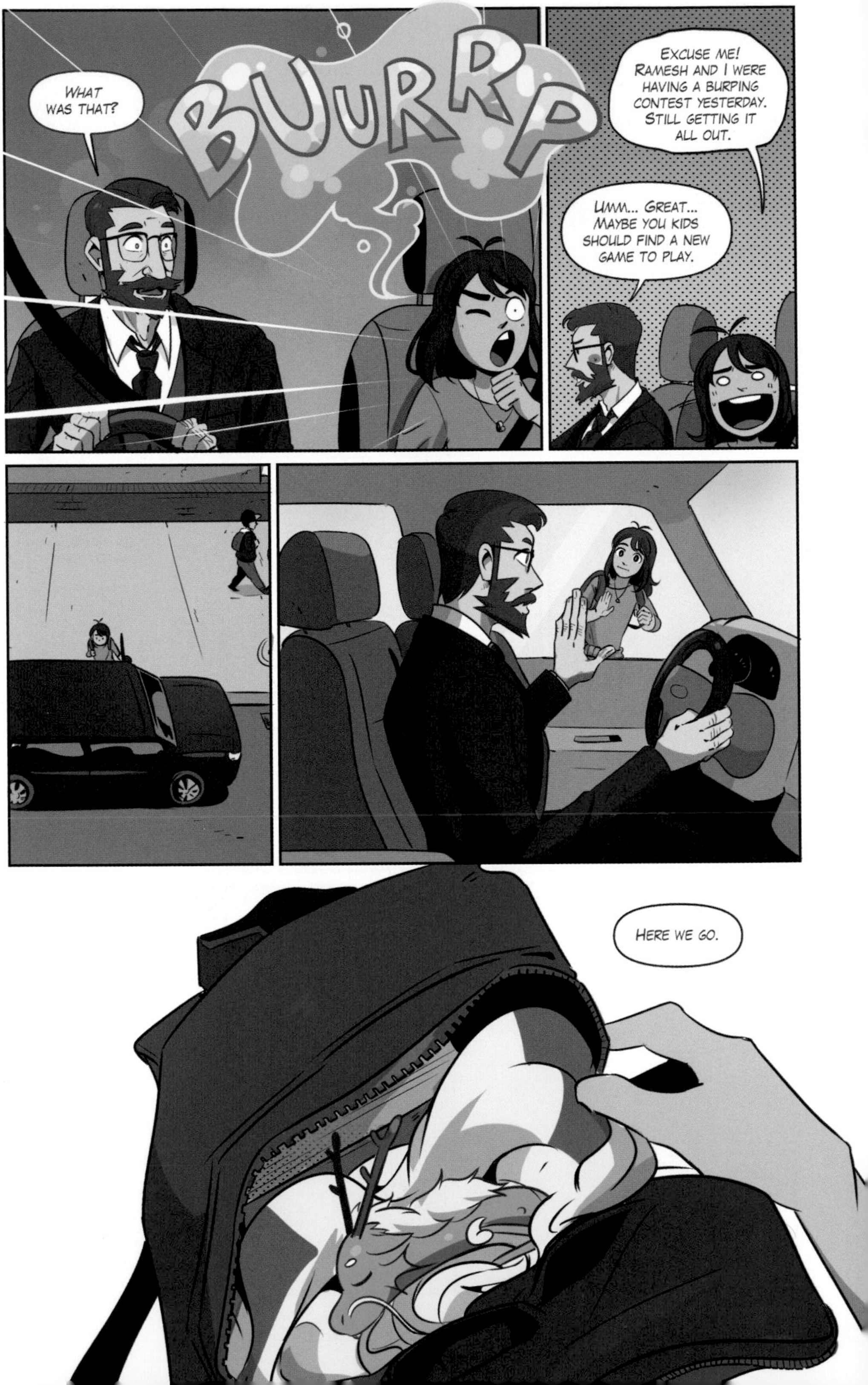

WHAT WAS THAT?
BUURRP
EXCUSE ME! RAMESH AND I WERE HAVING A BURPING CONTEST YESTERDAY. STILL GETTING IT ALL OUT.
UMM... GREAT... MAYBE YOU KIDS SHOULD FIND A NEW GAME TO PLAY.
HERE WE GO.

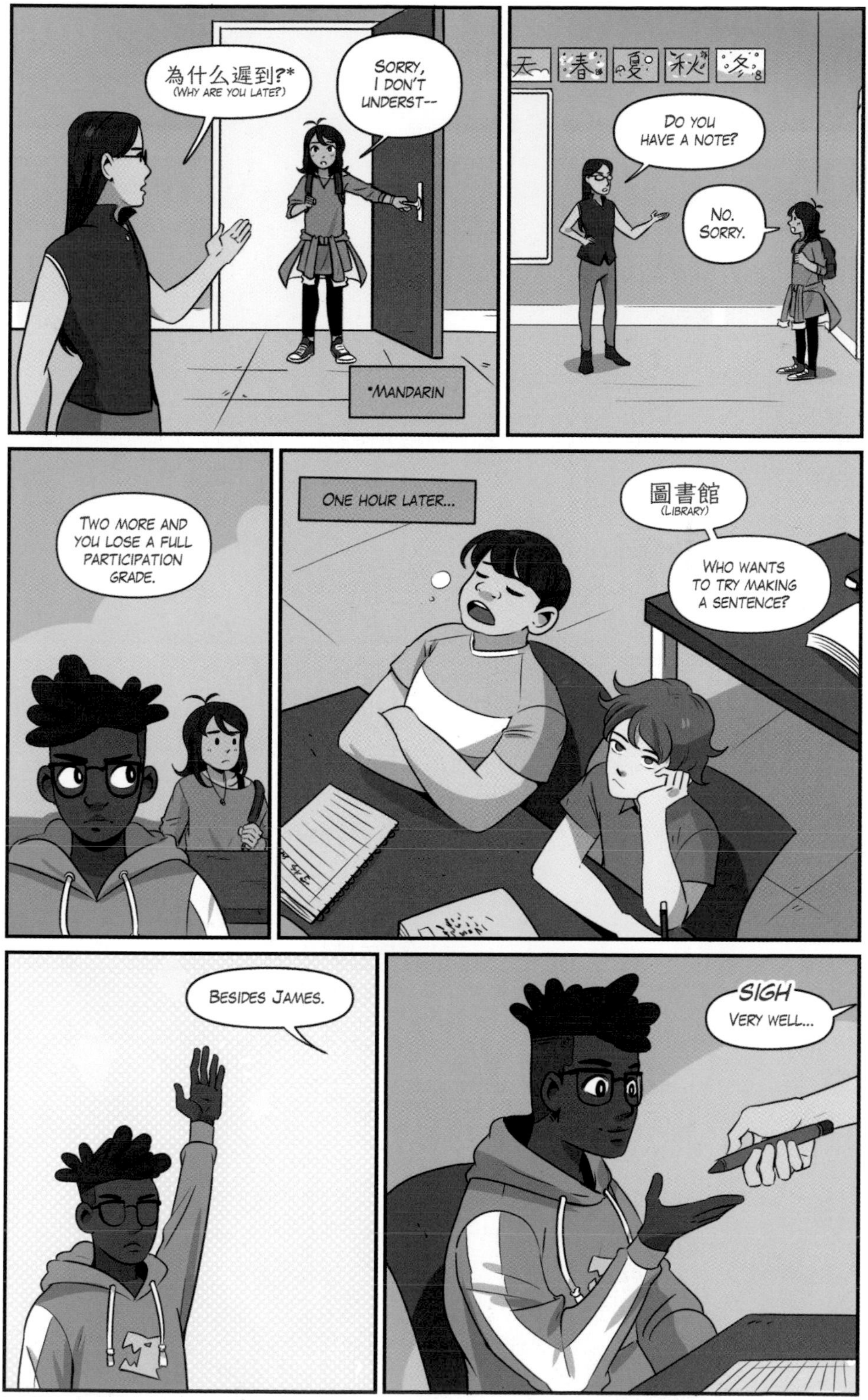

為什么遲到?*
(WHY ARE YOU LATE?)
SORRY, I DON'T UNDERST--
*MANDARIN
DO YOU HAVE A NOTE?
NO. SORRY.
TWO MORE AND YOU LOSE A FULL PARTICIPATION GRADE.
ONE HOUR LATER...
圖書館
(LIBRARY)
WHO WANTS TO TRY MAKING A SENTENCE?
BESIDES JAMES.
SIGH
VERY WELL...

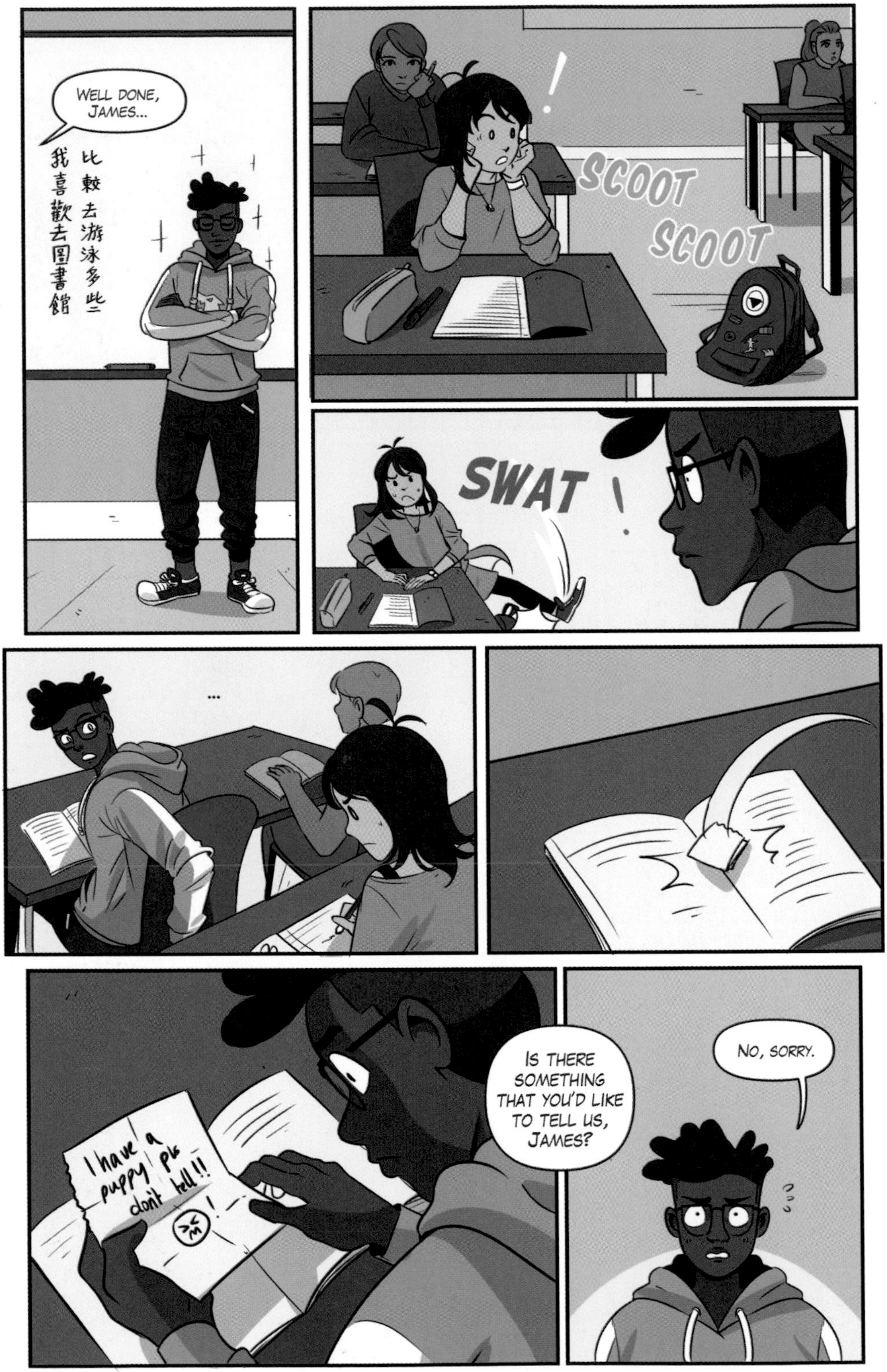
WELL DONE, JAMES...
比較去游泳多些
我喜歡去圖書館
!
SCOOT
SCOOT
SWAT
!
...
I have a puppy pls don't tell!!
IS THERE SOMETHING THAT YOU'D LIKE TO TELL US, JAMES?
NO, SORRY.

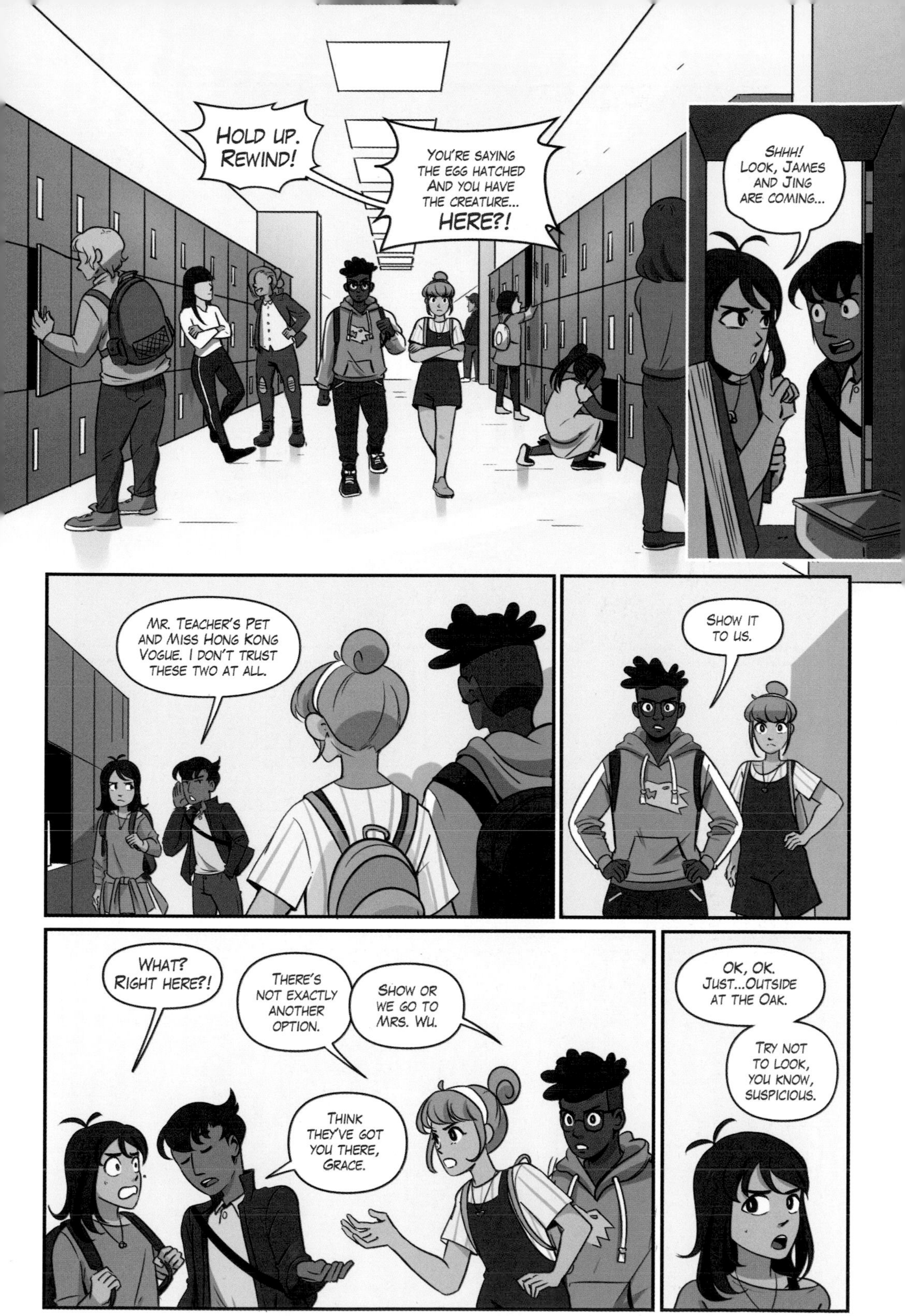
HOLD UP. REWIND!
YOU'RE SAYING THE EGG HATCHED AND YOU HAVE THE CREATURE... HERE?!
SHHH! LOOK, JAMES AND JING ARE COMING...
MR. TEACHER'S PET AND MISS HONG KONG VOGUE. I DON'T TRUST THESE TWO AT ALL.
SHOW IT TO US.
WHAT? RIGHT HERE?!
THERE'S NOT EXACTLY ANOTHER OPTION.
SHOW OR WE GO TO MRS. WU.
THINK THEY'VE GOT YOU THERE, GRACE.
OK, OK. JUST...OUTSIDE AT THE OAK.
TRY NOT TO LOOK, YOU KNOW, SUSPICIOUS.

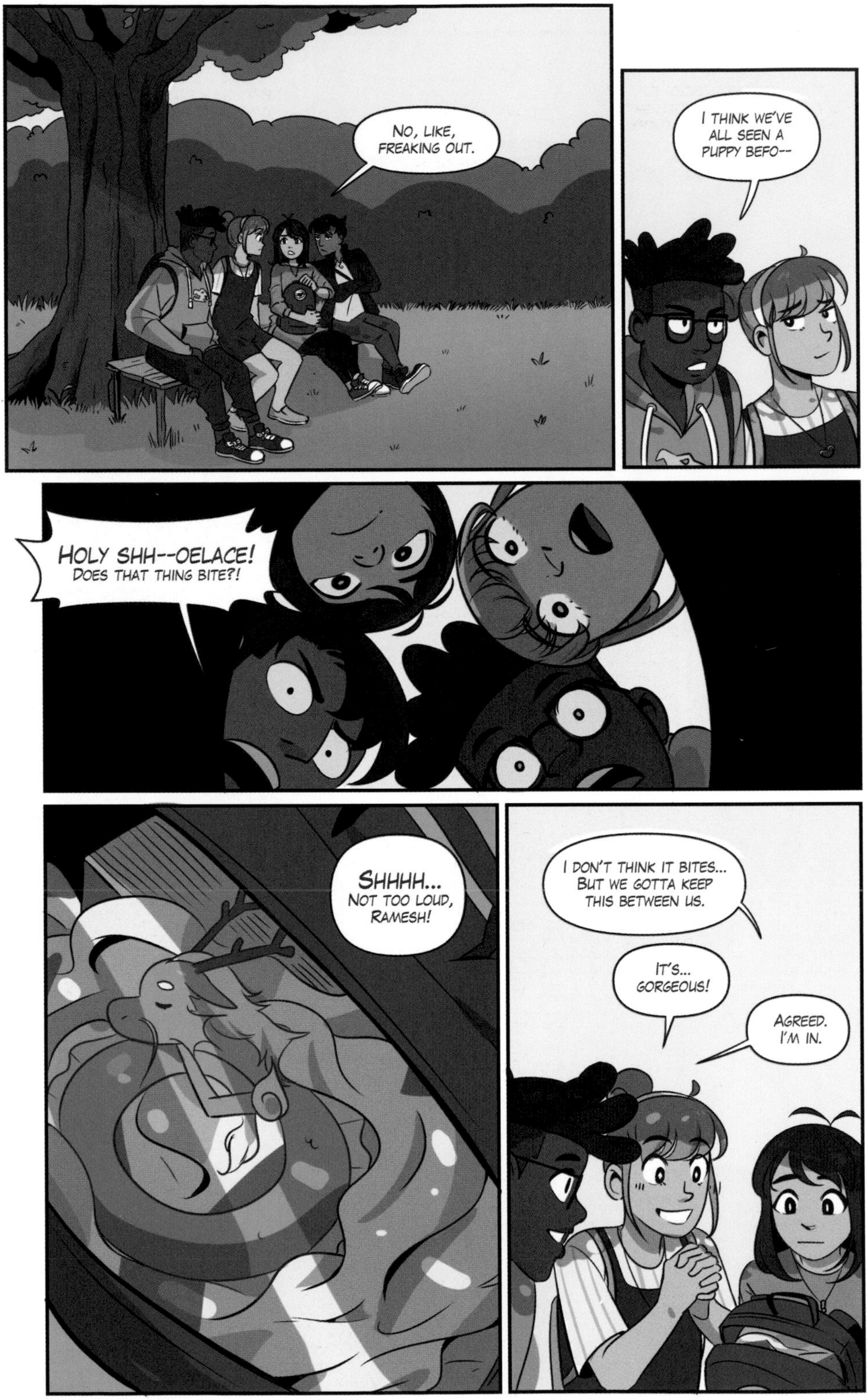
NO, LIKE, FREAKING OUT.
I THINK WE'VE ALL SEEN A PUPPY BEFO--
HOLY SHH--OELACE! DOES THAT THING BITE?!
SHHHH... NOT TOO LOUD, RAMESH!
I DON'T THINK IT BITES... BUT WE GOTTA KEEP THIS BETWEEN US.
IT'S... GORGEOUS!
AGREED. I'M IN.

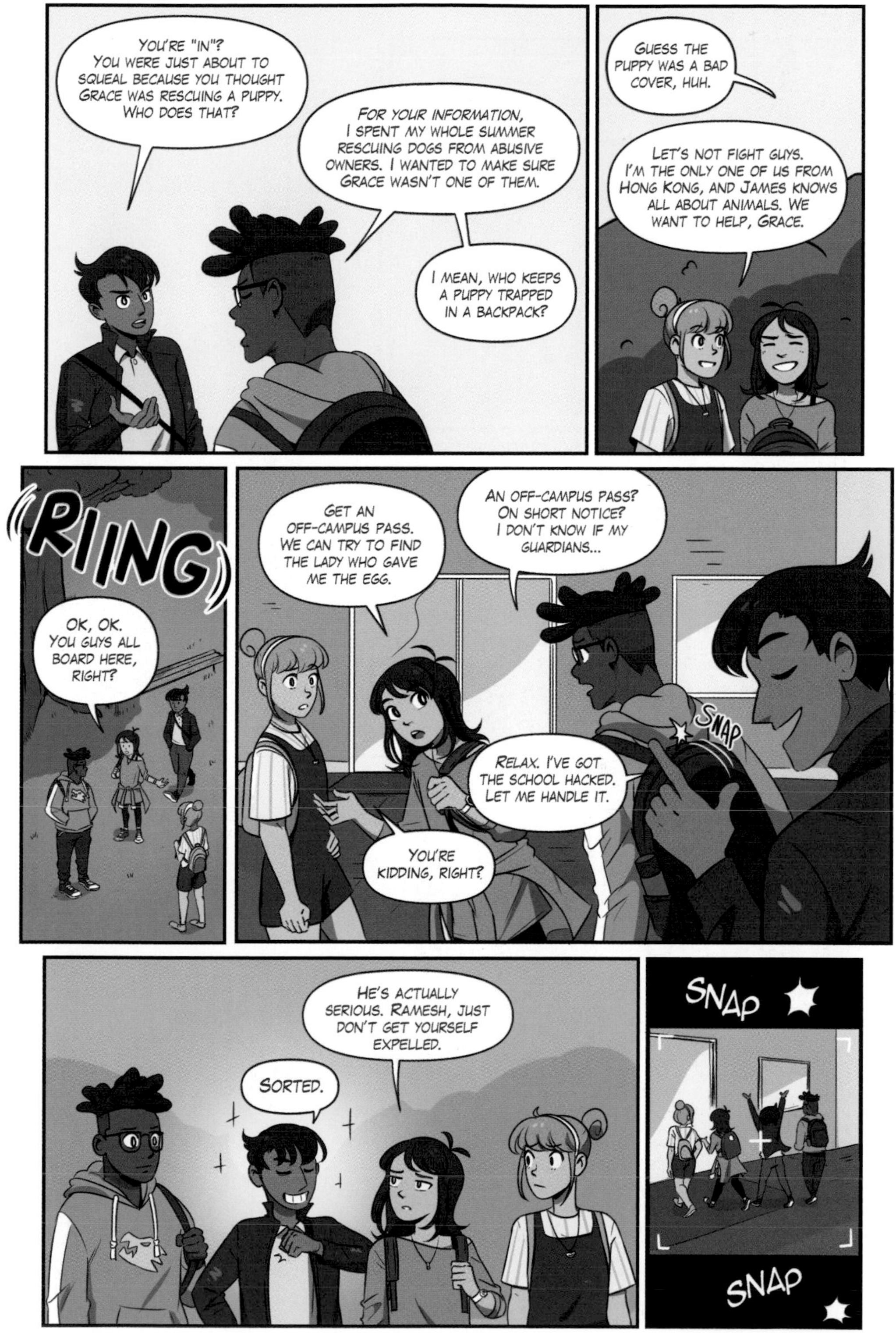
YOU'RE "IN"? YOU WERE JUST ABOUT TO SQUEAL BECAUSE YOU THOUGHT GRACE WAS RESCUING A PUPPY. WHO DOES THAT?
FOR YOUR INFORMATION, I SPENT MY WHOLE SUMMER RESCUING DOGS FROM ABUSIVE OWNERS. I WANTED TO MAKE SURE GRACE WASN'T ONE OF THEM.
I MEAN, WHO KEEPS A PUPPY TRAPPED IN A BACKPACK?
GUESS THE PUPPY WAS A BAD COVER, HUH.
LET'S NOT FIGHT GUYS. I'M THE ONLY ONE OF US FROM HONG KONG, AND JAMES KNOWS ALL ABOUT ANIMALS. WE WANT TO HELP, GRACE.
RIING
OK, OK. YOU GUYS ALL BOARD HERE, RIGHT?
GET AN OFF-CAMPUS PASS. WE CAN TRY TO FIND THE LADY WHO GAVE ME THE EGG.
AN OFF-CAMPUS PASS? ON SHORT NOTICE? I DON'T KNOW IF MY GUARDIANS...
SNAP
RELAX. I'VE GOT THE SCHOOL HACKED. LET ME HANDLE IT.
YOU'RE KIDDING, RIGHT?
HE'S ACTUALLY SERIOUS. RAMESH, JUST DON'T GET YOURSELF EXPELLED.
SORTED.
SNAP
SNAP

WELL, IT'S NOT A DRACO VOLANS.

DRACO WHAT?

I'M AUSTRALIAN. I KNOW SOMETHING ABOUT REPTILES.

PLUS WE SEARCHED BLUE LIZARDS ONLINE DURING MATH.

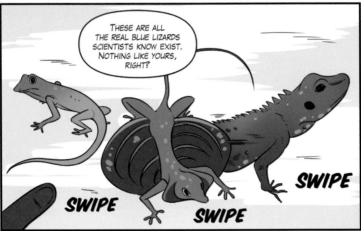

THESE ARE ALL THE REAL BLUE LIZARDS SCIENTISTS KNOW EXIST. NOTHING LIKE YOURS, RIGHT?

SWIPE

SWIPE

SWIPE

THEN I FOUND THIS. I SAW IT IN A MUSEUM WHEN I WAS LITTLE, AND IT JUST POPPED INTO MY HEAD.

"IT'S A CHINESE WATER DRAGON. THEY'RE SAID TO, LIKE, INFLUENCE WEATHER AND STUFF LIKE THAT."

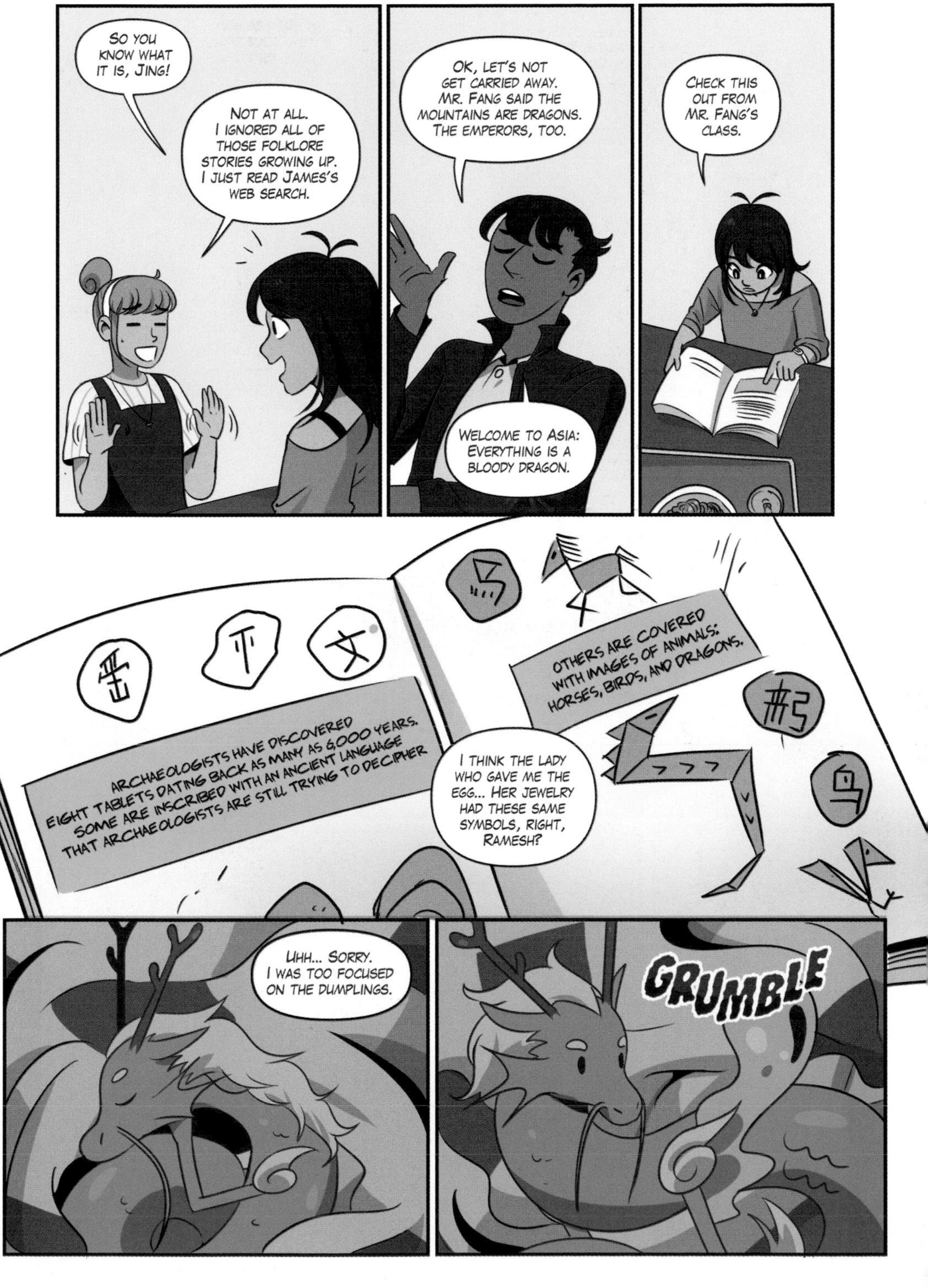

So you know what it is, Jing!
Not at all. I ignored all of those folklore stories growing up. I just read James's web search.
OK, let's not get carried away. Mr. Fang said the mountains are dragons. The emperors, too.
Welcome to Asia: Everything is a bloody dragon.
Check this out from Mr. Fang's class.
Archaeologists have discovered eight tablets dating back as many as 6,000 years. Some are inscribed with an ancient language that archaeologists are still trying to decipher
Others are covered with images of animals: horses, birds, and dragons.
I think the lady who gave me the egg... Her jewelry had these same symbols, right, Ramesh?
Uhh... Sorry. I was too focused on the dumplings.
GRUMBLE

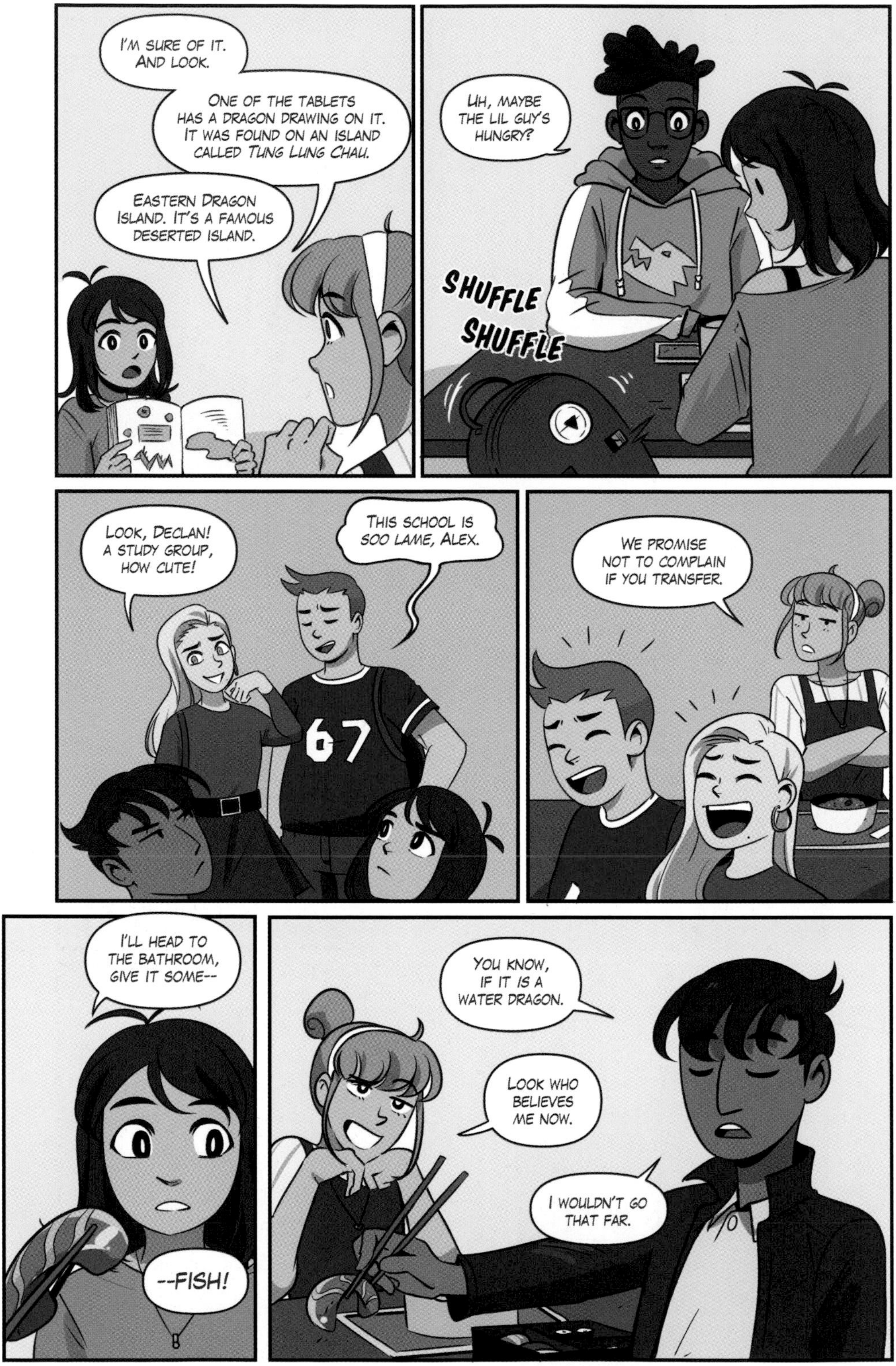
I'M SURE OF IT. AND LOOK.
ONE OF THE TABLETS HAS A DRAGON DRAWING ON IT. IT WAS FOUND ON AN ISLAND CALLED *TUNG LUNG CHAU*.
EASTERN DRAGON ISLAND. IT'S A FAMOUS DESERTED ISLAND.
UH, MAYBE THE LIL GUY'S HUNGRY?
SHUFFLE
SHUFFLE
LOOK, DECLAN! A STUDY GROUP, HOW CUTE!
THIS SCHOOL IS SOO LAME, ALEX.
WE PROMISE NOT TO COMPLAIN IF YOU TRANSFER.
I'LL HEAD TO THE BATHROOM, GIVE IT SOME--
--FISH!
YOU KNOW, IF IT IS A WATER DRAGON.
LOOK WHO BELIEVES ME NOW.
I WOULDN'T GO THAT FAR.

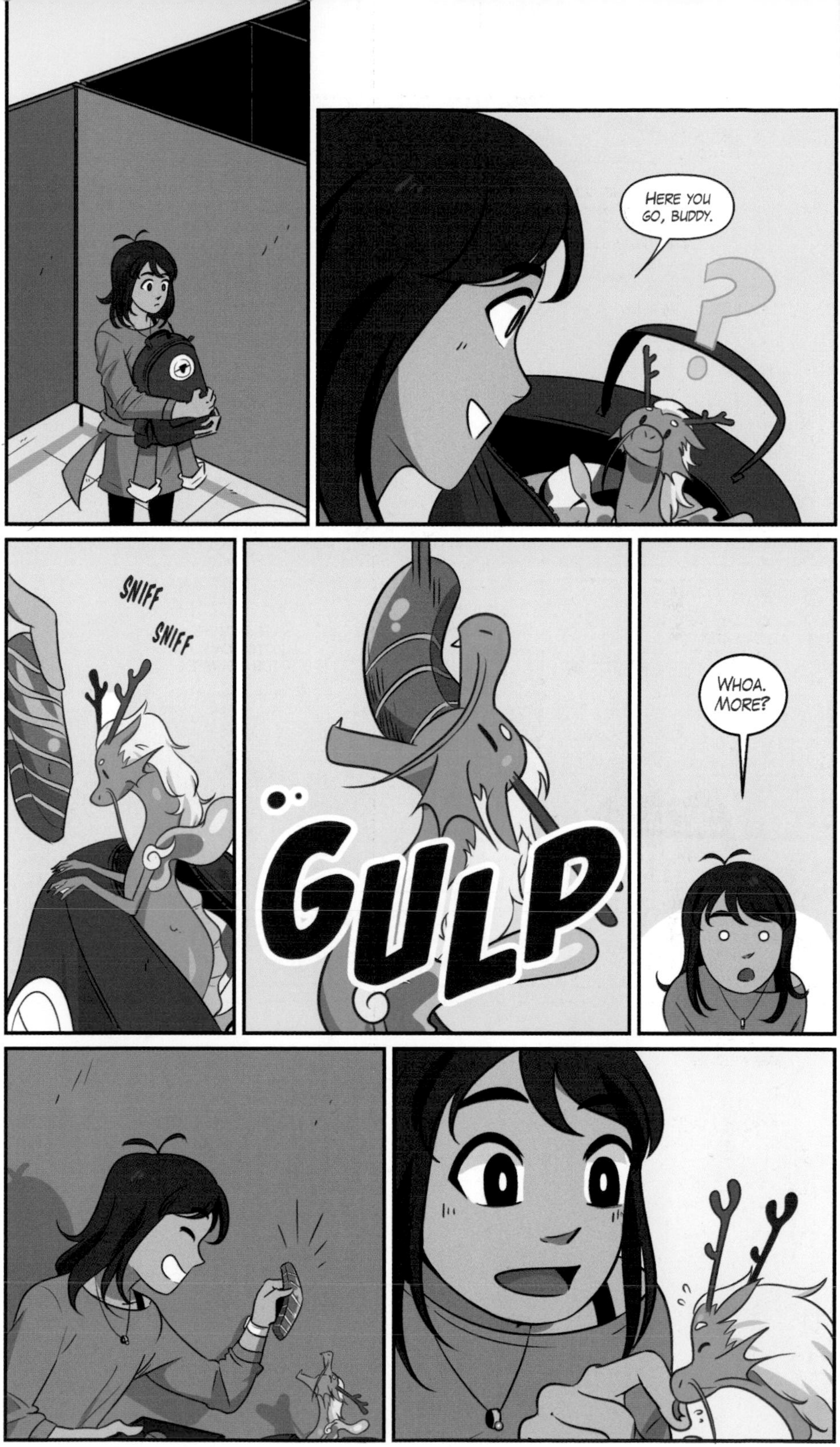
HERE YOU GO, BUDDY.
?
SNIFF
SNIFF
GULP
WHOA. MORE?

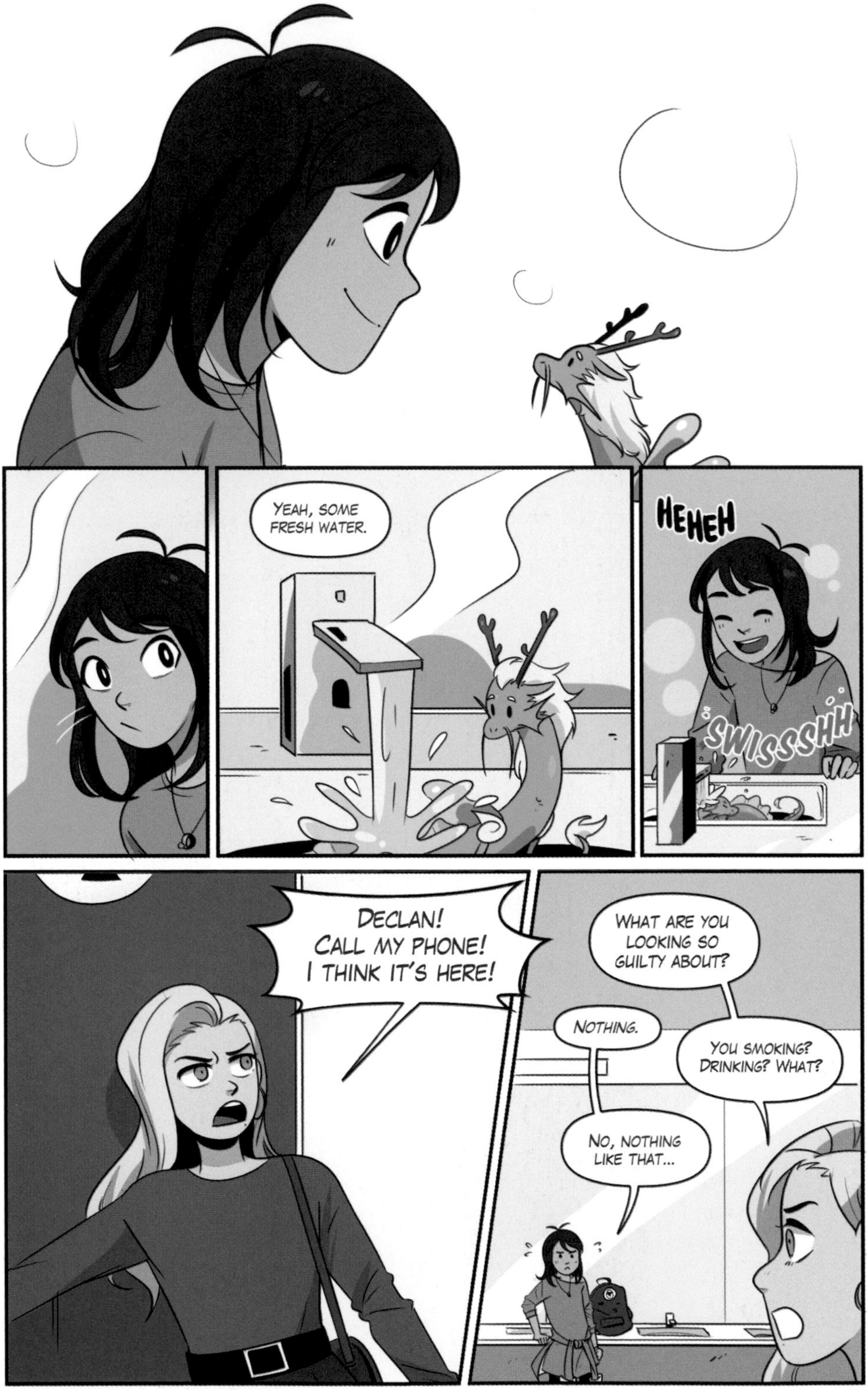
YEAH, SOME FRESH WATER.
HEHEH
SWISSSHH
DECLAN! CALL MY PHONE! I THINK IT'S HERE!
WHAT ARE YOU LOOKING SO GUILTY ABOUT?
NOTHING.
YOU SMOKING? DRINKING? WHAT?
NO, NOTHING LIKE THAT...

WELL, IT DOESN'T LOOK LIKE NOTHING. WHAT'VE YOU GOT THERE?

OK, YEAH, YOU CAUGHT ME. IT'S THIS...UM, CAFFEINE PILL. I CAN BARELY GET THROUGH MY CLASSES TODAY.

WELL, SHARE THE WEALTH THEN, I'VE GOT MRS. LI NEXT PERIOD.

YEAH, YEAH, I WOULD BUT YOU DON'T WANT THIS...

IF IT'S HELLA STRONG CAFFEINE THEN I DO, I'M GONNA PASS OUT FROM BOREDOM.

I WOULD...BUT THESE ARE, YOU KNOW, FISH...OIL...CAFFEINE PILLS...!

THEY'RE CALLED, UM, "CAFFEINE COD-LIVER" SO IF YOU EAT 'EM YOU'LL SMELL, YOU KNOW, LIKE CODFISH ALL DAY.

IT'S...A LITTLE EMBARRASSING, ACTUALLY.

YEAH, YEAH, I CAN SMELL IT. THIS WHOLE BATHROOM STINKS LIKE FISH!

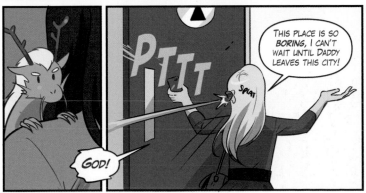

PTTT

THIS PLACE IS SO BORING, I CAN'T WAIT UNTIL DADDY LEAVES THIS CITY!

SPLAT

GOD!

CLICK CLICK

NICE ONE!

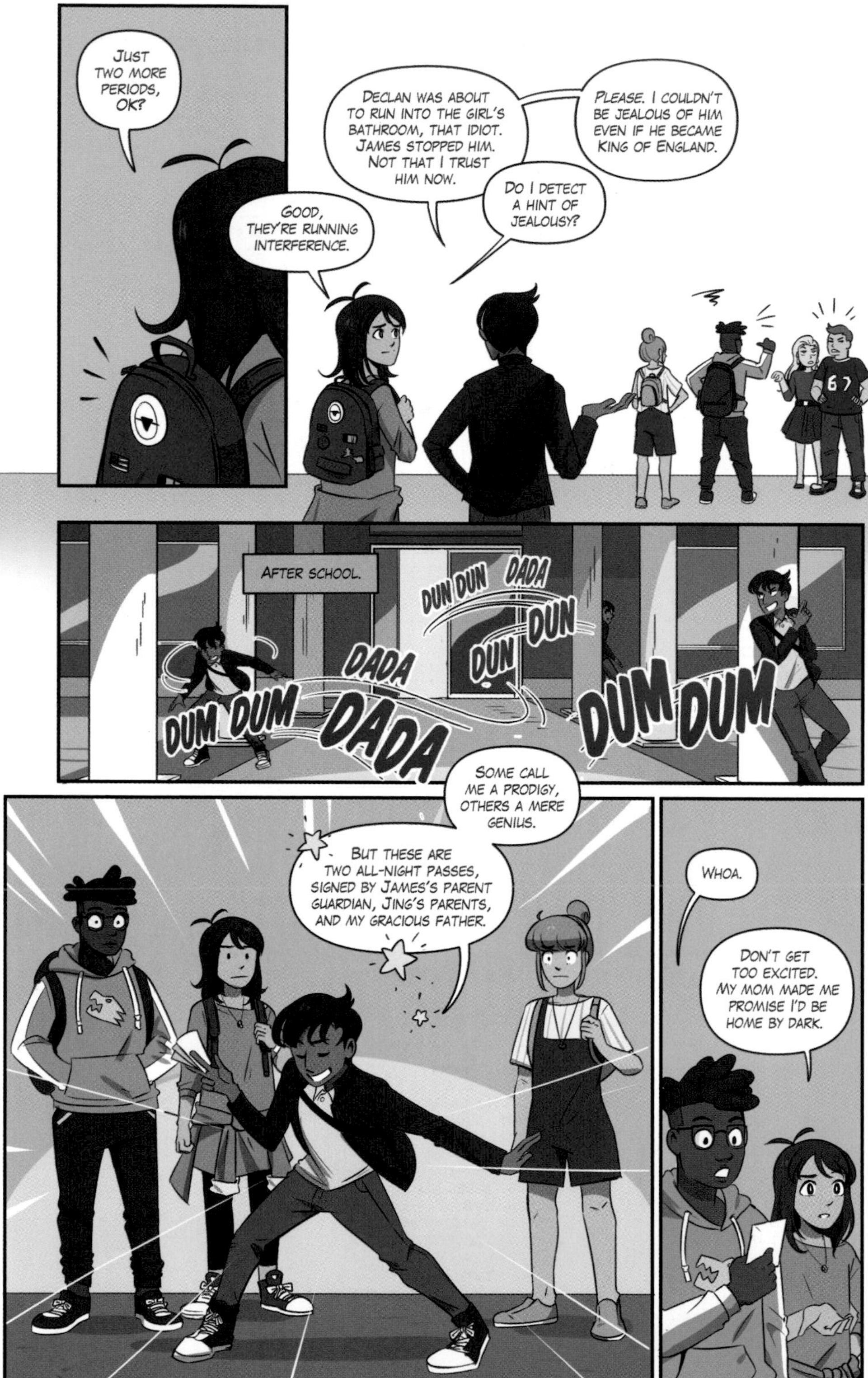
Just two more periods, OK?
Good, they're running interference.
Declan was about to run into the girl's bathroom, that idiot. James stopped him. Not that I trust him now.
Do I detect a hint of jealousy?
Please. I couldn't be jealous of him even if he became King of England.
After school.
DUN DUN DADA
DUN DUN
DADA
DUM DUM DADA
DUM DUM
Some call me a prodigy, others a mere genius.
But these are two all-night passes, signed by James's parent guardian, Jing's parents, and my gracious father.
Whoa.
Don't get too excited. My mom made me promise I'd be home by dark.

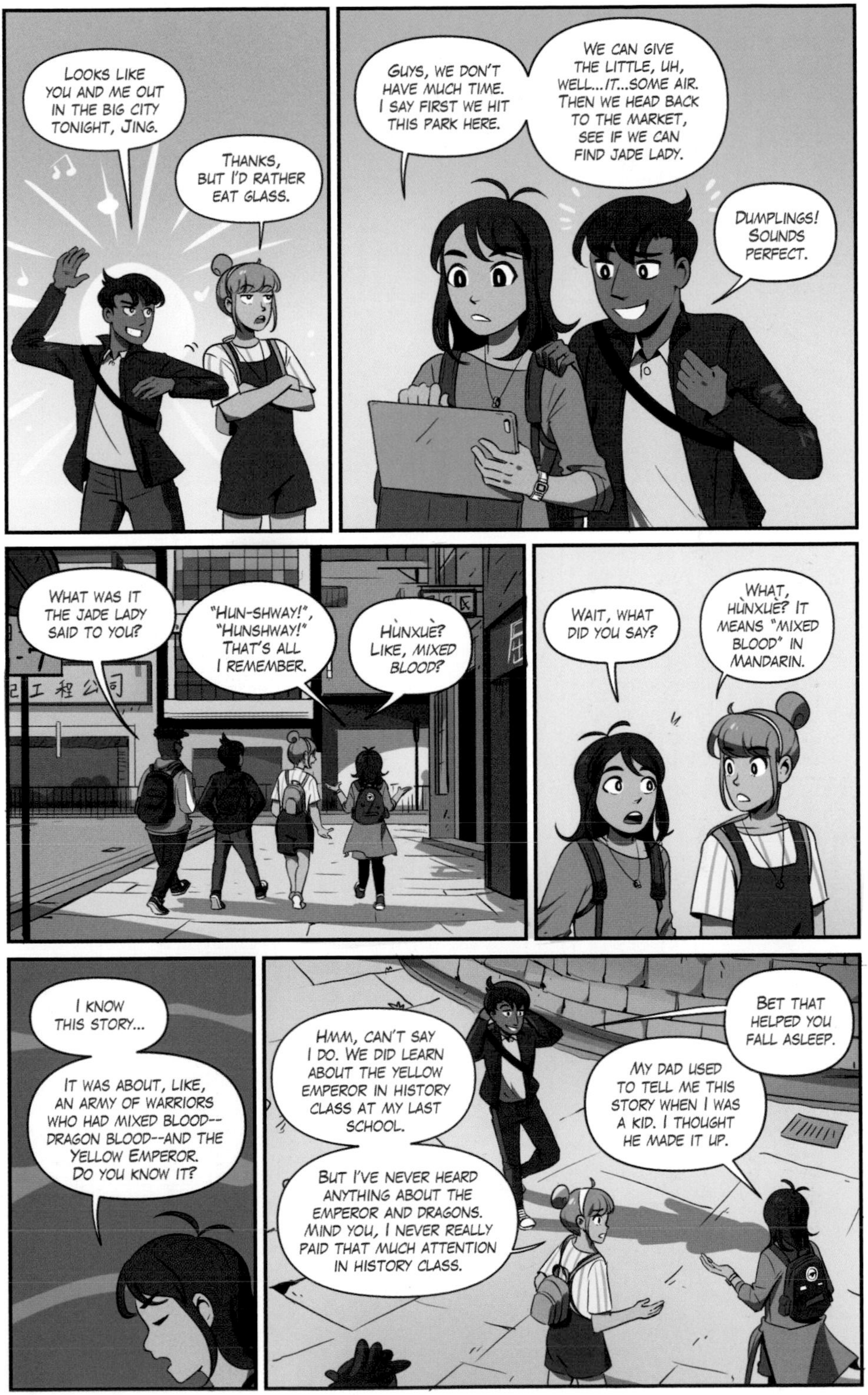
LOOKS LIKE YOU AND ME OUT IN THE BIG CITY TONIGHT, JING.
THANKS, BUT I'D RATHER EAT GLASS.
GUYS, WE DON'T HAVE MUCH TIME. I SAY FIRST WE HIT THIS PARK HERE.
WE CAN GIVE THE LITTLE, UH, WELL...IT...SOME AIR. THEN WE HEAD BACK TO THE MARKET, SEE IF WE CAN FIND JADE LADY.
DUMPLINGS! SOUNDS PERFECT.
WHAT WAS IT THE JADE LADY SAID TO YOU?
"HUN-SHWAY!", "HUNSHWAY!" THAT'S ALL I REMEMBER.
HÙNXUÈ? LIKE, MIXED BLOOD?
WAIT, WHAT DID YOU SAY?
WHAT, HÙNXUÈ? IT MEANS "MIXED BLOOD" IN MANDARIN.
I KNOW THIS STORY...
IT WAS ABOUT, LIKE, AN ARMY OF WARRIORS WHO HAD MIXED BLOOD--DRAGON BLOOD--AND THE YELLOW EMPEROR. DO YOU KNOW IT?
HMM, CAN'T SAY I DO. WE DID LEARN ABOUT THE YELLOW EMPEROR IN HISTORY CLASS AT MY LAST SCHOOL.
BUT I'VE NEVER HEARD ANYTHING ABOUT THE EMPEROR AND DRAGONS. MIND YOU, I NEVER REALLY PAID THAT MUCH ATTENTION IN HISTORY CLASS.
MY DAD USED TO TELL ME THIS STORY WHEN I WAS A KID. I THOUGHT HE MADE IT UP.
BET THAT HELPED YOU FALL ASLEEP.

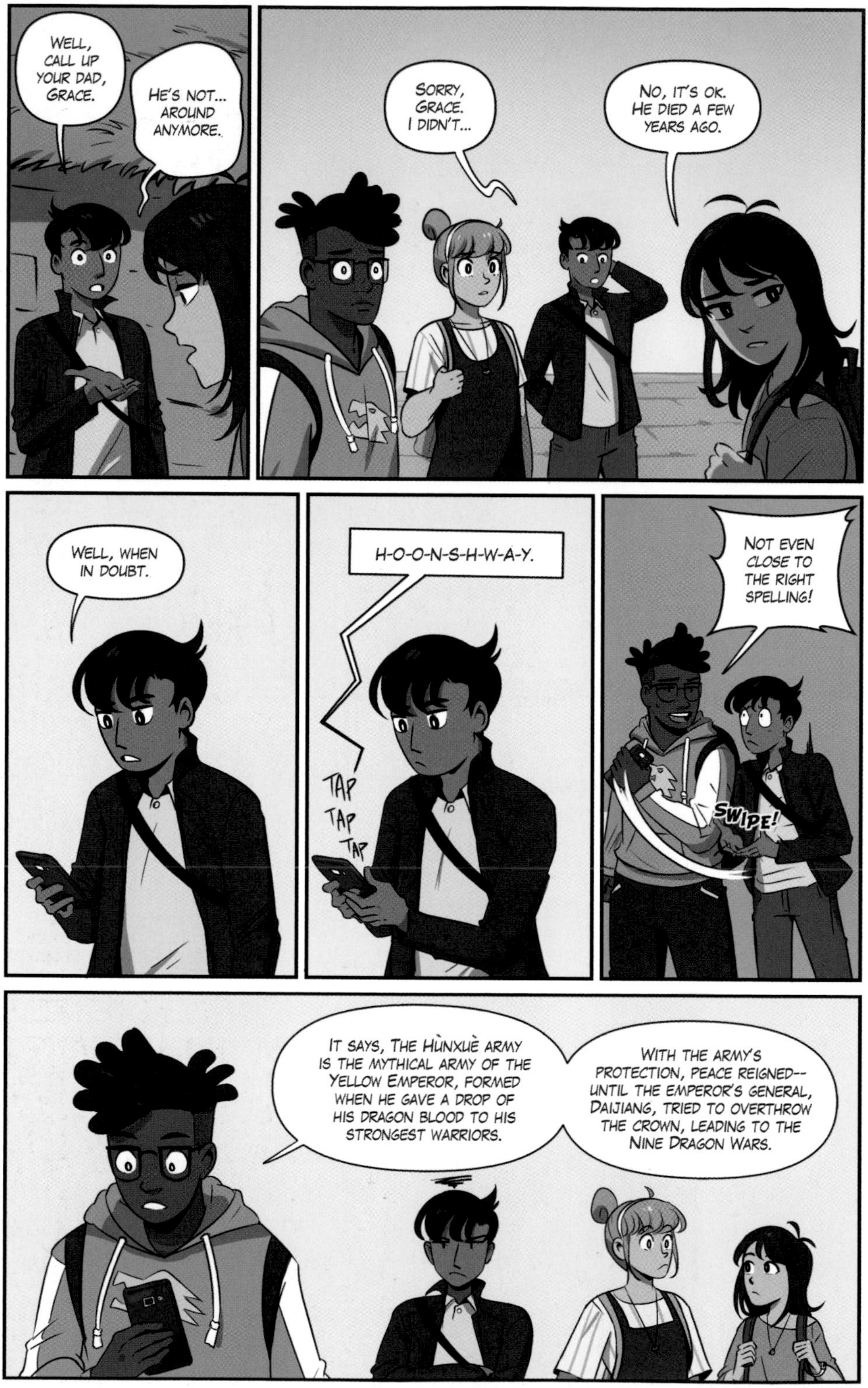

WELL, CALL UP YOUR DAD, GRACE.
HE'S NOT... AROUND ANYMORE.
SORRY, GRACE. I DIDN'T...
NO, IT'S OK. HE DIED A FEW YEARS AGO.
WELL, WHEN IN DOUBT.
H-O-O-N-S-H-W-A-Y.
TAP TAP TAP
NOT EVEN CLOSE TO THE RIGHT SPELLING!
SWIPE!
IT SAYS, THE HÙNXUÈ ARMY IS THE MYTHICAL ARMY OF THE YELLOW EMPEROR, FORMED WHEN HE GAVE A DROP OF HIS DRAGON BLOOD TO HIS STRONGEST WARRIORS.
WITH THE ARMY'S PROTECTION, PEACE REIGNED-- UNTIL THE EMPEROR'S GENERAL, DAIJIANG, TRIED TO OVERTHROW THE CROWN, LEADING TO THE NINE DRAGON WARS.

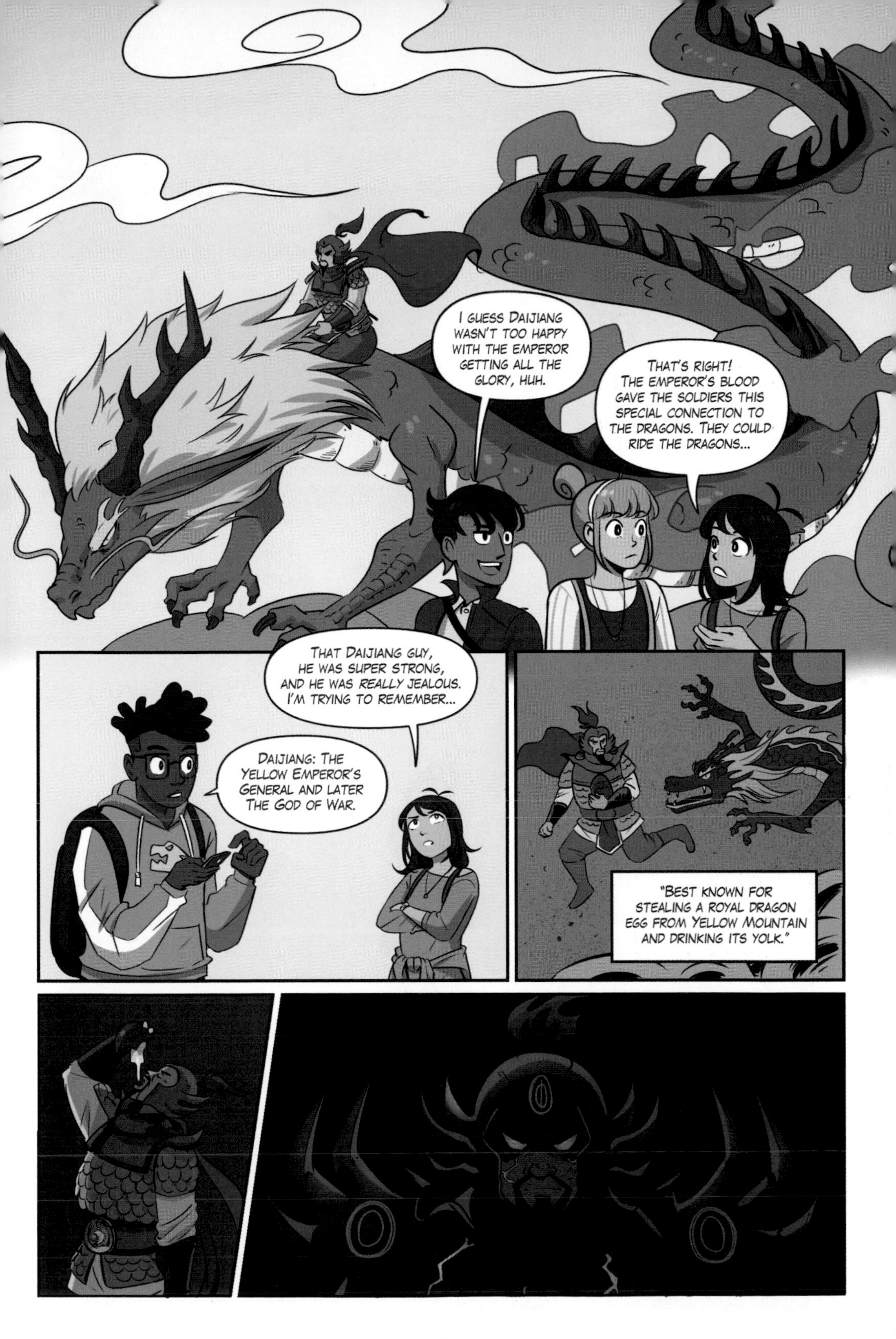
I GUESS DAIJIANG WASN'T TOO HAPPY WITH THE EMPEROR GETTING ALL THE GLORY, HUH.
THAT'S RIGHT! THE EMPEROR'S BLOOD GAVE THE SOLDIERS THIS SPECIAL CONNECTION TO THE DRAGONS. THEY COULD RIDE THE DRAGONS...
THAT DAIJIANG GUY, HE WAS SUPER STRONG, AND HE WAS *REALLY* JEALOUS. I'M TRYING TO REMEMBER...
DAIJIANG: THE YELLOW EMPEROR'S GENERAL AND LATER THE GOD OF WAR.
"BEST KNOWN FOR STEALING A ROYAL DRAGON EGG FROM YELLOW MOUNTAIN AND DRINKING ITS YOLK."

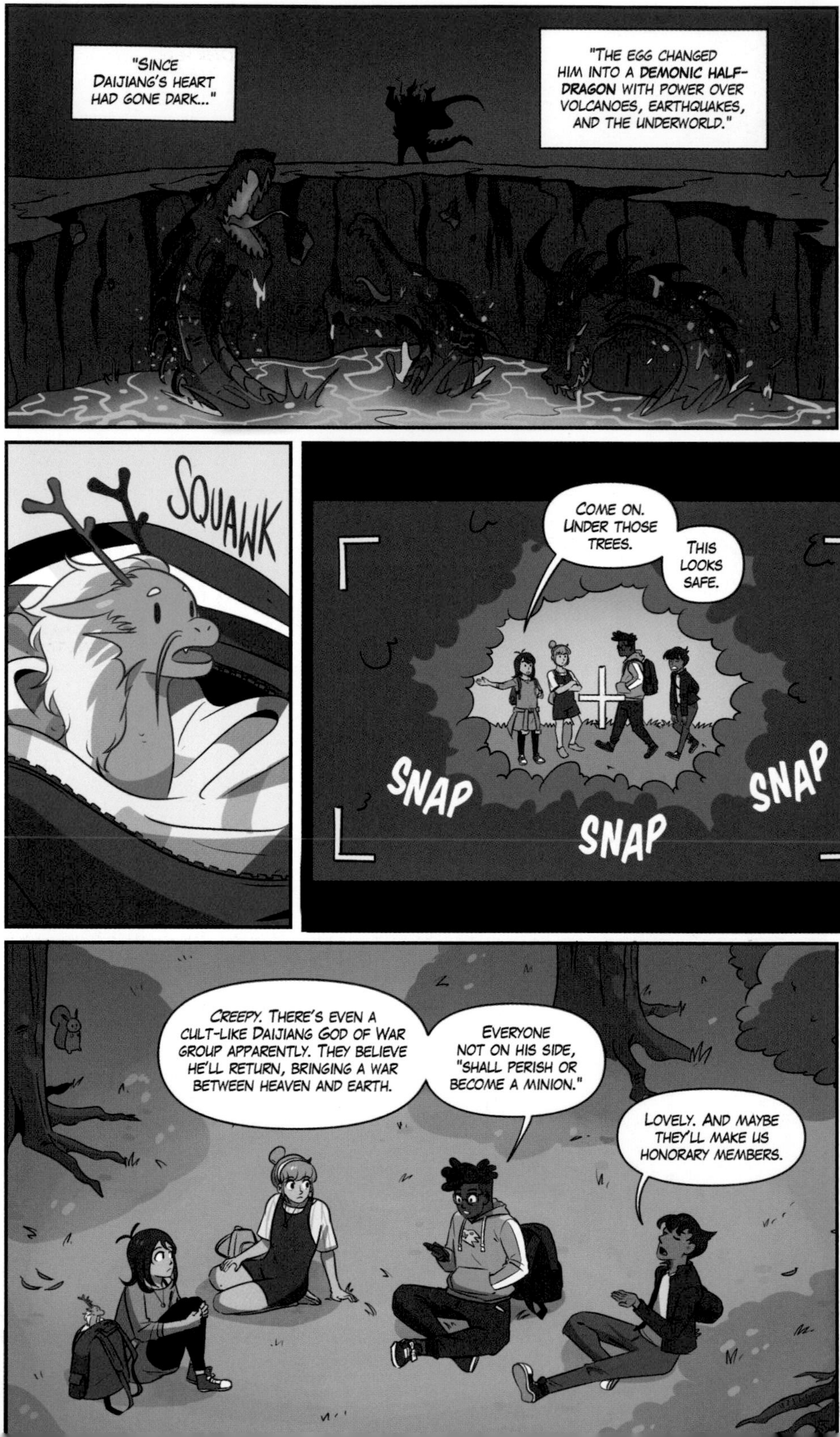
"Since Daijiang's heart had gone dark..."
"The egg changed him into a demonic half-dragon with power over volcanoes, earthquakes, and the underworld."
SQUAWK
Come on. Under those trees.
This looks safe.
SNAP
SNAP
SNAP
Creepy. There's even a cult-like Daijiang God of War group apparently. They believe he'll return, bringing a war between heaven and earth.
Everyone not on his side, "shall perish or become a minion."
Lovely. And maybe they'll make us honorary members.

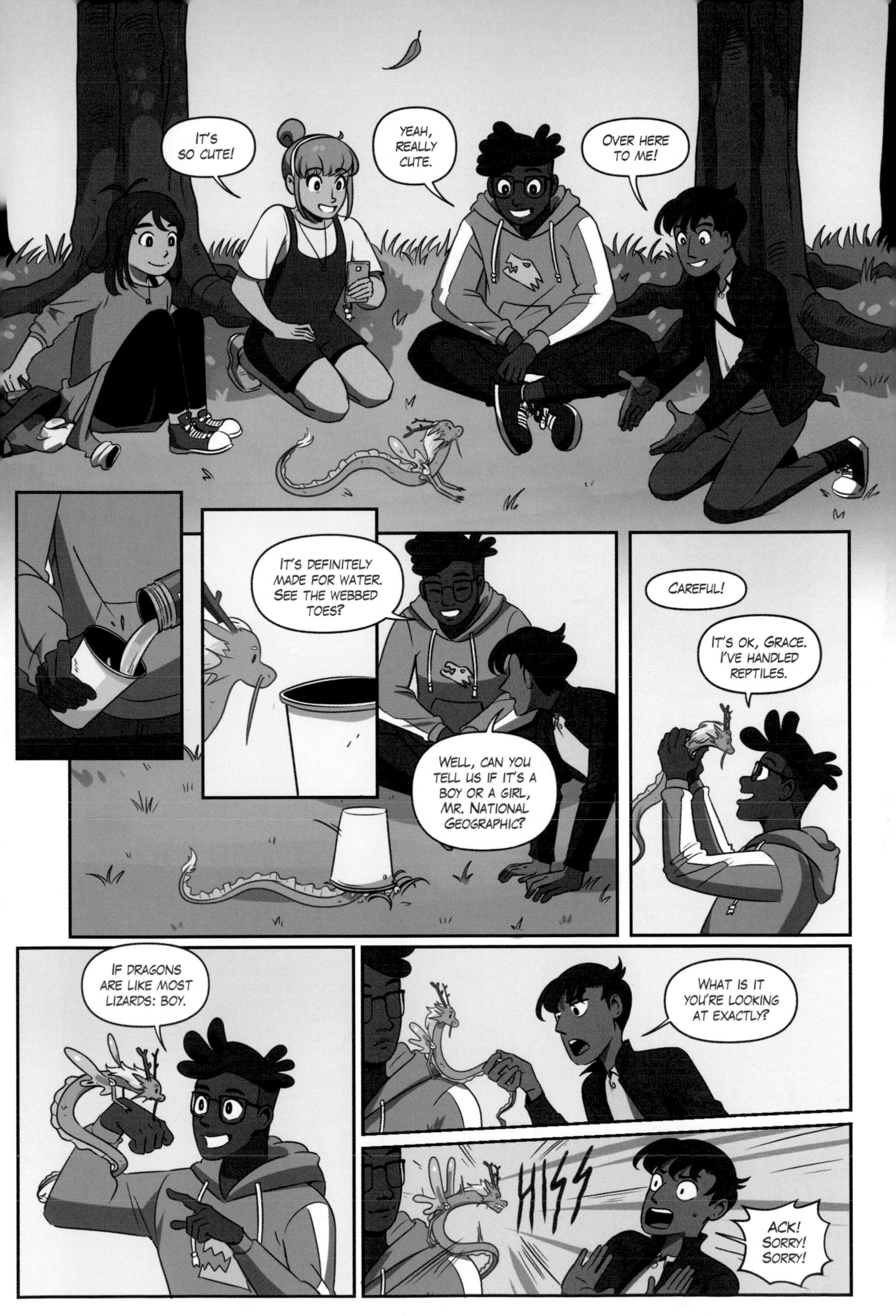
IT'S SO CUTE!
YEAH, REALLY CUTE.
OVER HERE TO ME!
IT'S DEFINITELY MADE FOR WATER. SEE THE WEBBED TOES?
WELL, CAN YOU TELL US IF IT'S A BOY OR A GIRL, MR. NATIONAL GEOGRAPHIC?
CAREFUL!
IT'S OK, GRACE. I'VE HANDLED REPTILES.
IF DRAGONS ARE LIKE MOST LIZARDS: BOY.
WHAT IS IT YOU'RE LOOKING AT EXACTLY?
HISS
ACK! SORRY! SORRY!

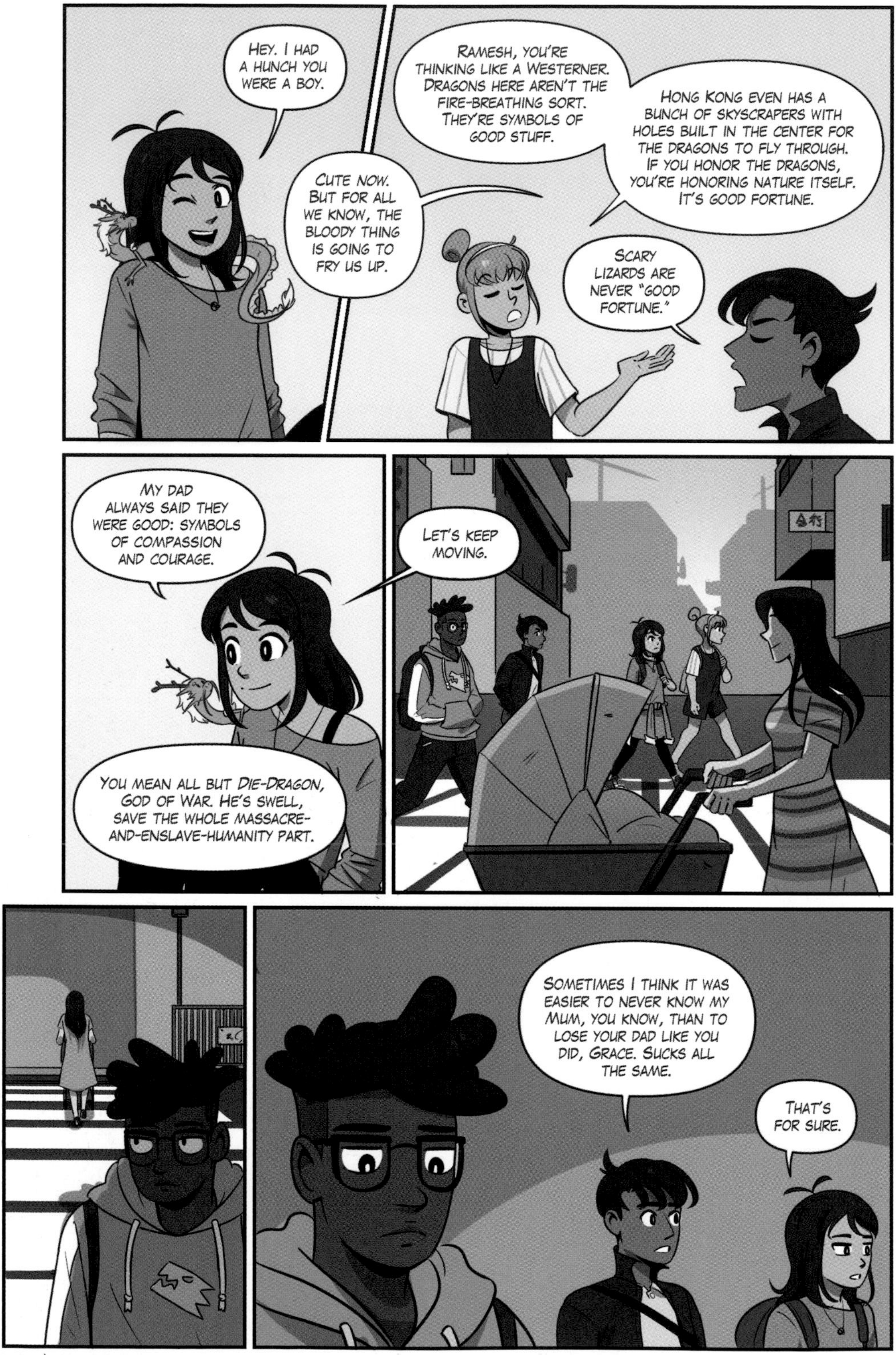
HEY. I HAD A HUNCH YOU WERE A BOY.
CUTE NOW. BUT FOR ALL WE KNOW, THE BLOODY THING IS GOING TO FRY US UP.
RAMESH, YOU'RE THINKING LIKE A WESTERNER. DRAGONS HERE AREN'T THE FIRE-BREATHING SORT. THEY'RE SYMBOLS OF GOOD STUFF.
HONG KONG EVEN HAS A BUNCH OF SKYSCRAPERS WITH HOLES BUILT IN THE CENTER FOR THE DRAGONS TO FLY THROUGH. IF YOU HONOR THE DRAGONS, YOU'RE HONORING NATURE ITSELF. IT'S GOOD FORTUNE.
SCARY LIZARDS ARE NEVER "GOOD FORTUNE."
MY DAD ALWAYS SAID THEY WERE GOOD: SYMBOLS OF COMPASSION AND COURAGE.
YOU MEAN ALL BUT *DIE-DRAGON*, GOD OF WAR. HE'S SWELL, SAVE THE WHOLE MASSACRE-AND-ENSLAVE-HUMANITY PART.
LET'S KEEP MOVING.
SOMETIMES I THINK IT WAS EASIER TO NEVER KNOW MY MUM, YOU KNOW, THAN TO LOSE YOUR DAD LIKE YOU DID, GRACE. SUCKS ALL THE SAME.
THAT'S FOR SURE.

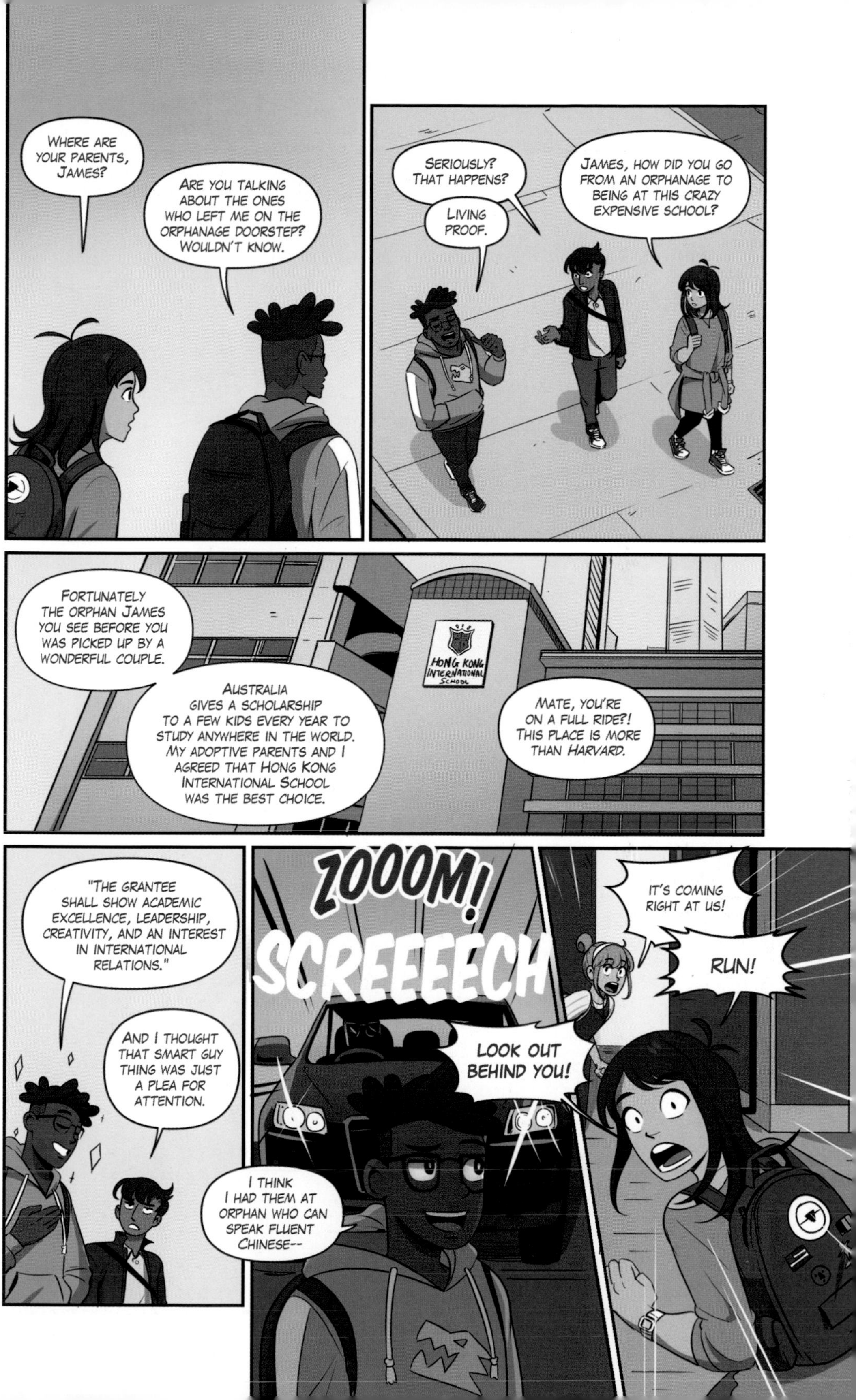
WHERE ARE YOUR PARENTS, JAMES?
ARE YOU TALKING ABOUT THE ONES WHO LEFT ME ON THE ORPHANAGE DOORSTEP? WOULDN'T KNOW.
SERIOUSLY? THAT HAPPENS?
LIVING PROOF.
JAMES, HOW DID YOU GO FROM AN ORPHANAGE TO BEING AT THIS CRAZY EXPENSIVE SCHOOL?
FORTUNATELY THE ORPHAN JAMES YOU SEE BEFORE YOU WAS PICKED UP BY A WONDERFUL COUPLE.
HONG KONG INTERNATIONAL SCHOOL
AUSTRALIA GIVES A SCHOLARSHIP TO A FEW KIDS EVERY YEAR TO STUDY ANYWHERE IN THE WORLD. MY ADOPTIVE PARENTS AND I AGREED THAT HONG KONG INTERNATIONAL SCHOOL WAS THE BEST CHOICE.
MATE, YOU'RE ON A FULL RIDE?! THIS PLACE IS MORE THAN HARVARD.
"THE GRANTEE SHALL SHOW ACADEMIC EXCELLENCE, LEADERSHIP, CREATIVITY, AND AN INTEREST IN INTERNATIONAL RELATIONS."
AND I THOUGHT THAT SMART GUY THING WAS JUST A PLEA FOR ATTENTION.
ZOOOM!
SCREEEECH
IT'S COMING RIGHT AT US!
RUN!
LOOK OUT BEHIND YOU!
I THINK I HAD THEM AT ORPHAN WHO CAN SPEAK FLUENT CHINESE--

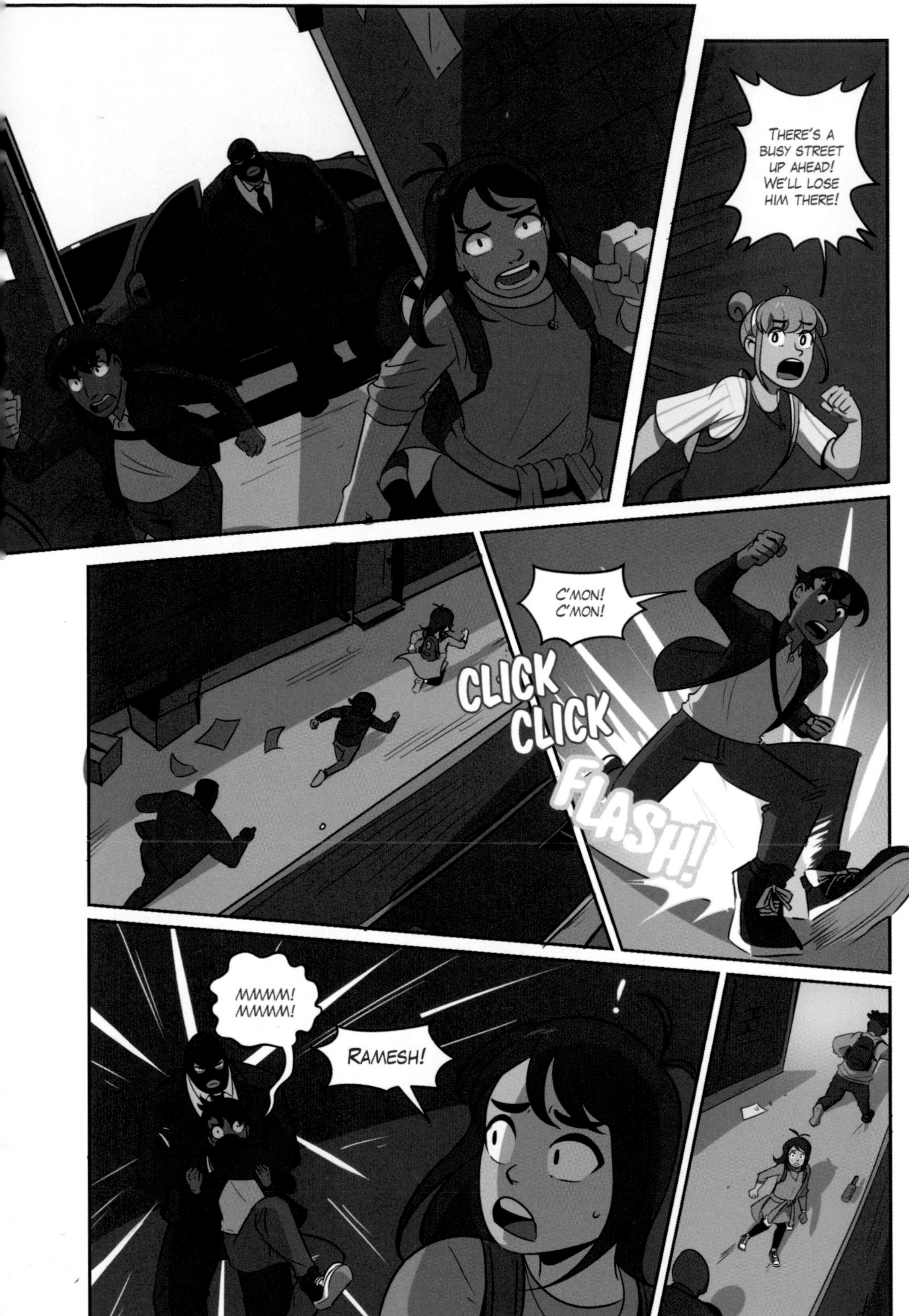
THERE'S A BUSY STREET UP AHEAD! WE'LL LOSE HIM THERE!
C'MON! C'MON!
CLICK
CLICK
FLASH!
MMMM! MMMM!
RAMESH!
!

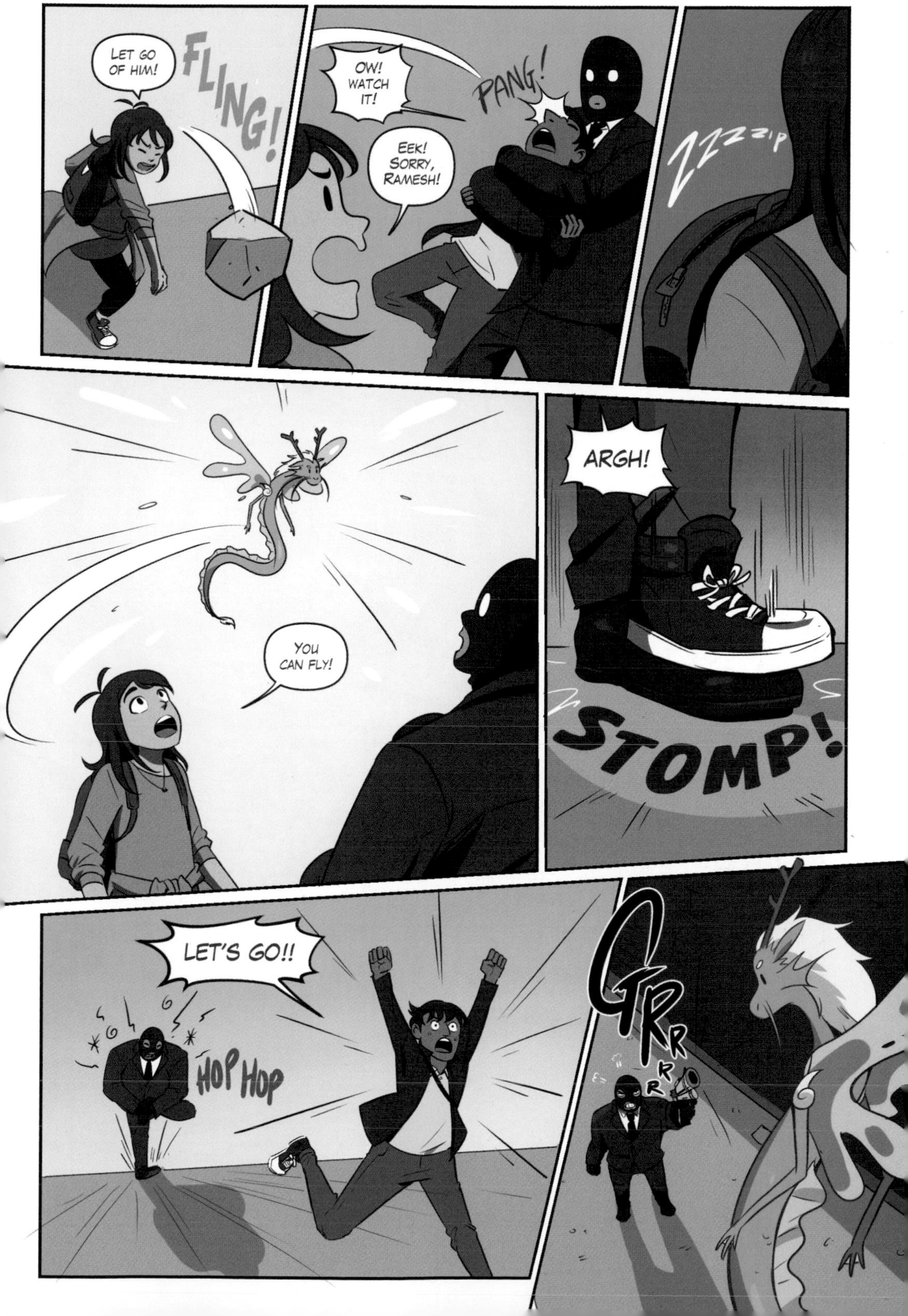

LET GO OF HIM!
FLING!
OW! WATCH IT!
PANG!
EEK! SORRY, RAMESH!
ZZZZZIP
YOU CAN FLY!
ARGH!
STOMP!
LET'S GO!!
HOP HOP
GRRRR

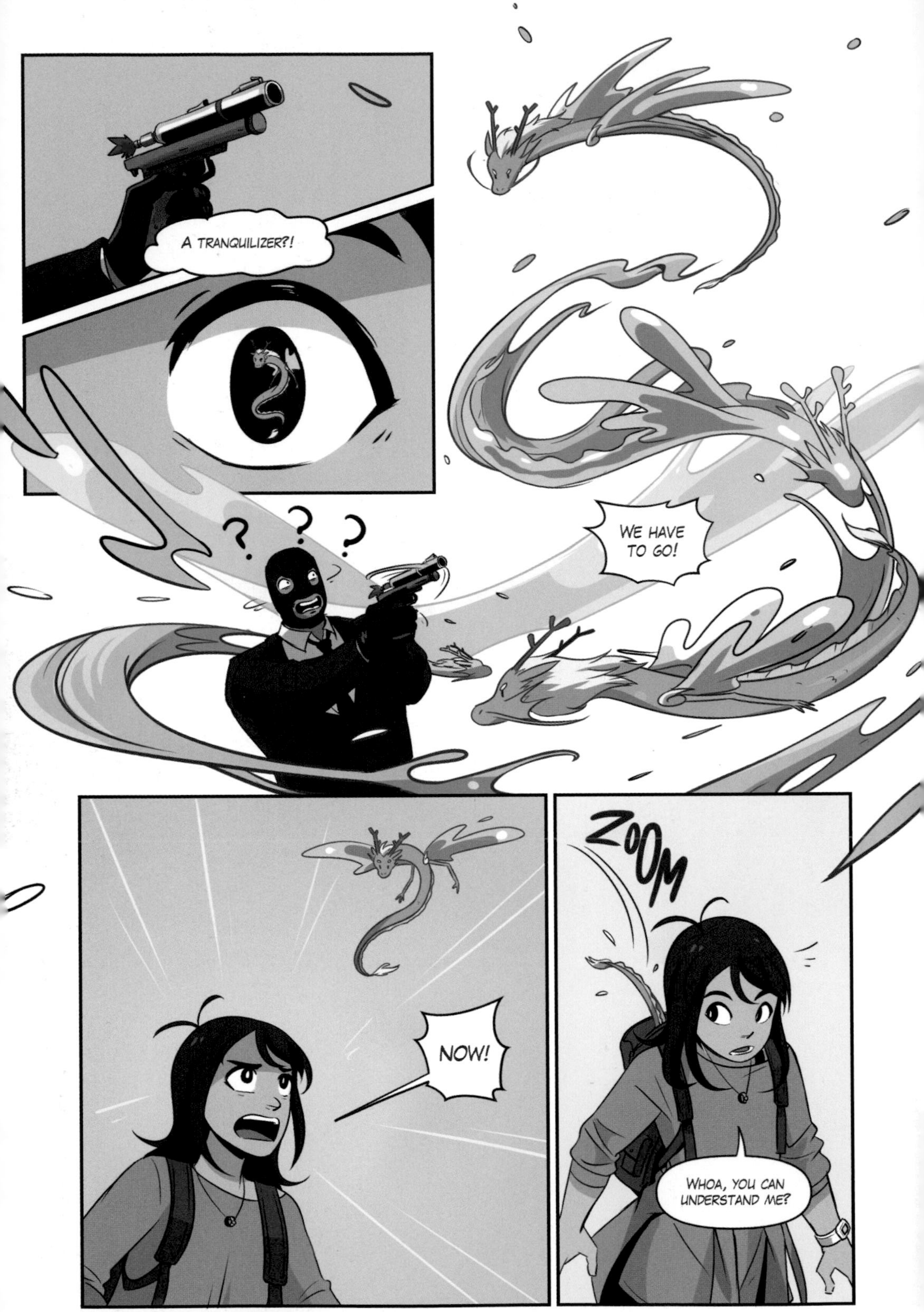
A TRANQUILIZER?!
?
?
?
WE HAVE TO GO!
NOW!
ZOOM
WHOA, YOU CAN UNDERSTAND ME?

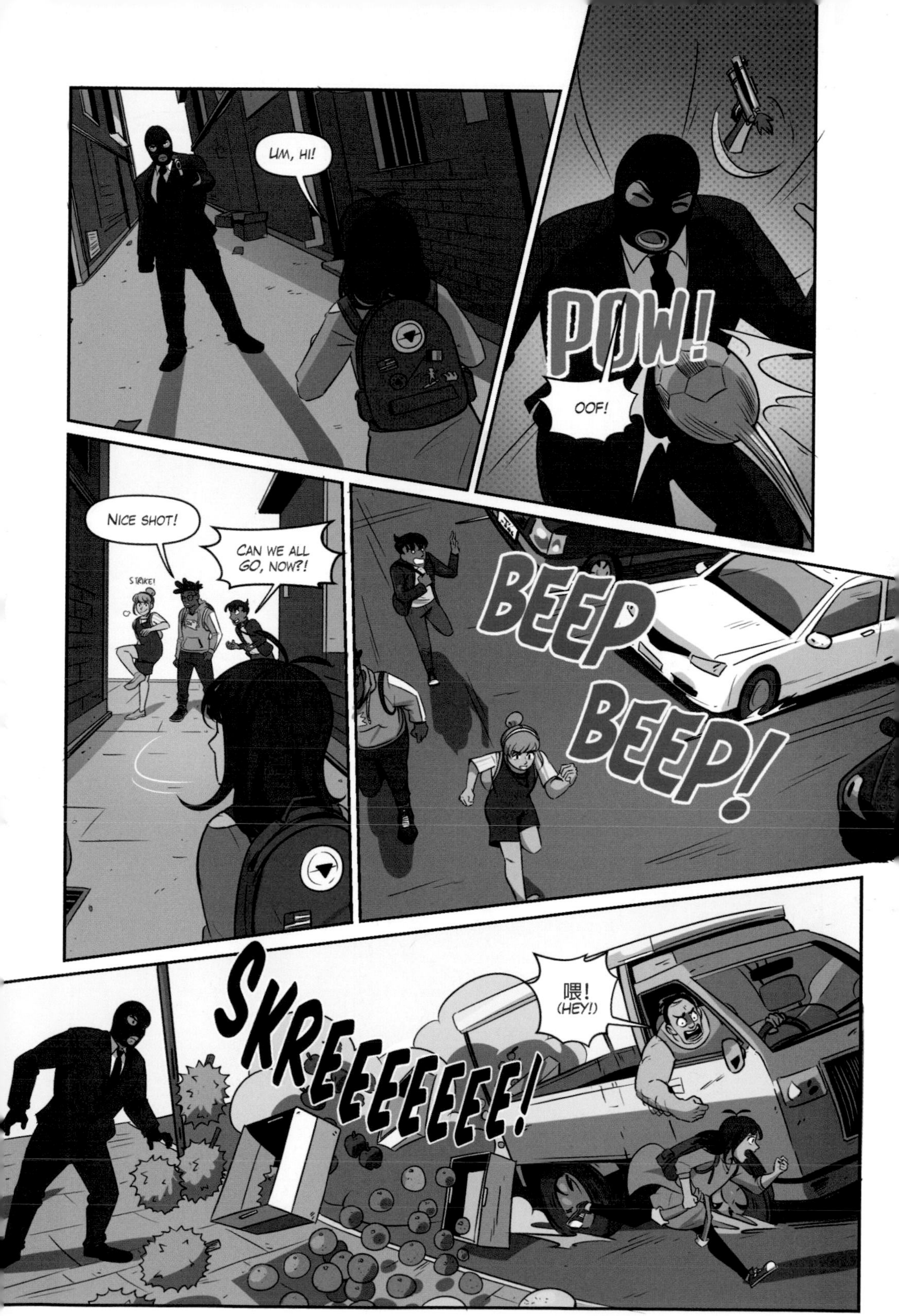
UM, HI!
POW!
OOF!
NICE SHOT!
STRIKE!
CAN WE ALL GO, NOW?!
BEEP BEEP!
SKREEEEEEEE!
喂!
(HEY!)

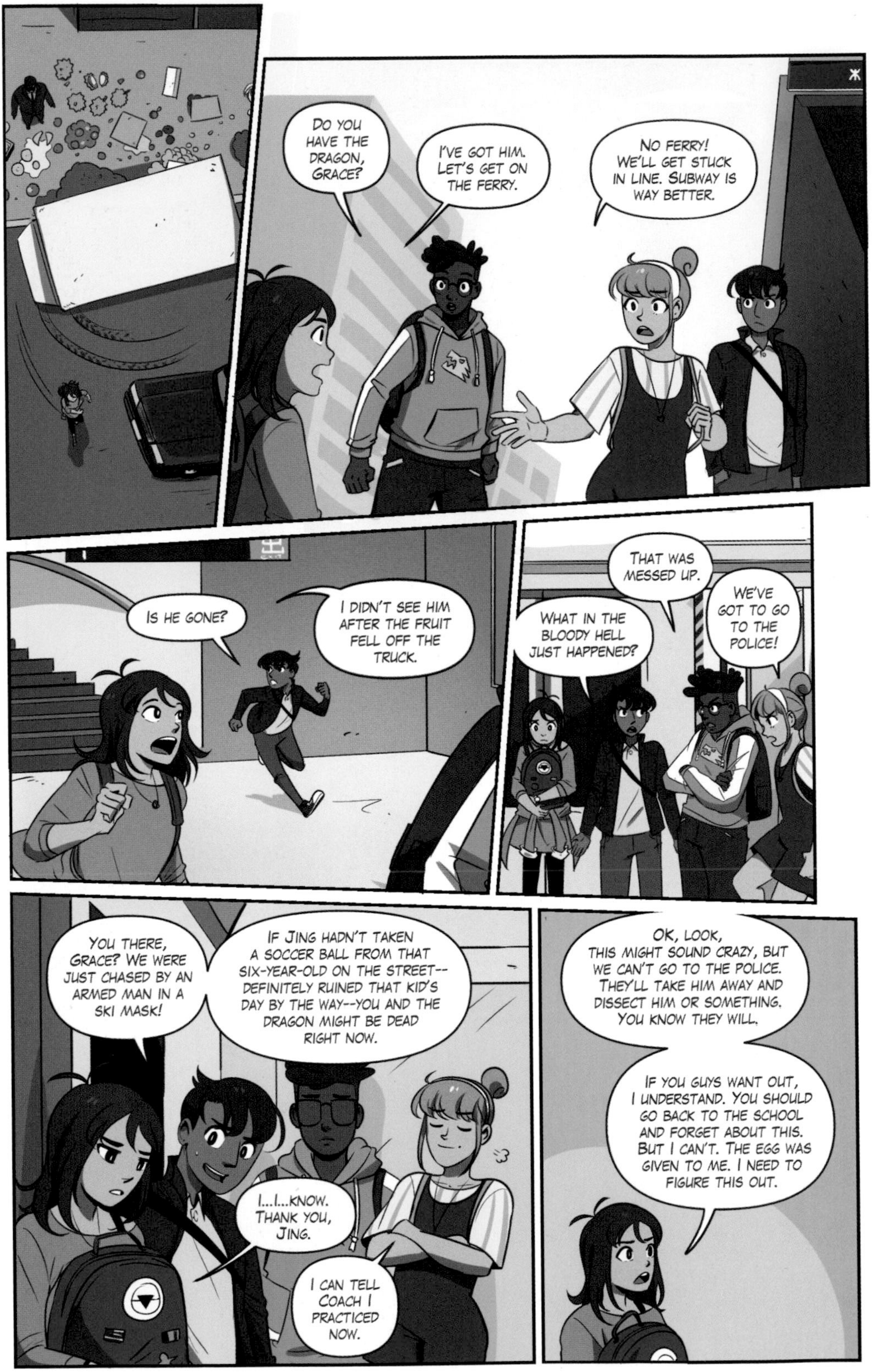
DO YOU HAVE THE DRAGON, GRACE?
I'VE GOT HIM. LET'S GET ON THE FERRY.
NO FERRY! WE'LL GET STUCK IN LINE. SUBWAY IS WAY BETTER.
IS HE GONE?
I DIDN'T SEE HIM AFTER THE FRUIT FELL OFF THE TRUCK.
WHAT IN THE BLOODY HELL JUST HAPPENED?
THAT WAS MESSED UP.
WE'VE GOT TO GO TO THE POLICE!
YOU THERE, GRACE? WE WERE JUST CHASED BY AN ARMED MAN IN A SKI MASK!
IF JING HADN'T TAKEN A SOCCER BALL FROM THAT SIX-YEAR-OLD ON THE STREET--DEFINITELY RUINED THAT KID'S DAY BY THE WAY--YOU AND THE DRAGON MIGHT BE DEAD RIGHT NOW.
I...I...KNOW. THANK YOU, JING.
I CAN TELL COACH I PRACTICED NOW.
OK, LOOK, THIS MIGHT SOUND CRAZY, BUT WE CAN'T GO TO THE POLICE. THEY'LL TAKE HIM AWAY AND DISSECT HIM OR SOMETHING. YOU KNOW THEY WILL.
IF YOU GUYS WANT OUT, I UNDERSTAND. YOU SHOULD GO BACK TO THE SCHOOL AND FORGET ABOUT THIS. BUT I CAN'T. THE EGG WAS GIVEN TO ME. I NEED TO FIGURE THIS OUT.

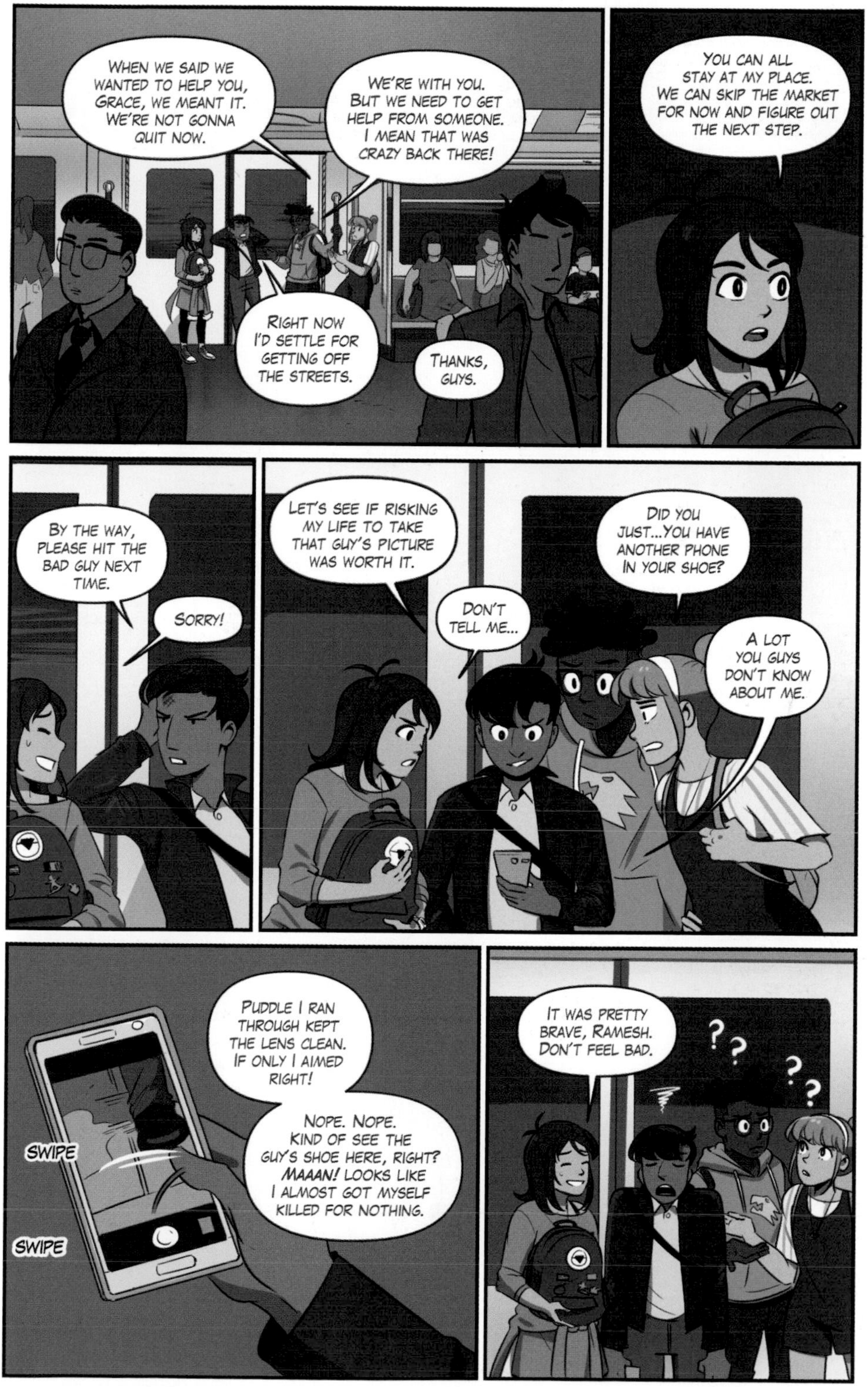

When we said we wanted to help you, Grace, we meant it. We're not gonna quit now.
We're with you. But we need to get help from someone. I mean that was crazy back there!
Right now I'd settle for getting off the streets.
Thanks, guys.
You can all stay at my place. We can skip the market for now and figure out the next step.
By the way, please hit the bad guy next time.
Sorry!
Let's see if risking my life to take that guy's picture was worth it.
Don't tell me...
Did you just...You have another phone in your shoe?
A lot you guys don't know about me.
Puddle I ran through kept the lens clean. If only I aimed right!
Nope. Nope. Kind of see the guy's shoe here, right? *Maaan!* Looks like I almost got myself killed for nothing.
SWIPE
SWIPE
It was pretty brave, Ramesh. Don't feel bad.
? ?
? ?

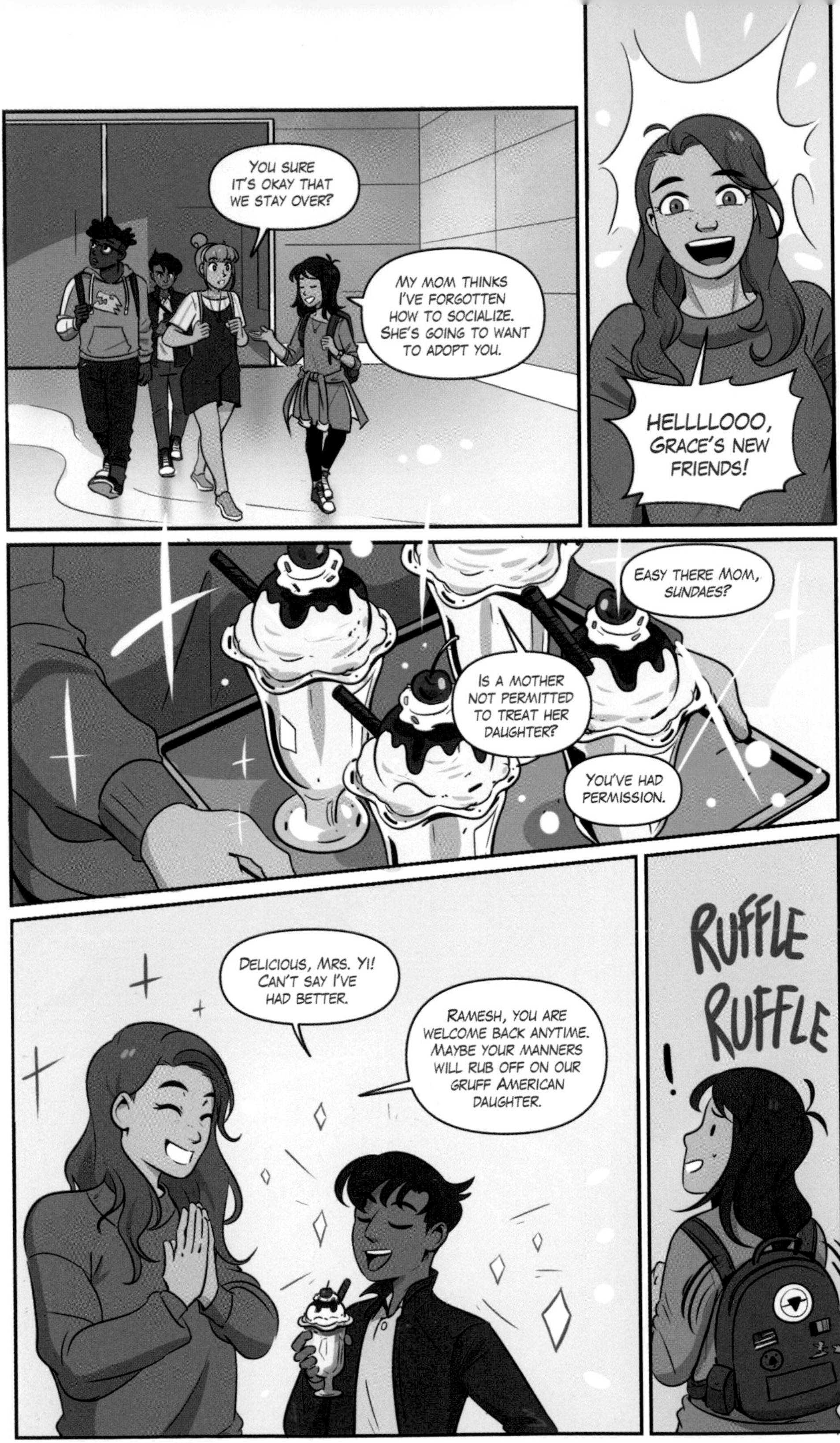
YOU SURE IT'S OKAY THAT WE STAY OVER?
MY MOM THINKS I'VE FORGOTTEN HOW TO SOCIALIZE. SHE'S GOING TO WANT TO ADOPT YOU.
HELLLLOOO, GRACE'S NEW FRIENDS!
EASY THERE MOM, SUNDAES?
IS A MOTHER NOT PERMITTED TO TREAT HER DAUGHTER?
YOU'VE HAD PERMISSION.
DELICIOUS, MRS. YI! CAN'T SAY I'VE HAD BETTER.
RAMESH, YOU ARE WELCOME BACK ANYTIME. MAYBE YOUR MANNERS WILL RUB OFF ON OUR GRUFF AMERICAN DAUGHTER.
RUFFLE
RUFFLE
!

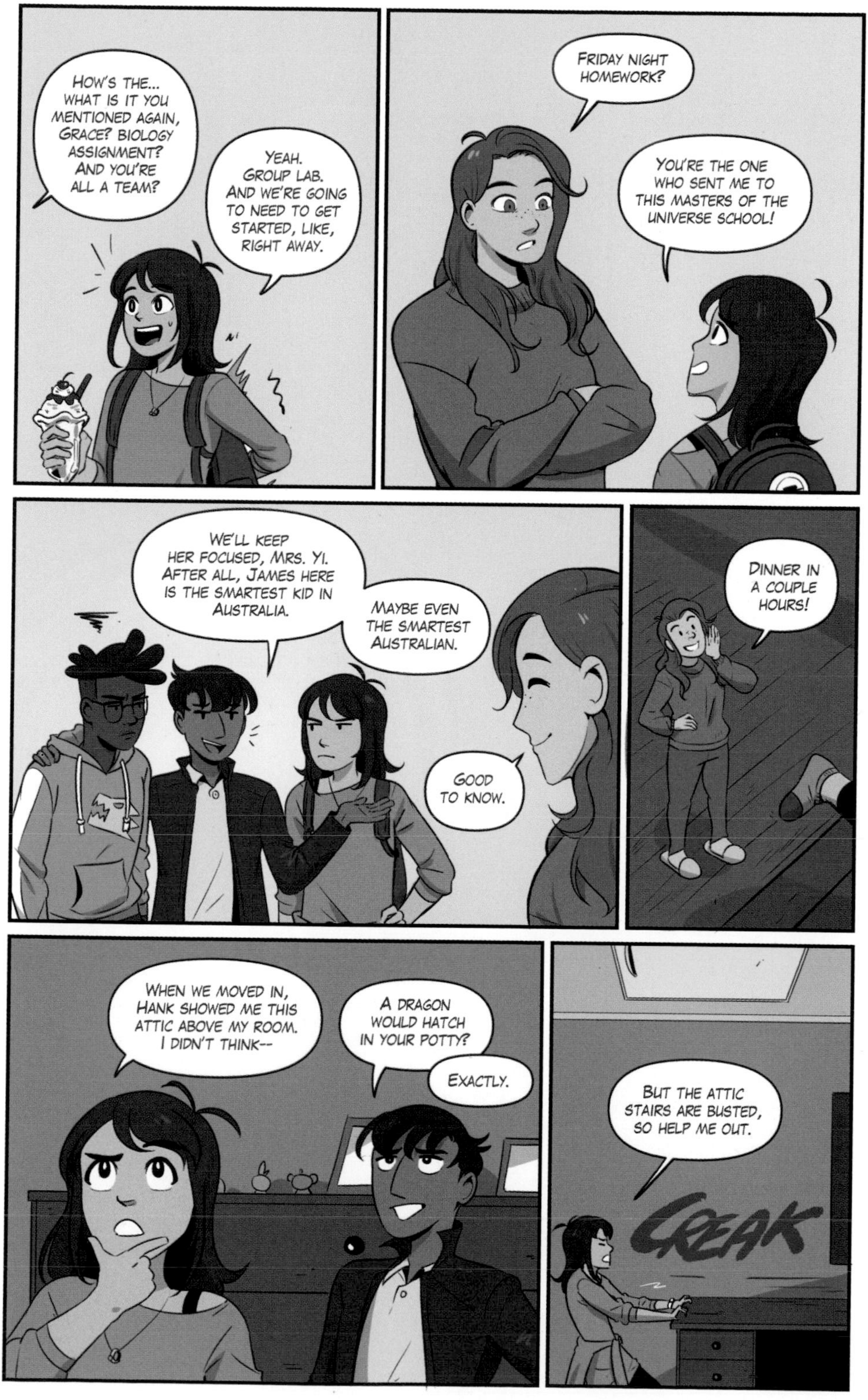
How's the... what is it you mentioned again, Grace? Biology assignment? And you're all a team?
Yeah. Group lab. And we're going to need to get started, like, right away.
Friday night homework?
You're the one who sent me to this Masters of the Universe school!
We'll keep her focused, Mrs. Yi. After all, James here is the smartest kid in Australia.
Maybe even the smartest Australian.
Good to know.
Dinner in a couple hours!
When we moved in, Hank showed me this attic above my room. I didn't think--
A dragon would hatch in your potty?
Exactly.
But the attic stairs are busted, so help me out.
CREAK

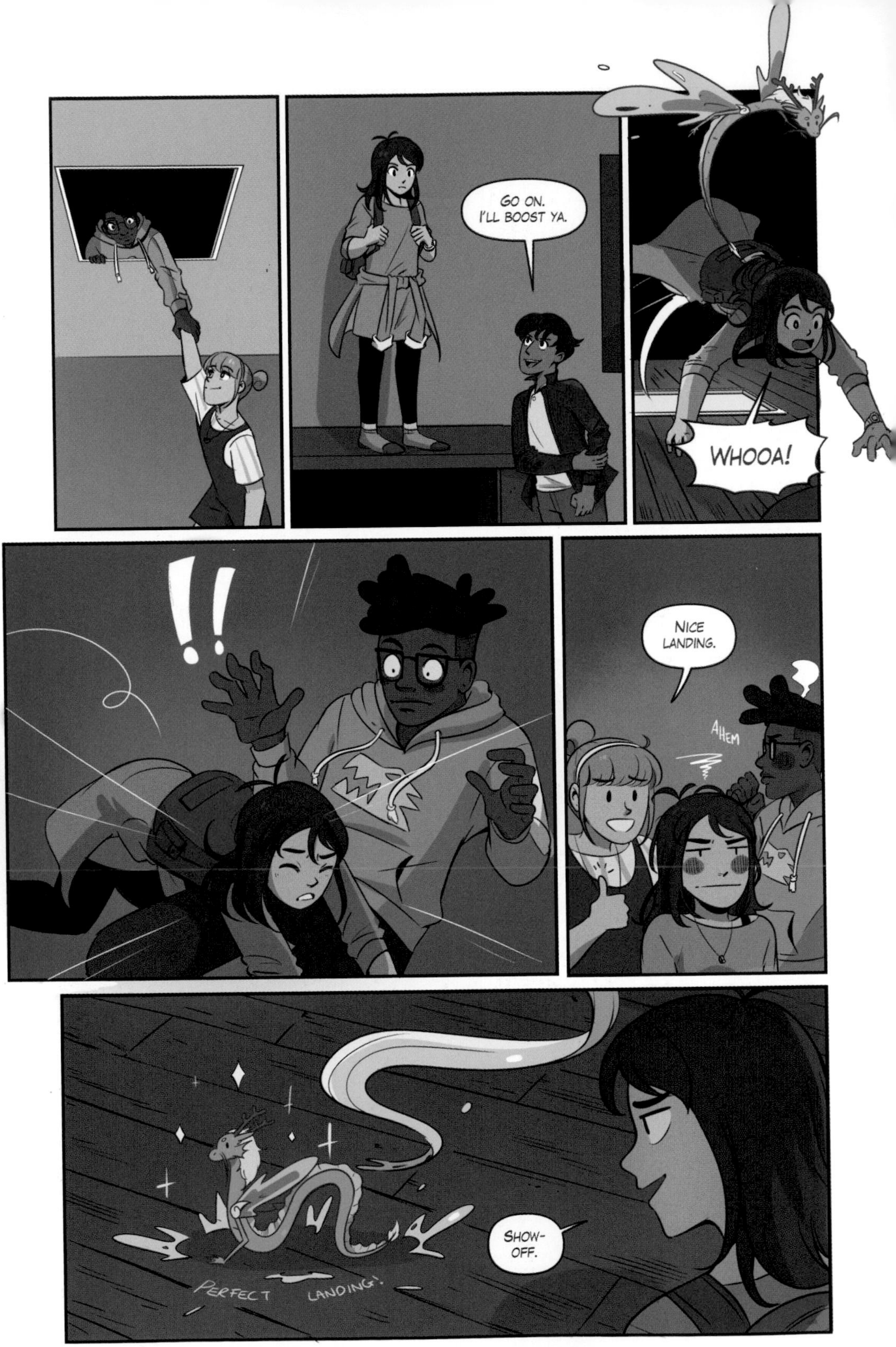
GO ON.
I'LL BOOST YA.
WHOOA!
!!
NICE
LANDING.
AHEM
SHOW-
OFF.
PERFECT LANDING!

DON'T WORRY ABOUT ME. I GOT THIS.

OKAY, I'VE GOT IT. I'VE GOT IT.

I DON'T THINK YOU DO!

I BROUGHT SOME EXTRA SNACKS FROM LUNCH.

SO FAR DRAGONS AREN'T PICKY EATERS.

I GUESS WE HAVE TO FIND A PLACE TO RELEASE HIM INTO THE WILD.

YEAH. TEACH HIM TO HUNT UNICORNS. IT'LL BE GRAND.

FIRST, WE NEED TO FIND OUT WHY HE'S BEING HUNTED.

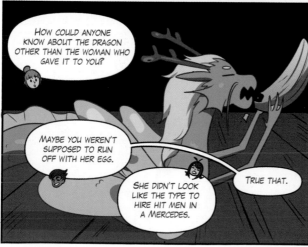

HOW COULD ANYONE KNOW ABOUT THE DRAGON OTHER THAN THE WOMAN WHO GAVE IT TO YOU?

MAYBE YOU WEREN'T SUPPOSED TO RUN OFF WITH HER EGG.

SHE DIDN'T LOOK LIKE THE TYPE TO HIRE HIT MEN IN A MERCEDES.

TRUE THAT.

I WISH DAD WERE HERE. HE'D BE ABLE TO HELP.

GRACE, YOU DON'T HAVE TO SAY, BUT WHAT... HAPPENED TO HIM, YOUR DAD?

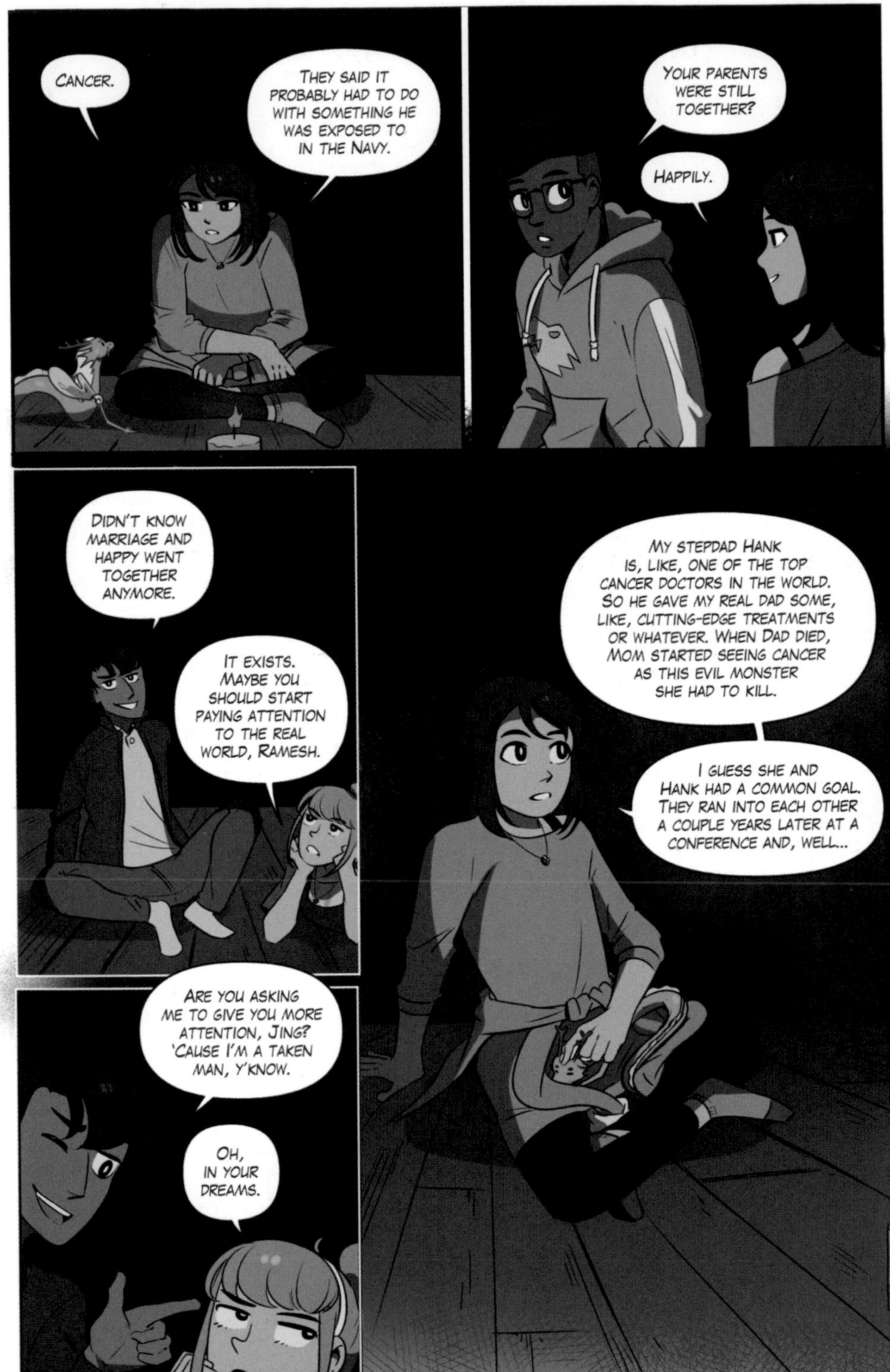
CANCER.
THEY SAID IT PROBABLY HAD TO DO WITH SOMETHING HE WAS EXPOSED TO IN THE NAVY.
YOUR PARENTS WERE STILL TOGETHER?
HAPPILY.
DIDN'T KNOW MARRIAGE AND HAPPY WENT TOGETHER ANYMORE.
IT EXISTS. MAYBE YOU SHOULD START PAYING ATTENTION TO THE REAL WORLD, RAMESH.
ARE YOU ASKING ME TO GIVE YOU MORE ATTENTION, JING? 'CAUSE I'M A TAKEN MAN, Y'KNOW.
OH, IN YOUR DREAMS.
MY STEPDAD HANK IS, LIKE, ONE OF THE TOP CANCER DOCTORS IN THE WORLD. SO HE GAVE MY REAL DAD SOME, LIKE, CUTTING-EDGE TREATMENTS OR WHATEVER. WHEN DAD DIED, MOM STARTED SEEING CANCER AS THIS EVIL MONSTER SHE HAD TO KILL.
I GUESS SHE AND HANK HAD A COMMON GOAL. THEY RAN INTO EACH OTHER A COUPLE YEARS LATER AT A CONFERENCE AND, WELL...

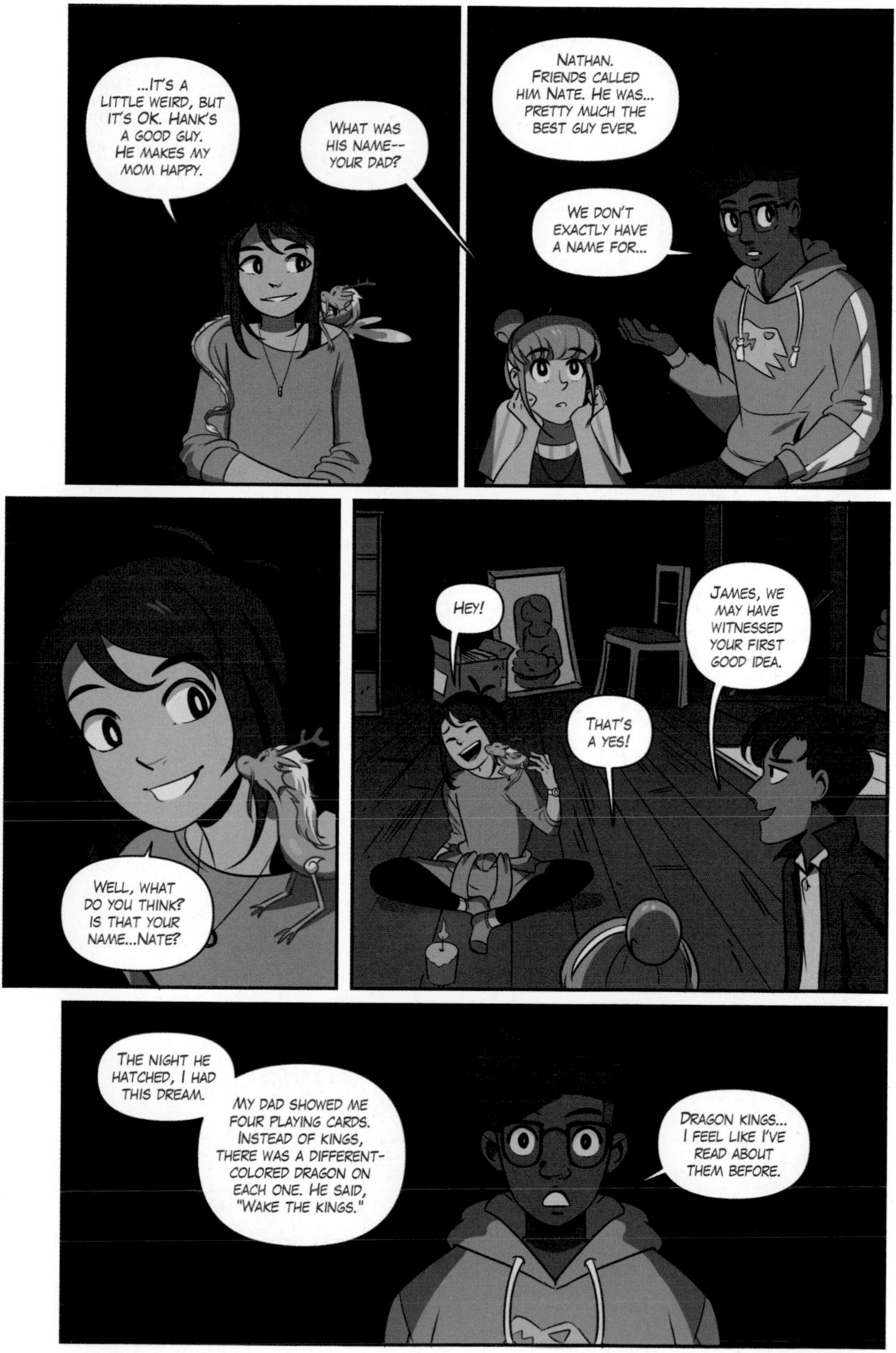
...IT'S A LITTLE WEIRD, BUT IT'S OK. HANK'S A GOOD GUY. HE MAKES MY MOM HAPPY.
WHAT WAS HIS NAME-- YOUR DAD?
NATHAN. FRIENDS CALLED HIM NATE. HE WAS... PRETTY MUCH THE BEST GUY EVER.
WE DON'T EXACTLY HAVE A NAME FOR...
WELL, WHAT DO YOU THINK? IS THAT YOUR NAME...NATE?
HEY!
JAMES, WE MAY HAVE WITNESSED YOUR FIRST GOOD IDEA.
THAT'S A YES!
THE NIGHT HE HATCHED, I HAD THIS DREAM.
MY DAD SHOWED ME FOUR PLAYING CARDS. INSTEAD OF KINGS, THERE WAS A DIFFERENT-COLORED DRAGON ON EACH ONE. HE SAID, "WAKE THE KINGS."
DRAGON KINGS... I FEEL LIKE I'VE READ ABOUT THEM BEFORE.

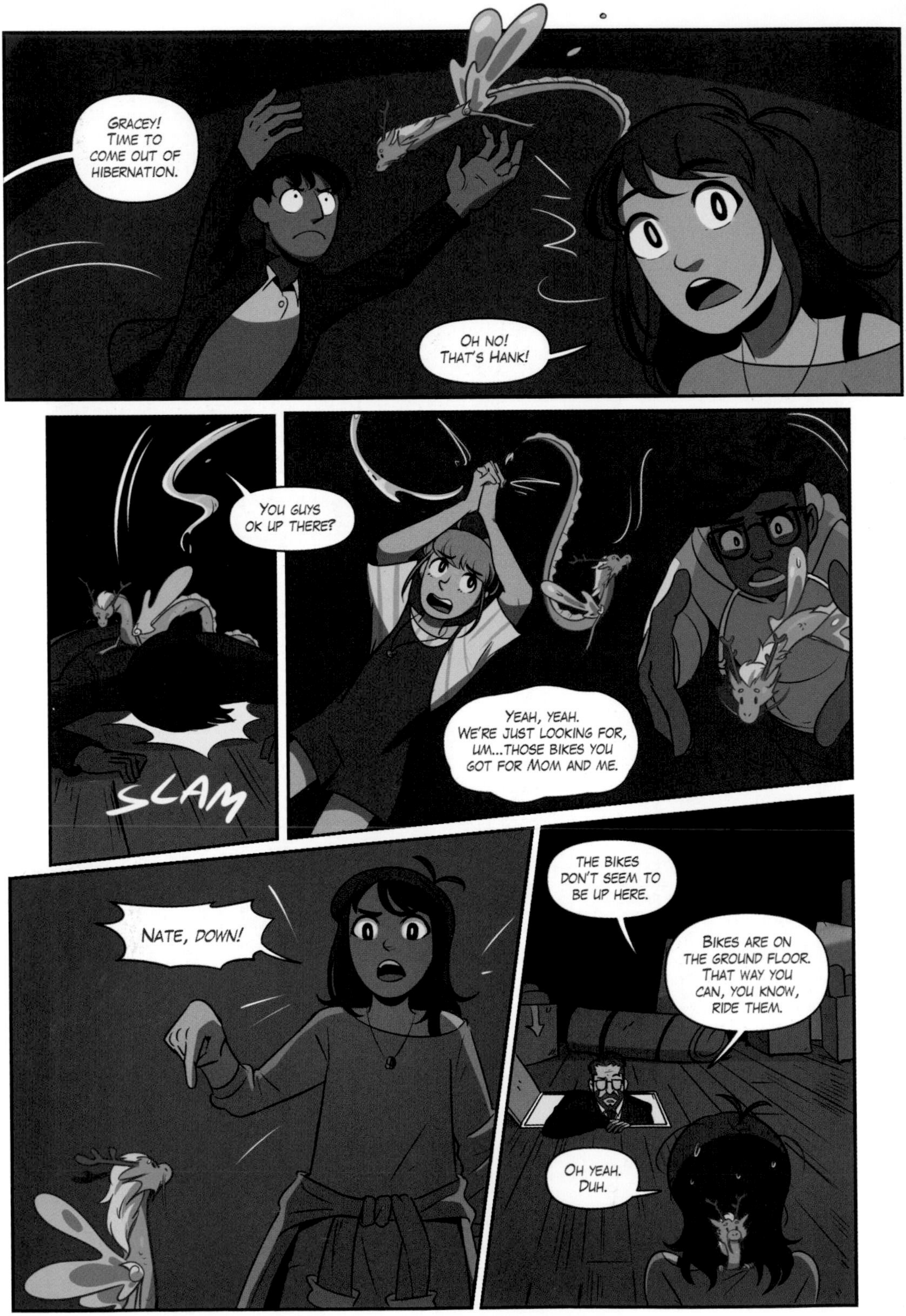
GRACEY! TIME TO COME OUT OF HIBERNATION.
OH NO! THAT'S HANK!
YOU GUYS OK UP THERE?
SLAM
YEAH, YEAH. WE'RE JUST LOOKING FOR, UM...THOSE BIKES YOU GOT FOR MOM AND ME.
NATE, DOWN!
THE BIKES DON'T SEEM TO BE UP HERE.
BIKES ARE ON THE GROUND FLOOR. THAT WAY YOU CAN, YOU KNOW, RIDE THEM.
OH YEAH. DUH.

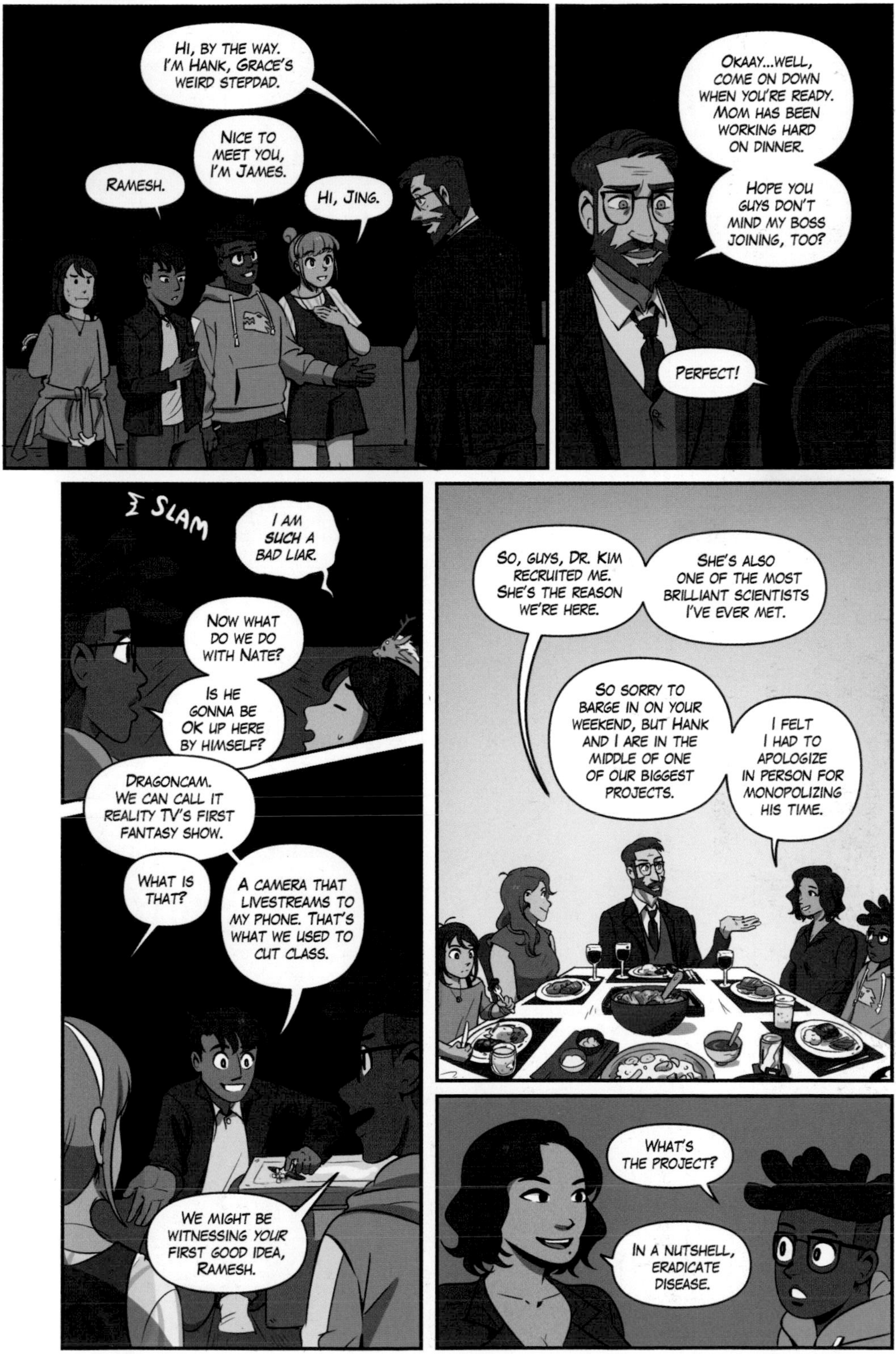
HI, BY THE WAY. I'M HANK, GRACE'S WEIRD STEPDAD.
RAMESH.
NICE TO MEET YOU, I'M JAMES.
HI, JING.
OKAAY...WELL, COME ON DOWN WHEN YOU'RE READY. MOM HAS BEEN WORKING HARD ON DINNER.
HOPE YOU GUYS DON'T MIND MY BOSS JOINING, TOO?
PERFECT!
SLAM
I AM SUCH A BAD LIAR.
NOW WHAT DO WE DO WITH NATE?
IS HE GONNA BE OK UP HERE BY HIMSELF?
DRAGONCAM. WE CAN CALL IT REALITY TV'S FIRST FANTASY SHOW.
WHAT IS THAT?
A CAMERA THAT LIVESTREAMS TO MY PHONE. THAT'S WHAT WE USED TO CUT CLASS.
WE MIGHT BE WITNESSING YOUR FIRST GOOD IDEA, RAMESH.
SO, GUYS, DR. KIM RECRUITED ME. SHE'S THE REASON WE'RE HERE.
SHE'S ALSO ONE OF THE MOST BRILLIANT SCIENTISTS I'VE EVER MET.
SO SORRY TO BARGE IN ON YOUR WEEKEND, BUT HANK AND I ARE IN THE MIDDLE OF ONE OF OUR BIGGEST PROJECTS.
I FELT I HAD TO APOLOGIZE IN PERSON FOR MONOPOLIZING HIS TIME.
WHAT'S THE PROJECT?
IN A NUTSHELL, ERADICATE DISEASE.

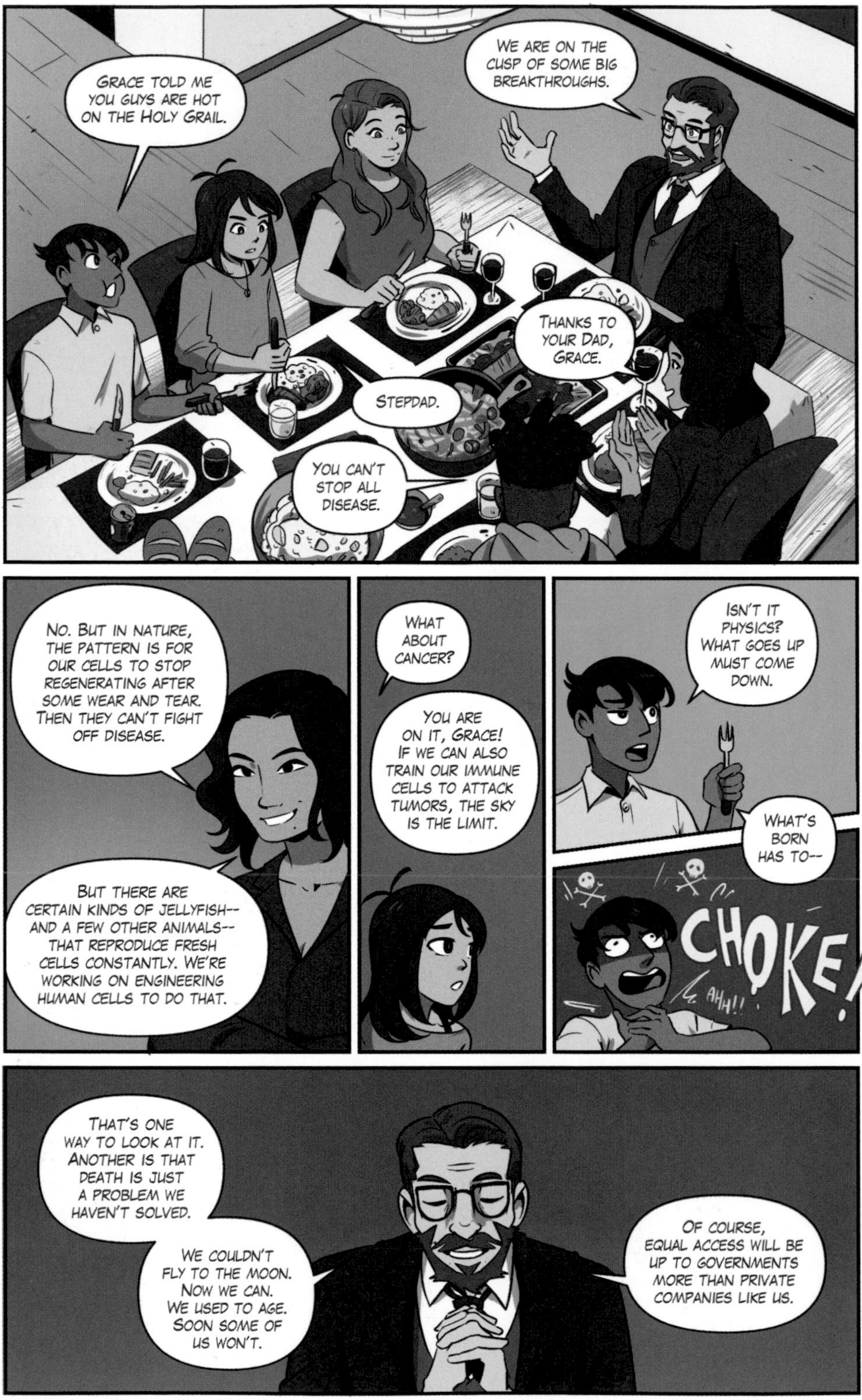
GRACE TOLD ME YOU GUYS ARE HOT ON THE HOLY GRAIL.
WE ARE ON THE CUSP OF SOME BIG BREAKTHROUGHS.
THANKS TO YOUR DAD, GRACE.
STEPDAD.
YOU CAN'T STOP ALL DISEASE.
NO. BUT IN NATURE, THE PATTERN IS FOR OUR CELLS TO STOP REGENERATING AFTER SOME WEAR AND TEAR. THEN THEY CAN'T FIGHT OFF DISEASE.
BUT THERE ARE CERTAIN KINDS OF JELLYFISH-- AND A FEW OTHER ANIMALS-- THAT REPRODUCE FRESH CELLS CONSTANTLY. WE'RE WORKING ON ENGINEERING HUMAN CELLS TO DO THAT.
WHAT ABOUT CANCER?
YOU ARE ON IT, GRACE! IF WE CAN ALSO TRAIN OUR IMMUNE CELLS TO ATTACK TUMORS, THE SKY IS THE LIMIT.
ISN'T IT PHYSICS? WHAT GOES UP MUST COME DOWN.
WHAT'S BORN HAS TO--
CHOKE!
AHH!!
THAT'S ONE WAY TO LOOK AT IT. ANOTHER IS THAT DEATH IS JUST A PROBLEM WE HAVEN'T SOLVED.
WE COULDN'T FLY TO THE MOON. NOW WE CAN. WE USED TO AGE. SOON SOME OF US WON'T.
OF COURSE, EQUAL ACCESS WILL BE UP TO GOVERNMENTS MORE THAN PRIVATE COMPANIES LIKE US.

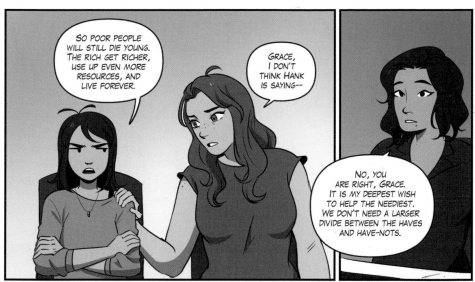

SO POOR PEOPLE WILL STILL DIE YOUNG. THE RICH GET RICHER, USE UP EVEN MORE RESOURCES, AND LIVE FOREVER.

GRACE, I DON'T THINK HANK IS SAYING--

NO, YOU ARE RIGHT, GRACE. IT IS MY DEEPEST WISH TO HELP THE NEEDIEST. WE DON'T NEED A LARGER DIVIDE BETWEEN THE HAVES AND HAVE-NOTS.

I S'POSE IT WOULD BE COOL IF YOU COULD STAY LOOKING GOOD FOREVER.

BUT IF EVERYONE'S JUST GONNA GET MORE WRINKLED AND FLABBY, BUT STILL BE HERE AND TAKING UP SPACE, THAT'D BE TRAGIC.

RAMESH, WE MIGHT HAVE TO BRING YOU IN FOR SOME CONSULTING!

HAHA

I'LL REQUIRE A WATCH, THANKS.

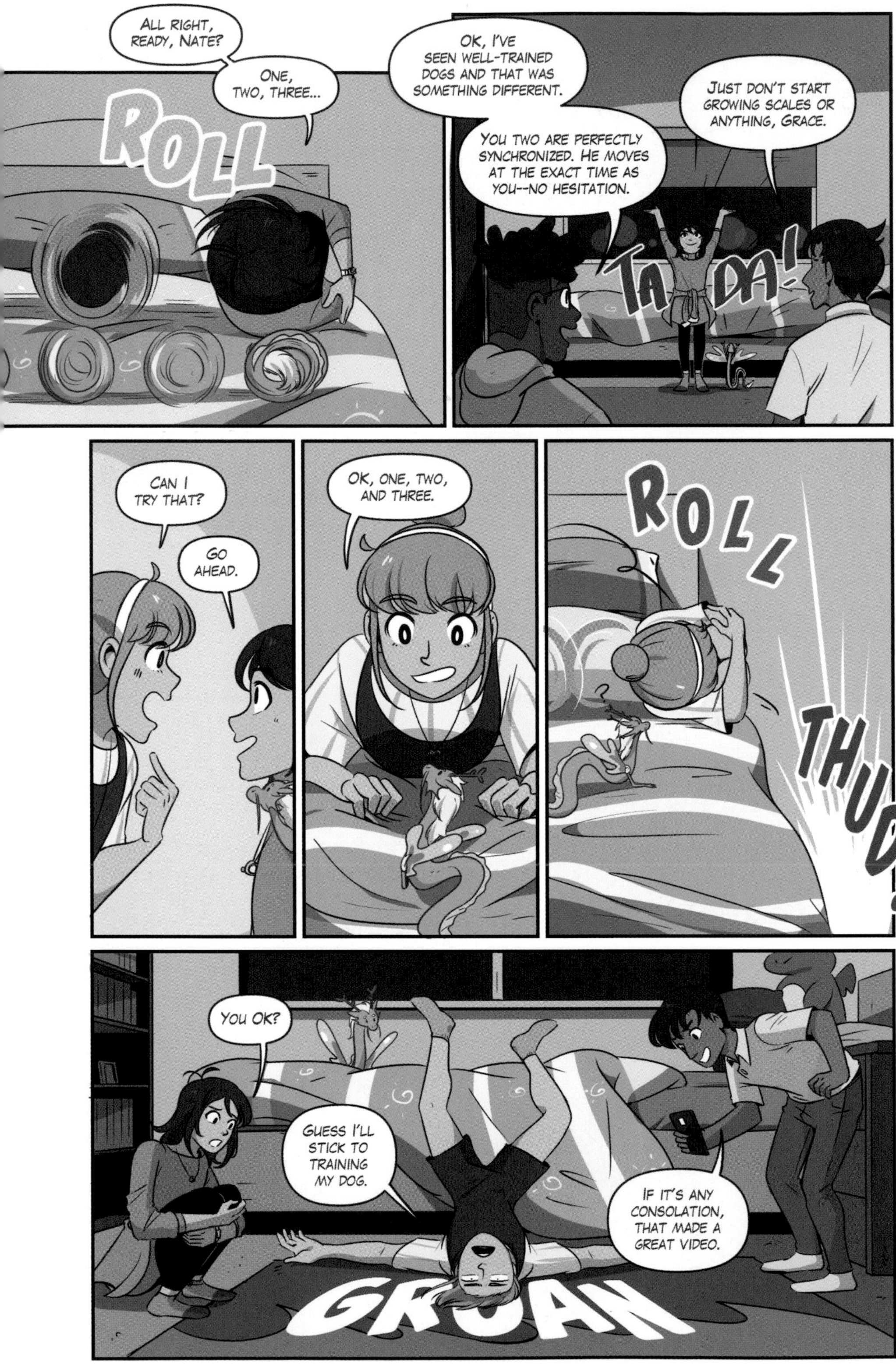
ALL RIGHT, READY, NATE?
ONE, TWO, THREE...
ROLL
OK, I'VE SEEN WELL-TRAINED DOGS AND THAT WAS SOMETHING DIFFERENT.
YOU TWO ARE PERFECTLY SYNCHRONIZED. HE MOVES AT THE EXACT TIME AS YOU--NO HESITATION.
JUST DON'T START GROWING SCALES OR ANYTHING, GRACE.
TA DA!
CAN I TRY THAT?
GO AHEAD.
OK, ONE, TWO, AND THREE.
ROLL
THUD!
YOU OK?
GUESS I'LL STICK TO TRAINING MY DOG.
IF IT'S ANY CONSOLATION, THAT MADE A GREAT VIDEO.
GROAN

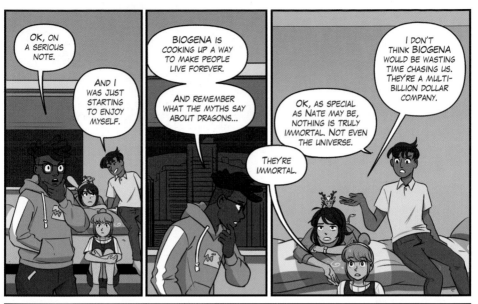

OK, ON A SERIOUS NOTE.

AND I WAS JUST STARTING TO ENJOY MYSELF.

BIOGENA IS COOKING UP A WAY TO MAKE PEOPLE LIVE FOREVER.

AND REMEMBER WHAT THE MYTHS SAY ABOUT DRAGONS...

THEY'RE IMMORTAL.

OK, AS SPECIAL AS NATE MAY BE, NOTHING IS TRULY IMMORTAL. NOT EVEN THE UNIVERSE.

I DON'T THINK BIOGENA WOULD BE WASTING TIME CHASING US. THEY'RE A MULTI-BILLION DOLLAR COMPANY.

UNLESS THEY THOUGHT THEY NEEDED THE DRAGON FOR TESTING.

YOU HEARD DR. KIM: "CERTAIN KINDS OF JELLYFISH AND OTHER ANIMALS." I HAD GOOSE BUMPS.

LET'S JUST SAY IT IS BIOGENA, WOULD YOUR STEPDAD KNOW ANYTHING ABOUT IT, GRACE?

BOUNCE

HANK WON'T EVEN JAYWALK. IF HE THOUGHT DR. KIM WAS CORRUPT, HE'D DO SOMETHING ABOUT IT. HE'S ALWAYS TALKING ABOUT "TRYING TO SAVE MANKIND."

I TRUST HIM. I THINK HE WAS SERIOUS ABOUT THE CONSULTING OFFER.

WELL THIS MIGHT SOUND PARANOID, BUT WHEN I WENT TO THE BATHROOM AT DINNER, I LOOKED DR. KIM UP ON THE NET.

CHECKING IF SHE WAS SINGLE? THINK YOU'RE A BIT YOUNG FOR HER, JAMES.

SHE'S FROM MONGOLIA.

I'M NOT SEEING THE CONNECTION.

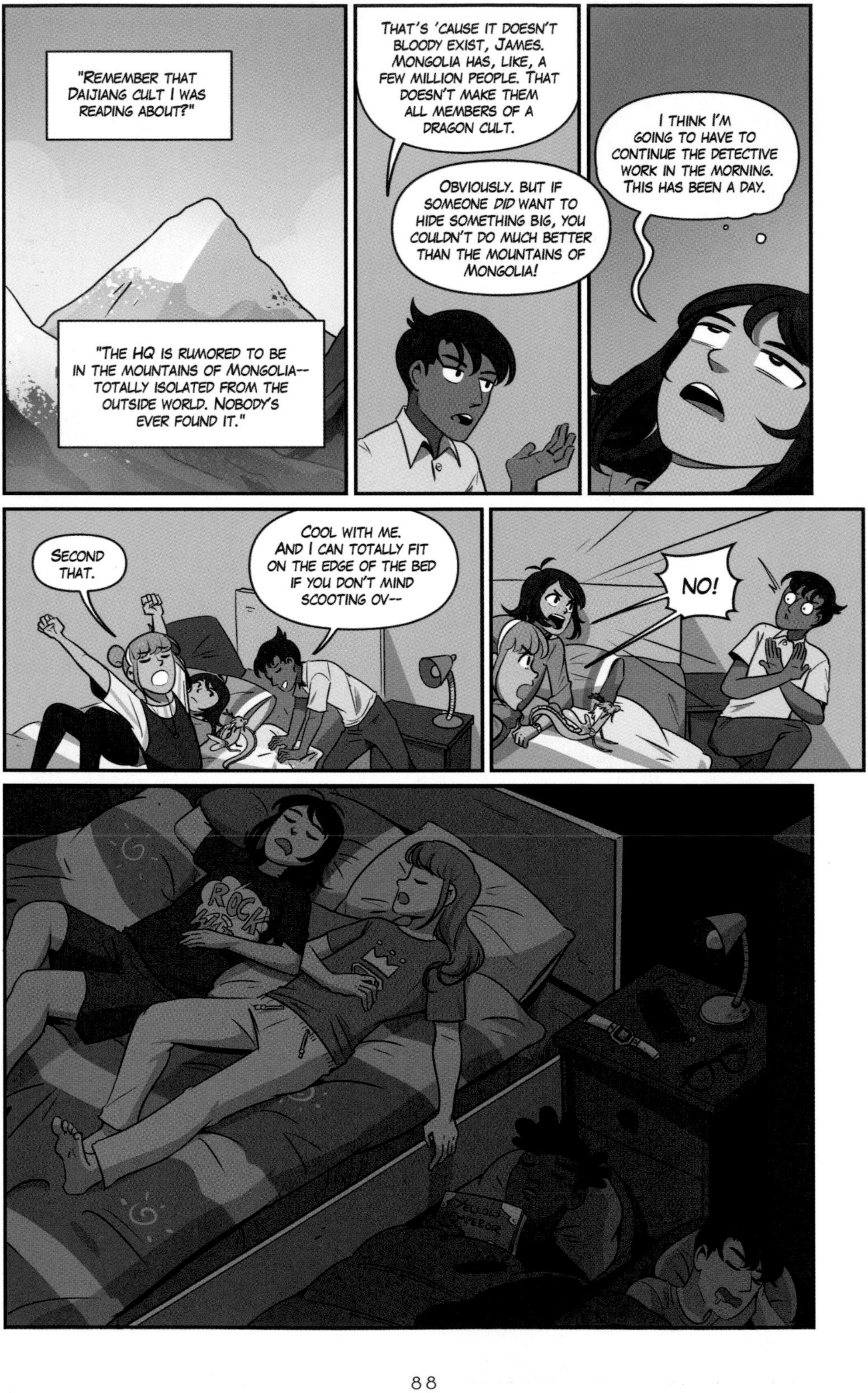
"REMEMBER THAT DAIJIANG CULT I WAS READING ABOUT?"
"THE HQ IS RUMORED TO BE IN THE MOUNTAINS OF MONGOLIA-- TOTALLY ISOLATED FROM THE OUTSIDE WORLD. NOBODY'S EVER FOUND IT."
THAT'S 'CAUSE IT DOESN'T BLOODY EXIST, JAMES. MONGOLIA HAS, LIKE, A FEW MILLION PEOPLE. THAT DOESN'T MAKE THEM ALL MEMBERS OF A DRAGON CULT.
OBVIOUSLY. BUT IF SOMEONE *DID* WANT TO HIDE SOMETHING BIG, YOU COULDN'T DO MUCH BETTER THAN THE MOUNTAINS OF MONGOLIA!
I THINK I'M GOING TO HAVE TO CONTINUE THE DETECTIVE WORK IN THE MORNING. THIS HAS BEEN A DAY.
SECOND THAT.
COOL WITH ME. AND I CAN TOTALLY FIT ON THE EDGE OF THE BED IF YOU DON'T MIND SCOOTING OV--
NO!

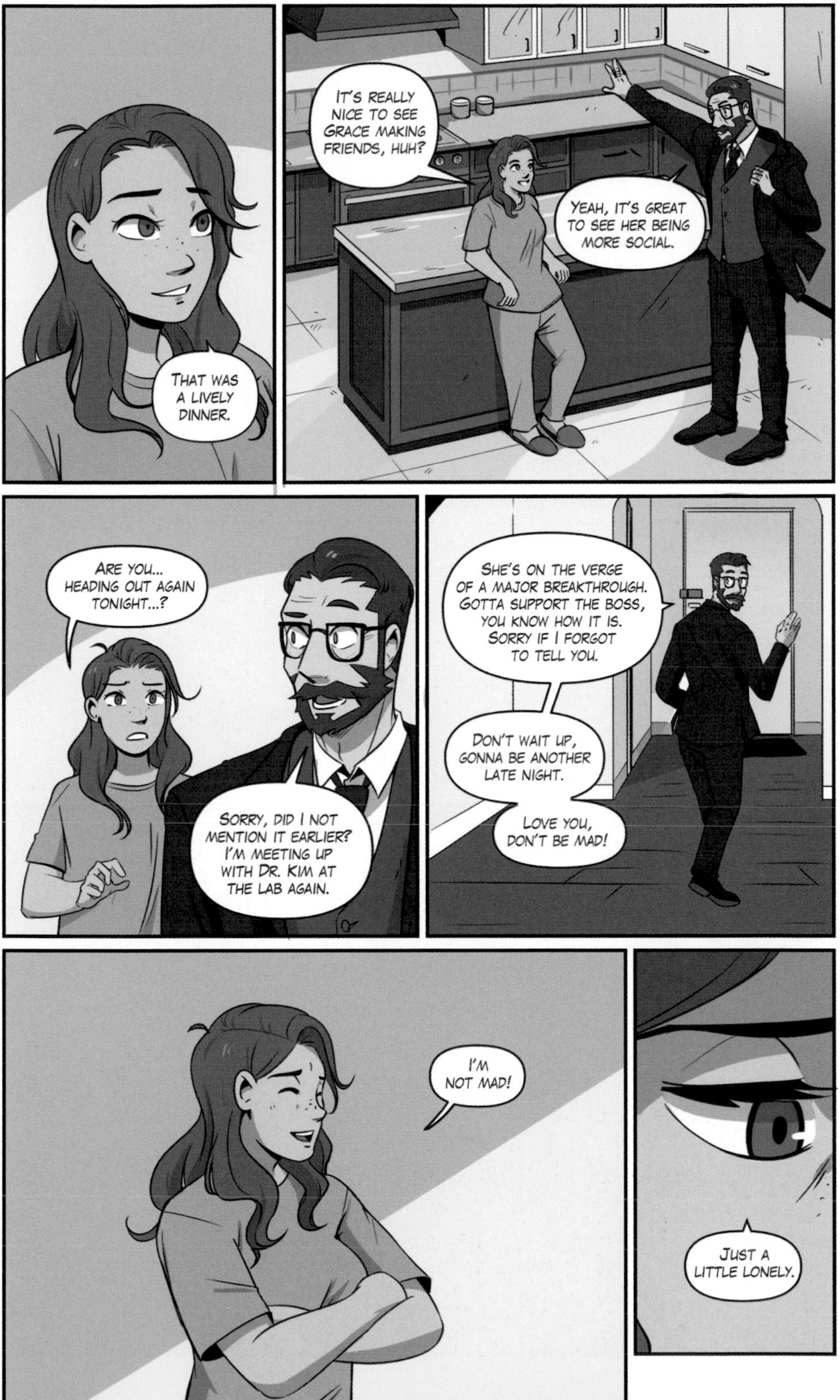
THAT WAS A LIVELY DINNER.
IT'S REALLY NICE TO SEE GRACE MAKING FRIENDS, HUH?
YEAH, IT'S GREAT TO SEE HER BEING MORE SOCIAL.
ARE YOU... HEADING OUT AGAIN TONIGHT...?
SORRY, DID I NOT MENTION IT EARLIER? I'M MEETING UP WITH DR. KIM AT THE LAB AGAIN.
SHE'S ON THE VERGE OF A MAJOR BREAKTHROUGH. GOTTA SUPPORT THE BOSS, YOU KNOW HOW IT IS. SORRY IF I FORGOT TO TELL YOU.
DON'T WAIT UP, GONNA BE ANOTHER LATE NIGHT.
LOVE YOU, DON'T BE MAD!
I'M NOT MAD!
JUST A LITTLE LONELY.

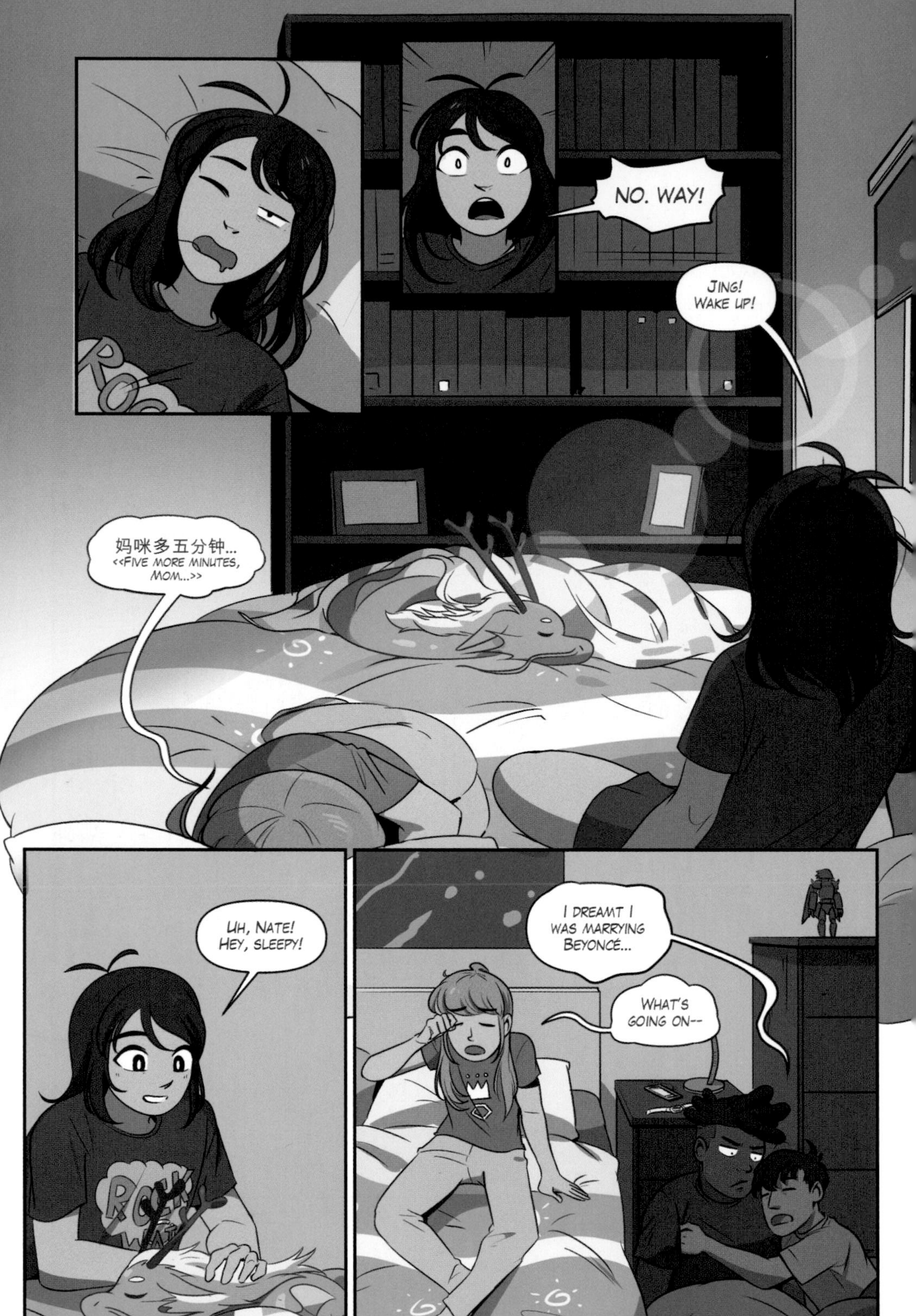
NO. WAY!
JING! WAKE UP!
妈咪多五分钟...
<<FIVE MORE MINUTES, MOM...>>
UH, NATE! HEY, SLEEPY!
I DREAMT I WAS MARRYING BEYONCÉ...
WHAT'S GOING ON--

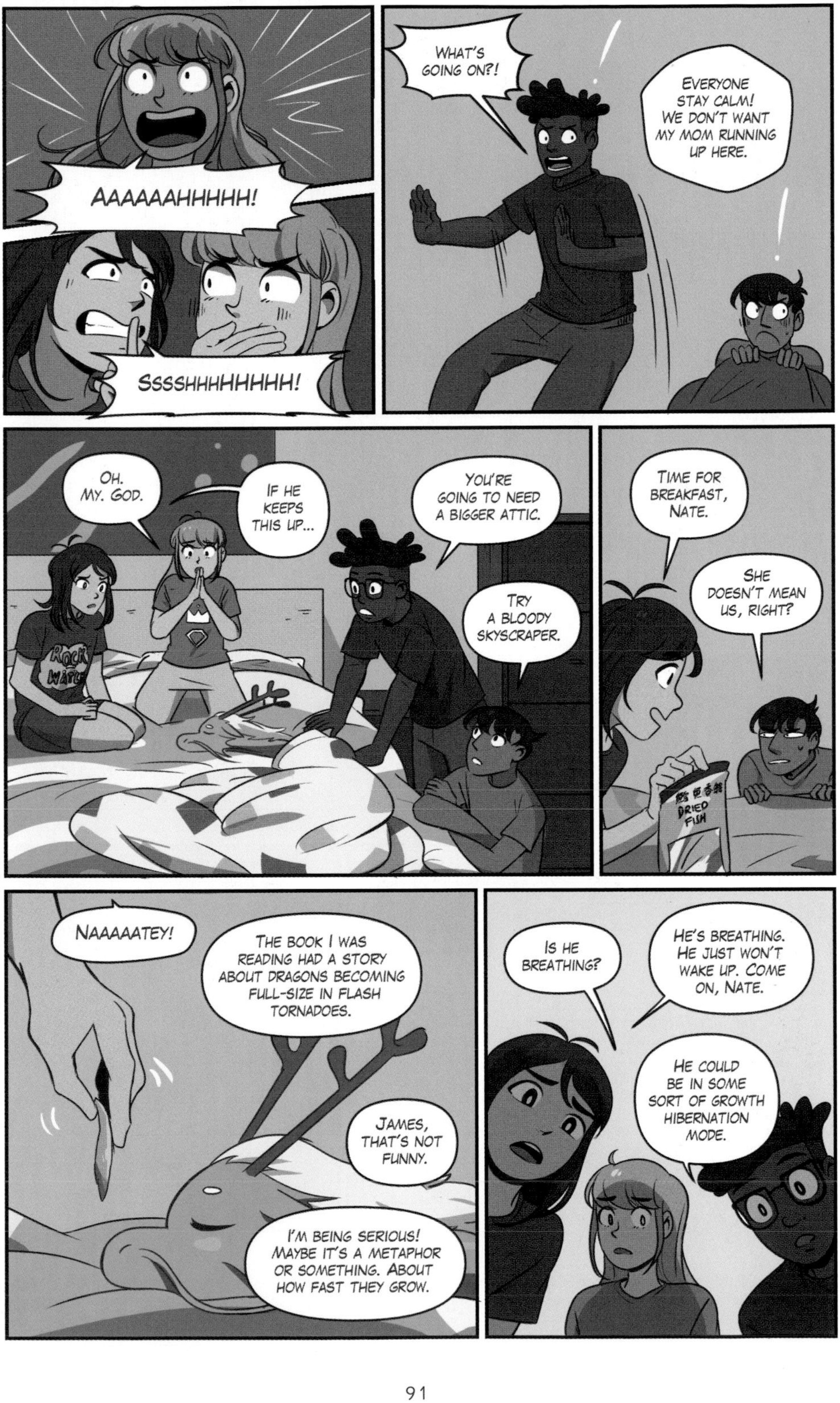
AAAAAAHHHHH!
SSSSHHHHHHHH!
WHAT'S GOING ON?!
EVERYONE STAY CALM! WE DON'T WANT MY MOM RUNNING UP HERE.
OH. MY. GOD.
IF HE KEEPS THIS UP...
YOU'RE GOING TO NEED A BIGGER ATTIC.
TRY A BLOODY SKYSCRAPER.
ROCK WATER
TIME FOR BREAKFAST, NATE.
SHE DOESN'T MEAN US, RIGHT?
DRIED FISH
NAAAAATEY!
THE BOOK I WAS READING HAD A STORY ABOUT DRAGONS BECOMING FULL-SIZE IN FLASH TORNADOES.
JAMES, THAT'S NOT FUNNY.
I'M BEING SERIOUS! MAYBE IT'S A METAPHOR OR SOMETHING. ABOUT HOW FAST THEY GROW.
IS HE BREATHING?
HE'S BREATHING. HE JUST WON'T WAKE UP. COME ON, NATE.
HE COULD BE IN SOME SORT OF GROWTH HIBERNATION MODE.

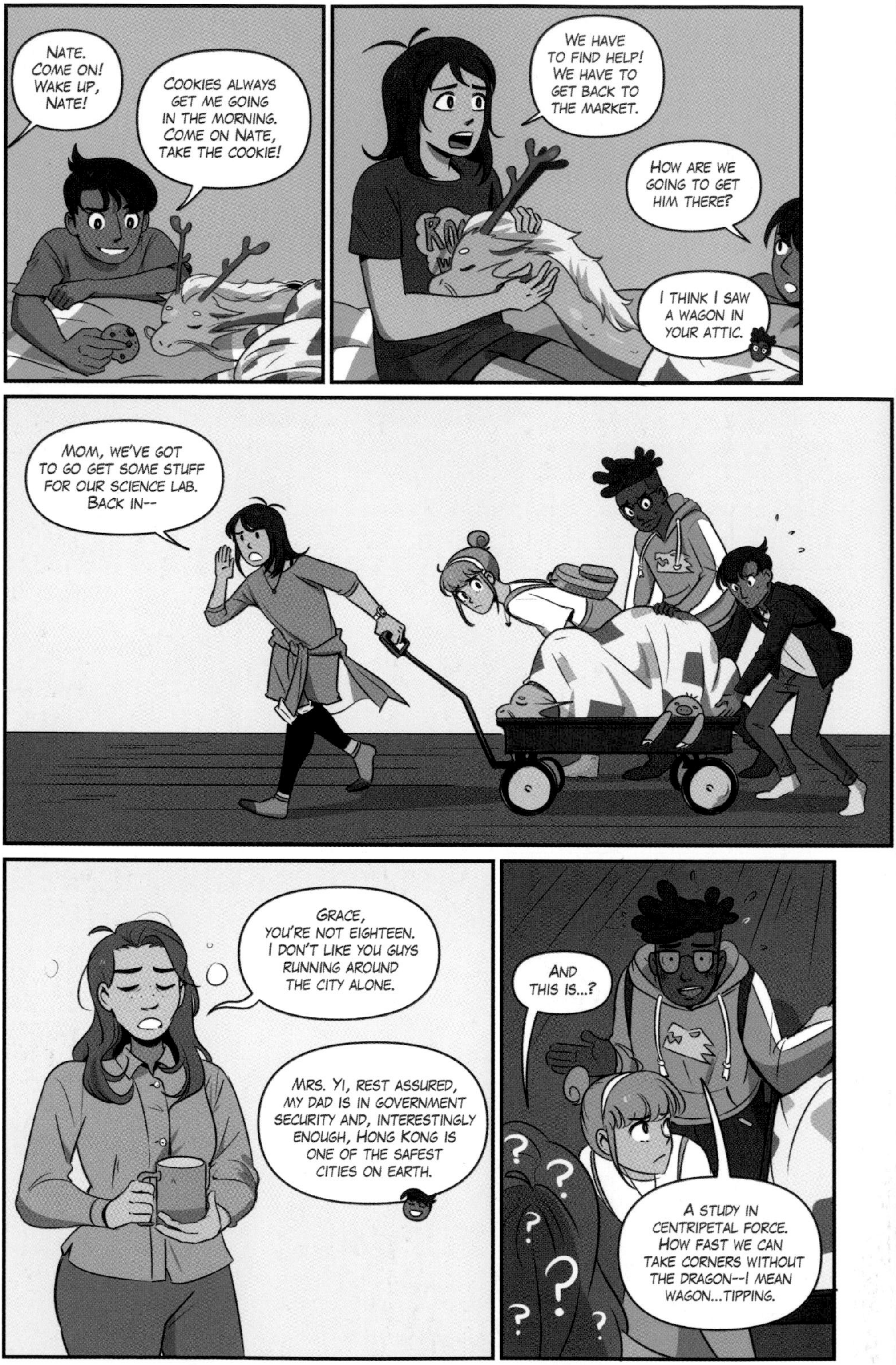

NATE. COME ON! WAKE UP, NATE!
COOKIES ALWAYS GET ME GOING IN THE MORNING. COME ON NATE, TAKE THE COOKIE!
WE HAVE TO FIND HELP! WE HAVE TO GET BACK TO THE MARKET.
HOW ARE WE GOING TO GET HIM THERE?
I THINK I SAW A WAGON IN YOUR ATTIC.
MOM, WE'VE GOT TO GO GET SOME STUFF FOR OUR SCIENCE LAB. BACK IN--
GRACE, YOU'RE NOT EIGHTEEN. I DON'T LIKE YOU GUYS RUNNING AROUND THE CITY ALONE.
MRS. YI, REST ASSURED, MY DAD IS IN GOVERNMENT SECURITY AND, INTERESTINGLY ENOUGH, HONG KONG IS ONE OF THE SAFEST CITIES ON EARTH.
AND THIS IS...?
A STUDY IN CENTRIPETAL FORCE. HOW FAST WE CAN TAKE CORNERS WITHOUT THE DRAGON--I MEAN WAGON...TIPPING.

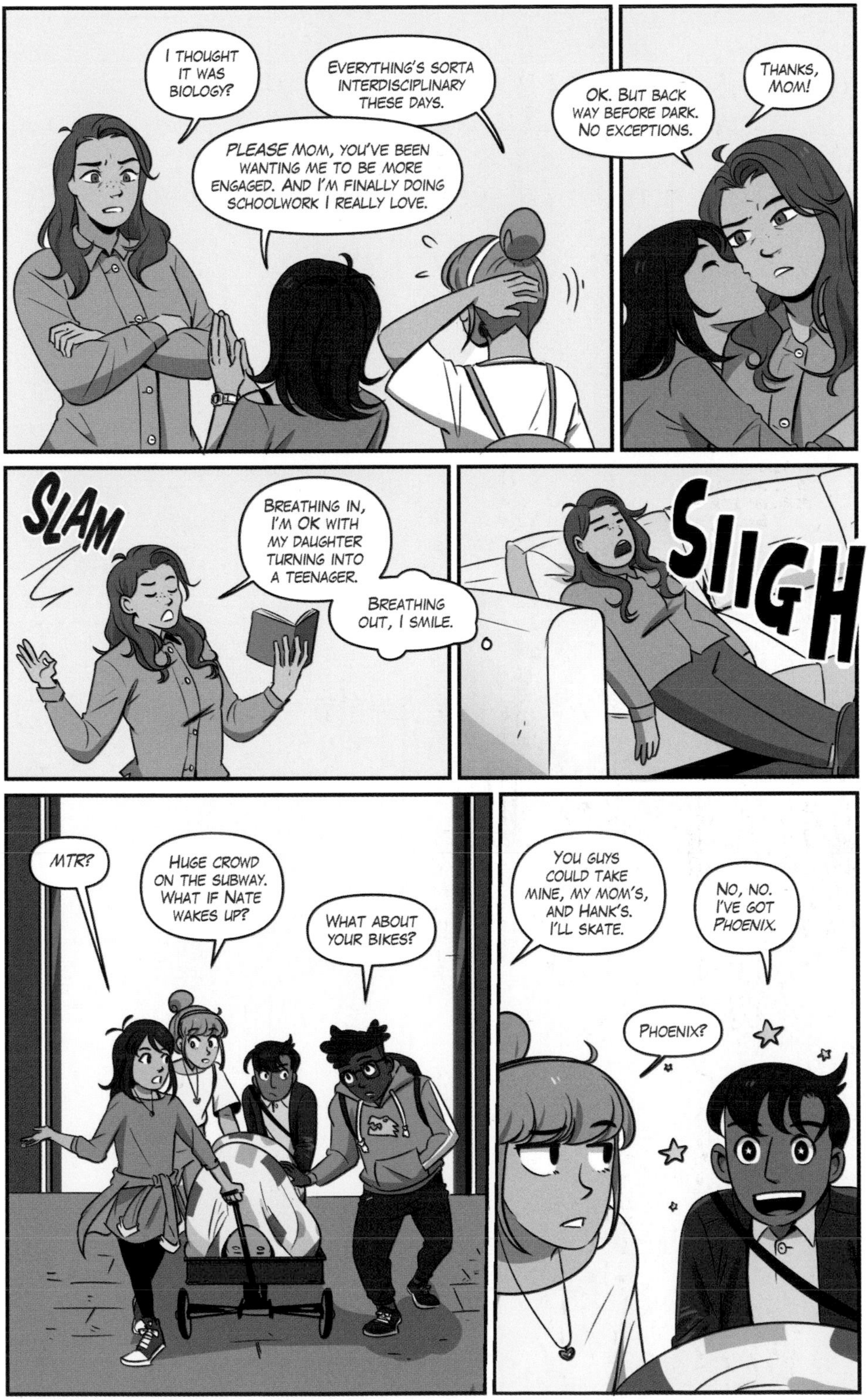

I THOUGHT IT WAS BIOLOGY?
EVERYTHING'S SORTA INTERDISCIPLINARY THESE DAYS.
PLEASE MOM, YOU'VE BEEN WANTING ME TO BE MORE ENGAGED. AND I'M FINALLY DOING SCHOOLWORK I REALLY LOVE.
OK. BUT BACK WAY BEFORE DARK. NO EXCEPTIONS.
THANKS, MOM!
SLAM
BREATHING IN, I'M OK WITH MY DAUGHTER TURNING INTO A TEENAGER.
BREATHING OUT, I SMILE.
SIIGH
MTR?
HUGE CROWD ON THE SUBWAY. WHAT IF NATE WAKES UP?
WHAT ABOUT YOUR BIKES?
YOU GUYS COULD TAKE MINE, MY MOM'S, AND HANK'S. I'LL SKATE.
NO, NO. I'VE GOT PHOENIX.
PHOENIX?

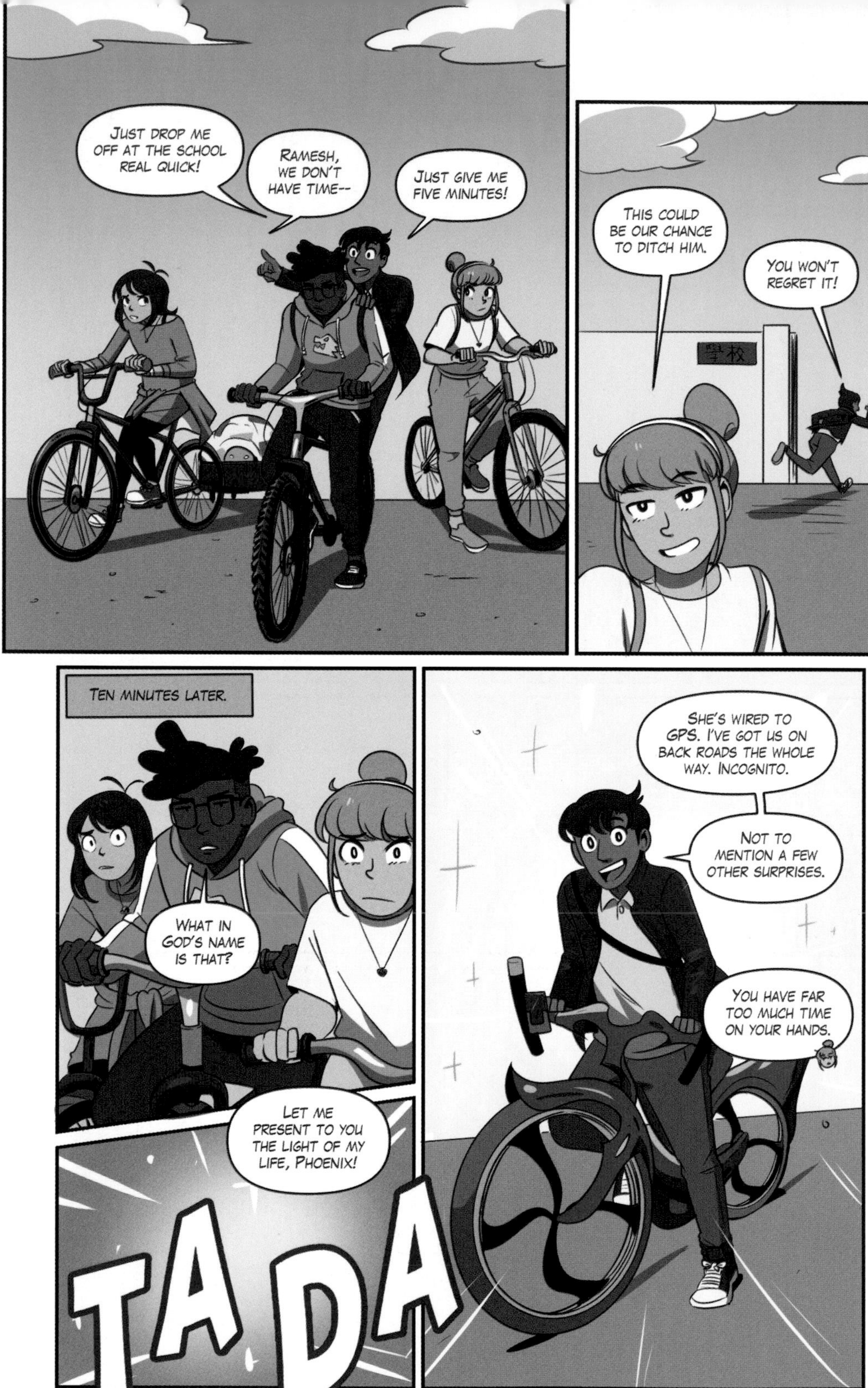
JUST DROP ME OFF AT THE SCHOOL REAL QUICK!
RAMESH, WE DON'T HAVE TIME--
JUST GIVE ME FIVE MINUTES!
THIS COULD BE OUR CHANCE TO DITCH HIM.
YOU WON'T REGRET IT!
学校
TEN MINUTES LATER.
WHAT IN GOD'S NAME IS THAT?
LET ME PRESENT TO YOU THE LIGHT OF MY LIFE, PHOENIX!
TA DA
SHE'S WIRED TO GPS. I'VE GOT US ON BACK ROADS THE WHOLE WAY. INCOGNITO.
NOT TO MENTION A FEW OTHER SURPRISES.
YOU HAVE FAR TOO MUCH TIME ON YOUR HANDS.

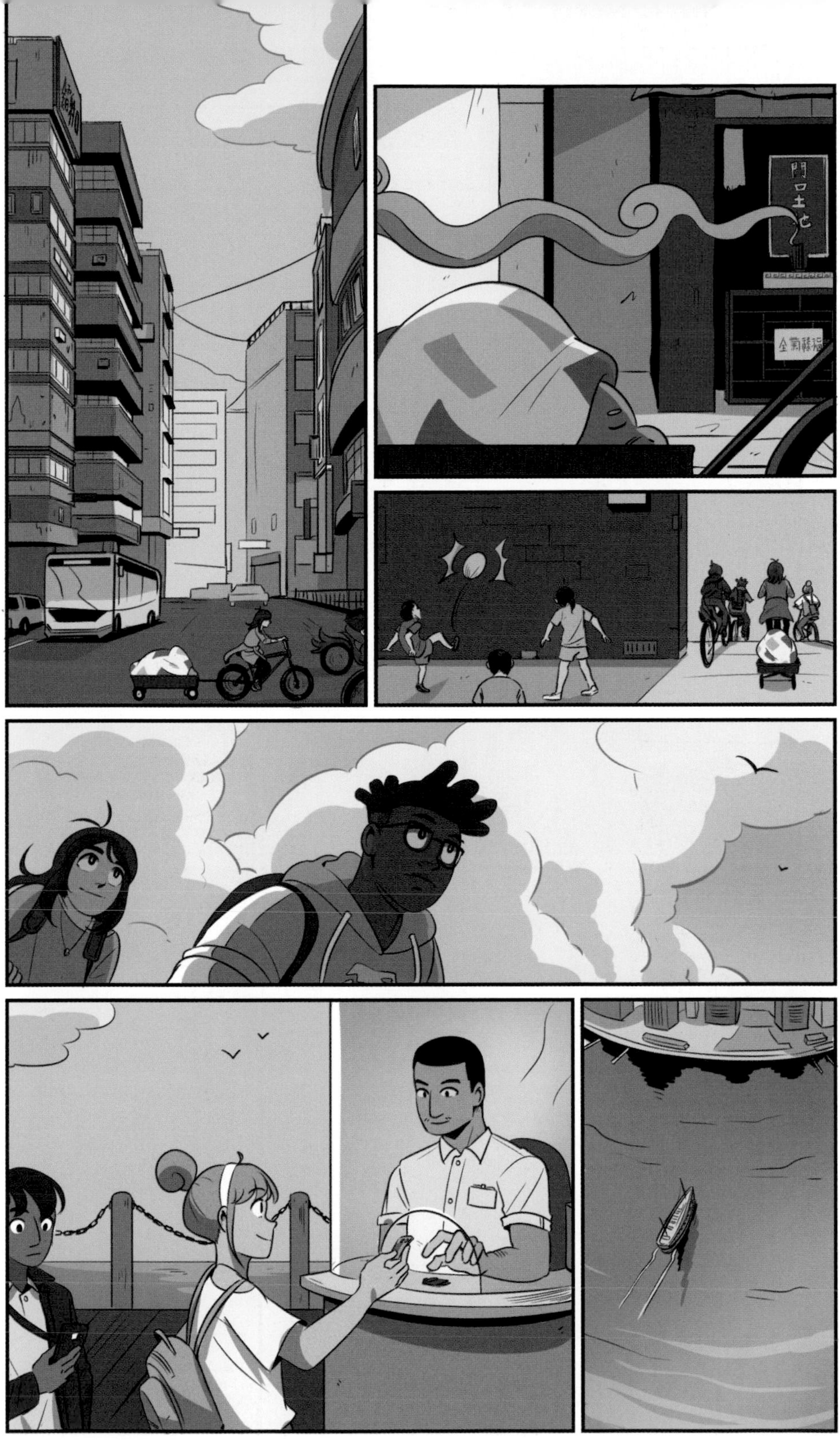

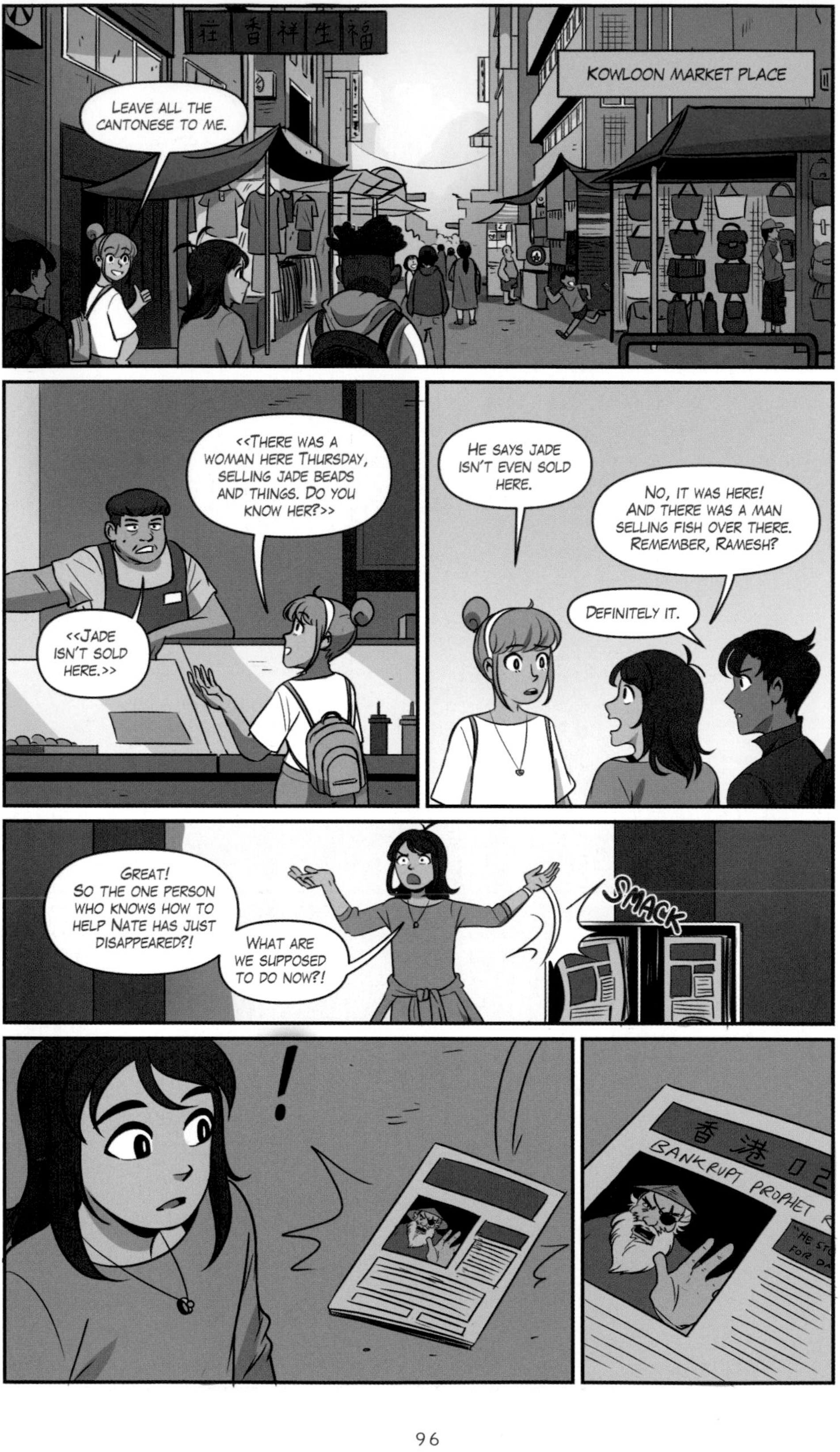
KOWLOON MARKET PLACE
LEAVE ALL THE CANTONESE TO ME.
<<THERE WAS A WOMAN HERE THURSDAY, SELLING JADE BEADS AND THINGS. DO YOU KNOW HER?>>
<<JADE ISN'T SOLD HERE.>>
HE SAYS JADE ISN'T EVEN SOLD HERE.
NO, IT WAS HERE! AND THERE WAS A MAN SELLING FISH OVER THERE. REMEMBER, RAMESH?
DEFINITELY IT.
GREAT! SO THE ONE PERSON WHO KNOWS HOW TO HELP NATE HAS JUST DISAPPEARED?!
WHAT ARE WE SUPPOSED TO DO NOW?!
SMACK
!
香港
BANKRUPT PROPHET

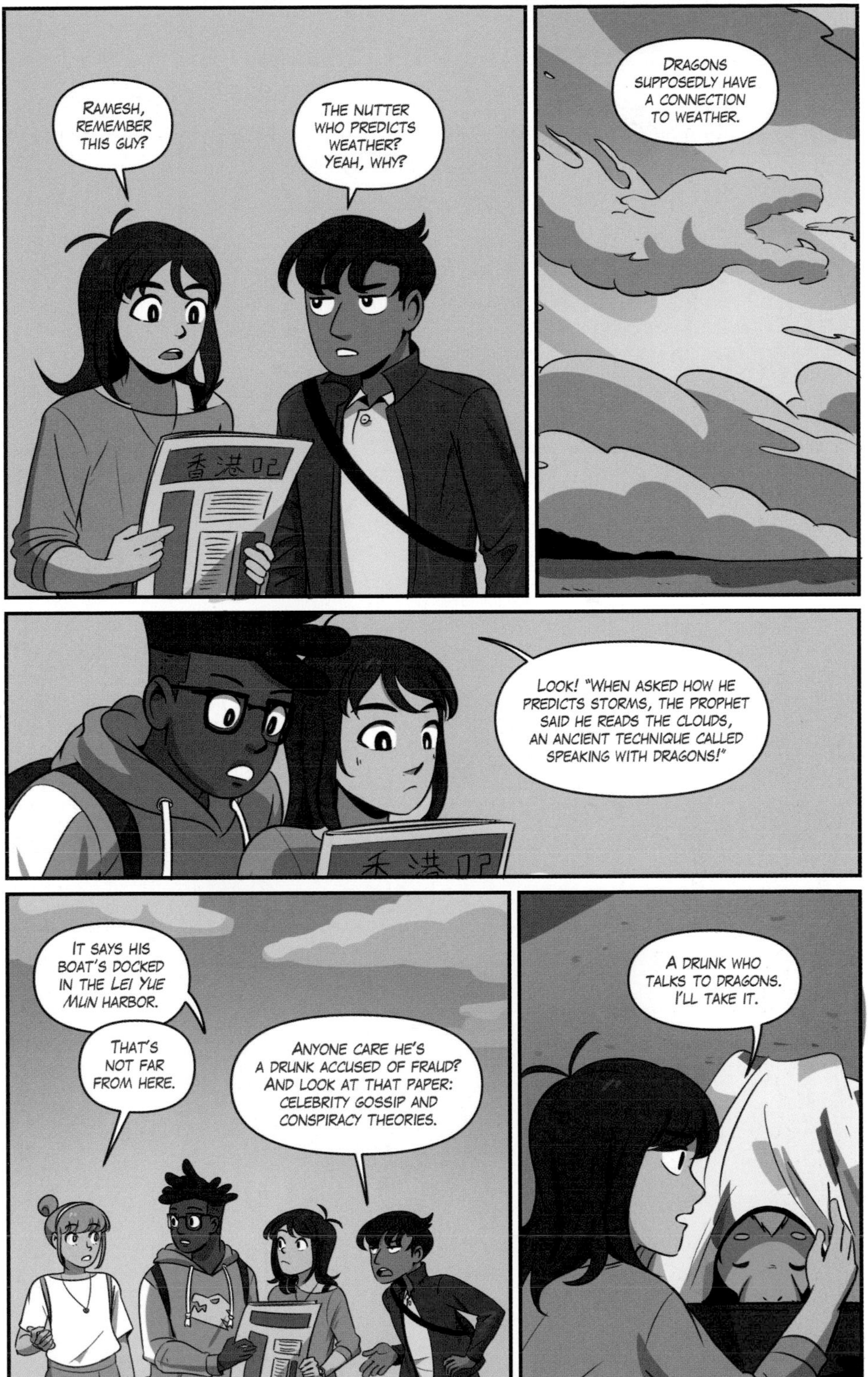
RAMESH, REMEMBER THIS GUY?
THE NUTTER WHO PREDICTS WEATHER? YEAH, WHY?
香港叱
DRAGONS SUPPOSEDLY HAVE A CONNECTION TO WEATHER.
LOOK! "WHEN ASKED HOW HE PREDICTS STORMS, THE PROPHET SAID HE READS THE CLOUDS, AN ANCIENT TECHNIQUE CALLED SPEAKING WITH DRAGONS!"
IT SAYS HIS BOAT'S DOCKED IN THE *LEI YUE MUN* HARBOR.
THAT'S NOT FAR FROM HERE.
ANYONE CARE HE'S A DRUNK ACCUSED OF FRAUD? AND LOOK AT THAT PAPER: CELEBRITY GOSSIP AND CONSPIRACY THEORIES.
A DRUNK WHO TALKS TO DRAGONS. I'LL TAKE IT.

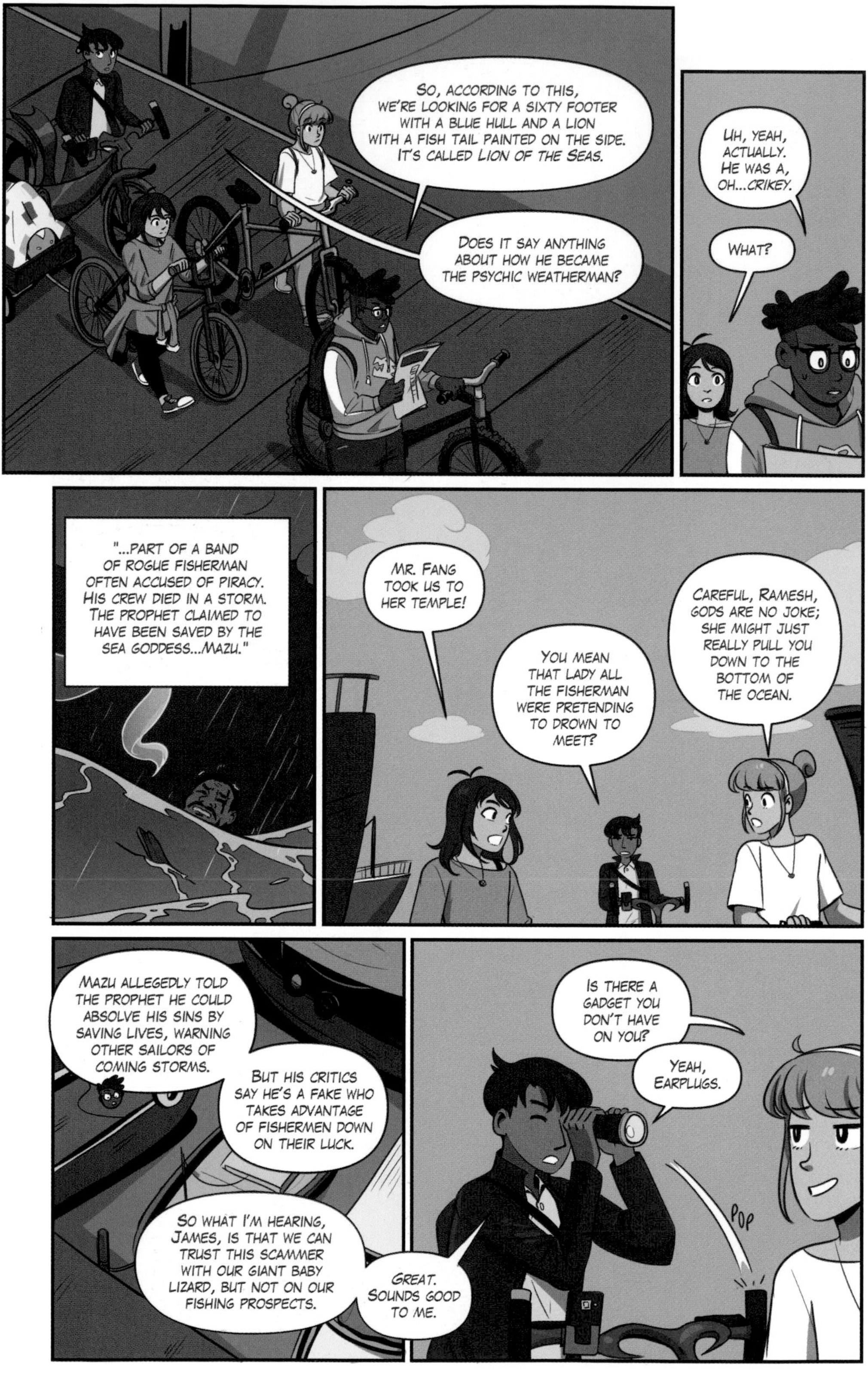
SO, ACCORDING TO THIS, WE'RE LOOKING FOR A SIXTY FOOTER WITH A BLUE HULL AND A LION WITH A FISH TAIL PAINTED ON THE SIDE. IT'S CALLED *LION OF THE SEAS*.
DOES IT SAY ANYTHING ABOUT HOW HE BECAME THE PSYCHIC WEATHERMAN?
UH, YEAH, ACTUALLY. HE WAS A, OH...CRIKEY.
WHAT?
"...PART OF A BAND OF ROGUE FISHERMAN OFTEN ACCUSED OF PIRACY. HIS CREW DIED IN A STORM. THE PROPHET CLAIMED TO HAVE BEEN SAVED BY THE SEA GODDESS...MAZU."
MR. FANG TOOK US TO HER TEMPLE!
YOU MEAN THAT LADY ALL THE FISHERMAN WERE PRETENDING TO DROWN TO MEET?
CAREFUL, RAMESH, GODS ARE NO JOKE; SHE MIGHT JUST REALLY PULL YOU DOWN TO THE BOTTOM OF THE OCEAN.
MAZU ALLEGEDLY TOLD THE PROPHET HE COULD ABSOLVE HIS SINS BY SAVING LIVES, WARNING OTHER SAILORS OF COMING STORMS.
BUT HIS CRITICS SAY HE'S A FAKE WHO TAKES ADVANTAGE OF FISHERMEN DOWN ON THEIR LUCK.
SO WHAT I'M HEARING, JAMES, IS THAT WE CAN TRUST THIS SCAMMER WITH OUR GIANT BABY LIZARD, BUT NOT ON OUR FISHING PROSPECTS.
GREAT. SOUNDS GOOD TO ME.
IS THERE A GADGET YOU DON'T HAVE ON YOU?
YEAH, EARPLUGS.
POP

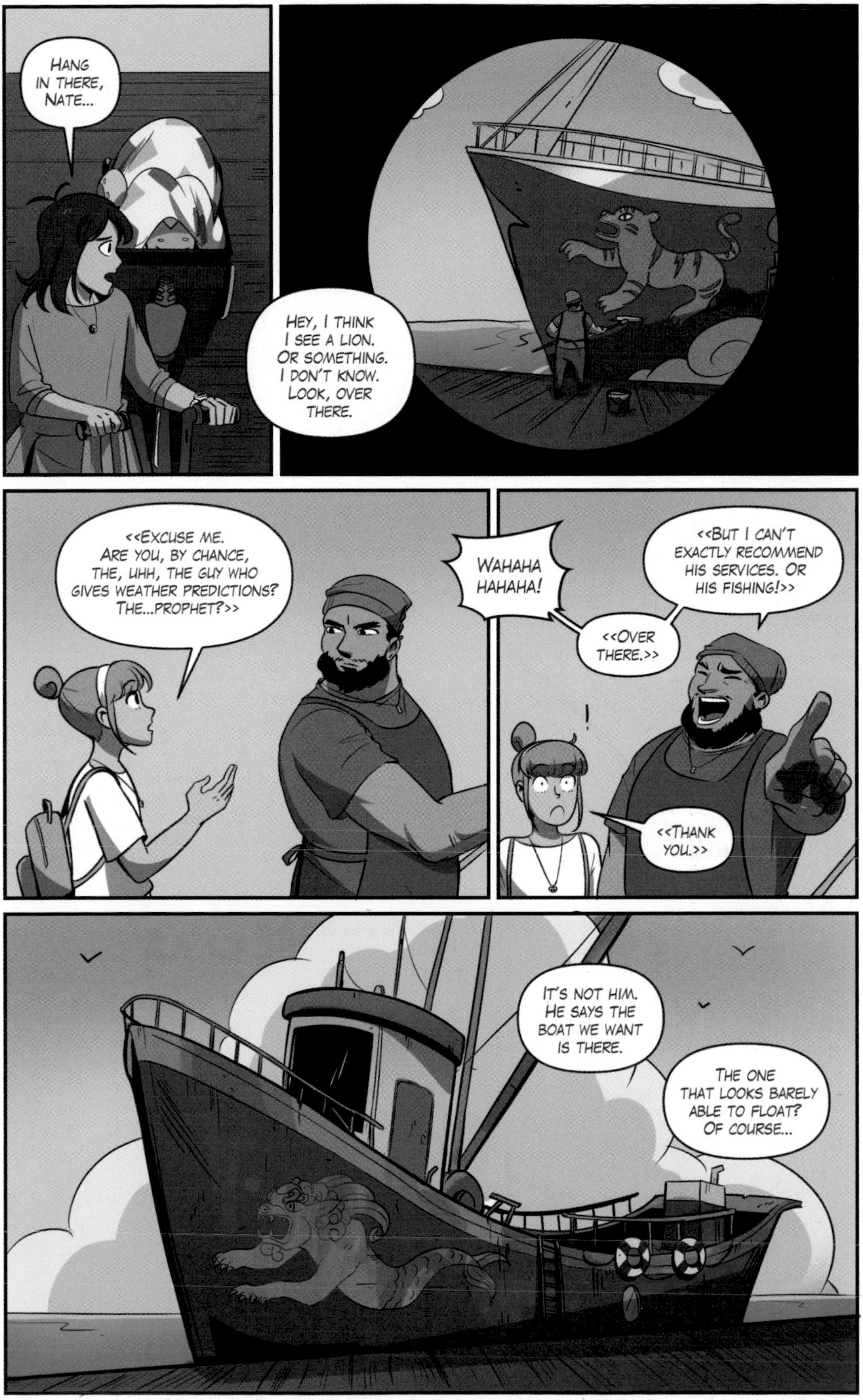
HANG IN THERE, NATE...
HEY, I THINK I SEE A LION. OR SOMETHING. I DON'T KNOW. LOOK, OVER THERE.
<<EXCUSE ME. ARE YOU, BY CHANCE, THE, UHH, THE GUY WHO GIVES WEATHER PREDICTIONS? THE...PROPHET?>>
WAHAHA HAHAHA!
<<OVER THERE.>>
<<BUT I CAN'T EXACTLY RECOMMEND HIS SERVICES. OR HIS FISHING!>>
!
<<THANK YOU.>>
IT'S NOT HIM. HE SAYS THE BOAT WE WANT IS THERE.
THE ONE THAT LOOKS BARELY ABLE TO FLOAT? OF COURSE...

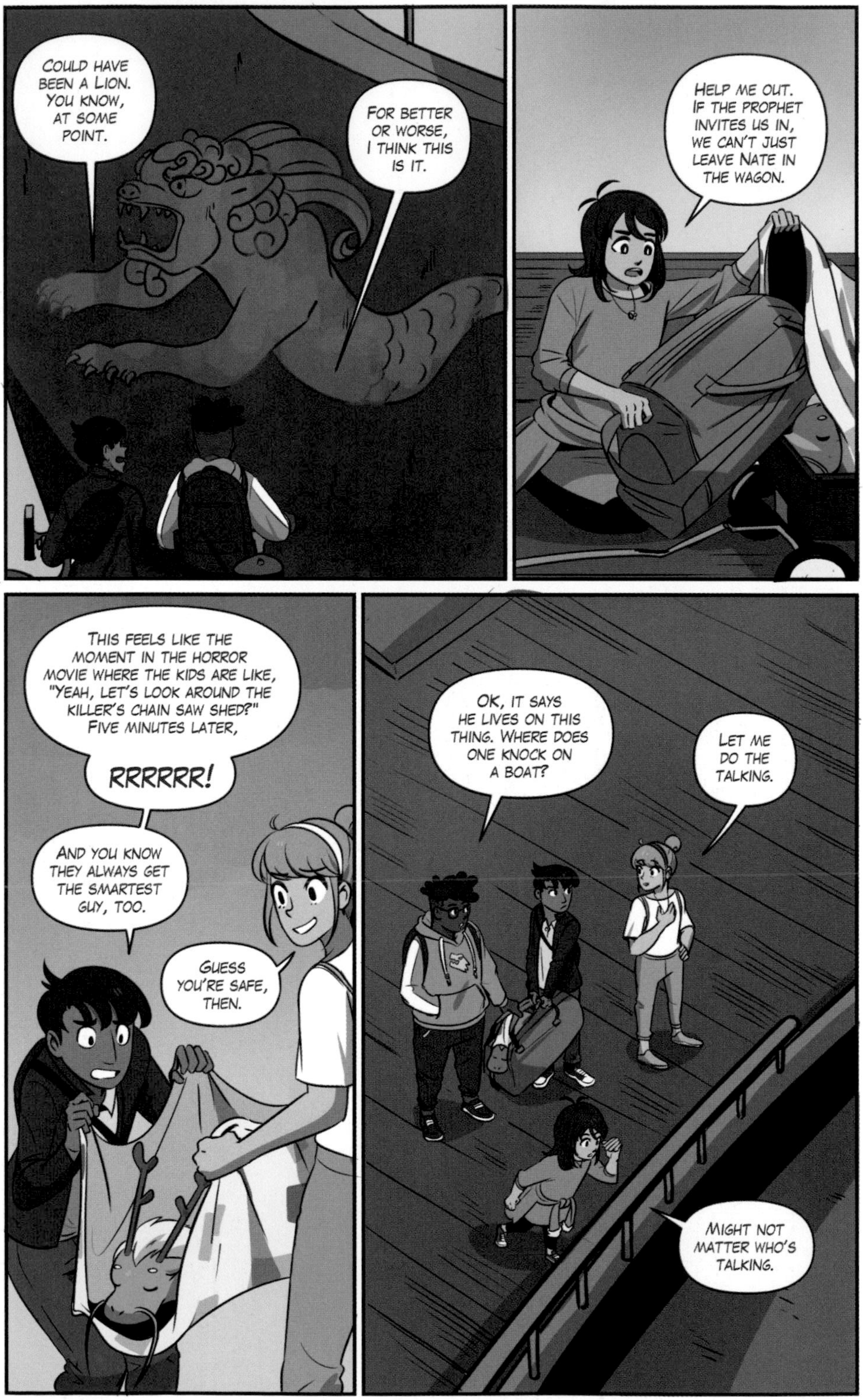

COULD HAVE BEEN A LION. YOU KNOW, AT SOME POINT.
FOR BETTER OR WORSE, I THINK THIS IS IT.
HELP ME OUT. IF THE PROPHET INVITES US IN, WE CAN'T JUST LEAVE NATE IN THE WAGON.
THIS FEELS LIKE THE MOMENT IN THE HORROR MOVIE WHERE THE KIDS ARE LIKE, "YEAH, LET'S LOOK AROUND THE KILLER'S CHAIN SAW SHED?" FIVE MINUTES LATER,
RRRRRR!
AND YOU KNOW THEY ALWAYS GET THE SMARTEST GUY, TOO.
GUESS YOU'RE SAFE, THEN.
OK, IT SAYS HE LIVES ON THIS THING. WHERE DOES ONE KNOCK ON A BOAT?
LET ME DO THE TALKING.
MIGHT NOT MATTER WHO'S TALKING.

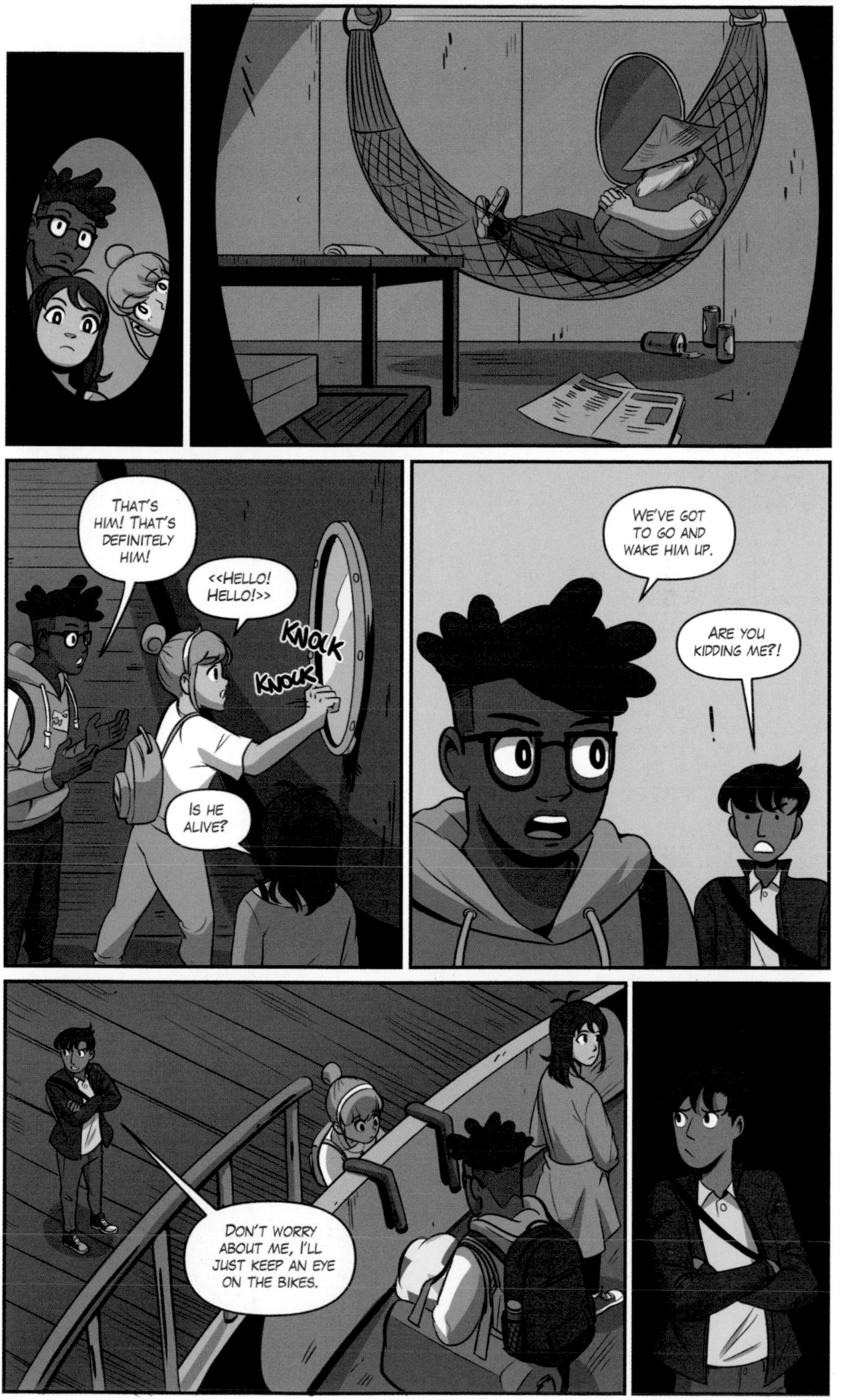
THAT'S HIM! THAT'S DEFINITELY HIM!
<<HELLO! HELLO!>>
KNOCK
KNOCK
IS HE ALIVE?
WE'VE GOT TO GO AND WAKE HIM UP.
ARE YOU KIDDING ME?!
!
DON'T WORRY ABOUT ME, I'LL JUST KEEP AN EYE ON THE BIKES.

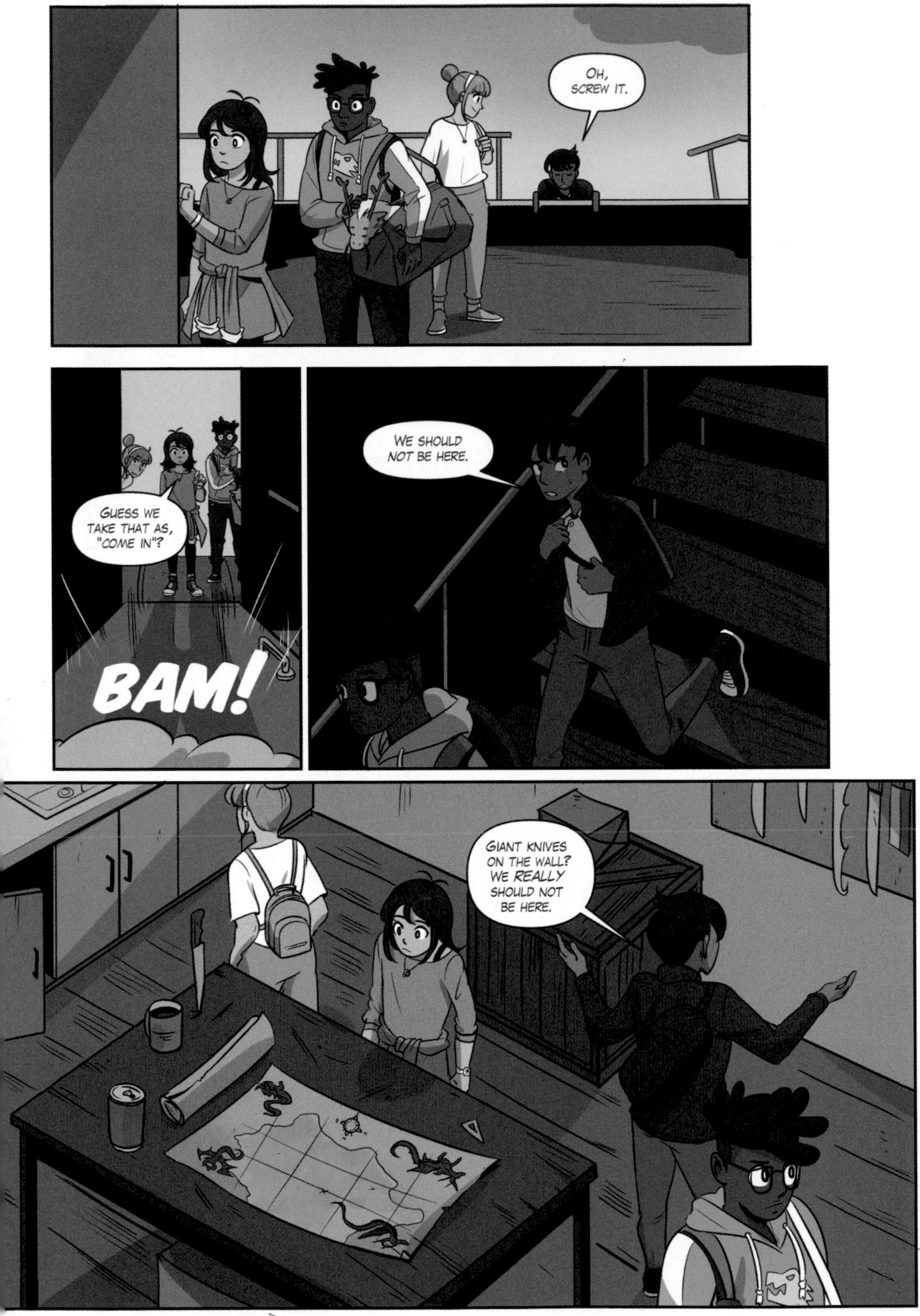
OH, SCREW IT.
GUESS WE TAKE THAT AS, "COME IN"?
BAM!
WE SHOULD NOT BE HERE.
GIANT KNIVES ON THE WALL? WE REALLY SHOULD NOT BE HERE.

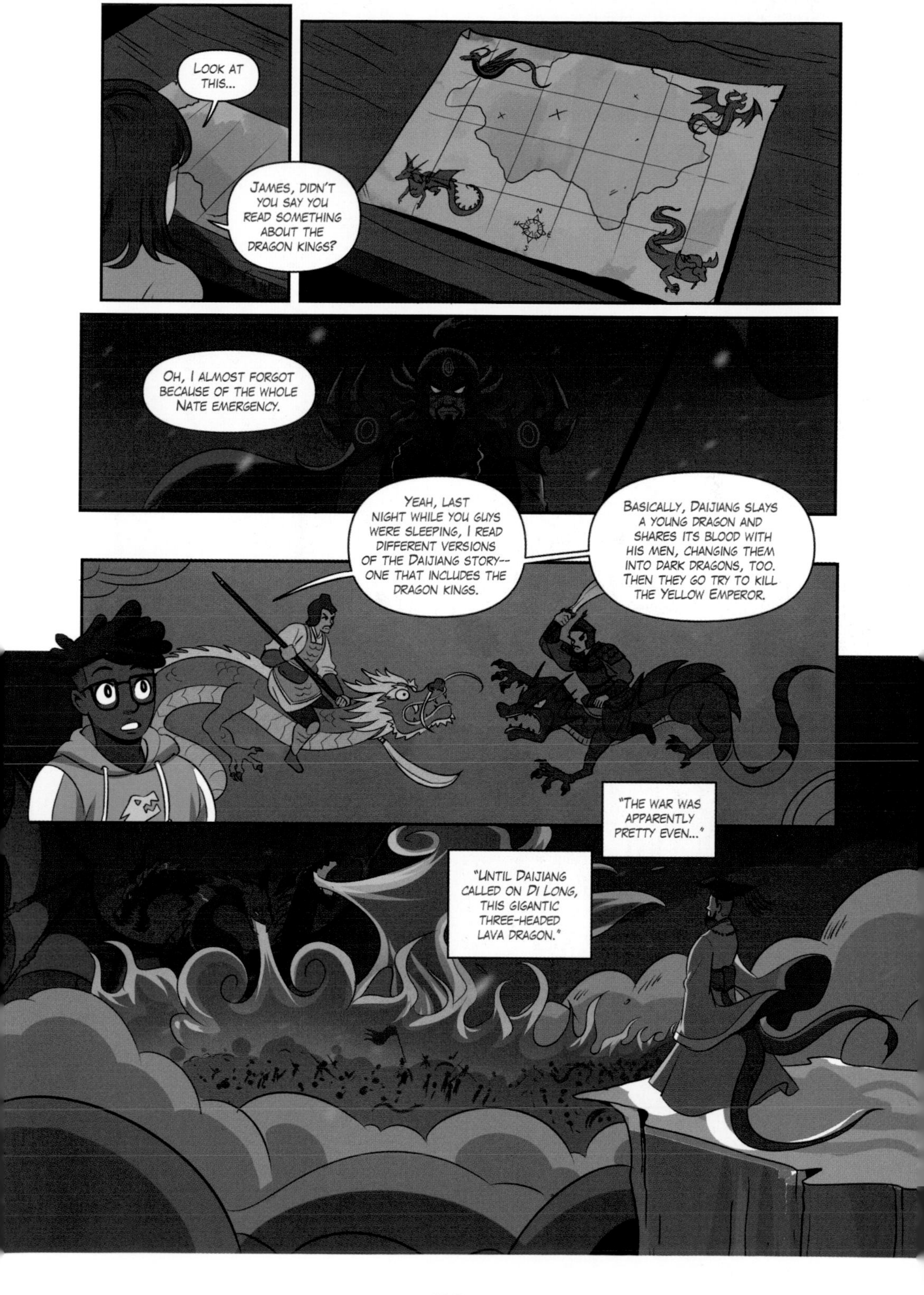
LOOK AT THIS...
JAMES, DIDN'T YOU SAY YOU READ SOMETHING ABOUT THE DRAGON KINGS?
OH, I ALMOST FORGOT BECAUSE OF THE WHOLE NATE EMERGENCY.
YEAH, LAST NIGHT WHILE YOU GUYS WERE SLEEPING, I READ DIFFERENT VERSIONS OF THE DAIJIANG STORY-- ONE THAT INCLUDES THE DRAGON KINGS.
BASICALLY, DAIJIANG SLAYS A YOUNG DRAGON AND SHARES ITS BLOOD WITH HIS MEN, CHANGING THEM INTO DARK DRAGONS, TOO. THEN THEY GO TRY TO KILL THE YELLOW EMPEROR.
"THE WAR WAS APPARENTLY PRETTY EVEN..."
"UNTIL DAIJIANG CALLED ON DI LONG, THIS GIGANTIC THREE-HEADED LAVA DRAGON."

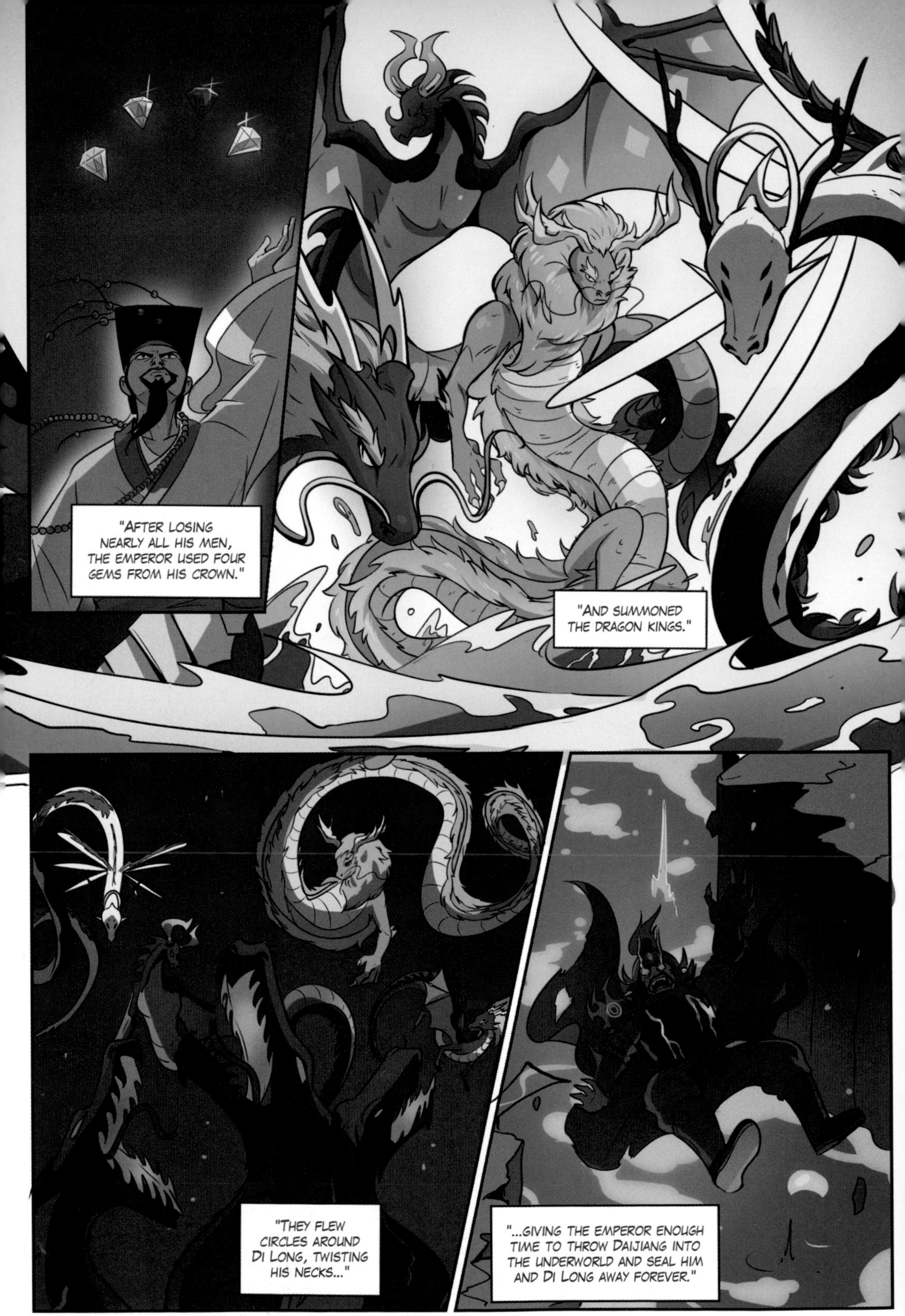
"After losing nearly all his men, the Emperor used four gems from his crown."
"And summoned the Dragon Kings."
"They flew circles around Di Long, twisting his necks..."
"...giving the Emperor enough time to throw Daijiang into the underworld and seal him and Di Long away forever."

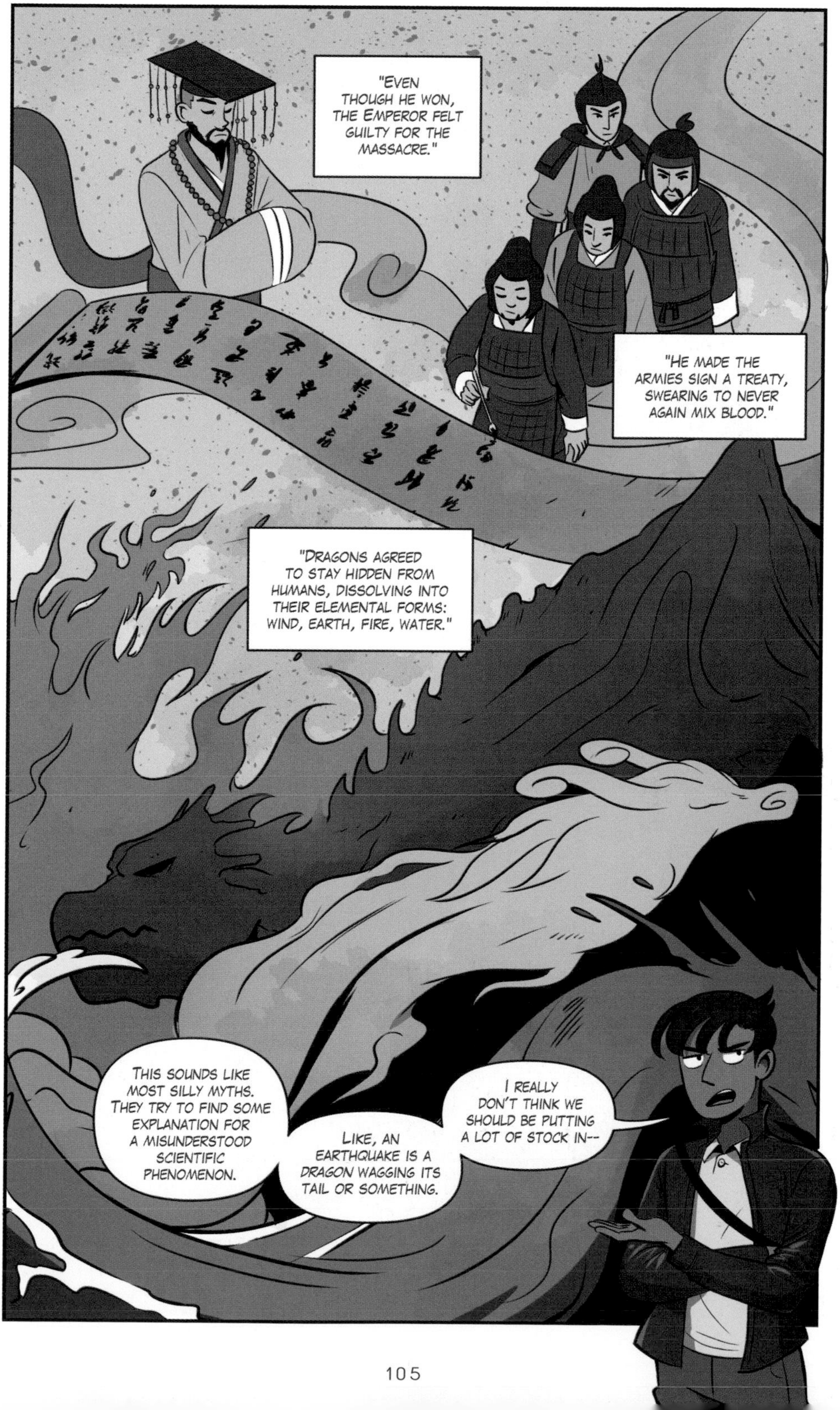
"EVEN THOUGH HE WON, THE EMPEROR FELT GUILTY FOR THE MASSACRE."
"HE MADE THE ARMIES SIGN A TREATY, SWEARING TO NEVER AGAIN MIX BLOOD."
"DRAGONS AGREED TO STAY HIDDEN FROM HUMANS, DISSOLVING INTO THEIR ELEMENTAL FORMS: WIND, EARTH, FIRE, WATER."
THIS SOUNDS LIKE MOST SILLY MYTHS. THEY TRY TO FIND SOME EXPLANATION FOR A MISUNDERSTOOD SCIENTIFIC PHENOMENON.
LIKE, AN EARTHQUAKE IS A DRAGON WAGGING ITS TAIL OR SOMETHING.
I REALLY DON'T THINK WE SHOULD BE PUTTING A LOT OF STOCK IN--

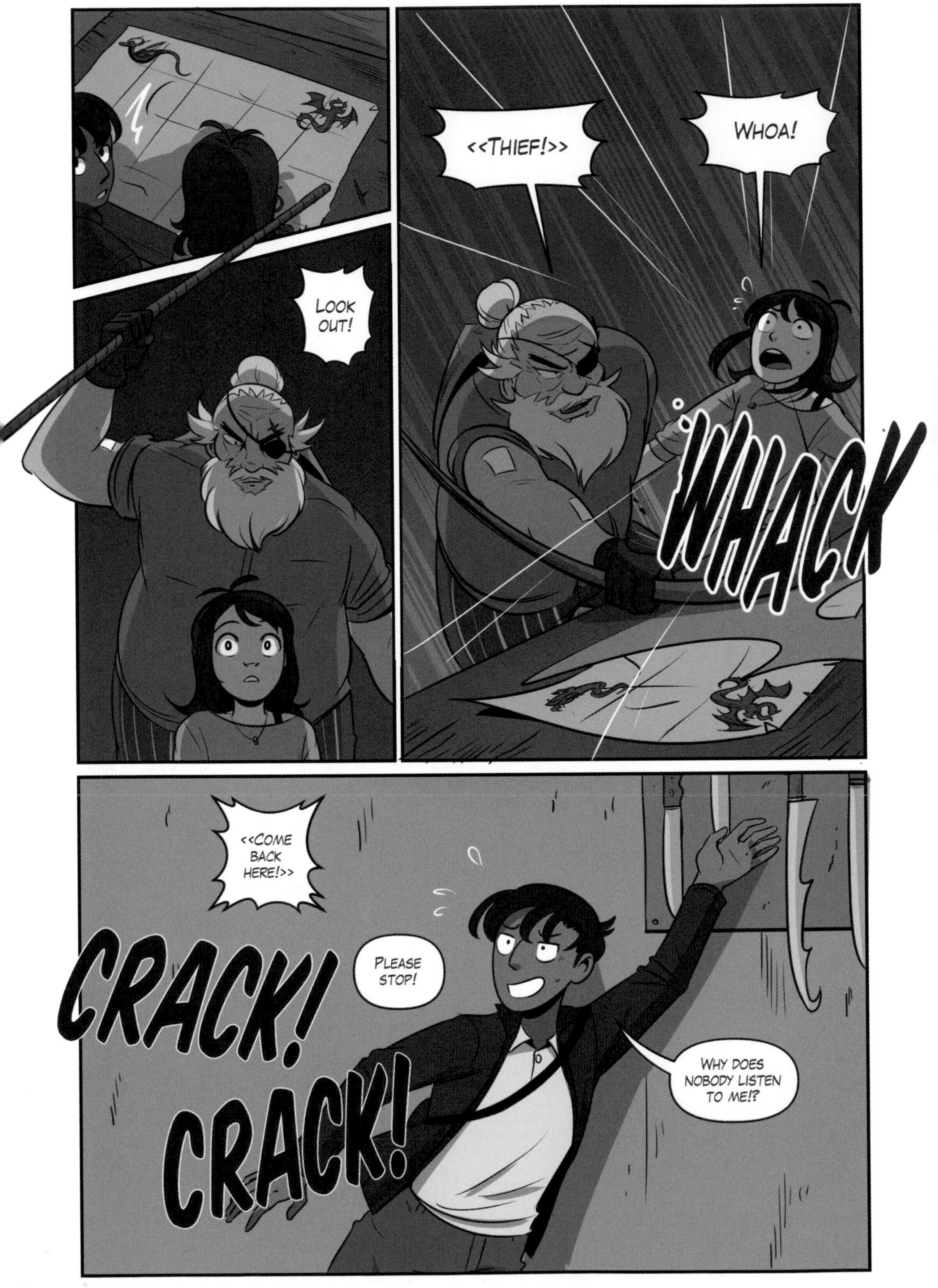
LOOK OUT!
<<THIEF!>>
WHOA!
WHACK
<<COME BACK HERE!>>
CRACK!
CRACK!
PLEASE STOP!
WHY DOES NOBODY LISTEN TO ME!?

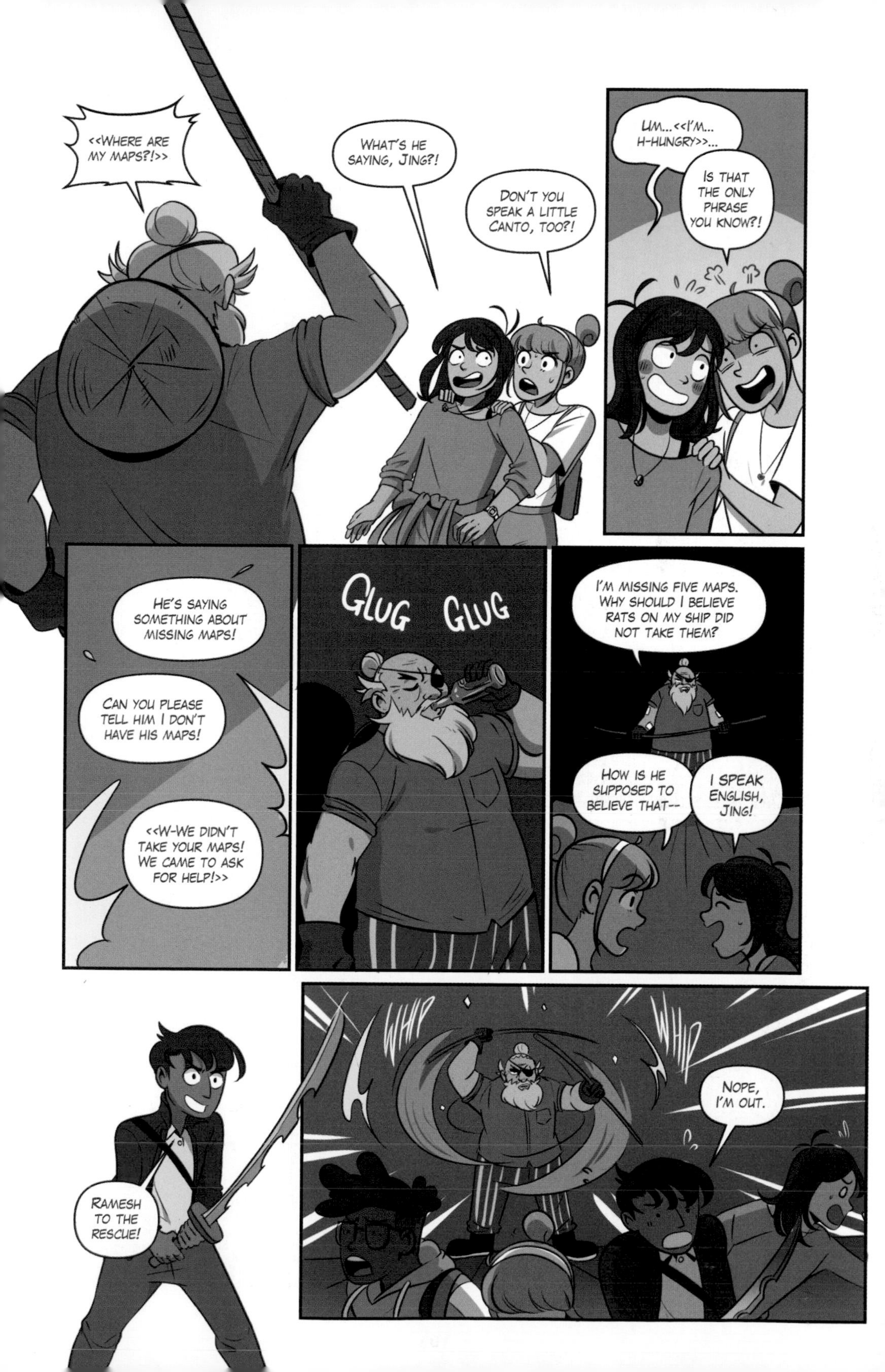
<<WHERE ARE MY MAPS?!>>
WHAT'S HE SAYING, JING?!
DON'T YOU SPEAK A LITTLE CANTO, TOO?!
UM...<<I'M... H-HUNGRY>>...
IS THAT THE ONLY PHRASE YOU KNOW?!
HE'S SAYING SOMETHING ABOUT MISSING MAPS!
CAN YOU PLEASE TELL HIM I DON'T HAVE HIS MAPS!
<<W-WE DIDN'T TAKE YOUR MAPS! WE CAME TO ASK FOR HELP!>>
GLUG GLUG
I'M MISSING FIVE MAPS. WHY SHOULD I BELIEVE RATS ON MY SHIP DID NOT TAKE THEM?
HOW IS HE SUPPOSED TO BELIEVE THAT--
I SPEAK ENGLISH, JING!
RAMESH TO THE RESCUE!
WHIP
WHIP
NOPE, I'M OUT.

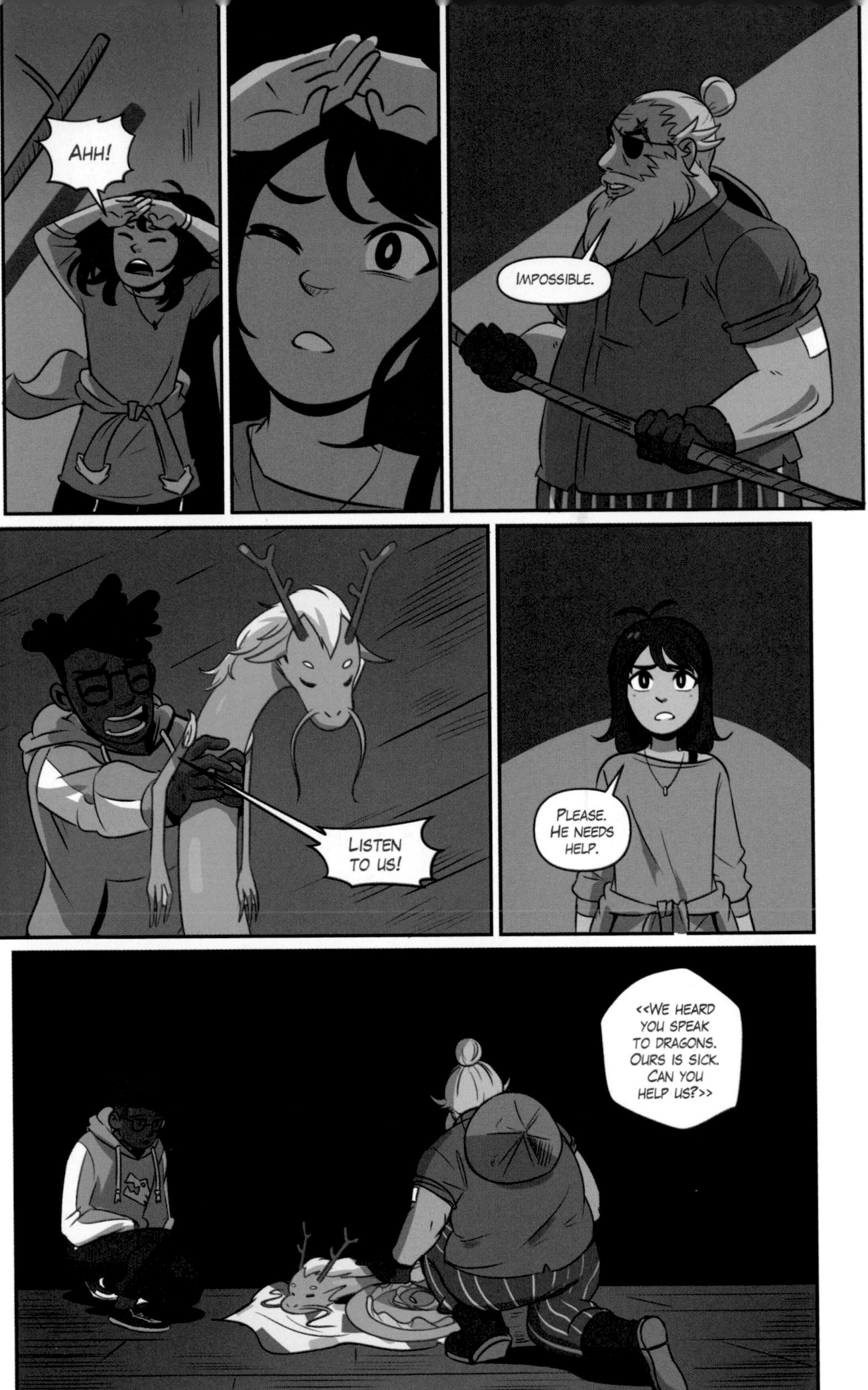
AHH!
IMPOSSIBLE.
LISTEN TO US!
PLEASE. HE NEEDS HELP.
<<WE HEARD YOU SPEAK TO DRAGONS. OURS IS SICK. CAN YOU HELP US?>>

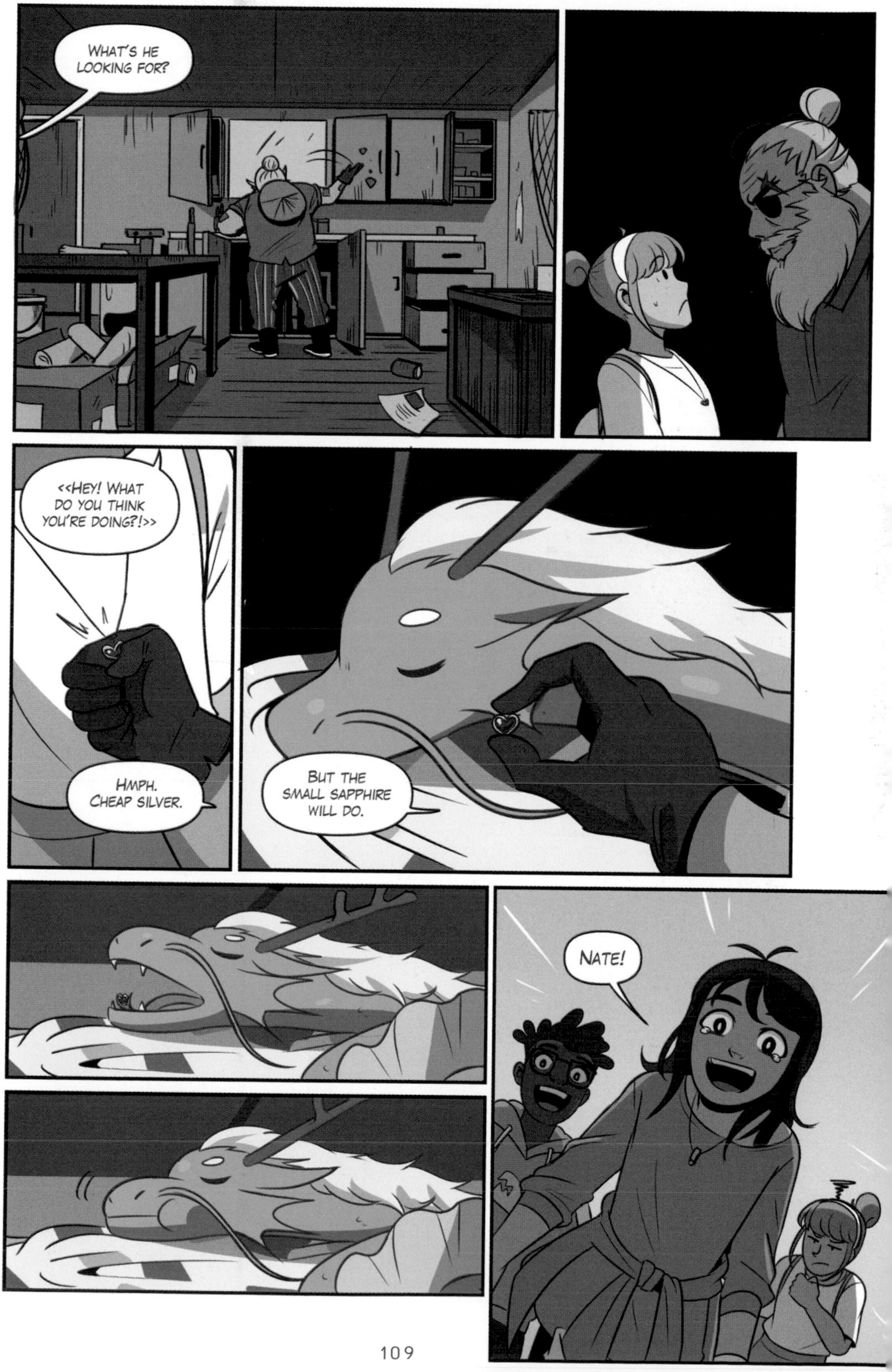
WHAT'S HE LOOKING FOR?
<<HEY! WHAT DO YOU THINK YOU'RE DOING?!>>
HMPH. CHEAP SILVER.
BUT THE SMALL SAPPHIRE WILL DO.
NATE!

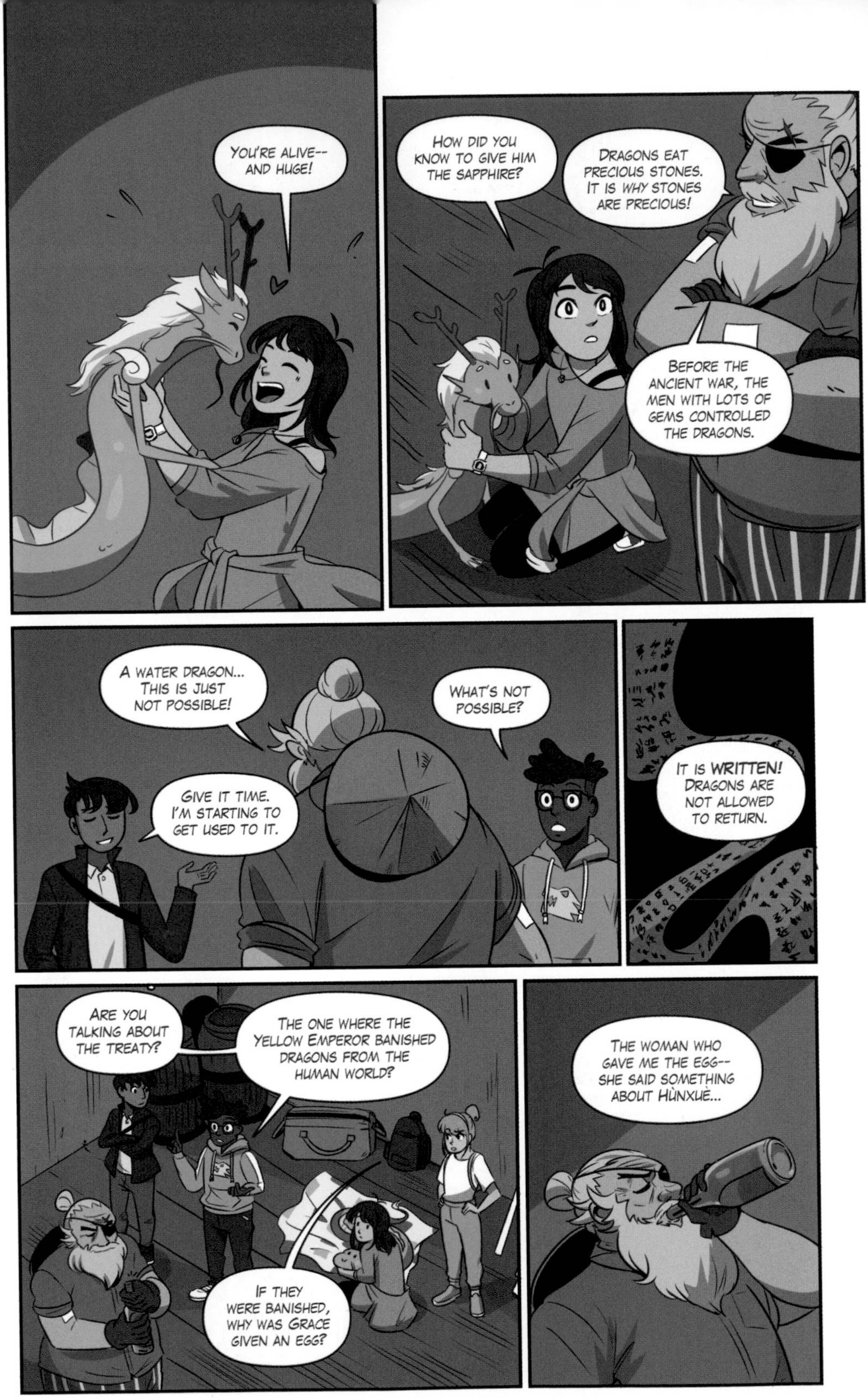
You're alive--
and huge!
How did you know to give him the sapphire?
Dragons eat precious stones. It is why stones are precious!
Before the ancient war, the men with lots of gems controlled the dragons.
A water dragon... This is just not possible!
What's not possible?
Give it time. I'm starting to get used to it.
It is WRITTEN! Dragons are not allowed to return.
Are you talking about the treaty?
The one where the Yellow Emperor banished dragons from the human world?
If they were banished, why was Grace given an egg?
The woman who gave me the egg-- she said something about Hùnxuè...

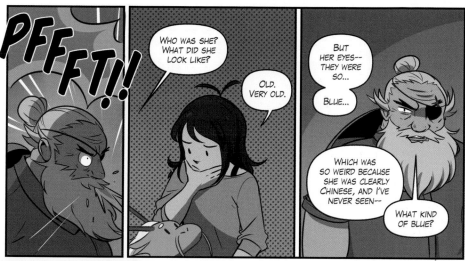

PFFFT!!

WHO WAS SHE? WHAT DID SHE LOOK LIKE?

OLD. VERY OLD.

BUT HER EYES-- THEY WERE SO...

BLUE...

WHICH WAS SO WEIRD BECAUSE SHE WAS CLEARLY CHINESE, AND I'VE NEVER SEEN--

WHAT KIND OF BLUE?

UH, BLUE BLUE?

NO. YOU'RE RIGHT. THEY WERE KIND OF...

...LIKE THE SEA.

DO YOU KNOW HER?

IF MAZU GAVE YOU A DRAGON, IT CAN'T BE A GOOD SIGN.

MAZU? THE ONE WHO SAVED YOU?

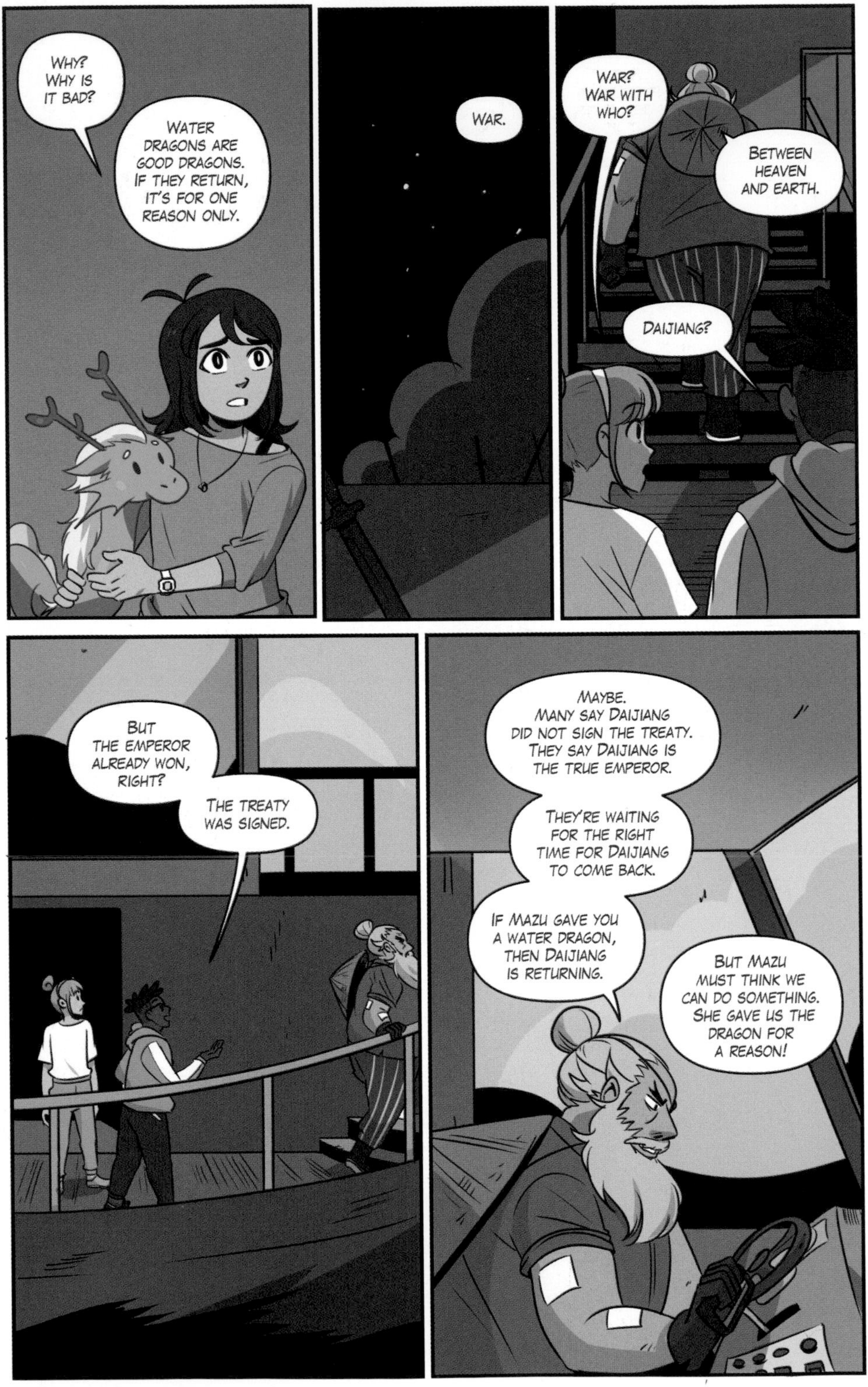
WHY? WHY IS IT BAD?
WATER DRAGONS ARE GOOD DRAGONS. IF THEY RETURN, IT'S FOR ONE REASON ONLY.
WAR.
WAR? WAR WITH WHO?
BETWEEN HEAVEN AND EARTH.
DAIJIANG?
BUT THE EMPEROR ALREADY WON, RIGHT?
THE TREATY WAS SIGNED.
MAYBE. MANY SAY DAIJIANG DID NOT SIGN THE TREATY. THEY SAY DAIJIANG IS THE TRUE EMPEROR.
THEY'RE WAITING FOR THE RIGHT TIME FOR DAIJIANG TO COME BACK.
IF MAZU GAVE YOU A WATER DRAGON, THEN DAIJIANG IS RETURNING.
BUT MAZU MUST THINK WE CAN DO SOMETHING. SHE GAVE US THE DRAGON FOR A REASON!

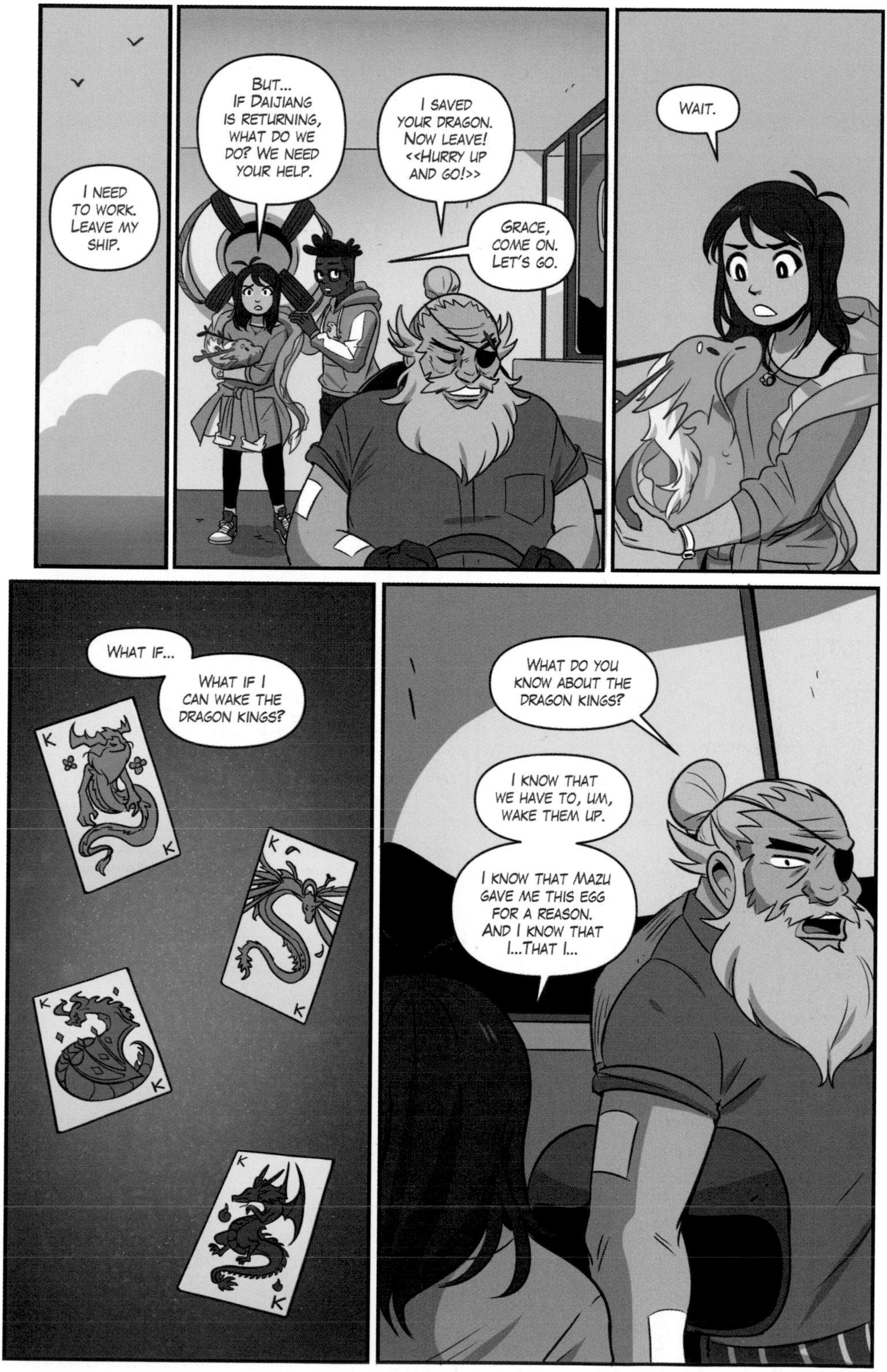
I NEED TO WORK. LEAVE MY SHIP.
BUT... IF DAIJIANG IS RETURNING, WHAT DO WE DO? WE NEED YOUR HELP.
I SAVED YOUR DRAGON. NOW LEAVE! <<HURRY UP AND GO!>>
GRACE, COME ON. LET'S GO.
WAIT.
WHAT IF...
WHAT IF I CAN WAKE THE DRAGON KINGS?
K
K
K
K
K
K
K
K
WHAT DO YOU KNOW ABOUT THE DRAGON KINGS?
I KNOW THAT WE HAVE TO, UM, WAKE THEM UP.
I KNOW THAT MAZU GAVE ME THIS EGG FOR A REASON. AND I KNOW THAT I...THAT I...

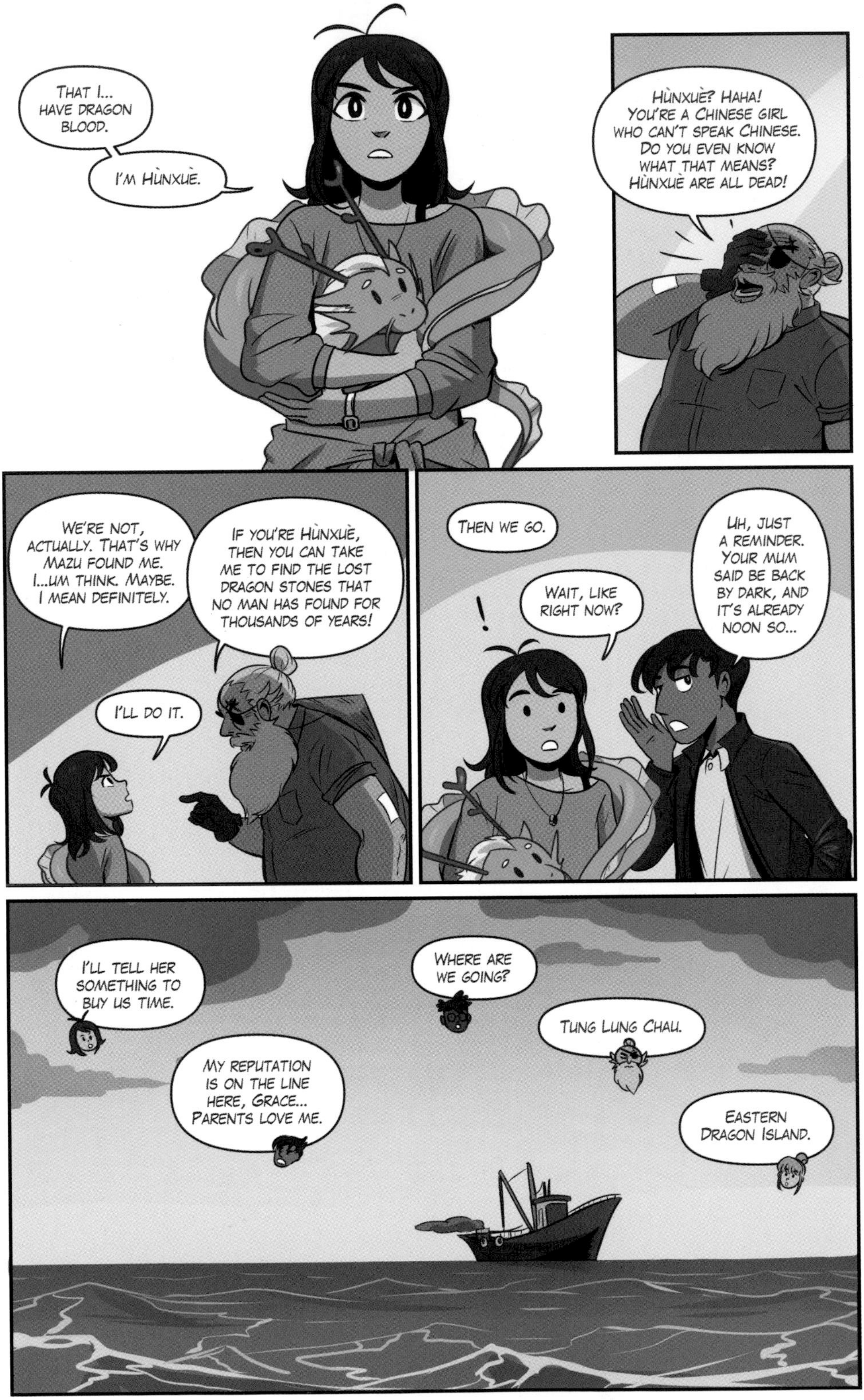
THAT I... HAVE DRAGON BLOOD.
I'M HÙNXUÈ.
HÙNXUÈ? HAHA! YOU'RE A CHINESE GIRL WHO CAN'T SPEAK CHINESE. DO YOU EVEN KNOW WHAT THAT MEANS? HÙNXUÈ ARE ALL DEAD!
WE'RE NOT, ACTUALLY. THAT'S WHY MAZU FOUND ME. I...UM THINK. MAYBE. I MEAN DEFINITELY.
IF YOU'RE HÙNXUÈ, THEN YOU CAN TAKE ME TO FIND THE LOST DRAGON STONES THAT NO MAN HAS FOUND FOR THOUSANDS OF YEARS!
I'LL DO IT.
THEN WE GO.
!
WAIT, LIKE RIGHT NOW?
UH, JUST A REMINDER. YOUR MUM SAID BE BACK BY DARK, AND IT'S ALREADY NOON SO...
I'LL TELL HER SOMETHING TO BUY US TIME.
MY REPUTATION IS ON THE LINE HERE, GRACE... PARENTS LOVE ME.
WHERE ARE WE GOING?
TUNG LUNG CHAU.
EASTERN DRAGON ISLAND.

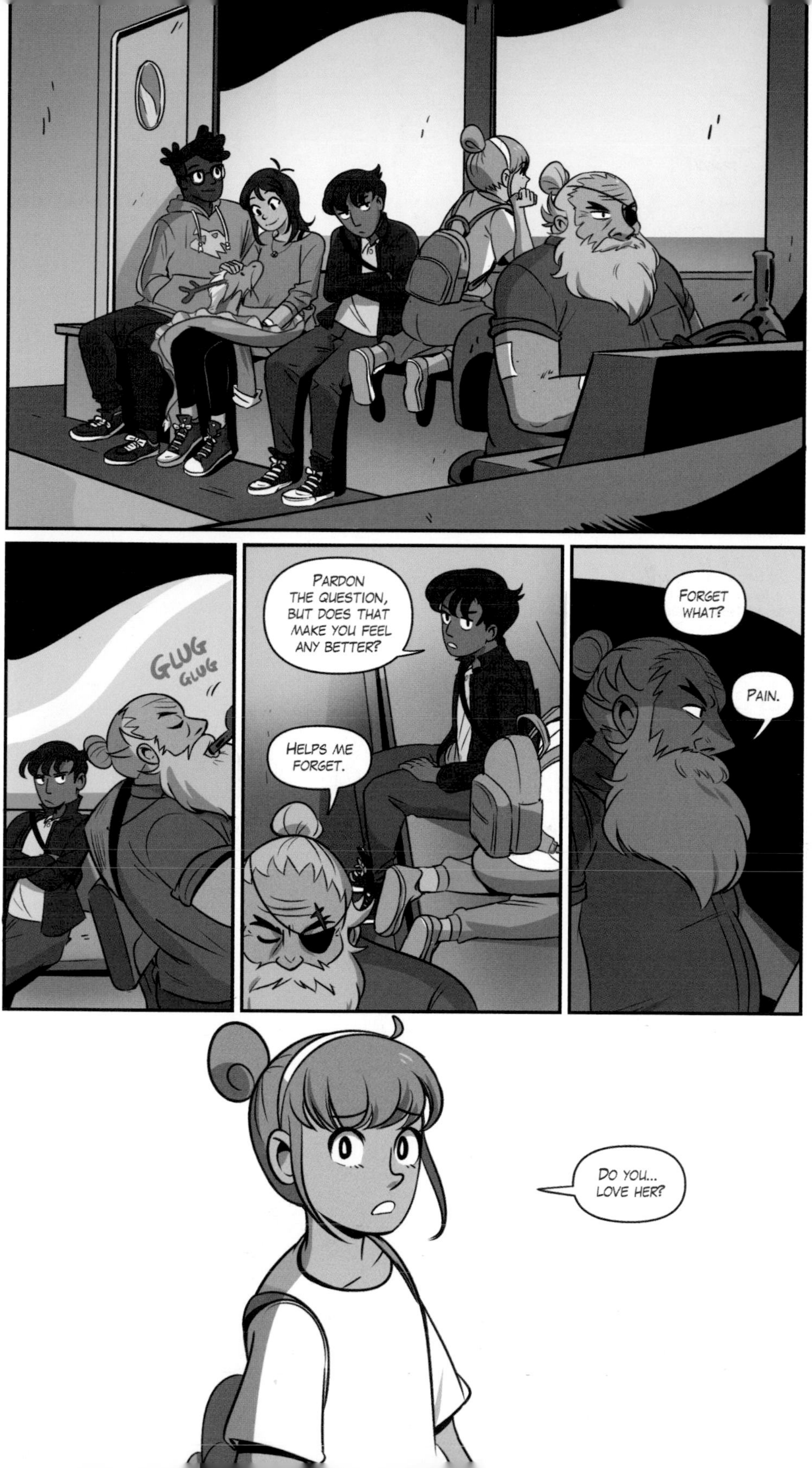
GLUG GLUG
PARDON THE QUESTION, BUT DOES THAT MAKE YOU FEEL ANY BETTER?
HELPS ME FORGET.
FORGET WHAT?
PAIN.
DO YOU... LOVE HER?

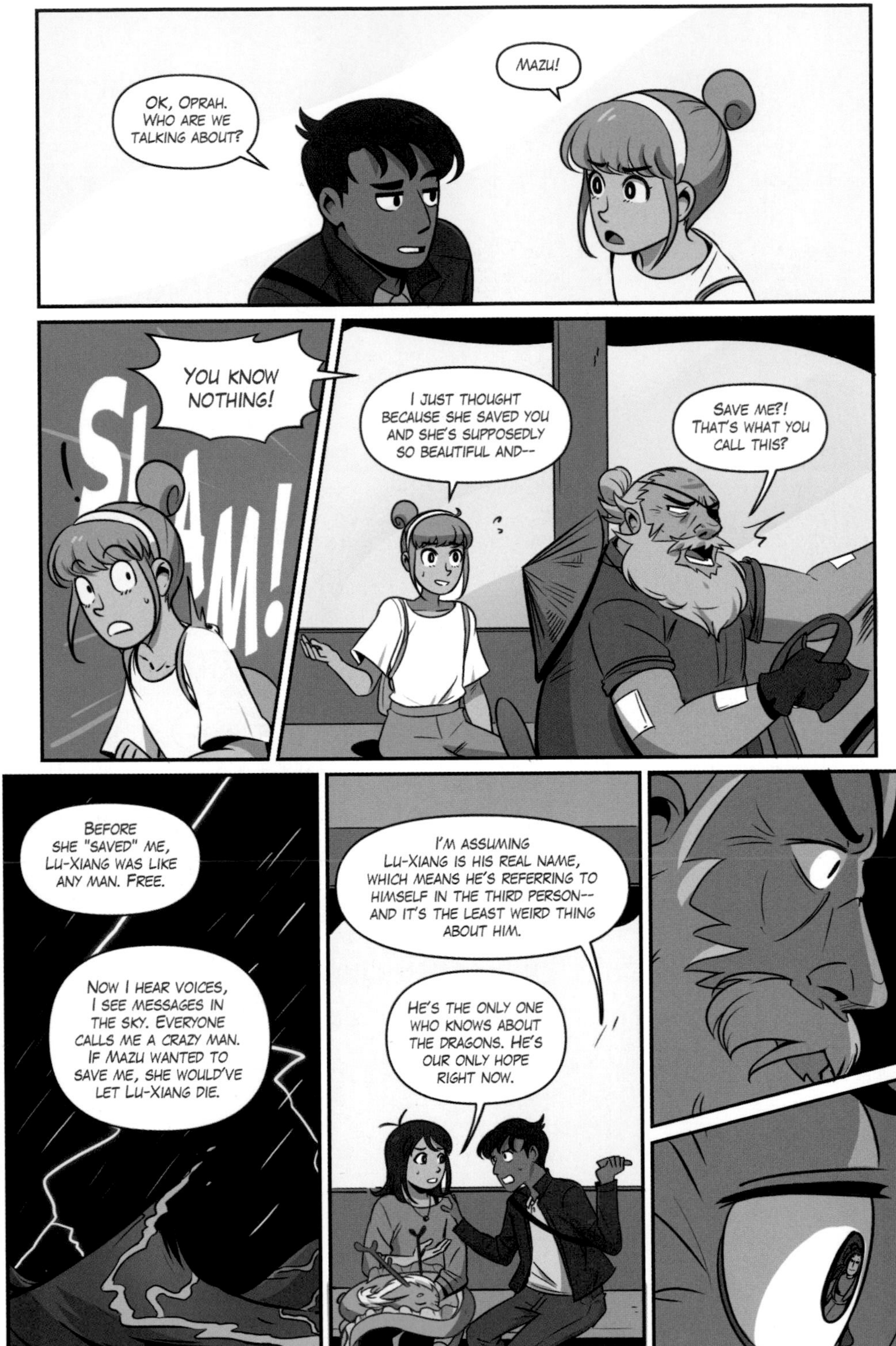
OK, OPRAH. WHO ARE WE TALKING ABOUT?
MAZU!
YOU KNOW NOTHING!
SLAM!
I JUST THOUGHT BECAUSE SHE SAVED YOU AND SHE'S SUPPOSEDLY SO BEAUTIFUL AND--
SAVE ME?! THAT'S WHAT YOU CALL THIS?
BEFORE SHE "SAVED" ME, LU-XIANG WAS LIKE ANY MAN. FREE.
NOW I HEAR VOICES, I SEE MESSAGES IN THE SKY. EVERYONE CALLS ME A CRAZY MAN. IF MAZU WANTED TO SAVE ME, SHE WOULD'VE LET LU-XIANG DIE.
I'M ASSUMING LU-XIANG IS HIS REAL NAME, WHICH MEANS HE'S REFERRING TO HIMSELF IN THE THIRD PERSON-- AND IT'S THE LEAST WEIRD THING ABOUT HIM.
HE'S THE ONLY ONE WHO KNOWS ABOUT THE DRAGONS. HE'S OUR ONLY HOPE RIGHT NOW.

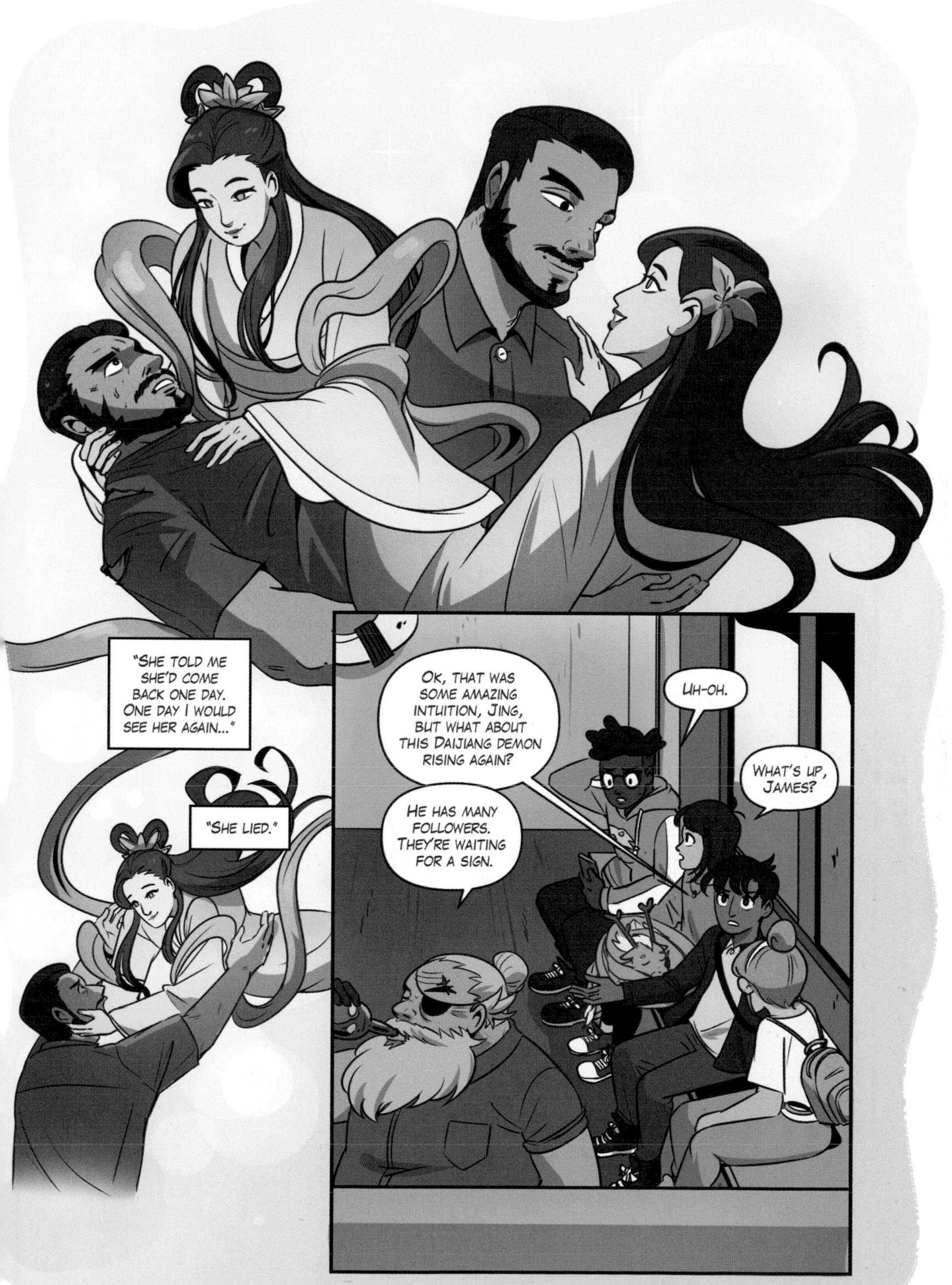
"She told me she'd come back one day. One day I would see her again..."
"She lied."
Ok, that was some amazing intuition, Jing, but what about this Daijiang demon rising again?
He has many followers. They're waiting for a sign.
Uh-oh.
What's up, James?

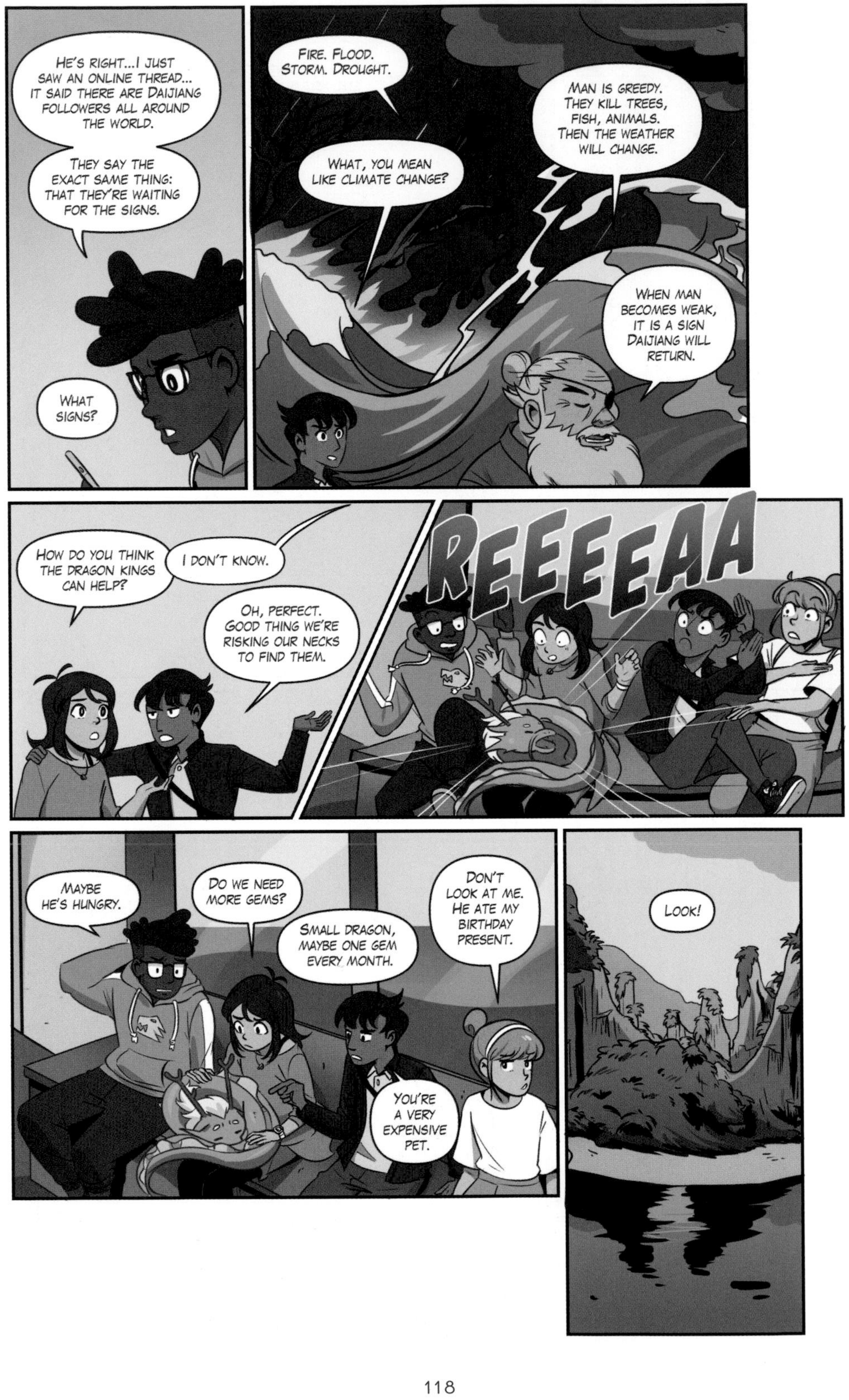
HE'S RIGHT...I JUST SAW AN ONLINE THREAD... IT SAID THERE ARE DAIJIANG FOLLOWERS ALL AROUND THE WORLD.
THEY SAY THE EXACT SAME THING: THAT THEY'RE WAITING FOR THE SIGNS.
WHAT SIGNS?
FIRE. FLOOD. STORM. DROUGHT.
WHAT, YOU MEAN LIKE CLIMATE CHANGE?
MAN IS GREEDY. THEY KILL TREES, FISH, ANIMALS. THEN THE WEATHER WILL CHANGE.
WHEN MAN BECOMES WEAK, IT IS A SIGN DAIJIANG WILL RETURN.
HOW DO YOU THINK THE DRAGON KINGS CAN HELP?
I DON'T KNOW.
OH, PERFECT. GOOD THING WE'RE RISKING OUR NECKS TO FIND THEM.
REEEEEAA
MAYBE HE'S HUNGRY.
DO WE NEED MORE GEMS?
SMALL DRAGON, MAYBE ONE GEM EVERY MONTH.
DON'T LOOK AT ME. HE ATE MY BIRTHDAY PRESENT.
YOU'RE A VERY EXPENSIVE PET.
LOOK!

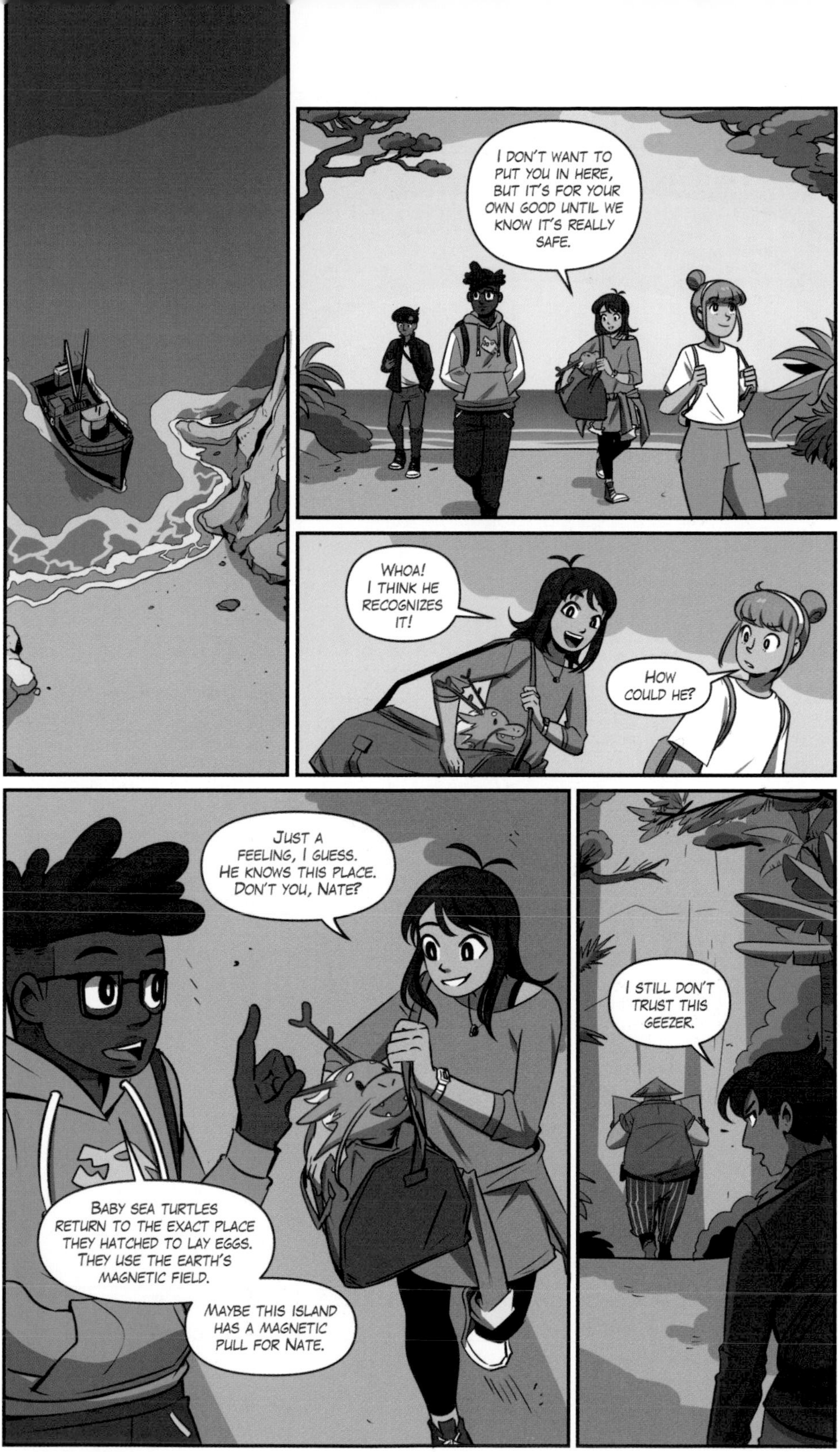
I DON'T WANT TO PUT YOU IN HERE, BUT IT'S FOR YOUR OWN GOOD UNTIL WE KNOW IT'S REALLY SAFE.
WHOA! I THINK HE RECOGNIZES IT!
HOW COULD HE?
JUST A FEELING, I GUESS. HE KNOWS THIS PLACE. DON'T YOU, NATE?
BABY SEA TURTLES RETURN TO THE EXACT PLACE THEY HATCHED TO LAY EGGS. THEY USE THE EARTH'S MAGNETIC FIELD.
MAYBE THIS ISLAND HAS A MAGNETIC PULL FOR NATE.
I STILL DON'T TRUST THIS GEEZER.

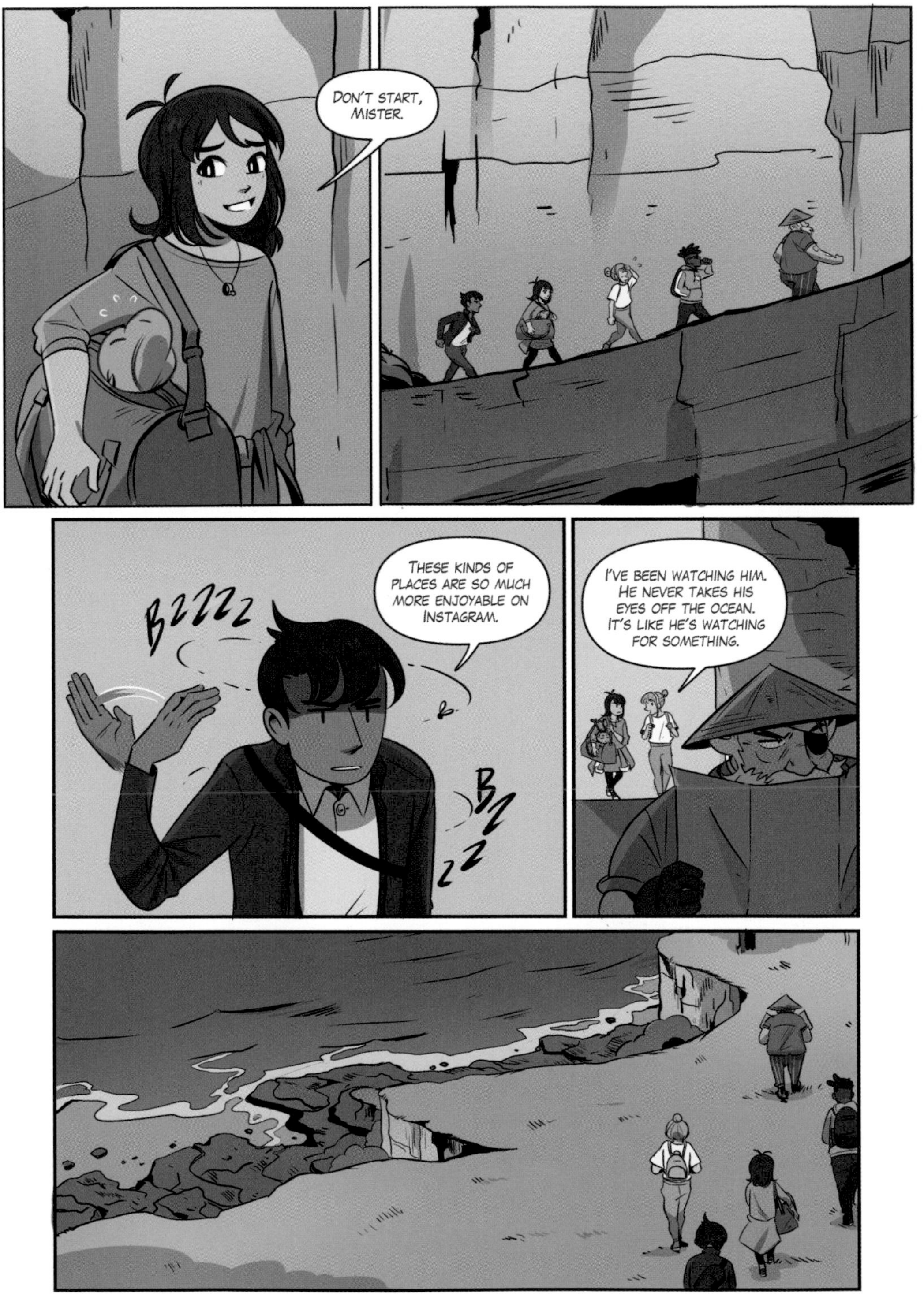
DON'T START, MISTER.
BZZZZ
THESE KINDS OF PLACES ARE SO MUCH MORE ENJOYABLE ON INSTAGRAM.
BZZZ
I'VE BEEN WATCHING HIM. HE NEVER TAKES HIS EYES OFF THE OCEAN. IT'S LIKE HE'S WATCHING FOR SOMETHING.

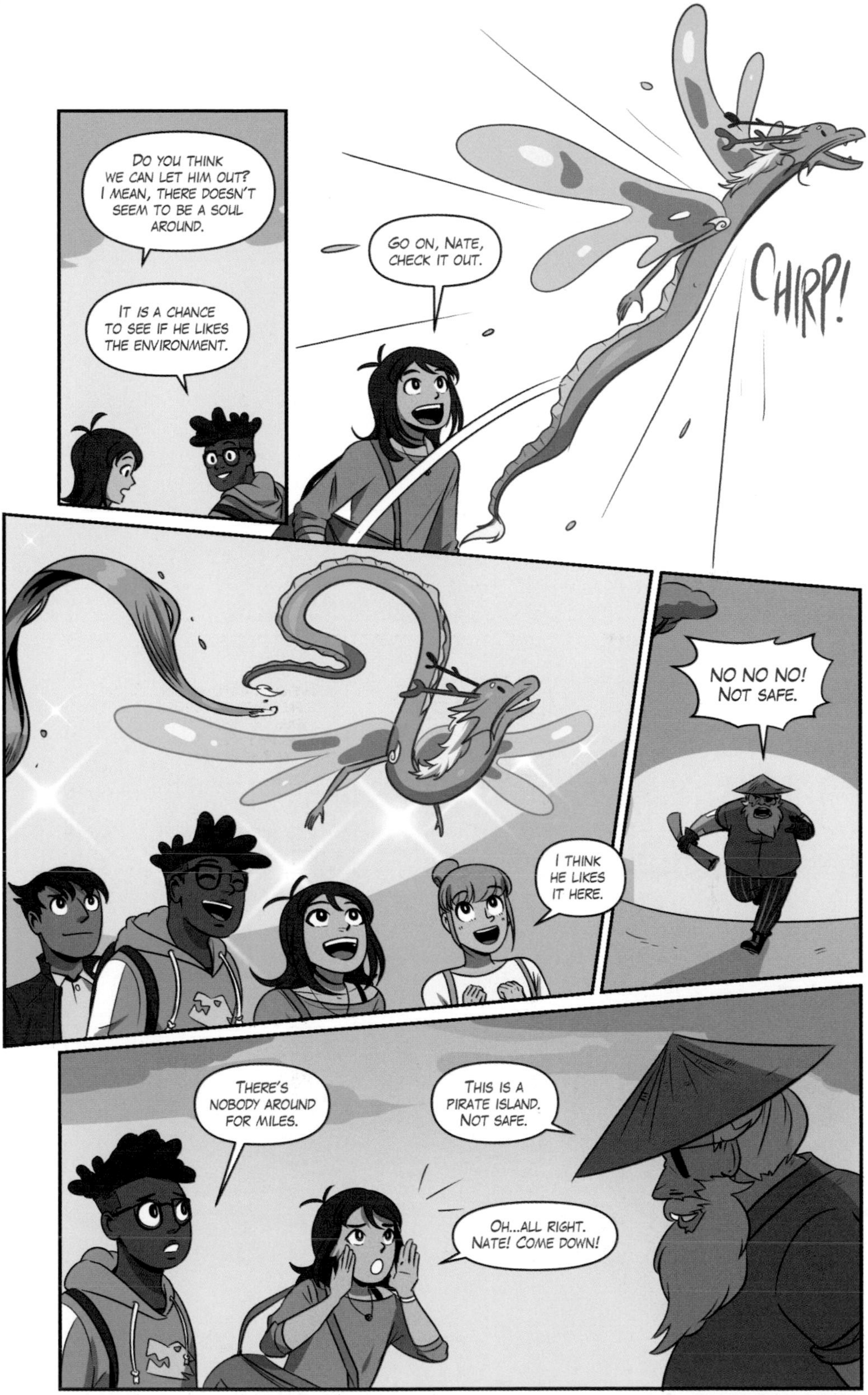
DO YOU THINK WE CAN LET HIM OUT? I MEAN, THERE DOESN'T SEEM TO BE A SOUL AROUND.
IT IS A CHANCE TO SEE IF HE LIKES THE ENVIRONMENT.
GO ON, NATE, CHECK IT OUT.
CHIRP!
I THINK HE LIKES IT HERE.
NO NO NO! NOT SAFE.
THERE'S NOBODY AROUND FOR MILES.
THIS IS A PIRATE ISLAND. NOT SAFE.
OH...ALL RIGHT. NATE! COME DOWN!

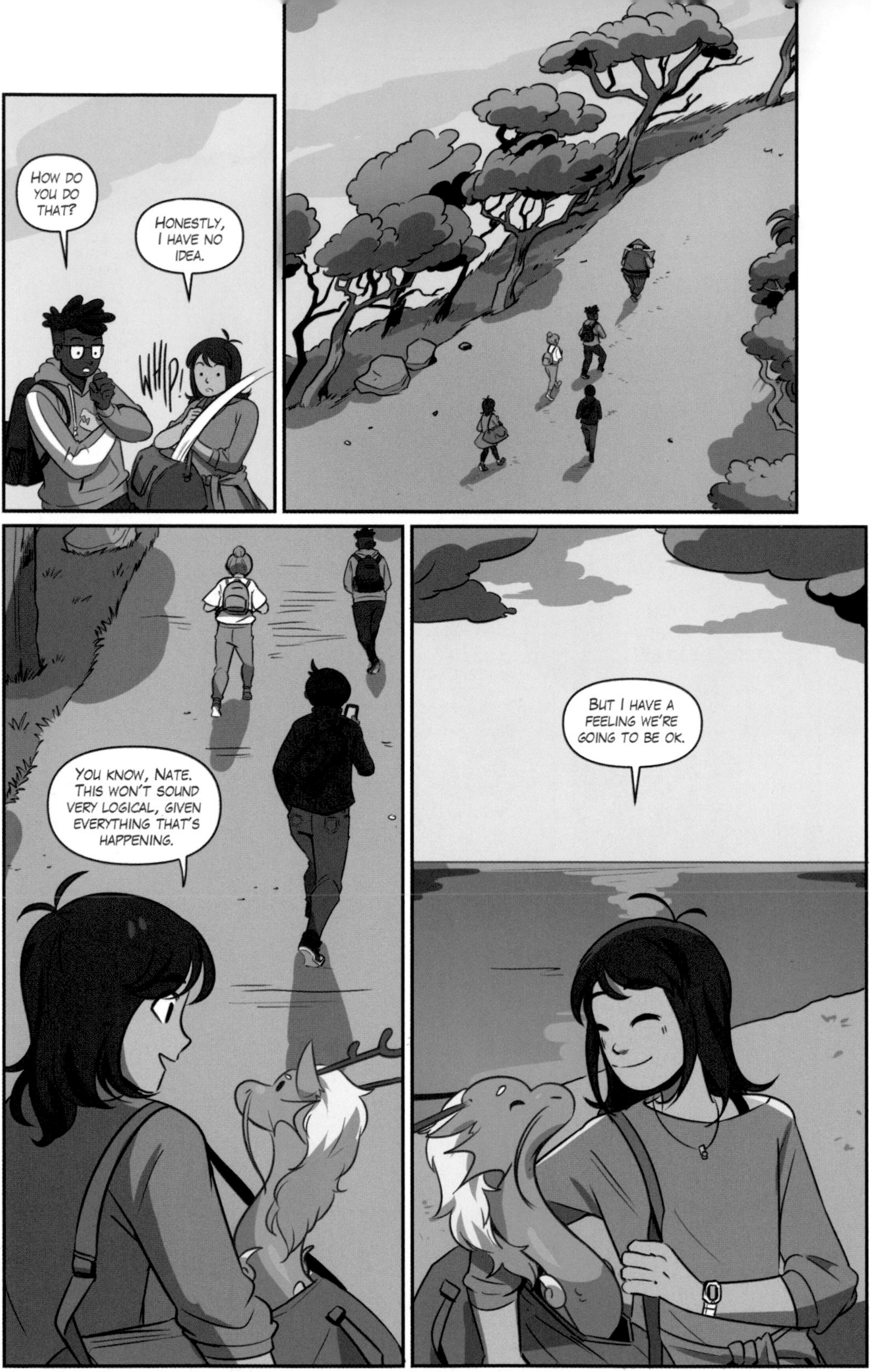
How do you do that?
Honestly, I have no idea.
WHIP!
You know, Nate. This won't sound very logical, given everything that's happening.
But I have a feeling we're going to be OK.

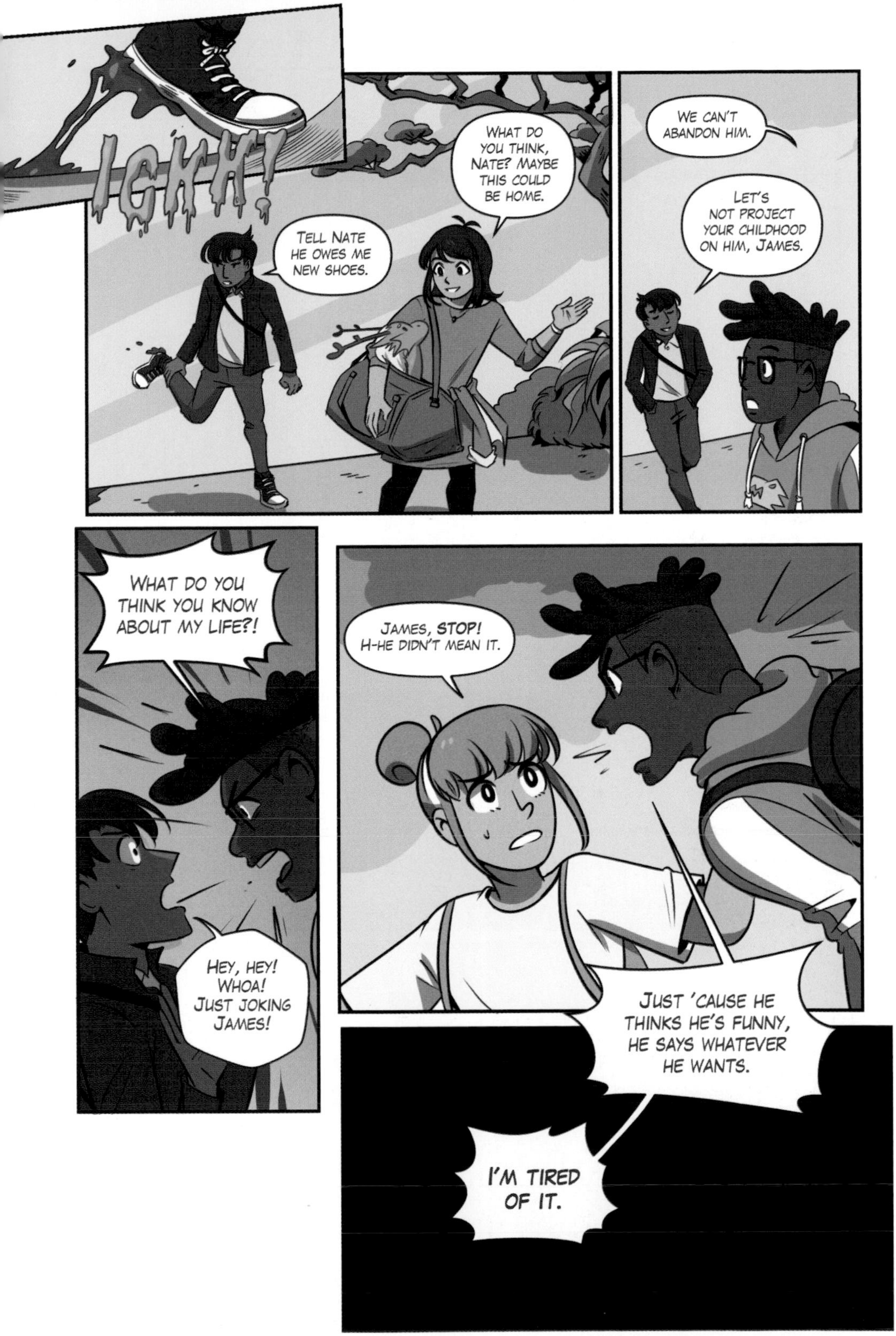
IGKH!
TELL NATE HE OWES ME NEW SHOES.
WHAT DO YOU THINK, NATE? MAYBE THIS COULD BE HOME.
WE CAN'T ABANDON HIM.
LET'S NOT PROJECT YOUR CHILDHOOD ON HIM, JAMES.
WHAT DO YOU THINK YOU KNOW ABOUT MY LIFE?!
HEY, HEY! WHOA! JUST JOKING JAMES!
JAMES, STOP! H-HE DIDN'T MEAN IT.
JUST 'CAUSE HE THINKS HE'S FUNNY, HE SAYS WHATEVER HE WANTS.
I'M TIRED OF IT.

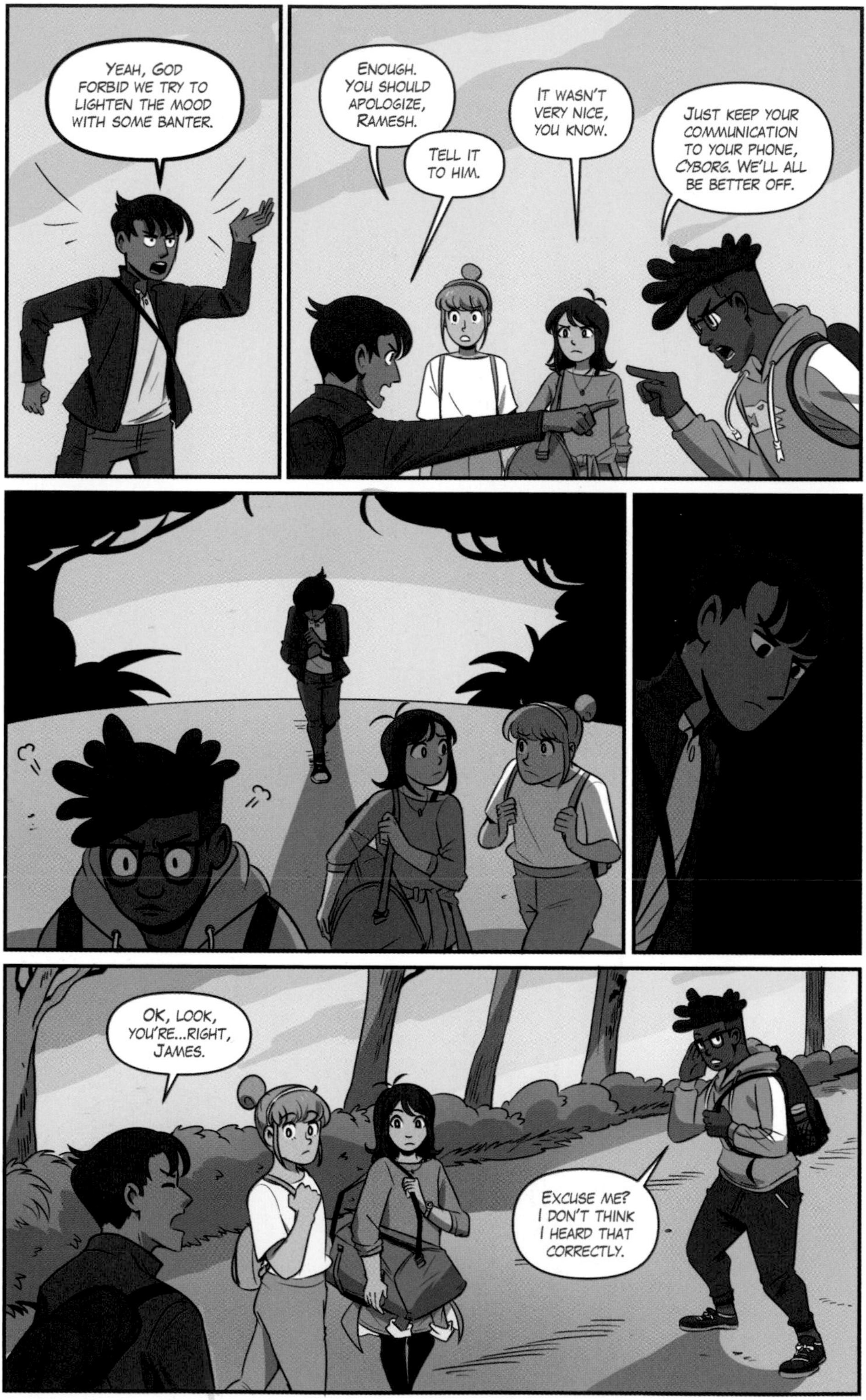
YEAH, GOD FORBID WE TRY TO LIGHTEN THE MOOD WITH SOME BANTER.
ENOUGH. YOU SHOULD APOLOGIZE, RAMESH.
TELL IT TO HIM.
IT WASN'T VERY NICE, YOU KNOW.
JUST KEEP YOUR COMMUNICATION TO YOUR PHONE, CYBORG. WE'LL ALL BE BETTER OFF.
OK, LOOK, YOU'RE...RIGHT, JAMES.
EXCUSE ME? I DON'T THINK I HEARD THAT CORRECTLY.

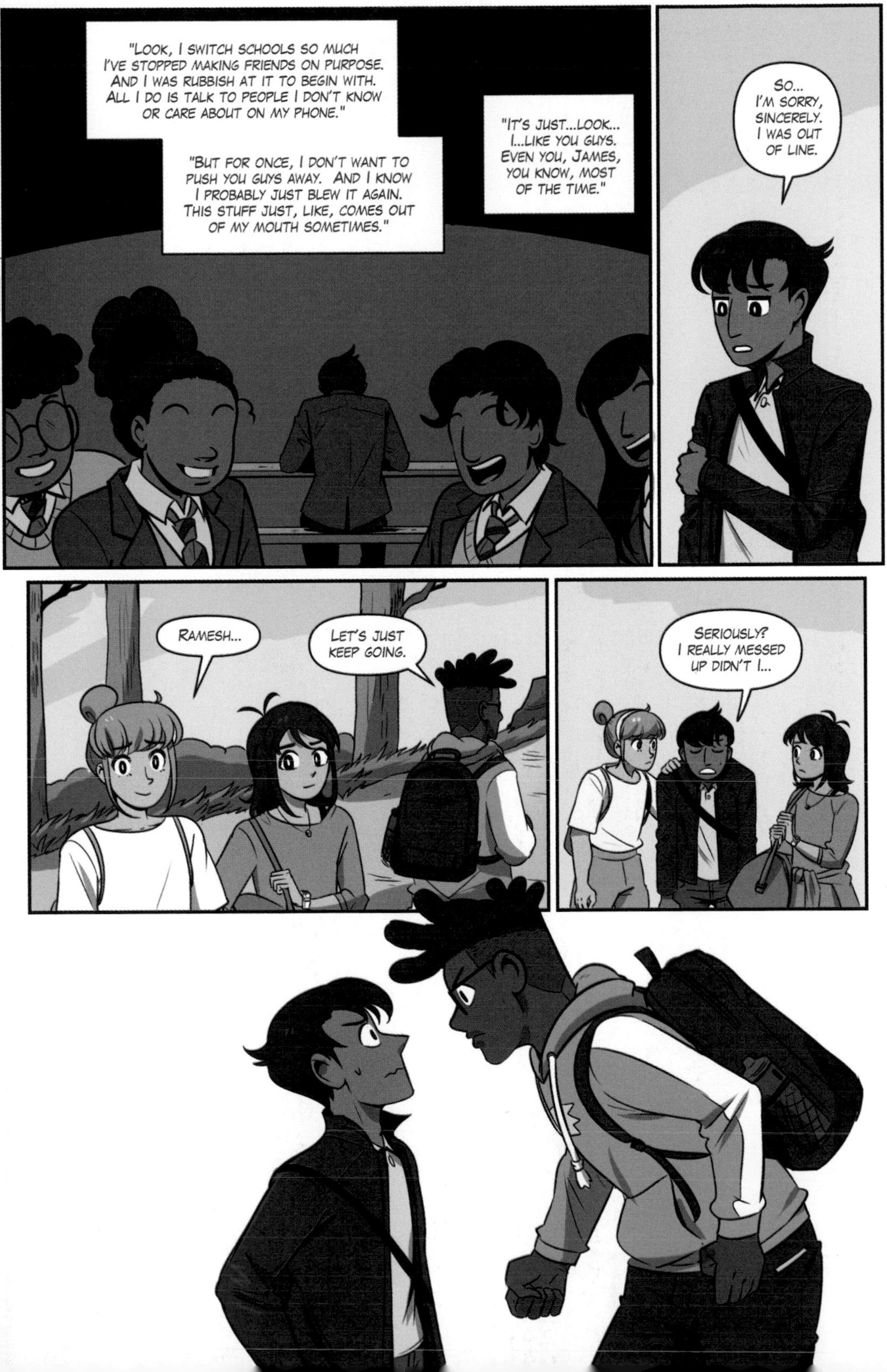
"LOOK, I SWITCH SCHOOLS SO MUCH I'VE STOPPED MAKING FRIENDS ON PURPOSE. AND I WAS RUBBISH AT IT TO BEGIN WITH. ALL I DO IS TALK TO PEOPLE I DON'T KNOW OR CARE ABOUT ON MY PHONE."
"BUT FOR ONCE, I DON'T WANT TO PUSH YOU GUYS AWAY. AND I KNOW I PROBABLY JUST BLEW IT AGAIN. THIS STUFF JUST, LIKE, COMES OUT OF MY MOUTH SOMETIMES."
"IT'S JUST...LOOK... I...LIKE YOU GUYS. EVEN YOU, JAMES, YOU KNOW, MOST OF THE TIME."
SO... I'M SORRY, SINCERELY. I WAS OUT OF LINE.
RAMESH...
LET'S JUST KEEP GOING.
SERIOUSLY? I REALLY MESSED UP DIDN'T I...

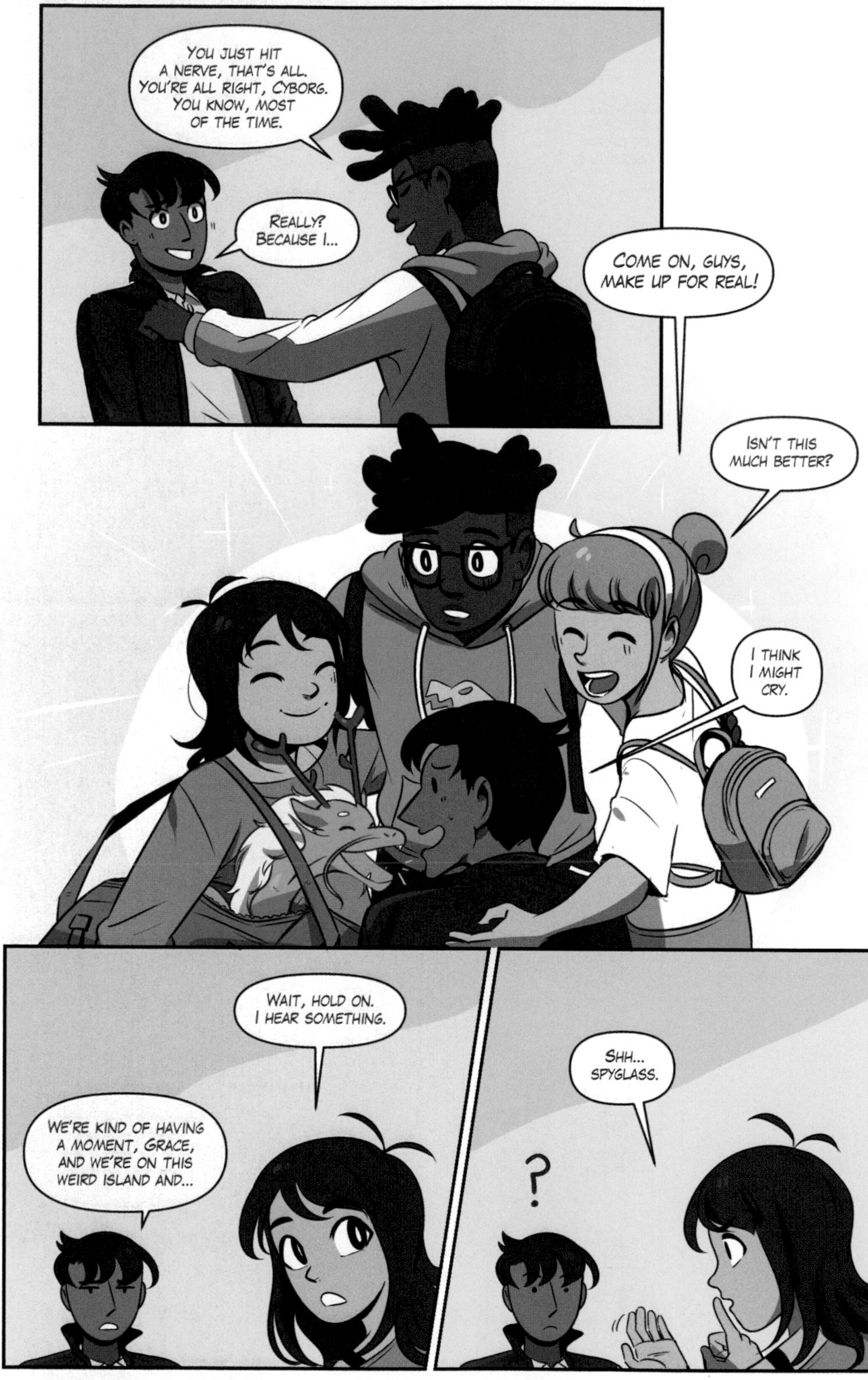
YOU JUST HIT A NERVE, THAT'S ALL. YOU'RE ALL RIGHT, CYBORG. YOU KNOW, MOST OF THE TIME.
REALLY? BECAUSE I...
COME ON, GUYS, MAKE UP FOR REAL!
ISN'T THIS MUCH BETTER?
I THINK I MIGHT CRY.
WAIT, HOLD ON. I HEAR SOMETHING.
WE'RE KIND OF HAVING A MOMENT, GRACE, AND WE'RE ON THIS WEIRD ISLAND AND...
SHH... SPYGLASS.
?

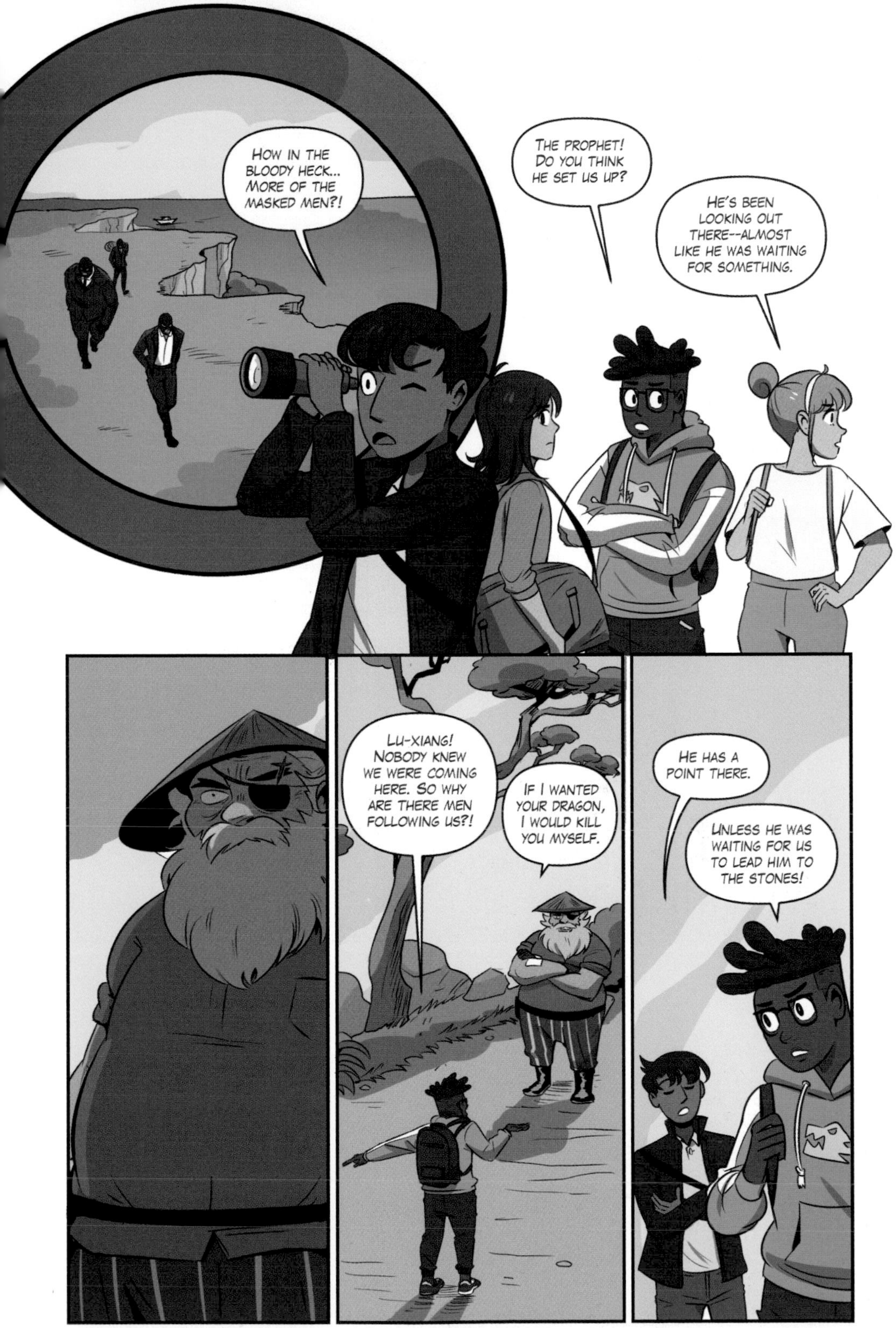
HOW IN THE BLOODY HECK... MORE OF THE MASKED MEN?!
THE PROPHET! DO YOU THINK HE SET US UP?
HE'S BEEN LOOKING OUT THERE--ALMOST LIKE HE WAS WAITING FOR SOMETHING.
LU-XIANG! NOBODY KNEW WE WERE COMING HERE. SO WHY ARE THERE MEN FOLLOWING US?!
IF I WANTED YOUR DRAGON, I WOULD KILL YOU MYSELF.
HE HAS A POINT THERE.
UNLESS HE WAS WAITING FOR US TO LEAD HIM TO THE STONES!

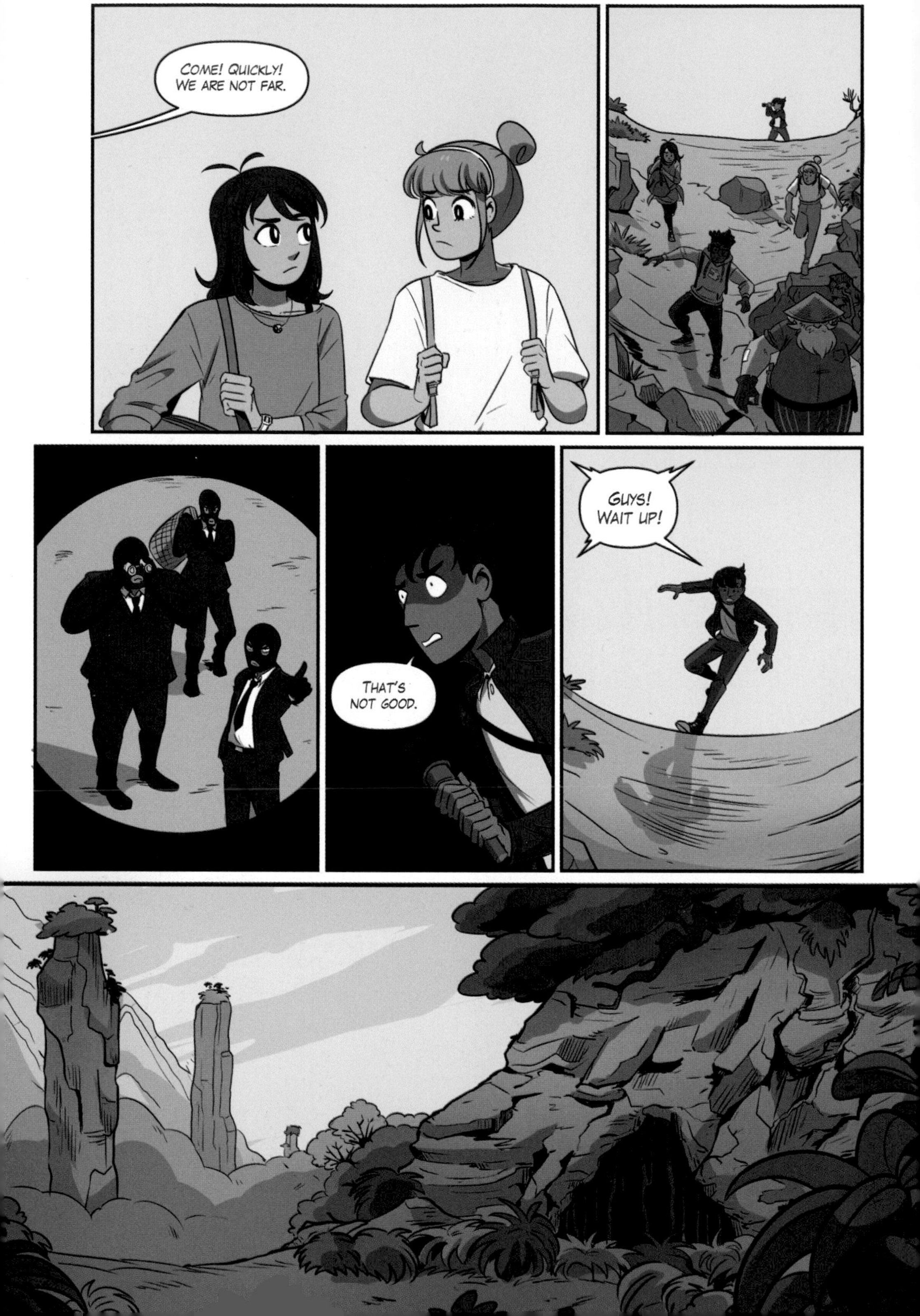
COME! QUICKLY! WE ARE NOT FAR.
THAT'S NOT GOOD.
GUYS! WAIT UP!

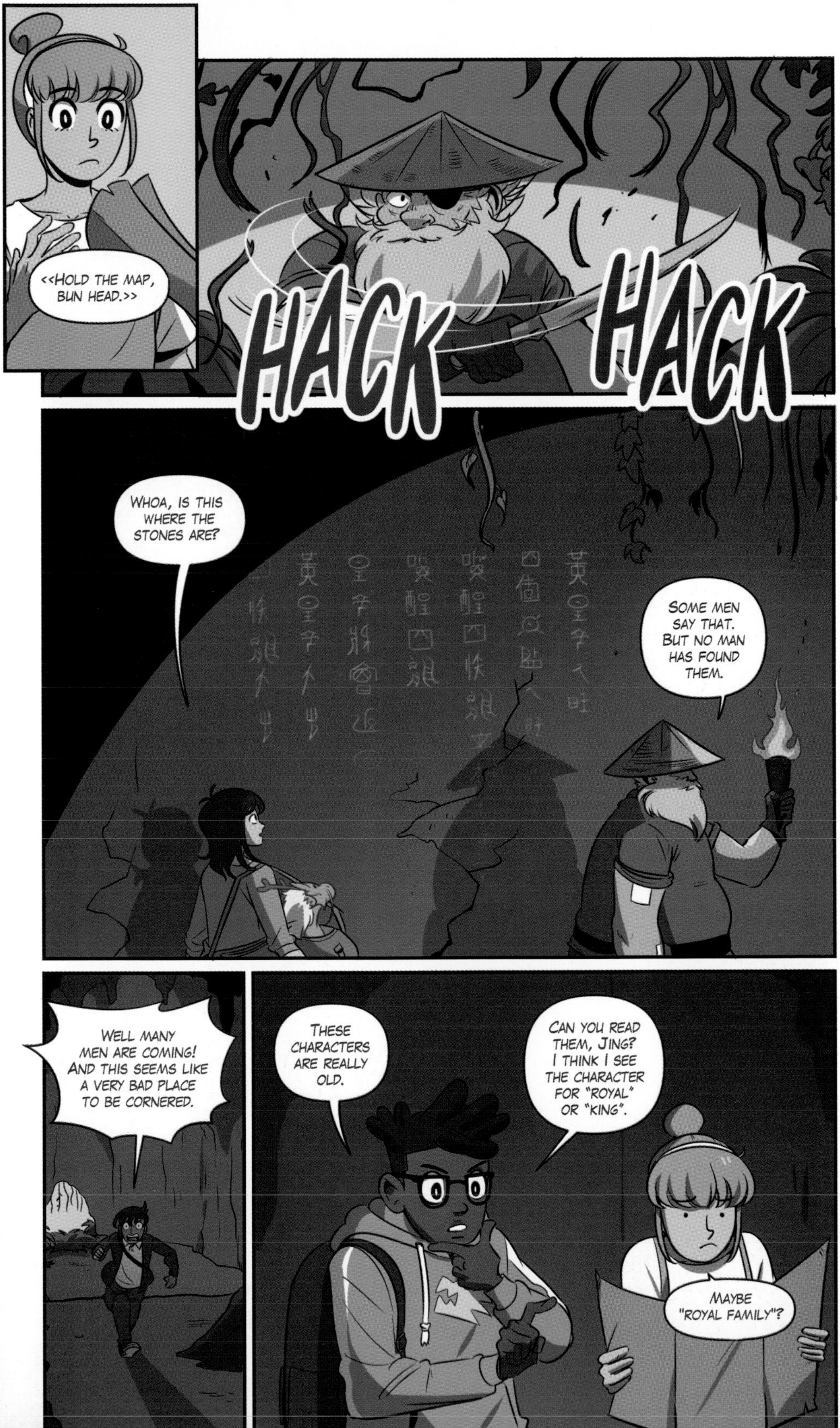
<<HOLD THE MAP, BUN HEAD.>>
HACK HACK
WHOA, IS THIS WHERE THE STONES ARE?
SOME MEN SAY THAT. BUT NO MAN HAS FOUND THEM.
WELL MANY MEN ARE COMING! AND THIS SEEMS LIKE A VERY BAD PLACE TO BE CORNERED.
THESE CHARACTERS ARE REALLY OLD.
CAN YOU READ THEM, JING? I THINK I SEE THE CHARACTER FOR "ROYAL" OR "KING".
MAYBE "ROYAL FAMILY"?

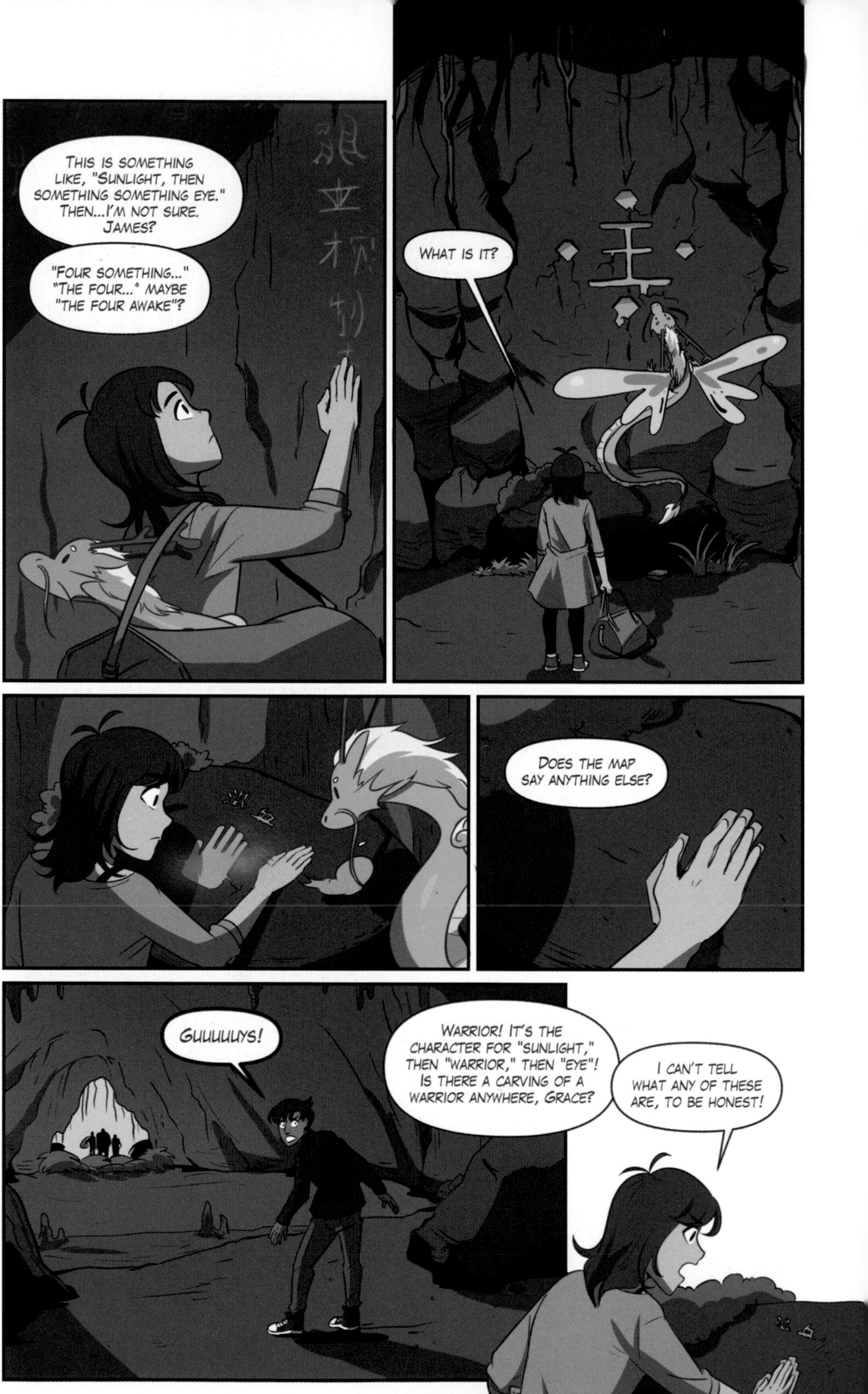

THIS IS SOMETHING LIKE, "SUNLIGHT, THEN SOMETHING SOMETHING EYE." THEN...I'M NOT SURE. JAMES?
"FOUR SOMETHING..." "THE FOUR..." MAYBE "THE FOUR AWAKE"?
WHAT IS IT?
DOES THE MAP SAY ANYTHING ELSE?
GUUUUUYS!
WARRIOR! IT'S THE CHARACTER FOR "SUNLIGHT," THEN "WARRIOR," THEN "EYE"! IS THERE A CARVING OF A WARRIOR ANYWHERE, GRACE?
I CAN'T TELL WHAT ANY OF THESE ARE, TO BE HONEST!

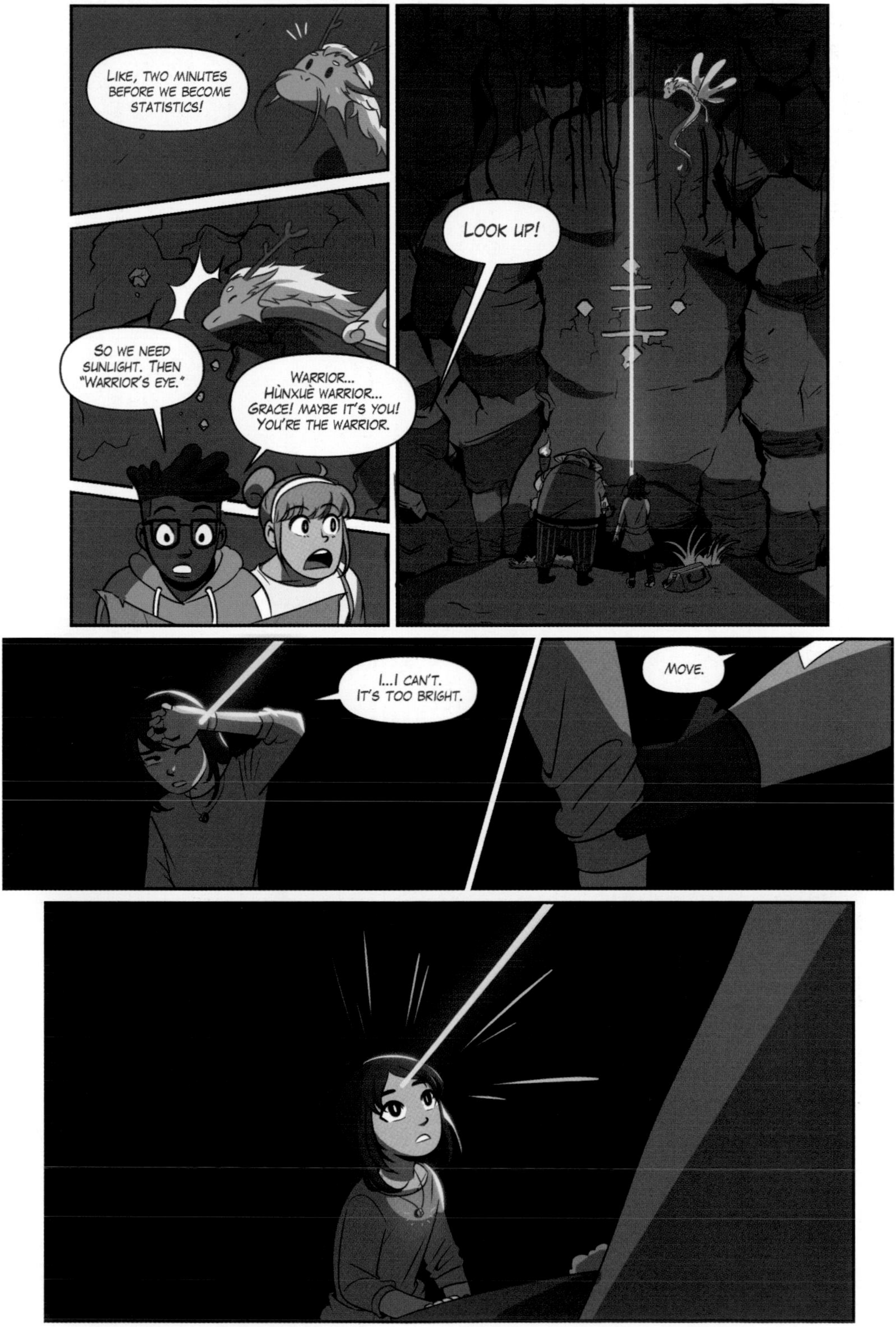
LIKE, TWO MINUTES BEFORE WE BECOME STATISTICS!
SO WE NEED SUNLIGHT. THEN "WARRIOR'S EYE."
WARRIOR... HÙNXUÈ WARRIOR... GRACE! MAYBE IT'S YOU! YOU'RE THE WARRIOR.
LOOK UP!
I...I CAN'T. IT'S TOO BRIGHT.
MOVE.

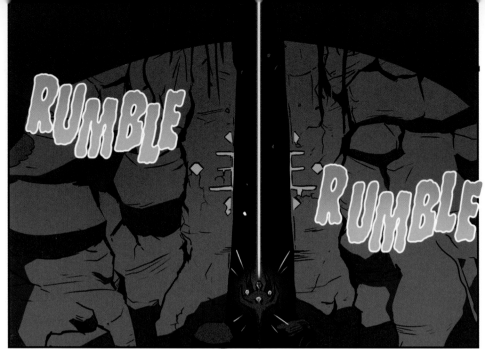

THE FOUR!

TAKE THAT!

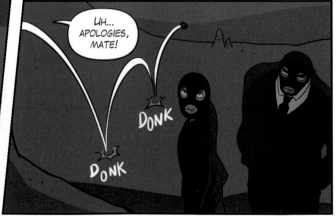

UH... APOLOGIES, MATE!

DONK

DONK

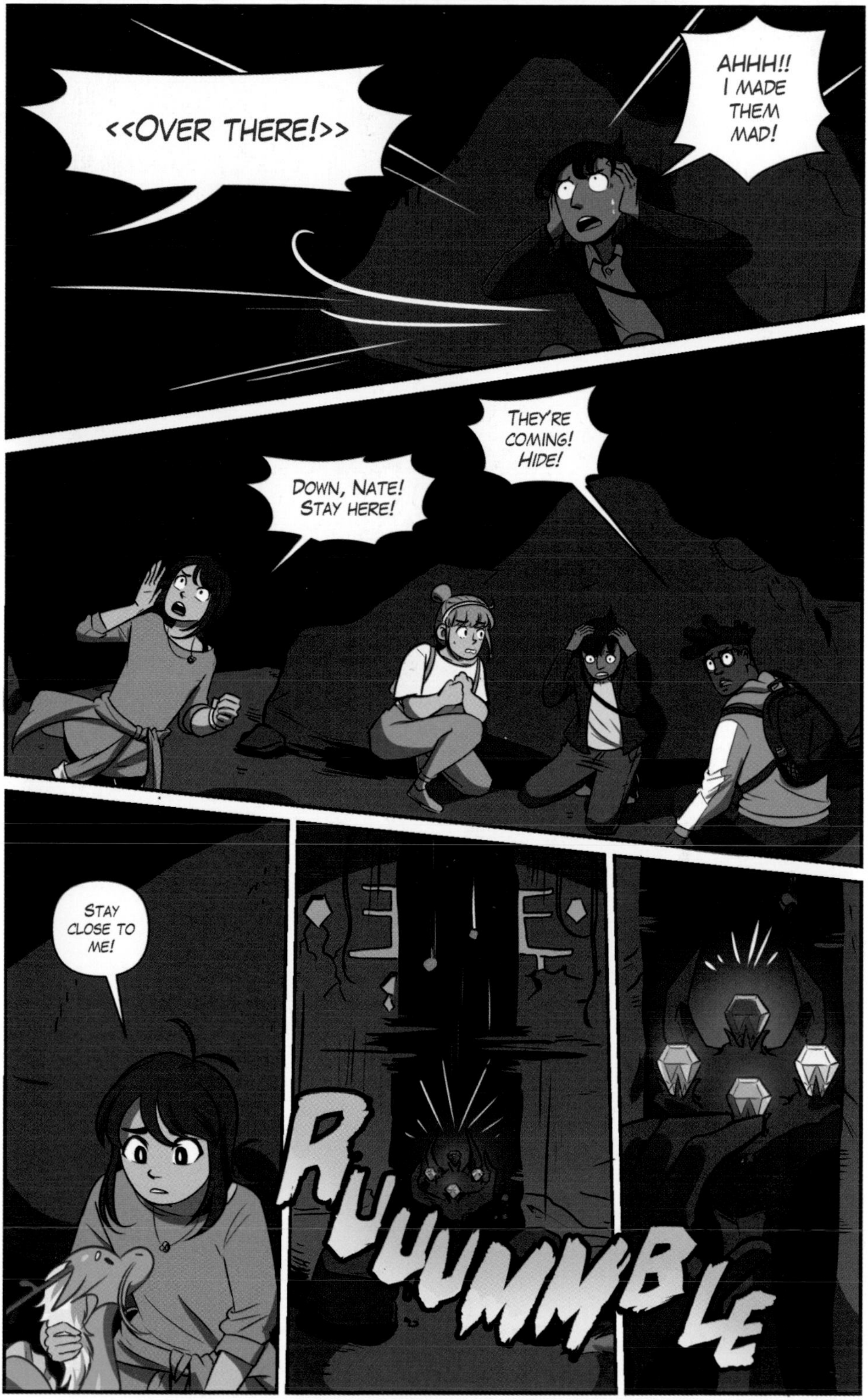
<<OVER THERE!>>
AHHH!! I MADE THEM MAD!
THEY'RE COMING! HIDE!
DOWN, NATE! STAY HERE!
STAY CLOSE TO ME!
RUUUMMBLE

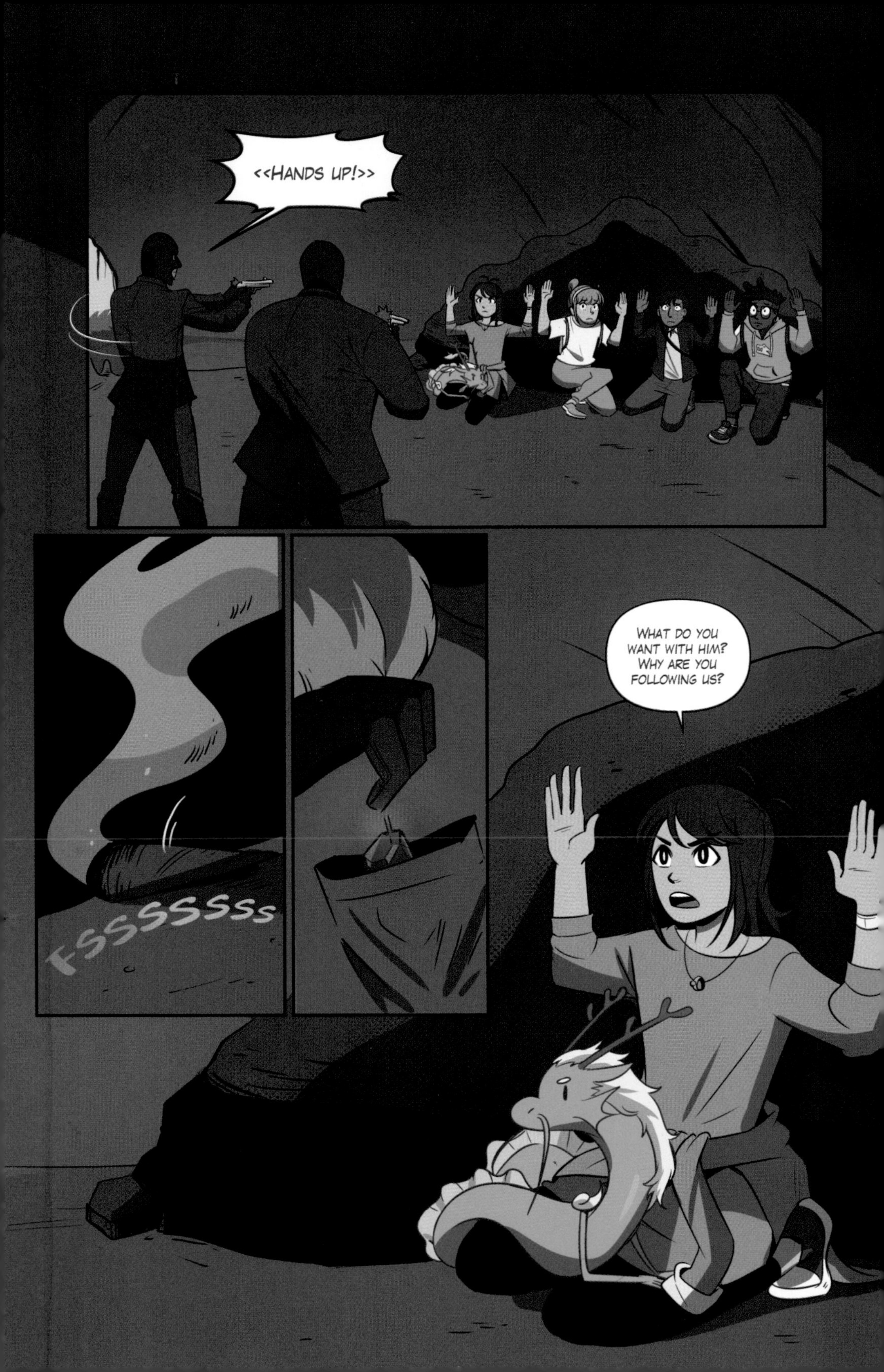
<<HANDS UP!>>
FSSSSSSSs
WHAT DO YOU WANT WITH HIM? WHY ARE YOU FOLLOWING US?

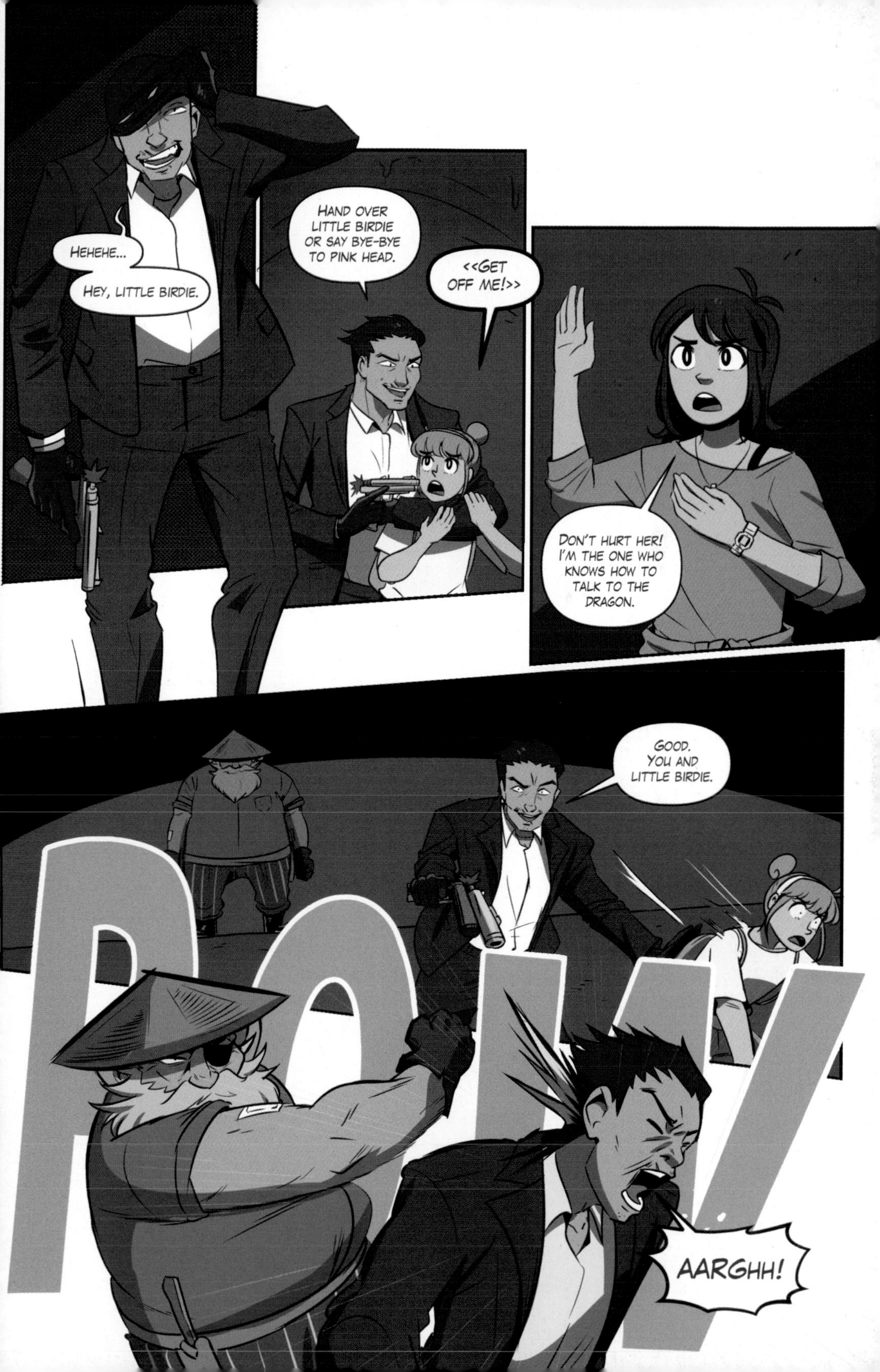
HEHEHE...
HEY, LITTLE BIRDIE.
HAND OVER LITTLE BIRDIE OR SAY BYE-BYE TO PINK HEAD.
<<GET OFF ME!>>
DON'T HURT HER! I'M THE ONE WHO KNOWS HOW TO TALK TO THE DRAGON.
GOOD. YOU AND LITTLE BIRDIE.
AARGHH!

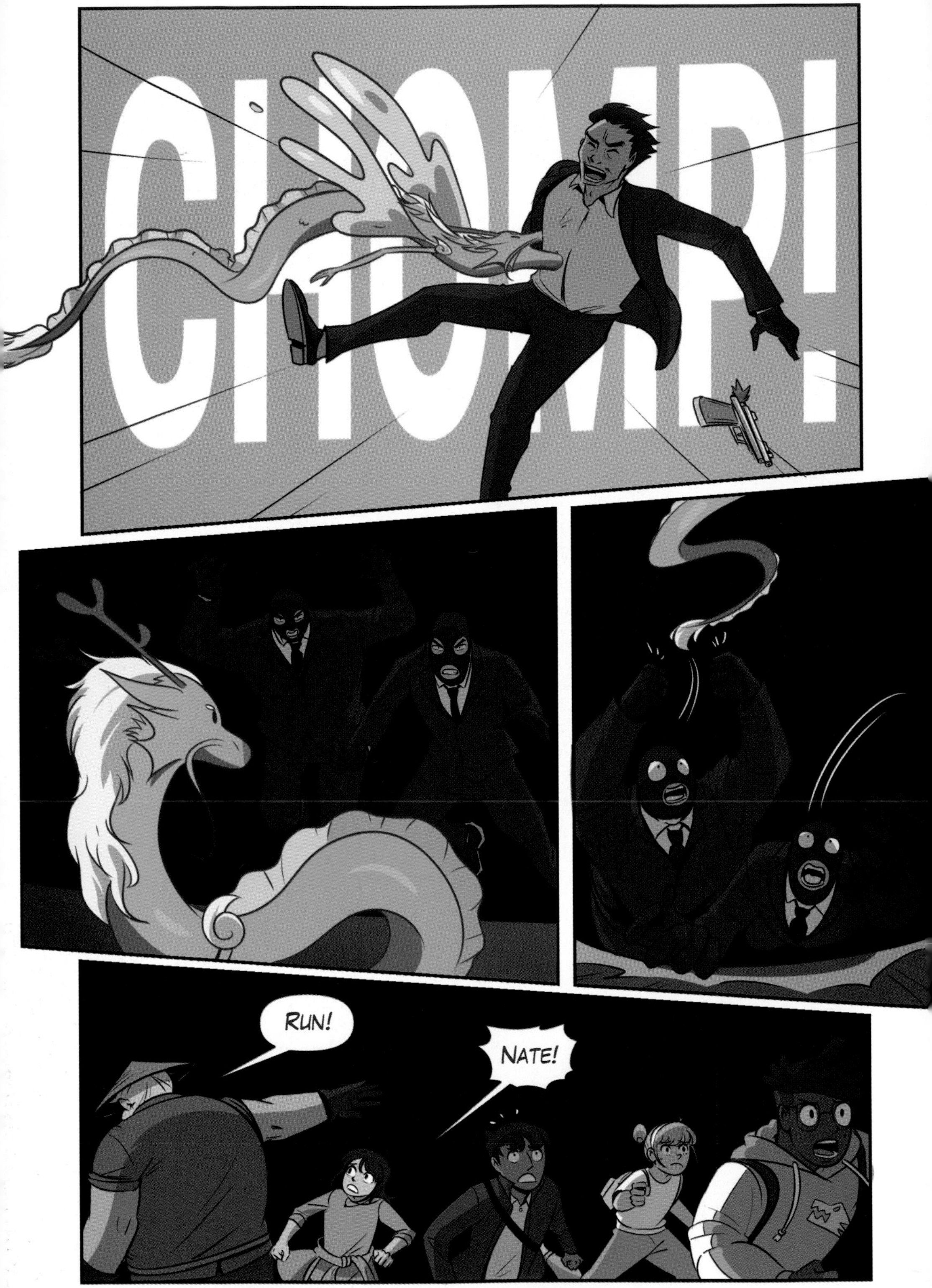
CHOMP!
RUN!
NATE!

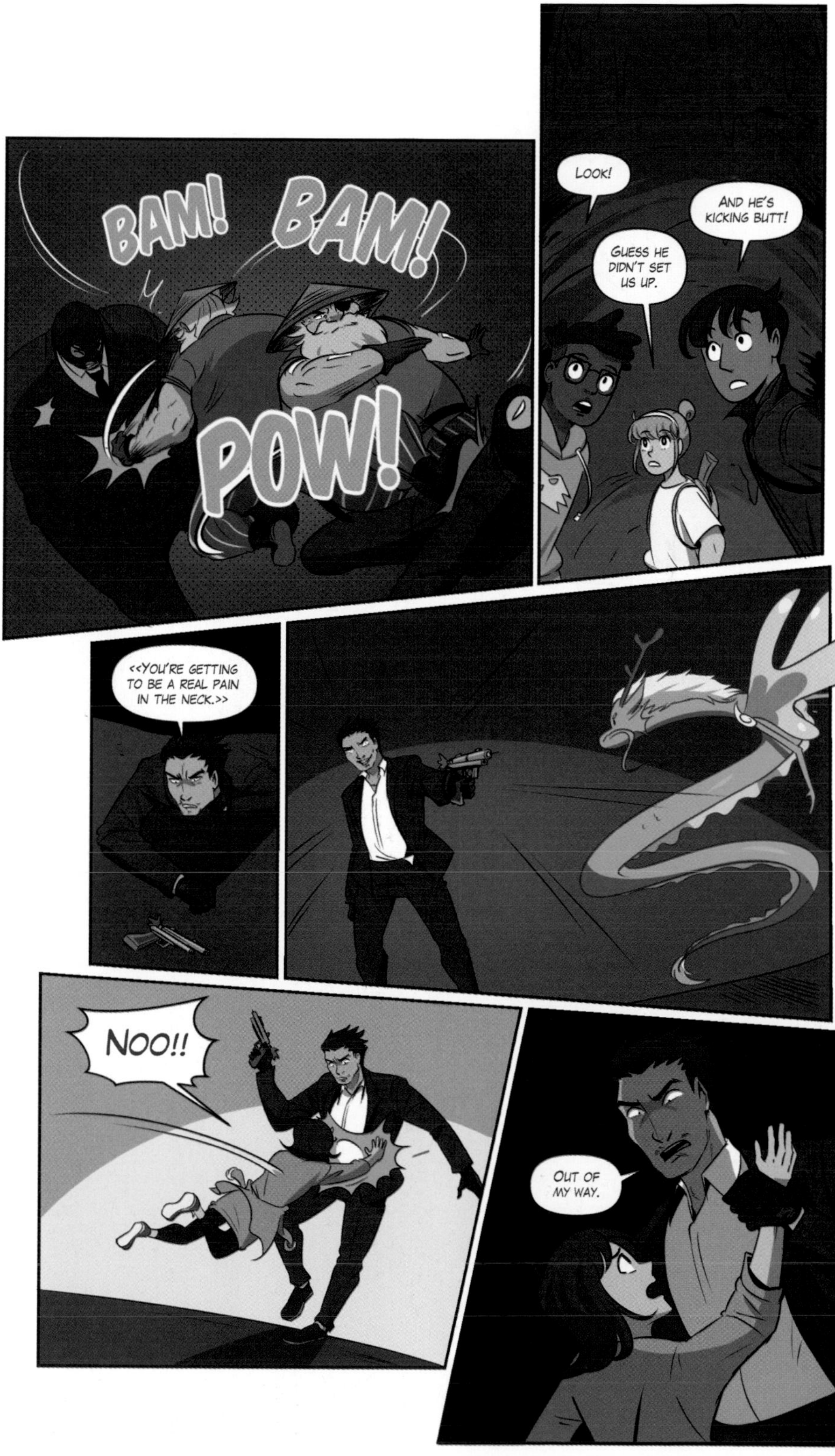
BAM! BAM!
POW!
LOOK!
GUESS HE DIDN'T SET US UP.
AND HE'S KICKING BUTT!
<<YOU'RE GETTING TO BE A REAL PAIN IN THE NECK.>>
NOO!!
OUT OF MY WAY.

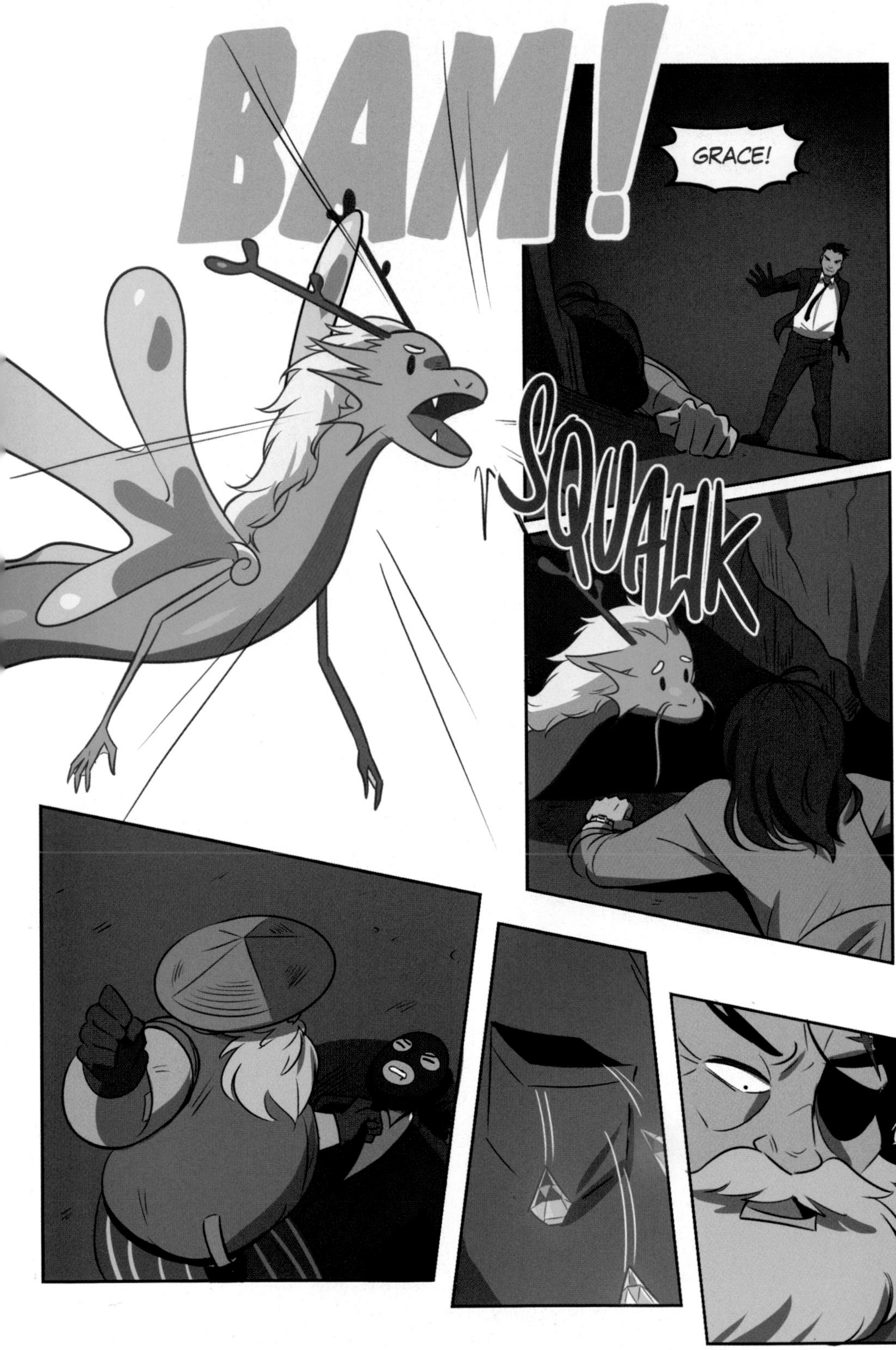
BAM!
GRACE!
SQUAWK

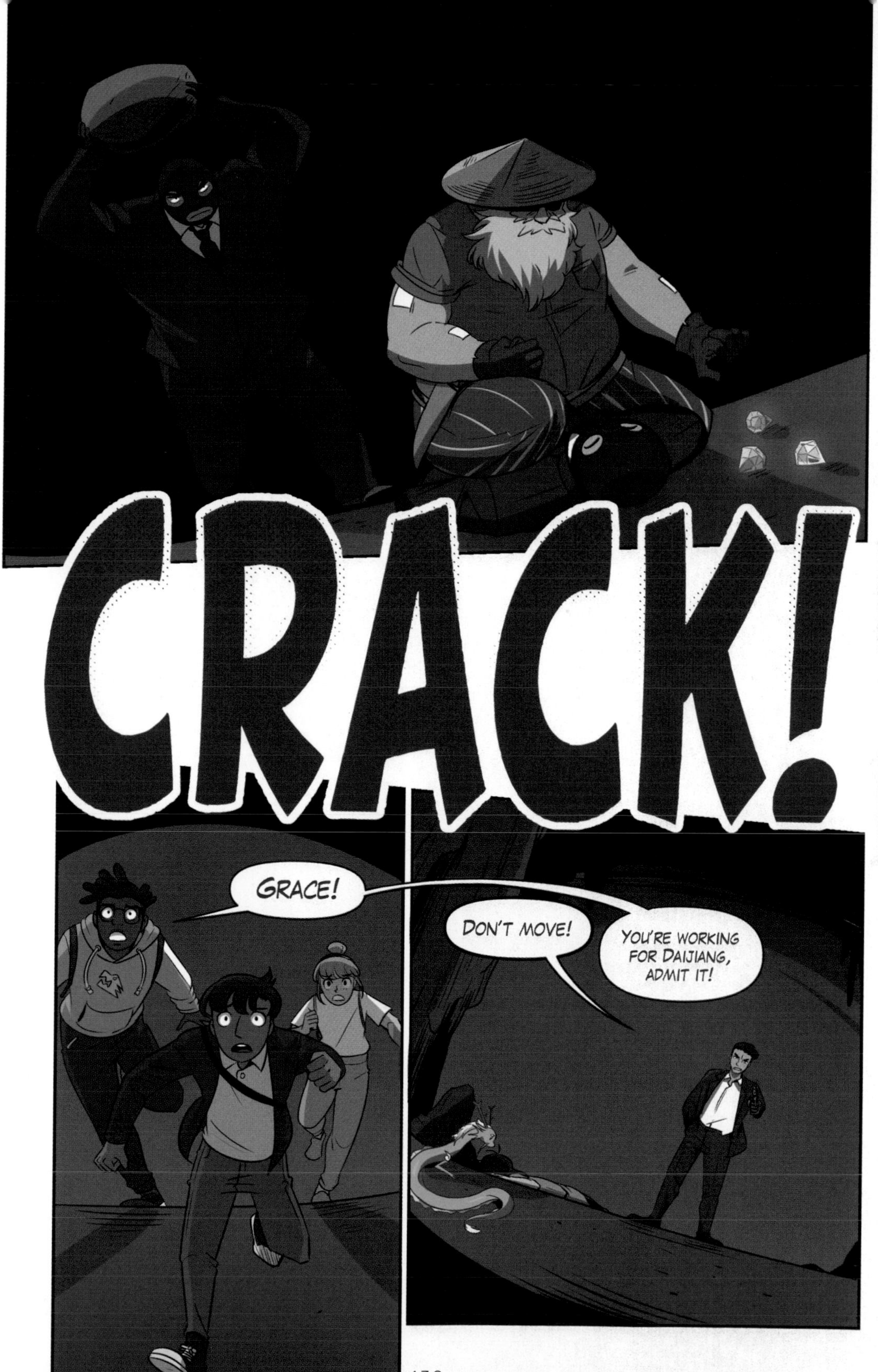
CRACK!
GRACE!
DON'T MOVE!
YOU'RE WORKING FOR DAIJIANG, ADMIT IT!

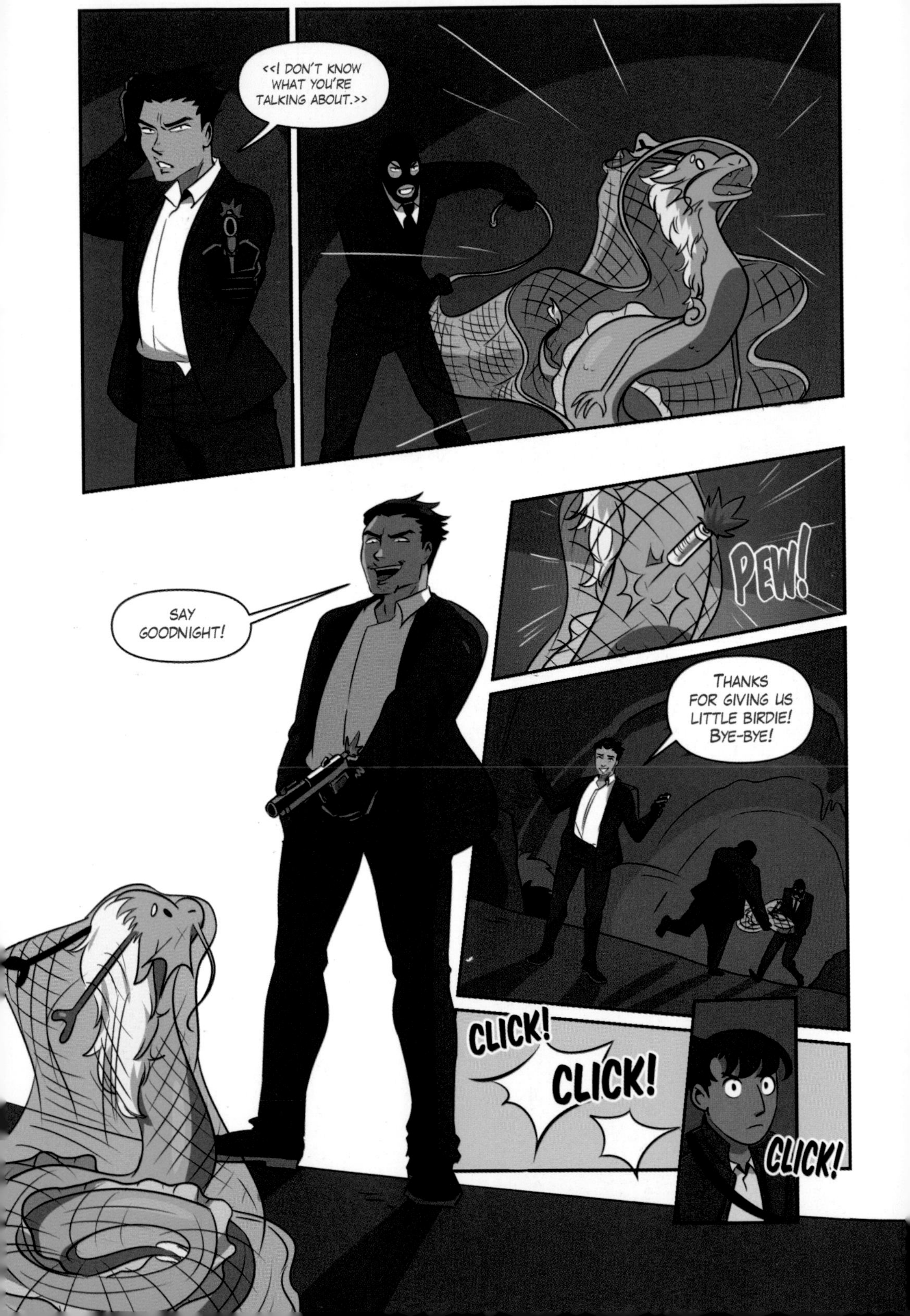
<<I DON'T KNOW WHAT YOU'RE TALKING ABOUT.>>
SAY GOODNIGHT!
PEW!
THANKS FOR GIVING US LITTLE BIRDIE! BYE-BYE!
CLICK!
CLICK!
CLICK!

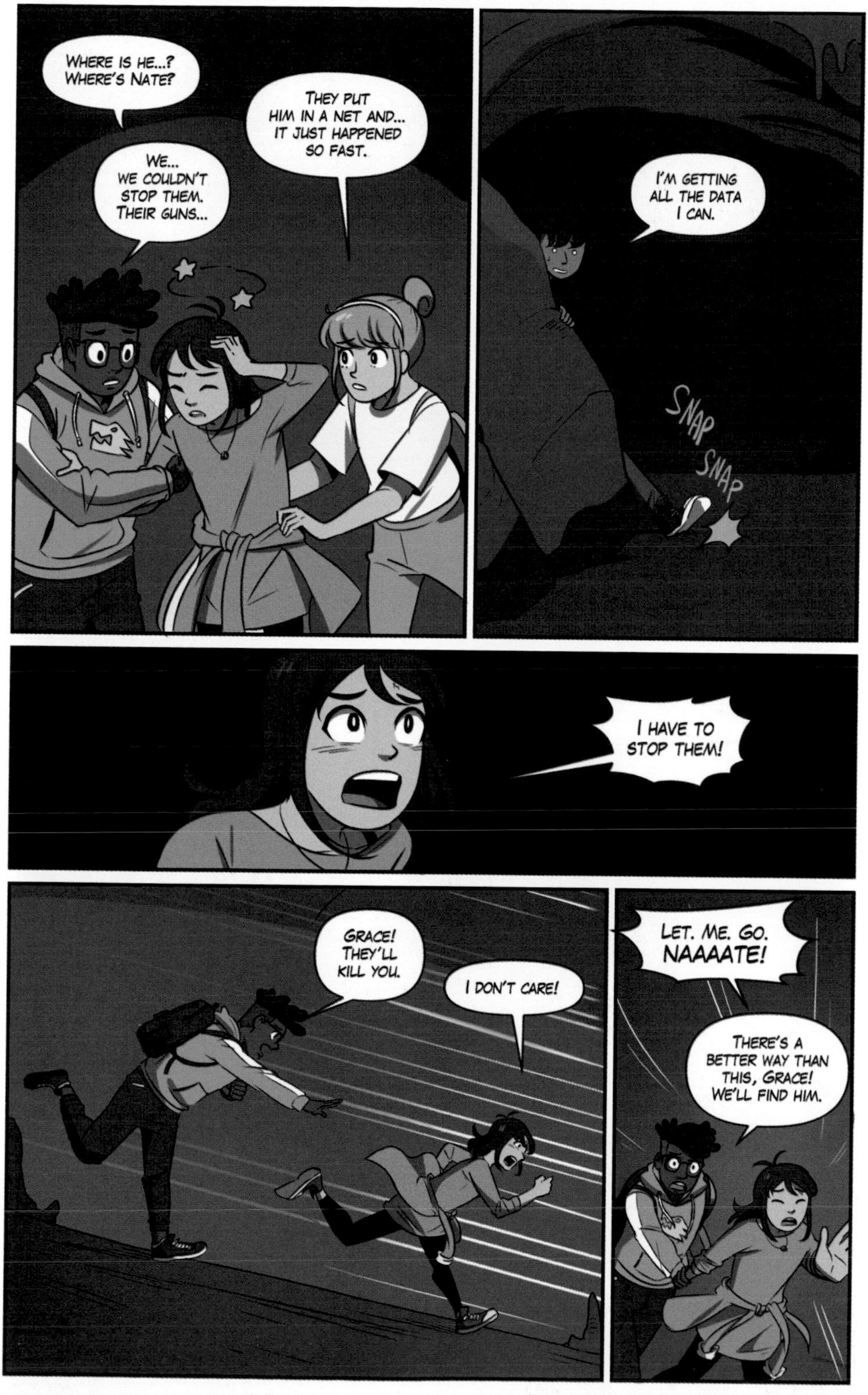
WHERE IS HE...? WHERE'S NATE?
WE... WE COULDN'T STOP THEM. THEIR GUNS...
THEY PUT HIM IN A NET AND... IT JUST HAPPENED SO FAST.
I'M GETTING ALL THE DATA I CAN.
SNAP
SNAP
I HAVE TO STOP THEM!
GRACE! THEY'LL KILL YOU.
I DON'T CARE!
LET. ME. GO. NAAAATE!
THERE'S A BETTER WAY THAN THIS, GRACE! WE'LL FIND HIM.

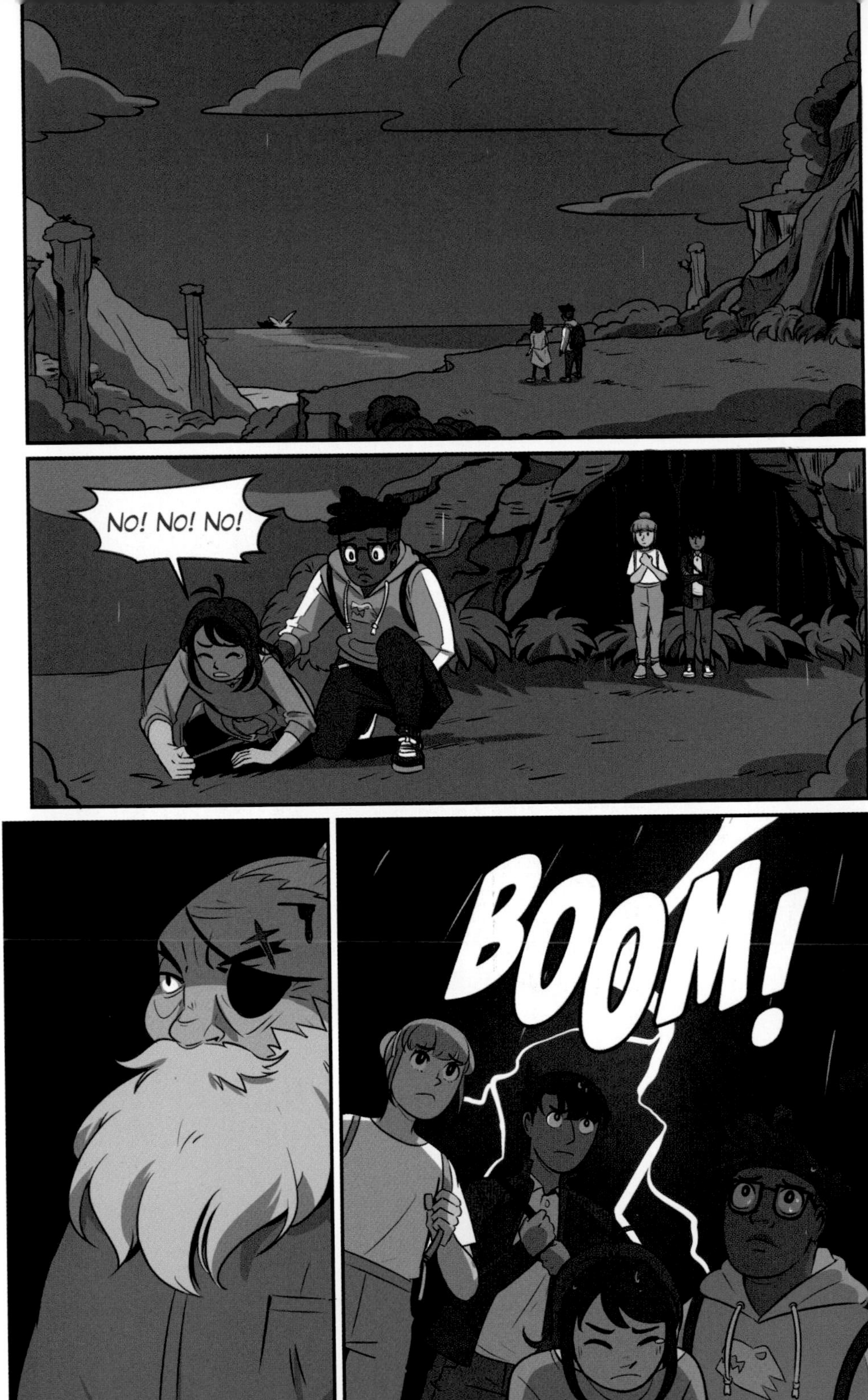

NO! NO! NO!
BOOM!

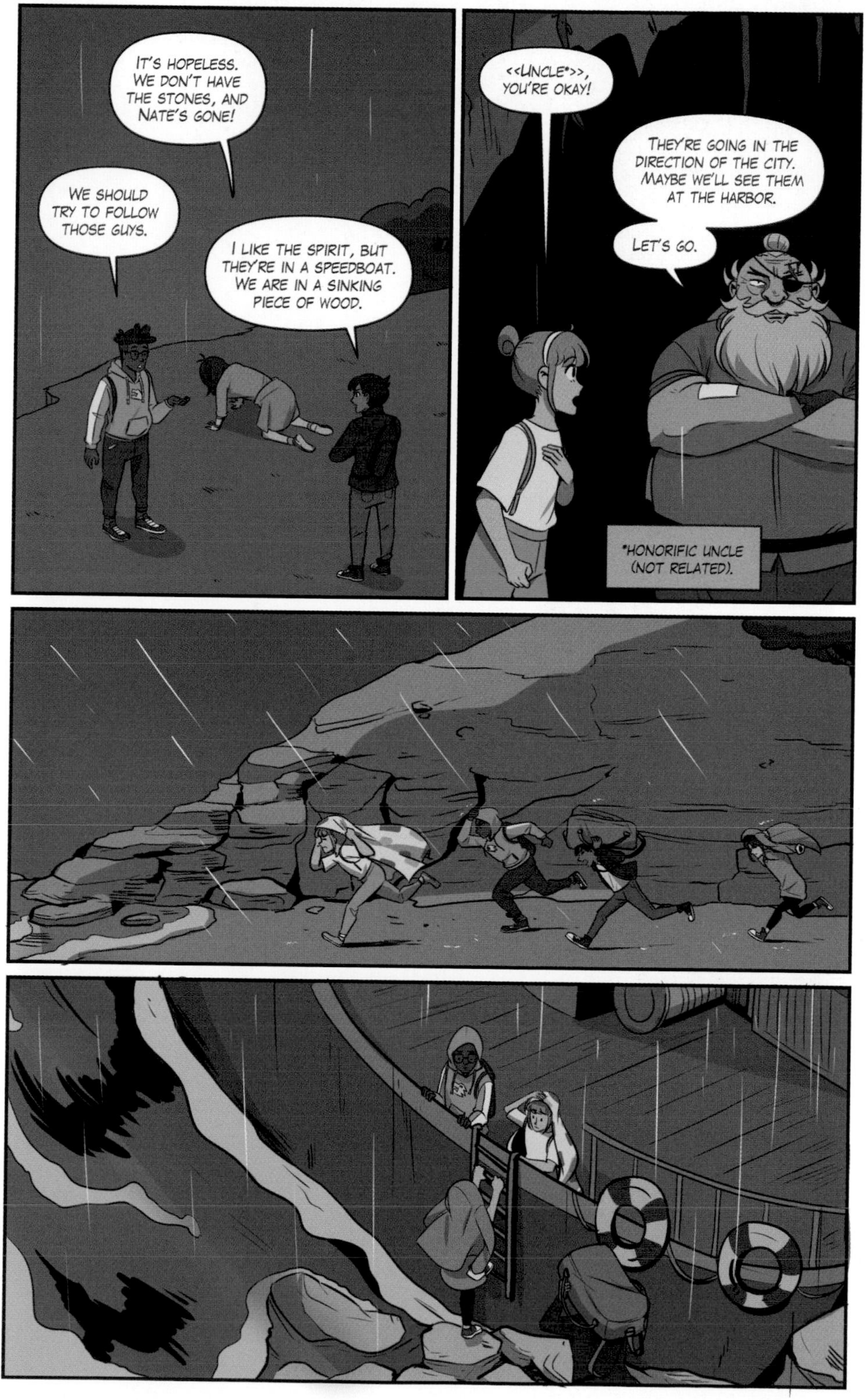
IT'S HOPELESS. WE DON'T HAVE THE STONES, AND NATE'S GONE!
WE SHOULD TRY TO FOLLOW THOSE GUYS.
I LIKE THE SPIRIT, BUT THEY'RE IN A SPEEDBOAT. WE ARE IN A SINKING PIECE OF WOOD.
<<UNCLE*>>, YOU'RE OKAY!
THEY'RE GOING IN THE DIRECTION OF THE CITY. MAYBE WE'LL SEE THEM AT THE HARBOR.
LET'S GO.
*HONORIFIC UNCLE (NOT RELATED).

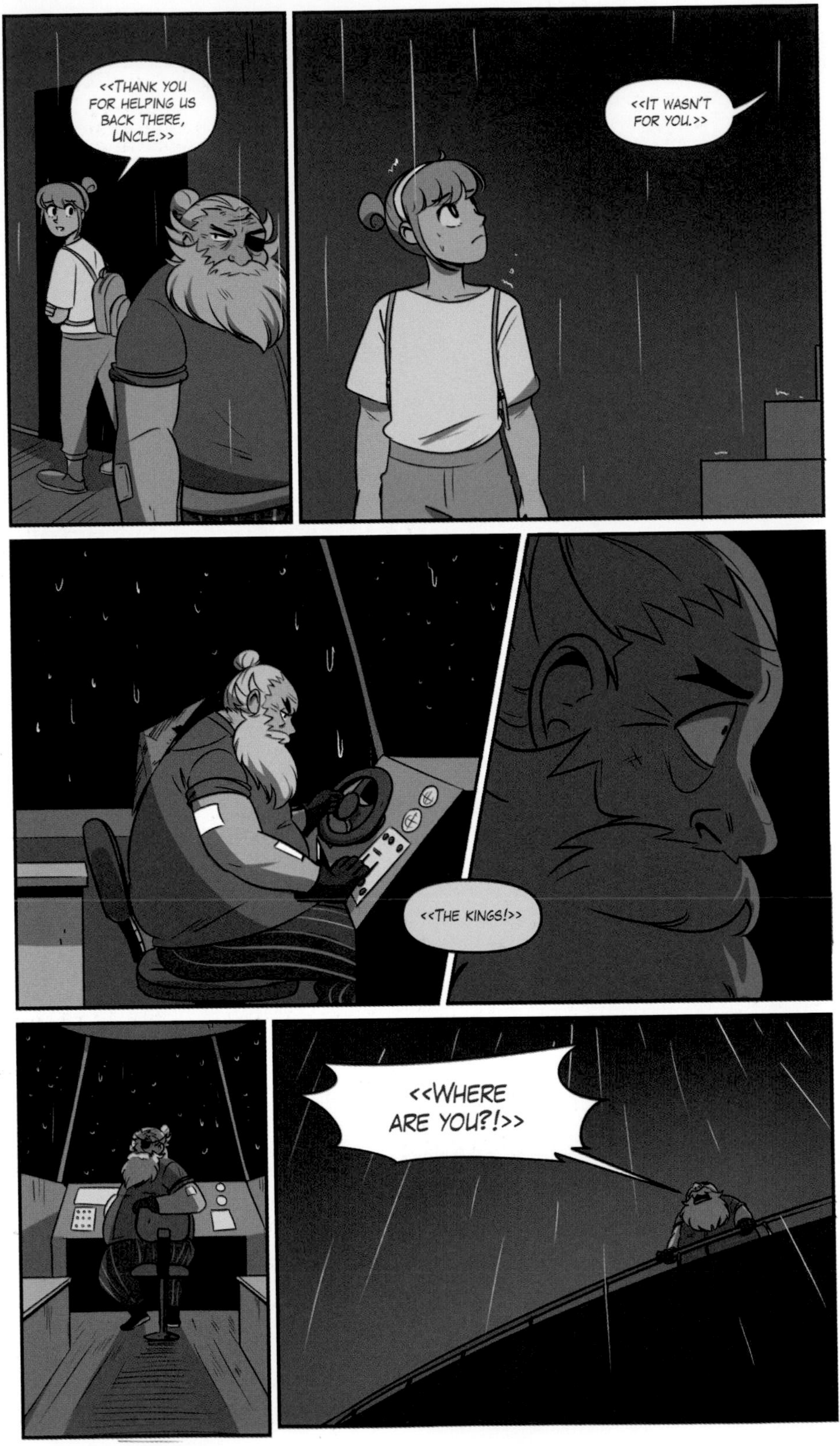
<<THANK YOU FOR HELPING US BACK THERE, UNCLE.>>
<<IT WASN'T FOR YOU.>>
<<THE KINGS!>>
<<WHERE ARE YOU?!>>

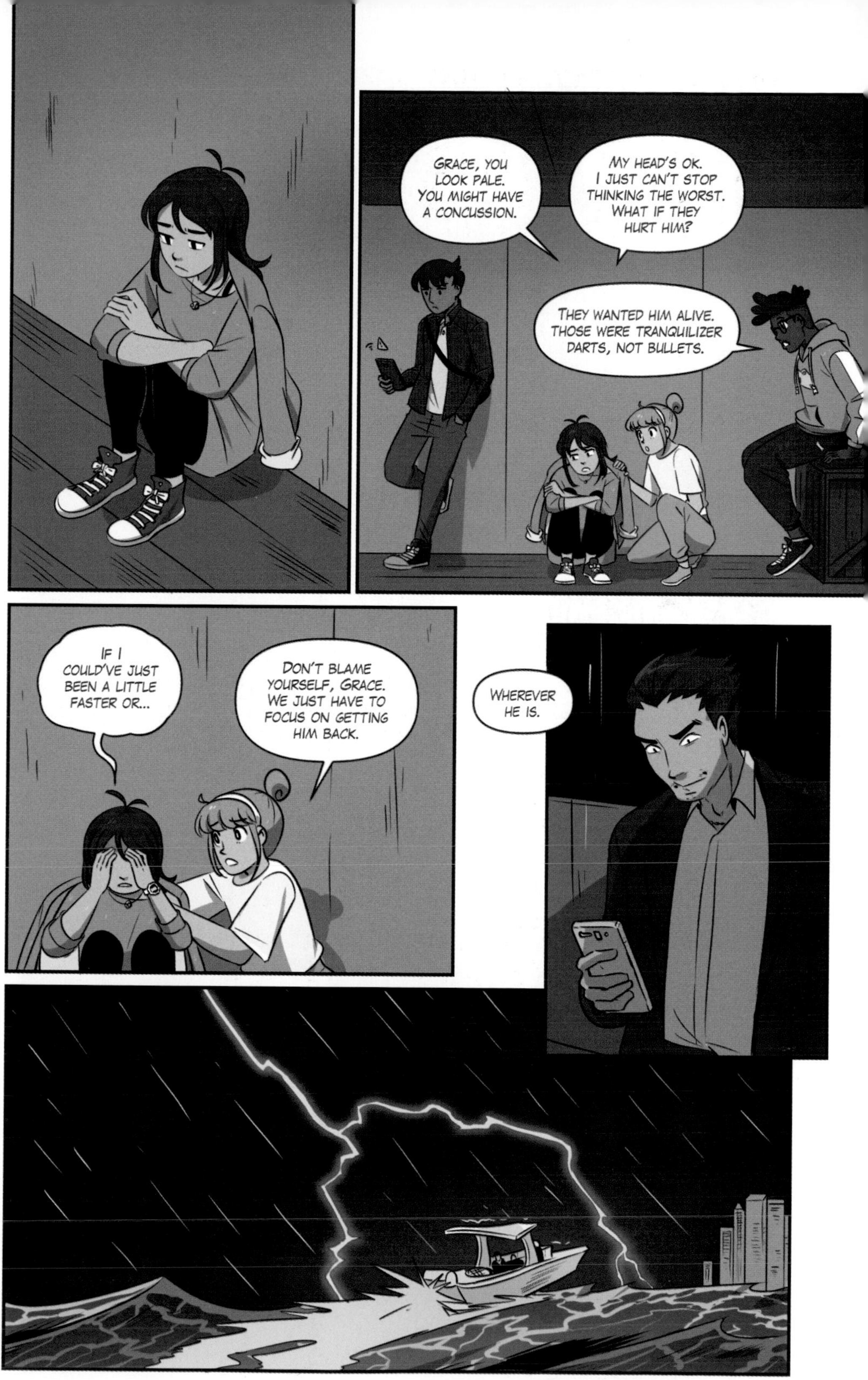
GRACE, YOU LOOK PALE. YOU MIGHT HAVE A CONCUSSION.
MY HEAD'S OK. I JUST CAN'T STOP THINKING THE WORST. WHAT IF THEY HURT HIM?
THEY WANTED HIM ALIVE. THOSE WERE TRANQUILIZER DARTS, NOT BULLETS.
IF I COULD'VE JUST BEEN A LITTLE FASTER OR...
DON'T BLAME YOURSELF, GRACE. WE JUST HAVE TO FOCUS ON GETTING HIM BACK.
WHEREVER HE IS.

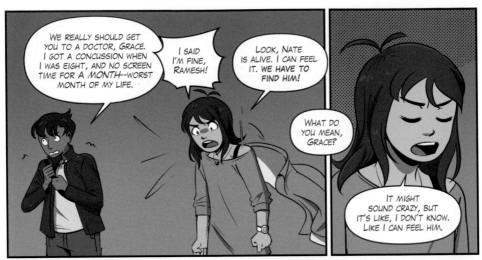

WE REALLY SHOULD GET YOU TO A DOCTOR, GRACE. I GOT A CONCUSSION WHEN I WAS EIGHT, AND NO SCREEN TIME FOR A *MONTH*--WORST MONTH OF MY LIFE.

I SAID I'M FINE, RAMESH!

LOOK, NATE IS ALIVE. I CAN FEEL IT. WE HAVE TO FIND HIM!

WHAT DO YOU MEAN, GRACE?

IT MIGHT SOUND CRAZY, BUT IT'S LIKE, I DON'T KNOW. LIKE I CAN FEEL HIM.

I'VE READ ABOUT *HÙNXUÈ* COMMUNICATING TELEPATHICALLY WITH DRAGONS.

DO YOU THINK THAT'S WHAT YOU'RE FEELING RIGHT NOW?

WHILE YOU GUYS MULL OVER THAT...

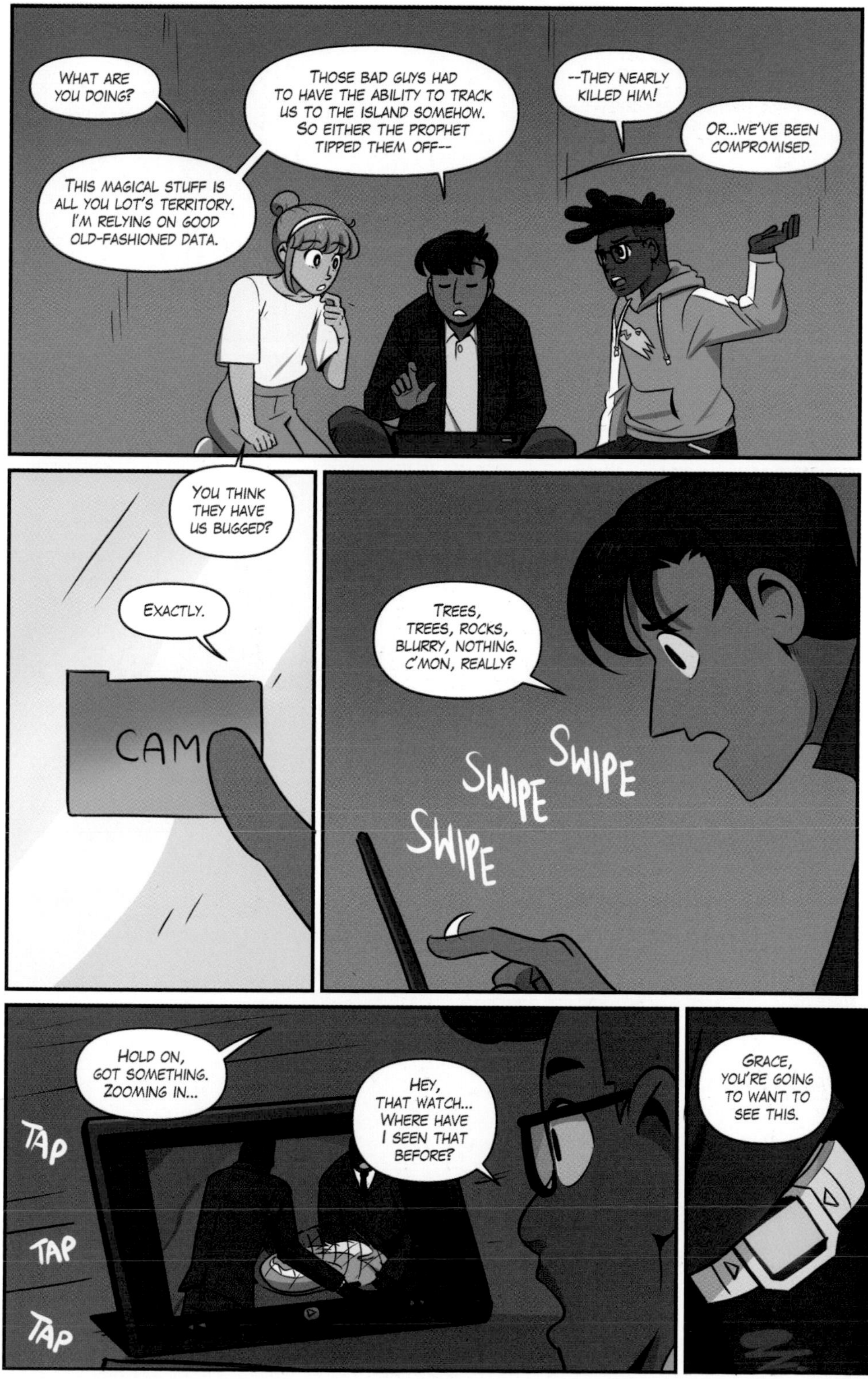
WHAT ARE YOU DOING?
THIS MAGICAL STUFF IS ALL YOU LOT'S TERRITORY. I'M RELYING ON GOOD OLD-FASHIONED DATA.
THOSE BAD GUYS HAD TO HAVE THE ABILITY TO TRACK US TO THE ISLAND SOMEHOW. SO EITHER THE PROPHET TIPPED THEM OFF--
--THEY NEARLY KILLED HIM!
OR...WE'VE BEEN COMPROMISED.
YOU THINK THEY HAVE US BUGGED?
EXACTLY.
CAM
TREES, TREES, ROCKS, BLURRY, NOTHING. C'MON, REALLY?
SWIPE
SWIPE
SWIPE
HOLD ON, GOT SOMETHING. ZOOMING IN...
TAP
TAP
TAP
HEY, THAT WATCH... WHERE HAVE I SEEN THAT BEFORE?
GRACE, YOU'RE GOING TO WANT TO SEE THIS.

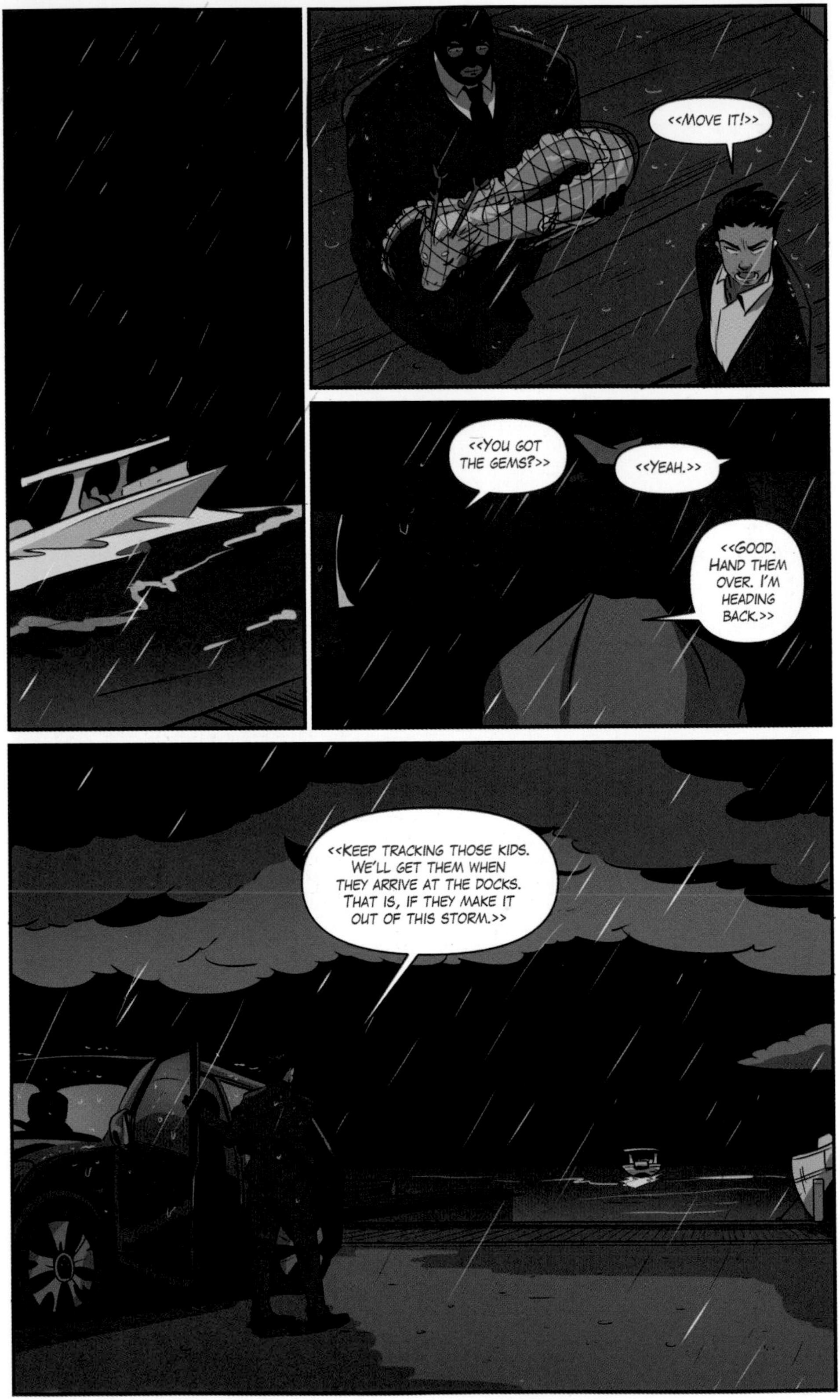
<<MOVE IT!>>
<<YOU GOT THE GEMS?>>
<<YEAH.>>
<<GOOD. HAND THEM OVER. I'M HEADING BACK.>>
<<KEEP TRACKING THOSE KIDS. WE'LL GET THEM WHEN THEY ARRIVE AT THE DOCKS. THAT IS, IF THEY MAKE IT OUT OF THIS STORM.>>

THE ONLY OTHER PEOPLE I'VE SEEN WITH A WATCH LIKE THAT ARE DR. KIM AND YOUR STEPDAD.

DO YOU THINK SHE REALLY COULD BE BEHIND THIS? I MEAN, WHY DID SHE SHOW UP FOR DINNER THE VERY NIGHT WE BROUGHT NATE? AND THE MONGOLIA CONNECTION...

I DON'T KNOW! I CAN'T THINK STRAIGHT.

I KEEP GETTING FLASHES OF NATE.

FULL BARS! I COULD KISS THE 5G GODS.

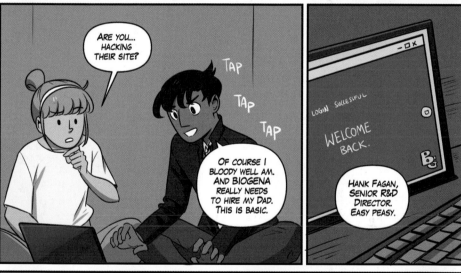

ARE YOU... HACKING THEIR SITE?

TAP
TAP
TAP

OF COURSE I BLOODY WELL AM. AND BIOGENA REALLY NEEDS TO HIRE MY DAD. THIS IS BASIC.

LOGIN SUCCESSFUL

WELCOME BACK.

B G

HANK FAGAN, SENIOR R&D DIRECTOR. EASY PEASY.

OK, CODING I CAN HANDLE. THESE MEDICAL STUDIES, NOT SO MUCH.

STEM CELLS, TELOMERES... IMPRESSIVE. ALL ANTI-AGING STUFF, NO SURPRISE.

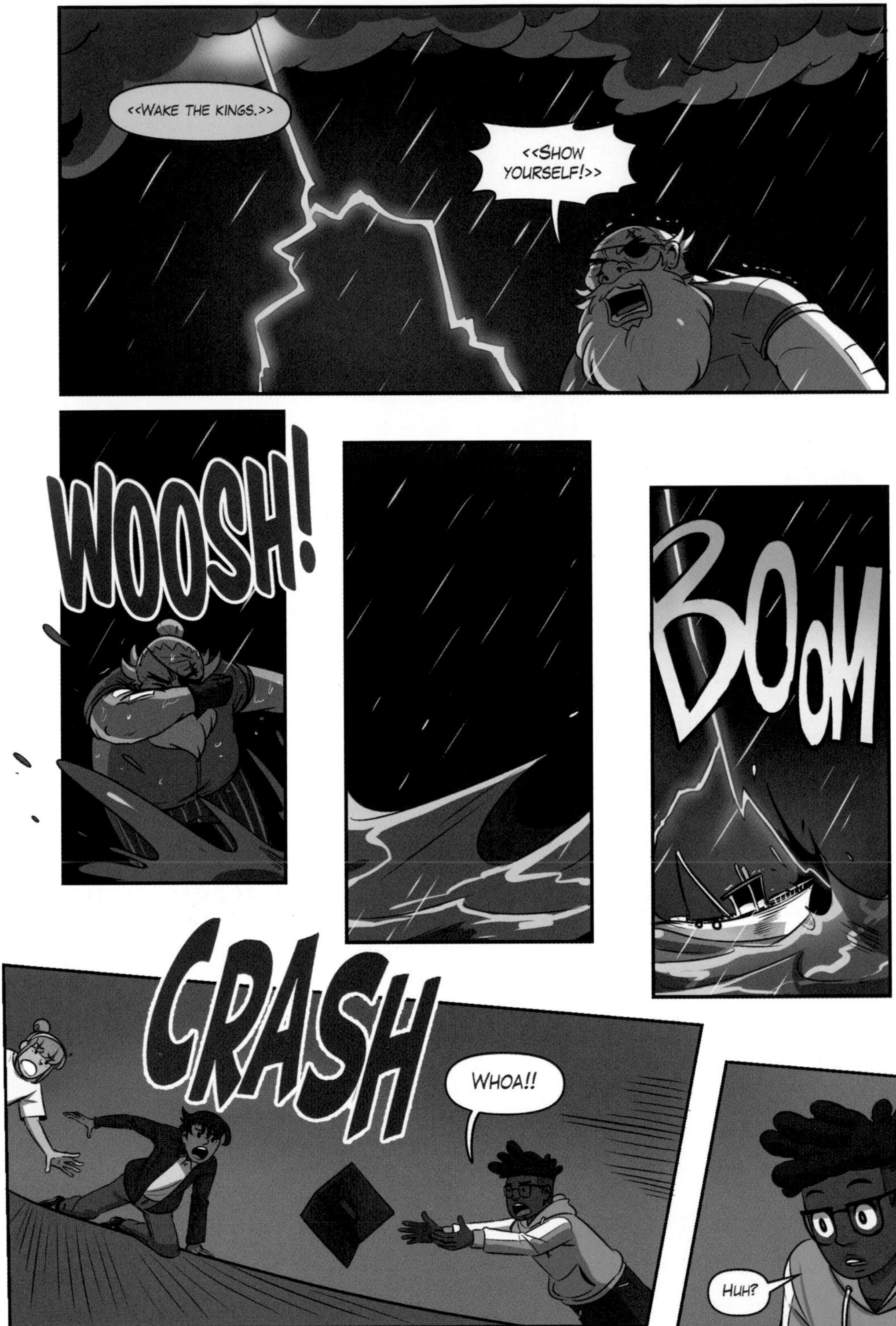
<<WAKE THE KINGS.>>
<<SHOW YOURSELF!>>
WOOSH!
BOOM
CRASH
WHOA!!
HUH?

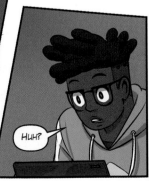

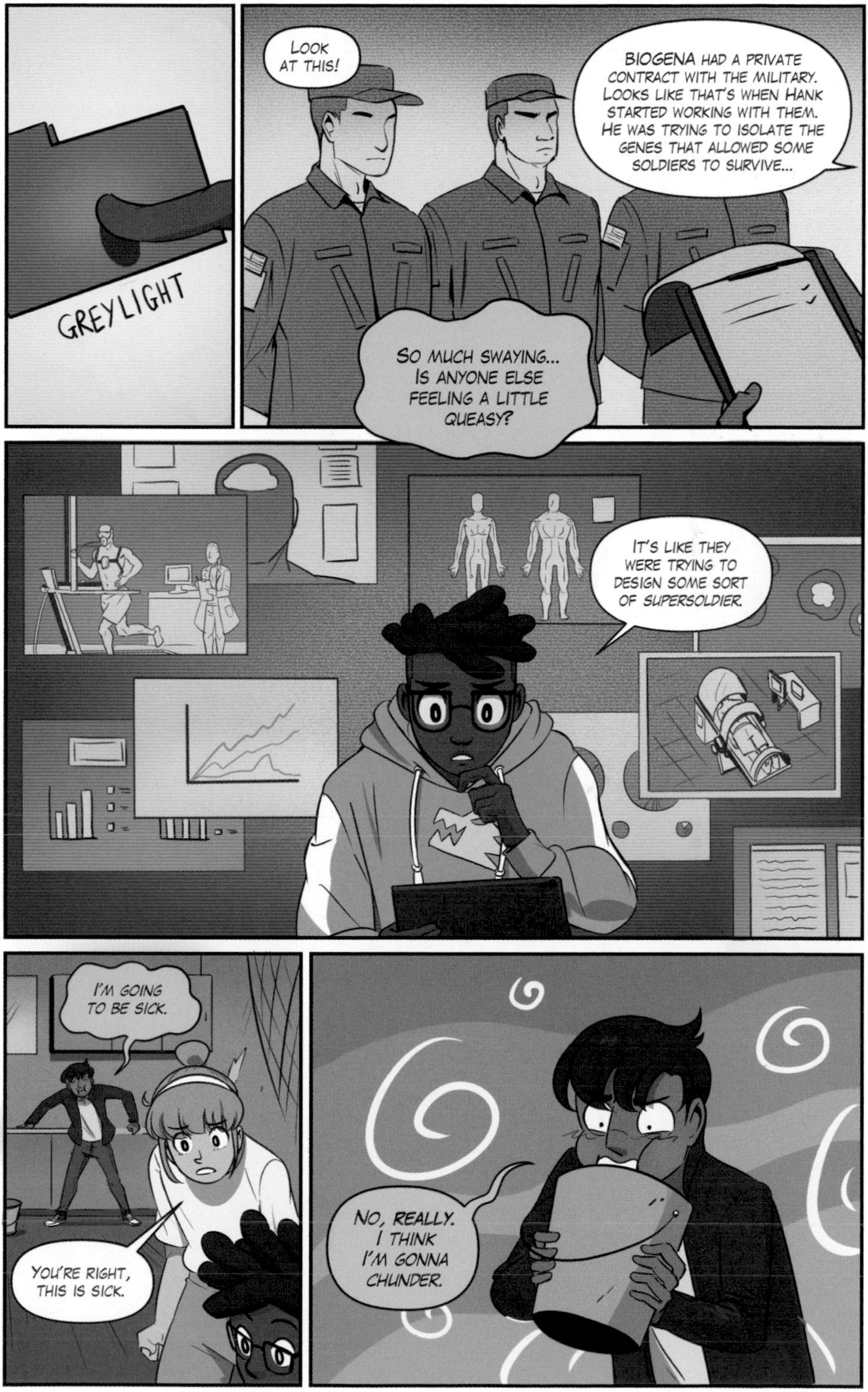
GREYLIGHT
LOOK AT THIS!
BIOGENA HAD A PRIVATE CONTRACT WITH THE MILITARY. LOOKS LIKE THAT'S WHEN HANK STARTED WORKING WITH THEM. HE WAS TRYING TO ISOLATE THE GENES THAT ALLOWED SOME SOLDIERS TO SURVIVE...
SO MUCH SWAYING... IS ANYONE ELSE FEELING A LITTLE QUEASY?
IT'S LIKE THEY WERE TRYING TO DESIGN SOME SORT OF SUPERSOLDIER.
I'M GOING TO BE SICK.
YOU'RE RIGHT, THIS IS SICK.
NO, REALLY. I THINK I'M GONNA CHUNDER.

THIS IS SO WEIRD AND CREEPY.

EMAIL ALL THE FILES TO US, JAMES. IF THE SITE DETECTS A SECURITY BREACH, THEY MIGHT SUDDENLY LOCK US OUT.

RIGHT... SENDING.

WAIT! JAMES, GO BACK!

IT CAN'T BE...

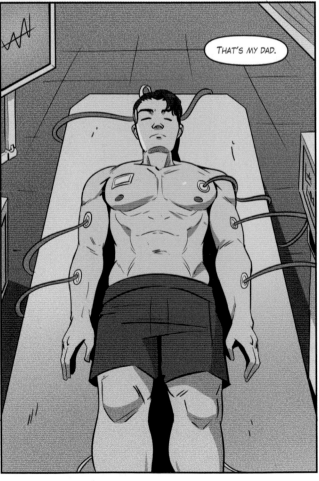

THAT'S MY DAD.

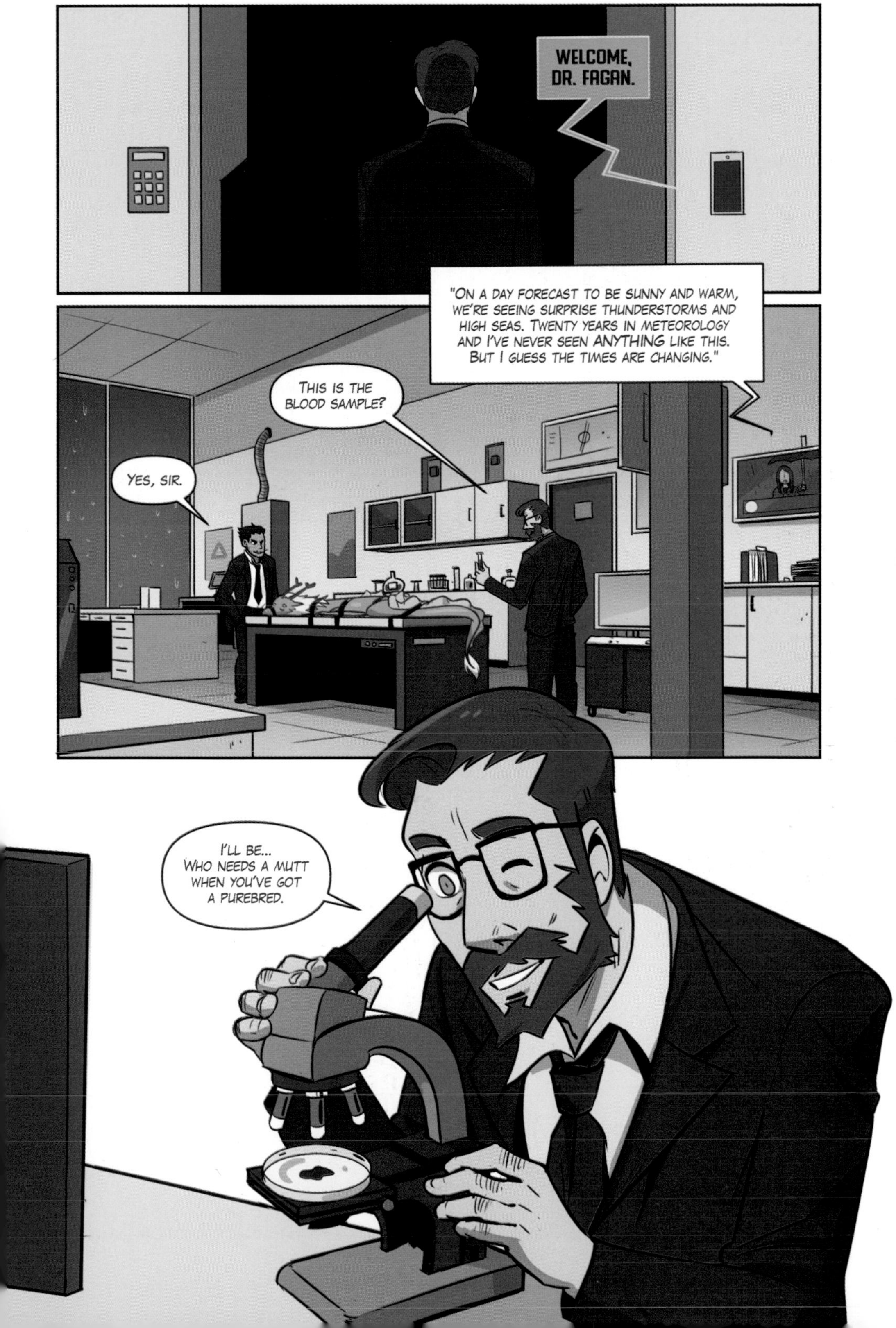
WELCOME, DR. FAGAN.
"ON A DAY FORECAST TO BE SUNNY AND WARM, WE'RE SEEING SURPRISE THUNDERSTORMS AND HIGH SEAS. TWENTY YEARS IN METEOROLOGY AND I'VE NEVER SEEN ANYTHING LIKE THIS. BUT I GUESS THE TIMES ARE CHANGING."
THIS IS THE BLOOD SAMPLE?
YES, SIR.
I'LL BE... WHO NEEDS A MUTT WHEN YOU'VE GOT A PUREBRED.

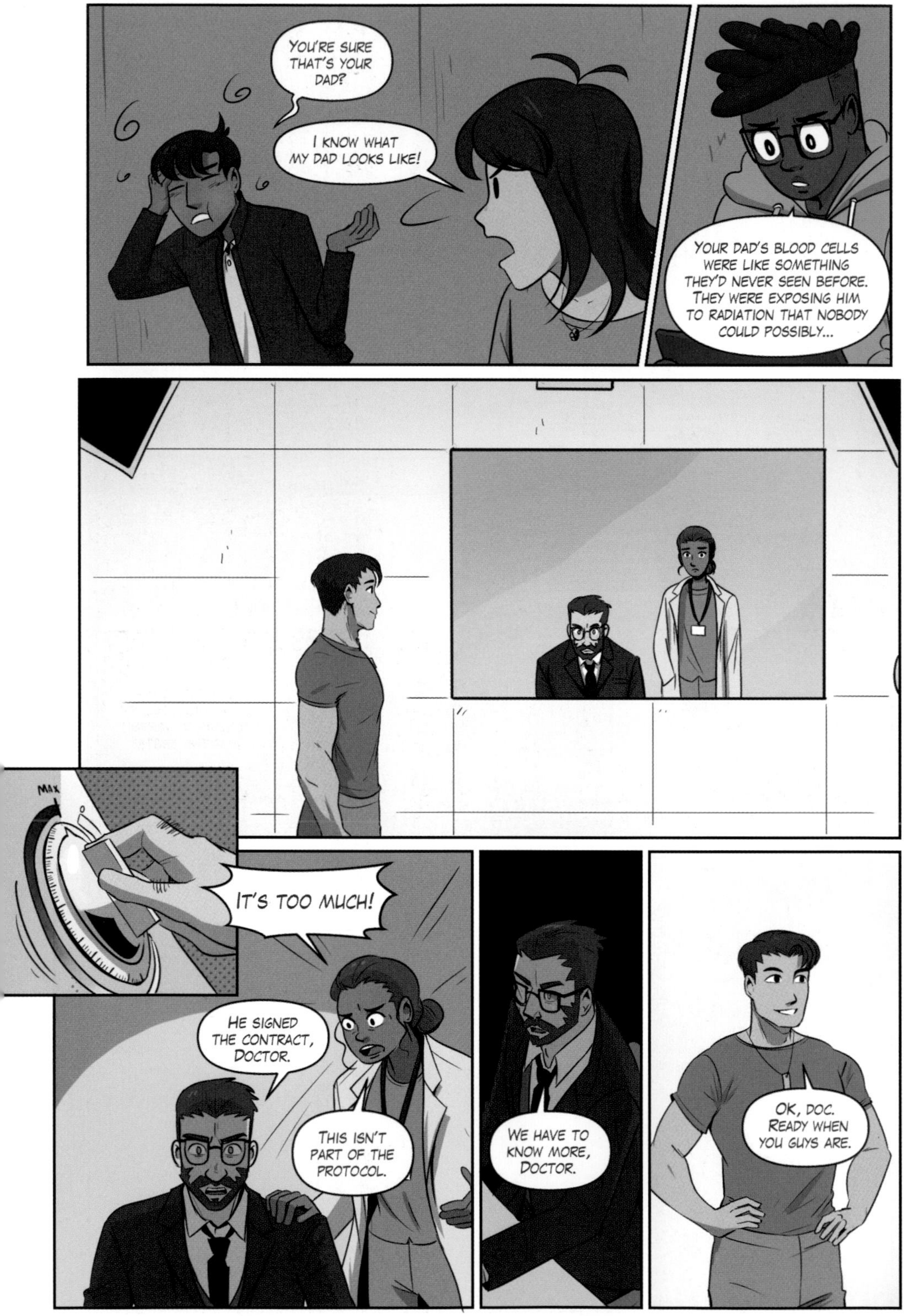

YOU'RE SURE THAT'S YOUR DAD?
I KNOW WHAT MY DAD LOOKS LIKE!
YOUR DAD'S BLOOD CELLS WERE LIKE SOMETHING THEY'D NEVER SEEN BEFORE. THEY WERE EXPOSING HIM TO RADIATION THAT NOBODY COULD POSSIBLY...
MAX
IT'S TOO MUCH!
HE SIGNED THE CONTRACT, DOCTOR.
THIS ISN'T PART OF THE PROTOCOL.
WE HAVE TO KNOW MORE, DOCTOR.
OK, DOC. READY WHEN YOU GUYS ARE.

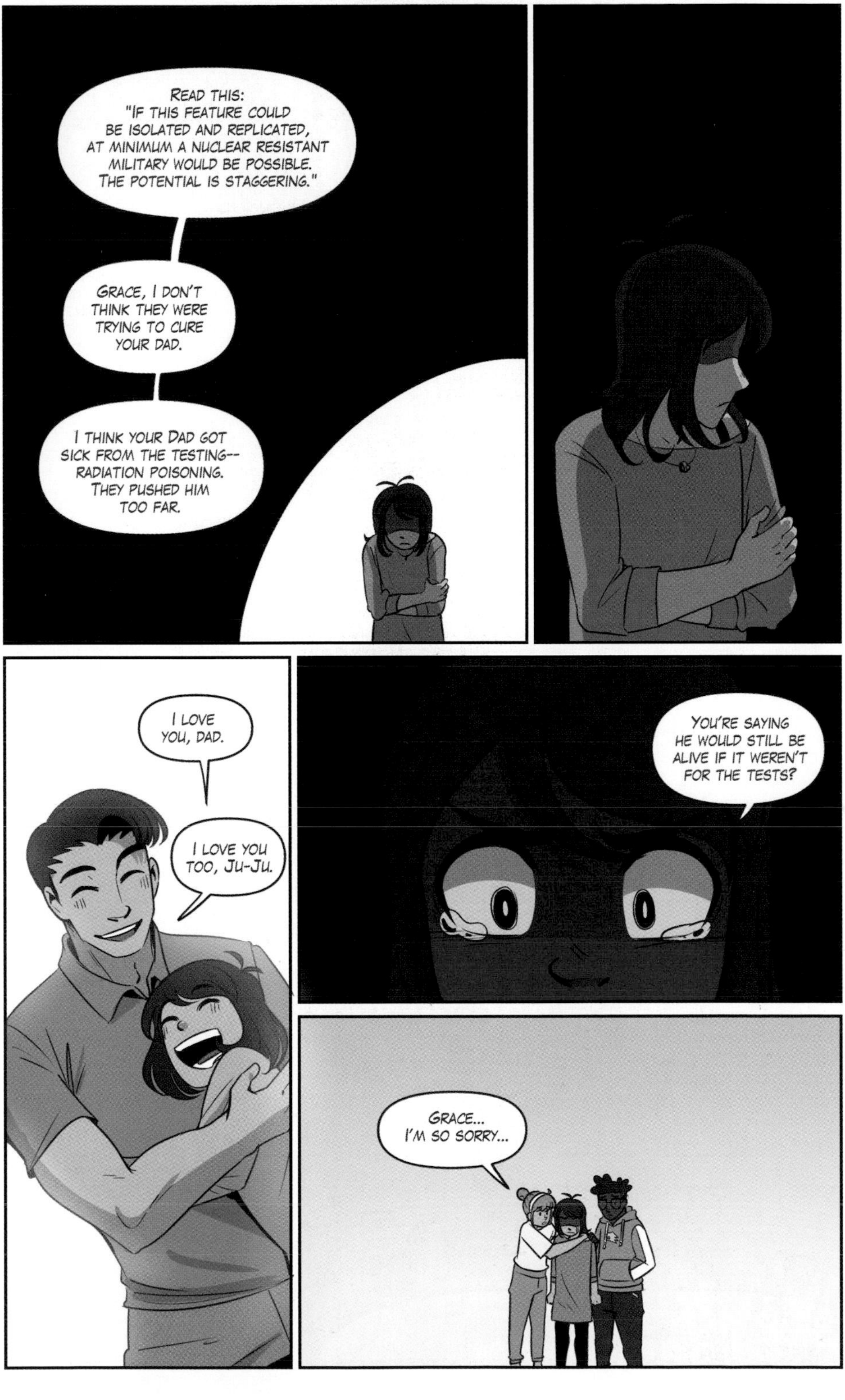
READ THIS: "IF THIS FEATURE COULD BE ISOLATED AND REPLICATED, AT MINIMUM A NUCLEAR RESISTANT MILITARY WOULD BE POSSIBLE. THE POTENTIAL IS STAGGERING."
GRACE, I DON'T THINK THEY WERE TRYING TO CURE YOUR DAD.
I THINK YOUR DAD GOT SICK FROM THE TESTING--RADIATION POISONING. THEY PUSHED HIM TOO FAR.
I LOVE YOU, DAD.
I LOVE YOU TOO, JU-JU.
YOU'RE SAYING HE WOULD STILL BE ALIVE IF IT WEREN'T FOR THE TESTS?
GRACE... I'M SO SORRY...

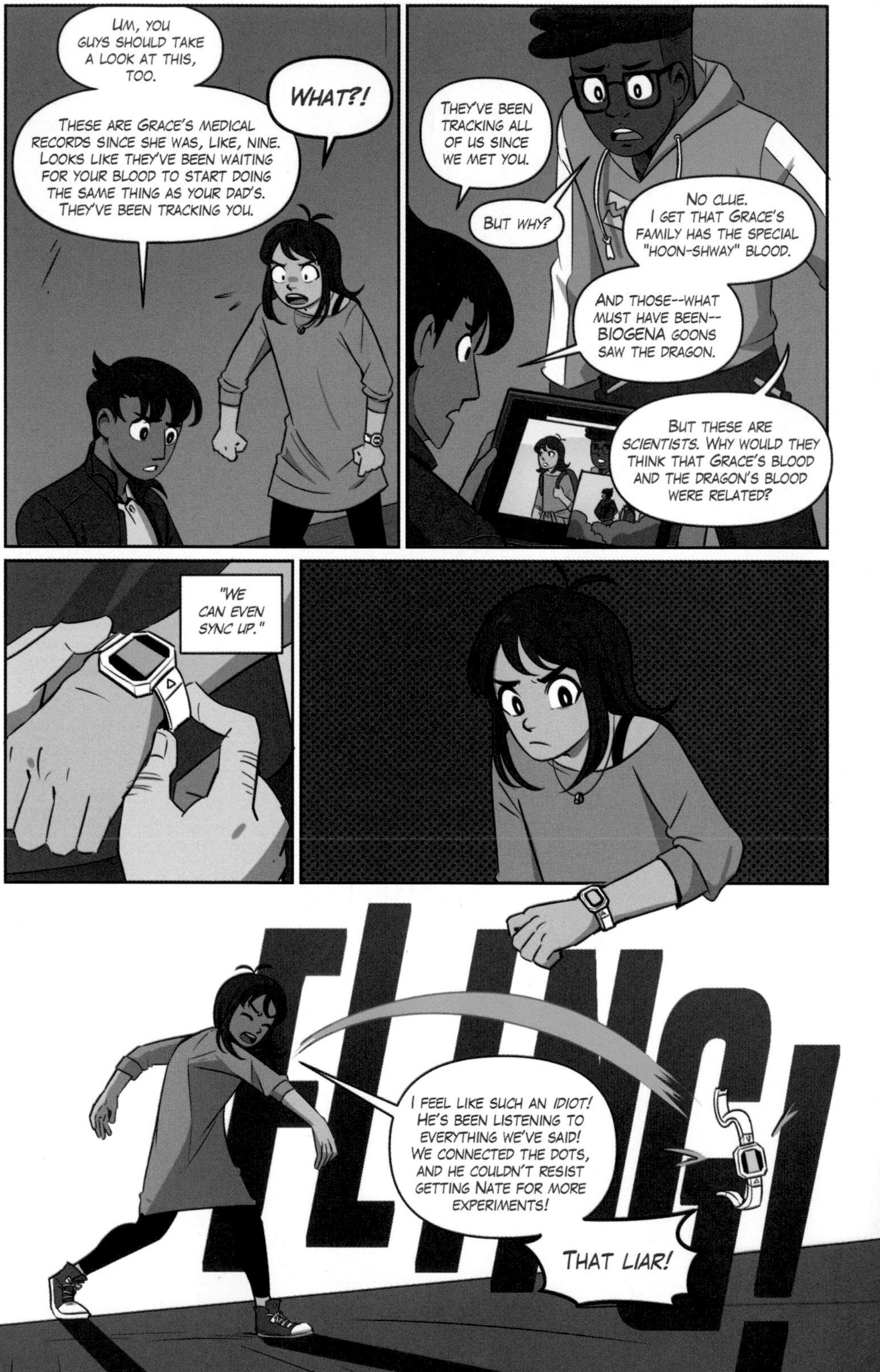
Um, you guys should take a look at this, too.
These are Grace's medical records since she was, like, nine. Looks like they've been waiting for your blood to start doing the same thing as your dad's. They've been tracking you.
What?!
They've been tracking all of us since we met you.
But why?
No clue. I get that Grace's family has the special "hoon-shway" blood.
And those--what must have been--BIOGENA goons saw the dragon.
But these are scientists. Why would they think that Grace's blood and the dragon's blood were related?
"We can even sync up."
FLING!
I feel like such an idiot! He's been listening to everything we've said! We connected the dots, and he couldn't resist getting Nate for more experiments!
That liar!

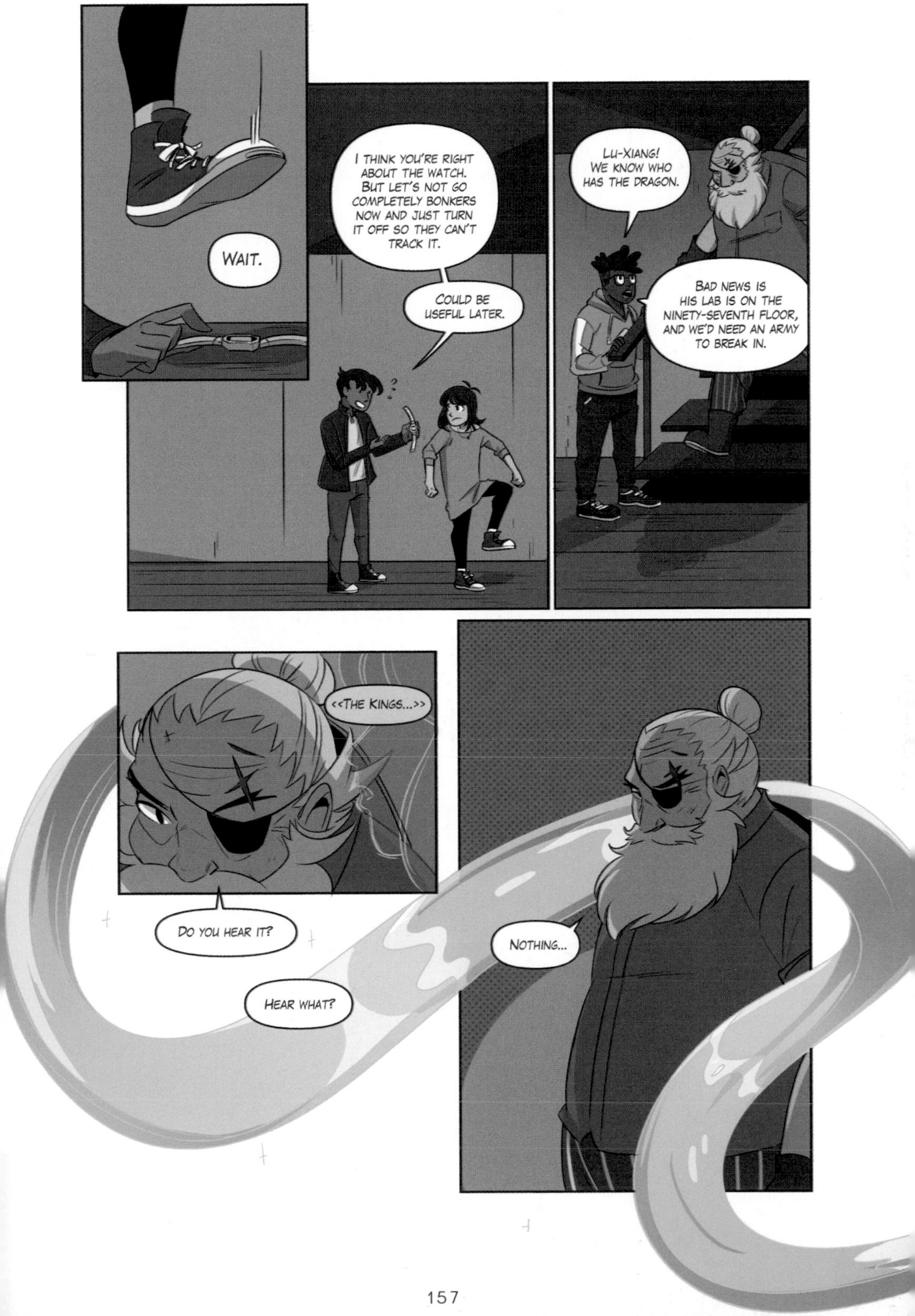
WAIT.
I THINK YOU'RE RIGHT ABOUT THE WATCH. BUT LET'S NOT GO COMPLETELY BONKERS NOW AND JUST TURN IT OFF SO THEY CAN'T TRACK IT.
COULD BE USEFUL LATER.
?
LU-XIANG! WE KNOW WHO HAS THE DRAGON.
BAD NEWS IS HIS LAB IS ON THE NINETY-SEVENTH FLOOR, AND WE'D NEED AN ARMY TO BREAK IN.
<<THE KINGS...>>
DO YOU HEAR IT?
HEAR WHAT?
NOTHING...

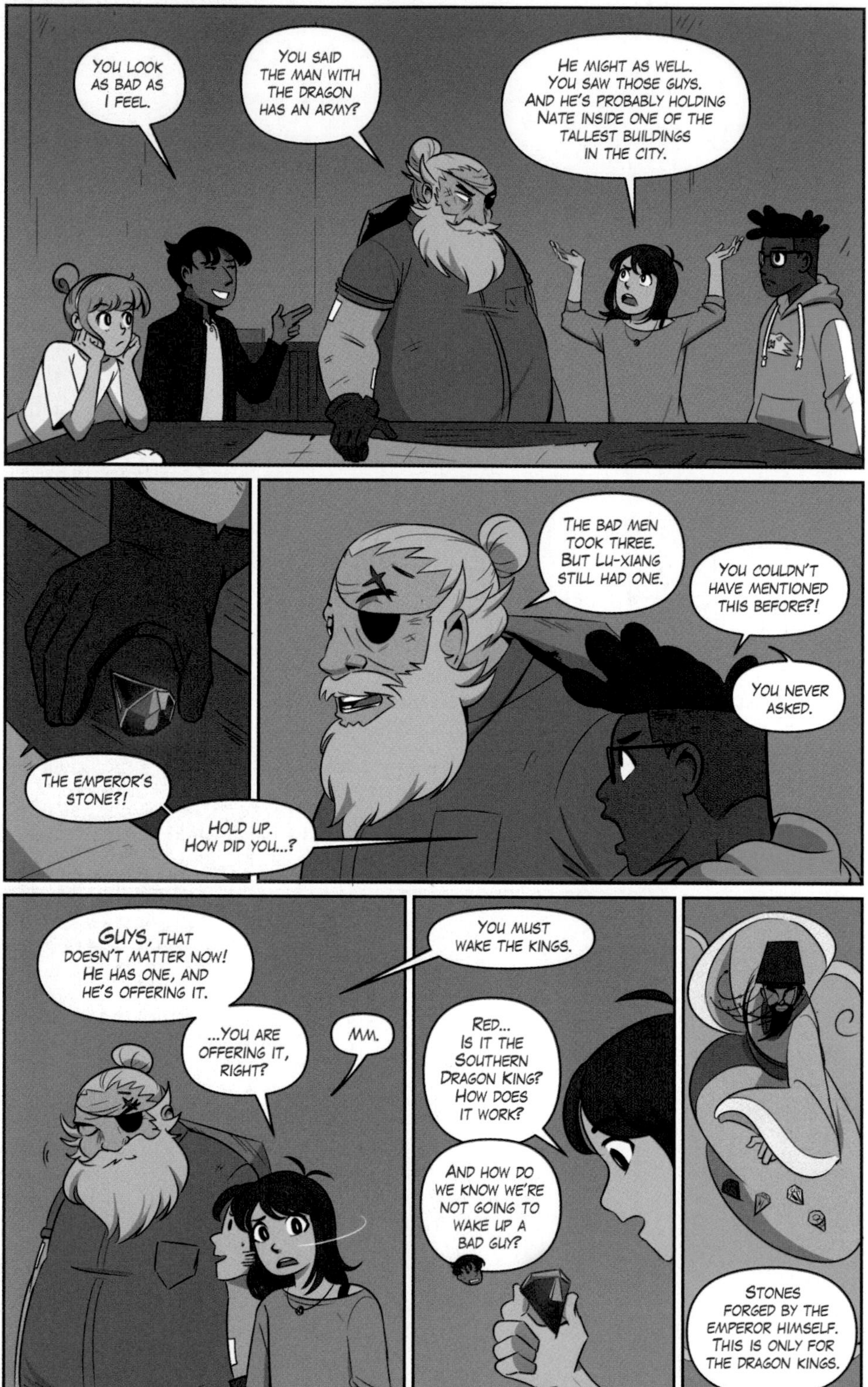
YOU LOOK AS BAD AS I FEEL.
YOU SAID THE MAN WITH THE DRAGON HAS AN ARMY?
HE MIGHT AS WELL. YOU SAW THOSE GUYS. AND HE'S PROBABLY HOLDING NATE INSIDE ONE OF THE TALLEST BUILDINGS IN THE CITY.
THE EMPEROR'S STONE?!
HOLD UP. HOW DID YOU...?
THE BAD MEN TOOK THREE. BUT LU-XIANG STILL HAD ONE.
YOU COULDN'T HAVE MENTIONED THIS BEFORE?!
YOU NEVER ASKED.
GUYS, THAT DOESN'T MATTER NOW! HE HAS ONE, AND HE'S OFFERING IT.
...YOU ARE OFFERING IT, RIGHT?
MM.
YOU MUST WAKE THE KINGS.
RED... IS IT THE SOUTHERN DRAGON KING? HOW DOES IT WORK?
AND HOW DO WE KNOW WE'RE NOT GOING TO WAKE UP A BAD GUY?
STONES FORGED BY THE EMPEROR HIMSELF. THIS IS ONLY FOR THE DRAGON KINGS.

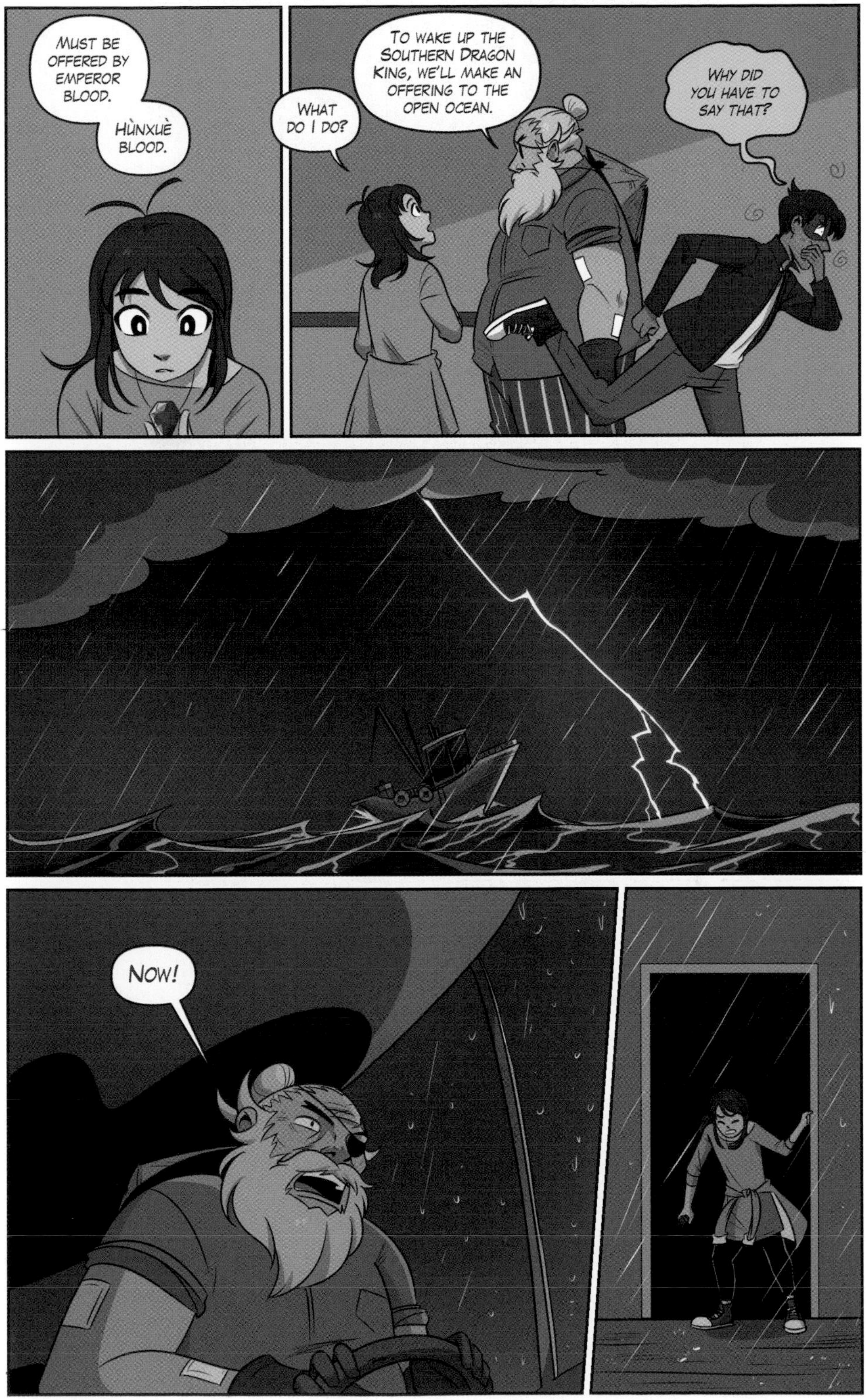
MUST BE OFFERED BY EMPEROR BLOOD.
HÙNXUÈ BLOOD.
WHAT DO I DO?
TO WAKE UP THE SOUTHERN DRAGON KING, WE'LL MAKE AN OFFERING TO THE OPEN OCEAN.
WHY DID YOU HAVE TO SAY THAT?
NOW!

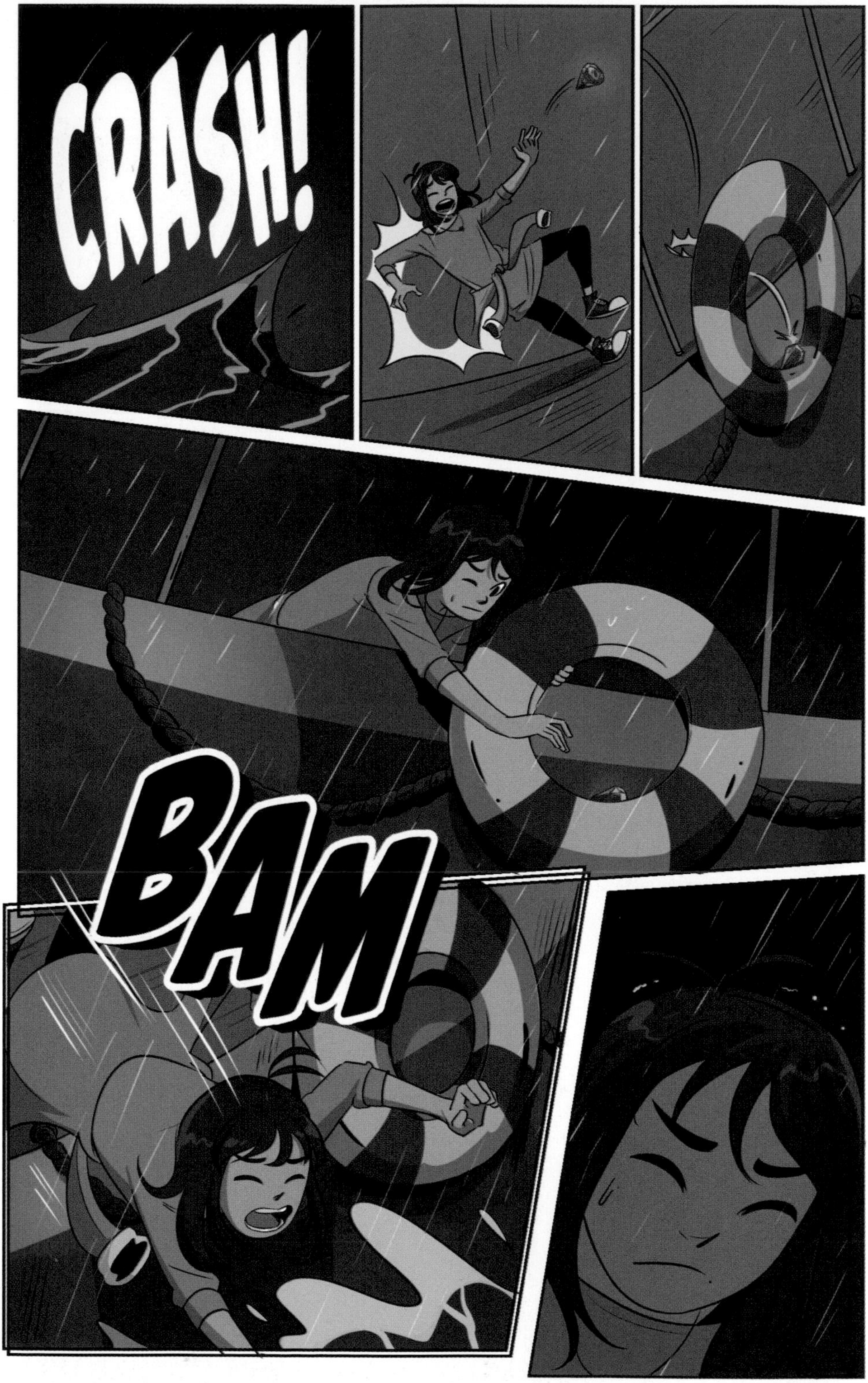
CRASH!
BAM

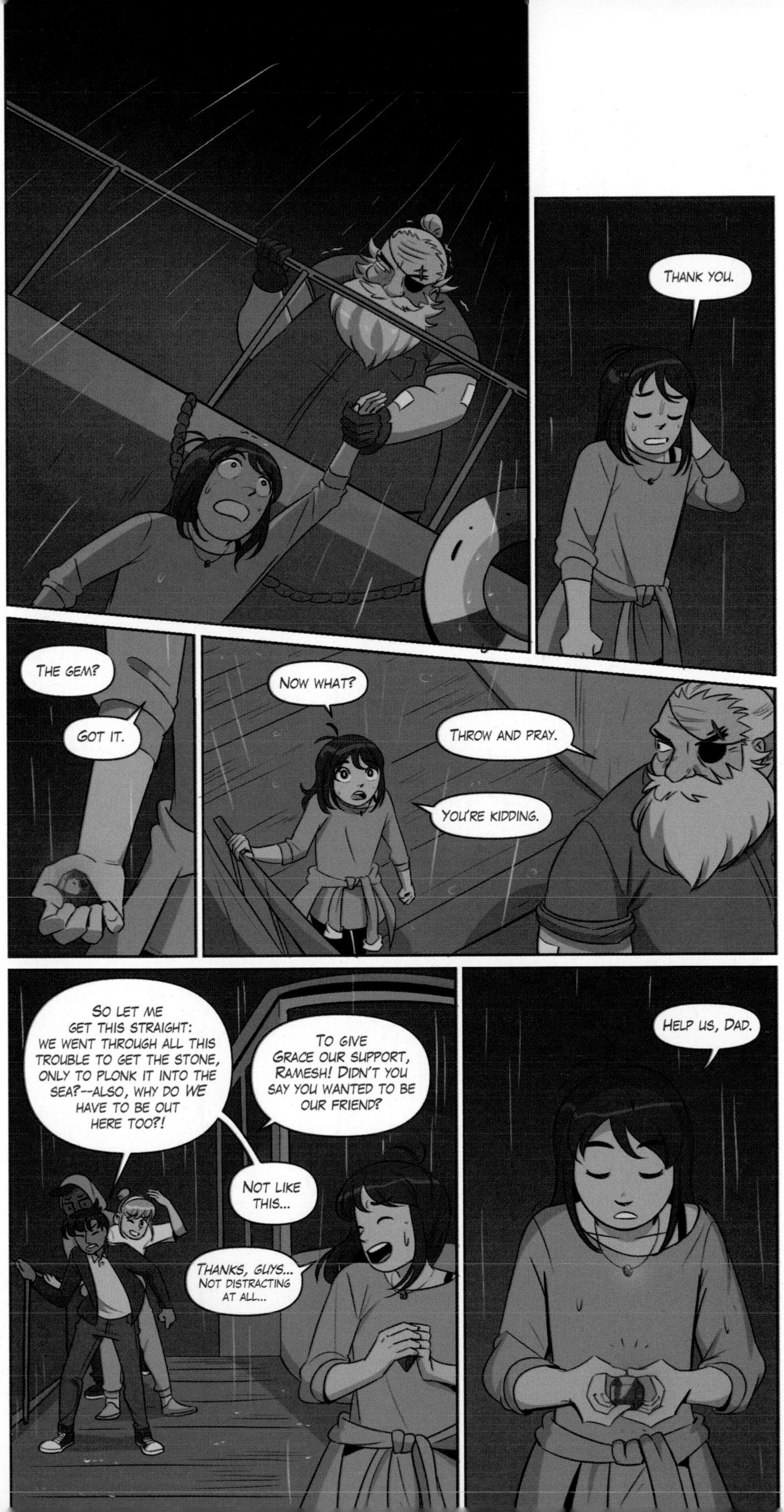
THANK YOU.
THE GEM?
GOT IT.
NOW WHAT?
THROW AND PRAY.
YOU'RE KIDDING.
SO LET ME GET THIS STRAIGHT: WE WENT THROUGH ALL THIS TROUBLE TO GET THE STONE, ONLY TO PLONK IT INTO THE SEA?--ALSO, WHY DO WE HAVE TO BE OUT HERE TOO?!
TO GIVE GRACE OUR SUPPORT, RAMESH! DIDN'T YOU SAY YOU WANTED TO BE OUR FRIEND?
NOT LIKE THIS...
THANKS, GUYS... NOT DISTRACTING AT ALL...
HELP US, DAD.

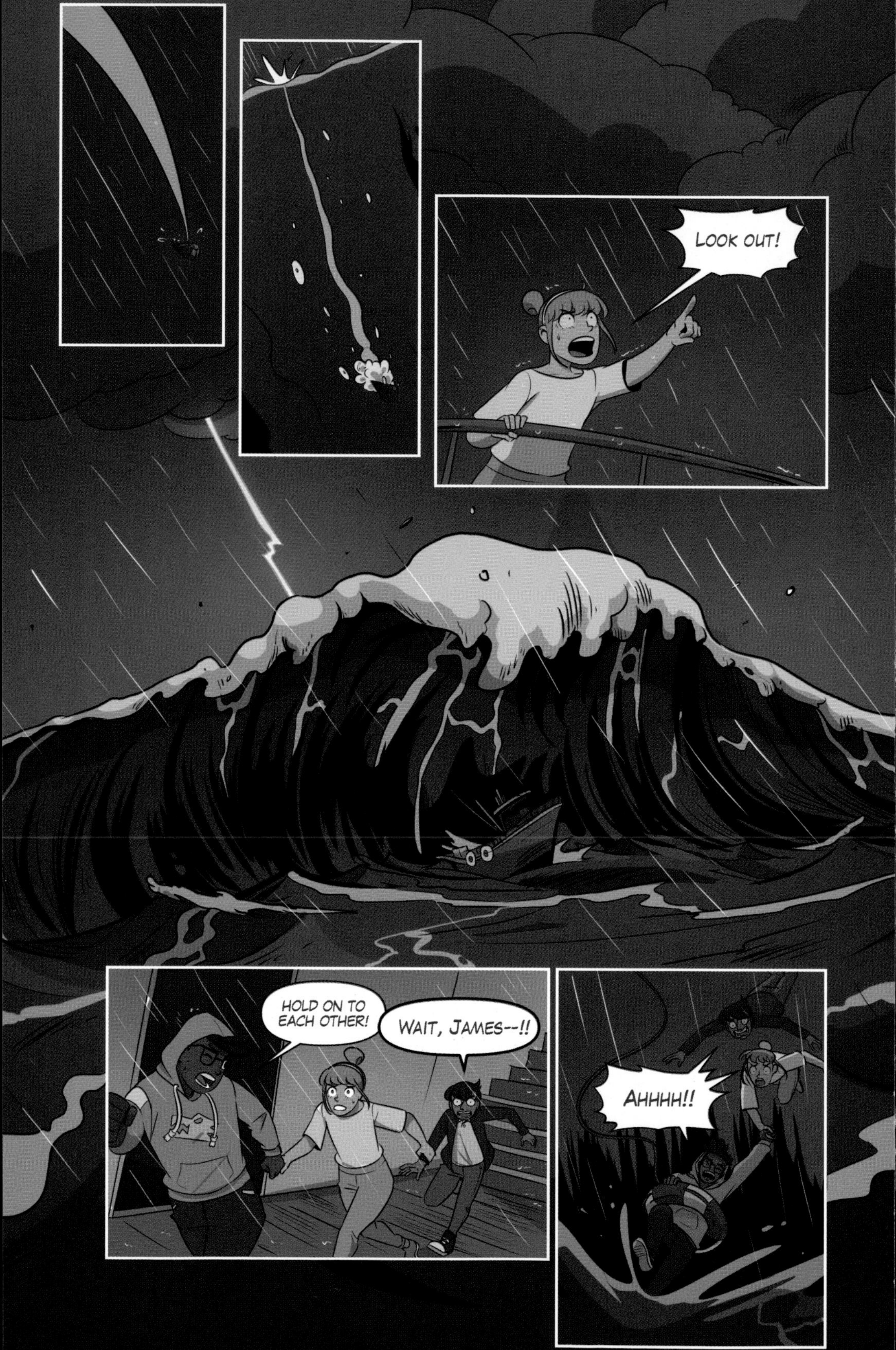
LOOK OUT!
HOLD ON TO EACH OTHER!
WAIT, JAMES--!!
AHHHH!!

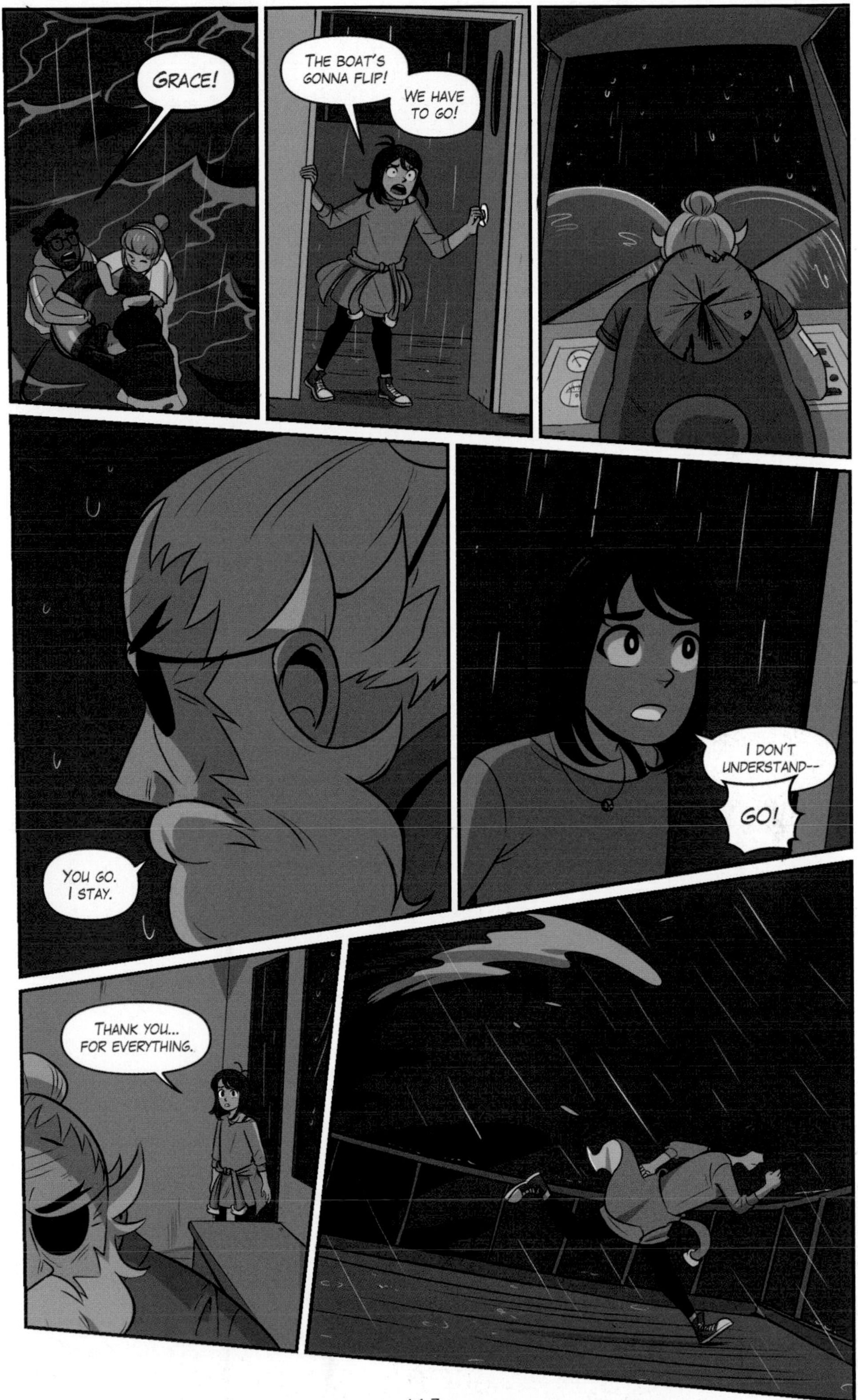
GRACE!
THE BOAT'S GONNA FLIP!
WE HAVE TO GO!
YOU GO. I STAY.
I DON'T UNDERSTAND--
GO!
THANK YOU... FOR EVERYTHING.

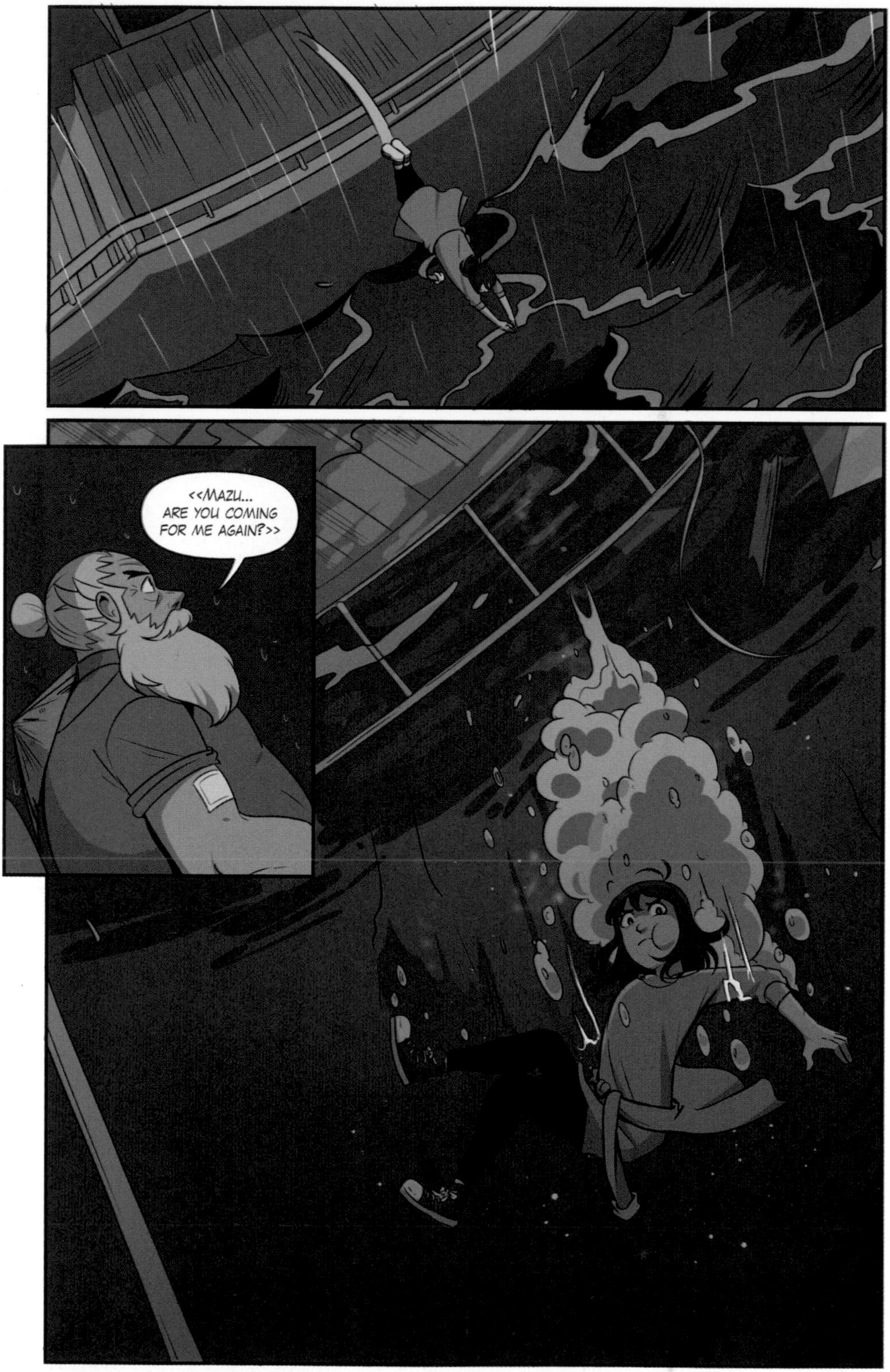

<<MAZU... ARE YOU COMING FOR ME AGAIN?>>

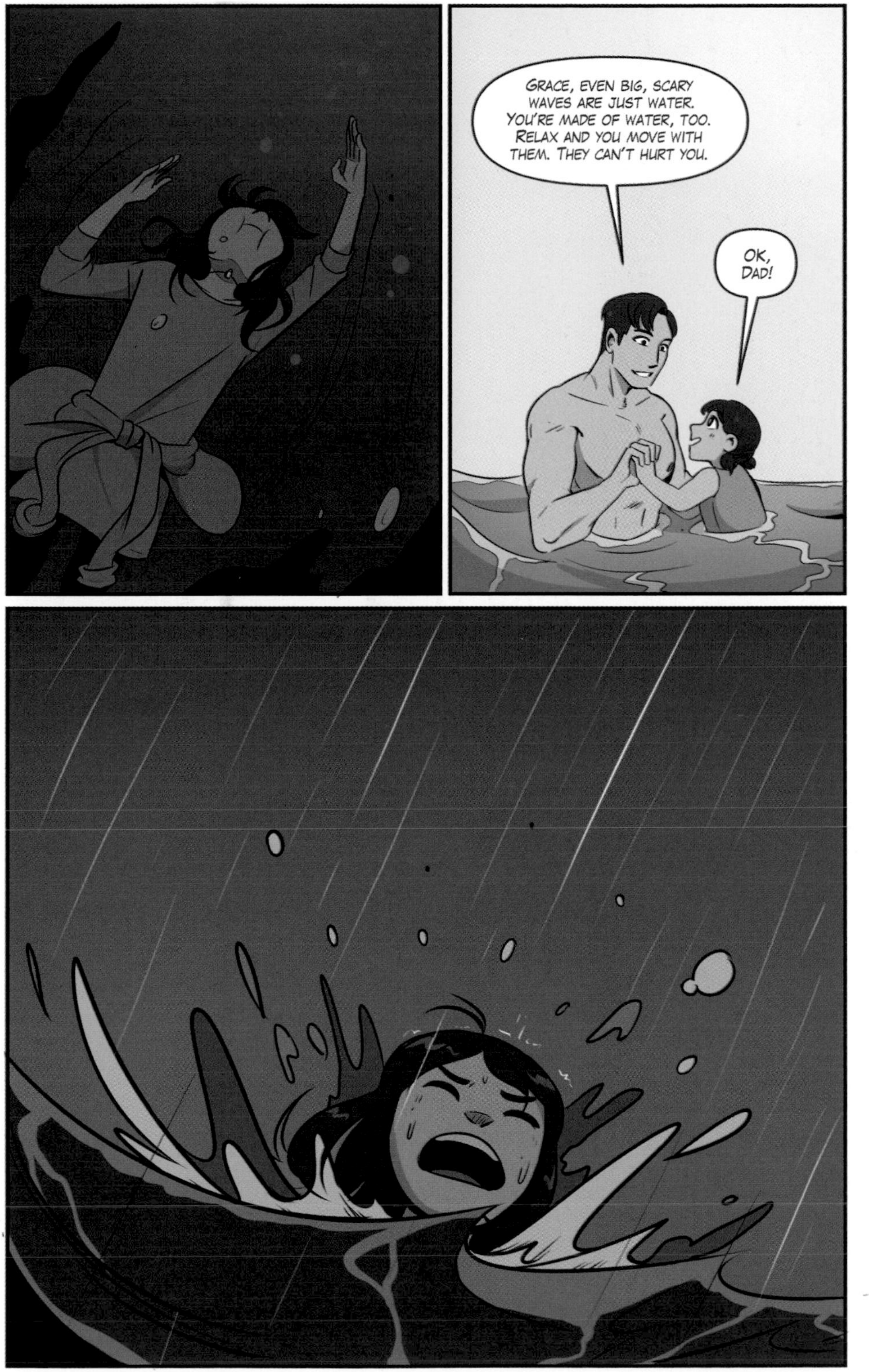
GRACE, EVEN BIG, SCARY WAVES ARE JUST WATER. YOU'RE MADE OF WATER, TOO. RELAX AND YOU MOVE WITH THEM. THEY CAN'T HURT YOU.
OK, DAD!

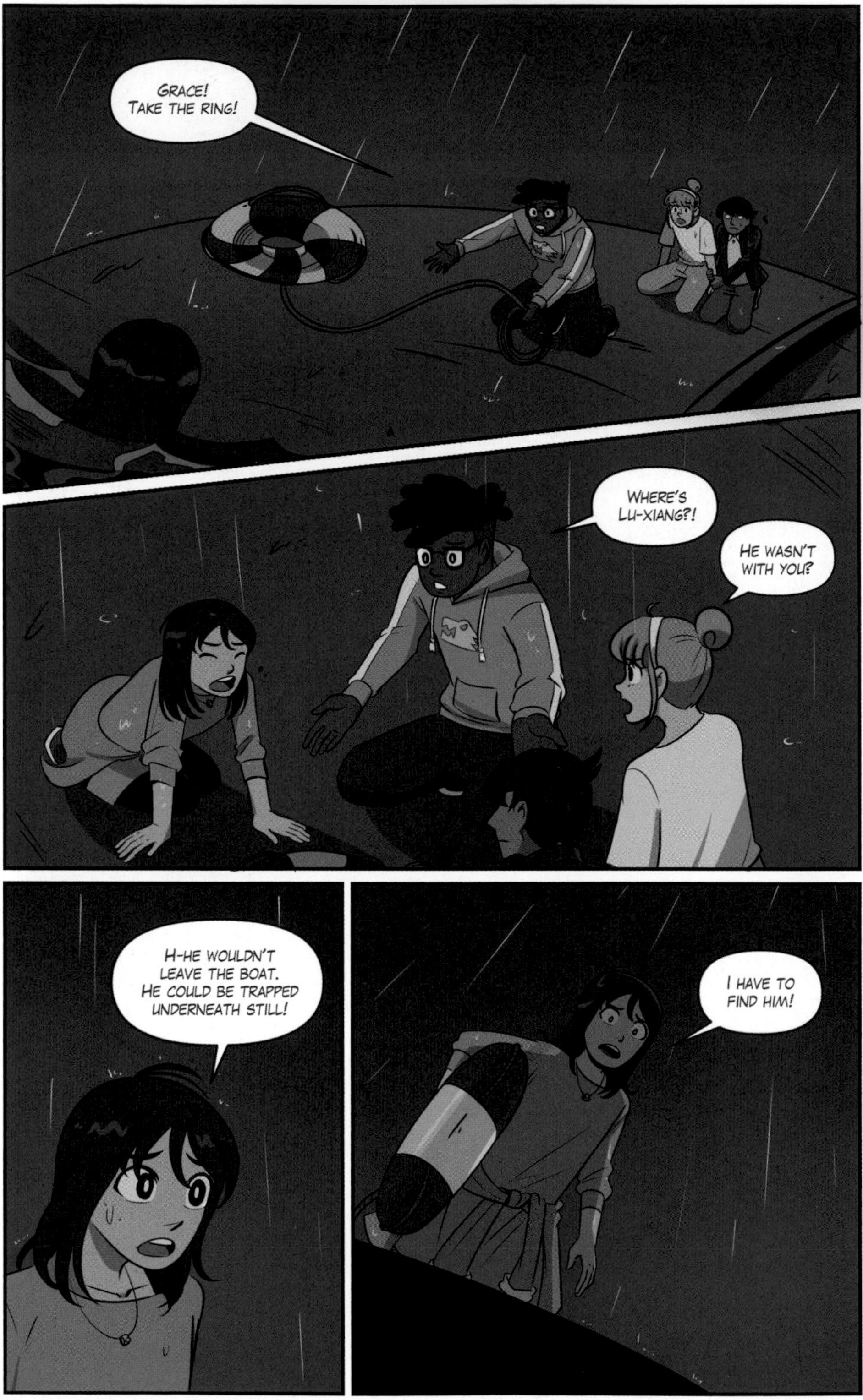
GRACE! TAKE THE RING!
WHERE'S LU-XIANG?!
HE WASN'T WITH YOU?
H-HE WOULDN'T LEAVE THE BOAT. HE COULD BE TRAPPED UNDERNEATH STILL!
I HAVE TO FIND HIM!

GRACE, WAIT!

THE BOAT SUCTION COULD PULL YOU DOWN!

GRACE! THANK GOD!

SO? DID YOU SEE HIM?

NO, I LOOKED EVERYWHERE. HE'S NOT IN THERE.

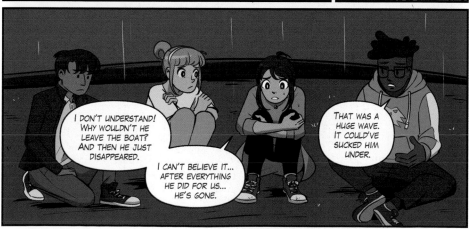

I DON'T UNDERSTAND! WHY WOULDN'T HE LEAVE THE BOAT? AND THEN HE JUST DISAPPEARED.

I CAN'T BELIEVE IT... AFTER EVERYTHING HE DID FOR US... HE'S GONE.

THAT WAS A HUGE WAVE. IT COULD'VE SUCKED HIM UNDER.

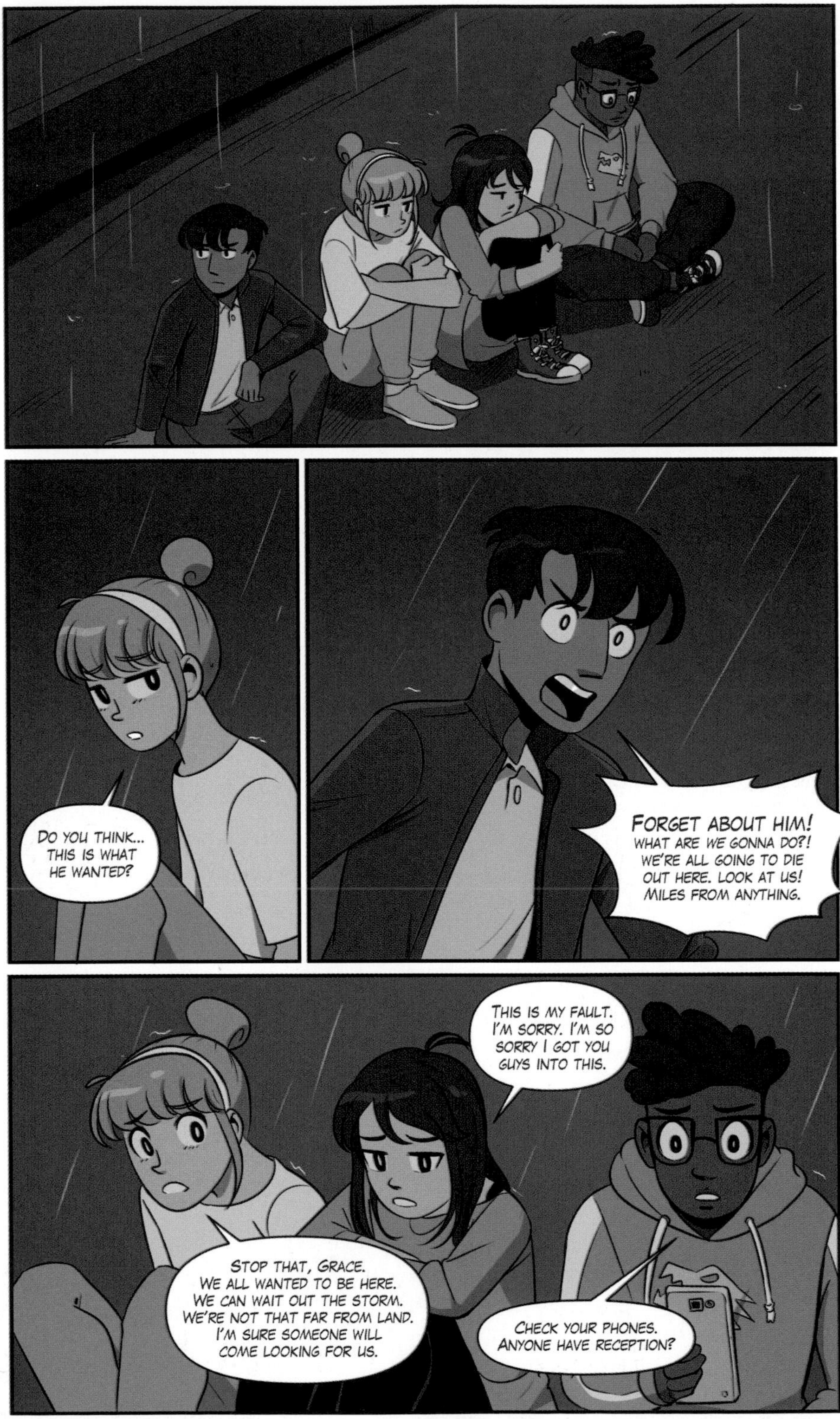

DO YOU THINK... THIS IS WHAT HE WANTED?
FORGET ABOUT HIM! WHAT ARE WE GONNA DO?! WE'RE ALL GOING TO DIE OUT HERE. LOOK AT US! MILES FROM ANYTHING.
THIS IS MY FAULT. I'M SORRY. I'M SO SORRY I GOT YOU GUYS INTO THIS.
STOP THAT, GRACE. WE ALL WANTED TO BE HERE. WE CAN WAIT OUT THE STORM. WE'RE NOT THAT FAR FROM LAND. I'M SURE SOMEONE WILL COME LOOKING FOR US.
CHECK YOUR PHONES. ANYONE HAVE RECEPTION?

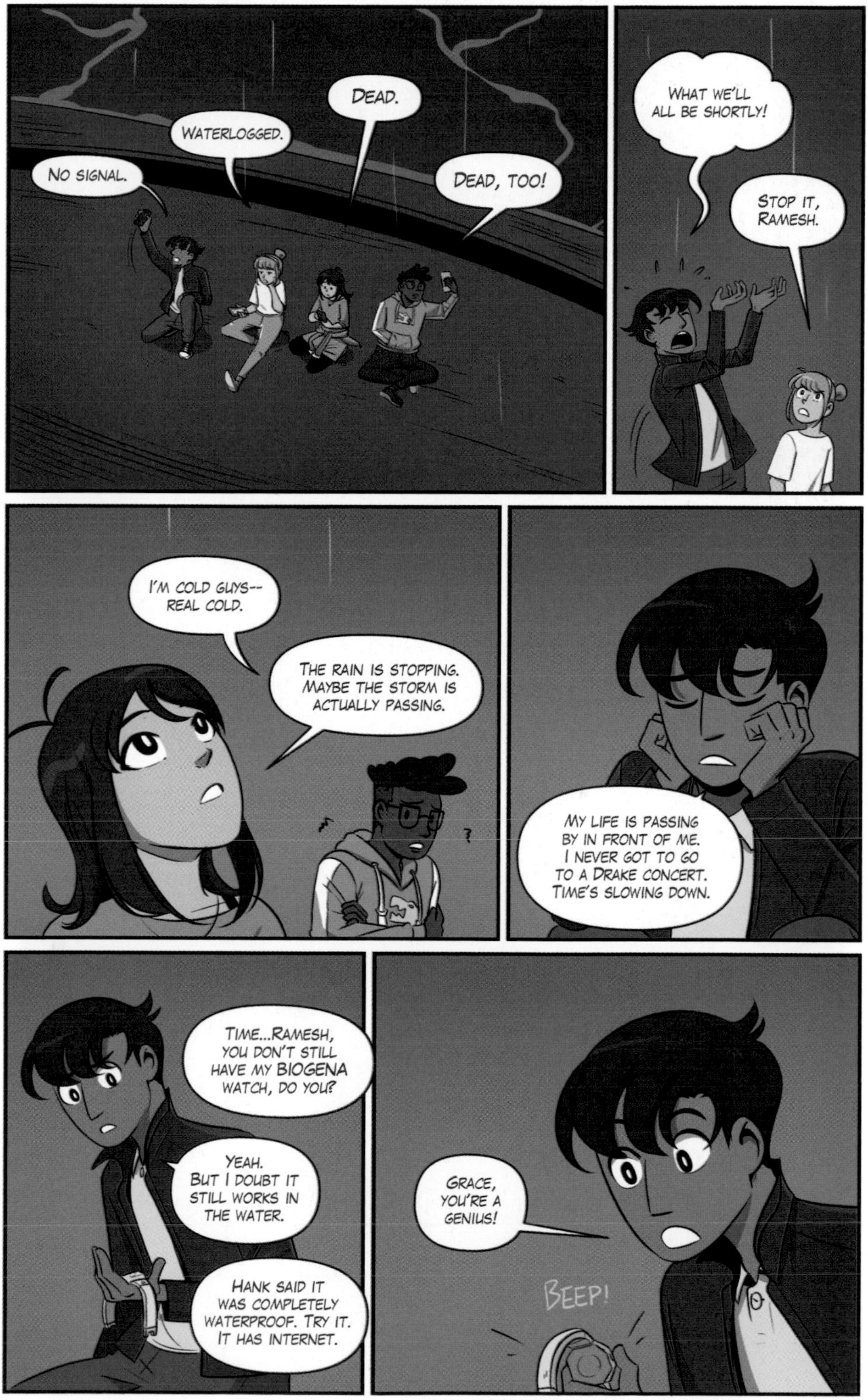
No signal.
Waterlogged.
Dead.
Dead, too!
What we'll all be shortly!
Stop it, Ramesh.
I'm cold guys-- real cold.
The rain is stopping. Maybe the storm is actually passing.
My life is passing by in front of me. I never got to go to a Drake concert. Time's slowing down.
Time...Ramesh, you don't still have my BIOGENA watch, do you?
Yeah. But I doubt it still works in the water.
Hank said it was completely waterproof. Try it. It has internet.
Grace, you're a genius!
BEEP!

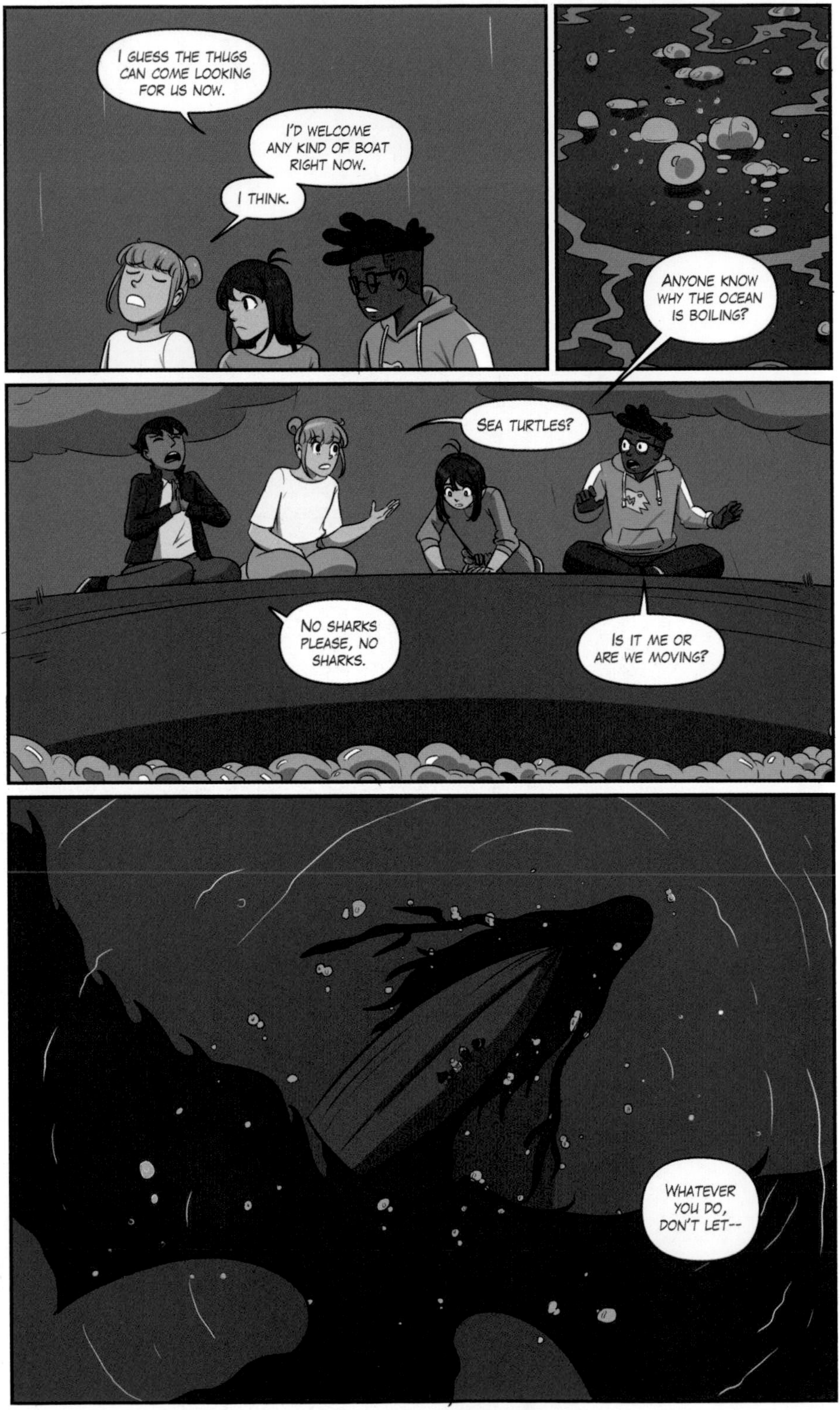
I GUESS THE THUGS CAN COME LOOKING FOR US NOW.
I'D WELCOME ANY KIND OF BOAT RIGHT NOW.
I THINK.
ANYONE KNOW WHY THE OCEAN IS BOILING?
SEA TURTLES?
NO SHARKS PLEASE, NO SHARKS.
IS IT ME OR ARE WE MOVING?
WHATEVER YOU DO, DON'T LET--

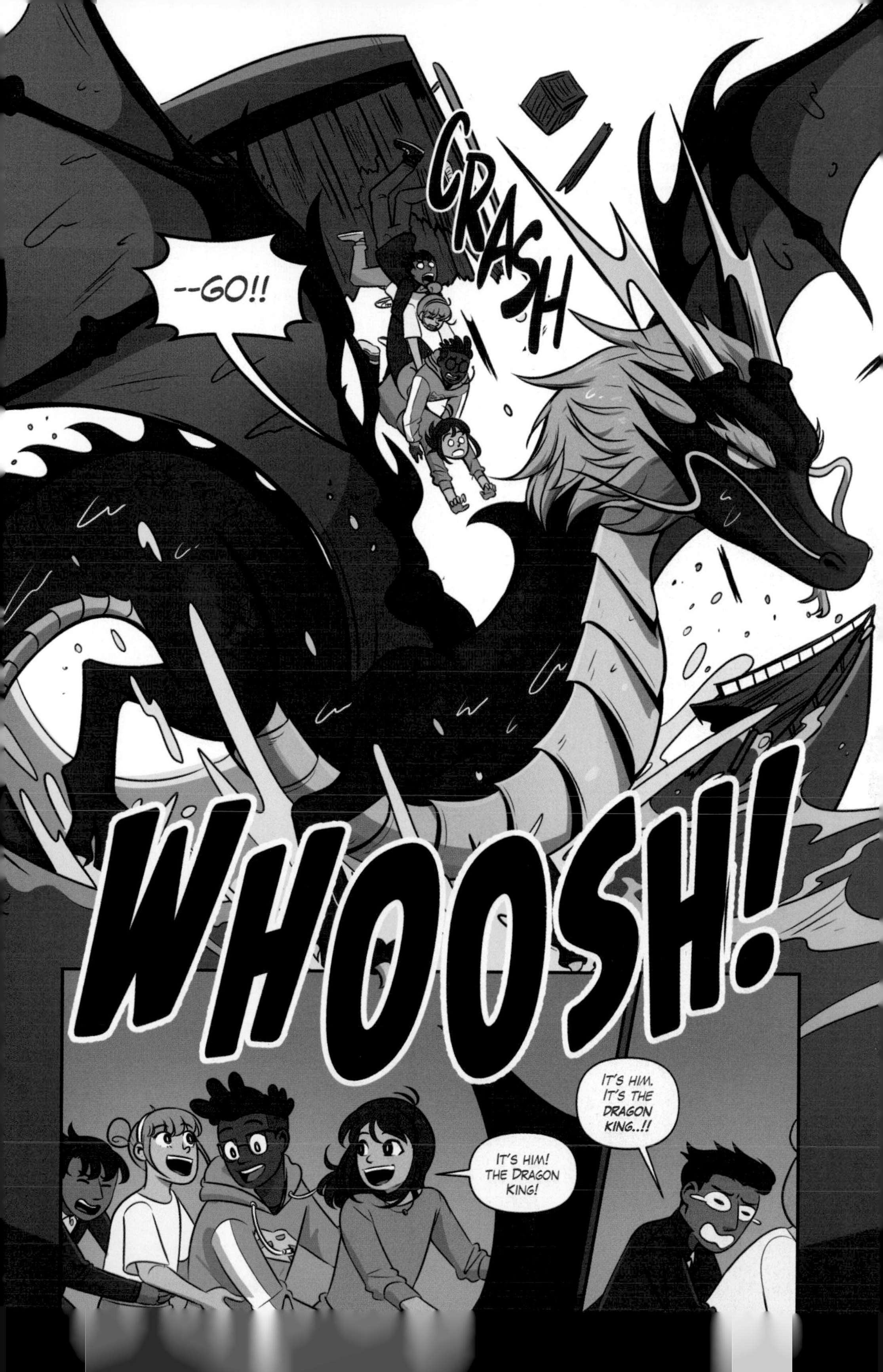
--GO!!
CRASH
WHOOSH!
IT'S HIM! THE DRAGON KING!
IT'S HIM. IT'S THE DRAGON KING..!!

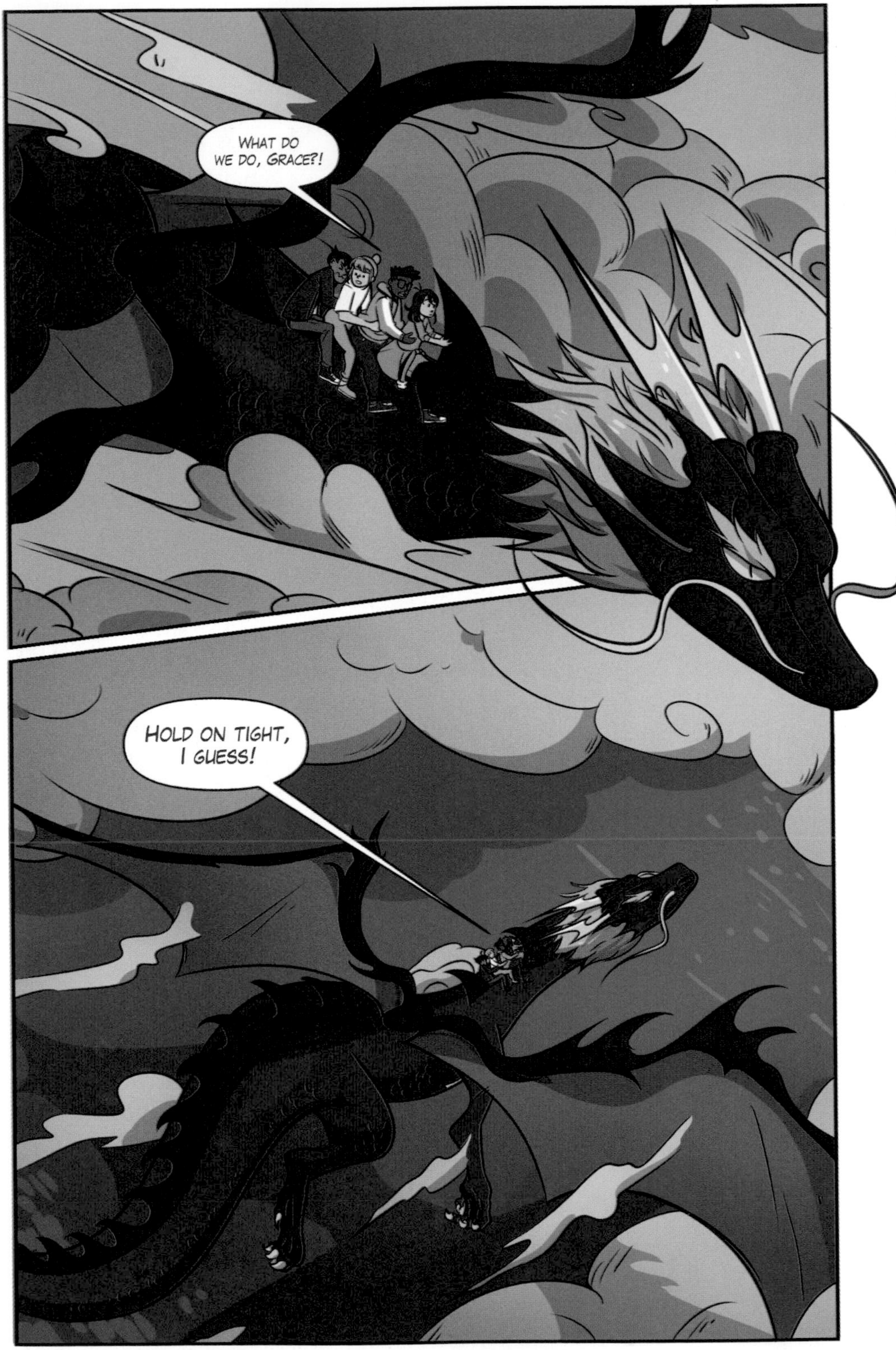
WHAT DO WE DO, GRACE?!
HOLD ON TIGHT, I GUESS!

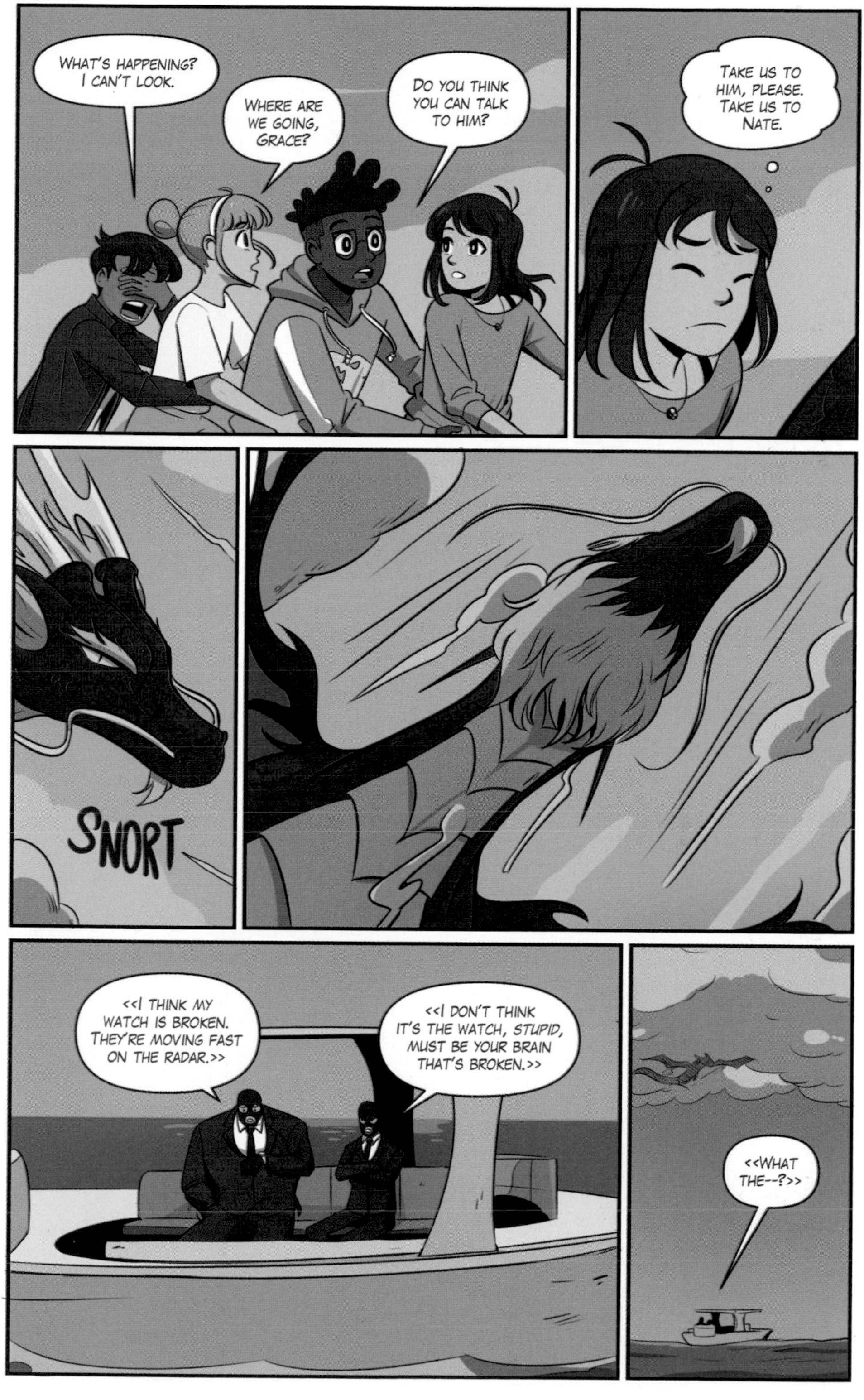
WHAT'S HAPPENING? I CAN'T LOOK.
WHERE ARE WE GOING, GRACE?
DO YOU THINK YOU CAN TALK TO HIM?
TAKE US TO HIM, PLEASE. TAKE US TO NATE.
SNORT
<<I THINK MY WATCH IS BROKEN. THEY'RE MOVING FAST ON THE RADAR.>>
<<I DON'T THINK IT'S THE WATCH, STUPID, MUST BE YOUR BRAIN THAT'S BROKEN.>>
<<WHAT THE--?>>

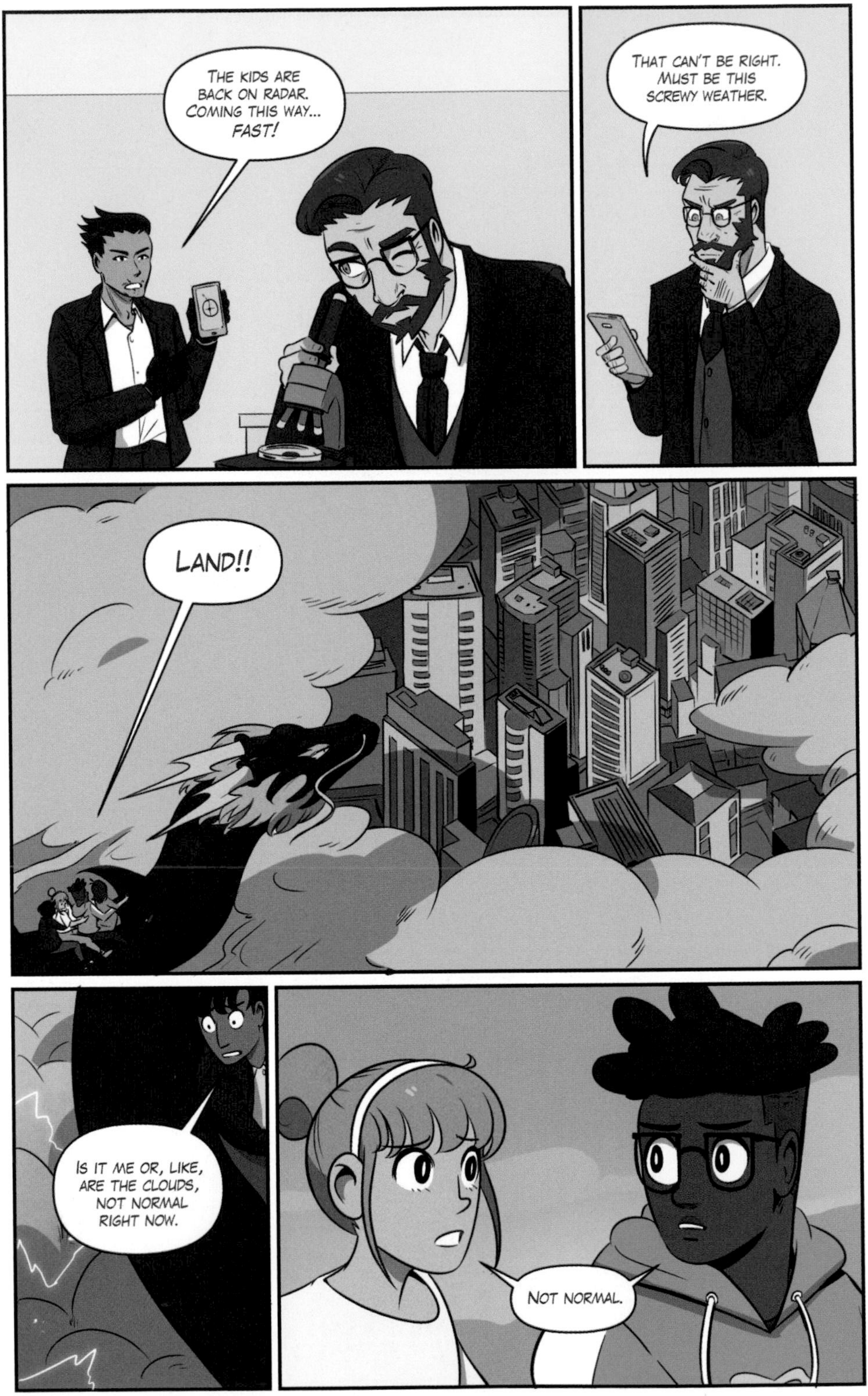
The kids are back on radar. Coming this way... *fast!*
That can't be right. Must be this screwy weather.
LAND!!
Is it me or, like, are the clouds, not normal right now.
Not normal.

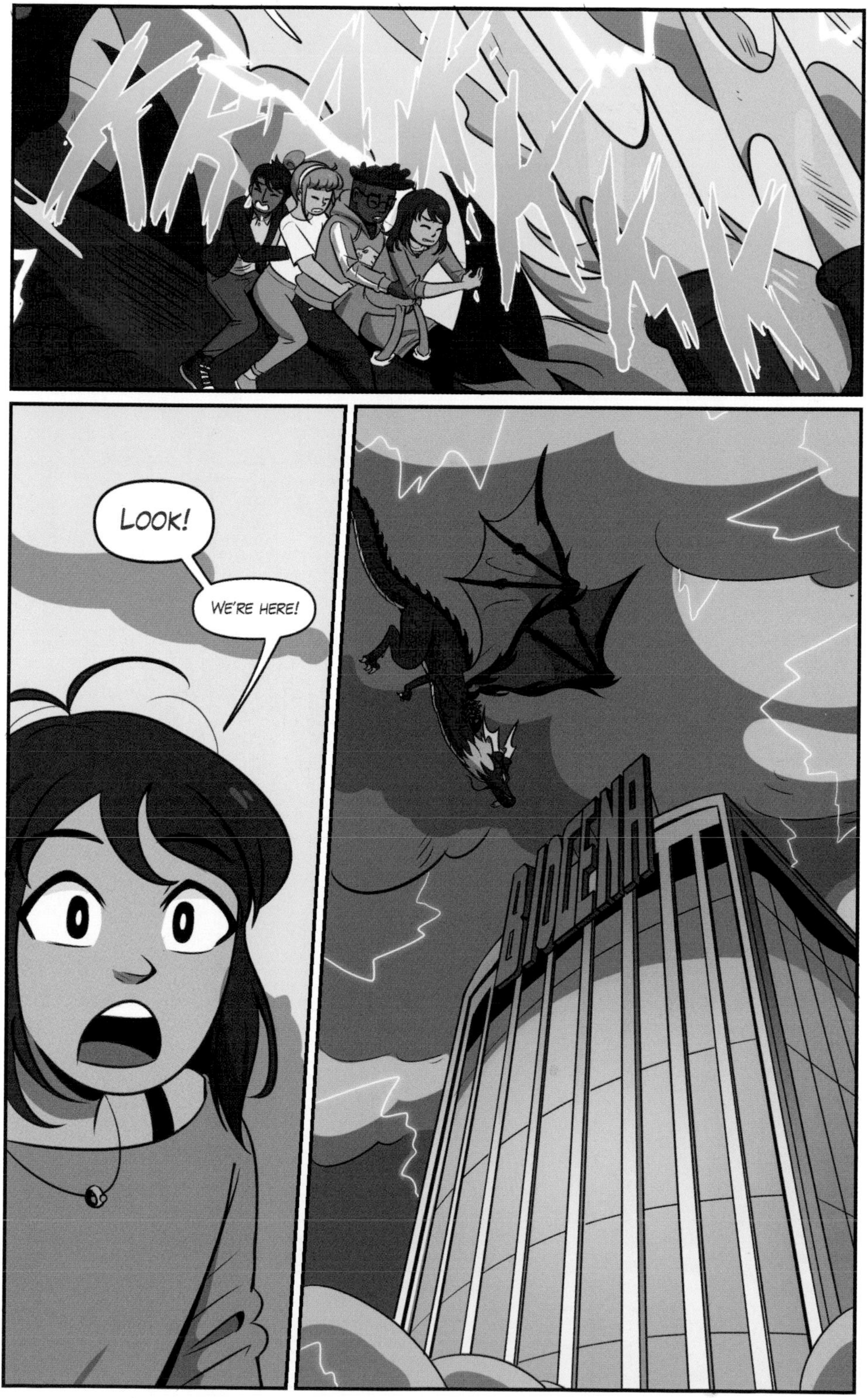
KRAAKKKKK
LOOK!
WE'RE HERE!
BIOGENA

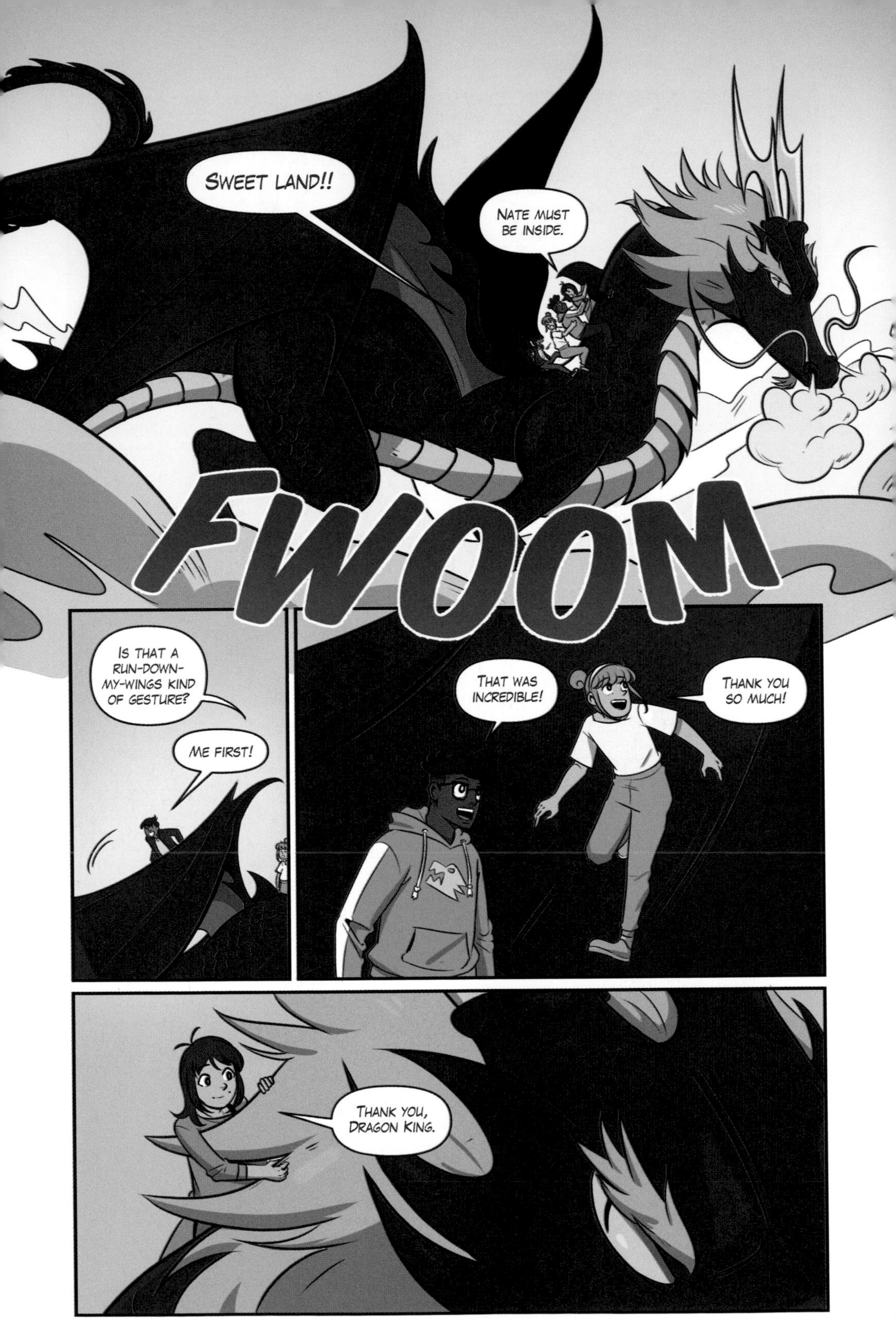
SWEET LAND!!
NATE MUST BE INSIDE.
FWOOM
IS THAT A RUN-DOWN-MY-WINGS KIND OF GESTURE?
ME FIRST!
THAT WAS INCREDIBLE!
THANK YOU SO MUCH!
THANK YOU, DRAGON KING.

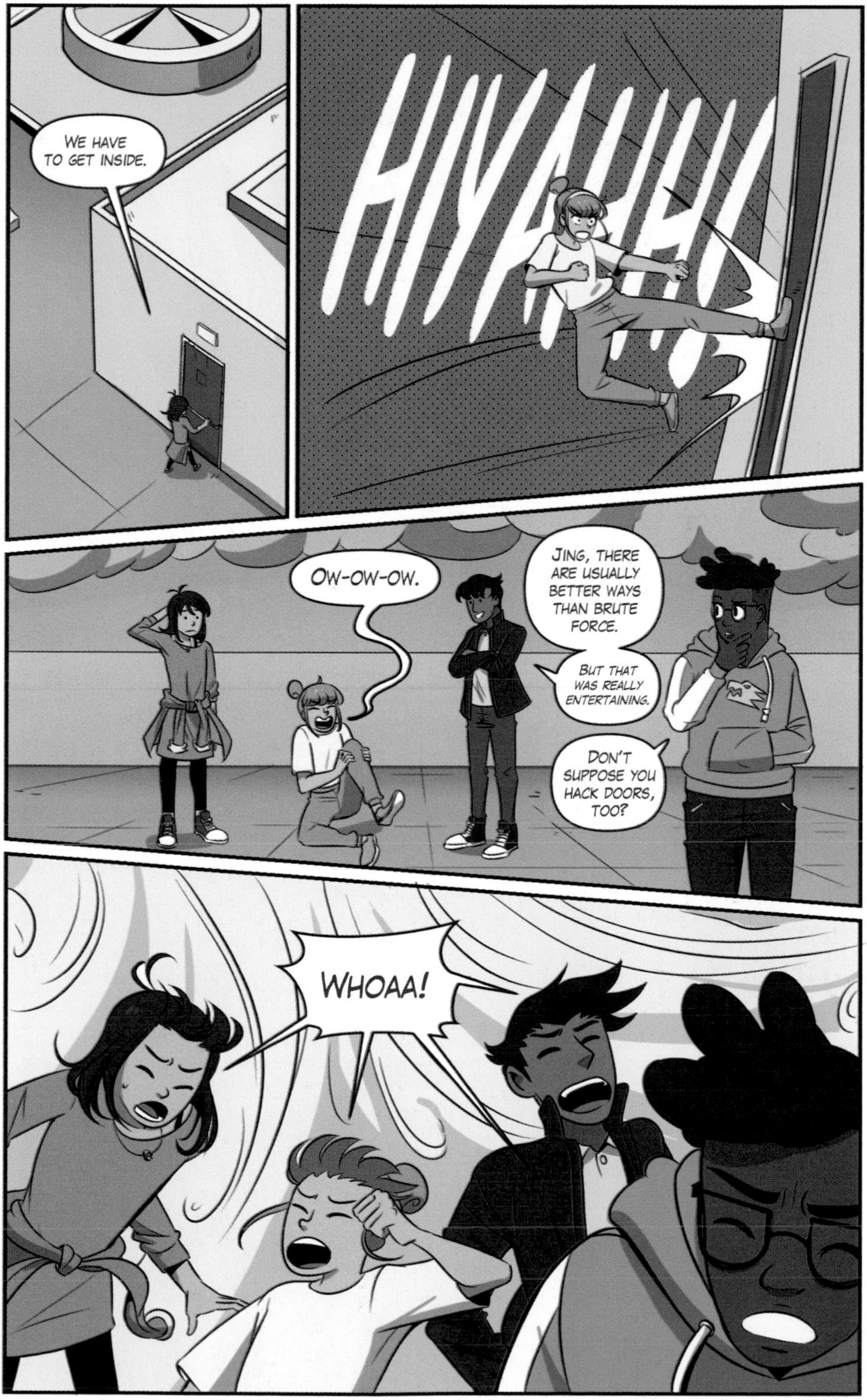
WE HAVE TO GET INSIDE.
HIYAHH!
OW-OW-OW.
JING, THERE ARE USUALLY BETTER WAYS THAN BRUTE FORCE.
BUT THAT WAS REALLY ENTERTAINING.
DON'T SUPPOSE YOU HACK DOORS, TOO?
WHOAA!

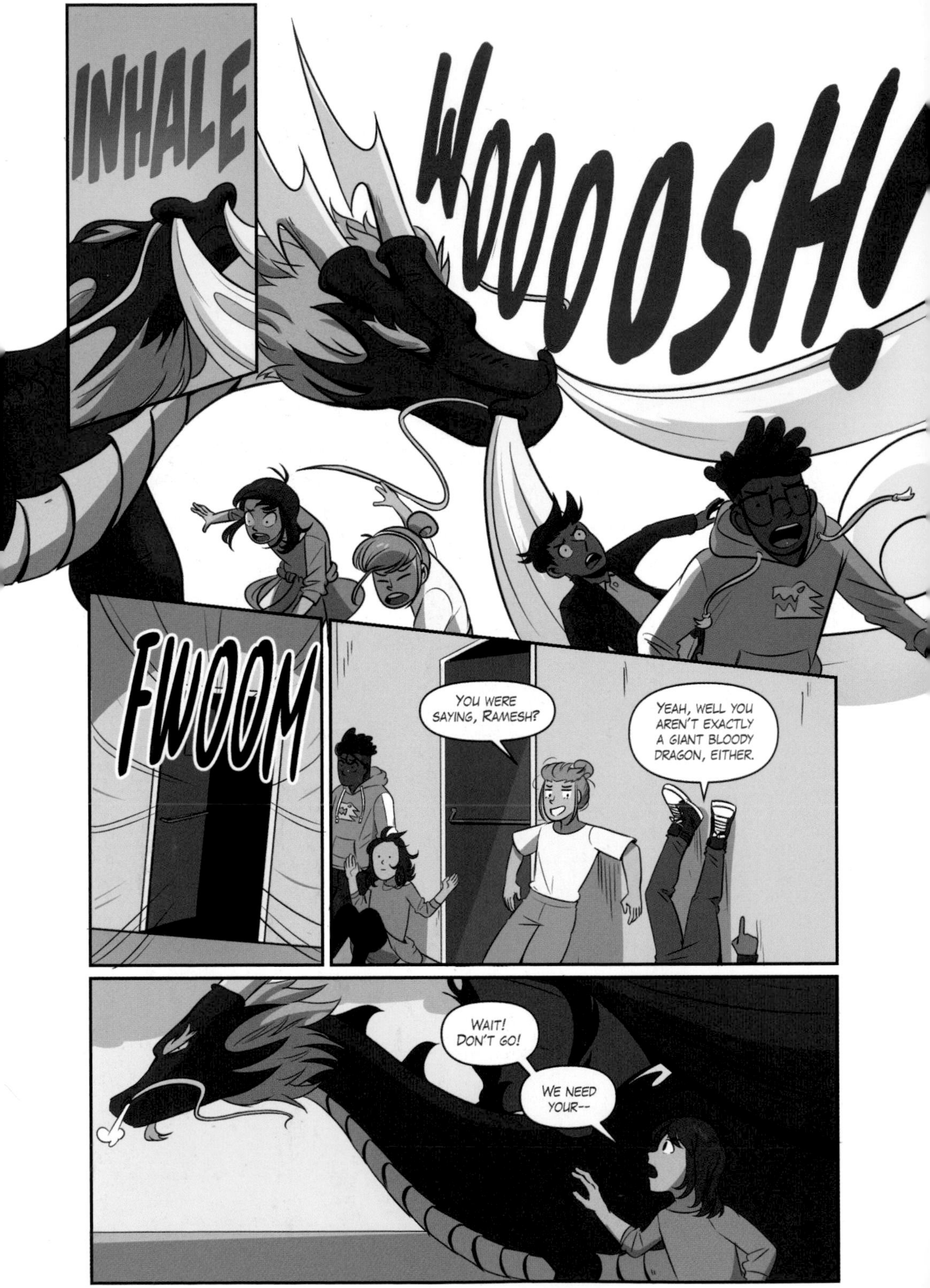
INHALE
WOOOOSH!
FWOOM
YOU WERE SAYING, RAMESH?
YEAH, WELL YOU AREN'T EXACTLY A GIANT BLOODY DRAGON, EITHER.
WAIT! DON'T GO!
WE NEED YOUR--

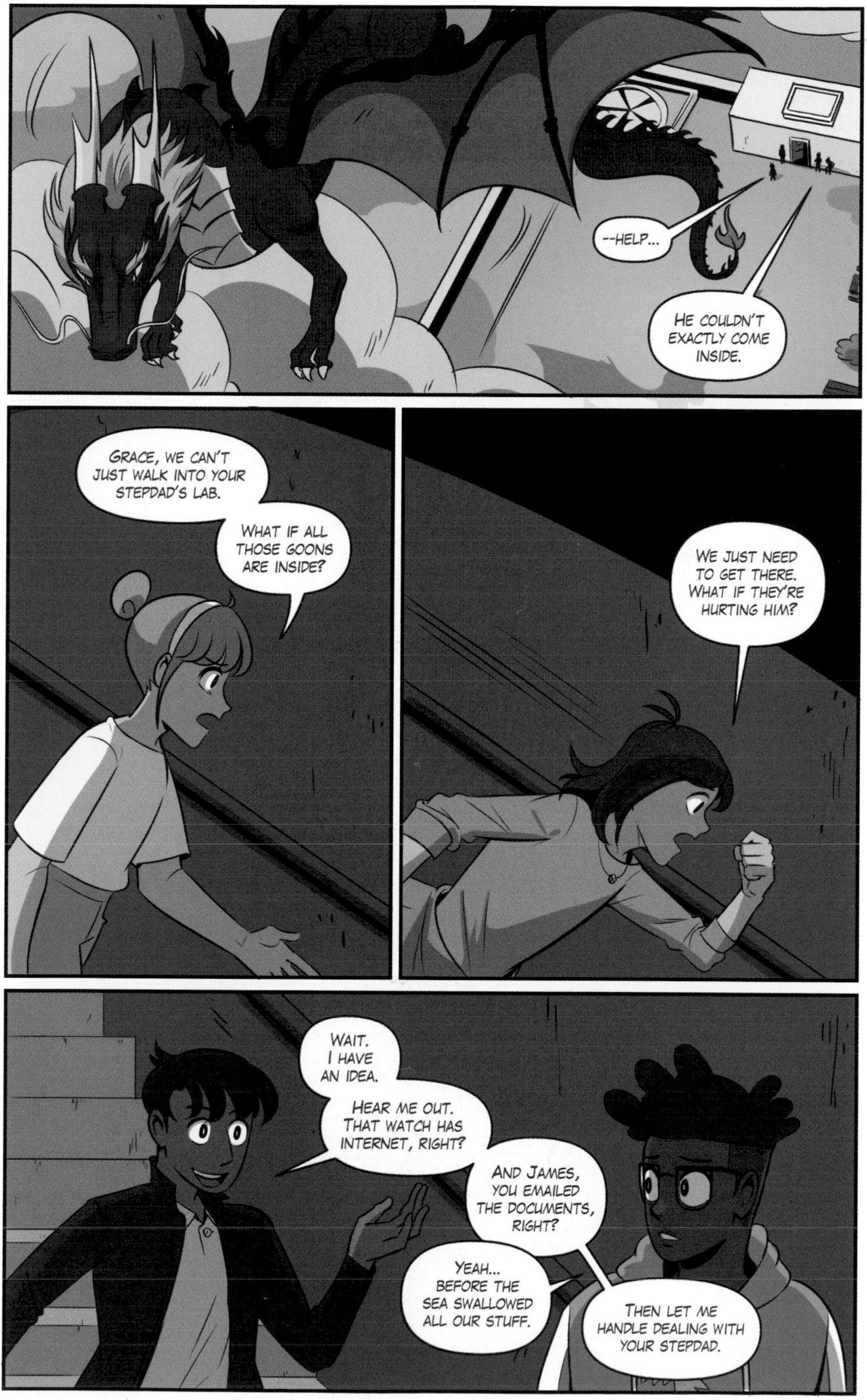
--HELP...
HE COULDN'T EXACTLY COME INSIDE.
GRACE, WE CAN'T JUST WALK INTO YOUR STEPDAD'S LAB.
WHAT IF ALL THOSE GOONS ARE INSIDE?
WE JUST NEED TO GET THERE. WHAT IF THEY'RE HURTING HIM?
WAIT. I HAVE AN IDEA.
HEAR ME OUT. THAT WATCH HAS INTERNET, RIGHT?
AND JAMES, YOU EMAILED THE DOCUMENTS, RIGHT?
YEAH... BEFORE THE SEA SWALLOWED ALL OUR STUFF.
THEN LET ME HANDLE DEALING WITH YOUR STEPDAD.

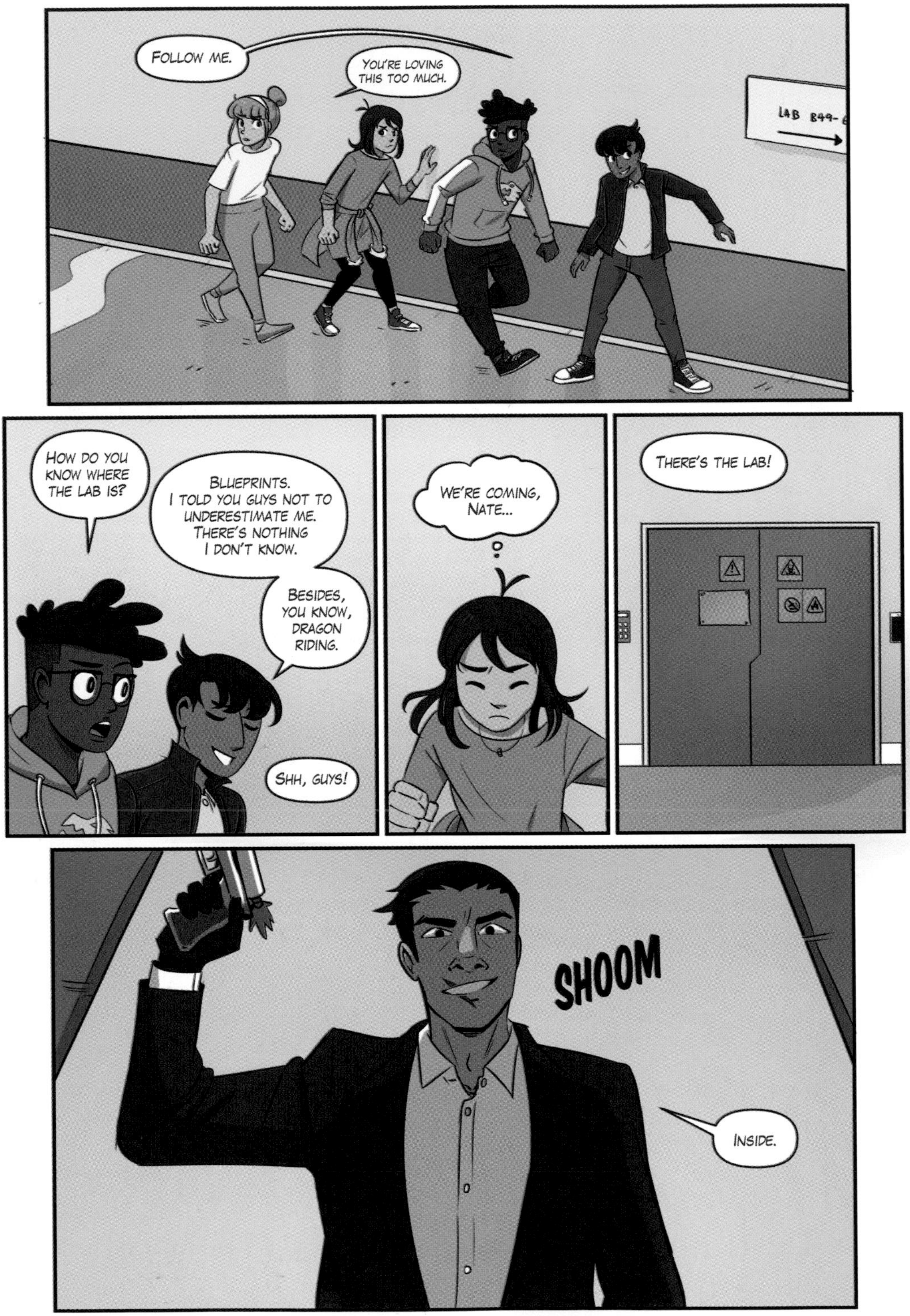
FOLLOW ME.
YOU'RE LOVING THIS TOO MUCH.
LAB B49-
HOW DO YOU KNOW WHERE THE LAB IS?
BLUEPRINTS. I TOLD YOU GUYS NOT TO UNDERESTIMATE ME. THERE'S NOTHING I DON'T KNOW.
BESIDES, YOU KNOW, DRAGON RIDING.
SHH, GUYS!
WE'RE COMING, NATE...
THERE'S THE LAB!
SHOOM
INSIDE.

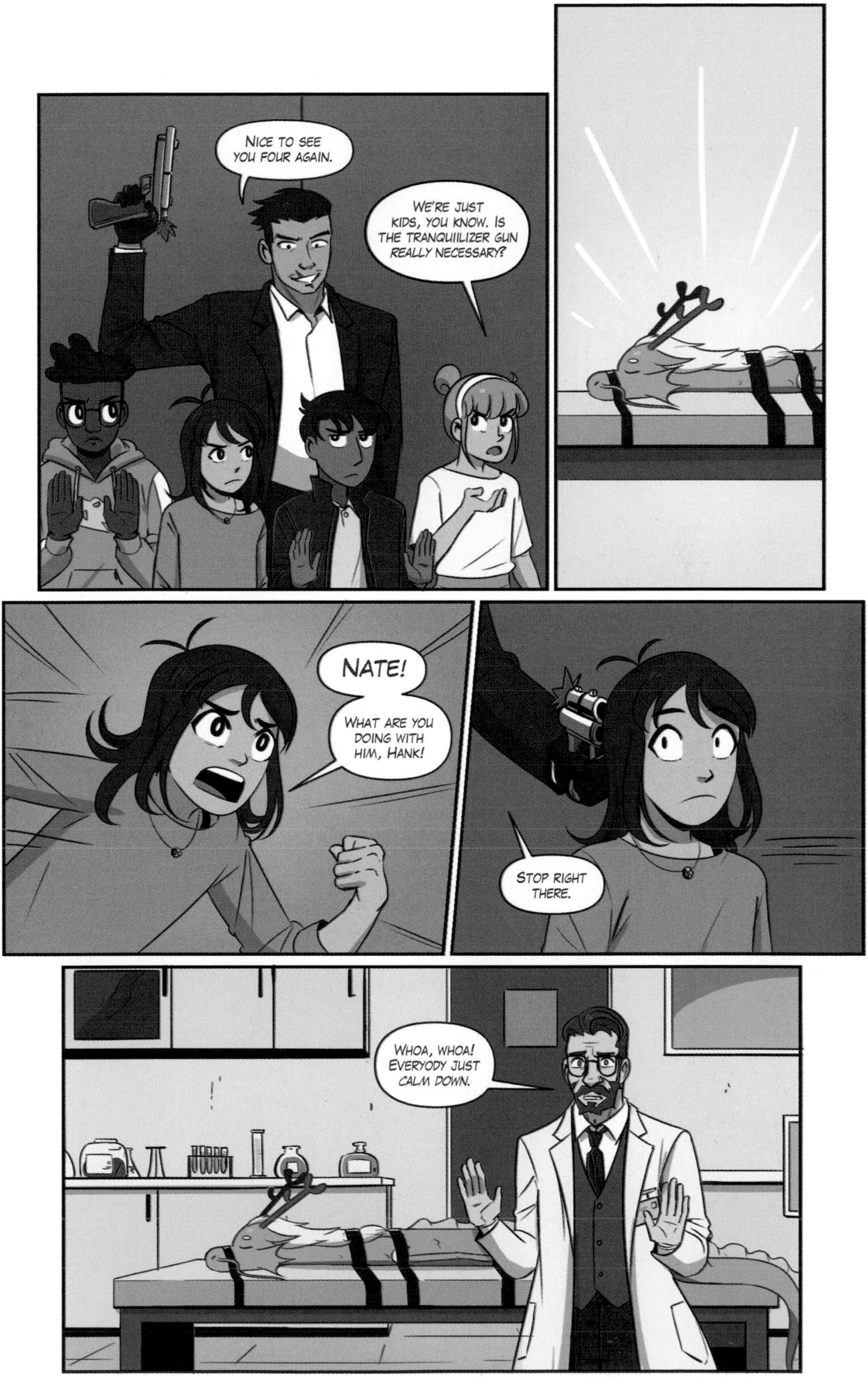
NICE TO SEE YOU FOUR AGAIN.
WE'RE JUST KIDS, YOU KNOW. IS THE TRANQUIILIZER GUN REALLY NECESSARY?
NATE!
WHAT ARE YOU DOING WITH HIM, HANK!
STOP RIGHT THERE.
WHOA, WHOA! EVERYODY JUST CALM DOWN.

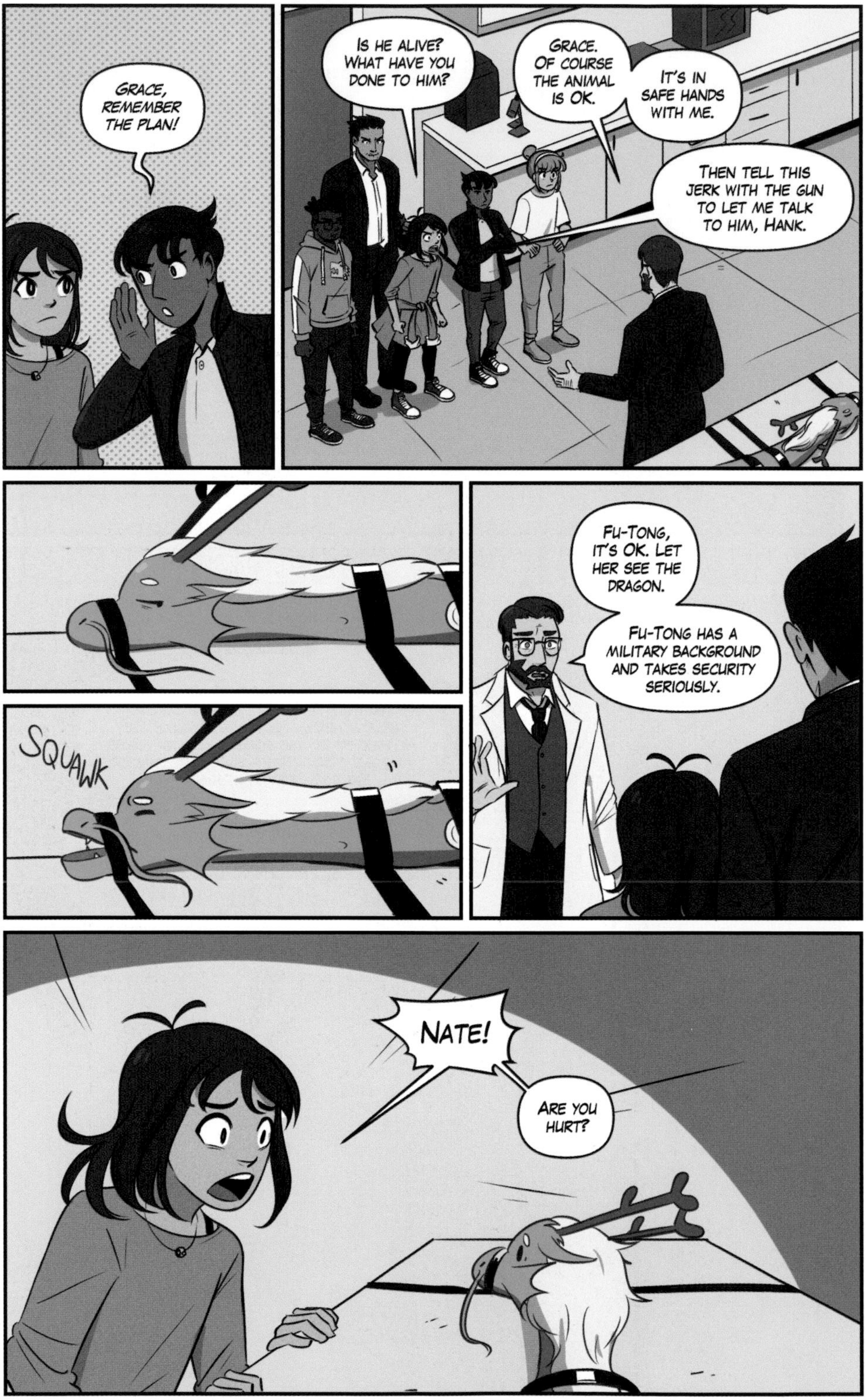
GRACE, REMEMBER THE PLAN!
IS HE ALIVE? WHAT HAVE YOU DONE TO HIM?
GRACE. OF COURSE THE ANIMAL IS OK.
IT'S IN SAFE HANDS WITH ME.
THEN TELL THIS JERK WITH THE GUN TO LET ME TALK TO HIM, HANK.
SQUAWK
FU-TONG, IT'S OK. LET HER SEE THE DRAGON.
FU-TONG HAS A MILITARY BACKGROUND AND TAKES SECURITY SERIOUSLY.
NATE!
ARE YOU HURT?

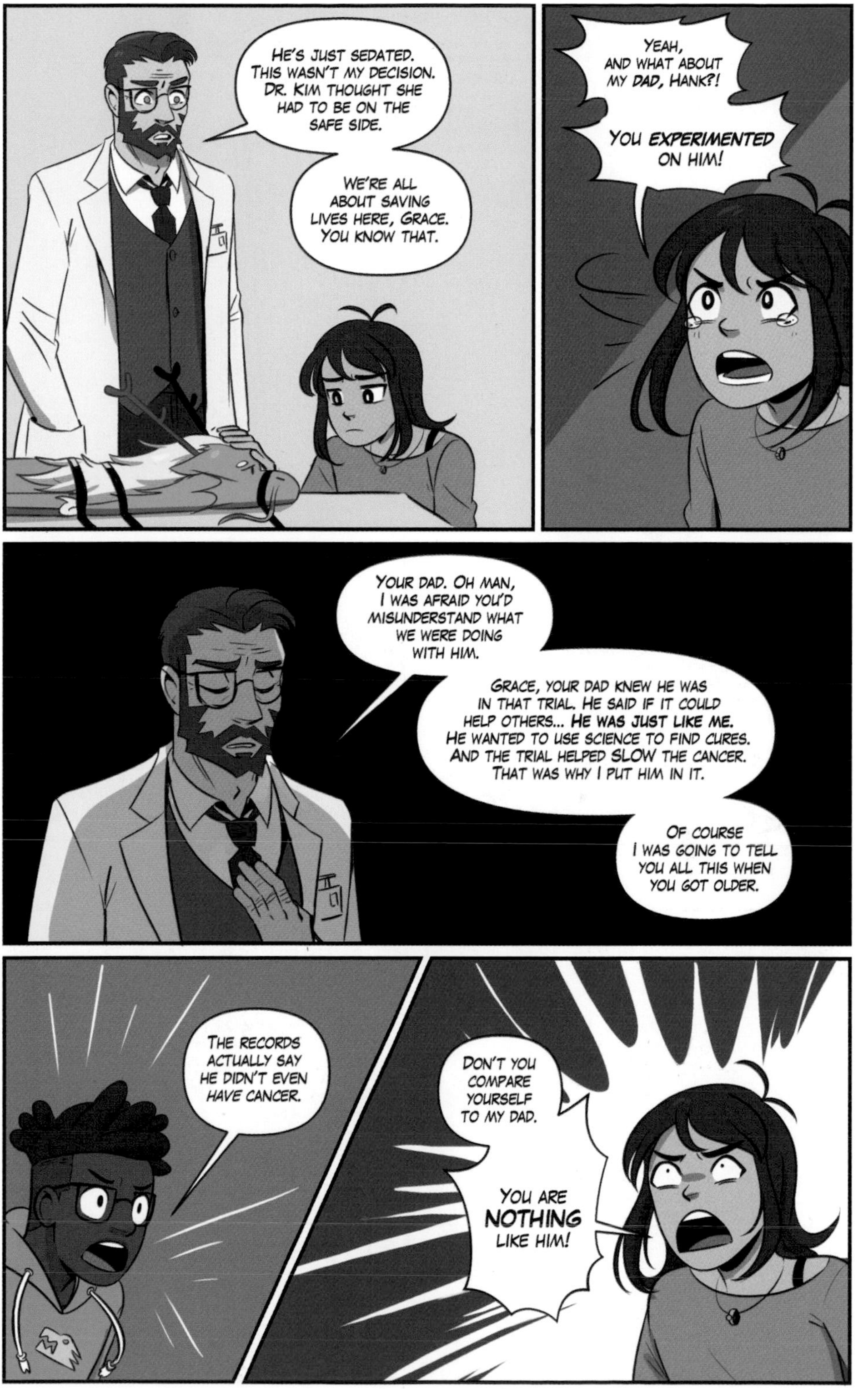
HE'S JUST SEDATED. THIS WASN'T MY DECISION. DR. KIM THOUGHT SHE HAD TO BE ON THE SAFE SIDE.
WE'RE ALL ABOUT SAVING LIVES HERE, GRACE. YOU KNOW THAT.
YEAH, AND WHAT ABOUT MY DAD, HANK?!
YOU EXPERIMENTED ON HIM!
YOUR DAD. OH MAN, I WAS AFRAID YOU'D MISUNDERSTAND WHAT WE WERE DOING WITH HIM.
GRACE, YOUR DAD KNEW HE WAS IN THAT TRIAL. HE SAID IF IT COULD HELP OTHERS... HE WAS JUST LIKE ME. HE WANTED TO USE SCIENCE TO FIND CURES. AND THE TRIAL HELPED SLOW THE CANCER. THAT WAS WHY I PUT HIM IN IT.
OF COURSE I WAS GOING TO TELL YOU ALL THIS WHEN YOU GOT OLDER.
THE RECORDS ACTUALLY SAY HE DIDN'T EVEN HAVE CANCER.
DON'T YOU COMPARE YOURSELF TO MY DAD.
YOU ARE NOTHING LIKE HIM!

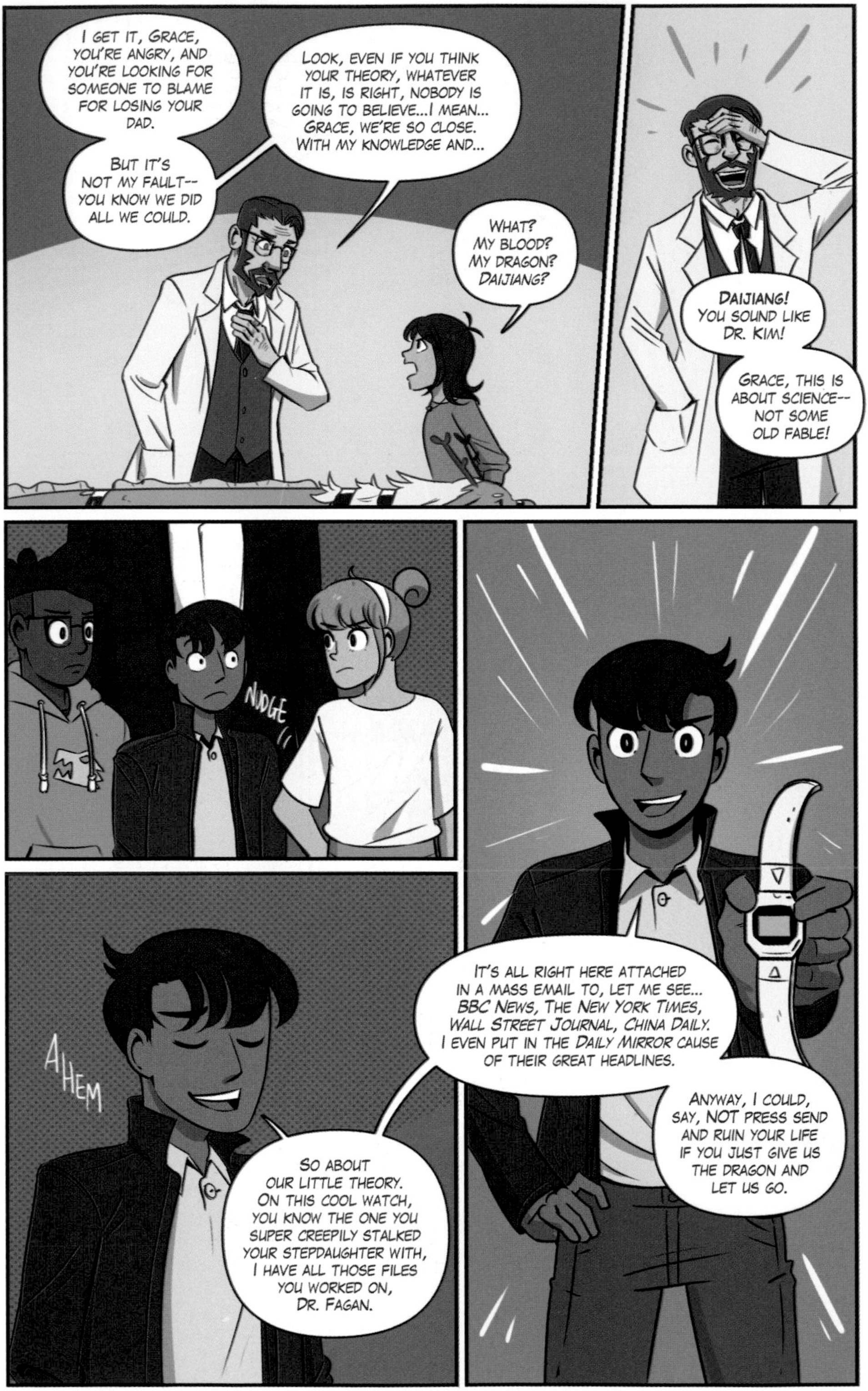
I GET IT, GRACE, YOU'RE ANGRY, AND YOU'RE LOOKING FOR SOMEONE TO BLAME FOR LOSING YOUR DAD.
BUT IT'S NOT MY FAULT-- YOU KNOW WE DID ALL WE COULD.
LOOK, EVEN IF YOU THINK YOUR THEORY, WHATEVER IT IS, IS RIGHT, NOBODY IS GOING TO BELIEVE...I MEAN... GRACE, WE'RE SO CLOSE. WITH MY KNOWLEDGE AND...
WHAT? MY BLOOD? MY DRAGON? DAIJIANG?
DAIJIANG! YOU SOUND LIKE DR. KIM!
GRACE, THIS IS ABOUT SCIENCE-- NOT SOME OLD FABLE!
NUDGE
AHEM
SO ABOUT OUR LITTLE THEORY. ON THIS COOL WATCH, YOU KNOW THE ONE YOU SUPER CREEPILY STALKED YOUR STEPDAUGHTER WITH, I HAVE ALL THOSE FILES YOU WORKED ON, DR. FAGAN.
IT'S ALL RIGHT HERE ATTACHED IN A MASS EMAIL TO, LET ME SEE... BBC NEWS, THE NEW YORK TIMES, WALL STREET JOURNAL, CHINA DAILY. I EVEN PUT IN THE DAILY MIRROR CAUSE OF THEIR GREAT HEADLINES.
ANYWAY, I COULD, SAY, NOT PRESS SEND AND RUIN YOUR LIFE IF YOU JUST GIVE US THE DRAGON AND LET US GO.

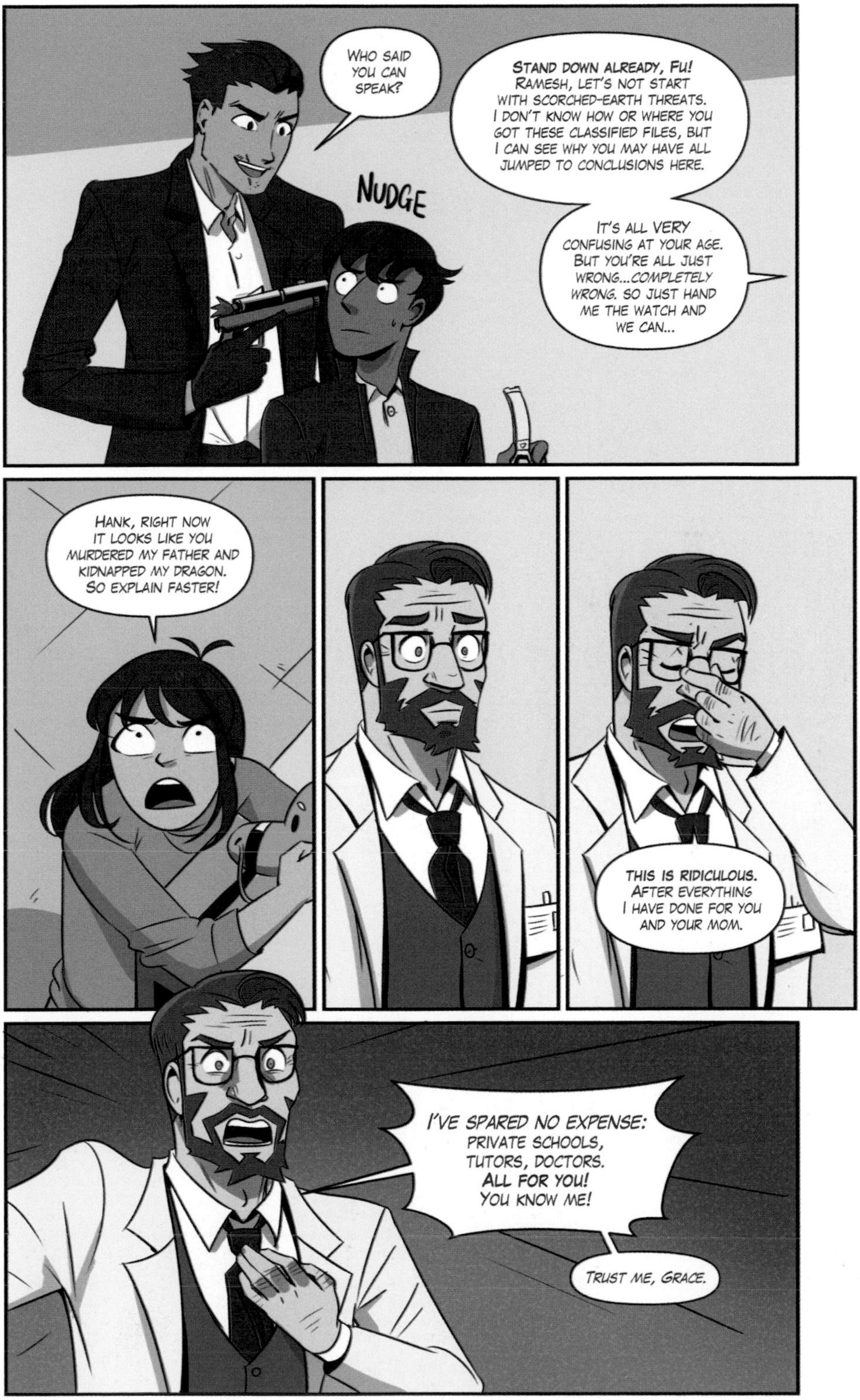
WHO SAID YOU CAN SPEAK?
STAND DOWN ALREADY, FU! RAMESH, LET'S NOT START WITH SCORCHED-EARTH THREATS. I DON'T KNOW HOW OR WHERE YOU GOT THESE CLASSIFIED FILES, BUT I CAN SEE WHY YOU MAY HAVE ALL JUMPED TO CONCLUSIONS HERE.
NUDGE
IT'S ALL VERY CONFUSING AT YOUR AGE. BUT YOU'RE ALL JUST WRONG...COMPLETELY WRONG. SO JUST HAND ME THE WATCH AND WE CAN...
HANK, RIGHT NOW IT LOOKS LIKE YOU MURDERED MY FATHER AND KIDNAPPED MY DRAGON. SO EXPLAIN FASTER!
THIS IS RIDICULOUS. AFTER EVERYTHING I HAVE DONE FOR YOU AND YOUR MOM.
I'VE SPARED NO EXPENSE: PRIVATE SCHOOLS, TUTORS, DOCTORS. ALL FOR YOU! YOU KNOW ME!
TRUST ME, GRACE.

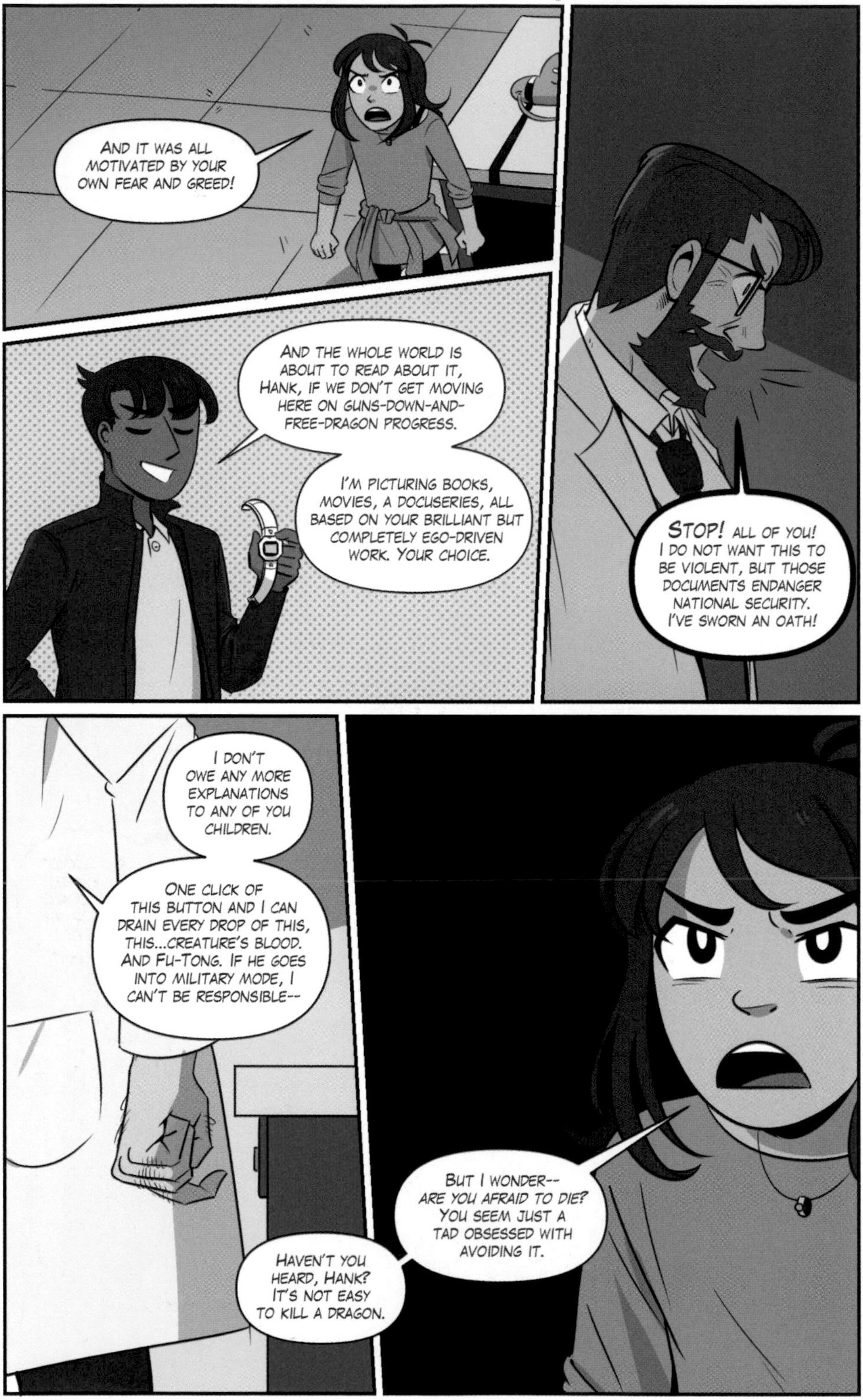
AND IT WAS ALL MOTIVATED BY YOUR OWN FEAR AND GREED!
AND THE WHOLE WORLD IS ABOUT TO READ ABOUT IT, HANK, IF WE DON'T GET MOVING HERE ON GUNS-DOWN-AND-FREE-DRAGON PROGRESS.
I'M PICTURING BOOKS, MOVIES, A DOCUSERIES, ALL BASED ON YOUR BRILLIANT BUT COMPLETELY EGO-DRIVEN WORK. YOUR CHOICE.
STOP! ALL OF YOU! I DO NOT WANT THIS TO BE VIOLENT, BUT THOSE DOCUMENTS ENDANGER NATIONAL SECURITY. I'VE SWORN AN OATH!
I DON'T OWE ANY MORE EXPLANATIONS TO ANY OF YOU CHILDREN.
ONE CLICK OF THIS BUTTON AND I CAN DRAIN EVERY DROP OF THIS, THIS...CREATURE'S BLOOD. AND FU-TONG. IF HE GOES INTO MILITARY MODE, I CAN'T BE RESPONSIBLE--
BUT I WONDER-- ARE YOU AFRAID TO DIE? YOU SEEM JUST A TAD OBSESSED WITH AVOIDING IT.
HAVEN'T YOU HEARD, HANK? IT'S NOT EASY TO KILL A DRAGON.

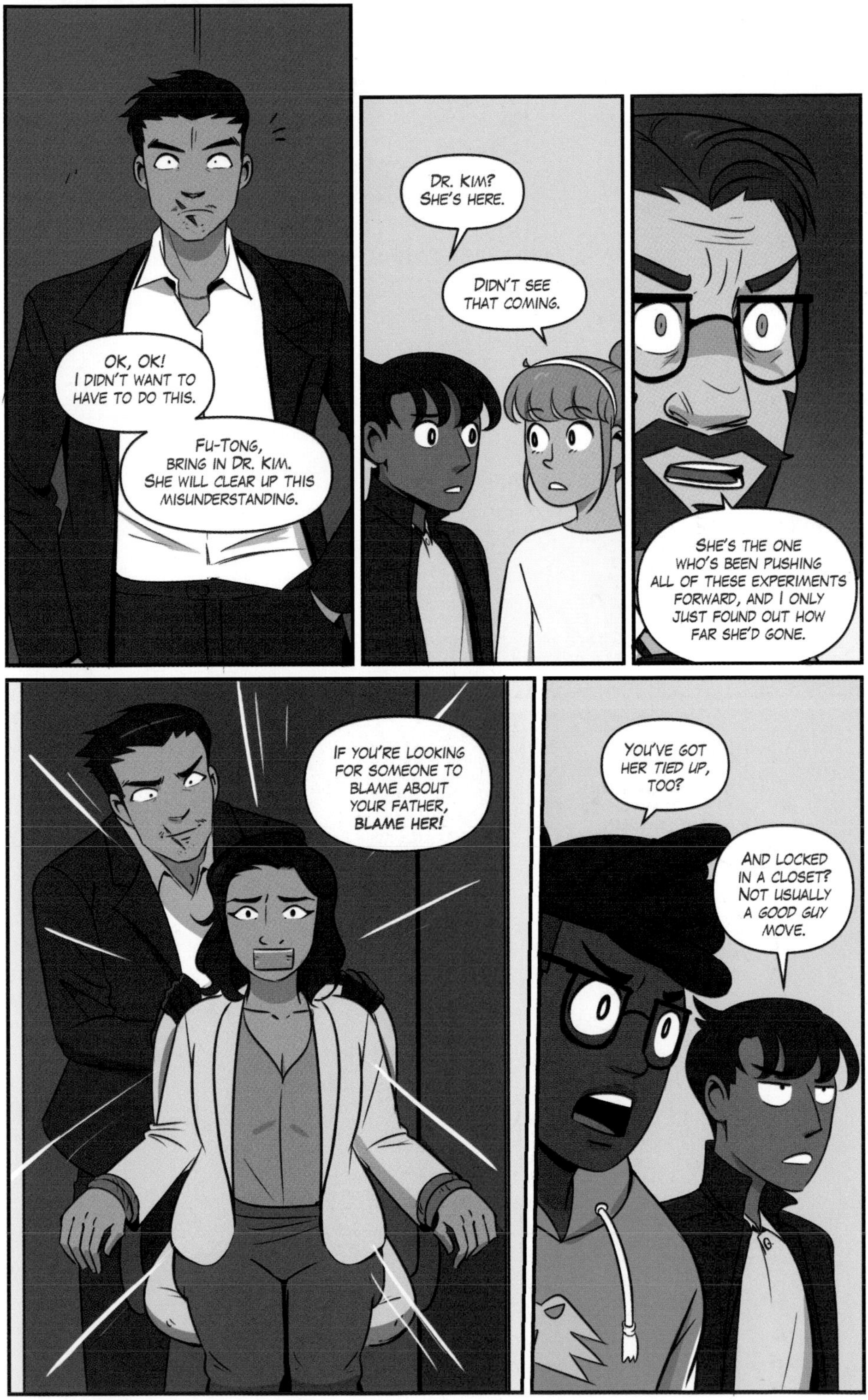
OK, OK! I DIDN'T WANT TO HAVE TO DO THIS.
FU-TONG, BRING IN DR. KIM. SHE WILL CLEAR UP THIS MISUNDERSTANDING.
DR. KIM? SHE'S HERE.
DIDN'T SEE THAT COMING.
SHE'S THE ONE WHO'S BEEN PUSHING ALL OF THESE EXPERIMENTS FORWARD, AND I ONLY JUST FOUND OUT HOW FAR SHE'D GONE.
IF YOU'RE LOOKING FOR SOMEONE TO BLAME ABOUT YOUR FATHER, **BLAME HER!**
YOU'VE GOT HER *TIED UP*, TOO?
AND LOCKED IN A CLOSET? NOT USUALLY A GOOD GUY MOVE.

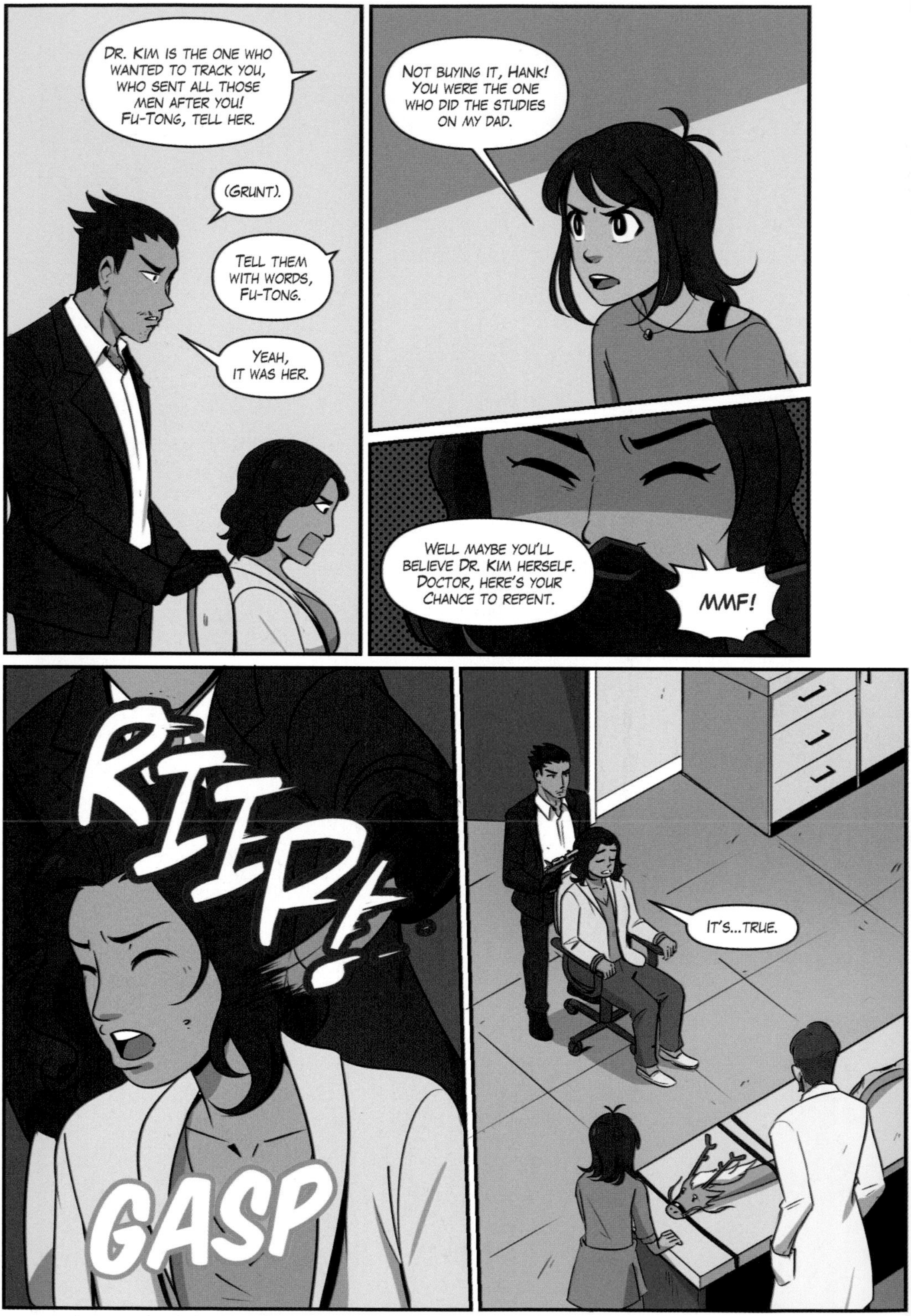
DR. KIM IS THE ONE WHO WANTED TO TRACK YOU, WHO SENT ALL THOSE MEN AFTER YOU! FU-TONG, TELL HER.
(GRUNT).
TELL THEM WITH WORDS, FU-TONG.
YEAH, IT WAS HER.
NOT BUYING IT, HANK! YOU WERE THE ONE WHO DID THE STUDIES ON MY DAD.
WELL MAYBE YOU'LL BELIEVE DR. KIM HERSELF. DOCTOR, HERE'S YOUR CHANCE TO REPENT.
MMF!
RIIIP!
GASP
IT'S...TRUE.

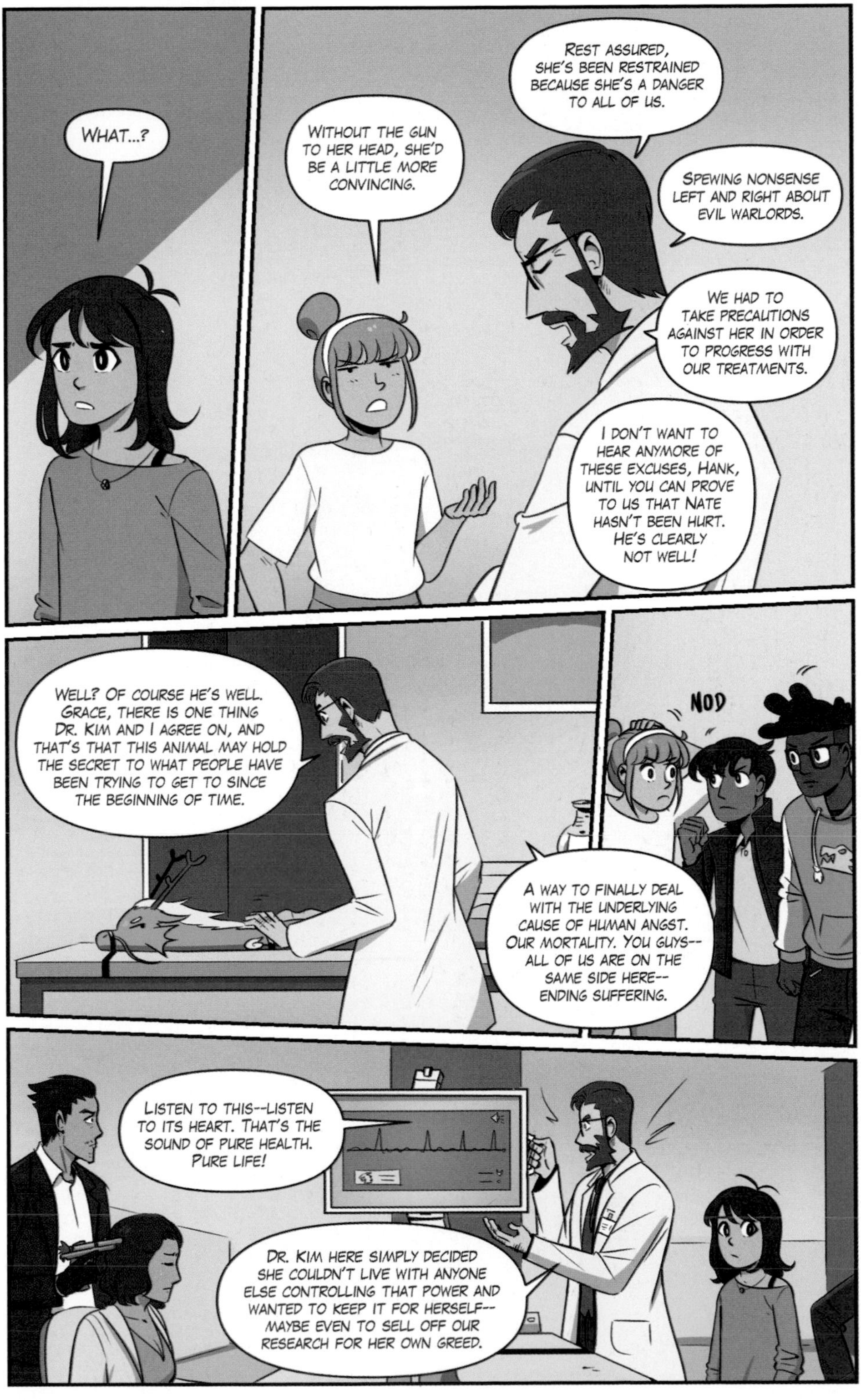
WHAT...?
WITHOUT THE GUN TO HER HEAD, SHE'D BE A LITTLE MORE CONVINCING.
REST ASSURED, SHE'S BEEN RESTRAINED BECAUSE SHE'S A DANGER TO ALL OF US.
SPEWING NONSENSE LEFT AND RIGHT ABOUT EVIL WARLORDS.
WE HAD TO TAKE PRECAUTIONS AGAINST HER IN ORDER TO PROGRESS WITH OUR TREATMENTS.
I DON'T WANT TO HEAR ANYMORE OF THESE EXCUSES, HANK, UNTIL YOU CAN PROVE TO US THAT NATE HASN'T BEEN HURT. HE'S CLEARLY NOT WELL!
WELL? OF COURSE HE'S WELL. GRACE, THERE IS ONE THING DR. KIM AND I AGREE ON, AND THAT'S THAT THIS ANIMAL MAY HOLD THE SECRET TO WHAT PEOPLE HAVE BEEN TRYING TO GET TO SINCE THE BEGINNING OF TIME.
NOD
A WAY TO FINALLY DEAL WITH THE UNDERLYING CAUSE OF HUMAN ANGST. OUR MORTALITY. YOU GUYS-- ALL OF US ARE ON THE SAME SIDE HERE-- ENDING SUFFERING.
LISTEN TO THIS--LISTEN TO ITS HEART. THAT'S THE SOUND OF PURE HEALTH. PURE LIFE!
DR. KIM HERE SIMPLY DECIDED SHE COULDN'T LIVE WITH ANYONE ELSE CONTROLLING THAT POWER AND WANTED TO KEEP IT FOR HERSELF-- MAYBE EVEN TO SELL OFF OUR RESEARCH FOR HER OWN GREED.

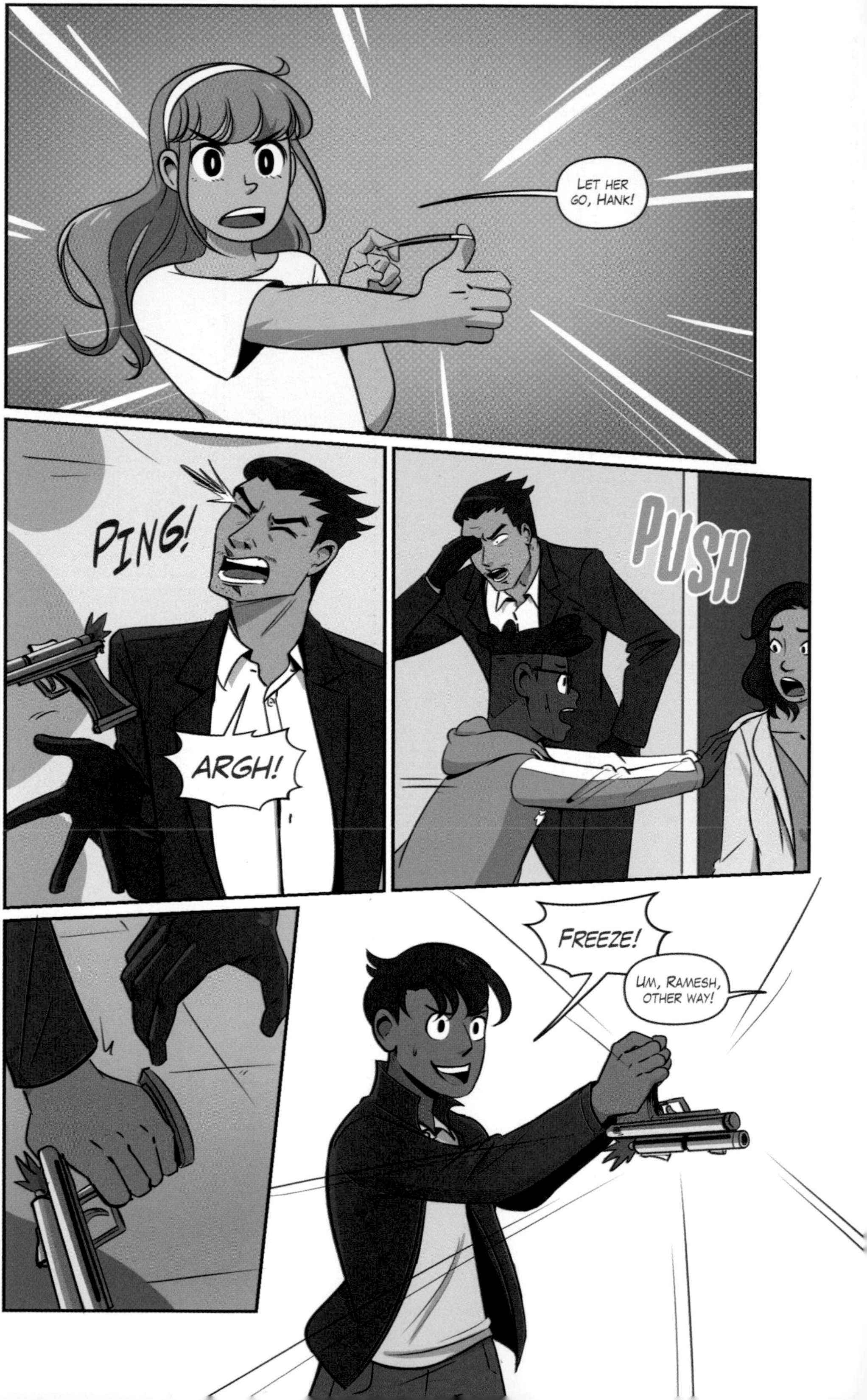
LET HER GO, HANK!
PING!
ARGH!
PUSH
FREEZE!
UM, RAMESH, OTHER WAY!

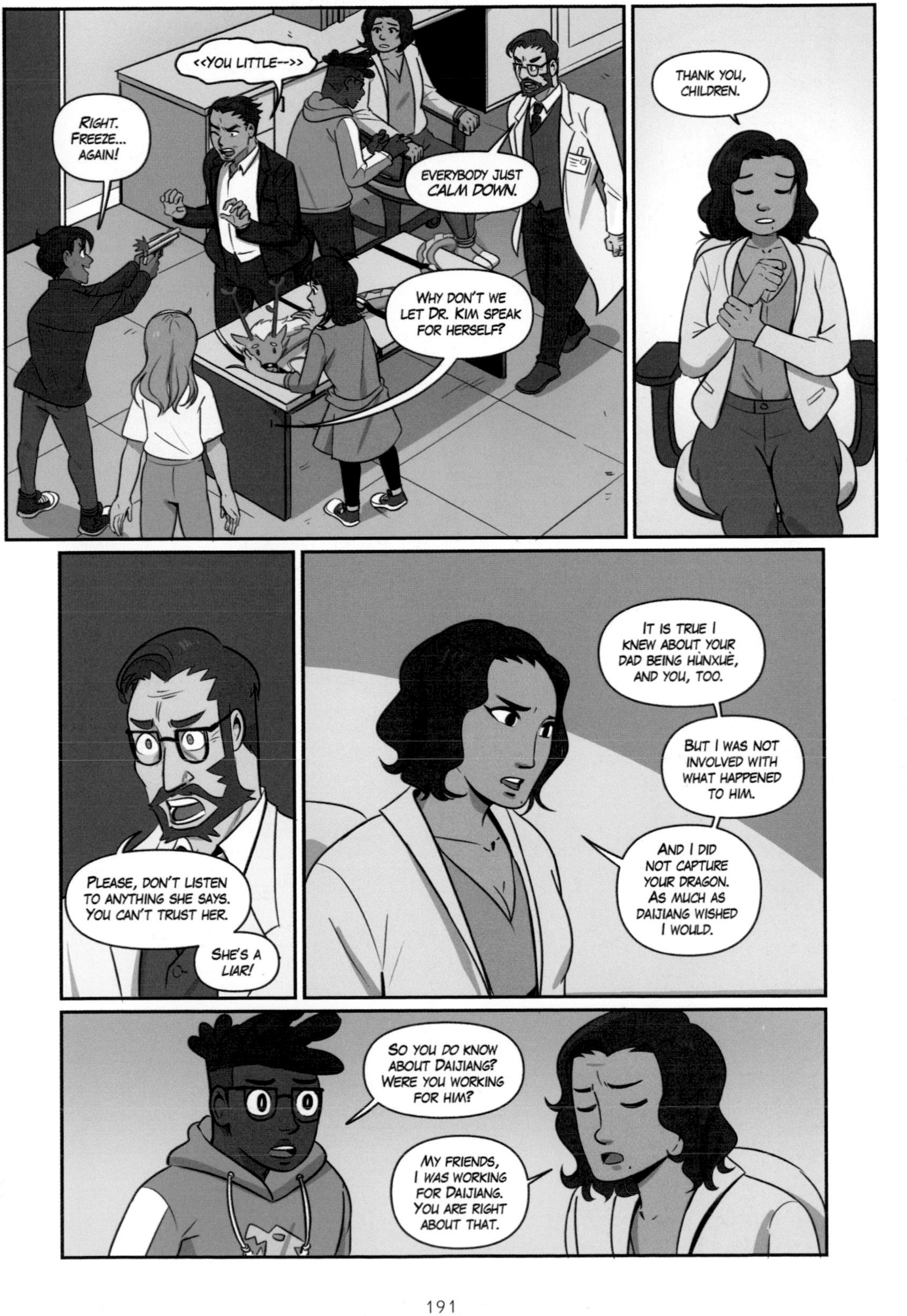
RIGHT. FREEZE... AGAIN!
<<YOU LITTLE-->>
EVERYBODY JUST CALM DOWN.
WHY DON'T WE LET DR. KIM SPEAK FOR HERSELF?
THANK YOU, CHILDREN.
PLEASE, DON'T LISTEN TO ANYTHING SHE SAYS. YOU CAN'T TRUST HER.
SHE'S A LIAR!
IT IS TRUE I KNEW ABOUT YOUR DAD BEING HÙNXUÈ, AND YOU, TOO.
BUT I WAS NOT INVOLVED WITH WHAT HAPPENED TO HIM.
AND I DID NOT CAPTURE YOUR DRAGON. AS MUCH AS DAIJIANG WISHED I WOULD.
SO YOU DO KNOW ABOUT DAIJIANG? WERE YOU WORKING FOR HIM?
MY FRIENDS, I WAS WORKING FOR DAIJIANG. YOU ARE RIGHT ABOUT THAT.

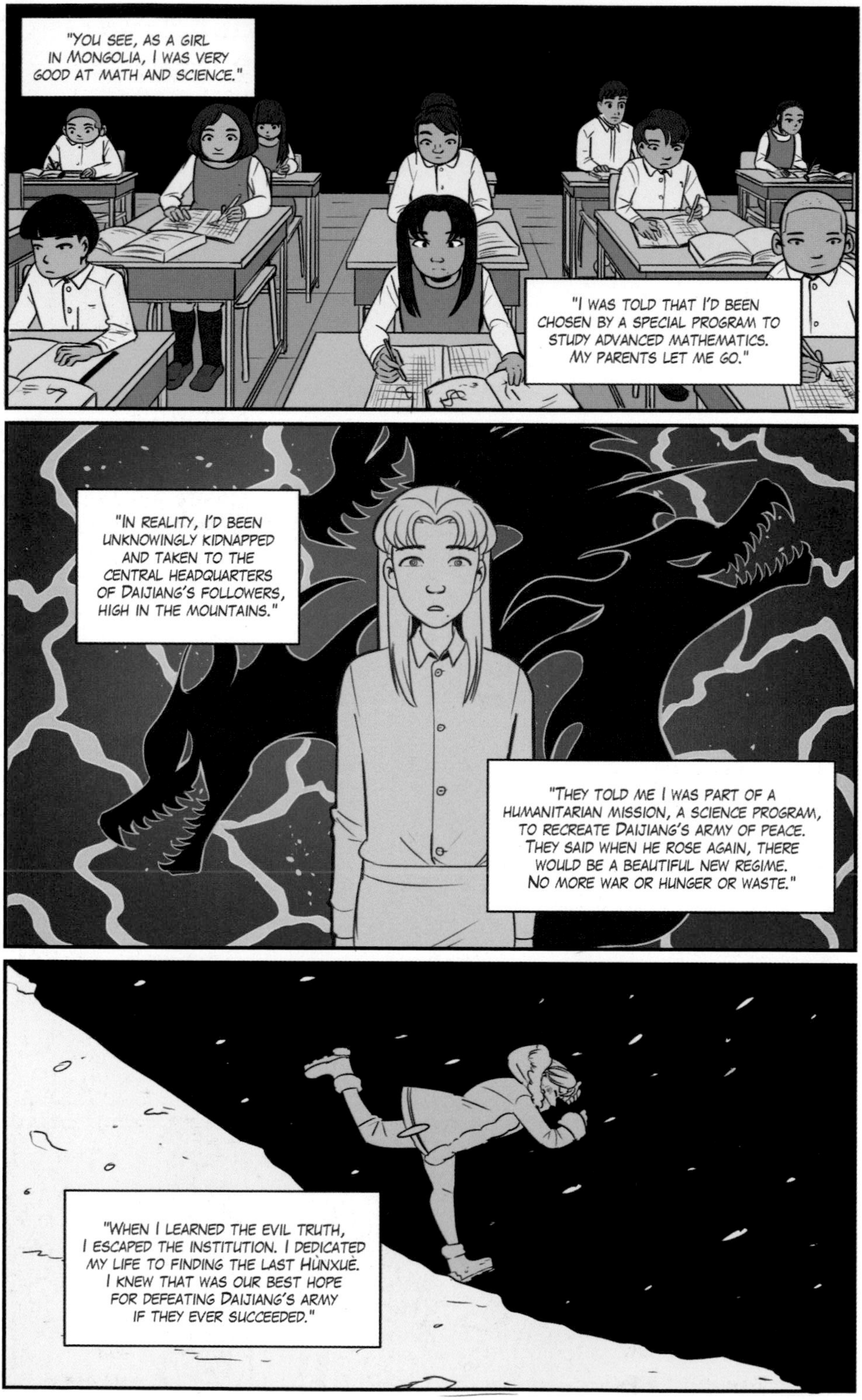
"YOU SEE, AS A GIRL IN MONGOLIA, I WAS VERY GOOD AT MATH AND SCIENCE."
"I WAS TOLD THAT I'D BEEN CHOSEN BY A SPECIAL PROGRAM TO STUDY ADVANCED MATHEMATICS. MY PARENTS LET ME GO."
"IN REALITY, I'D BEEN UNKNOWINGLY KIDNAPPED AND TAKEN TO THE CENTRAL HEADQUARTERS OF DAIJIANG'S FOLLOWERS, HIGH IN THE MOUNTAINS."
"THEY TOLD ME I WAS PART OF A HUMANITARIAN MISSION, A SCIENCE PROGRAM, TO RECREATE DAIJIANG'S ARMY OF PEACE. THEY SAID WHEN HE ROSE AGAIN, THERE WOULD BE A BEAUTIFUL NEW REGIME. NO MORE WAR OR HUNGER OR WASTE."
"WHEN I LEARNED THE EVIL TRUTH, I ESCAPED THE INSTITUTION. I DEDICATED MY LIFE TO FINDING THE LAST HÚNXUÈ. I KNEW THAT WAS OUR BEST HOPE FOR DEFEATING DAIJIANG'S ARMY IF THEY EVER SUCCEEDED."

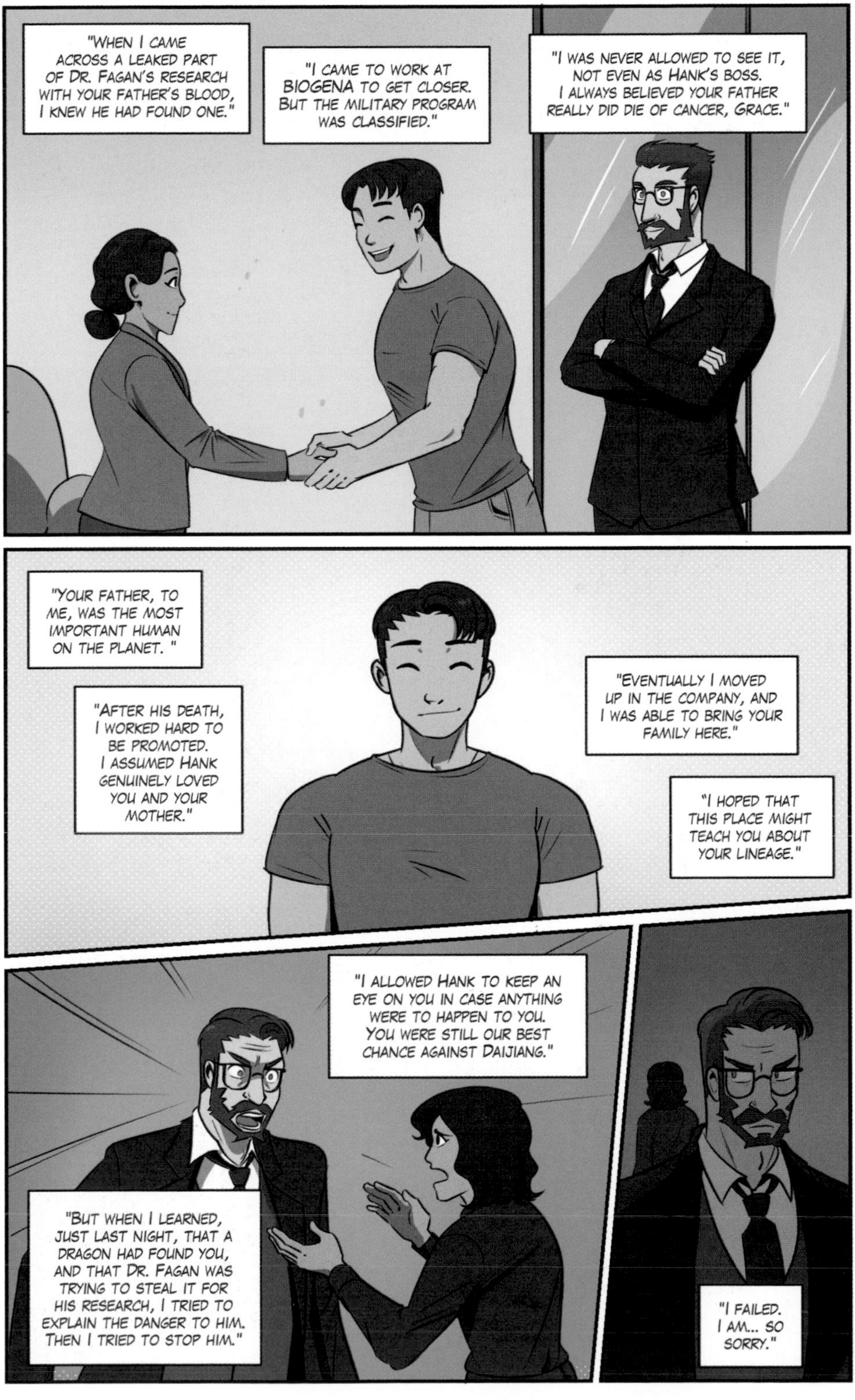
"WHEN I CAME ACROSS A LEAKED PART OF DR. FAGAN'S RESEARCH WITH YOUR FATHER'S BLOOD, I KNEW HE HAD FOUND ONE."
"I CAME TO WORK AT BIOGENA TO GET CLOSER. BUT THE MILITARY PROGRAM WAS CLASSIFIED."
"I WAS NEVER ALLOWED TO SEE IT, NOT EVEN AS HANK'S BOSS. I ALWAYS BELIEVED YOUR FATHER REALLY DID DIE OF CANCER, GRACE."
"YOUR FATHER, TO ME, WAS THE MOST IMPORTANT HUMAN ON THE PLANET. "
"AFTER HIS DEATH, I WORKED HARD TO BE PROMOTED. I ASSUMED HANK GENUINELY LOVED YOU AND YOUR MOTHER."
"EVENTUALLY I MOVED UP IN THE COMPANY, AND I WAS ABLE TO BRING YOUR FAMILY HERE."
"I HOPED THAT THIS PLACE MIGHT TEACH YOU ABOUT YOUR LINEAGE."
"I ALLOWED HANK TO KEEP AN EYE ON YOU IN CASE ANYTHING WERE TO HAPPEN TO YOU. YOU WERE STILL OUR BEST CHANCE AGAINST DAIJIANG."
"BUT WHEN I LEARNED, JUST LAST NIGHT, THAT A DRAGON HAD FOUND YOU, AND THAT DR. FAGAN WAS TRYING TO STEAL IT FOR HIS RESEARCH, I TRIED TO EXPLAIN THE DANGER TO HIM. THEN I TRIED TO STOP HIM."
"I FAILED. I AM... SO SORRY."

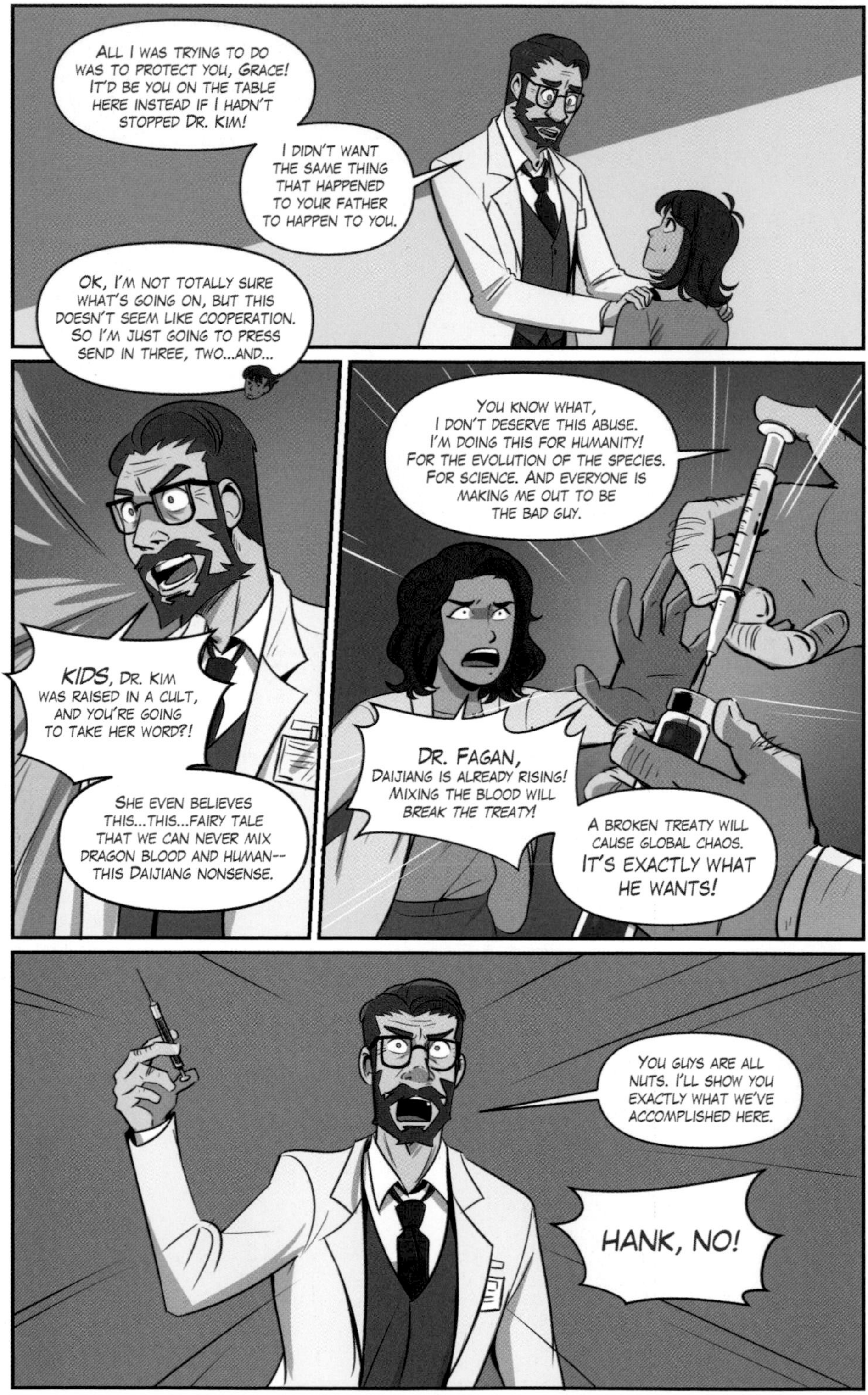
ALL I WAS TRYING TO DO WAS TO PROTECT YOU, GRACE! IT'D BE YOU ON THE TABLE HERE INSTEAD IF I HADN'T STOPPED DR. KIM!
I DIDN'T WANT THE SAME THING THAT HAPPENED TO YOUR FATHER TO HAPPEN TO YOU.
OK, I'M NOT TOTALLY SURE WHAT'S GOING ON, BUT THIS DOESN'T SEEM LIKE COOPERATION. SO I'M JUST GOING TO PRESS SEND IN THREE, TWO...AND...
KIDS, DR. KIM WAS RAISED IN A CULT, AND YOU'RE GOING TO TAKE HER WORD?!
SHE EVEN BELIEVES THIS...THIS...FAIRY TALE THAT WE CAN NEVER MIX DRAGON BLOOD AND HUMAN--THIS DAIJIANG NONSENSE.
YOU KNOW WHAT, I DON'T DESERVE THIS ABUSE. I'M DOING THIS FOR HUMANITY! FOR THE EVOLUTION OF THE SPECIES. FOR SCIENCE. AND EVERYONE IS MAKING ME OUT TO BE THE BAD GUY.
DR. FAGAN, DAIJIANG IS ALREADY RISING! MIXING THE BLOOD WILL BREAK THE TREATY!
A BROKEN TREATY WILL CAUSE GLOBAL CHAOS. IT'S EXACTLY WHAT HE WANTS!
YOU GUYS ARE ALL NUTS. I'LL SHOW YOU EXACTLY WHAT WE'VE ACCOMPLISHED HERE.
HANK, NO!

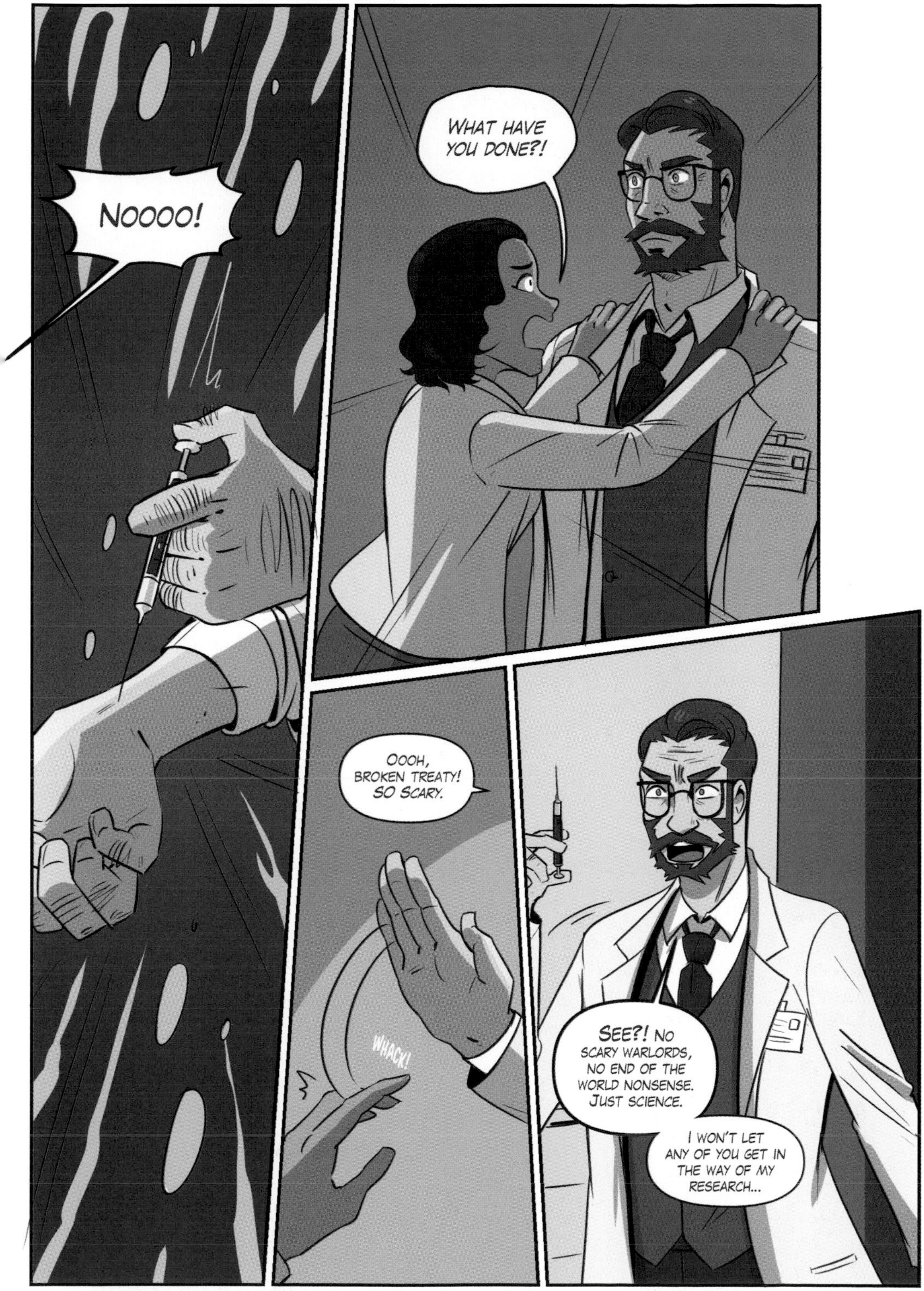
NOOOO!
WHAT HAVE YOU DONE?!
OOOH, BROKEN TREATY! SO SCARY.
WHACK!
SEE?! NO SCARY WARLORDS, NO END OF THE WORLD NONSENSE. JUST SCIENCE.
I WON'T LET ANY OF YOU GET IN THE WAY OF MY RESEARCH...

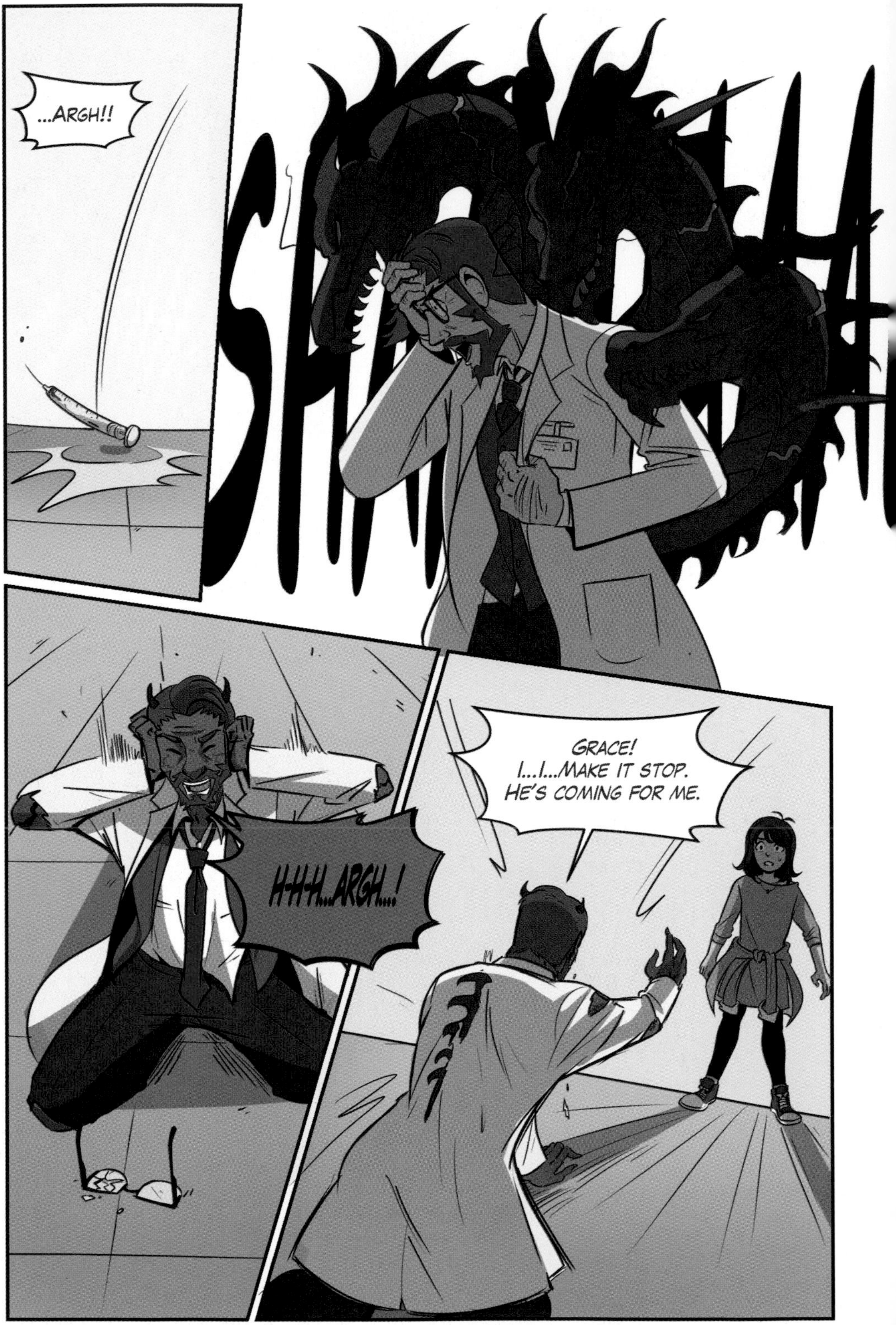
...ARGH!!
SPHAA
H-H-H...ARGH...!
GRACE!
I...I...MAKE IT STOP.
HE'S COMING FOR ME.

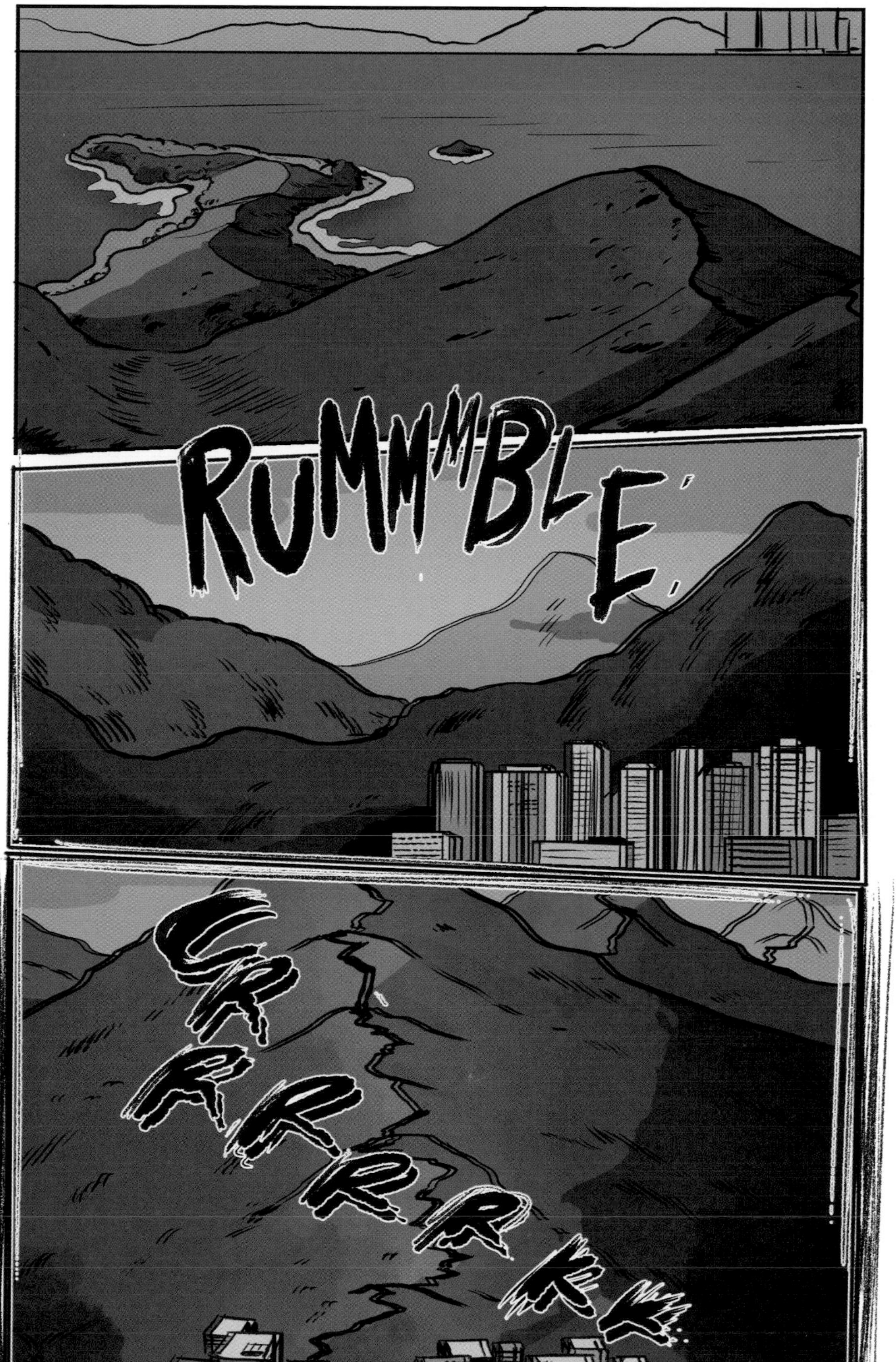
RUMMMBLE
CRRRRRKK

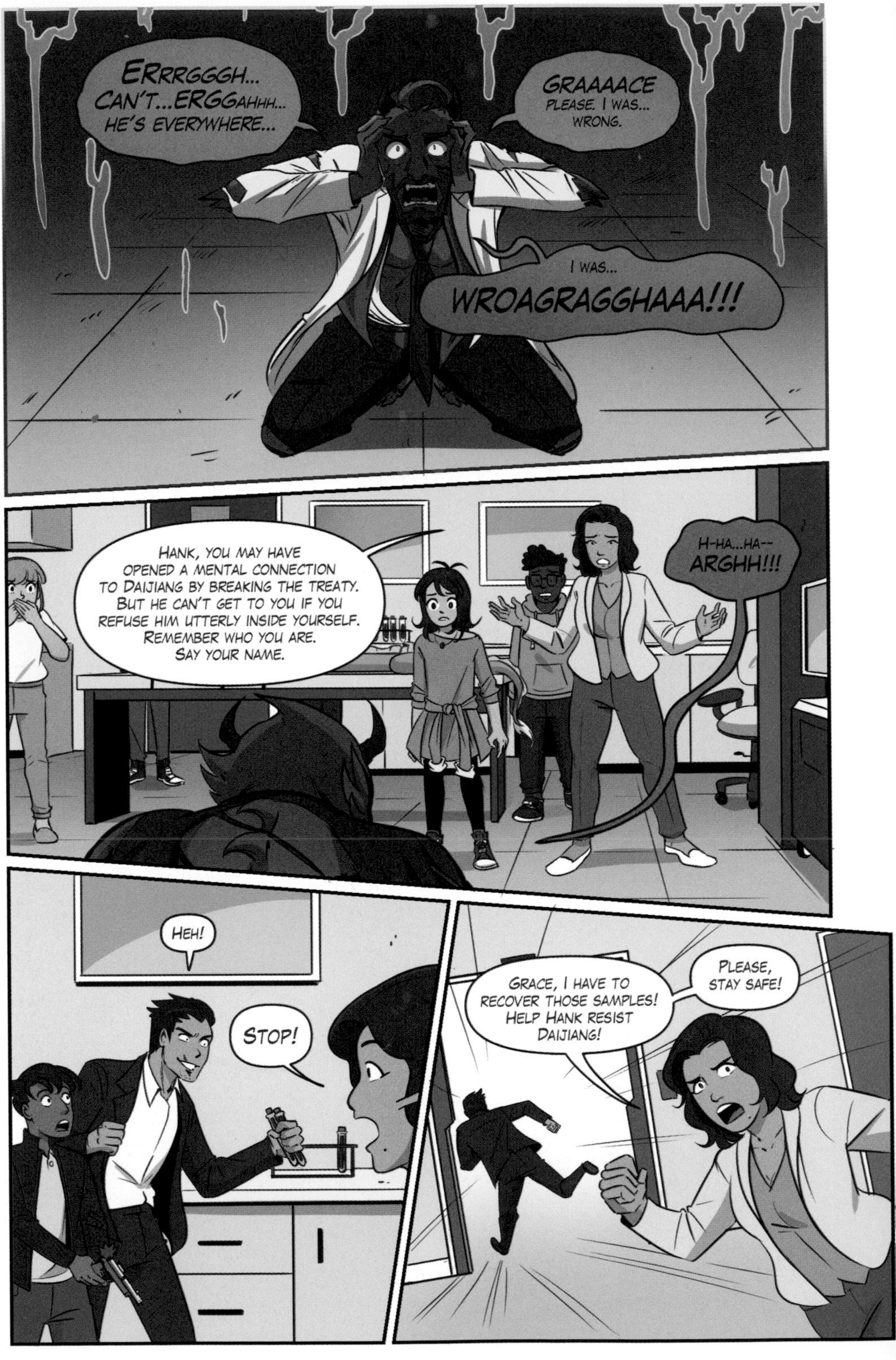
ERRRGGGH... CAN'T...ERGGAHHH... HE'S EVERYWHERE...
GRAAAACE PLEASE. I WAS... WRONG.
I WAS... WROAGRAGGHAAA!!!
HANK, YOU MAY HAVE OPENED A MENTAL CONNECTION TO DAIJIANG BY BREAKING THE TREATY. BUT HE CAN'T GET TO YOU IF YOU REFUSE HIM UTTERLY INSIDE YOURSELF. REMEMBER WHO YOU ARE. SAY YOUR NAME.
H-HA...HA-- ARGHH!!!
HEH!
STOP!
GRACE, I HAVE TO RECOVER THOSE SAMPLES! HELP HANK RESIST DAIJIANG!
PLEASE, STAY SAFE!

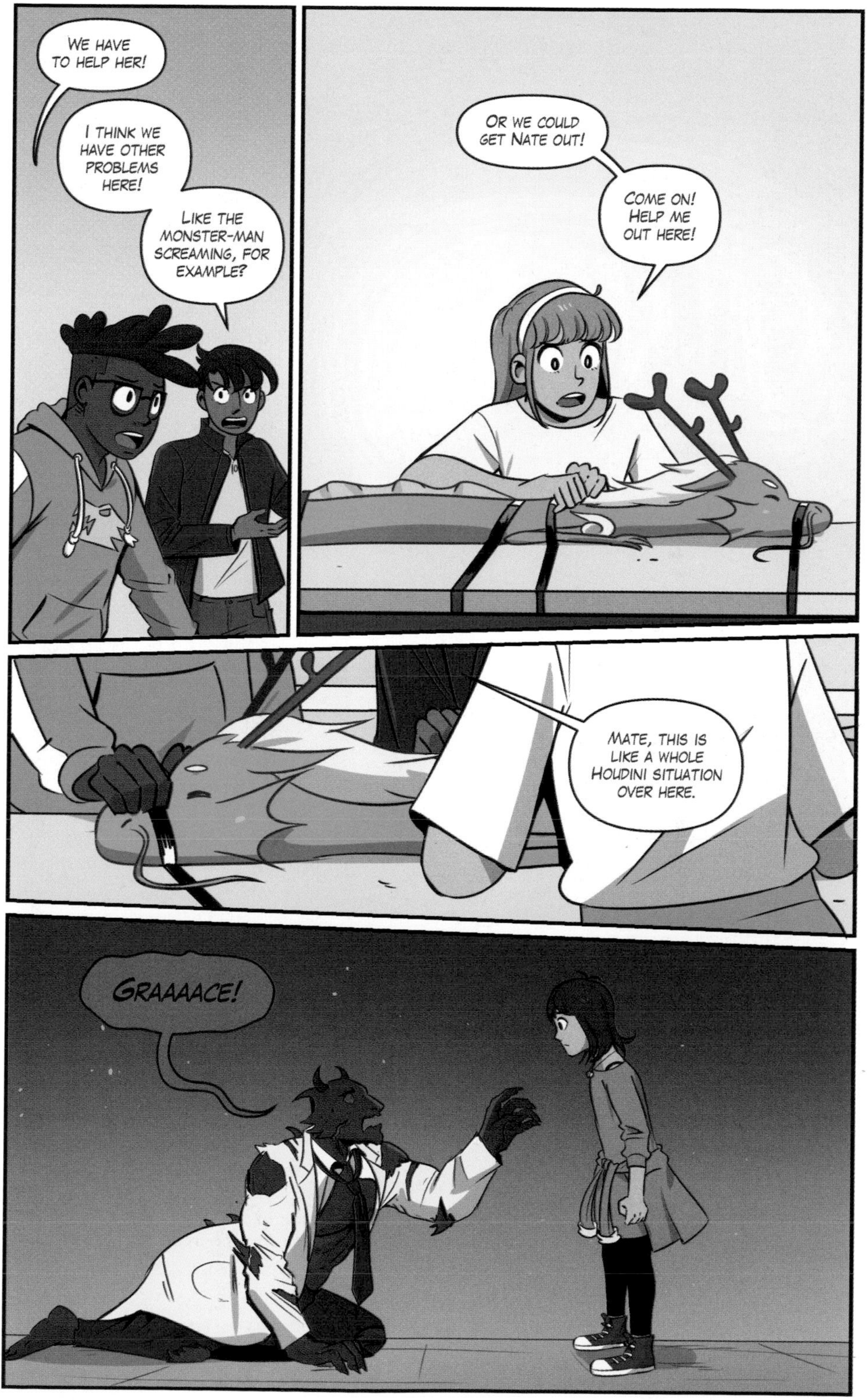
WE HAVE TO HELP HER!
I THINK WE HAVE OTHER PROBLEMS HERE!
LIKE THE MONSTER-MAN SCREAMING, FOR EXAMPLE?
OR WE COULD GET NATE OUT!
COME ON! HELP ME OUT HERE!
MATE, THIS IS LIKE A WHOLE HOUDINI SITUATION OVER HERE.
GRAAAACE!

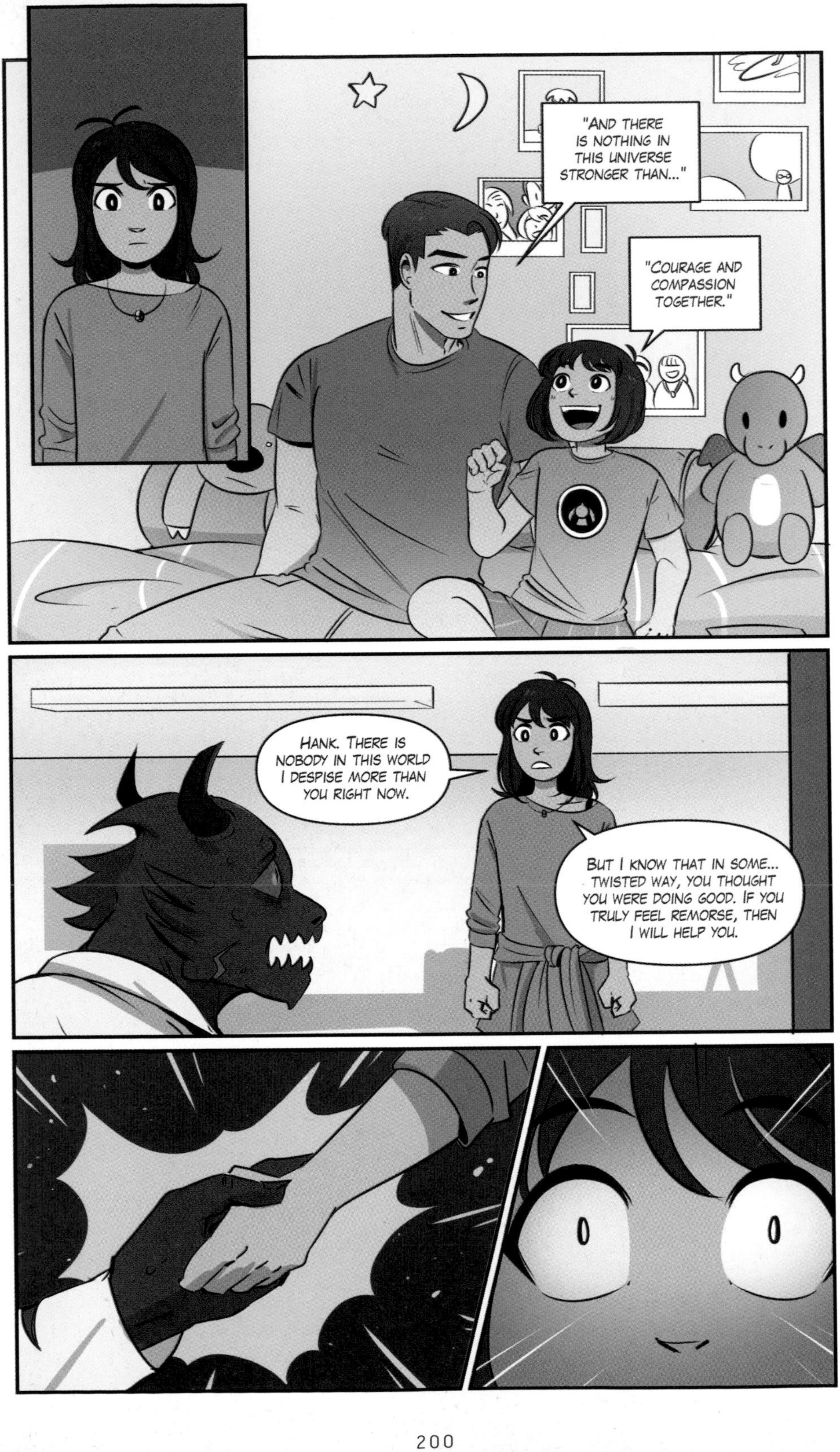
"AND THERE IS NOTHING IN THIS UNIVERSE STRONGER THAN..."
"COURAGE AND COMPASSION TOGETHER."
HANK. THERE IS NOBODY IN THIS WORLD I DESPISE MORE THAN YOU RIGHT NOW.
BUT I KNOW THAT IN SOME... TWISTED WAY, YOU THOUGHT YOU WERE DOING GOOD. IF YOU TRULY FEEL REMORSE, THEN I WILL HELP YOU.

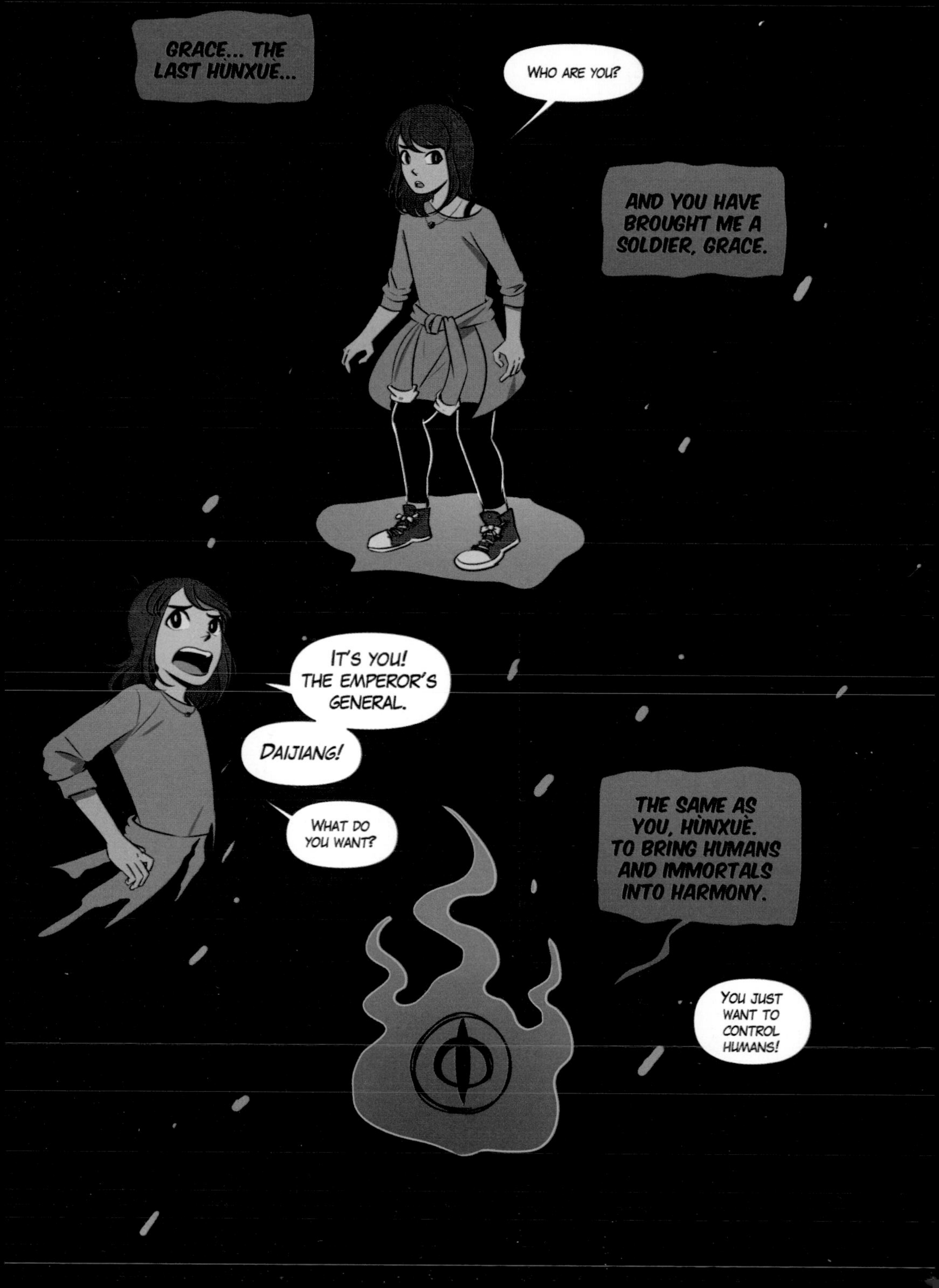
GRACE... THE LAST HÙNXUÈ...
WHO ARE YOU?
AND YOU HAVE BROUGHT ME A SOLDIER, GRACE.
IT'S YOU! THE EMPEROR'S GENERAL.
DAIJIANG!
WHAT DO YOU WANT?
THE SAME AS YOU, HÙNXUÈ. TO BRING HUMANS AND IMMORTALS INTO HARMONY.
YOU JUST WANT TO CONTROL HUMANS!

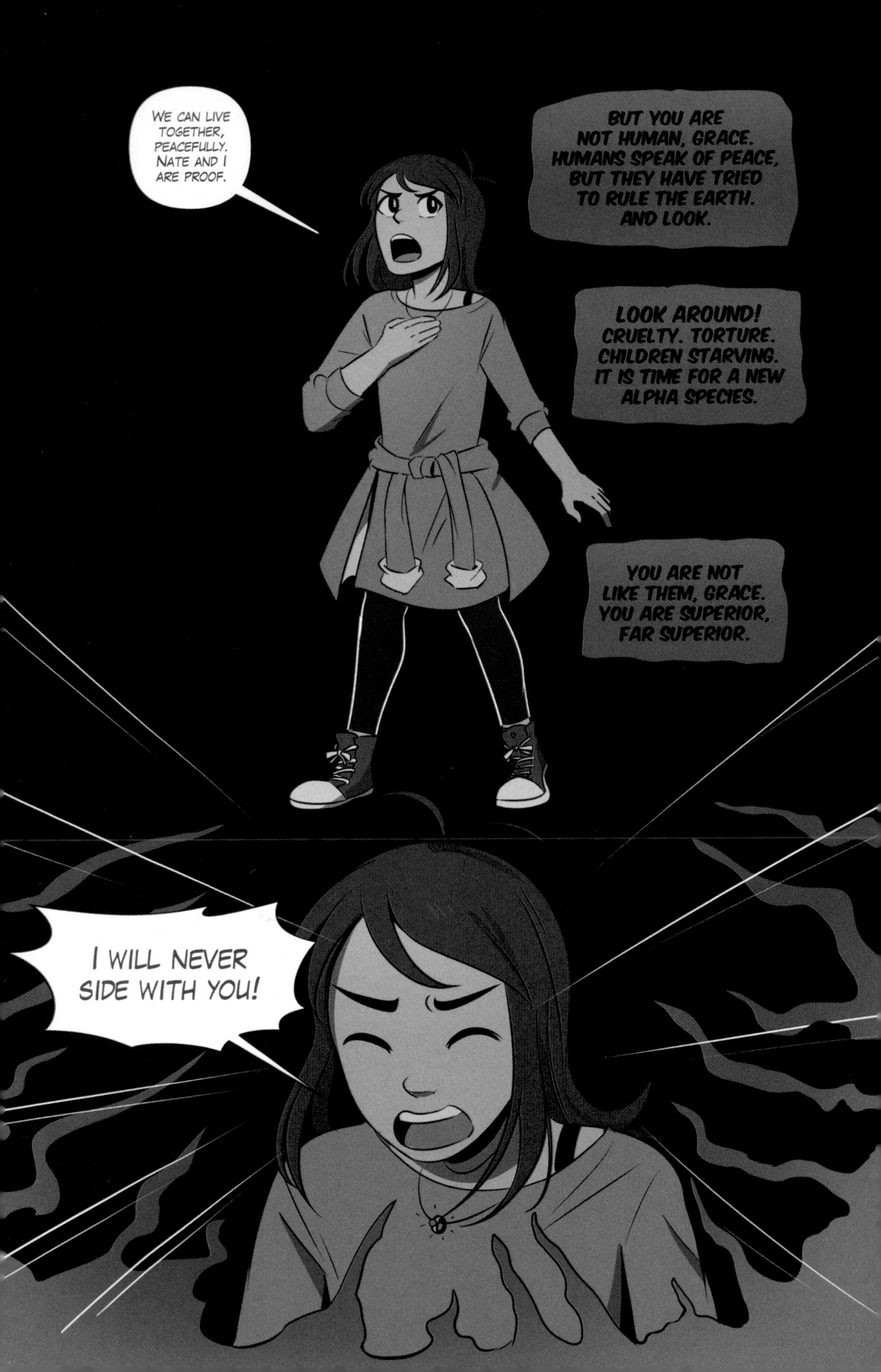
WE CAN LIVE TOGETHER, PEACEFULLY. NATE AND I ARE PROOF.
BUT YOU ARE NOT HUMAN, GRACE. HUMANS SPEAK OF PEACE, BUT THEY HAVE TRIED TO RULE THE EARTH. AND LOOK.
LOOK AROUND! CRUELTY. TORTURE. CHILDREN STARVING. IT IS TIME FOR A NEW ALPHA SPECIES.
YOU ARE NOT LIKE THEM, GRACE. YOU ARE SUPERIOR, FAR SUPERIOR.
I WILL NEVER SIDE WITH YOU!

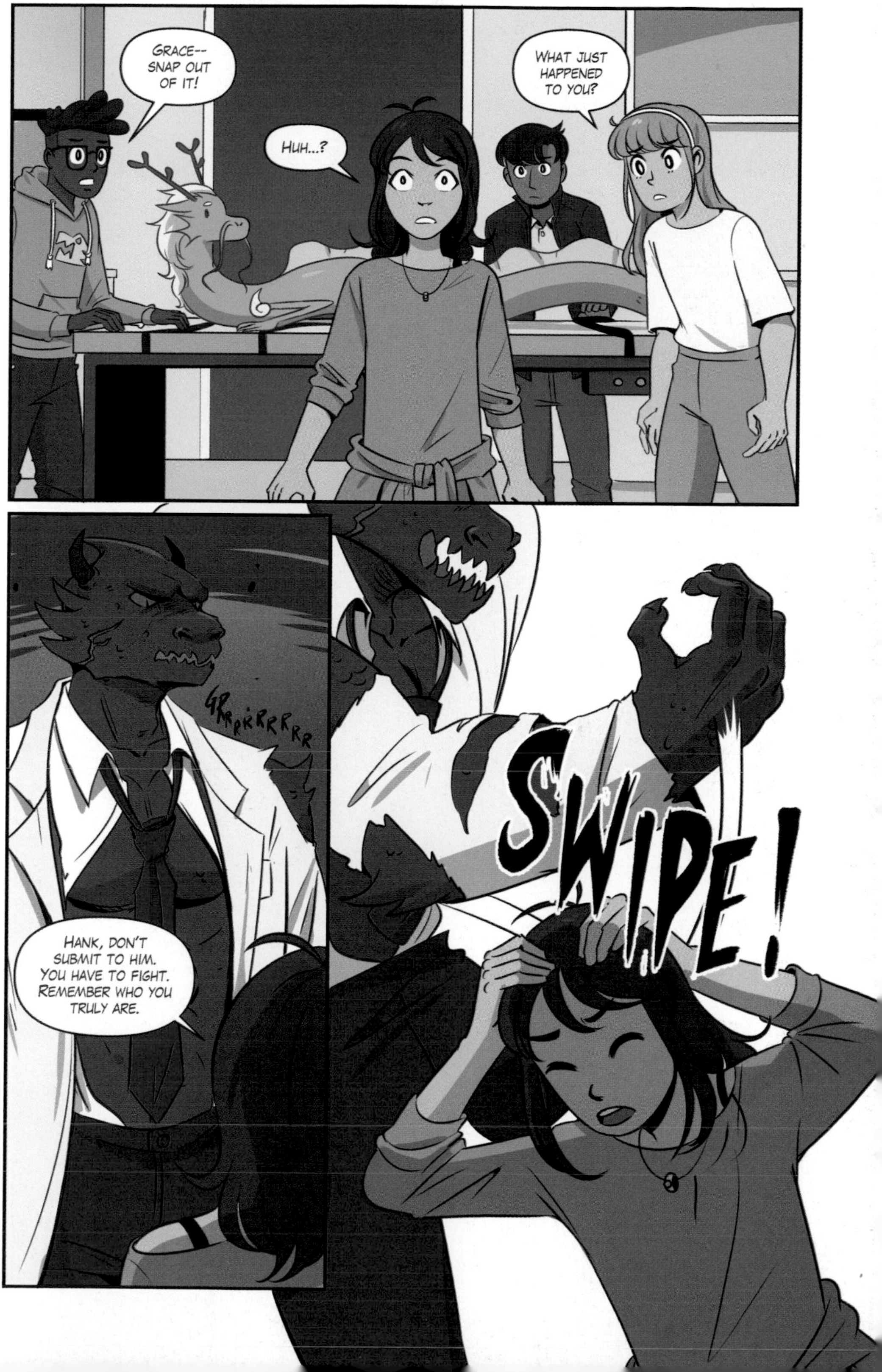
GRACE--
SNAP OUT
OF IT!
HUH...?
WHAT JUST
HAPPENED
TO YOU?
GRRRRRRRRRR
HANK, DON'T
SUBMIT TO HIM.
YOU HAVE TO FIGHT.
REMEMBER WHO YOU
TRULY ARE.
SWIPE!

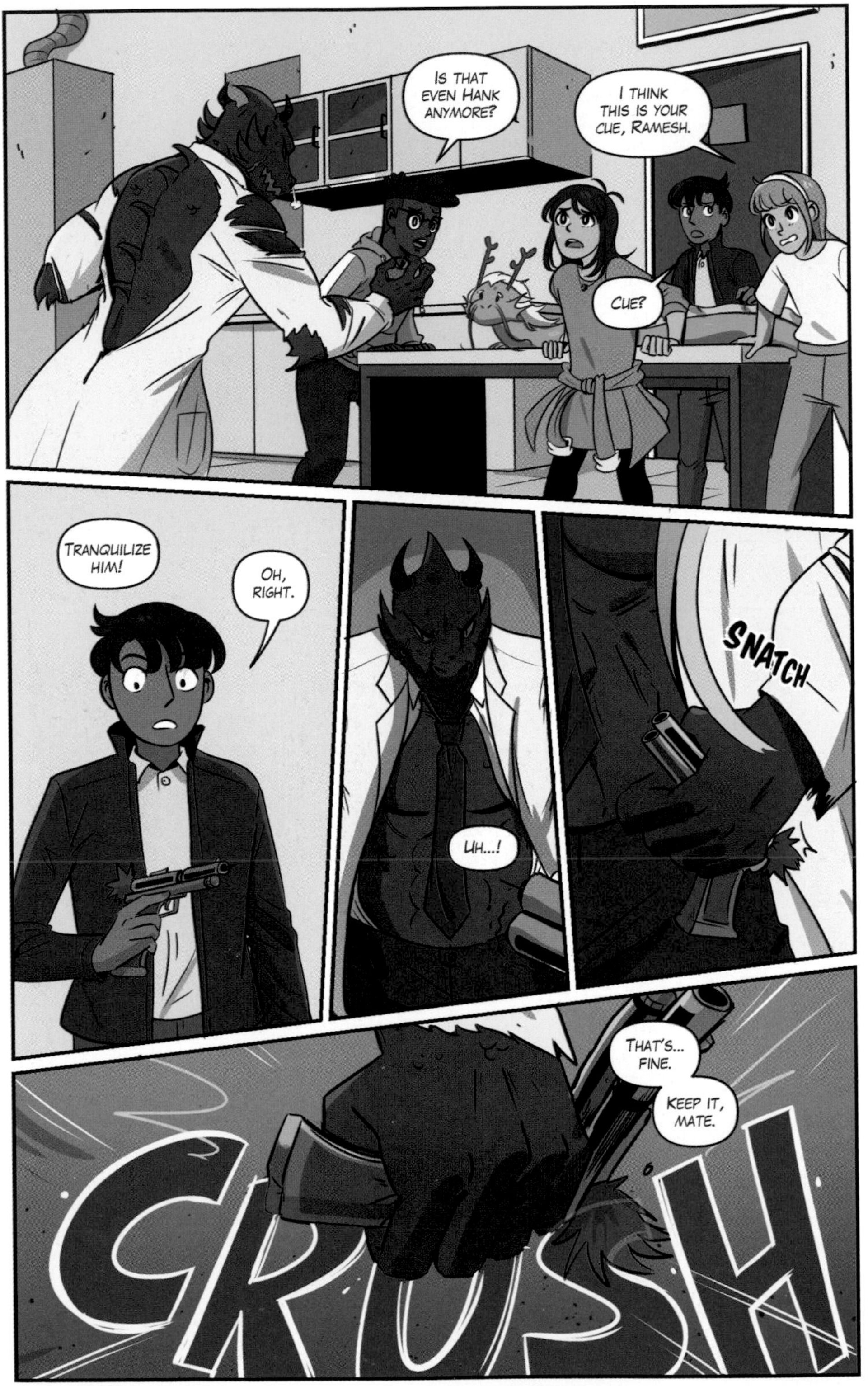

Is that even Hank anymore?
I think this is your cue, Ramesh.
Cue?
Tranquilize him!
Oh, right.
Uh...!
SNATCH
That's... fine.
Keep it, mate.
CRUSH

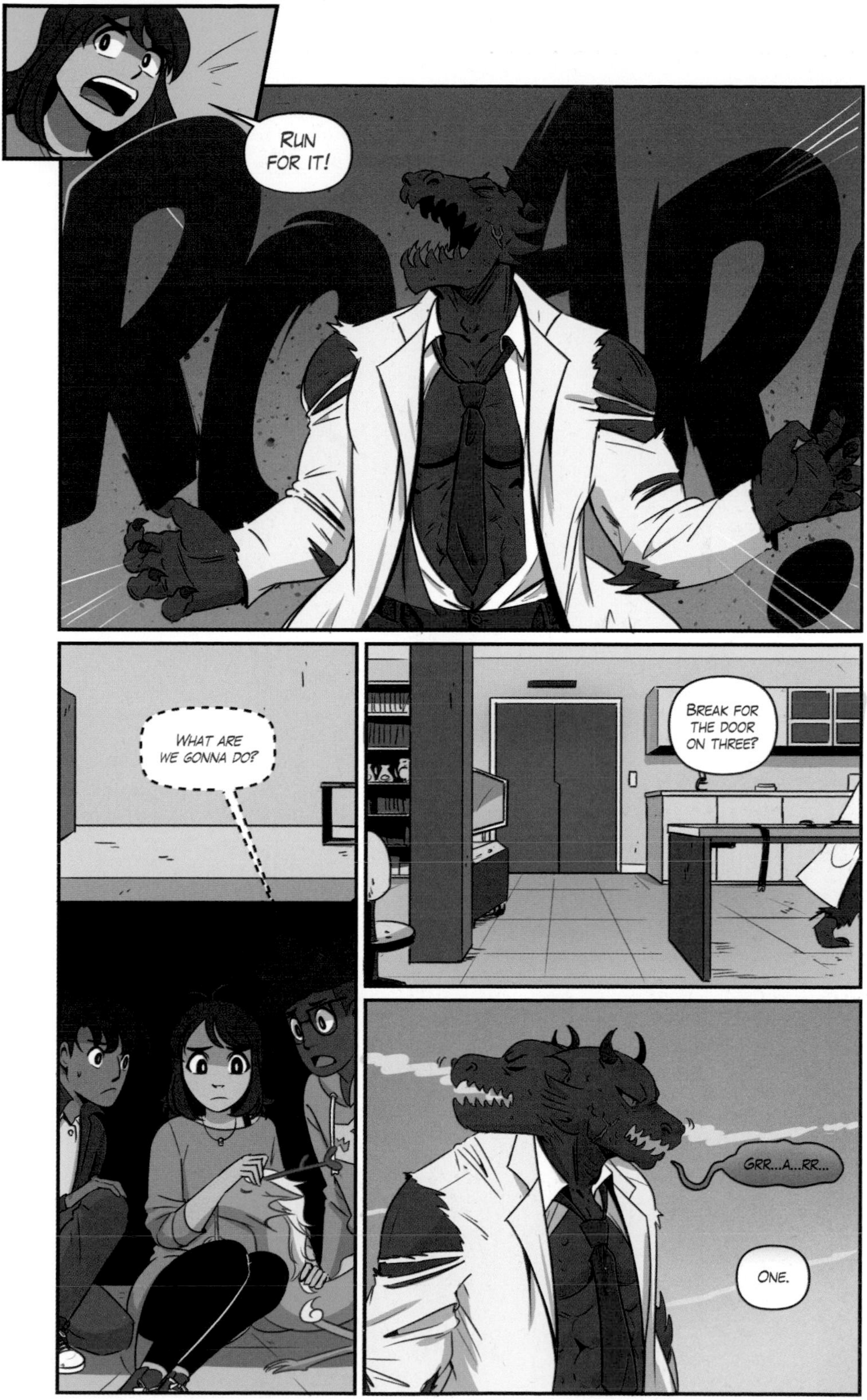
RUN FOR IT!
ROAR!
WHAT ARE WE GONNA DO?
BREAK FOR THE DOOR ON THREE?
GRR...A...RR...
ONE.

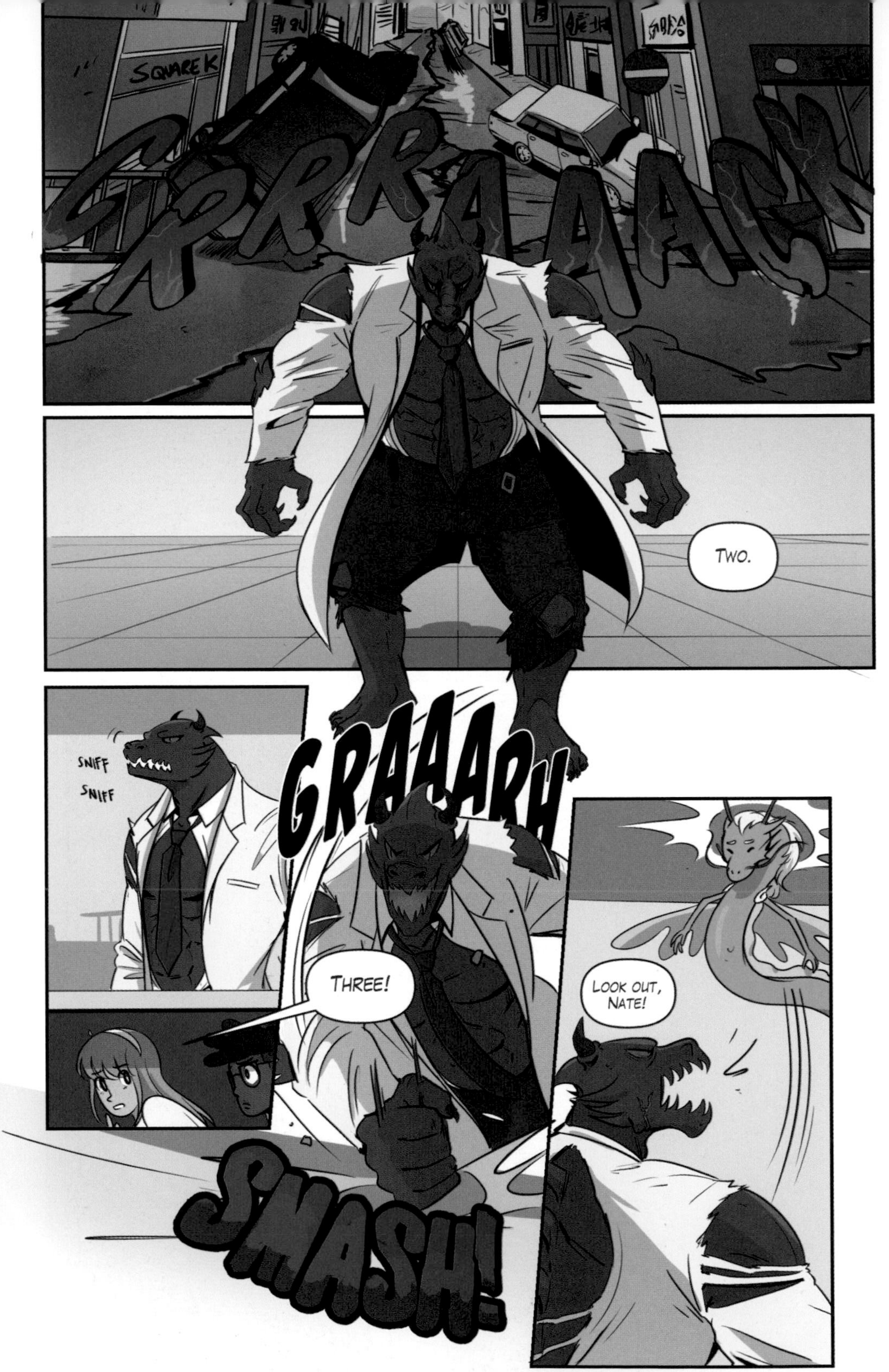
SQUARE K
CRRRAAACK
TWO.
SNIFF
SNIFF
GRAAARH
THREE!
LOOK OUT, NATE!
SMASH!

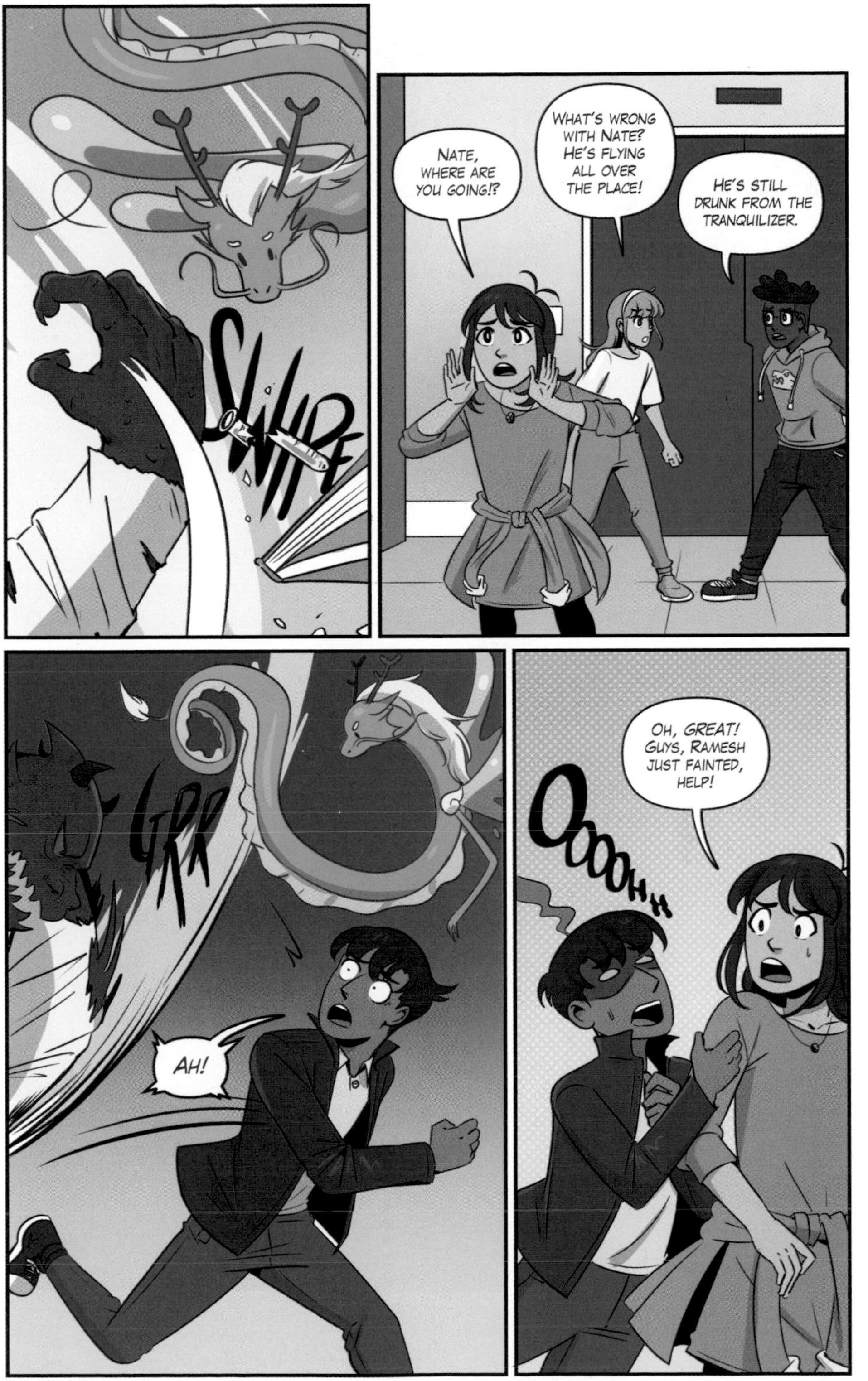
SWIPE
NATE, WHERE ARE YOU GOING!?
WHAT'S WRONG WITH NATE? HE'S FLYING ALL OVER THE PLACE!
HE'S STILL DRUNK FROM THE TRANQUILIZER.
GRR
AH!
OOOOHH
OH, GREAT! GUYS, RAMESH JUST FAINTED, HELP!

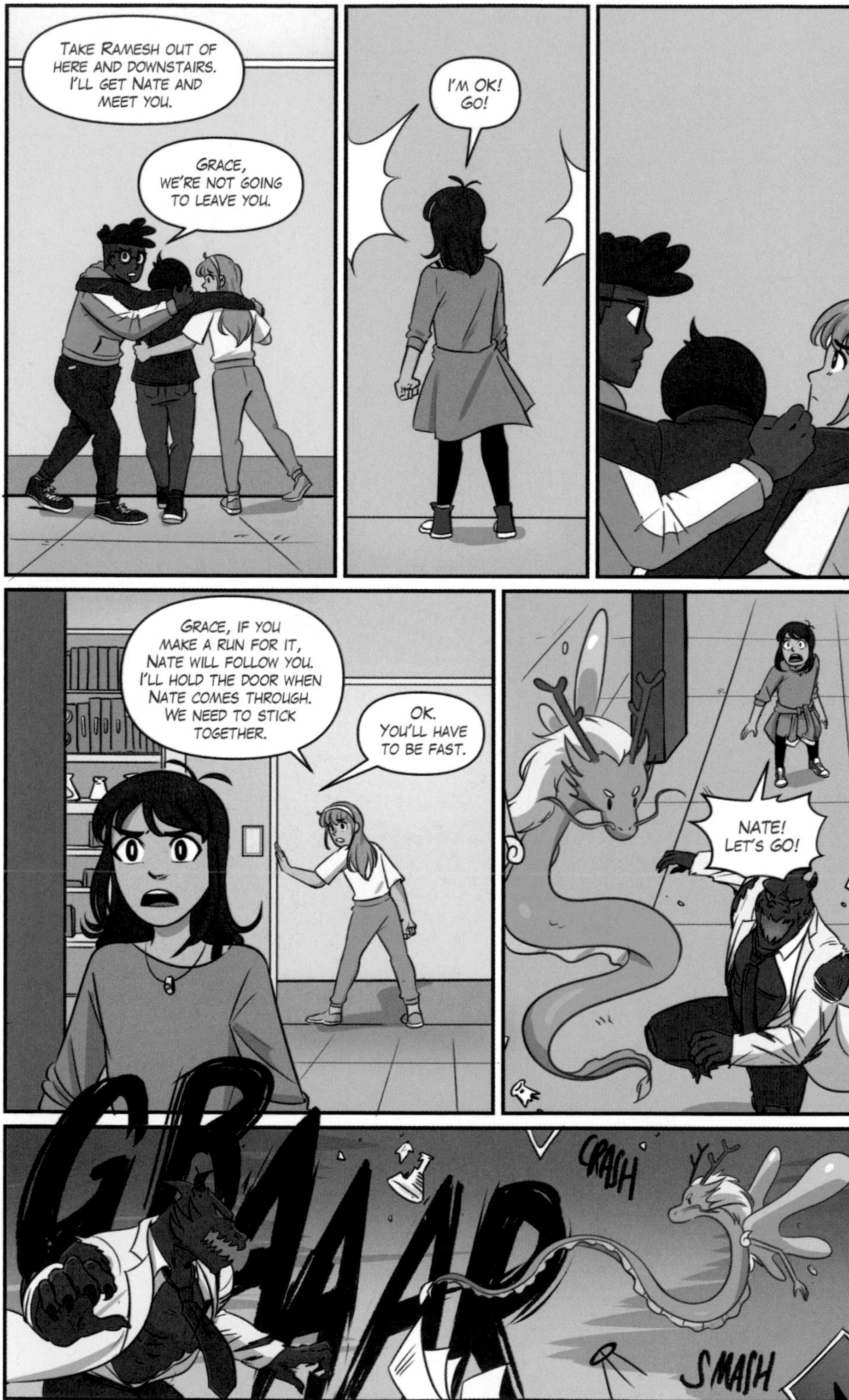
TAKE RAMESH OUT OF HERE AND DOWNSTAIRS. I'LL GET NATE AND MEET YOU.
GRACE, WE'RE NOT GOING TO LEAVE YOU.
I'M OK! GO!
GRACE, IF YOU MAKE A RUN FOR IT, NATE WILL FOLLOW YOU. I'LL HOLD THE DOOR WHEN NATE COMES THROUGH. WE NEED TO STICK TOGETHER.
OK. YOU'LL HAVE TO BE FAST.
NATE! LET'S GO!
GRAAAR
CRASH
SMASH

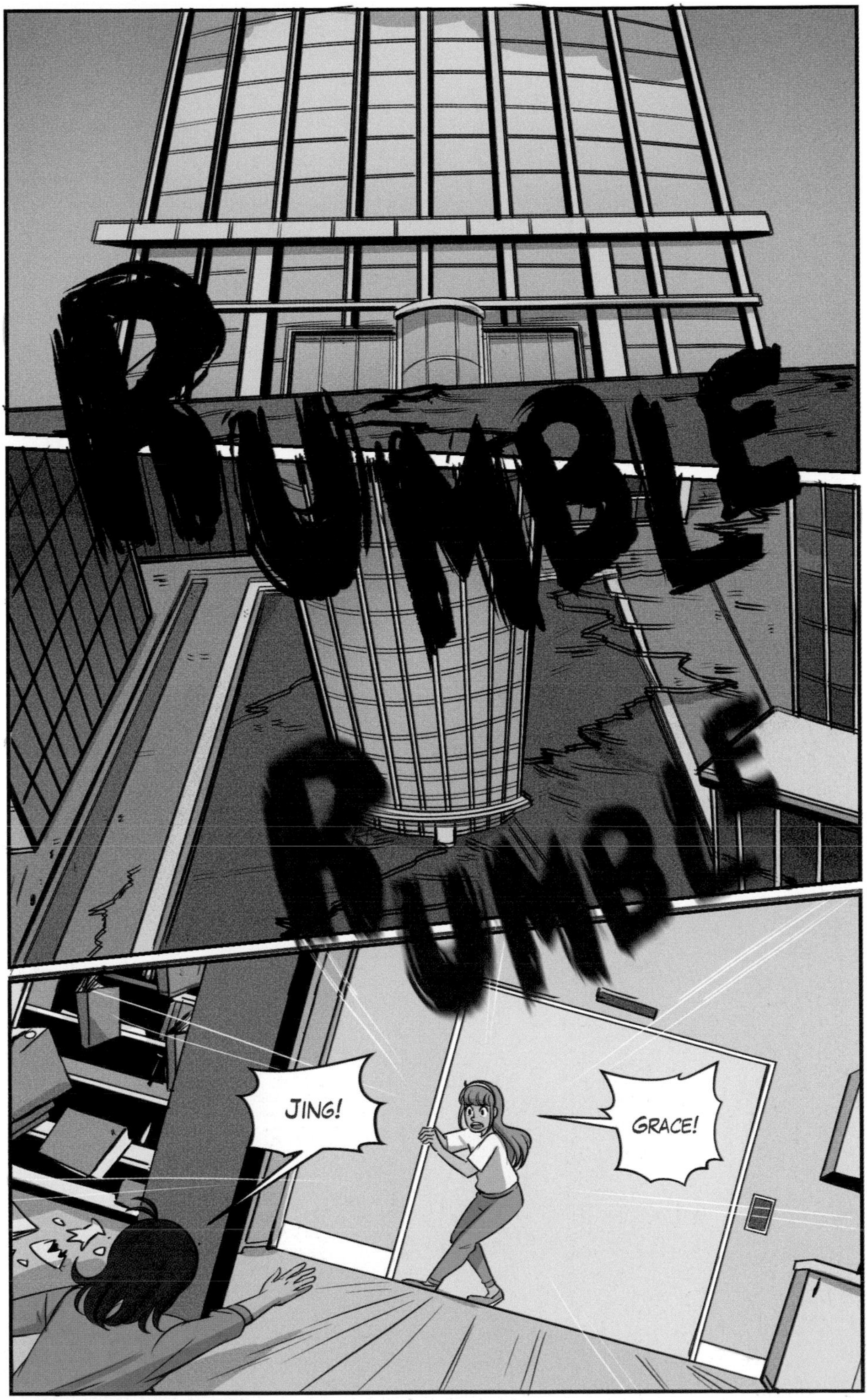
RUMBLE
RUMBLE
JING!
GRACE!

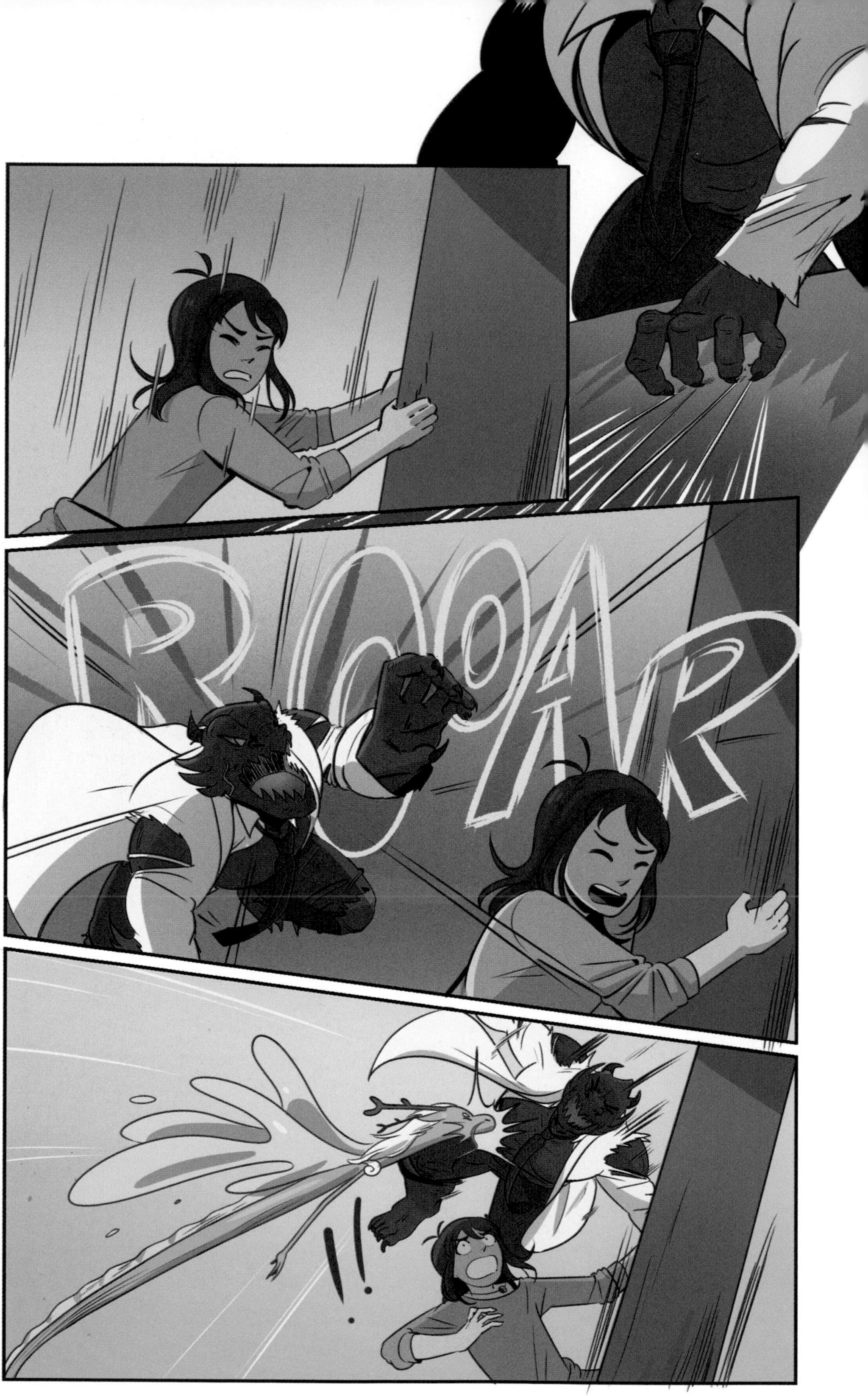
ROOAR
!!

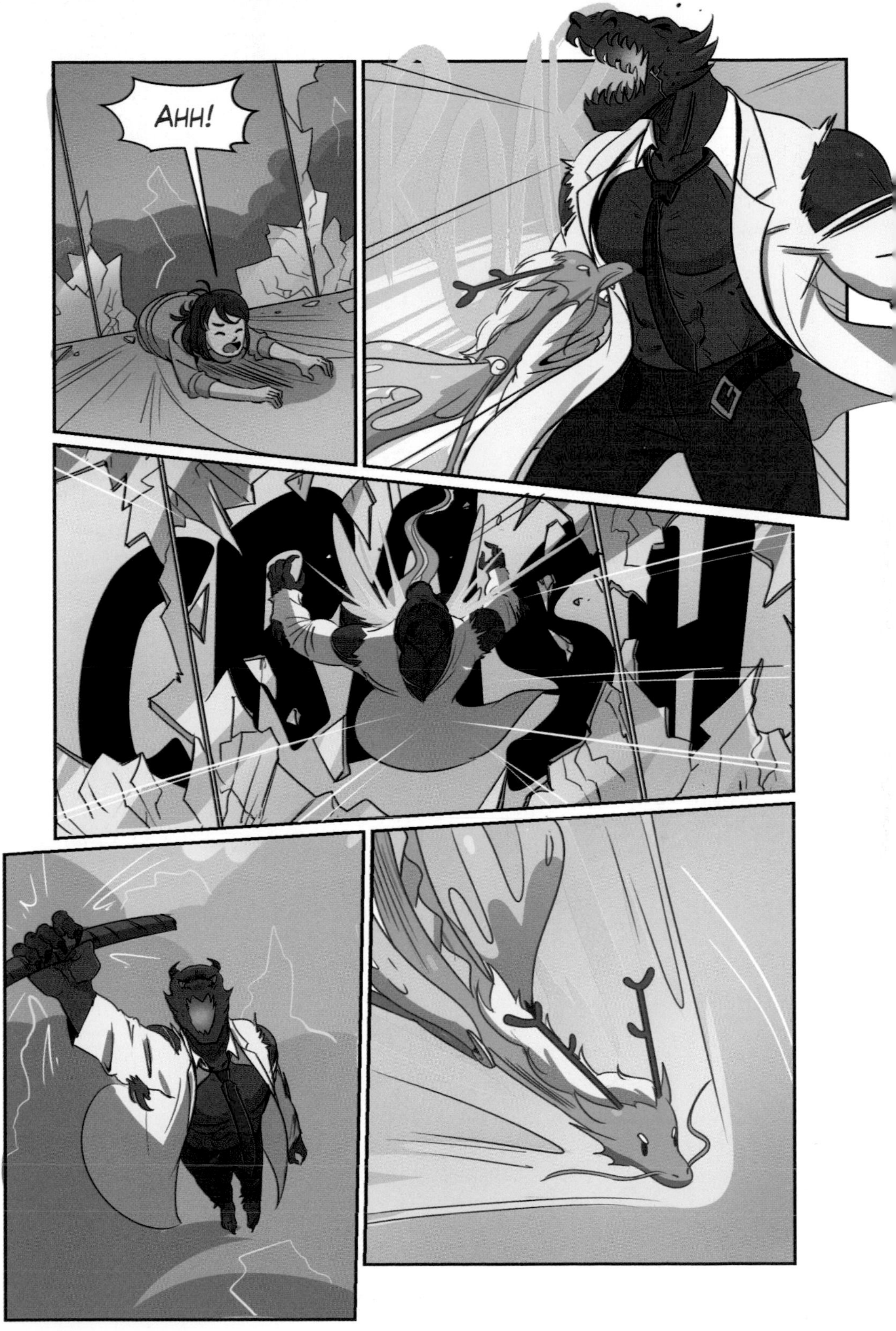
AHH!
ROAR
CRASH

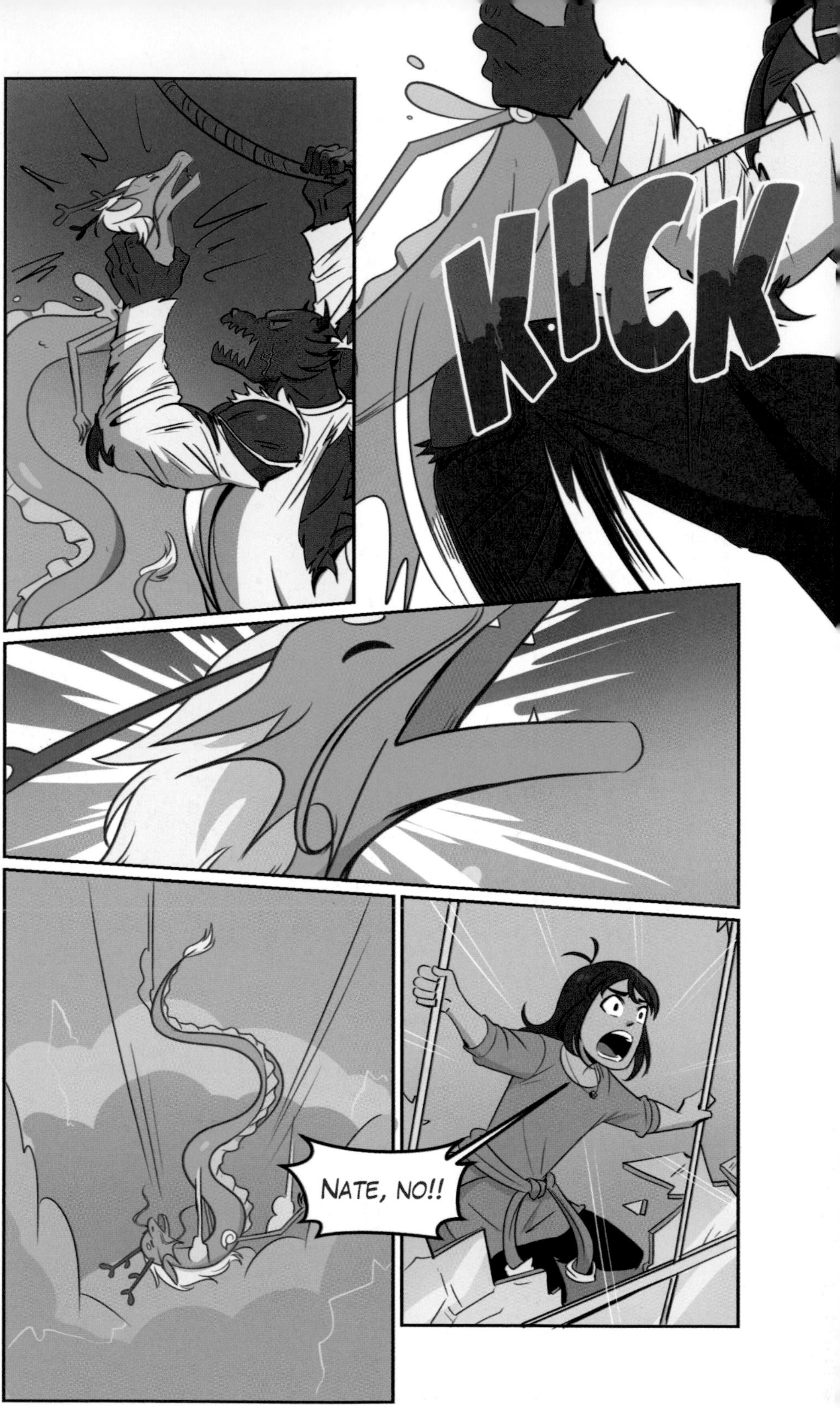
KICK
NATE, NO!!

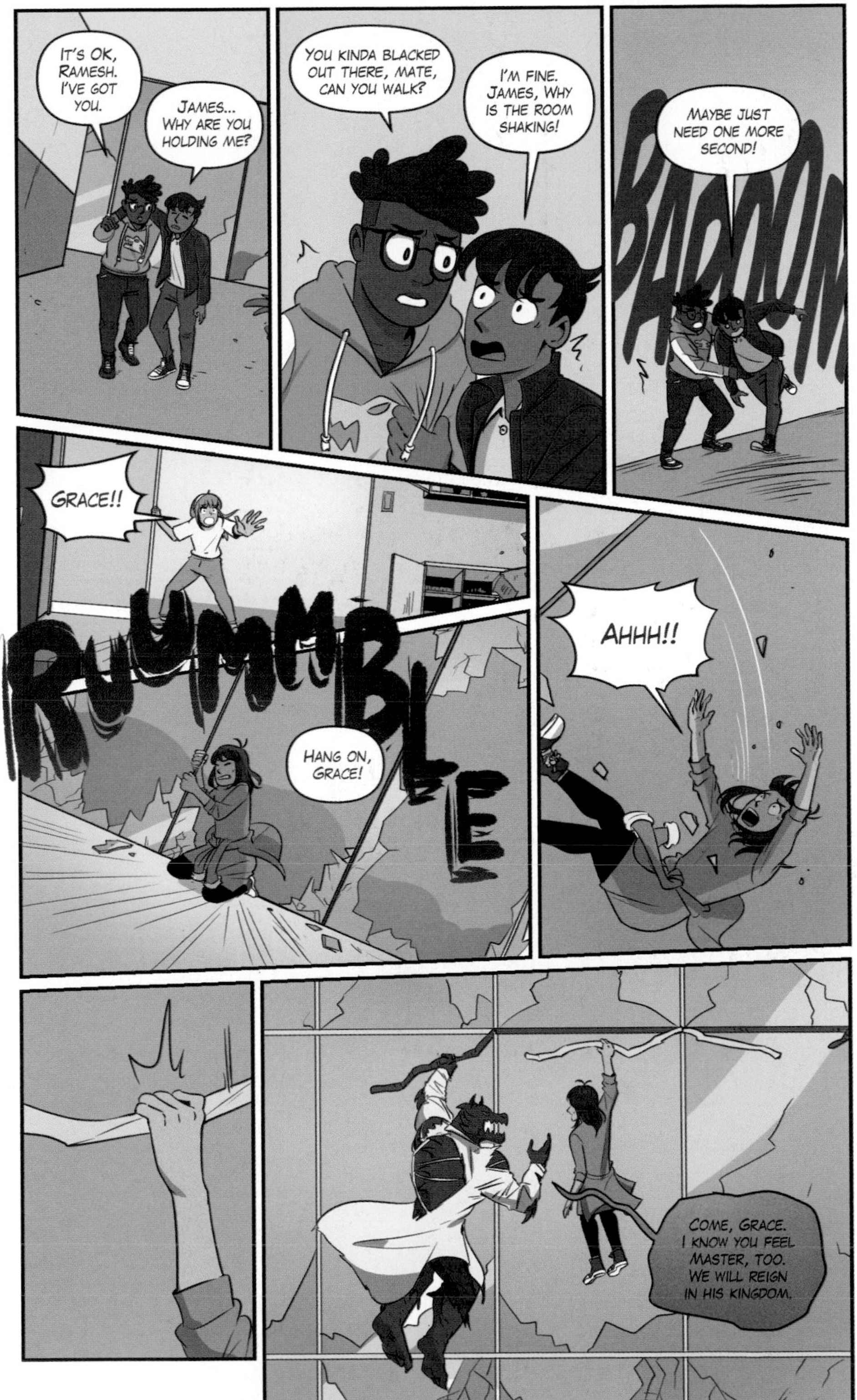
IT'S OK, RAMESH. I'VE GOT YOU.
JAMES... WHY ARE YOU HOLDING ME?
YOU KINDA BLACKED OUT THERE, MATE, CAN YOU WALK?
I'M FINE. JAMES, WHY IS THE ROOM SHAKING!
MAYBE JUST NEED ONE MORE SECOND!
BADOOM
GRACE!!
RUMMBLE
HANG ON, GRACE!
AHHH!!
COME, GRACE. I KNOW YOU FEEL MASTER, TOO. WE WILL REIGN IN HIS KINGDOM.

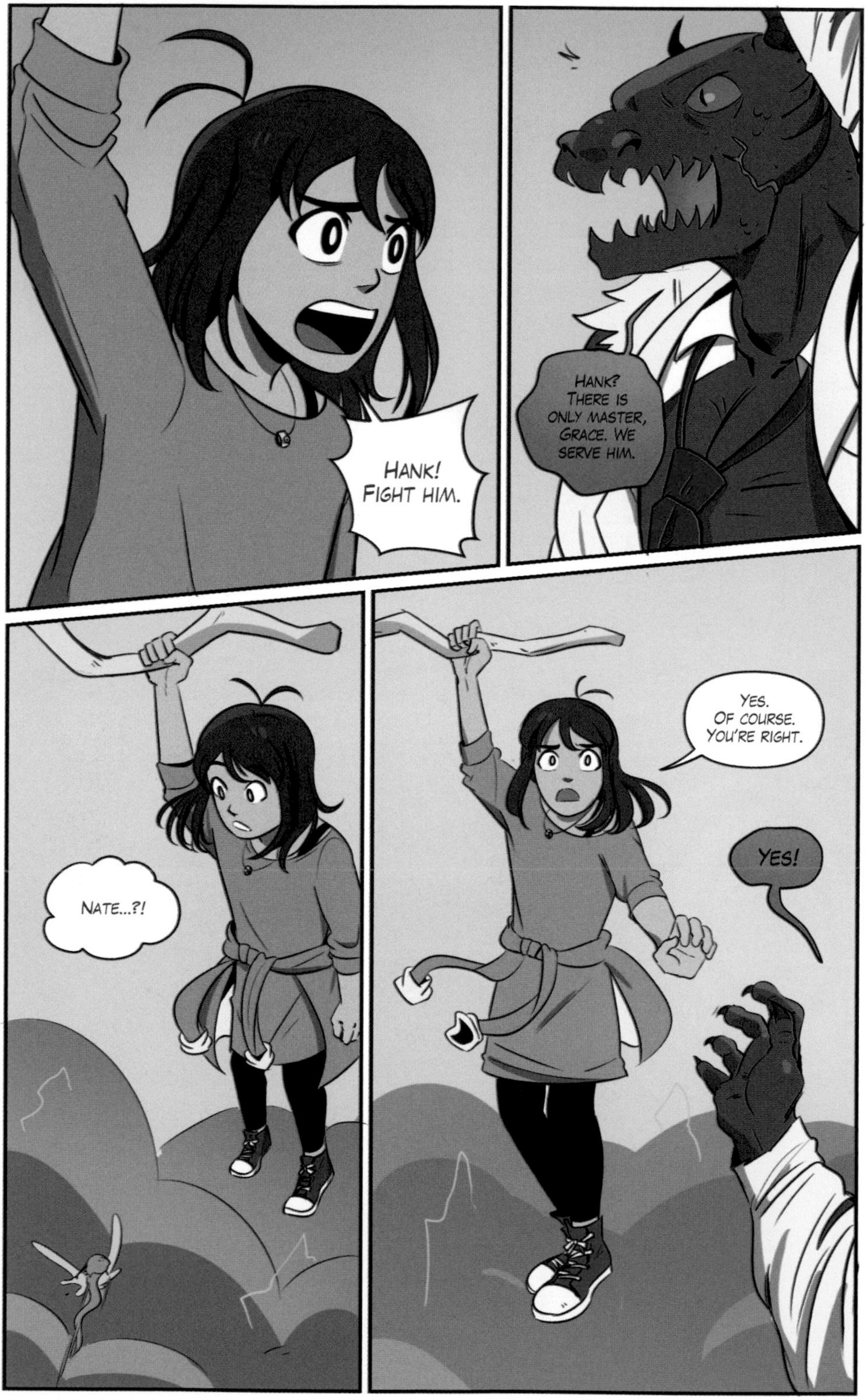
HANK! FIGHT HIM.
HANK? THERE IS ONLY MASTER, GRACE. WE SERVE HIM.
NATE...?!
YES. OF COURSE. YOU'RE RIGHT.
YES!

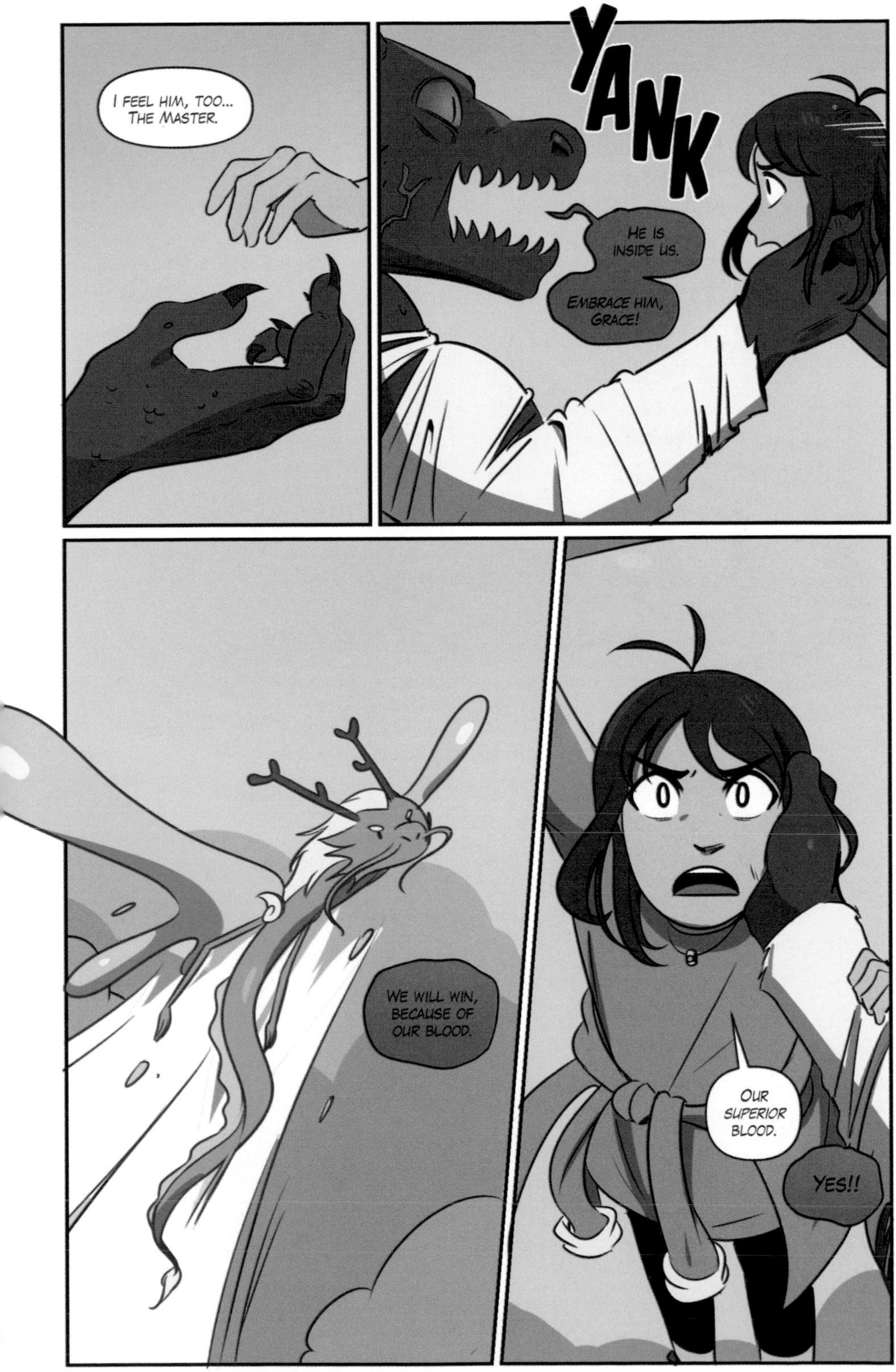
I FEEL HIM, TOO... THE MASTER.
YANK
HE IS INSIDE US.
EMBRACE HIM, GRACE!
WE WILL WIN, BECAUSE OF OUR BLOOD.
OUR SUPERIOR BLOOD.
YES!!

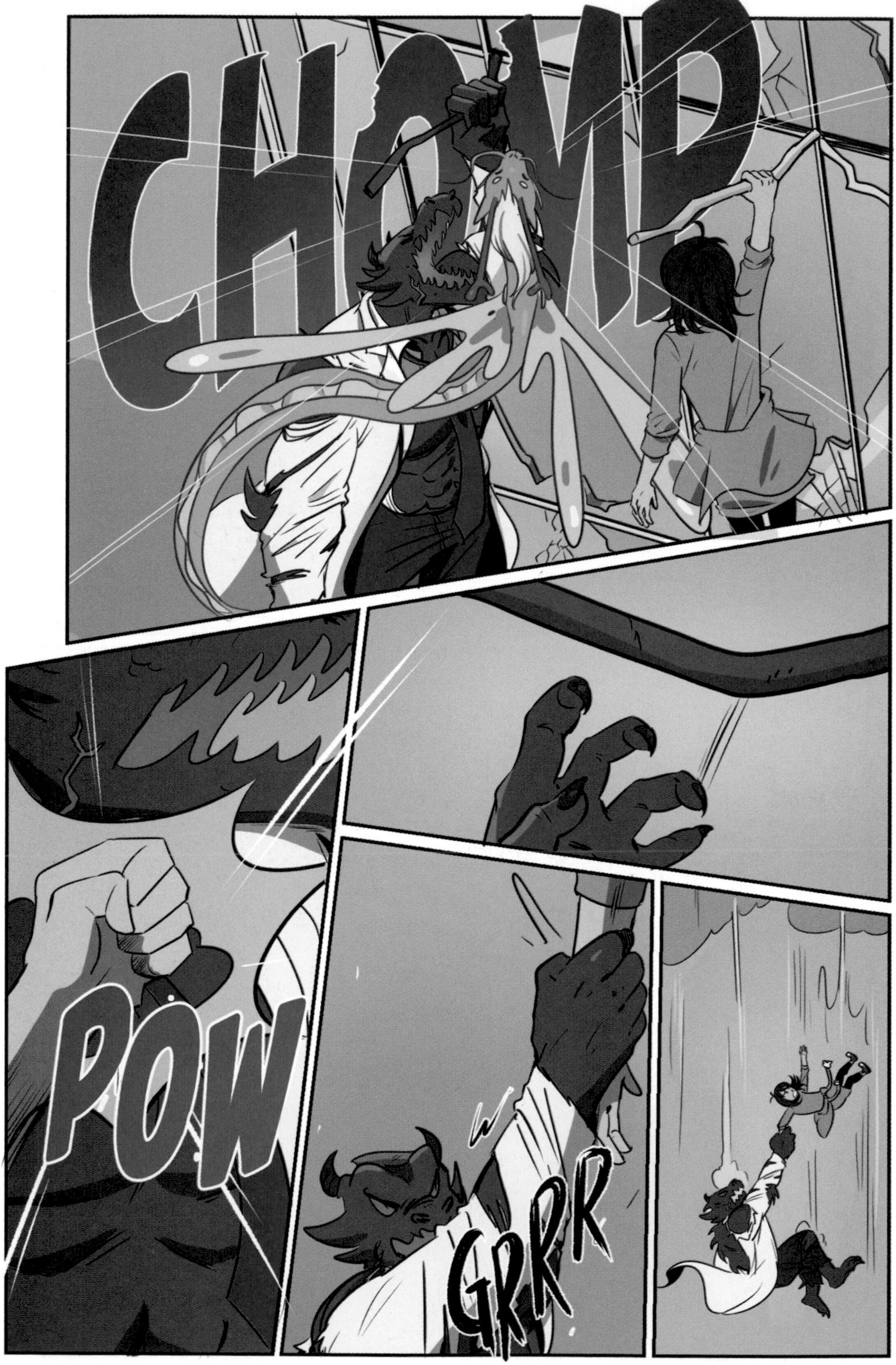
CHOMP
POW
GRRR

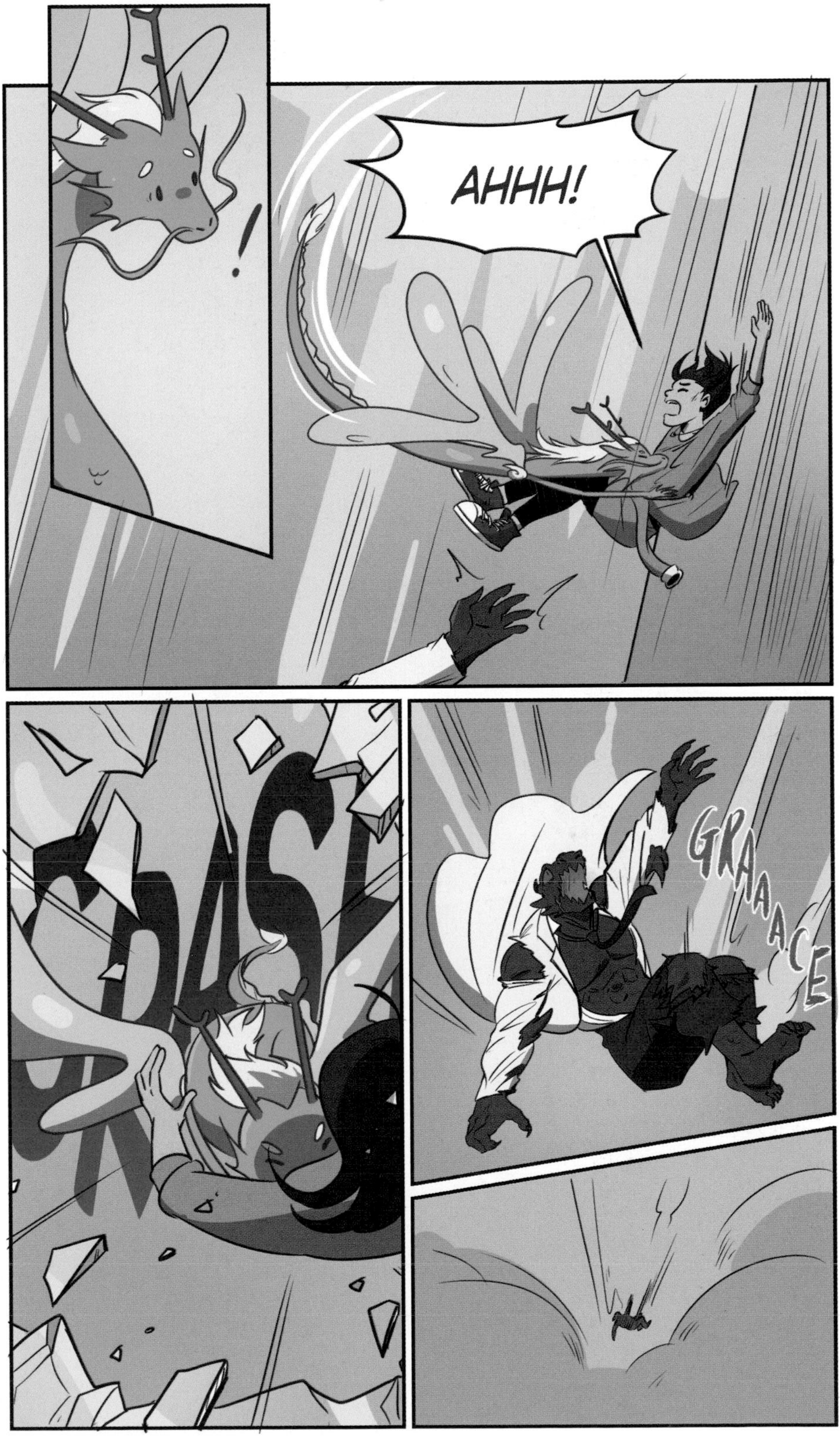
AHHH!
!
GRAAAACE

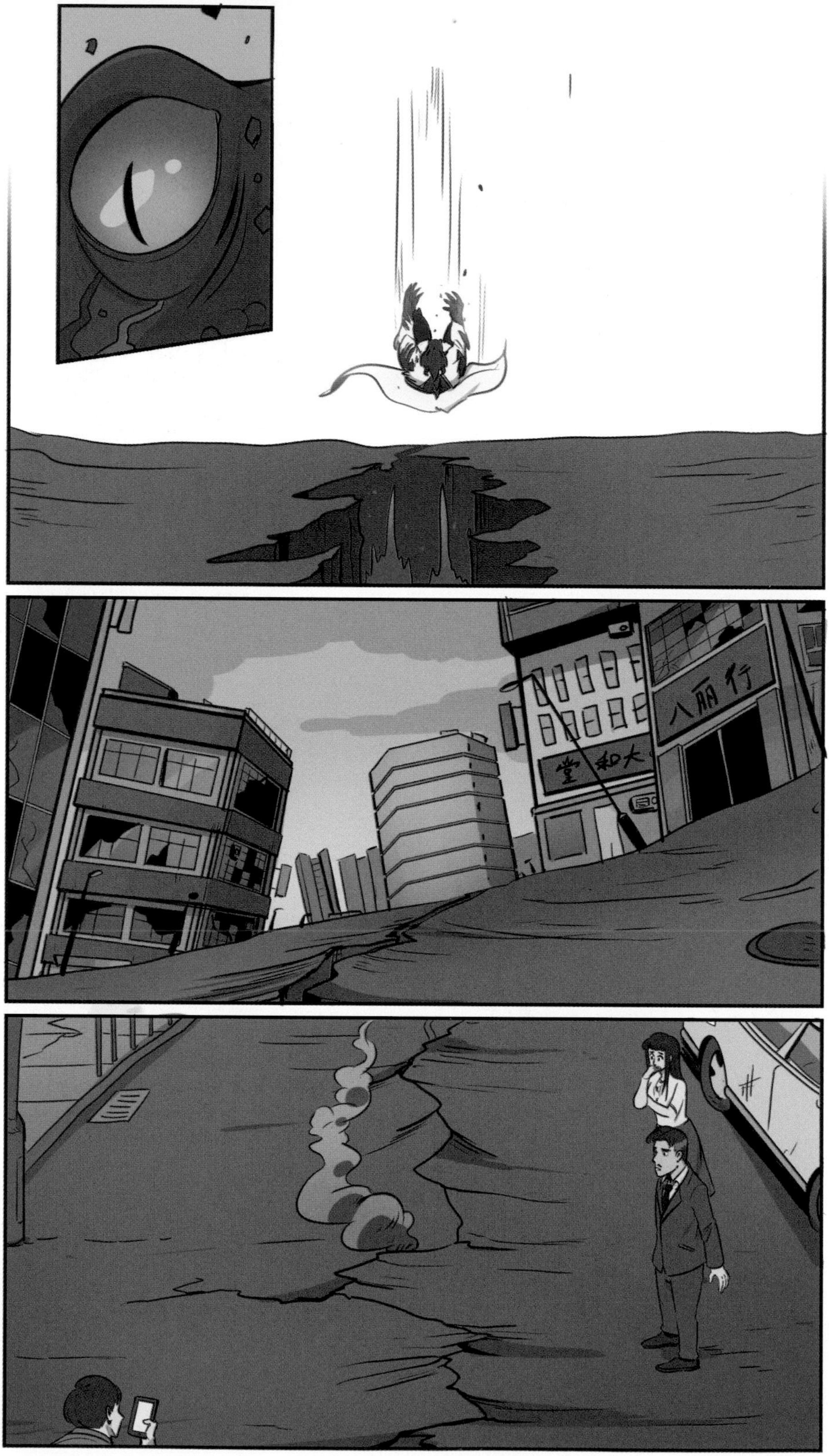
堂和大

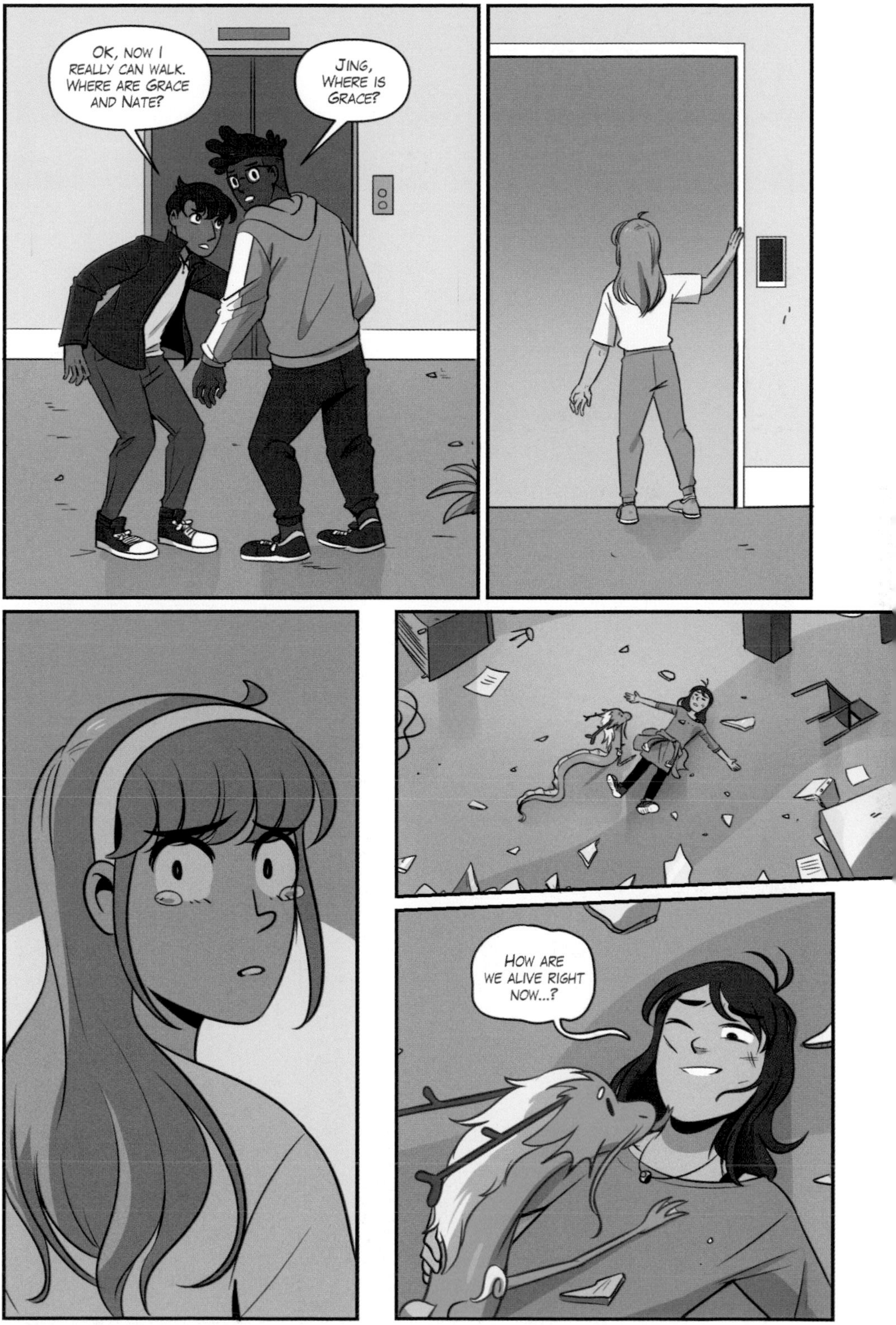
OK, NOW I REALLY CAN WALK. WHERE ARE GRACE AND NATE?
JING, WHERE IS GRACE?
HOW ARE WE ALIVE RIGHT NOW...?

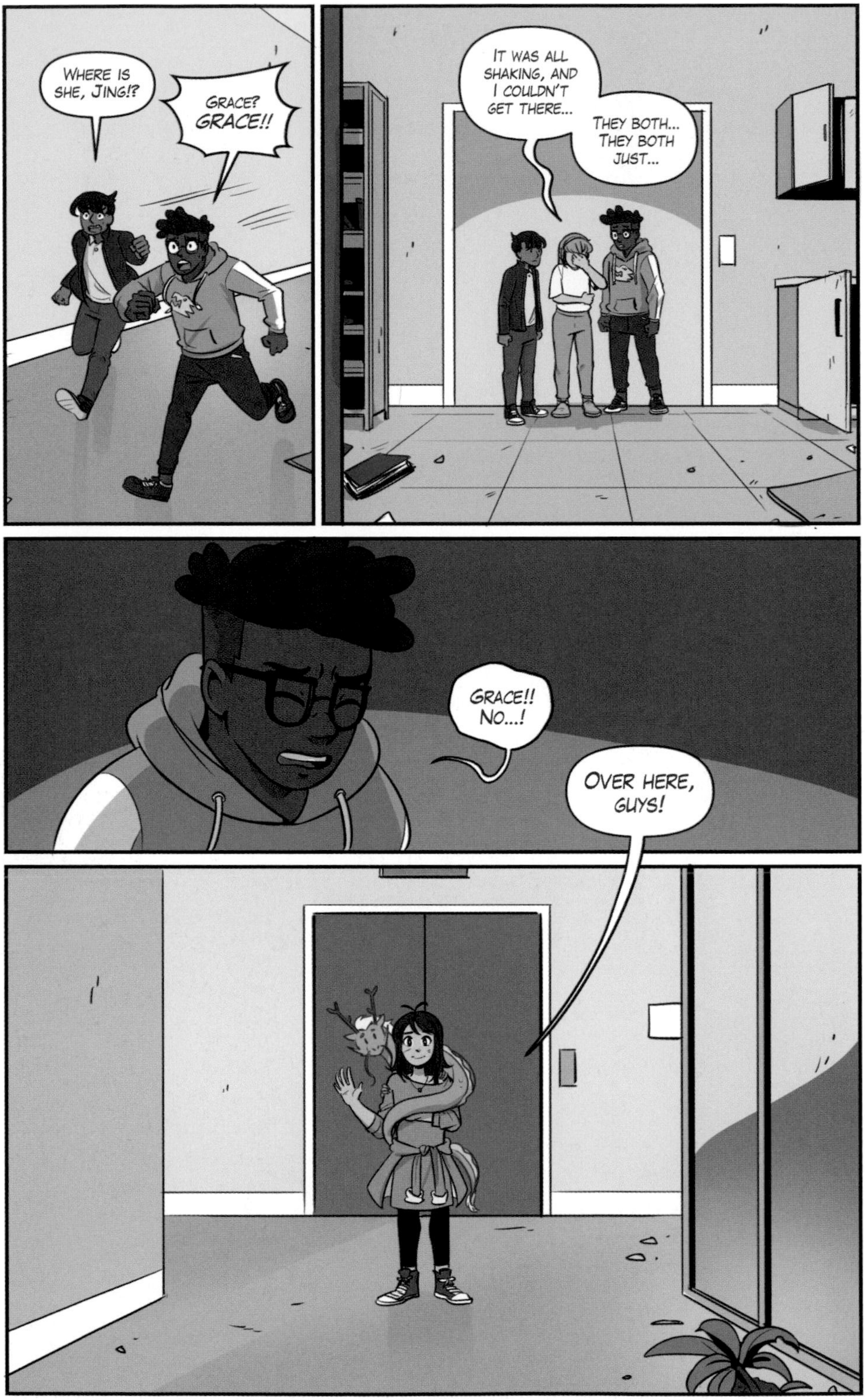
Where is she, Jing!?
Grace? GRACE!!
It was all shaking, and I couldn't get there...
They both... They both just...
Grace!! No...!
Over here, guys!

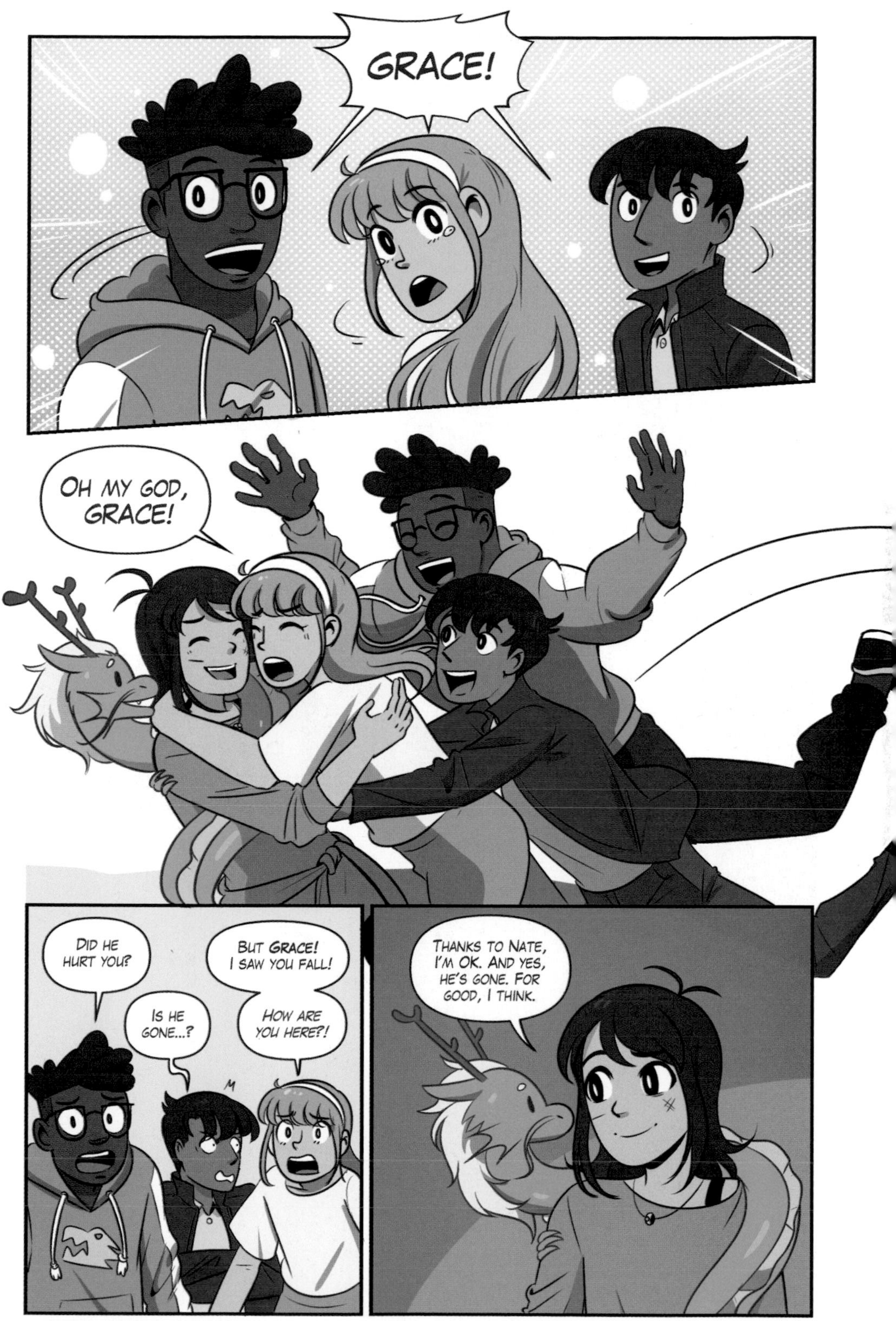
GRACE!
OH MY GOD, GRACE!
DID HE HURT YOU?
IS HE GONE...?
BUT GRACE! I SAW YOU FALL!
HOW ARE YOU HERE?!
THANKS TO NATE, I'M OK. AND YES, HE'S GONE. FOR GOOD, I THINK.

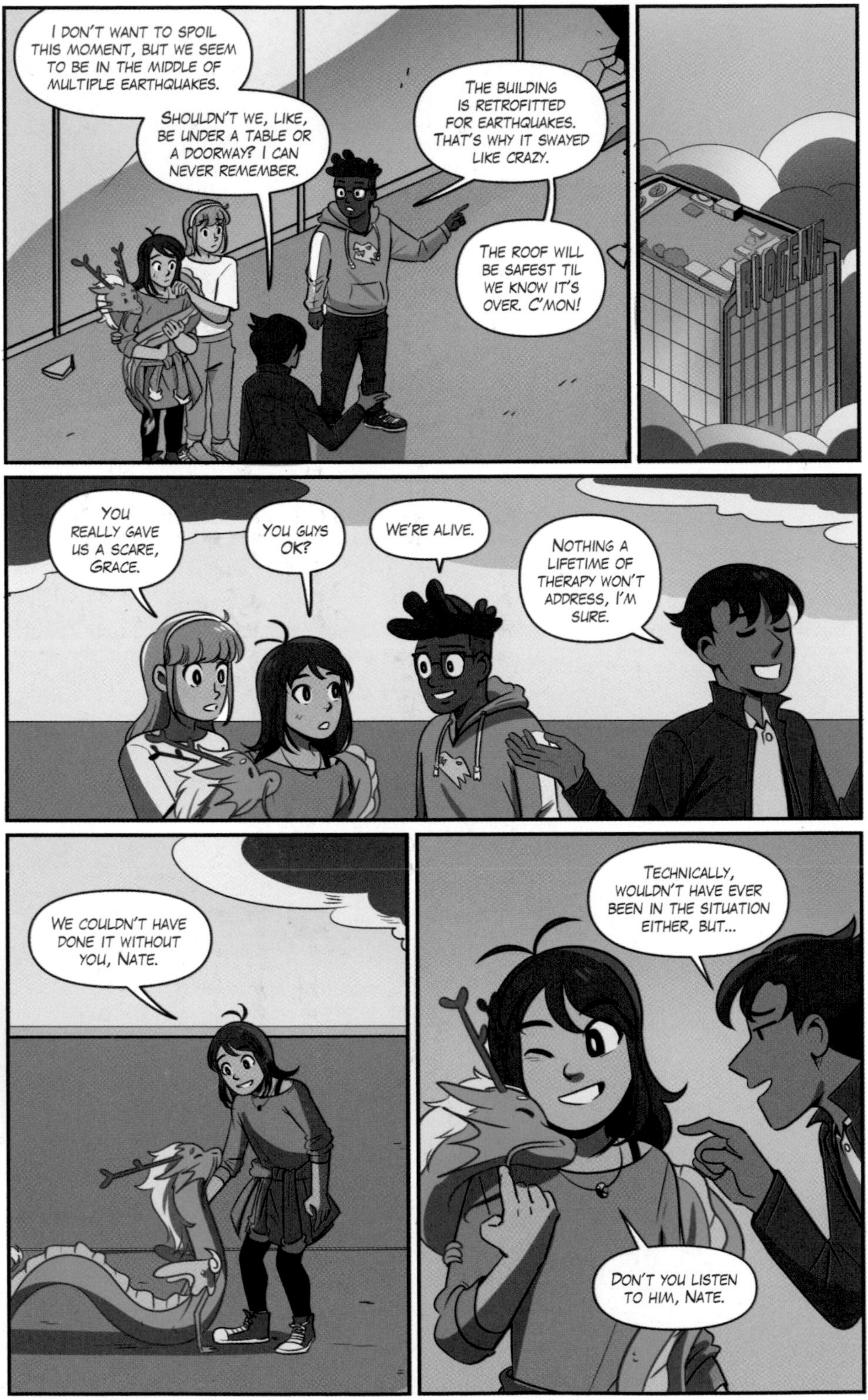
I DON'T WANT TO SPOIL THIS MOMENT, BUT WE SEEM TO BE IN THE MIDDLE OF MULTIPLE EARTHQUAKES.
SHOULDN'T WE, LIKE, BE UNDER A TABLE OR A DOORWAY? I CAN NEVER REMEMBER.
THE BUILDING IS RETROFITTED FOR EARTHQUAKES. THAT'S WHY IT SWAYED LIKE CRAZY.
THE ROOF WILL BE SAFEST TIL WE KNOW IT'S OVER. C'MON!
YOU REALLY GAVE US A SCARE, GRACE.
YOU GUYS OK?
WE'RE ALIVE.
NOTHING A LIFETIME OF THERAPY WON'T ADDRESS, I'M SURE.
WE COULDN'T HAVE DONE IT WITHOUT YOU, NATE.
TECHNICALLY, WOULDN'T HAVE EVER BEEN IN THE SITUATION EITHER, BUT...
DON'T YOU LISTEN TO HIM, NATE.

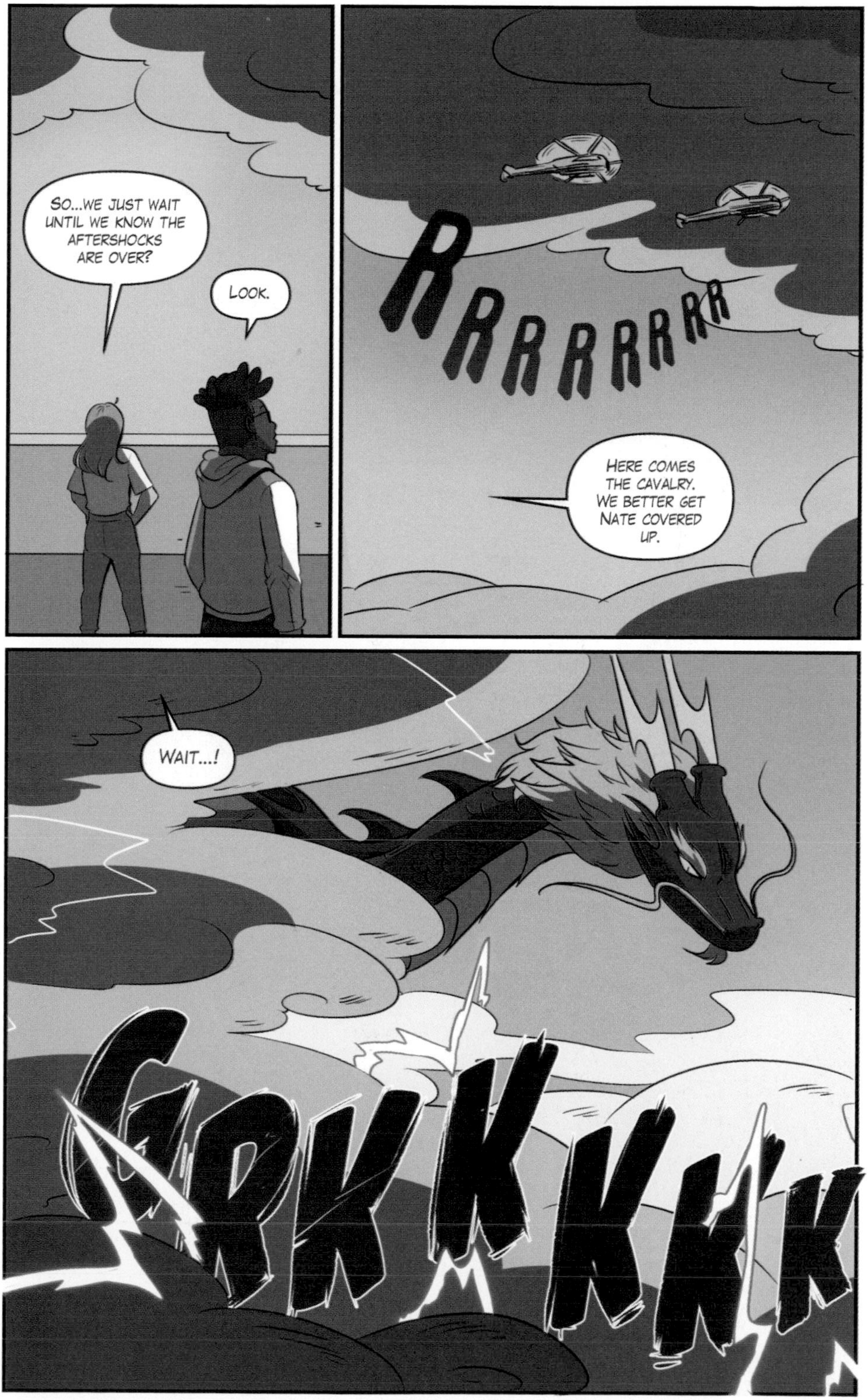
SO...WE JUST WAIT UNTIL WE KNOW THE AFTERSHOCKS ARE OVER?
LOOK.
RRRRRRRRR
HERE COMES THE CAVALRY. WE BETTER GET NATE COVERED UP.
WAIT...!
GRKKKKK

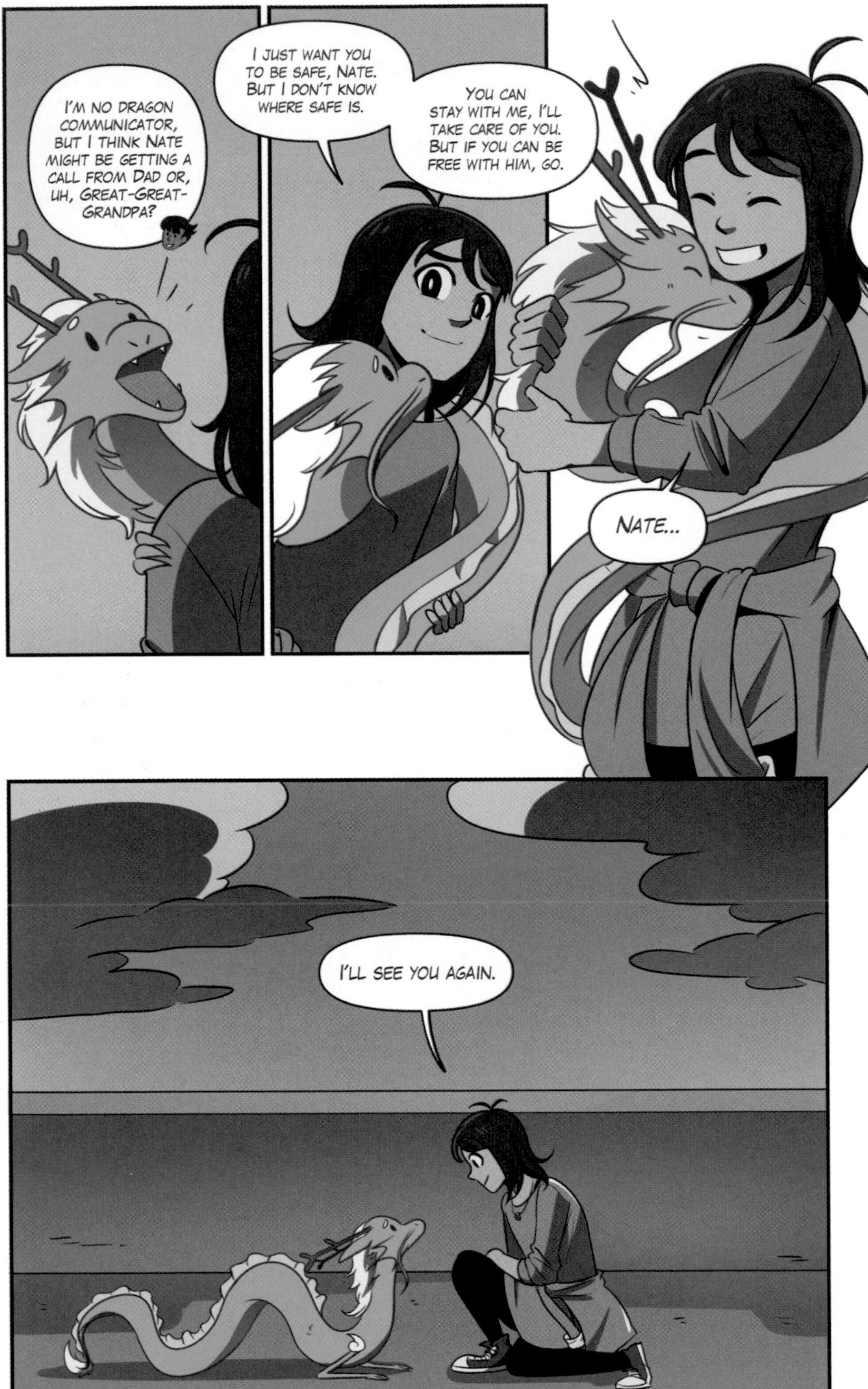
I'M NO DRAGON COMMUNICATOR, BUT I THINK NATE MIGHT BE GETTING A CALL FROM DAD OR, UH, GREAT-GREAT-GRANDPA?
I JUST WANT YOU TO BE SAFE, NATE. BUT I DON'T KNOW WHERE SAFE IS.
YOU CAN STAY WITH ME, I'LL TAKE CARE OF YOU. BUT IF YOU CAN BE FREE WITH HIM, GO.
NATE...
I'LL SEE YOU AGAIN.

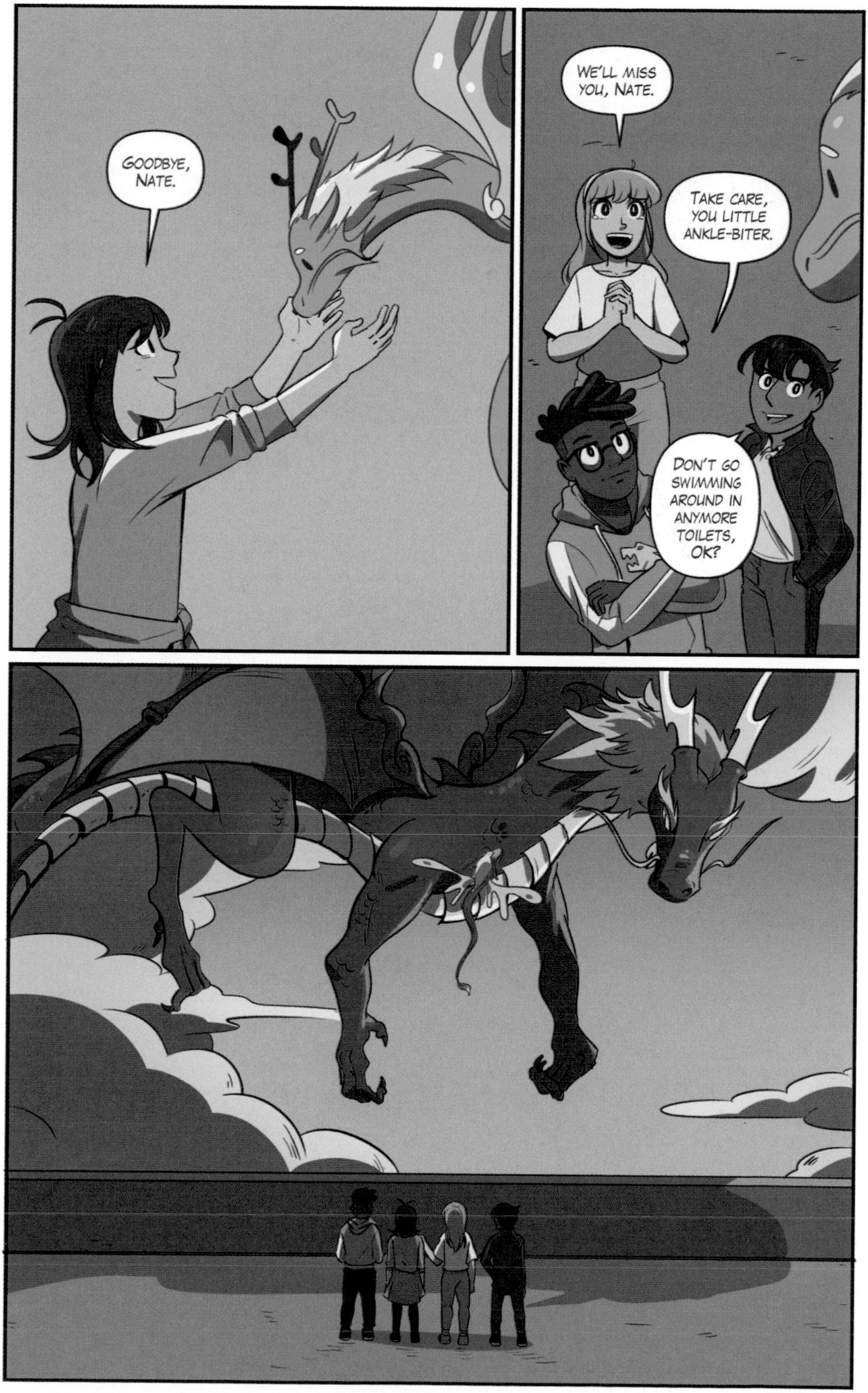
GOODBYE, NATE.
WE'LL MISS YOU, NATE.
TAKE CARE, YOU LITTLE ANKLE-BITER.
DON'T GO SWIMMING AROUND IN ANYMORE TOILETS, OK?

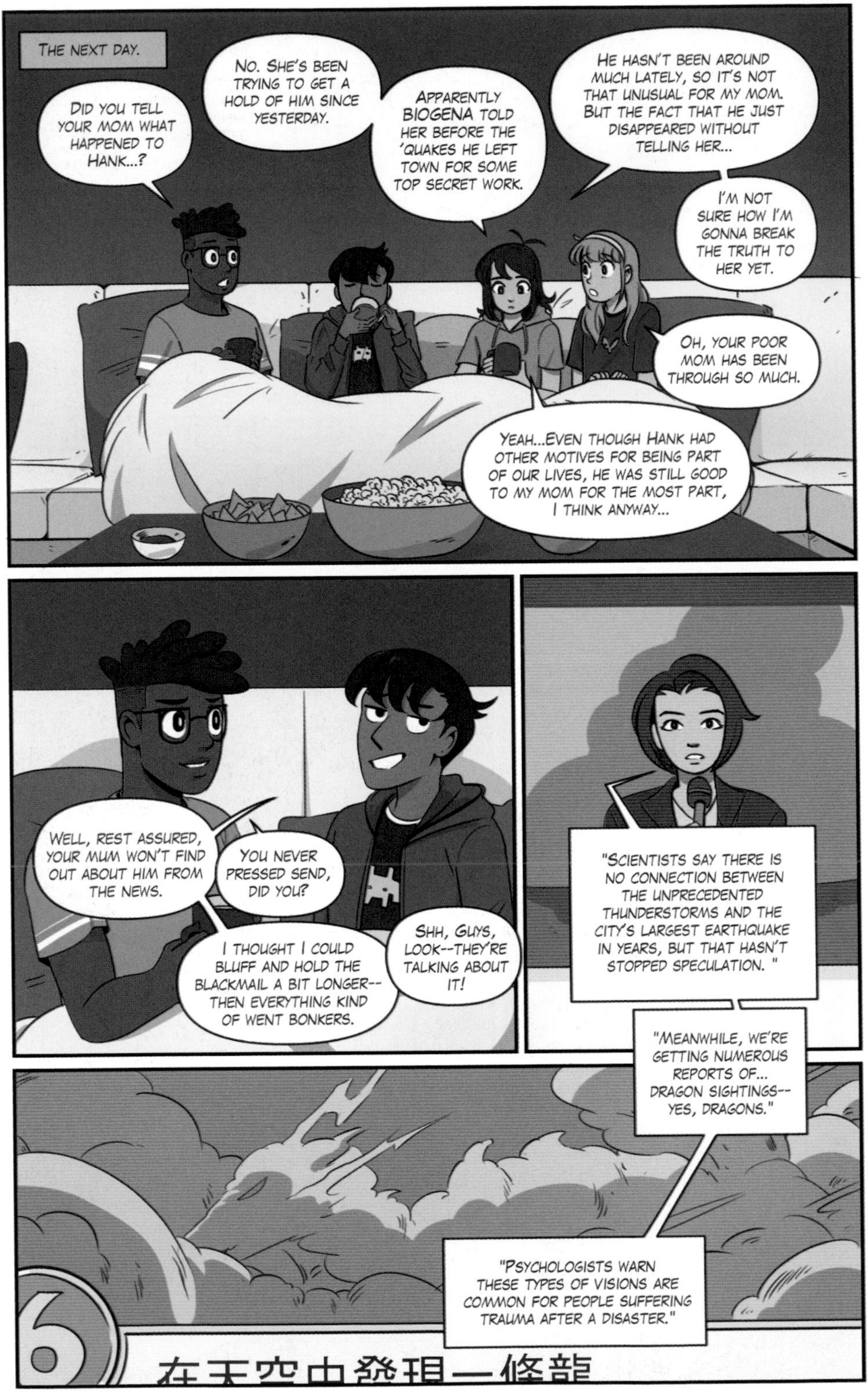

THE NEXT DAY.
DID YOU TELL YOUR MOM WHAT HAPPENED TO HANK...?
NO. SHE'S BEEN TRYING TO GET A HOLD OF HIM SINCE YESTERDAY.
APPARENTLY BIOGENA TOLD HER BEFORE THE 'QUAKES HE LEFT TOWN FOR SOME TOP SECRET WORK.
HE HASN'T BEEN AROUND MUCH LATELY, SO IT'S NOT THAT UNUSUAL FOR MY MOM. BUT THE FACT THAT HE JUST DISAPPEARED WITHOUT TELLING HER...
I'M NOT SURE HOW I'M GONNA BREAK THE TRUTH TO HER YET.
OH, YOUR POOR MOM HAS BEEN THROUGH SO MUCH.
YEAH...EVEN THOUGH HANK HAD OTHER MOTIVES FOR BEING PART OF OUR LIVES, HE WAS STILL GOOD TO MY MOM FOR THE MOST PART, I THINK ANYWAY...
WELL, REST ASSURED, YOUR MUM WON'T FIND OUT ABOUT HIM FROM THE NEWS.
YOU NEVER PRESSED SEND, DID YOU?
I THOUGHT I COULD BLUFF AND HOLD THE BLACKMAIL A BIT LONGER--THEN EVERYTHING KIND OF WENT BONKERS.
SHH, GUYS, LOOK--THEY'RE TALKING ABOUT IT!
"SCIENTISTS SAY THERE IS NO CONNECTION BETWEEN THE UNPRECEDENTED THUNDERSTORMS AND THE CITY'S LARGEST EARTHQUAKE IN YEARS, BUT THAT HASN'T STOPPED SPECULATION. "
"MEANWHILE, WE'RE GETTING NUMEROUS REPORTS OF... DRAGON SIGHTINGS--YES, DRAGONS."
"PSYCHOLOGISTS WARN THESE TYPES OF VISIONS ARE COMMON FOR PEOPLE SUFFERING TRAUMA AFTER A DISASTER."
6

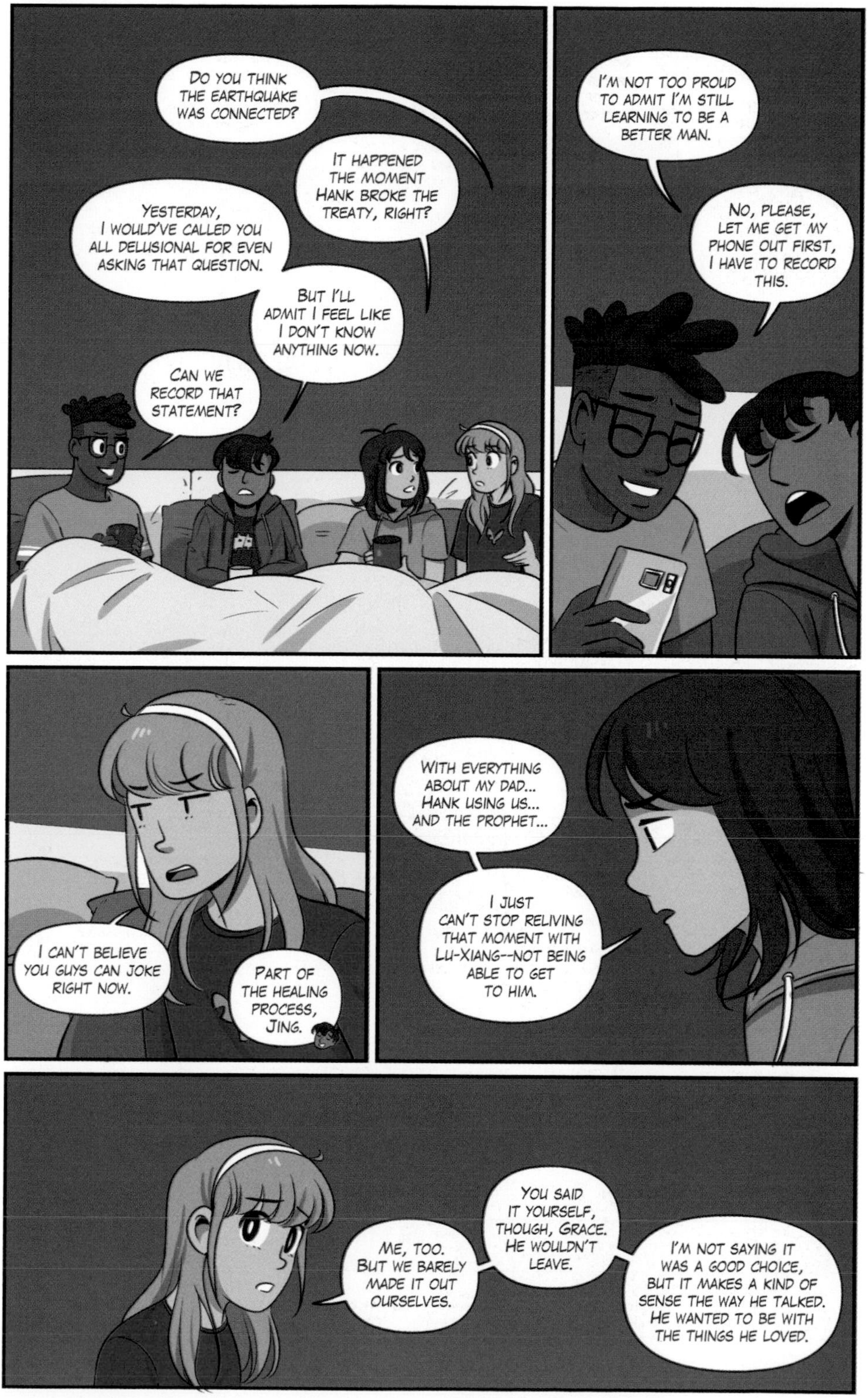
Do you think the earthquake was connected?
It happened the moment Hank broke the treaty, right?
Yesterday, I would've called you all delusional for even asking that question.
But I'll admit I feel like I don't know anything now.
Can we record that statement?
I'm not too proud to admit I'm still learning to be a better man.
No, please, let me get my phone out first, I have to record this.
I can't believe you guys can joke right now.
Part of the healing process, Jing.
With everything about my dad... Hank using us... and the prophet...
I just can't stop reliving that moment with Lu-Xiang--not being able to get to him.
Me, too. But we barely made it out ourselves.
You said it yourself, though, Grace. He wouldn't leave.
I'm not saying it was a good choice, but it makes a kind of sense the way he talked. He wanted to be with the things he loved.

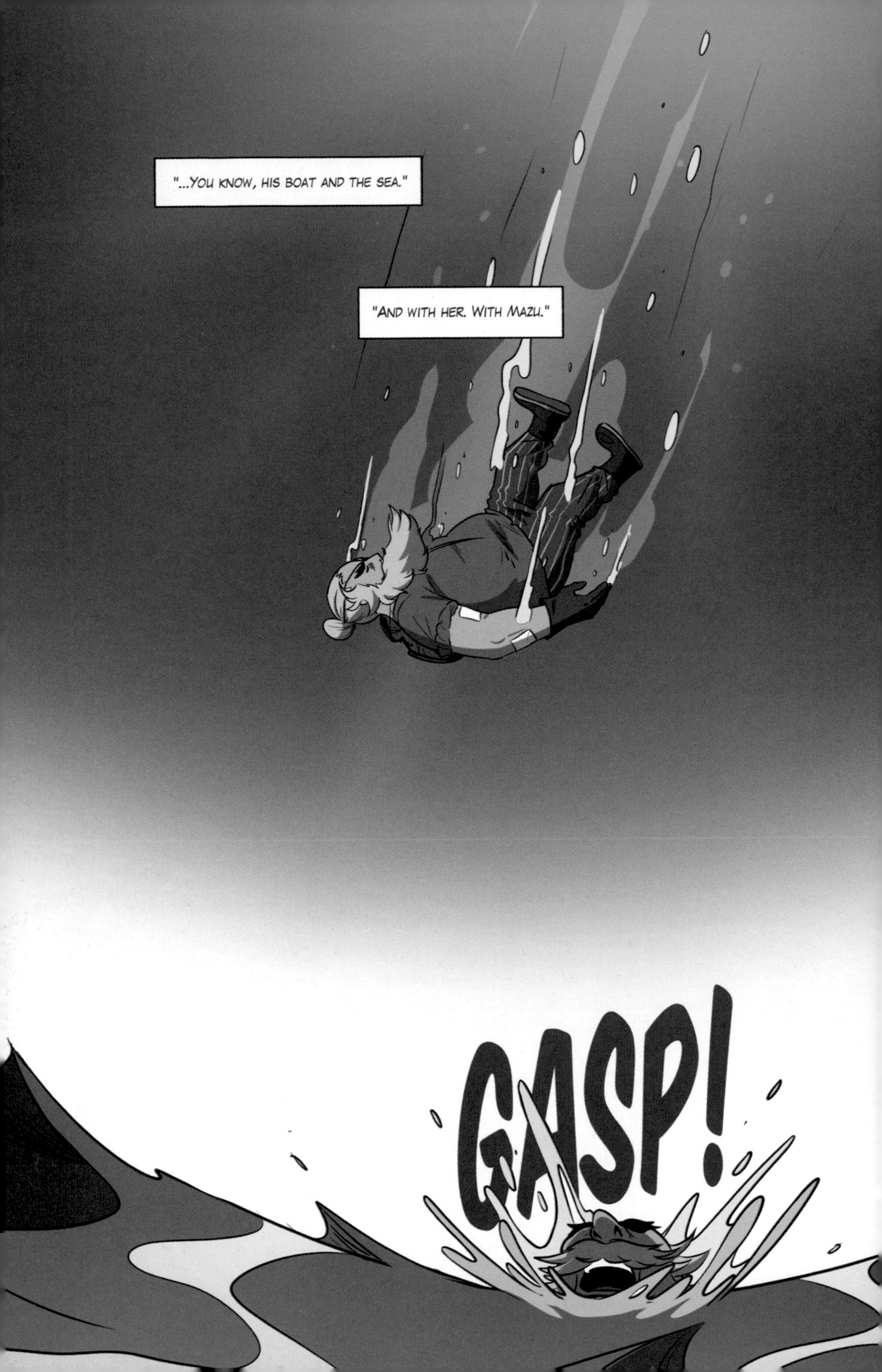
"...You know, his boat and the sea."
"And with her. With Mazu."
GASP!

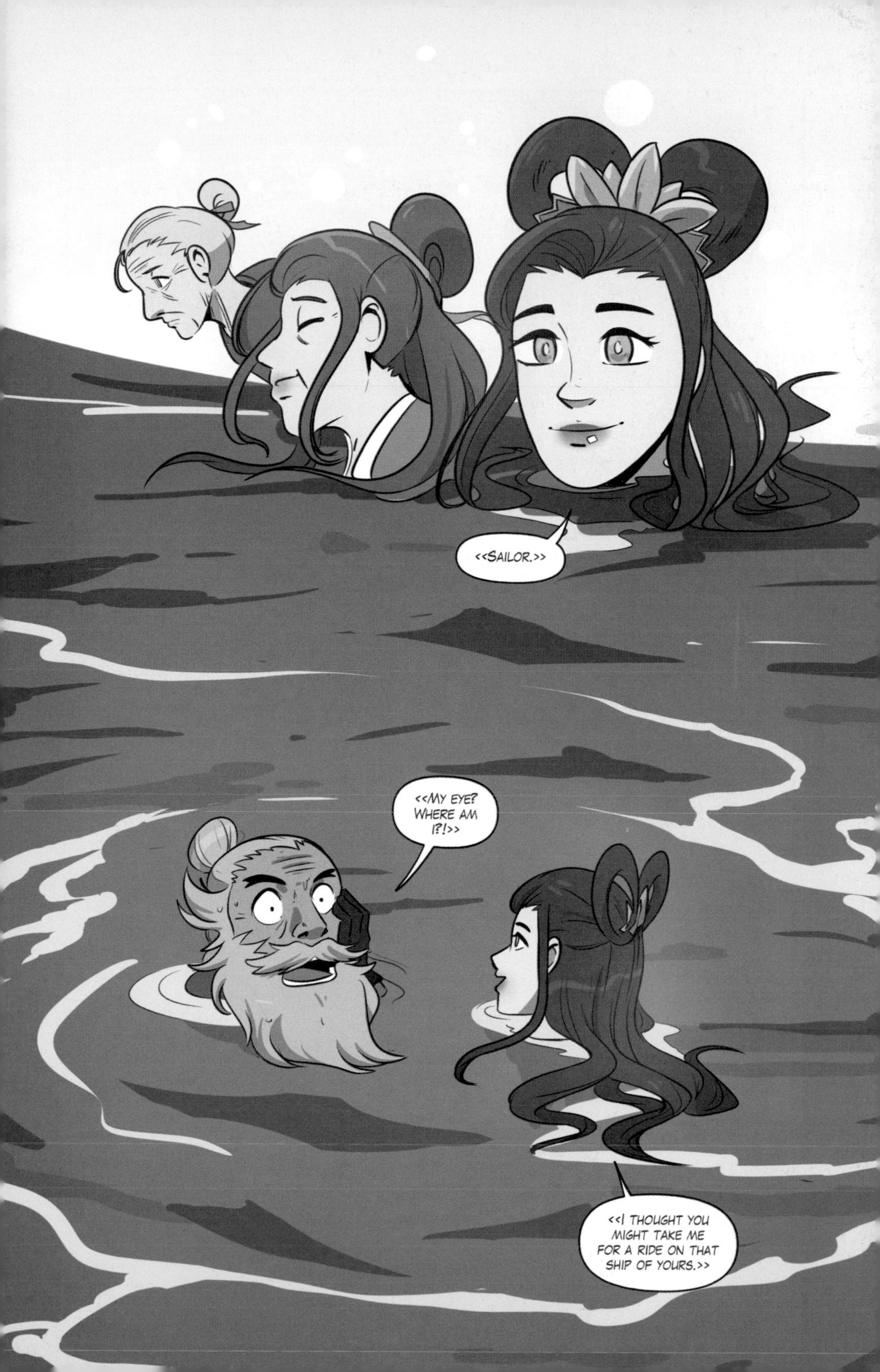
<<SAILOR.>>
<<MY EYE? WHERE AM I?!>>
<<I THOUGHT YOU MIGHT TAKE ME FOR A RIDE ON THAT SHIP OF YOURS.>>

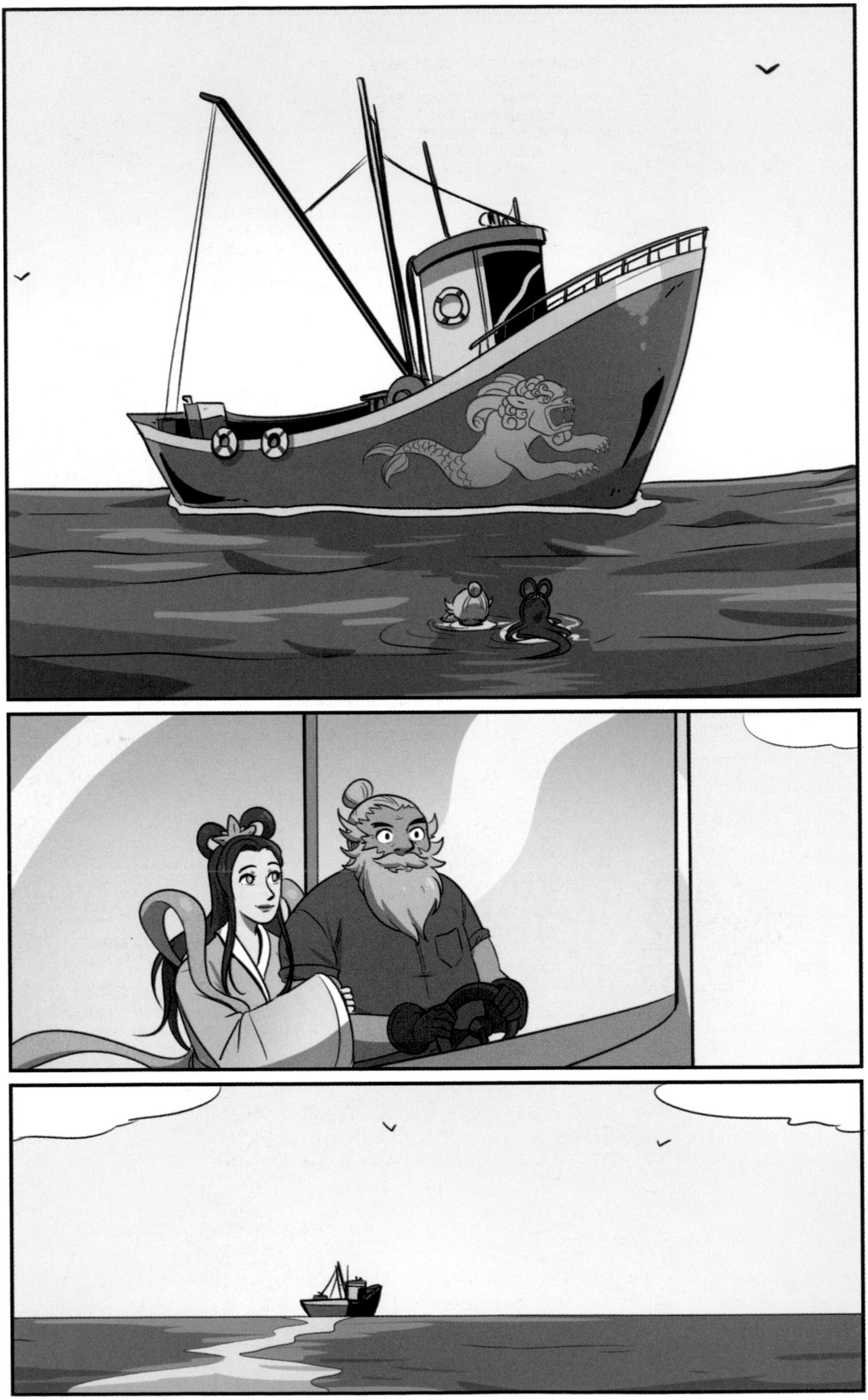

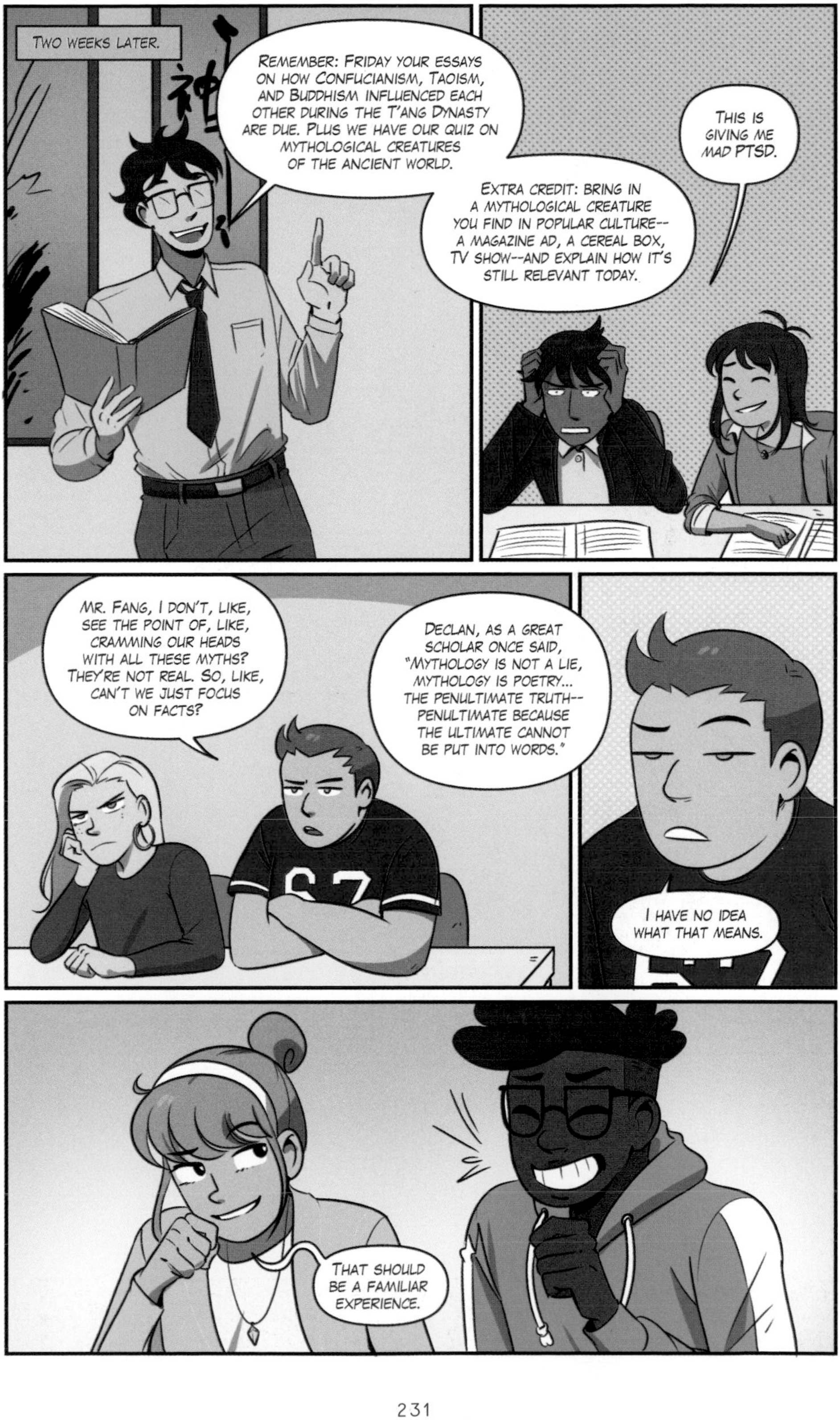
TWO WEEKS LATER.
REMEMBER: FRIDAY YOUR ESSAYS ON HOW CONFUCIANISM, TAOISM, AND BUDDHISM INFLUENCED EACH OTHER DURING THE T'ANG DYNASTY ARE DUE. PLUS WE HAVE OUR QUIZ ON MYTHOLOGICAL CREATURES OF THE ANCIENT WORLD.
EXTRA CREDIT: BRING IN A MYTHOLOGICAL CREATURE YOU FIND IN POPULAR CULTURE-- A MAGAZINE AD, A CEREAL BOX, TV SHOW--AND EXPLAIN HOW IT'S STILL RELEVANT TODAY.
THIS IS GIVING ME MAD PTSD.
MR. FANG, I DON'T, LIKE, SEE THE POINT OF, LIKE, CRAMMING OUR HEADS WITH ALL THESE MYTHS? THEY'RE NOT REAL. SO, LIKE, CAN'T WE JUST FOCUS ON FACTS?
DECLAN, AS A GREAT SCHOLAR ONCE SAID, "MYTHOLOGY IS NOT A LIE, MYTHOLOGY IS POETRY... THE PENULTIMATE TRUTH-- PENULTIMATE BECAUSE THE ULTIMATE CANNOT BE PUT INTO WORDS."
I HAVE NO IDEA WHAT THAT MEANS.
THAT SHOULD BE A FAMILIAR EXPERIENCE.

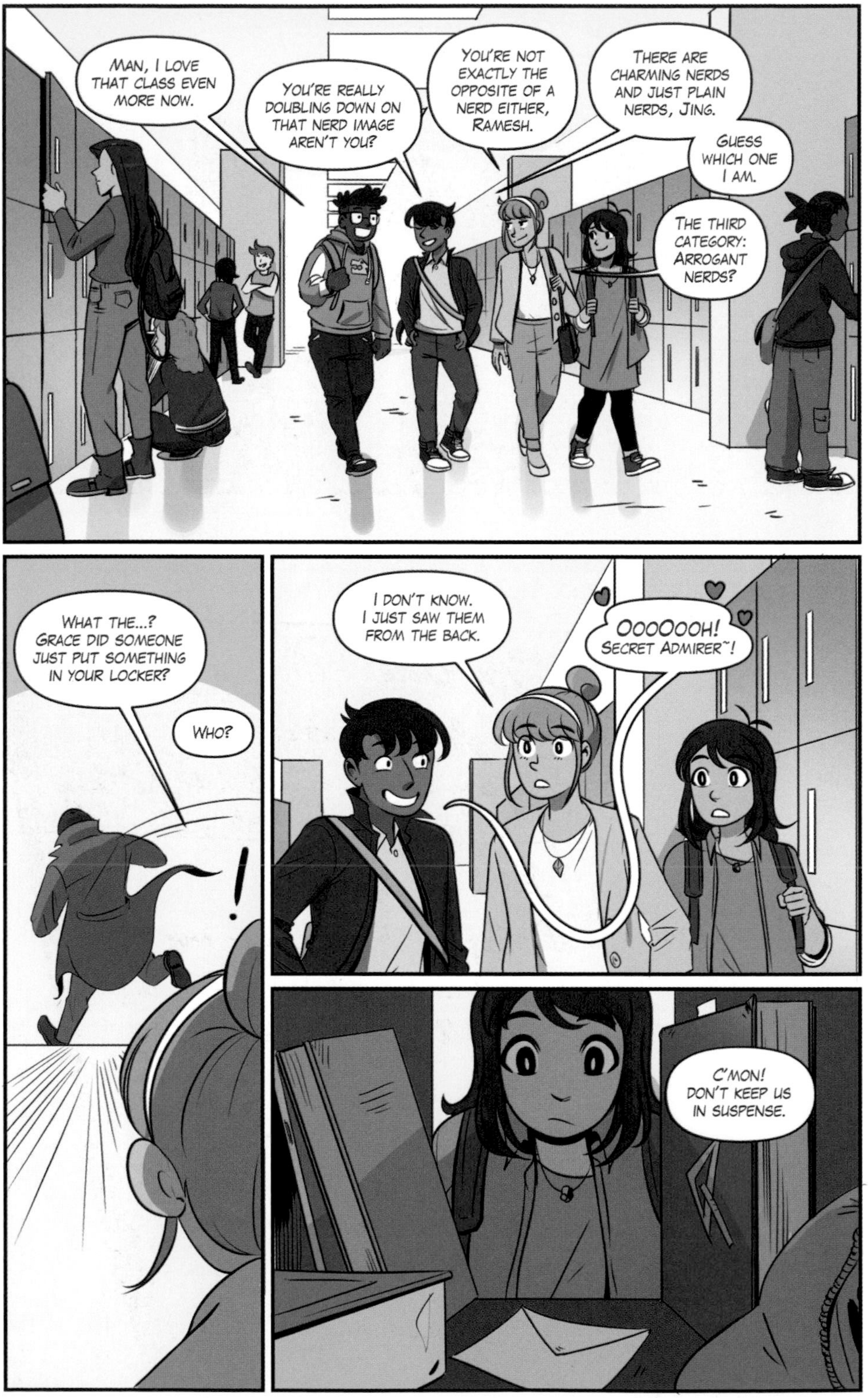

MAN, I LOVE THAT CLASS EVEN MORE NOW.
YOU'RE REALLY DOUBLING DOWN ON THAT NERD IMAGE AREN'T YOU?
YOU'RE NOT EXACTLY THE OPPOSITE OF A NERD EITHER, RAMESH.
THERE ARE CHARMING NERDS AND JUST PLAIN NERDS, JING.
GUESS WHICH ONE I AM.
THE THIRD CATEGORY: ARROGANT NERDS?
WHAT THE...? GRACE DID SOMEONE JUST PUT SOMETHING IN YOUR LOCKER?
WHO?
!
I DON'T KNOW. I JUST SAW THEM FROM THE BACK.
OOOOOOH! SECRET ADMIRER~!
C'MON! DON'T KEEP US IN SUSPENSE.

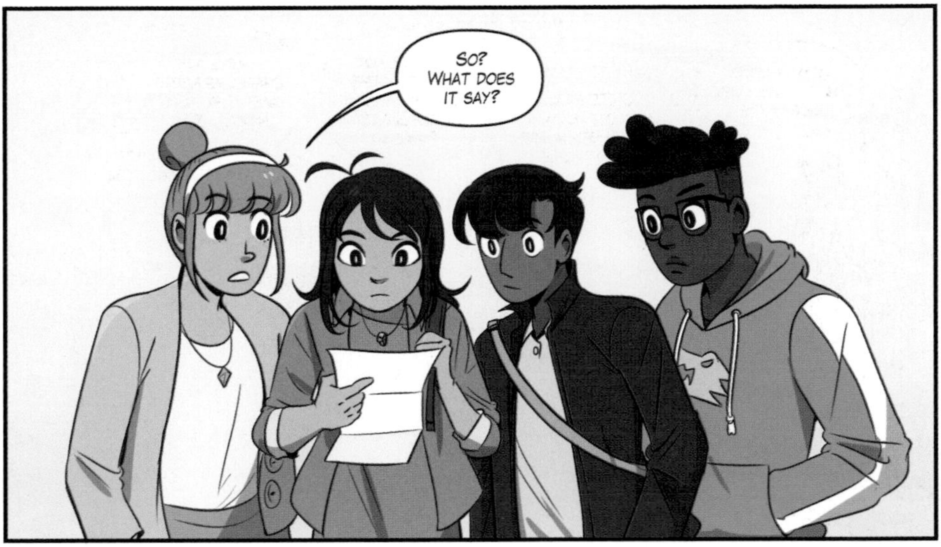
SO?
WHAT DOES
IT SAY?

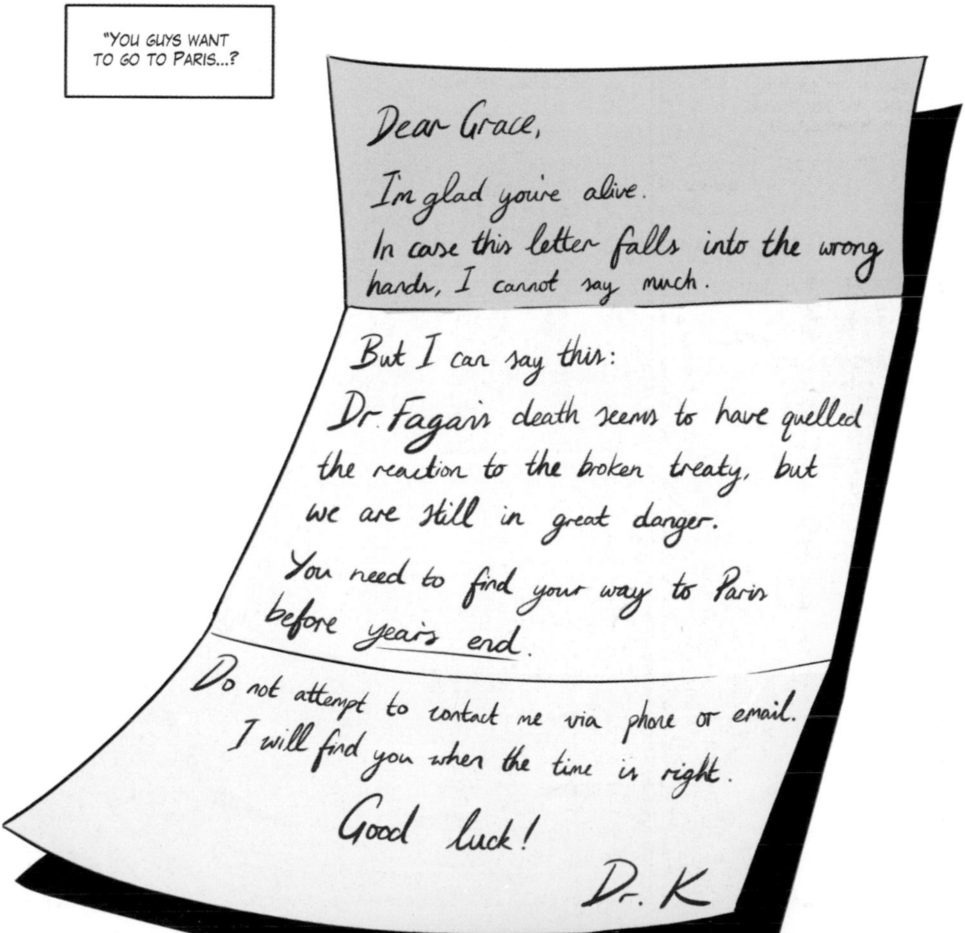
"YOU GUYS WANT
TO GO TO PARIS...?
Dear Grace,
I'm glad you're alive.
In case this letter falls into the wrong
hands, I cannot say much.
But I can say this:
Dr. Fagan's death seems to have quelled
the reaction to the broken treaty, but
we are still in great danger.
You need to find your way to Paris
before year's end.
Do not attempt to contact me via phone or email.
I will find you when the time is right.
Good luck!
Dr. K

ACKNOWLEDGMENTS

I am profoundly grateful to our stellar agent Mark Gottlieb and the Trident Media team, and of course to the magic makers at Scholastic / Graphix. David Saylor, Emily Nguyen, Phil Falco, Steve Ponzo — thank you for seeing this vision and for your steady, skillful guidance. Huge thanks, as well, to Randie Adler and ICM for believing in the big picture.

Space constraints won't let me name everyone who offered love and support along the way, but I need to squeeze in a few. Thank you to my amazing mom and sis, the whole DuRoss clan, Margaret Defayamoreau, the Klar and Walker fams, the Yogis-Fitzpatrick pirates, Jon Silk, Philip Cryan, Alexandre Megret, Jim Klar, Chloe Sladden and Kevin Mcelroy, Jake Lesnik and Laura Kahn, Carter Hall, Molli and Ella Bernard, Guido Rosei, Ashita Trikha and Noble Athimattathil, Heng Sure Fa Shr, Alex Fang, Noah and Kiki Klei-Borrero, Heather Kessinger, Bren Langlois, Chris Youngless, and Aryn Terese. And extra special thanks to Emily Melton, as well as the Goosby-Preston family — Jenckyn, Dean, Sky, Kira. Couldn't have done this without you!

Infinite thanks, as well, to my whole family, especially my wife, Amy, who, in addition to everything, puts up with me on grumpy days. To our boys, Eben, Fin, and Kaifas: You're as brave, creative, and kind as the heroes of this tale!

— Jaimal Yogis

Thank you to David Saylor, Emily Nguyen, Phil Falco, Steve Ponzo, the rest of the Scholastic team, and our agent Mark Gottlieb for making this graphic novel debut happen!

— Vivian Truong

Jaimal Yogis is the author of *Saltwater Buddha, The Fear Project, All Our Waves Are Water*, and the children's book series *Mop Rides the Waves of Life* and *Mop Rides the Waves of Change*. His writing has also appeared in *The Atlantic, ESPN Magazine*, and *The Washington Post*. He lives in San Francisco.

Vivian Truong is a comic artist who has created artwork for Riot Games, miHoYo, Rebellion, and more. Her work includes the Punches and Plants webcomic series for the popular MOBA game League of Legends. She also works as a storyboard artist for game studios, a digital production studio, and a children's book publisher. She currently lives in London.

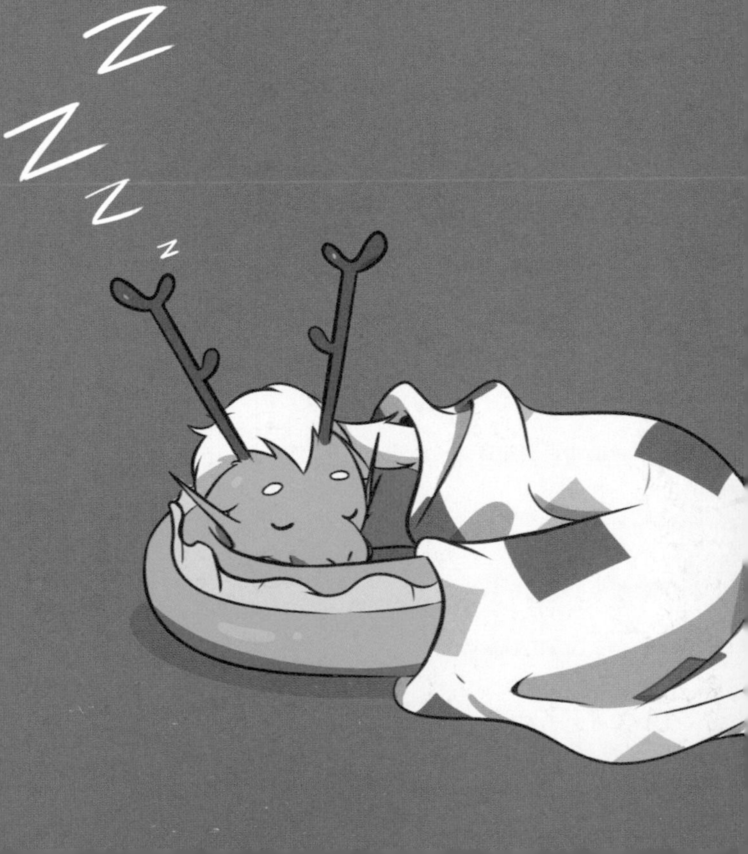
Z
Z
Z
z